IVANA

For Love Alone

TRUMP

POCKET STAR BOOKS

New York   London   Toronto   Sydney   Tokyo   Singapore

This book is a work of fiction. Names, characters, places and incidents are either products of the author's imagination or are used fictitiously. Any resemblance to actual events or locales or persons, living or dead, is entirely coincidental.

Author photograph by Christopher Makos; Hair by Maury Hopson for Louis Licari; Makeup by Vincent Longo

A Pocket Star Book published by
POCKET BOOKS, a division of Simon & Schuster Inc.
1230 Avenue of the Americas, New York, NY 10020

ISBN: 0-671-74369-4

First Pocket Books paperback printing February 1993

10 9 8 7 6 5 4 3 2 1

POCKET STAR BOOKS and colophon are registered trademarks of Simon & Schuster Inc.

Printed in the U.S.A.

IVANA TRUMP
FOR LOVE ALONE

Ivana Trump brings us a marvelous novel about a woman of charm and courage whose life surpassed the grandest fantasies; the man whose daring ambitions matched hers and made them the golden couple of the age; and her exclusive circle of friends, whose devotion was priceless . . .

Adam Graham: A vital, sexual man, his Midas touch had built his old-line shipping money into a huge personal fortune. With his gorgeous wife, Katrinka, at his side, Adam demanded the best . . .

Daisy Elliott: A fun-loving blue blood from old New York stock, she was about to give her friends the shock of their lives . . .

Lucia di Campo: The sultry, lavishly talented yacht designer was married to a slick lawyer with sinister connections . . .

Zuzka Havlíček: A Czech and fellow skier, her abundant sensuality led her into delicious sexual adventures . . .

Margo Jensen: The magazine editor and fashion doyenne had made herself, through sheer force of will, into the most interesting-looking woman in the world . . .

Alexandra Ogelvy: A striking society girl once enamored of Adam, she shone as the "trophy wife" of a Wall Street takeover king . . .

Natalie Bovier: French fashion wizard and tycoon's mistress, she was a seductress whose restless eroticism inspired a Saudi prince to promise endless Arabian nights . . .

In Loving Memory of My Beloved Father, Miloš

I would like to dedicate this book to my three wonderful children, Donny, Ivanka, and Eric, and to my dear mother, Maria.

I would like to thank my friend Camille Marchetta for helping me to tell Katrinka's story.

Acknowledgments

I would like to thank Bill Grose, Jack Romanos, Irwyn Applebaum, Anne Maitland, Kara Welsh, Barbara Buck, and the whole staff at Pocket Books for their strong belief, support, and enthusiasm.

I would also like to thank Robert Gottlieb, Pamela Bernstein, and Norman Brokaw from the William Morris Agency, who came to me with a firm idea and a contract from Pocket Books; and for their continuing support and friendship.

Many thanks to Billy Norwich for coming to me two years ago with the idea of writing a book.

Finally, I would like to thank my friend, business assistant, and public-relations representative, Lisa Calandra, for years of hard work and dedication.

Acknowledgments

I would like to thank Bill Grose, Jack Romanos, Irwyn Applebaum, Anne Maitland, Kara Welsh, Barbara Buck, and the whole staff at Pocket Books for their strong belief, support and enthusiasm.

I would also like to thank Robert Gottlieb, Pamela Bernstein, and Norman Brokaw from the William Morris Agency who came to me with a firm idea and a contract from Pocket Books and for their continuing support and friendship.

Many thanks to Bill Stordahl for coming to me two years ago with the idea of writing a book.

Finally I would like to thank my friend, business assistant, and public relations representative, Lisa Calandra, for years of hard work and dedication.

The
Present

—◆—

1991

One

We'll be in St. Moritz from the twenty-second," said Daisy, her elegant blond head cocked in Katrinka's direction as if expecting a refusal. In her opinion, Katrinka had been behaving very oddly of late. "Of course, if you want to go sooner, do. Just let me know when to tell the Meyerhofs to expect you." The Meyerhofs were the butler and housekeeper heading the staff of sixteen employed at the chalet to cater to the varying desires of assorted children, grandchildren, and guests, all of whom had been invited for Christmas.

Daisy was always lavish with invitations, but usually she was quite easy about whether or not they were accepted. This year, however, with Katrinka, she seemed determined to have her way. Because she's worried, of course, thought Katrinka, who nevertheless shook her head. "Thank you, Daisy," she said, her low-pitched voice colored by the hint of Middle European accent which changed *w* to *v*, *th* to *z*, and gave her sentences an occasional odd tilt, "but not this year."

Her friends waited for her to continue, to give a reason for her refusal that would reassure them, but when she didn't, Lucia asked, "Are you going to Czechoslovakia?" That was where Katrinka had spent the preceding Christmas.

"I don't think so."

"Aspen?" Alexandra asked hopefully.

"I did not decide yet what I will do," replied Katrinka, avoiding the eyes of her friends, not liking to be so vague

3

with them, though at the moment she felt she had little choice.

"What is this?" said Zuzka, speaking as always in a quick, staccato burst, her accent, after only six years of living in the United States, much more pronounced than Katrinka's. Friends from their university days, she and Katrinka had both been members of the Czechoslovakian national ski team. "You don't go skiing?" Katrinka shook her head and Zuzka frowned. If Katrinka didn't want to ski, she must be even more depressed than Zuzka had thought.

"You can't spend Christmas alone in that enormous apartment," said Margo in her determined, take-charge way. She, too, would be joining Daisy in St. Moritz.

"You'll make yourself ill," added Alexandra, extending an invitation for Katrinka to join her family for the usual round of Chanukah and Christmas festivities at their Pound Ridge estate and go on with them to Aspen for New Year's.

"You all worry about me too much," said Katrinka. "I'm fine now. Never better." And it was true, oddly enough, though her friends assumed her smile was still fake and her heart still broken. She would have liked to put their concern to rest, but only the truth would do that, and the truth was what she could not tell them, at least for a few more days.

Katrinka Graham, Zuzka Havlíček, Daisy Elliott, Margo Jensen, Alexandra Ogelvy, and Lucia di Campo lunched together often, whenever they happened to be in the same city, at Le Cirque as today, or at La Grenouille, or "21," the San Lorenzo in London, Maxim's in Paris, always the best or most charming restaurants in whatever interesting place in the world they happened to be. They dined together, as well, with current husbands or lovers or assorted escorts, went to the theater, the opera, to parties when parties used to be in vogue, even vacationed together. They had been doing this for so many years that, by now, there was little that they did not already know about one another's lives, and nothing new that they could not usually ferret out in the course of a meal. Which is why it surprised Katrinka that they could not sense the change that had taken place in her these past few months. These women had been so close to

4

her for so long, how could they not realize that at last she had no reason to fake, that finally she was happy again?

"Look who's just come in," whispered Daisy. The oldest of the friends, she was in her mid-fifties, a petite, elegant woman, her youthful appearance recently enhanced by the services of a famed Los Angeles plastic surgeon who had tautened her face, tucked her abdomen and butt, lifted her breasts just enough and no more.

Katrinka glanced up from her chicken paillard, past the mirrored columns, along the line of wall frescoed with French pastoral scenes and the tables brightened with small bunches of roses and orchids, to the front door where Betsy Bloomingdale was chatting with Calvin Klein while Ed McMahon stood taking off his coat. But surely Daisy wasn't referring to them?

"Bitch," hissed Margo.

And then Katrinka saw her, the awful Sabrina, following Sirio Maccioni, the restaurant's owner, across the room, stopping en route to greet acquaintances (Sabrina did not have any friends), dropping a kiss on a cheek, calling out a promise of future lunch. When she spotted the six women, an automatic smile curved her lips and she nodded, rather like the Queen of England on parade, but did not pause. Noting the moment, the tycoons suppressed grins and the matrons leaned their vast lacquered bouffant heads closer together to whisper. No one could remember when or why it had started, but Sabrina's vendetta against Katrinka Graham always made for interesting reading in the pages of *The Chronicle*.

"She has heart like prune," said Zuzka. "Dried prune."

Her progress completed, Sabrina allowed Sirio to seat her opposite Carolina Herrera, with whom—to everyone's surprise—she was apparently having lunch. They were an odd couple: the patrician designer with not a strand of her shining blond hair out of place, wearing an elegant plaid suit of her own design, and the international gossip columnist, her mouse-colored hair hanging limply to her shoulders, her de la Renta dress, though recognizably this season's, looking as if it had been fought over at a rummage sale. She had

5

small eyes set like raisins in a pasty face, a broad meandering nose, and a lopsided mouth filled with unpleasant yellow teeth. How she had come to wield so much power boggled the minds of all who met her, though no one would have missed reading her columns, and had them faxed when traveling in parts of the world (admittedly fewer every day) where there was no van Hollen newspaper available.

"God, doesn't she look awful?" whispered Alexandra, repressing a shudder. "She always reminds me of one of those puddings they used to serve for dessert at Farmington." Tall, with luxurious red hair, perfect features, and a body to match, Alexandra had the impatience of many beautiful women with those less fortunate than themselves, as if ugliness were a moral failing rather than a joke of nature.

"She could make an effort," said Margo disapprovingly. A homely child, through acquired style and sheer force of will she had managed to convince a dubious world that her dramatic face with its pale, perfect skin, deep-set smoky eyes, prominent beak of a nose, full mouth painted always bright red, the whole set against a backdrop of frizzed charcoal hair, was stunningly attractive. Moving from Scarsdale to Sarah Lawrence College to a secretarial position at a women's magazine, she had slowly conquered Manhattan, securing one of the top positions at *Chic,* from where, until recently, she had reigned as New York's arbiter of taste and fashion, trendsetter, maker and breaker of designers and models, capable of being either a good friend or a bitter enemy. Almost from their first meeting, she had been one of Katrinka's best friends.

"That's the problem coming here," said Alexandra. "You run into everyone."

"That's the fun," said Daisy, who was fearless, and for good reason. From the top of her dyed-by-Kenneth hair to the tips of her Manolo Blahnik shoes, Daisy was every inch an aristocrat, tracing her ancestry on both sides back to colonial settlers. And if she was no longer the wealthiest among the friends, her social position remained unchallenged because her money was the oldest and (since time erases the memory of all sins) the purest, coming from

Yankee trading in the 1790s, not corporate raiding and other excesses of greed in the 1980s.

"I could never stop coming here and give up this bread," said Margo, who had already finished a Brie twist and was now breaking into a small loaf of brown bread, smearing it with butter, and biting into it, a smile of almost orgiastic pleasure on her face.

"Margo, butter!" said Alexandra, horrified. How on earth could Margo remain a size six the way she ate?

"My only remaining vice," said Margo. "At least where food is concerned," she added.

"I eat everything," said Zuzka, the largest of the women and still only a size eight. Tall, with a mane of golden hair, large brown eyes, and clear skin masked by only a light cover of makeup, Zuzka had the natural beauty, the healthy good looks of an athlete, despite the twenty years or so that had passed since she had taken any sport seriously.

"I used to. I don't dare anymore," said Lucia, her large chestnut eyes looking longingly at the bread. She had gone up two dress sizes a few years ago and had fought too hard to regain her slender figure to jeopardize it again, no matter what the provocation. Not that she had any at the moment. Though it had been months since she had designed her last yacht and, given the condition of the world's economy in this December of 1991, she was not expecting any new commissions for a while, Lucia wasn't worried. The combination of savings and family money would see her through until some billionaire somewhere decided to splurge. And, meanwhile, she had a beautiful home, a beautiful daughter, and a handsome man in love with her, which, given her tendency to attract men with no redeeming qualities *but* their looks, perhaps ought to have worried her at least a little.

Daisy was not paying any attention at all to her food, pushing the chicken salad absentmindedly around the Limoges plate, her gaze returning again and again to Sabrina. "I'll never understand why Mark van Hollen continues to employ her," she said finally.

"She sells papers," said Katrinka, who over the years had suffered the most from Sabrina's acid pen.

7

"Well, she can be amusing, I suppose," said Daisy grudgingly, "but whatever happened to good taste and journalistic standards?"

"They're not as important as profit margins," replied Katrinka, smiling. Due in large part to its controversial columnists, foremost of whom was Sabrina, *The Chronicle* was the only one of the New York tabloids thought likely to survive the economic crunch.

"How can you defend Mark, or her, after that column this morning?" said Alexandra, earning immediate glares from Daisy and Margo for having brought the subject up. The column had contained a short piece on Natalie Bovier, who not too long ago would have been the seventh at lunch. Now, none of them spoke to her; at least, not unless absolutely necessary.

"Piece of shit," said Zuzka, meaning either the article or Natalie. No one was certain which.

Most of the item had been unremarkable, a recounting of the amazing success—despite the recession—of Natalie's West Coast boutiques. The stinger had been in the implied accusation that Katrinka had used her influence to stop the French retail magnate Jean-Claude Gillette from going ahead with his plan to acquire the boutiques, thus doing Natalie out of millions of dollars in profits. "You did read it, didn't you?" Alexandra continued unrepentantly.

Katrinka nodded. "Five copies came by fax, by eight this morning. Sent by friends," she added dryly, though she did not in fact consider the senders particularly malicious; they simply loved gossip and could not resist passing it on, whatever the consequences.

In this case, the consequences had not been very great. Over the years, Katrinka had developed thick skin where Sabrina's barbs were concerned. They still pricked, but it was a long time since they had been able to draw blood. And though it irritated her to think some people would believe her capable of the pettiness, the vindictiveness, necessary to ruin Natalie's chances (her *business* chances, at any rate), Katrinka consoled herself with the fact that those who knew her well knew better.

"As if you, of all people, would do a thing like that," said Daisy, echoing Katrinka's thoughts.

"Or, for that matter," said the practical Margo, "that Jean-Claude would pay any attention to you where Natalie is concerned."

"Why didn't Sabrina put *that* in her column?" said Alexandra, meaning that Jean-Claude and Natalie had once been lovers, as everyone knew, and had continued over the years to be good friends. "Since she's so interested in raking over dirt."

"I hope Mark van Hollen had the grace to apologize," said Daisy.

"Yes," replied Katrinka, "but I did tell him really no apology was necessary."

He had been the first to tell her about the column, preparing her for the arrival of the faxes. "I'm sorry," he had said, "but there's nothing I can do. I don't interfere with my journalists." That wasn't quite true. Mark van Hollen's name was rarely mentioned in his own newspapers, no matter what he was up to. When Katrinka had once pointed that out to him, Mark had insisted it was due to the discretion of his senior editors, not to any direct intervention by him. That, she supposed, was a question of how you defined influence.

"But, you know," said Lucia, "being realistic about this, any hint that you and he are lovers could cause you a lot of trouble."

"Who?" said Katrinka, startled.

"You and Jean-Claude," replied Margo impatiently.

"You're not, are you?" asked Daisy.

"It is nonsense," said Katrinka, annoyed now. "All nonsense."

"Who would blame you?" said Zuzka, who had harbored the same suspicion. "Nobody. You deserve him."

"A cutthroat businessman, with no morals," said Katrinka, with a laugh. "Unfaithful to his wife *and* his mistress. You do think I'm *so* crazy?"

Zuzka smiled. "You do know what I say."

"Well," said Daisy defensively, "there's definitely some-

9

thing very odd about you lately, Katrinka, my dear. And I can't quite put my finger on it."

"I tell you what it is," said Katrinka. "I stopped being heartbroken. It was *so* boring." Her friends laughed, and again she felt that small twinge of guilt at not being able to tell them the whole truth. Oh, well, she consoled herself, just a few more days.

The busboy cleared away the luncheon plates and the waiter appeared carrying desserts: a chocolate gateau under an elaborate spun-sugar cage, fruit tarts, a crème brûlée, a strawberry shortcake. "With the compliments of the pastry chef," he said, knowing that otherwise they would be refused.

Katrinka's name was written in chocolate around the edge of the plate. She knew she should not eat it, but recently she was having a hard time saying no to food. *"Ay yi yi yi,"* she murmured as she picked up her fork and took a piece of the gateau, "am I in trouble?"

"Dead," said Zuzka appreciatively, her mouth closing around a bite of strawberry shortcake.

"I'm over my limit," said Margo, looking regretfully at the crème brûlée. "Very definitely over the top."

"No dinner for me tonight," said Alexandra, taking a bite of apple tart. "Neil is out of town, thank God."

Lucia pushed hers reluctantly away, resisting the urge to dump salt on it (the best deterrent to temptation), and Daisy said, "I can't eat another bite. I don't care whose feelings are hurt."

There was a flurry of activity at the door and an expectant hush fell upon the room, as in a theater when the lights dim and the curtain begins slowly to rise. All eyes focused on the entrance, where Adam Graham, apparently oblivious to the attention, stood divesting himself of his charcoal-gray cashmere coat, chatting with Sam Lowenthal, his lawyer, and Sirio Maccioni, Le Cirque's dapper owner. And then the hubbub resumed, people absentmindedly returning to their conversations all the while watching to see what would happen next. The Grahams, Adam and Katrinka both, were an endless source of interest to the public, even to this public, which equaled them in wealth. The Grahams had something more than money—they had glamour, and that provided a good show wherever they went.

"Well, he is certainly gorgeous," said Daisy.

"You know what they say, gorgeous is as gorgeous does," said Alexandra.

"The sonovabitch," muttered Margo. "Did you know he was lunching here?"

Katrinka nodded. "His secretary did phone me this morning."

"Well, you're a cool one," said Margo.

"What it does matter?" said Katrinka, shrugging, inverting words, a sign that she was perhaps not so calm as she appeared.

Katrinka watched her husband as he crossed the room toward her. He was over six feet tall, with a slender, well-exercised body; thick, straight salt-and-pepper hair, brush cut; a long, thin face; large brown eyes set too close together over a prominent nose—not individually the features of a handsome man, yet somehow they combined in a way that made Adam always too attractive to women. Daisy was right, conceded Katrinka, he is gorgeous. But at least the thought did not any longer cause her heart to go thump in her breast.

He stopped at their table, said hello to each of the women and kissed Katrinka briefly on her mouth, causing Sabrina to add yet another stain to the skirt of her de la Renta. "I didn't know you'd be here today," he said to Katrinka, lying through his teeth.

"Your secretary did forget to tell you," she replied sweetly.

Adam smiled. "I don't know what's wrong with her lately."

"High-pressure jobs," said Margo. "They pickle everybody's brains sooner or later." She pulled a small gold-plated Canovas compact and bright red lipstick from her purse and began carefully to repaint her mouth.

Adam watched her a moment, wondering what bliss that mouth and thick pink tongue might provide if he could coax her into a brief fling. Then he turned his attention back to Katrinka.

Only recently had he begun to pay attention again to the way Katrinka looked, and Adam found himself thinking, as he too often did these days, that she was beautiful. She was wearing a Dior suit he had bought her in Paris two or three years before. It was in a rich, deep blue that complemented her pale azure eyes, brought out the creamy texture of her skin and the highlights in her dark straight hair. In her ears were the sapphires set with diamonds he had given her for Christmas the year before. On her lapel was a pin he did not recognize, a diamond leopard with sapphire spots and ruby eyes. He made a mental note to have his accountant check to see when and how she had been buying jewelry. She wore no rings. The only word to describe her, he thought with an unexpected pang, was radiant. "I better go," he said, inclining his head in the direction of the corner table where his chubby gray-haired lawyer waited for him. "Sam charges even when I pay for lunch," he added with a grin that again, to her relief, did not cause, as it once had, Katrinka's heart to beat faster. "Will you be home later?"

"After four," said Katrinka.

"I'll call you," he said. "We should talk."

Katrinka watched him as he walked away, thinking, with more regret than she expected, that it was, of course, much too late to talk.

"What was that about?" asked Sam as Adam slid into the seat opposite him.

"I was just being pleasant."

"Don't be. You'll encourage her to up the ante."

"No," said Adam, with the confident smile of an empire builder. It always surprised him when people, especially someone as astute as his lawyer, got that one basic fact of negotiating wrong. "People only up the ante when they're mad."

$\mathcal{A}$s the friends came out of Le Cirque into the bleak
New York afternoon, Daisy turned to Katrinka, who was
immediately behind her, and, gesturing to the gray
Mercedes sedan where a driver in a navy suit and peaked
cap stood waiting for her, said, "Do you want a lift home,
darling?"

When they were in New York, the six lived within a few
blocks of each other: Zuzka and Lucia, who spent little time
in the city, kept small apartments in the upper East Fifties;
Daisy, though her primary home was now in Italy, had an
apartment on Fifth Avenue at Sixty-third Street, where
Margo was also staying; Katrinka's duplex penthouse was
two blocks farther north; and Alexandra's town house was
on Sixty-sixth Street between Madison and Park.

"No, thank you," said Katrinka. "I'm going only to the
Praha. It's not far."

"You'll freeze in that thing," said Margo, referring to
Katrinka's short full coat, which, flaring just above her
knees, left her long legs bare to their high-heeled pumps.
The others were bundled into furs.

"Nonsense," said Katrinka, turning to Zuzka with a
laugh. "You know they never did ski mornings on the High
Tatra if they think this is cold."

Zuzka, who was leaving town the next day, hugged her
good-bye. "I wish I could stay, but . . ." She shrugged.
"When you're in love . . ."

13

"I know," said Katrinka. "Don't worry. I feel fantastic. Really."

Still doubtful, Zuzka hugged her again and was about to hail a cab when Alexandra insisted on dropping her and Lucia.

"That would be great," said Lucia, quickly kissing the others and following Zuzka into Alexandra's black Mercedes. "See you next week," she called, waving good-bye. Katrinka was giving a small dinner party in ten days' time and all except Zuzka expected to see each other there, though it was quite likely some of them might meet for lunch or dinner again in the meantime.

Margo, of course, was going with Daisy, who said, "Promise me you'll think about joining us at St. Moritz," just before the driver closed her door.

"I will," said Katrinka, not able to think of any other polite reply.

Her appointments for the day finished, Katrinka had sent her own driver home when he had dropped her at Le Cirque for lunch. It was a way of compensating him for the late nights he sometimes worked, waiting for her outside theaters, restaurants, sometimes (though less and less frequently now) discotheques, where she loved to dance into the early hours of the morning. Except for skiing, there was for Katrinka no better way in the world to ward off a bad mood than dancing.

The day was overcast, a gray mist softening the edges of the city. There was a bite in the air. Snow had been promised for evening. A security guard in plain clothes beside her, Katrinka walked quickly, her head down, careful not to meet the eyes of passersby who might recognize her from the photographs that appeared frequently in newspapers and magazines. Those who did usually just smiled in greeting, but occasionally some wanted to talk, and that was at best awkward and sometimes frightening. Entering Bloomingdale's one day several months before, she had been accosted by a man wearing a shirt, tie, and Burberry trench coat. His eyes glazed with drugs, he had muttered obscenities at her and grabbed her arm so hard it had left a bruise. Luckily, Luther, her driver, had been nearby. The man got away before the police had arrived, of course, which was just as well. That kind of publicity was not what she needed. The next morning Katrinka had hired a firm of security specialists to provide round-the-clock protection.

When she reached the corner of Sixty-fifth and Madison, Katrinka stopped, waiting for the light to change, looking across the street to the Praha, feeling the same surge of pride and pleasure she always got when confronted with its exuberant baroque facade, now in excellent repair, its trim neatly painted. Built in 1922 by Schultze and Weaver, the Praha, with its sixty-four rooms, was Katrinka's first hotel in New York, her flagship enterprise, the jewel in her crown. She had fallen in love with it at first sight, when it had summoned up for her happy memories of the buildings she had known in her youth, in Prague. At the time she had bought it, it had not been in such good shape. That had been accomplished only with months of exhausting work. But now, for the fifth year in a row, the Praha had been voted best small luxury hotel in North America.

The light changed and Katrinka crossed the street, smiling at a gray-haired woman who had managed after all to catch her eye, and hurried to the entrance of the hotel, where the doorman greeted her by name as he ushered her respectfully inside. "Hello, Luis," she said, returning his greeting. "How you doing today?"

The lobby was small and luxurious, its baroque furniture kept to a minimum so as not to overwhelm the space. As she entered, Katrinka paused briefly, enjoying the sudden warmth, taking in every detail: the seating area to the right with its gilded sofa covered in blue damask, the matching curtains, the two petit-point bergères, the carved wood tables, Meissen lamps, Aubusson carpet, French landscape paintings on the patterned silk wall. Between it and the concierge's desk was a Louis XIV buhl cabinet on top of which was a Baccarat vase with an arrangement of enormous red roses by Salou, one of New York's leading florists. Opposite the desk was the VIP "room," an alcove set off by blue damask curtains tied back with gold fringe, furnished with Louis XIV chairs and an escritoire holding another, smaller Salou arrangement of orchids; on the wall behind hung a copy of Watteau's *Embarkation for Cythera*. Beyond the alcove was the elevator. Some of the furnishings were genuine antiques; most were extremely good copies. The restaurant to the left of the entrance was done in the lighter Louis XV style, as was the dining room on the second floor.

"Good afternoon, Mrs. Graham," said the concierge, a dark-haired man in his late twenties.

"Good afternoon, Rinaldo. Would you tell housekeeping, please, there's a stain on the carpet, in front of the sofa?"

"They've already been notified, Mrs. Graham. Someone's on the way."

Pleased, Katrinka smiled at him. "Good," she said. Both of them knew that it was thanks to Rinaldo and the rest of the staff that the Praha was able to maintain the standard of luxury for which it had become known, attracting a varied clientele from movie and rock stars who required discreet service to European aristocrats who liked privacy.

Not that Katrinka was shy about acknowledging her own part in her hotel's success. False modesty seemed to her as silly (if not usually so dangerous) as the rampant egotism that was unable to admit to any help up the ladder, or concede anyone else a share in the spotlight. Katrinka was well aware of her own contribution to the Praha and to the New York and London Grahams, all three of which were always numbered among the best hotels of their size. Not only had she overseen every detail of their renovation, she had been smart enough to hire good management, energetic enough to keep them on their toes, and secure enough to allow them the freedom they needed to operate efficiently. She had, in addition, devoted enormous time and energy to promoting them, as a result of which there were few travelers left, from Brasilia to Tokyo, who did not know the name and reputation of at least one, and probably more, of the Graham hotels.

The executive offices were on the second floor in a suite of rooms across the lobby from the Koruna, the less expensive of the hotel's two restaurants, serving breakfast, lunch, afternoon tea, and a light supper on Wedgwood china in a pretty peach-and-white rococo room. The staff was setting up for tea as Katrinka got off the elevator and stopped to talk for a minute with the Koruna's hostess, who supplied her with a rundown of the week's business. Given the state of the economy, it had not been bad.

The entrance into the executive suite was through an anteroom. "Hello, Dennis," said Katrinka to the receptionist as she walked past him through the door leading to the inner office.

"Good afternoon," the young man responded, smiling nervously. He was a little afraid of her, though he wasn't sure why. She had always been nice to him.

Unlike the rest of the hotel, the executive suite was the epitome of high-tech style, secretaries and assistants seated at workstations carefully designed to avoid the stresses and plagues of modern technology. Each had a computer linked to a central laser printer and at least four phone lines. The requisite fax machine occupied a corner and the two executive offices had television monitors and VCRs. There was a small kitchenette with a coffee maker and electric kettle, mini-refrigerator and microwave. Sharing the suite with Katrinka was Michael Ferrante, the hotel's general manager, their secretaries, Katrinka's assistant, and a clerk.

Katrinka's own office, decorated in soft peach tones, was in a more traditional style, with an antique partner's desk flanked by Queen Anne chairs and a seating area composed of two facing sofas upholstered in a Fortuny print and separated by an Italian glass table.

What did he want to talk about? she wondered as she sat behind her desk, remembering Adam's parting words to her. Whatever it was, she promised herself, she would not get upset.

"Katrinka?" Her assistant, Robin Dougherty, was standing beside her, a folder in her hand. "Are you all right?"

"Yes, fine," said Katrinka, though she jumped a bit. She had not heard Robin come in.

"You had such a funny look on your face," said Robin. Now in her mid-twenties, Robin had worked for Katrinka for over seven years, was privy to most (though not all) of what went on in Katrinka's life, and was devoted to her. A pretty redhead with a smattering of freckles across her snub nose, Robin—to the dismay of her Irish Catholic family—had recently moved into her boyfriend's Brooklyn apartment: to cut expenses, they said. They were planning to marry as soon as they had saved enough money for a down payment on a house, which, Katrinka conceded, was very practical if not at all romantic. She herself had a very strong romantic streak, though at the moment she was trying hard to follow Robin's example and let her mind for once overrule her heart.

"I'm a little tired," said Katrinka, feeling suddenly exhausted. These waves of fatigue were happening too frequently of late, and she found them more annoying than worrying. She took the folder from Robin and began to review her mail, most of it invitations to attend various events and to chair others, all of which she would refuse politely, pleading prior engagements: her schedule for the next few months was too uncertain for her to be able to commit herself to anything, which would surprise the people who said, with good reason, that they could always count on Katrinka Graham. These same people would make assumptions about why she was refusing, and would be wrong.

The one invitation she did tell Robin to accept was for a photo layout in *Town and Country.* It would be good publicity, and, though business had picked up from the early part of the year when it had been devastated by the effects of the Gulf War, still it was far from healthy. Photographs of her in next March's edition, working out (if she could convince the editor) in the specially designed exercise suites in the Praha and the Graham—her hotel on Seventy-third Street between Madison and Park—would result, she knew, in a substantial increase in bookings for April and May. But the layout would have to be done quickly, or it would be too late. "If *Town and Country* don't want it," she told Robin, "call Alice Zucker at *Chic.* She will love it." Since Alice had replaced Margo Jensen as fashion editor, she had been trying hard to establish the same kind of close relationship with Katrinka as her predecessor had enjoyed. But, from the start, Margo and Katrinka had been more than business associates (that is, people who used each other for mutual

18

advancement), they had been friends, though in New York the distinction was always hard to detect.

Finished with the mail, Katrinka reviewed the package deal she had worked out with the CEO of Adam's cruise-ship line. It was similar to others the two companies had had in effect for years and looked fine to her, but perhaps the agreement was what Adam wanted to discuss? She searched the document but, though she had developed a keen instinct these past few months for second-guessing her husband, could find nothing to which he might object. She pushed the papers to the side and began returning her phone calls, taking them in order, proceeding down the page from first to last, ticking each one off as she completed it, never leaving the office until she had returned them all. When she saw her mother-in-law's name, she groaned. Today she was not in the mood to deal with Nina Graham. In truth, she was never in the mood to deal with her. Nevertheless, Katrinka dutifully dialed the Newport number and waited as the phone rang, feeling the anxiety that only Nina Graham could produce in her begin to knot in her stomach. What could she want *now?* wondered Katrinka. But the elder Mrs. Graham was not then at home, announced Edward, her butler, to Katrinka's relief. "Tell her I did call back, please," said Katrinka, supplying no helpful information about her own availability. "Bye, Edward."

"Busy?" said Michael Ferrante from the doorway. He was a good-looking man in his late forties, with large brown eyes, a long straight nose, generous mouth, and a mop of curly dark hair that New York's finest hairdressers had failed to tame. It added to his charm somehow, complementing rather than detracting from the perfect tailoring of his charcoal pin-striped Canali suit and the brilliant shine of his Ralph Lauren shoes. He had worked as an assistant manager at the Carlyle before Katrinka had tempted him away to help her with the Praha. Somehow she had convinced him that the untidy heap of rubble he was looking at would one day be a first-class hotel. His wife had thought him crazy to take a chance on what seemed such a long shot. She had imagined their brand-new house in Teaneck reclaimed by the bank, their daughters condemned to go without Nikes and college educations. What good was a raise in salary, she argued, if you were out of a job in a year? Happily, she had been wrong, which, since she was a good if timid person, she now cheerfully admitted. "Michael never listens to me," she announced often, adding, with a laugh, "thank God."

Katrinka motioned him in and Michael sank into one of the Queen Anne chairs opposite her. "Problems?" she asked.

"The GP," he replied, using a code that was alternately explained as meaning either the "German Prince" or the "German Prick," depending on with whom they happened to be discussing the matter. Both names aptly described the person in question.

"He still did not pay his bill?"

"He hasn't even offered an excuse."

Normally a problem of nonpayment would not have filtered so far up the chain of command before being turned over to collectors, but this minor member of the former German royal family was, if not exactly a friend of the Grahams, at least a close acquaintance. They ran in the same circles, attended the same parties, skied the same slopes.

"Is he broke?" asked Michael.

"No," said Katrinka. "He did make a killing on the last KKR takeover. Millions. He's just cheap. How much does he owe?"

"He had the penthouse suite for over a week. Plus food, drinks." Michael referred to the sheaf of papers in his hand. "Nineteen thousand, six hundred."

"No way we write that off." She sat quietly for a moment, thinking, then she smiled. "I tell you what we do," she said. "We leak the story to Sabrina."

"How?" said Michael. "You know she won't print anything we give her."

"Don't worry. I'll find a way." Maybe Mark would do it as a favor? After all, he owed her one. Then she changed her mind. "Who needs Sabrina? Rick Colins will help." Rick, in addition to being a free-lance journalist and a friend, had a cable network show, a combination of gossip and inter-

20

views, which everyone (well, everyone who counted) watched.

"I don't see what good it will do even if he does use the item."

"It's simple. When it appears, I do call the GP to apologize, saying I don't know how the story got out. He asks me to deny it. I say I will, of course, no problem. The check will come Federal Express. Guaranteed."

"How can you be so sure?"

"I do know him. He has an ego this big," she said, extending her arms. "He hates to be embarrassed."

Michael laughed. "What a devious mind you've got."

"If he had no money," she said, "that would be a different story." Katrinka would not have been capable of dunning anyone in real financial trouble. But she had been raised to despise those who shirked their responsibilities, who were lazy, who lied their way out of difficulties, who did not always do their best, who had no consideration for others. People, she believed, should do what they said and pay what they owed. Even after years of living in New York, it still sometimes surprised her when they did not.

Her business with Michael completed, Katrinka spent a few minutes on the phone with the manager of the Graham, then left her office, walking the short distance home to her Fifth Avenue apartment, accompanied as always by the security guard. They chatted as they walked, but Katrinka's mind was not on the conversation. It was dusk already and the temperature had dropped, the chill settling in her bones. Suddenly, she felt as if a belt of ice around her chest was being drawn tighter and tighter. She was afraid, she realized. Terrified. But of what? Not of Adam, surely. Nor of anything else she could name—except perhaps that, as before, this new happiness of hers might be snatched abruptly, terribly, away.

21

Three

"ea, Anna," Katrinka said to her housekeeper as the woman helped her out of her coat. "Chamomile, please. It did turn so nasty. I am chilled to the bone."

"Mr. Graham called. He said he would call again later," said Anna, her tone neutral. She had never cared for Adam but, even now, was reluctant to make her dislike obvious.

Katrinka looked at her watch. It was only five past four. Calling promptly. That was a new departure for Adam. "I'll be in the library," she said.

"Yes, Mrs. Graham." A plump, pretty gray-haired widow with two daughters, Anna Bubeník had emigrated to the United States with her husband after the communist take-over in Czechoslovakia in 1948. She had been with the Grahams since shortly after their marriage and had grown very attached to Katrinka, tending to worry about her as much as she did her own children. Now, as she folded the coat neatly and laid it across one of the tall MacIntosh armchairs in the hall—she would hang it up later, after getting Katrinka her tea—Anna watched Katrinka moving quickly across the living room to the library. The poor thing looked exhausted, she thought, and hurried downstairs to the kitchen to put the kettle on. Too much work, too much travel, too many late nights, that was the problem.

Anna took a dainty Spode cup and saucer from the cabinet, put the chamomile teabag into a matching china pot, poured in the boiling water, and placed everything on a silver tray, which she picked up with a sigh. She wished

Katrinka would take better care of herself, especially now, she thought, as she entered the library and found Katrinka sitting in the window seat, staring out at Central Park, across to where the pond should be, invisible now because of the mist. Only the street lamps, which had just come on, interrupted the dark with halos of faint light.

"Your tea, Mrs. Graham."

"Thank you, Anna," said Katrinka, turning away from the window and adjusting her vision to the room's interior. She got up, turned on another lamp, then sat on the quilted beige banquette that ran along the wall under the Chinese screen.

"Will you be having dinner in this evening?"

"Yes. And tonight it will be just me."

"Would you like some swordfish?"

"That would be fine, grilled. And some vegetables, whatever there is." Katrinka had let the chef go earlier in the year. The former live-in staff of five had been reduced to just Anna. A housemaid came in daily to help with the cleaning, and a laundress twice a week. When she had people to dinner, Katrinka now used caterers, and a seamstress she had employed for years was on call to attend to clothing repairs and alterations when needed.

"Yes, Mrs. Graham," said Anna, turning to leave, then remembering. "You have mail, on your desk. And a Federal Express letter. It arrived about an hour ago."

"Thank you," said Katrinka. Left alone, she drank her tea, leafing as she did so through the latest copy of *W*. She read several newspapers every day—*The New York Times, The Wall Street Journal, The Chronicle*—and skimmed *The Daily News, The Post, Newsday, Women's Wear Daily,* and the periodicals as they arrived. What she missed seeing herself, friends inevitably sent faxes of, as she did to them when she noticed articles she thought might interest them. Books she read evenings when she was at home and on vacation, light fiction usually, for entertainment, and some biography, though she never missed a work by Kundera and liked to reread Kafka's *The Castle* from time to time. It had been one of her mother's favorite books and reading it made Katrinka feel close to her.

Katrinka finished the tea and closed the paper. She felt better now, the chill gone from her body as well as that strange flash of fear. Leaving the tea tray for Anna to clear away, she went along the corridor to her study to have a look at her mail.

The apartment was a duplex consisting of six bedrooms, a sitting room, library, and dining room all on the top level, with a kitchen, butler's pantry, five staff rooms, and a laundry room on the lower. The rooms, except for the library, were large, with high ceilings—it was a prewar building—and that, combined with the terrace that ran around the entire upper floor, gave the apartment a feeling of great spaciousness.

Katrinka had decorated to please Adam, softening the high-tech minimalist style of his bachelor pad without retreating into the fussy traditional look of his parents' Newport home. Working with Carlos Medina, a young designer most people credited her with discovering, she had used neutral tones and beautiful woods, overstuffed furniture and antique accents, a Biedermeier chest, a Charles X pedestal table, a Degas bronze in a corner, Adam's collection of modern paintings on the walls, creating a contemporary home of elegant simplicity. Adam had loved it. But then he had loved everything she did.

Katrinka switched on the light in her study, crossed to her desk, and picked up the Federal Express envelope that lay on top of the pile of mail, ignoring the rest as well as the coil of paper her fax machine had spit out in her absence. She read the name of the sender and felt, as always of late, a spasm of despair grip her stomach. Zeiss Associates.

For so many years now, she had opened one kind of envelope or another from Zeiss, and always, no matter what information the enclosed report contained, it had ended with the same disappointing phrase: "We deeply regret that our efforts on your behalf have so far been unsuccessful . . ." This one would be no different, she was sure. Ripping open the cardboard Federal Express envelope and the manila one inside, she removed the sheaf of papers and began to read.

"Oh, my God," she murmured once, softly. She read through to the end, then, sitting down in her desk chair, she switched on the lamp and read the report again, to be sure she had understood correctly.

She felt the tears running down her face and brushed them away. After so many years, for this to happen now. It was unbelievable, bewildering, terrifying. It would change everything. Everything.

"Oh, my God," she murmured once, softly. She read through to the end, then, sitting down in her desk chair, she switched on the lamp and read the report again, to be sure she had understood correctly.

She felt the tears running down her face and brushed them away. After so many years, for this to happen now. It was unbelievable, bewildering, terrifying. It would change everything. Everything.

The
Past

---◆---

1953 – 1971

Four

JUANA TRUMP

$\mathcal{K}$atrinka was four years old and skiing down a mountain that to her seemed very steep, its base out of sight beyond the curving downhill terrain. She had had her first lesson at the beginning of October, and now, a month later, though the skis already felt familiar, she knew she could still not get them always to do what she wanted, as her father could.

"Weight on your left foot," she heard him call. He was skiing in front of her, looking back over his shoulder to be sure she was all right.

She shifted her weight onto her left foot and began the turn to the right, back across the hill.

"Good," her father called. "Remember, keep your skis parallel."

That was easier said than done. Her face puckered in concentration as she tried to flatten her right ski, which insisted for some reason on turning into its edge.

"Now, weight on your right foot," called her father.

Again and again, following her father's instructions, Katrinka shifted her weight from ski to ski, traversing the hill, feeling more and more sure of herself. Her mother had been worried that this slope was too advanced and had tried to talk her father out of letting her try. But Katrinka had been sure she could do it, and she had been right. The problem was that her mother was not at all athletic.

It was a clear, cold morning, early enough so that the slopes were not yet crowded. The few skiers who went past, leaving a plume of snow in their wake, were all much older than she, Katrinka was happy to note. The little kids would come out later, and most would stay at the bottom of the hill, on the kindergarten slopes, where the terrain was broader and not so steep. That's where Katrinka had skied until this morning.

"Katrinka, flatten your left ski," called her father.

It was on its edge again. "Stupid ski," she muttered impatiently. Then, suddenly, instead of traversing, she was schussing straight down the hill. Katrinka's heart began to pound with excitement. She felt wonderful, as if she were flying. She wanted to laugh. But only for a moment, until she realized she could not stop. Terror gripped her. *"Taťi,"* she shouted.

Turning, Jirka Kovář saw his four-year-old daughter, looking like a small red ball in her bulky red sweater and ski pants, hurtling toward him, her dark braid whipping out in the wind behind, ski tips on the fall line increasing her speed down the icy slope. His immediate response was a fear almost as great as Katrinka's. But she was in no real danger, he assessed quickly, positioning himself to catch her if she could not stop herself. "Snowplow," he called calmly. "Tips together, tails apart to slow down."

Katrinka tried to do as he said, but she was not slowing down at all, she knew, but moving faster and faster forward. Soon, as the terrain curved, she would zoom past her father and run straight over the edge of the cliff. *"Taťi,"* she shouted again.

"You'll be all right," he said reassuringly. "Just snowplow, Katrinka."

What did he think she was trying to do? It wasn't her fault her stupid skis wouldn't listen. Then she remembered what he had taught her during her first lesson and let herself go limp, flopping down into the snow and sliding a few feet on the slick surface before coming to a stop.

"Katrinka, are you all right?" Now, for the first time, she could hear the worry in her father's voice.

The wind had been knocked out of her and she had banged her head as well as her bottom. For an instant Katrinka was tempted to cry, then reconsidered. If she did

30

that, maybe her father would never let her ski again. And what if her mother found out and thought she had been hurt? She sat up and reached for the pointed red wool cap, which had fallen off into the snow. "Yes," she called as she pulled it down over her ears.

As he began the laborious climb up toward the bright red mark in the white hillside, Jirka saw his friend Ota Černý schuss down and flip to a stop beside Katrinka.

"I fell down," she said.

"So I see," he replied. He was a good-looking man an inch or so taller than her father, with fair hair, hazel eyes, and the perennially tanned skin of the sportsman. "Can you get up?" he asked.

"Oh, yes," she said eagerly, wanting to show off her expertise, her fear totally forgotten.

Watching from where he had stopped on the hillside, Jirka saw his daughter pull herself skillfully to a standing position. She really does handle herself well, he thought proudly.

"Very good," said Ota, smiling down at her fondly.

"Yesterday, I fell all the time," she admitted. "Today I'm much better. I never cry," she added.

He reached out and tugged her dark braid, regretting—as always when he was with Katrinka—that he and Olga had no child of their own.

"Ready, Katrinka?" called Jirka.

"Coming, Tati," she called, arranging her body in the proper position, leaning forward, knees relaxed, feet at an angle. Using her poles, she pushed off. "Bye," she called to Ota.

After a moment, Ota too pushed off, schussing down, lifting a ski pole in salute as he sped past first the little girl, then her father. "See you later," he called.

Mimicking him, Katrinka lifted a ski pole, but the unfamiliar movement cost her control of the turn. Her right ski rolled inward, and she thought she was going to fall again.

"Concentrate," called her father.

Determined not to go down again quite yet, frowning with the effort of it, Katrinka flattened her ski and turned into the hillside, recovering, before changing edges for the next turn.

"Good girl," said Jirka.

Looking back over his shoulder at her, Ota smiled.

The two families, the Kovářs and the Černýs, were friends, though the wives did not have much in common. Like her husband, Olga Černý was an athlete; and like him, too, her hopes of competing in the Olympics had been dashed by the war.

Milena Kovář was not at all athletic. Just the opposite, in fact. People teased her about being an intellectual, though of course she knew she was not. Great thoughts and original ideas did not crowd her mind, though she loved to read, not only Kafka and Häsek but Bohumil Říha and Jan Očenášek, the popular novelists who managed somehow to circumvent government restrictions. She had worked as a librarian before Katrinka was born, and, if there was not another child soon, she would return to it when Katrinka started school.

The Kovářs and the Černýs came from Svitov, which used to be called something else before the communists took over in 1948 and changed everything, including place names. The city, once the largest manufacturer of crystal in the world, was in the province of Moravia, Czechoslovakia's garden, producer of the best fruits and vegetables, the best wines in the country—or so the Moravians thought. Jirka Kovář was an assistant manager at the city's sports complex, and Ota Černý taught physical education at the technical college and coached the local ski team as well, a job which kept him occupied most winter weekends. Both men earned salaries good enough to cover luxuries like inexpensive holidays and, because Olga worked too, the Černýs could afford a car, a small Škoda. She taught languages at the gymnasium: Russian, which every Czech schoolchild now had to learn, and French, only God knew why, since almost no one but diplomats could get a visa for France.

This weekend, in the Černýs' Škoda, the two families had driven to Nový Smokovec, a sprawling resort in the High Tatra Mountains of Slovakia. The Apollo, where they were staying, was a small timbered inn, only thirteen rooms, with views of snow-covered mountains quilted with patches of dense pine forests. Far from luxurious, the inn was scrupulously clean and comfortable, with simple pine furniture in the rooms and a bathroom and WC on each floor. Worn upholstered sofas and chairs formed seating areas in the lounge, where a fire blazed in an enormous hearth. Another hearth, even larger, was the central feature of the paneled dining room, where, at night, the plain wood tables were covered with carefully ironed linen cloths.

"You should come with us tomorrow," urged Jirka, who never stopped trying to interest his wife in his favorite pastime.

Milena shook her red head and laughed. "Not me. I'll stay here warm and comfortable and happy, thank you very much." She never minded when the others went off and left her. It allowed her long uninterrupted hours to read, to work on her needlepoint, to knit. Even as a child she had enjoyed her solitude, never getting bored, always finding ways to keep herself amused.

"It's fun, *Mami,*" said Katrinka. "When you don't fall." The grown-ups laughed and Katrinka smiled, delighted, wondering what she could have said to amuse them.

They had just finished dinner, potato soup, which Katrinka did not like, followed by meat loaf with three kinds of meat, which she did, and for dessert, her favorite *palačinky,* thin raspberry-filled crepes covered with hot chocolate, almonds, and whipped cream. Now the grown-ups lingered over big cups of strong Turkish coffee, and Katrinka tried to hide a yawn because she was not yet ready to be banished to the cot set up for her in her parents' room.

"Ready for bed, *andeličku?*" asked her mother, stubbing out her cigarette in the ashtray nearest her.

Katrinka shook her head.

"We have to be up early in the morning," said Jirka, who preferred to coax rather than order.

"You spoil her," said Olga.

A short, plain woman, Olga had fallen in love, during the war, with a boy who was later executed by the Nazis for his involvement with Obrana nafoda, one of the four major Czech resistance groups. Only sixteen, pregnant, devastated by her lover's death, Olga had terminated the pregnancy.

When she met Ota, at a World Cup skiing competition in 1947, she thought she had been given a second chance at life. But a year or so after her marriage, when she visited a doctor to see why she had not yet become pregnant, she learned that her self-induced abortion had so damaged her that she would never have a child.

Torn between longing and resentment, Olga reached out a hand to stroke Katrinka's shiny dark head. "Children need discipline," she said.

Ota looked at Katrinka's plump, sleepy face, her skin as soft as a rose petal, her high cheekbones, her slanted eyes the light, brilliant color of turquoises. She was wearing a ruffled blue wool dress Milena had made for her. "She looks like an angel in that dress," he said indulgently.

"Not quite," said Jirka, laughing. As much as he loved his daughter, he had quite an accurate reading of her character: loving, intelligent, and courageous without doubt, but headstrong and impetuous as well. "There are no wings yet on this little girl."

"I felt like I had wings," said Katrinka, interrupting, remembering the heady sensation of speeding down the mountain in those few wonderful moments before the panic had set in. "I felt like I was flying."

"To me," said Ota, "you looked like you were crashlanding."

"Oh," said Katrinka, crestfallen.

"Did she take a bad fall?" asked Milena. "I knew that trail was too advanced for her." She turned accusingly to Jirka.

"I didn't get hurt, *Mami,*" said Katrinka, sensing trouble.

"It was nothing," added Jirka.

"Children are so flexible," consoled Olga. "They don't get hurt as easily as adults."

"Katrinka's strong," said Ota. "She has courage. And she doesn't have bad form for such a little peanut. In fact," he continued, turning to Jirka, "I think you should enroll in the ski club and let Katrinka start racing." It was from the local ski clubs that young athletes, if they were good enough, progressed to the provincial, then the national, then to World Cup and Olympic competitions.

"Racing?" said Milena. "She's only four!"

"She'll be five in December," said Olga.

"Katrinka could be good, I think. Very good," said Ota. "And for a champion athlete, the sooner training starts, the better."

"She's too young," said Milena firmly.

"It would be good for her, Milena," said Olga.

"Really? And how many broken bones do you have in your body?"

"The issue isn't danger," interrupted Jirka, who had been weighing the advantages and disadvantages. "A broken bone here and there, what does it matter?"

"How can you say that, Jirka?" Milena looked at her daughter, imagining a chubby little arm or leg, with its deliciously soft skin, broken and in a cast.

"But even for the little children," continued Jirka, "the clubs are very competitive. I don't know that I like that."

"It's good for them," said Ota. "Competition builds character." He waved his cigarette. "Look at what's happening to this country. We're an industrious people and we're going soft and lazy."

Olga looked around nervously, checking to see if anyone was within earshot. But the dining room was emptying out, the waiters were busy clearing tables, and the few people who, like them, were lingering over coffee seemed to be deep in their own conversations and not paying any attention to the Kovářs and the Černýs. "Ota, not so loud," cautioned Olga.

"I'm only saying what's true," said Ota, nevertheless lowering his voice and leaning closer to Jirka. "Nobody wants to work hard anymore. And why should they? Do they get paid any more for working hard than for taking it easy, for doing a good job not a bad one?"

"I work hard," said Jirka. "And so do you. So do all of us."

"We're exceptions."

"As usual, Ota, you're exaggerating," said Milena.

"I am? What about your parents?"

"What about them?"

"Ota, please," said Olga. "Why argue?"

"I'm trying to make a point," said Ota stubbornly. "Your parents still have their orchard, right?" he asked Milena.

"Yes, of course. You know they do."

"Lucky for them, they slipped through a crack in the collectivization system. Too small for anybody to care about."

Milena shrugged. "As you say. Lucky for them."

"So they work from dawn to dusk every day. They study the best methods of cultivation, look for innovations to produce better fruit, they worry about sun and drought and pests, and, when after months of backbreaking labor they finally manage to produce a good crop and harvest it, what do they do?"

"They sell it."

"Yes, sell it to the state collective, for a price set artificially low. No profit to put back into the land to improve production, let alone provide them a better life. They just scrape by, year after year. Is it any wonder most people refuse to work that hard?"

"You're saying it's pointless?"

"No, I'm saying it's wonderful. To know the value of hard work is a beautiful thing. They're lucky. But in Katrinka's generation, very few will have that opportunity. And most will be athletes. Because they're the ones who will have to learn that winning requires hard work and discipline. Something we all knew before the war and have forgotten since," he added bitterly.

From 1918 Czechoslovakia had been a democracy, but, after the Nazi invasion of 1939, a totalitarian regime was established, all signs of resistance ruthlessly stamped out, schools and universities closed, all non-war-related industry prohibited, thirty thousand Czechs transported to work in Germany, and as many as fifty-six thousand political prisoners killed in concentration camps along with the Jewish population, which was virtually annihilated.

Farming was considered an essential war industry, so Milena's parents were allowed to stay on their land, along with Milena and her sister, who had been sent home from university. A son was deported to Germany and killed, so

36

the family was eventually notified, in an Allied bombing raid. The Kovářs, too, lost a son in Germany, though the circumstances of his death remained unclear, but Jirka was sent home from university to work in the local glass factory, which had been converted to military use. His father, a carpentry teacher at the local school, was allowed to continue training students who would later be put to work building for the Reich. Ota had worked in a coal mine with his father, who was killed in an accident a few months before the war ended. Now Ota spent every possible moment of his life outdoors.

Despite massive retaliation, Czech resistance to the Nazis continued throughout the war. When leaders were imprisoned or killed, the various groups reorganized, their primary activity in the early years to gather intelligence to be forwarded to London or Moscow. Toward the end of the war, guerrilla units were formed to carry out acts of sabotage, and it was these groups that later took over the administration of towns as the liberating armies expelled the Germans. The most militant of these groups was the Communist Party, the KSC, and, after the war, when Czechoslovakia remained in the Soviet sphere of influence, it was rewarded with positions in the government. Within a short time, the KSC had secured key posts, including the Ministry of Interior, giving them control of the police and security forces, which were then used to suppress dissidents. The coup, when it came in 1948, was bloodless.

And now, five years later, with gratitude toward their liberators wiped out by years of oppression, people like the Kovářs and the Černýs hated the native communists as much as they ever had the Nazi invaders, but kept their heads down and their mouths shut, making the best of a situation they believed they could not change. "At least no one is going hungry," they said, trying to console themselves for the liberty they had lost.

"Sorry," said Ota, standing up, taking another Sparta cigarette from its soft white package with its red-and-blue logo. "Beer always makes me talk too much."

"What you say," said Jirka, "makes a lot of sense."

"A smart guy, drunk or sober, eh?"

Milena opened her mouth as if about to say something, then shut it again.

"Too smart for your own good," said Olga.

"What do you think, little one?" said Ota, swinging Katrinka up into his arms to give her a good-night hug.

Katrinka's heavy eyes snapped wide open. "You smell of beer," she said.

"What did I tell you?" laughed Ota.

"Out of the mouths of babes," said Olga.

"Katrinka, mind your manners," said Milena sternly.

"Give me a kiss," said Ota.

"And one for me," said Olga.

Katrinka obliged, kissing their cheeks, and Ota then set her down on her feet. "I want to join the ski club," she said.

They all looked at her, astounded.

"Here I thought she was asleep," said Milena, looking accusingly at Ota, "and she was listening to every word we said."

"Can I?"

"No," said Milena.

"We'll see," said Jirka simultaneously. He picked her up and Katrinka smiled. She did love to ski, she thought as she fell asleep against her father's shoulder.

Five

*A*fraid of waking Katrinka, her parents postponed their argument about the ski club for another time. Instead, when they got back to their room, they laid their daughter on her cot, made hurried trips down the hall to the WC, slipped between the rough cotton sheets of their bed, and made love quietly so as not to disturb her.

The subject of the ski club was also not mentioned on the drive back to Svitov the next morning. In fact, there was little conversation of any kind, all the occupants of the Černýs' car being preoccupied with thoughts of what they had to do that day.

On either side of the two-lane road was forest, slender birches at the perimeter and, behind them, tall pines, their wide branches draped in white, their silhouettes like those of the elegant eighteenth-century court ladies in Katrinka's book of fairy tales. Snow had begun to fall, and she sat peering into the forest's dim interior, planning the ice fort she was going to build in the back garden of her grandparents' house, where she and her parents lived. Maybe she would even let Slávka, her friend from next door, help—if she promised not to complain all the time about the cold or cry when she fell down. Slávka was one of the primary reasons why Katrinka did not at all like playing with girls.

But later that day, just when Milena had begun to believe the issue completely forgotten, Katrinka, who was standing on a stool at the kitchen counter, holding a long wooden spoon, carefully stirring the contents of a large, brightly patterned pottery bowl, turned to her grandmother and said confidently, "I'm going to join the ski club."

Dana Kovář finished putting the chicken in the oven, then turned and looked at her granddaughter. "Pay attention to what you're doing," she said, in the same tone of voice that Jirka used when he was teaching someone to do something. Although Jirka looked more like his father, Honza, with the same stocky frame, dark hair, and brown eyes, he had all the petite fair-haired Dana's expressions and mannerisms, so that there was never a doubt as to whose son he was.

"I am," said Katrinka, stirring conscientiously. She was allowed to help make dumplings, to add the milk to the blended shortening and flour, and sometimes even the eggs after her grandmother had broken them open into a cup. (Once she had, when her grandmother had turned away, tried breaking the eggs herself, but shells had fallen into the mixture, and she had been banished from the kitchen for the rest of the day.) She liked watching the dumplings boil in the giant pot on the old iron stove. And especially she liked eating them, hot, sprinkled with farmer cheese and sugar, a splash of melted butter poured over them.

With Dana working, Milena did most of the housekeeping for the family, but her mother-in-law still insisted on cooking every night and the kitchen remained her personal domain, with assistants drafted as needed. It was her way of letting everyone know it was still her house, and another of the reasons why Milena longed for one of her own, though, given how cramped they all were living together, they got along amazingly well.

Before their marriage, Jirka and Milena had put their name on the list for an apartment, but there was no telling how long they would have to wait, as adequate housing was always in short supply and the method of allocating available sites erratic. Favoritism was the rule, with Communist party members getting preference. Jirka and Milena had been married now for six years and, as far as they could tell, were no closer to having a home of their own.

Joining the KSČ certainly would have made life smoother for them all. For Honza, raises in salary at the school where

he still taught woodworking and carpentry would have come
more quickly, as would those for Dana, who worked as a
switchboard operator at the city hall. Jirka's promotion to
assistant manager at the sports complex had come as a
surprise last year, though there had been no one else the
manager, one of the laziest men in Svitov, could trust to
assume most of his workload without complaining. But
Jirka was getting paid less than a party member would have
been for the same job.

Many, certainly, joined the Communist party out of
conviction. But even more did it opportunistically, a fact
that gave rise to periodic purges, the party's attempts to
cleanse itself of all but true believers. For the Kovářs (along
with most of the population), joining was never a serious
consideration. They were not only devout Catholics but
fervent nationalists. Since before the founding of the state in
1918, the family had been firmly for a free and independent
Czechoslovakia.

No one talked about freedom much anymore, at least not
out loud, in public. No one went to church very much either,
as that too the government considered subversive. Though
the churches remained opened, the priests and their congre-
gations were subject to harassment and parishioners gradually fell into the habit of going only when necessary, for
christenings and burials usually. Nor did anyone complain
in public about lack of adequate housing. Families learned
to make do, sharing what accommodation was available.
The Kovářs lived better than most, in a three-bedroom,
semidetached red-brick house that the older couple had
bought in 1921, the year Jirka was born. The tiny front yard
was all paving stones and wildflowers, with an herb garden
along the fence. In the back, Dana grew roses in which she
took enormous pride, as well as vegetables to supplement
the supply at the markets.

"Are you hungry, *miláčku?*" asked Milena as she finished
peeling the homegrown carrots that were preserved for the
winter in a bed of sand in the cellar.

"No," admitted Katrinka, remembering the *koláčky*, the
miniature cakes, she and her friend Slávka had eaten earlier
in the afternoon. "But I love dumplings."

41

"You're a little dumpling," said her grandmother, pinching her cheek lightly, not enough to hurt. Taking the bowl and spoon from Katrinka, she blended the mixture a moment more, then went to the stove and began dropping spoonsful of dough into the pot of boiling water. "So you like skiing?" she said. Katrinka nodded solemnly. "I never did," continued Dana. "But your father and grandfather, that's a different story." She looked at Milena and smiled. "I guess we know who she takes after."

"Uncle Ota says I'm good at it," said Katrinka. "And Auntie Olga."

"Did they, now?" said Dana, enjoying Katrinka's chatter without paying much attention to it. She was more concerned with getting dinner on the table at a reasonable hour. "Well, they ought to know, champion skiers like them."

"Nothing's been decided," said Milena, hoping to put an end to the conversation.

"Yes," said Katrinka stubbornly. *"Táta* said so."

"Katrinka . . ." Milena's voice trailed off, leaving the threat implicit. Good little girls did not answer their parents back.

Hating to be scolded, Katrinka dropped her eyes and began to fidget with the things her grandmother had left on the countertop.

"There's no harm in it," said Dana, taking what she perceived to be Katrinka and Jirka's side. "Fresh air and exercise. It will be good for her."

Why did no one but her, wondered Milena, think about this in terms of broken bones? "We still haven't made a decision," said Milena firmly. It was from her that Katrinka had inherited her stubbornness.

"Look," said Katrinka, taking a handful of flour from a canister and tossing it into the air. "It's snowing."

"You little imp," said her grandmother.

"Katrinka, you are naughty. Very naughty," said Milena, embarrassed.

"Out of my kitchen, now!" said Dana, her face stern, worrying Katrinka.

"I didn't mean . . ."

"Out," ordered Dana, cutting off the apology. "Go pester your grandfather for a while."

"I'm so sorry," said Milena, beginning to wipe up the flour from the countertop and floor as Katrinka, knowing she had gone too far, scampered from the room, calling for her grandfather. "I don't know what gets into that child, sometimes."

Now that the offending villain was out of sight, Dana began to laugh. "Snow," she said fondly. "Snow. What will she think of next?"

Milena had been a delicate child, falling prey to one illness after another in childhood, the most serious of which had been pneumonia. She had come close to dying of it, and, since she continued to be subject to bouts of severe inflammation of the lungs, her parents had pampered her. Unlike her brother and sister, she was not expected to help with heavy work. While they harvested the fruit from the orchards, the most Milena was required to do was feed the chickens or milk the cow and help with the washing up after dinner. She spent most of her time lying on her bed, reading books from the local library or studying for school. She was considered the scholar in the family, and her parents happily sent her off to the university in Brno to study to be a librarian. Her brother went only as far as secondary school since he, before his death in the war, wanted nothing more than one day to take over the farm. And her sister, Zdeňka, fell in love and married before she had time to think seriously about what she meant to do with the rest of her life.

Though Milena's health improved as she grew up, the habit of worry persisted, and with it a sort of cowardice that she termed being careful. It was a habit she could not break with her daughter. Though Katrinka was a robust and healthy little girl, Milena could not forget the numbers of times she had miscarried, and how close she had come to losing Katrinka. That her daughter had held on, waiting for the eighth month to be born, seemed to her as much a miracle as her own survival of pneumonia. And so Milena imitated her parents and tried to coddle her daughter. But unlike her mother, Katrinka did not cooperate. She was not fragile and studious. She was sturdy and energetic and, most important of all, she was brave.

Later that night, when everyone else had gone to bed, Jirka and Milena sat in the living room. A small room filled with new, cheaply made furniture replacing what the Nazis had confiscated during the war, it was painted a bright sunny yellow, making it cheerful during the day and at night, in the lamplight, cozy. Milena, sipping a cup of hot chocolate, which she preferred to coffee at that hour, was sitting on the print sofa. Drinking a beer, which he hoped would help him to sleep, Jirka was in the armchair opposite her, frowning, replaying the problems of the day in his mind. An inspection of the spectator stands had shown some in need of immediate structural repair, and Jirka had suggested closing that particular facility until the work was done, but the manager and the rest of the committee had rejected this suggestion as too radical and had insisted on the season's going ahead as planned despite the danger. Now it was up to Jirka to figure out how to get the repairs done without interfering with the various events, at the same time making sure that no one was hurt during a match. And, if he failed, the responsibility for the resulting mess would surely fall on his shoulders, that being the way of the world in Svitov.

"You have to talk to Katrinka about the ski club," said Milena.

"Hmmn?" he murmured, returning his attention to his wife. How beautiful she was, he thought, her hair blazing like fire in the lamplight. She was tall, almost as tall as he, with a slender, youthful body and skin like silk. He had fallen in love with her the first time he had seen her, in the university library, when they were both students finishing their degrees after the war. Entranced by the fall of her red hair over the textbook on the table, he had sat staring at her, wanting to see her face. And when finally she had lifted her head, smoothing her hair back with one exquisitely delicate

44

hand, his breath had caught in his throat, she was so beautiful. She had a short, straight nose, high cheekbones, a full mouth, and eyes blue as cornflowers. But her face had had none of the arrogance of beauty. She looked sad and serious and even a little lonely, he thought, which was why he dared to wait for her on the steps of the library and ask her to go with him for a coffee. She had said no that time, but, after running into him here and there for a few weeks, finally she had smiled and agreed. She had a lovely smile, which Katrinka had inherited, too, like the high cheekbones and slanted eyes, though Katrinka's were a much paler blue. Only her dark hair came from Jirka. Katrinka. That's why Milena seemed so worried. "Why do I have to speak to Katrinka?"

"She thinks you promised she could join the ski club."

"I didn't promise."

"That's what I told her. But she won't listen to me."

Jirka took a sip of beer. "Well," he said, "I've been thinking."

"She can't get everything she wants, just because she wants it, Jirka," said Milena. "I've been thinking, too. Olga is right. We spoil her."

"She's a good girl."

"You wouldn't think so if you'd seen her tossing flour around your mother's kitchen tonight."

"Did she do that?"

Milena nodded. " 'It's snowing,' she said." Jirka laughed, and Milena's frown softened to a smile, as it often did when she looked at him. "You're as bad as your mother. You'll let her get away with anything." What had first attracted Milena to her husband was not his good looks, but his air of confidence, his high spirits, his energy, though sometimes, like now, she found his refusal to be worried by what worried her irritating, and his boundless energy exhausting.

"What do you have against the ski club?"

"For you, nothing. But Katrinka's too young." Milena was frowning again. "I thought you didn't like the idea either."

"I had some reservations."

"And you don't now?"

"As I said, I've been thinking." Jirka took another sip of beer. "About the advantages," he added.

"Advantages!"

"Think what this could mean if Ota is right and Katrinka could someday ski competitively."

"For God's sake, Jirka, the child is four years old."

"You heard Ota. The younger an athlete starts training, the better."

"She's a baby, not an athlete! You're letting your imagination run away with you."

It occurred to Jirka that Milena was possibly the only person in Czechoslovakia with whom he could be having this argument. The country was sports mad. Every city had a federation, SOKOL, an umbrella organization under which all the various sports clubs functioned. From these clubs the best athletes were chosen for teams to compete with other cities for provincial championships, then with other provinces for national championships. Those selected for the national team went on to the World Cup and the Olympic games. It was SOKOL that had built and now ran the sports complex where Jirka worked.

"No, I'm not," he said. "I'm just thinking ahead a little, planning for my family." He put the bottle of pilsen down on the table and moved from his chair to the sofa, to be closer to her. He wanted to take her hand but did not dare, she was glaring at him with such anger. "Milena, look, you see how things are now, how hard it is for anyone to get ahead, to get a decent job, earn good money."

"We do all right," she said stubbornly, not wanting to be convinced of whatever it was he was trying to tell her.

"Christ, we can't even get a house of our own!" He ran his hands through his hair, leaving it sticking up wildly all over his head.

Milena resisted the urge to smooth it back into place. "It's only a matter of time," she said, not really believing it.

"Time, and influence." He leaned back into the stiff horsehair sofa and said in a more reasonable tone, "You want the best for Katrinka, don't you?"

"How can you even ask?"

"Well, let's say Ota is right, and Katrinka turns out to be a good athlete. You know what communist countries are like, Milena. Nothing will be too good for her. She'll have the best food, the best clothing, the best education, freedom to travel, her living expenses will be paid, and when she's too old to race, she'll have money saved and a job as a trainer guaranteed. It would be a good life for her."

"And what if she's hurt?" wailed Milena, finally getting to what for her was the heart of the matter.

"You can't keep her wrapped in cotton forever," said Jirka angrily. "I won't let you. *She* won't let you."

Then both remembered Dana and Honza asleep upstairs and grew quiet, Milena stifling her sobs. "And you can't treat her like a son. She's not. She's your daughter."

"I'd never force Katrinka to do anything she doesn't want to do. You know that. But this is something, for now at least, she does want." Jirka leaned forward again and this time did take Milena's hand. "Why not give her the chance?"

Milena nodded. She really had no choice, no way of fighting a husband and child allied against her. Jirka tugged on her hand and pulled her across to him and settled her on his lap. "Do you mind very much that I can't give you a son?" she said. She had had one miscarriage before Katrinka and two afterward. The year before, there had been a stillborn boy.

"That's in God's hands," he replied. "Not yours." He kissed her. "I love Katrinka," he said. "I love you."

"Not here," she whispered as she felt his hands moving inside her dress.

"It's all right," he murmured reassuringly. "Everyone's asleep."

47

Six

The Kovářs paid the fee of five korunas each and joined the ski club, even Milena, who was not prepared to let her husband and daughter go off without her every weekend. On Friday afternoon, with the other members of the club, they boarded a bus in front of the sports complex—eighty people that weekend, men, women, and children, needing two buses to accommodate them all—and traveled to the club's lodge, called a *chata*, about half an hour away in the mountains near the provincial border with Slovakia. It was a jolly group, consisting mostly of families who had skied with each other for years and newcomers already known to one or several of the other members, so easy conversation alternated with song on the trip. Katrinka sang along with the others, traditional polkas like the *Poslední* or popular songs by Karel Gott and Jiří Korn, prompted by her mother when she forgot the words.

There were some small children, though few as young as Katrinka, and most of those were boys. The older children were more evenly mixed, as were the adults. The majority were recreational skiers of varying abilities. Some were members of the local ski team who trained with the club on weekends. A handful, like Milena, were there simply to accompany someone else.

A few miles from the lodge, the road came to an end. The buses pulled into a parking area, at the far end of which was a small hut with a phone, and the passengers disembarked to complete the journey on foot.

48

"We have to walk?" asked Katrinka, looking around her in dismay as everyone in sight seemed to be slipping into their backpacks. These contained provisions of food and clothing for the weekend, along with books and games to while away the time. Some people had musical instruments, guitars and harmonicas mostly, a few balalaikas. People here for the first time, like the Kovářs, had skis to carry as well.

"It's not that far," said Jirka reassuringly, though even to him the distance seemed formidable, seven kilometers through snow, uphill all the way. He helped Katrinka with her knapsack, then slipped into his own. "You can make it, can't you?"

Katrinka stared into the dusk. A narrow lane of virgin snow marked the road cut through the pine forest and her eyes followed it until it disappeared into a curve of the steeply rising mountain. "I don't see the *chata,*" she said, evading her father's question. This was not turning out to be as much fun as she had thought.

The trip was always difficult. In bad weather, it was dangerous. The phone in the hut was to alert staff at the lodge that a group was on the way. A safety precaution. If the group failed to appear in what was considered a reasonable amount of time, a search party was sent out.

It had snowed the day before and the accumulation lay knee high on the ground. Ota called the lodge, and the group began the climb, a straggling line in ski sweaters, parkas, and pointed woolen hats faded to gray by the failing light, kept to a semblance of order by the club's instructors, Ota leading the way, his flashlight setting the route, bulldozing a path as he walked. He was a powerful man, in peak physical condition, and the effort did not seem to tax him at all, despite the heavy knapsack. Occasionally, he would look back to be sure the group had not got away from him. "That's it," he called, his voice full of energy, spurring them on. "Not much farther now."

"What would it be like if it was snowing?" asked Milena.

"Hell," replied Olga, who had dropped back to walk with them. With her muscular legs in their tight ski pants sticking out from under a bulky quilted jacket, a pointed navy cap on

49

her head, Olga looked like a character from a set of children's blocks.

"How far is it?" asked Katrinka, a plaintive note creeping into her voice. Her feet in their snow boots were beginning to feel very heavy.

"A big girl like you doesn't want to be carried," said Olga.

Yes, she did, very much, but did not like to say so, at least not to Olga. Though Ota was always scolding her for one thing or another, it was Olga who seemed to Katrinka to be judging her, to be looking for some terrible flaw in her character. She turned around to her father, hoping he would sweep her off her feet and up onto his shoulders as he often did when she was tired. But this time he had enough to manage with the skis. He smiled at her. "That's the girl, Katrinka," he said encouragingly. "We're almost there."

There were, in fact, two *chatas*, the Rys and the Orlik, large wooden chalets with steeply pitched roofs set on adjacent snow-covered hills a short walk apart, each accommodating between forty and fifty people. Both had large kitchens, dining and recreation areas, and dormitory-style bedrooms with whitewashed walls, containing a coal stove, six cots (for one or two families depending on their size), and lockers where personal possessions could be stored between visits. The bathrooms and WCs were at the ends of the corridors. The Kovářs were assigned to the Orlik, to a room with another family, the Lukánskýs, who had two daughters, Olinka and Ilona, six and seven respectively. Both girls had skied the year before and, from the pinnacle of that vast experience, seemed to doubt Katrinka's estimate of her abilities.

"How old are you?" Ilona, the elder sister, asked.

"Four," said Katrinka, jumping up and down on her cot, trying to keep warm. Jirka had filled the coal stove and lit it, but the room was still icy cold. "But I'll be five in December. The end of December," she added to be accurate.

"I'll bet she can't ski," the girl whispered to her younger sister. "I'll bet she's lying."

"I can too," said Katrinka.

50

"Now, girls," said their mother. "Don't argue. You'll find out soon enough what's true."

"Stop jumping on the bed, Katrinka," warned Milena, who decided to be diplomatic. The two families would be spending many weekends together over the winter.

I'll show them, thought Katrinka.

Each family was responsible for preparing its own meals, and the common areas that night, as every night, were scenes of cheerful confusion, the smells of sausage and goulash and cabbage mingling with the sounds of laughter and children's games, adult chatter and childish squabbles. After dinner, people played chess, checkers, cards. Those who could picked out tunes on their guitars or played their harmonicas and balalaikas while others sang and sometimes danced in front of the fire. The mood was cheerful, festive. Exhausted, Katrinka fell asleep in her father's lap and Jirka carried her upstairs to bed.

When she awakened in the morning, Katrinka did not at first remember where she was, or why there were two strange girls sleeping in the beds next to her. It was cold, too, and she did not like being cold. One of the little girls, Olinka, opened her eyes, saw Katrinka, and stuck out her tongue. Then Katrinka remembered. All at once she felt happy, excited, as she always did before the start of an adventure. In response, she too stuck out her tongue and, for good measure, crossed her eyes.

An hour later she was on the ski slope, a beginner's slope, not with her father, as she had expected, but with one of the instructors, a young woman named Janička, who was not at all willing to take Katrinka's word concerning her skill. "We'll soon see what you can do," she said, checking the leather bindings on Katrinka's ski boots to make sure they had sufficient give. The last thing she wanted was this little daredevil ending her first lesson with a broken leg.

To Katrinka's annoyance, "I told you so" was written clearly on the faces of the Lukánský sisters, who were in a more advanced group. Katrinka was tempted to stick her tongue out again, but didn't. Janička would be sure to notice, which would just add to the embarrassment. Anyway, the Lukánskýs soon lost interest in her and Katrinka turned her attention to the novice skiers as they began the difficult task of learning to walk in their skis, trying to avoid tripping themselves and each other up. They looked awkward and unhappy, their skis flapping out of control as they tried to lift them. Katrinka was certain she had managed much better on her first try.

This was by now old hat to her, and she sidestepped up the small slope with relative ease, earning an approving look from Janička. And when she skied down again without mishap, coming to a neat stop before the slight natural rise at the bottom, the instructor smiled and asked her to do it again. When Katrinka had obliged, retracing her steps up the hill, skiing down, and stopping, Janička took her by the arm and led her in the direction of another group. "Milan," she called to a young man in his early twenties. "I have someone for you," she said, handing Katrinka over. "She can ski."

Katrinka looked back over her shoulder and saw the Lukánskýs watching her. Again she resisted the urge to stick out her tongue.

"What's your name?" asked Milan. Katrinka told him. "So you can ski, can you?" he said, sounding unimpressed. "Well, we'll soon see."

Katrinka sighed. She was learning already there always someone you had to convince.

Every weekend until late into the spring, the Kovářs went skiing, taking the club's bus to the *chata* on Friday afternoon and remaining there until Sunday evening, when the bus carried them back to Svitov.

While Katrinka took lessons with the children, graduating quickly from one group to the next, Jirka skied the difficult trails in endless variations with newfound friends and Milena—trying to control her anxiety about Katrinka's safety—sat in the *chata* reading or doing needlepoint, chatting with those who, for one reason or another, remained indoors. Sometimes on a sunny afternoon she would take a long walk through the pine-studded hillside, away from the complex network of lifts carrying skiers from one mountain to another, enjoying the quiet, the fresh air, the sky as light and clear as Katrinka's eyes, and the view of the snow-covered mountains of Slovakia—rounded humps in the foreground and, beyond them, towering peaks disappearing into the mist—appearing with startling beauty through sudden, unexpected gaps in the trees. On two occasions she agreed to have a skiing lesson. But she found that she was frightened all the time, and cold. She didn't like skiing at all, though she wished she did. Then, at least, she could ski back to the bus at the end of each visit like almost everyone else instead of having to walk down the hill to the parking lot.

"If you break, you'll mend," said Olga, who could not quite conceal her contempt.

"Leave her alone," said Ota, who liked to poke fun but all the same had a kind heart. "You're all thumbs with a needle," he added, pointing admiringly to the needlepoint Milena was close to finishing.

"I *hate* needlepoint," said Katrinka.

Everyone laughed and the tension dissipated.

"She's jealous of you," Jirka told Milena afterward, whispering so as not to wake Katrinka. "She's a good soul, but not what you'd call a pretty woman." He reached out and touched Milena's bright hair. "How could she help but be jealous?" he said. The door opened and the Lukánskýs entered, the parents and two children. Jirka's hand fell to his side.

"Quiet now," Mrs. Lukánský cautioned in hushed tones. "Katrinka's asleep."

The Kovářs celebrated Christmas quietly on the eve with Jirka's parents, then on Christmas day traveled to the *chata* to spend the week's holiday there. Following the Černýs' advice, they had, in the preceding month, gradually laid in extra provisions so that they had little more than usual in their knapsacks to carry up to the lodge, a bit of foresight for which they were grateful when they saw the snow begin to fall that morning. At Easter, they spent another week. These longer trips were difficult for Jirka. Sometimes he could convince Milena to join him in the bathroom and there, in the bathtub, the hot water splashing out onto the floor, they would make love quickly, silently. Sometimes someone would knock on the door and call for them to hurry, which would spoil Milena's pleasure. But not his. For Jirka, the presence outside the door made the lovemaking seem dangerous, illicit, and all the more exciting.

Whatever the inconveniences, there was never any question for Jirka of dropping out of the club. Katrinka, who had by now turned five, sometimes—like all children—protested about the cold, insisted she was tired, and sometimes even begged to remain at home with her grandparents for the weekend, but it was clear that she enjoyed the sport and was good at it. And even should she turn out not to be as good as Jirka hoped, still skiing with the club was excellent training for her. Unlike so many of the young people he saw every day, without ambition or hope, his daughter was learning to be disciplined, competitive, goal oriented, and hardworking. These qualities, coupled with the ones she was born with, intelligence and energy, a good nature and loving disposition, would help her, he was certain, make something of her life.

What Milena saw in Katrinka's future was not opportunity, but danger. Every time her daughter went off to ski, Milena imagined her carried back hurt, arms and legs broken, ribs cracked, fingers sprained, skull fractured. And it was not only paranoia, as she was well aware. She was there during the day, in the *chata,* when the injured were carried back from the slopes, faces pale, limbs twisted, groaning with pain. Jirka could laugh at her, could make fun of her fears, but Milena knew the danger was real.

Not that Milena complained. That was not her style. But Jirka could see the worry in her face and sometimes could not help asking if she wanted her daughter to grow up as timid as she.

"Would that be so terrible?" she would reply. "At least she'd be safe."

And Jirka would pull her into his arms and hold her. "You're frightened all the time. At least the brave *feel* safe. Isn't that better?"

No, she thought, it's not. What was the point, she wondered, of bringing a child into the world, if you could not keep it safe from all harm, forever?

That summer the Kovářs, like all members of the sports club, spent the requisite forty hours at the lodges getting the buildings and terrain into shape for the next season. The men cleared trees from the mountains to increase the number of trails, overhauled the lifts, repaired the plumbing and the electrical wiring, fixed the roof where it leaked, the window frames where they sagged. The women cleaned from top to bottom, mended the bed linens, made new curtains, re-covered the worn sofas in the lounge. Together they painted, inside and out. Those who refused to do their part, and there were not many, were expelled from the club.

Even children as young as Katrinka were expected to help, the girls given rags and told to dust, the boys handed buckets to carry the winter's supply of coal from the delivery truck to the storage area. Katrinka, set small chores to do at home by her mother and grandmother, had already decided that housework was no more fun than needlepoint. Bored with helping Milena, she wandered away, looking for something more interesting to do and found it when Milan, the young ski instructor, took a cigarette break, leaving his paintbrush in a bucket in one of the upstairs dormitory rooms. The temptation was irresistible and Katrinka had, before long, covered herself and the floor as well as the wall in white-wash. *"Mami,* look what Katrinka's doing," shouted one of the Lukánský sisters.

Milan, when he returned, looked ready to wring her neck,

fearing that somehow this would turn out to be his fault. "My God," he said, looking around in horror. "I was only gone long enough to have a cigarette."

"Katrinka, look at the mess you've made," said her mother angrily, when she was called to the scene. "How could you?"

"I was helping," explained Katrinka, beginning to cry, embarrassed to have behaved badly in front of Milan.

"You have to keep your eye on her every minute," said Olga, torn between exasperation and amusement.

"No dessert for you tonight," said Milena, dragging her daughter into the bathroom to clean her up.

"Don't tell *Tati*," pleaded Katrinka, heartbroken.

Of course Milena did, and Jirka volunteered to repair the damage his daughter had done. "Good intentions aren't enough," he told Katrinka. "Before you can do something, first you have to learn how. You have to start small and practice, just the way you learned to ski. That way, you have less chance of getting into trouble. Do you understand what I'm talking about?"

"Yes, *Tati*," she said, though she was still not quite sure where she had gone wrong. She had watched Milan for a long time, and painting had looked so easy.

In July, when Jirka had his summer vacation, the family went by train to visit Milena's parents in the north of Moravia. Katrinka had only the haziest memory of the trip the year before and so it seemed to her another new and exciting adventure. She sat by the window on the hard wood seat and looked out at the changing landscape, the pine forests, the green hills, the distant mountains, the occasional cluster of ochre-colored houses with their flat red-tiled roofs, the steeples of Gothic churches rising like exclamation marks above the trees. When she got bored with that, she played games with her parents, and when they were hungry, Milena opened the wicker hamper she had packed with cold meats, homemade cheese, crusty brown bread, buttermilk for Katrinka, and a bottle of Moravian wine for Jirka and herself. Afterward, they all felt drowsy and, lulled by the roll of the train on its tracks, dozed until awakened by the shrill whistle at the next stop.

They were met at the station by Milena's father, Pavel Novotný, a big man with a sun-weathered face and blue eyes the same shape and color as his daughter's. He shook Jirka's hand, kissed Milena, and swung Katrinka up in his arms. "Well, *miláčku,* you've grown so much your poor old grandad can hardly lift you."

"I can ski, *Děda.*"

"So I've heard," said Pavel as he kissed her soft cheek.

Jirka loaded the old leather suitcases into the trunk of the Škoda, which Pavel had owned for as long as anyone could remember: it was even too old to have been requisitioned by the Nazis during the war. They climbed inside, Katrinka riding up front with her grandfather, Jirka and Milena in the back.

The orchard was a fifteen-minute drive from the town, along a two-lane road lined with borders of long grass and buttercups beyond which the hills stretched lazily to the horizon. Just beyond the crossroads, where a field of daisies and bluebells grew wild, Pavel turned right and stopped, Jirka getting out to open the gate and close it again once the car had passed through. "I remember. I remember," said Katrinka excitedly. "There are chickens."

Alerted by the barking of the two German shepherds, Jirina, Milena's mother, came running from the house as the car came to a stop. A tall woman, as slender as her daughter, still graceful despite the toll of heavy farm work which she had done without complaint for years, she ran to the car and embraced them all as they got out, clucking contentedly to have them with her again.

The farm had belonged to the Novotný family for generations and, as Ota Černý had pointed out, had somehow escaped collectivization when the communists came to power. But continuing to run it as a private enterprise was not without its problems. Since they were forced to sell their produce to the state at a set price, even in good harvest years the Novotnýs never had enough money to make the necessary repairs, and the farm had begun to have a shabby, run-down appearance, which pained Milena, who remembered how, in her childhood, the rambling frame house and its outbuildings had always looked freshly painted, how gates were repaired as soon as they sagged, fences mended, leaking roofs replaced.

To Katrinka, however, the farm was the prettiest place in the world—and the most interesting. There were Rosa and Rudolph, the two dogs who followed her everywhere, licking her face when she stood still for a minute; and the chickens she helped Milena feed; the ripe, juicy peaches and the tart plums she could pick from the trees when Pavel held her in his arms; the lake where her father taught her to swim; and František and Oldřich, her Aunt Zdeňka's two sons. Aunt Zdeňka and her family lived on the farm and helped with the work, though her husband, also named Oldřich, had to supplement his income by working part-time with one of the local construction companies.

"I can ski," she told her cousins, hoping to impress them. She didn't.

"Bet you can't do this," František said, leaping from the top of a wall, grabbing onto a tree branch, swinging gently to and fro a moment, then falling lightly to the ground. A moment later, Oldřich followed him.

The distances looked vast to her. She stood on top of the wall, trembling, hoping they would not notice how frightened she was.

"You're scared," they said.

"I'm not," she insisted. She jumped, grabbed the branch, and fell, tumbling onto the soft earth.

"Look at you! What happened?" asked Milena when Katrinka appeared at the kitchen door, limping, leaves and twigs in her hair, her face streaked with dirt, her overalls splattered with mud.

"I was playing," she said.

"Did you hurt yourself?"

"No," said Katrinka, "I just fell."

Katrinka adored František and Oldřich and followed them everywhere. They teased her and she loved it. They taught her *kuličhky*, a cross between marbles and boules played with glass beads. They helped her to climb the trees and shake the branches until the ripe fruit fell to the ground, a prank for which their irate grandfather punished them all later. They played tag with her and hide-and-seek and took her fishing, showing her the best spots to find worms, and how to thread them on her hook. Whatever they caught, Jirina cooked for supper. Sometimes they ate chicken, or pork from the pig slaughtered earlier in the year, always with fresh vegetables from the garden and fruits from the orchard, eggs from the chickens, and milk and cheese from the two cows. There was rarely enough money for new clothes or household items, or even for new farm machinery when it was needed, but they were lucky, Jirina said: they always had plenty of food for the table. There were countries in the world, she told them, where people starved to death.

The rooster, crowing, woke Katrinka each dawn. And the days that followed were long and hot, mellow with sunlight and the drowsy hum of insects in the air. The nights were cool and bright with the light of a million stars shining like ice crystals in the heavens.

"I don't want the summer to end," she confided to her father.

"If it was always summer," he said, "think of all the things you couldn't do."

"Like what?"

"Well, ski."

"I don't care," she said, and, at that moment, she didn't.

The long, lazy days continued for Katrinka when the family returned to Svitov. She would go grocery shopping with her mother and swim at the sports complex where Jirka worked. Her grandfather Honza had let her help him plant the vegetable seeds in the spring. He had made her a small trowel and shovel and taught her how to weed carefully among the tender shoots of the plants as they crept through the earth. Now, each day, she helped him harvest the ripened plants. With her grandmother, she tended the flowers in their beds, except for the roses, which Dana

permitted no one but herself to touch. The other flowers—
the daffodils and sweet peas, the tulips and peonies—could
be cut for bouquets for the house, but not the roses. They
bloomed and died on their stems.

In the midst of the roses was a garden bench where Milena
sat sometimes, either reading or working at her needlepoint.
When she was tired of playing with Slávka, Katrinka,
carrying a book of illustrated fairy tales, would go to her
mother and beg her to read. "The Beast is just like *Babička*,"
she said one day, startling Milena in the middle of a story.
"He won't let anybody touch his roses."

The bench was Dana's, really, and, every day after work,
she would sit there, lost in thought. Katrinka asked her once
what she was thinking about. "Your uncle," replied her
grandmother.

Her uncle, Katrinka knew, had died in the war that had
happened before she was born. His picture was on the
mantel in the sitting room. In it, he was laughing and looked
like her father, except that he had a mustache. "He's been
away a long time," said Katrinka pragmatically.

"It doesn't matter how long," said Dana. "A child is a
part of you, like your arm, or your leg. Even more a part of
you. You never stop missing your child. Even if you live a
hundred years." She lifted Katrinka onto her lap and held
her tightly, stroking her dark hair. "One day you'll understand, *andelíčku*," she said. "When you have children of
your own."

One day late in August, as Milena was leaving the butcher
shop, she was approached by a man. Feeling pleased because
the straw basket over her arm contained, among other items,
a small piece of veal, a delicacy always in short supply, she
smiled, imagining Dana's surprise when she began to prepare dinner that night. She reached down with her free hand
and took hold of Katrinka's. "*Babička* is going to be very
happy about this veal," she said as they came out of the
store into the wide boulevard that was the city's main street.

"Is that your little girl?" the man asked, stopping in front
of them and pointing to Katrinka.

"Yes," said Milena, startled, wondering what mischief of Katrinka's had prompted the question. The child had not been out of her sight all morning.

"My name is Mirek Bartoš," he said. "I'm a film director."

"Yes?" said Milena, not understanding what this had to do with her or her daughter.

"I'm making a film at the moment, at the studio." Bartoš gestured vaguely in the direction of the film studio located on one of the mountains overlooking the city. Smaller than the Barrandov Studios in Prague, the one in Svitov still functioned, though on a very small scale, since production throughout the country had decreased to only five or six films a year thanks to the establishment of a centralized artistic council in 1948. "My staff and I, we've been talking to parents for days. The thing is, I'm looking for some children to be in a few scenes I'm shooting next week." He could see that Milena looked more puzzled than interested. "It's a mystery," he explained. "And I want to shoot some scenes in a school. So, you see, I need schoolchildren."

"Katrinka doesn't go to school yet," said Milena.

"She doesn't? Really?" He sounded surprised. "Well, that doesn't matter. She looks right. What do you say? She'll be paid, of course." He smiled. "Though not much."

"I don't know," said Milena, as always reluctant to set foot into unknown territory.

Mirek smiled again and, though Milena was very much in love with her husband, still she could not help responding. Mirek Bartoš was a big man, not tall so much as broad and powerful, with a craggy handsome face, long, dark, wavy hair, and compelling brown eyes, now alight with humor. He had enormous charm and the air of someone used to getting what he wanted. "The scene is new. One of my bright ideas. And if I take too much time trying to cast it, I'll be over budget and behind schedule. It's just for a few days," he coaxed, giving her the names of several children, including Katrinka's friend Slávka, whose parents had already agreed.

"I'll talk to my husband," said Milena, at last returning his smile.

62

What a beautiful woman, he thought. And then decided against pursuing the thought to its usual conclusion. He had enough problems at the moment.

"This is my number," he said, scribbling it on a piece of paper. "One of the secretaries will answer. She'll give you all the details." He reached down and tugged at Katrinka's dark braid, tied this morning with a bright scarlet ribbon. "You'd like to be in a movie, wouldn't you?"

"I'm not promising," said Milena.

"No," said Mirek, turning his smile on her again. "Of course not. We'll wait and see what your husband says."

Jirka, who happened to be a fan of Bartoš's films, said yes. "You remember, don't you?" he said to Milena. "We saw one of his films last winter. *Last Chance.*"

"Oh, yes," said Milena who never paid any attention to film credits. "That was a mystery, too. I liked it very much."

"Every movie he makes is a hit," said Honza, quoting Bartoš's success in Scandinavia and Germany, as well as throughout the Eastern bloc countries. One of the few directors in Czechoslovakia to have survived the arrival of the communists (not so much because his films were successful as because they were genre pieces, with no political references whatsoever), Bartoš was a national celebrity, responsible for substantial amounts of hard foreign currency entering the government coffers.

Everyone, as it turned out, had a favorite Bartoš film. So the next morning, Milena called the number that Mirek Bartoš had given her, made the necessary arrangements, and, on Monday of the following week, as instructed, delivered Katrinka to the studio at seven o'clock in the morning for makeup.

"Makeup?" said Milena, frowning as she regarded the long mirrored table and the row of chairs in front of it, each containing a small giggling girl having pancake and eyeliner and lipstick applied.

"Just a touch," reassured an assistant. "You'll hardly notice it. Now, if you'll excuse us," she said, ushering Milena out of the way.

The mothers were encouraged to leave and many had to because they were expected at work, but Milena stayed, assuring Slávka's mother and the others that she would keep an eye on the little girls. Warned not to make a sound and to keep out of the way, Milena stood in a dark corner and watched. In a way it was exciting, she conceded, so noisy, with so many people rushing here and there, though in truth it was hard to tell what any of them were doing. In the distance, she caught sight of Mirek Bartoš, dominating whatever group he was in, speaking rapidly, gesturing wildly with his expressive hands.

A set had been constructed to look like a schoolroom, except it had no ceiling and where the back wall should have been stood a camera and other equipment. Still, what there was of it was very realistic, Milena thought. Someone without costume or makeup stood doing sums at the blackboard. Someone else was arranging books on the rows of student desks. Eventually, the little girls appeared, in Milena's opinion in too much makeup, wearing some sort of school uniform, herded by assistants and placed behind the desks according to some pattern which Milena could not quite make out, and which Mirek Bartoš himself disrupted when he strolled onto the set a moment later and began moving children hither and thither, from this seat to that, until finally he nodded, apparently satisfied, though to Milena his rearrangement seemed to make no great difference. Backing up to survey the effect from another angle, he caught sight of her and smiled.

He's flirting with me, thought Milena, then put the thought from her mind. An important film director flirting with a housewife like her: the idea was absurd.

Bartoš walked to the front of the set, climbed up on the platform, stood behind the teacher's desk, and turned his smile on the children, welcoming them to the studio, impressing upon them the importance of doing exactly as they were told when they were told it, assuring them they would do it very well if they concentrated. He called for his script, studied the page for a moment, then walked up and down the aisles, looking at the faces of the children, stopping at first one, then another, asking each to repeat a line after him.

Katrinka watched him approach with apprehension. So far she was not enjoying herself at all. Putting on makeup, which at first had seemed like fun, had turned out to be boring because it required sitting still for so long. And now here she was, stuck behind a desk, which she did not at all like, with a strange man about to ask her to say something she did not quite understand. Bartoš stopped in front of Slávka, who was seated just ahead of Katrinka. "Try saying this just like me," he said. Obviously nervous, the little girl repeated the line, faltering twice. "Thank you," said Bartoš, with a slight shake of his head. Then he was standing in front of Katrinka. "Now you try," he said. He gave her the line and Katrinka repeated it after him, doing her best to mimic his inflections, concentrating hard, not wanting to repeat Slávka's mistakes. "Again," he said, and again a third time. He reached out and grabbed hold of her braid, giving it a little tug. "Blue ribbons today," he said. "They match your eyes. What's your name?" She told him, and he smiled. "Do you think you can remember that line for a little while, Katrinka?"

"Oh, yes," she said. "I can remember the names of all the vegetables in the garden."

"Good, good," said Bartoš, his attention beginning to wander. Now that he had got what he wanted, he was anxious to get on with the scene. "You watch me, and when I point my finger at you, say the line. All right?"

Katrinka nodded, and Bartoš walked away, moving off the set, stopping to confer for a moment with a young woman who soon took his place behind the teacher's desk. An actress, thought Milena, and was proved right when Bartoš called for a rehearsal of the scene to begin. Milena watched anxiously, until Bartoš pointed his finger and, exactly on cue, Katrinka repeated the line he had given her to say. Through all the rehearsals, Katrinka never missed once, nor did she during the filming of the scene or her close-up later, saying the line each time exactly as she had the first.

"Very good," said Bartoš. "Excellent, Katrinka. Now, we're going to do it all just one more time."

"Well, how do you like being a movie star?" asked her grandmother after the first day.

"I hate it," said Katrinka. "You have to sit still for so long. You can't do anything. The afternoon was better," she said, to be fair. "We had to run down a long hallway." Then she thought about it some more. "Over and over again. It wasn't fun after a while."

Milena, on the other hand, had enjoyed the day, the novelty of it, the look behind the scenes of a new world, one where she could sit apart and observe quietly, which was what she liked to do best. To Katrinka, who had not yet even seen a movie, the whole process was totally without interest. Only when she was waiting for Bartoš's finger to point in her direction did she feel any sense of anticipation, of anxiety, of excitement. Otherwise, it was all very boring. By the third morning, she was begging to be allowed to stay home. "When can I stop?" she asked.

"When you've finished," said Milena, which was always the answer she gave no matter what chore it was that Katrinka wanted to get out of.

"How many days?"

"Two."

"Two more days," said Katrinka, sighing.

"Enjoying yourself?" asked Bartoš, tugging at her braid as he walked past her one morning.

"No, thank you. Are you?" she added, trying to be polite.

Bartoš howled with laughter, which surprised Katrinka, who did not think she had said anything funny. "Yes," he replied. "Enormously."

Embarrassed, Milena took Katrinka's hand. "It's all very interesting," she said.

"Possibly to you." He was still smiling broadly. Usually, he did not like children at all, not even his own. "And certainly to me. But I do see that from her point of view it's all pretty dull stuff." He turned to Katrinka. "Do you like school?"

"I don't go to school yet," she said.

66

"Oh, yes, I forgot. Your mother told me."

"But I ski."

"You do? Well, then we have something in common. I ski, too."

"Are you good?" she said. "My father is."

Bartoš laughed again. "Well, I may not be as good as your father," he said. "What about you? Are you good?"

"Oh, yes," she said.

"She's a very active child," said Milena apologetically.

"And truthful." He tugged again at Katrinka's braid. "That's a luxury not many of us can afford," he said and walked away.

Eight

"We went to Yugoslavia this summer," said Ilona, the older Lukánský girl.

"We went swimming in the sea. The Adriatic," said Olinka.

"I know," said Katrinka.

"What?" Neither could imagine who had told Katrinka where they had been on holiday.

"That it's called the Adriatic," said Katrinka.

It had snowed most of the previous week, the first snow of the season, and on Friday afternoon the buses had once again picked up passengers outside the sports complex and carried them to the mountains for the weekend. For the whole bus ride, Katrinka had felt impatient and excited. "How much longer?" she kept asking her parents. "Can we go skiing this afternoon?" She wondered if she would be able to ski as well as she had at the end of last season, or if she would be wobbly and uncertain, as she had been at the beginning. There was no way, she vowed, that she would go back to the kindergarten slopes. It would be too embarrassing, especially with those awful Lukánský sisters watching her all the time. She hoped her family would not have to share a room again with theirs.

But all Katrinka's hopes were disappointed that day. It was, as usual, too late to ski when the Kovářs arrived at the lodge. And when they checked their dormitory assignments, just to make sure there had been no last-minute changes, sure enough the Lukánskýs and the Kovářs were together again for another season.

"What did you do?" asked Ilona.

Katrinka thought about all the wonderful things she had done that summer, about gardening with her grandparents, about the farm and how she had climbed trees with her cousins. She bet the Lukánský sisters would think František and Oldřich were great. "I was in a movie," she said finally.

"You weren't," said Ilona.

"You mean you *saw* a movie," said Olinka, the younger sister.

"No," insisted Katrinka. "I was *in* a movie. It was a mystery."

"You weren't," repeated Ilona.

"You're lying."

"I'm not," said Katrinka, outraged. "I don't tell lies."

"Yes, you do," they said. "You always tell lies, great big lies. Katrinka's a liar," they chanted. "Katrinka's a liar."

"I'm not," she said, beginning to feel tears pricking behind her eyelids. She wouldn't cry. She wouldn't give them the chance to call her a crybaby, too. "I'm not a liar," she said again.

They kept chanting, dancing in a circle around her. "Katrinka's a liar. Katrinka's a liar."

"Admit you're lying," said the older one finally, grabbing Katrinka's arm and twisting it.

"Stop it," said Katrinka, pulling away, refusing to cry but needing to do something, hurling herself into them, fists flying. Soon they were writhing together on the floor, three little furies, trying to hurt one another, though not succeeding to any great extent.

"What's going on here?" said Mrs. Lukánský, returning to the room from the kitchen where she had just finished a soothing cup of tea, needed after the long bus ride and strenuous climb with her complaining daughters.

"Katrinka hit me," said Olinka, crying.

"She called me a liar," said Katrinka belligerently.

"She said she was in a movie," declared Ilona.

"Well," said Mrs. Lukánský, turning to Katrinka. "It's not nice to tell stories, you know."

"It's true," insisted Katrinka.

Milena, who had been down the corridor in the WC, entered the room, saw two crying little girls and Katrinka still braced for conflict, legs spread, fists curled, and her heart sank. What a winter this was going to be! She crossed to Katrinka, put a restraining hand on her daughter's shoulder, and asked what had happened.

"She hit me," repeated Olinka.

"I told them I was in a movie this summer, and they didn't believe me," said Katrinka.

"You have to admit," said Mrs. Lukánský, trying to be diplomatic, "it's an unlikely story."

"But it's true," said Milena calmly.

"I told you!"

"Katrinka *was* in a movie," continued Milena, ignoring her daughter's interjection. "So were many other little girls from Svitov. There's a film studio there."

"I am sorry," said Mrs. Lukánský, embarrassed. "But, well, it did sound like such a tall tale."

"Katrinka doesn't lie," said Milena. Vindicated, Katrinka smiled. But Milena looked down at her, her face stern. "And she should know better than to hit anyone. Now, Katrinka, say you're sorry." Katrinka hesitated. Apologizing did not seem at all fair to her. She glared at the girl who had twisted her arm. "Say you're sorry," repeated Milena.

"I'm sorry," said Katrinka, finally.

Mrs. Lukánský turned to her daughters. "Now, it's your turn. Apologize for not believing Katrinka."

"You didn't believe her," replied Ilona, who never liked to give in.

"Do as you're told!" snapped the woman.

The Lukánský sisters apologized and the three girls were then made to shake hands as a sign that all was forgiven, though of course nothing was.

"Why didn't they believe me?" Katrinka asked her mother later, as Milena tucked her into her cot for the night.

How could she explain about envy, wondered Milena, so

that a five-year-old could understand it? The task defeated her. "Mrs. Lukánský was right, you know," she said instead. "It did sound like a very tall tale."

"But it was true."

Milena laughed. "I don't know what to tell you, Katrinka, except that, as you can see, the truth isn't always believed."

Then why did it matter if you lied? wondered Katrinka. But she suddenly felt too sleepy to pursue the matter. "I'm going to wake up early in the morning," she said, her thoughts turning again to her skiing lesson the next morning.

"I'm sure you are," said Milena, smiling. She leaned over and kissed Katrinka's cheek. "Good night, *miláčku.*"

"Good night, *Mami,*" replied Katrinka, her heavy eyelids slowly shutting out the light.

Milena sat on the edge of the cot, looking at Katrinka, watching her sleep, feeling that same habitual, nagging worry, that frustration at not being able to protect her daughter from hurt. People would always be envious of Katrinka, suspected Milena, not just because of her looks, or her intelligence—for every woman, no matter how beautiful, there is always another somewhere more beautiful, more talented, smarter—but because of the combination of qualities that was Katrinka, her vitality, her energy, her openness and warmth, her supreme self-confidence. She was a little wonder, thought Milena, certain that it was not just blind prejudice that made her think so. A wave of love for her daughter washed over her with such intensity that it left her shaken. She leaned over and once again kissed Katrinka's cheek, round and soft as one of her father's prize peaches, smooth as silk under her lips. "I love you," she whispered.

The next morning Katrinka found herself, once again, in Janička's group, just as she had been on her first morning the year before. She was about to protest, loudly, when Janička saw the belligerent look on her face and assured her that she was not with the beginners, but right where she belonged. The ski instructors, it seems, alternated groups according to some plan whose logic was lost on the club's members. "Come on," said Janička, as soon as she had finished checking the bindings on the children. "Let's see what you remember."

The children, waddling awkwardly, followed her over to the lift, which was a simple power-driven conveyor, each unit consisting of a wire with a hook at its end and a towrope feeding in and out of a drum at the top of the mountain. Katrinka was first in line, and Janička grabbed a swinging hook and attached it to Katrinka's belt. "Hold the rope tightly," she cautioned, "and wait for the rest of us at the top."

Katrinka did as she was told, holding tightly to the rope, feeling excited and anxious, wondering if she would remember what to do. Her father had assured her that she had not forgotten how to ski over the summer, but she was not at all sure.

The rope pulled her higher and higher up the slope, her arms fully extended, her body relaxed, her skis gliding along the thin crust of ice. It was a cold morning, with no sun and a sharp wind blowing down the mountain. To Katrinka's left was a forest of tall pines, their wide branches heavy with snow. On the right, the terrain extended for about twenty feet, then dropped away sharply. The trail was out of sight, on the other side of the mountain. She had never skied this one before and wondered what it was like, how sharp the turns, how steep the descent. There was a strange fluttery feeling in her stomach, which she did not want to admit was fear.

Behind the drum for the lift system, at the top of the slope, was a hut with windows overlooking the mountain. Katrinka was close enough now to see figures inside. As she put her hand on her belt, preparing to detach the hook, she saw a man come out, walk a few feet across the flattened landing area, and stand still to watch her. "Release the hook," he called.

Katrinka had used this sort of lift many times before and was familiar with the mechanism. Confidently, she squeezed the hook, preparing to sidestep quickly to be out of the way of the others coming up behind her. "Release the hook," the man called again. Again Katrinka squeezed, and again the hook failed to release.

The drum was getting closer. Katrinka could just see its dark interior and the giant rimmed wheel along which the tow rope ran. "The hook, you little idiot," shouted the man, both anger and fear in his voice. "Release the hook."

"I can't," cried Katrinka. "It's stuck." Frantically, her fingers played with the hook, trying to get it to release. She was terrified now, the yawning mouth of the drum looming closer and closer, the jagged edge of the wheel rim looking like giant teeth. She started to cry.

"Jesus Christ," the man muttered, as he raced across the few remaining feet of snow toward Katrinka. "Stop the tow," he shouted, hoping someone was looking out the window and could see the danger, praying his voice was not carried away by the wind. "Stop the tow!" He reached Katrinka and grabbed hold of her. "I've got you," he said, trying to drag back on the tow, knowing it was futile, trying frantically to release the hook before they were pulled into the drum. The kid was right: the hook was jammed. He swore again, under his breath. Quickly, he unbuckled her belt and let it drop. "Let go of the rope," he said. It felt as if her hands were frozen to it. "Let go," the man insisted, tugging at her fingers. Katrinka forced her hands open and immediately felt herself lifted up and off to the side. He steadied her on her feet, and turned to help the next child. Tears running down her cheeks, shaking with fear, Katrinka watched her belt continuing without her, moving relentlessly closer to the drum. Then, suddenly, with an enormous grinding of gears, the tow stopped and her belt, waving gently on its hook, hung suspended at the entrance.

All down the hill, the young skiers, caught off guard, lost their balance and fell. Turning around, Katrinka saw them and started to laugh, they looked so funny, like a row of pins knocked down by a ball.

Followed by the young boy who had been behind her on the tow, the man came back toward her. "That was a close one," he said. "You all right?" Katrinka wiped the tears from her cheeks and nodded. "Well, you must be, if you're laughing." Putting an arm around her shoulder, he smiled at her, his teeth looking big and white in his leathered face. "But that took ten years off my life."

The tow was soon repaired and operating again and the ski class assembled at the top. When Janička arrived and heard what had happened, she was frantic, clucking and flapping over Katrinka like one of the hens at her grandparents' farm. Katrinka enjoyed the attention. Everyone made her feel like a heroine, except for one boy who, fed up with all the fuss and wanting to get on with the day, pointed out that Katrinka hadn't done anything but get stuck. "That's not true," said the man who had rescued her. "She did more than that. She didn't panic. She showed great courage." Uncle Ota, suspected Katrinka, would agree with the boy when he heard. When he heard. That thought worried her. When he heard, so would her mother.

There was a discussion about whether or not to cancel the class, but since the only feasible way of getting everyone down the mountain was to have them ski, the decision was made finally to continue. "Think you can do it?" asked Janička, as if Katrinka had been injured and not merely frightened, suggesting that she might perhaps like to be taken to the bottom by sled.

Katrinka nodded. Her legs had stopped shaking. She no longer felt frightened. And she had not been skiing since last spring and was impatient to begin again.

"All right, let's go," said Janička, as she pushed off down the trail, her class following in her wake. Turning constantly, she watched them over her shoulder, calling out instructions as she went.

For a while, Katrinka concentrated on following Janička's lead, on not making a mistake, on weighting her skis properly in the turns, on trying to improve her form. But soon, as she gained confidence, this became automatic and she entered another sphere, Janička's voice coming to her now from a great distance. This was for her like no other feeling in the world. When she had leapt from the wall to the tree last summer, goaded by František and Oldřich, she had

74

merely been afraid. But now, gliding along the surface of the mountain, her fear was overlaid with excitement, with exhilaration. She was no longer cold; her body radiated heat. And the wind still blowing off the mountain, pushing into her back, seemed to lift her, carry her. She felt again as if she were flying, soaring like a bird, free and wild.

"Katrinka, slow down," yelled Janička.

Katrinka laughed. How could she slow down? Why should she slow down? But obediently she pushed her feet into a snowplow, a moment too late. She hit a mogul and felt her legs go out from under her.

"Are you all right?" called Janička.

Katrinka sat up in the snow, moving gently until she was sure nothing hurt. "Yes," she said, as she pushed her skis together and, using her poles, pulled herself upright.

"Now stay behind me, and do as I say," said Janička sternly. "And for pity's sake, concentrate."

When he heard what had happened, Jirka considered not telling Milena but quickly realized the futility of that. So many people had witnessed Katrinka's near-fatal encounter with the drum that she was sure to learn of it from someone or another. Better him, he decided.

To his surprise, Milena took the news well. She paled as she heard the story, but, though tears filled her eyes, she did not cry, or insist, as he had expected, that they pack up immediately, return home, and end once and for all their association with the ski club. When he thanked her for not making an issue of it, she smiled bleakly. "What good would it do me?" she asked, unable to keep the bitterness from her voice. "Would you listen?"

Jirka did speak to Ota Černý, though, and both pursued the issue, wanting to know what had caused the problem with the lift, if only to prevent something similar happening in the future. But their efforts, as they had expected, proved inconclusive. They themselves had helped to overhaul the lifts the previous summer, they were told. Nothing had been left undone. Accidents will happen.

Tramping across the frozen earth on their way back to the

chata, Ota turned to his friend. "They're right, you know," he said philosophically. "The only time you're safe from accidents is when you're dead."

"That's a hard truth to accept," replied Jirka, "about your own child."

"She'll be all right, that little one," said Ota.

"We worry," said Jirka, "perhaps too much. It's the miscarriages, I suppose. And the little boy we lost. And there were times, you know, when it was touch and go with Katrinka. The doctors weren't hopeful. None of us were. When she was born, at eight months, healthy and strong, it was like a miracle."

"That's what I mean," said Ota. "She held on. She's a fighter. Death won't have an easy time getting his hands on her."

"It's hard," said Jirka, "fighting the impulse to protect her. *Over*-protect," he corrected. "Maybe Milena is right and I go too far in the other direction."

"Olga can't have children," said Ota. "But if we could, we'd want a child like Katrinka, full of spirit, not some mama's girl, happy to sit in a corner all day."

"We're lucky, I know," said Jirka.

"You are," said Ota. "Very lucky, my friend."

So, much to Katrinka's surprise, no attempt was made to curtail her skiing. Each weekday now, since the start of school in September, she walked with her mother or father, or sometimes with Slávka and her mother, down the terraced steps that led through the wooded hillside to the valley where the city center lay, across the railroad tracks, to a large yellow stucco building, the same school where Jirka had once gone. Then, on Friday afternoons, she boarded the ski-club bus with her parents.

Katrinka enjoyed school, where her teacher, a thin, gray-haired woman much kinder than her fierce look suggested, taught her to read and do sums, to write the letters of the alphabet and spell all the words she knew. She liked learning so many new things, how to pronounce strange Russian words and find Moscow on a map. But the days of the week, however interesting they might be, could not compete with Saturday and Sunday for excitement.

All season Katrinka continued to make rapid progress, each week gaining in endurance and skill. She was promoted out of Janička's group up to the next one, where she held her own against boys and girls several years older. That made her feel, at times, confident and proud. Mostly, though, she was aware of how many skiers were better than she.

The younger Lukánský sister, Olinka, had no athletic ability at all, but the older one, Ilona, did. She was now eight and in the same group as Katrinka. "You think you're so wonderful, don't you?" she said, whispering in Katrinka's ear, standing behind her as they waited for the ski lift.

"I don't," said Katrinka.

"You think you're better than everybody," insisted Ilona, reaching out and pinching Katrinka's thigh. She was a tall thin girl, very pale, with white-blond hair, watery gray eyes, and a flat face. Katrinka thought she looked like a fish.

"Stop that," squealed Katrinka.

"Girls," said Josef, one of the ski coaches. "Pay attention. It's your turn next, Katrinka." He grabbed a hook and attached it to her belt. "Remember to release it as soon as you hit the landing stage." He doubted the damn lift would jam again. Still, he couldn't help worrying.

"I will," said Katrinka. Gratefully, she reached out and took hold of the rope, letting it pull her away, out of Ilona's vicious reach.

Katrinka wanted to tell her parents about the way Ilona tormented her so they would make her stop. But telling tales seemed wrong to her. It violated a code of behavior she had learned from her cousins, František and Oldřich, a code recently confirmed in the schoolroom and which extended, she was sure, to the ski slopes. Instead, she kept as much as possible out of Ilona's way, careful never to be alone with her and her sister in their room and to stay close to Josef, the coach, during lessons.

"You never want to play with the little Lukánský girls," said Milena, always observant where Katrinka was concerned.

"I don't like them," said Katrinka, resisting the temptation to say why.

"You should make an effort to get along with everyone," said Milena, who did not like them either and felt a little ashamed of herself for it. They were, after all, only children, if thoroughly unpleasant ones.

Rivalry between the club's two lodges, the Rys and the Orlik, was encouraged, and races were organized weekly with teams from each competing against the other. Since many of the club's members were competition skiers—on teams for their town or province or, in some cases, their country—the rivalry though basically friendly was nevertheless taken seriously, with everyone investing a great deal of effort and energy in winning.

Katrinka was no exception, and, over the winter, she had steadily improved, finishing tenth out of fifteen children in her first race, then fifth, then third. But no matter how well she did, Ilona always did better.

Katrinka had heard her father and Ota Černý talk about team spirit, but only dimly did she understand its importance. Yes, she wanted her team to win. But what she wanted most of all was to ski better and faster than anyone else; or, if that was not possible, at least to come in ahead of Ilona Lukánský.

Again the Kovářs spent their Christmas week holiday at the *chata* and every day Katrinka practiced, concentrating harder than she ever had before, listening carefully to Josef's every instruction, trying to improve her control and her speed, determined to win the next race, which was scheduled for New Year's Day, the day after her sixth birthday. But it seemed to her that she fell more often than usual, that Josef lost patience with her more frequently. Frustrated, she was tempted to cry, but remembered Ilona was nearby and didn't. At the end of the day, her legs and arms ached from the effort she was making, but she was afraid to complain for fear that Milena would insist she rest. Katrinka couldn't rest. Ilona, who was older and taller and heavier, remained faster than she, and Katrinka was beginning to be afraid there was no way in the world she could beat her.

On New Year's Eve, the Kovářs celebrated Katrinka's sixth birthday. Milena made strawberry dumplings, Katrinka's favorite dessert, and the other children were invited to share. Ota and Olga Černý gave her a ski cap and scarf and mittens, knitted by Olga in bright blue wool. From her parents, Katrinka received a new set of skis, also blue, made at Mittersill, purchased by Jirka while on a business trip to Austria for the sports complex with money he and Milena had saved by skimping for months on their living expenses. Katrinka thought they were the most wonderful gift she had ever received.

"For you to use tomorrow," said Milena.

Katrinka looked at the obvious envy on Ilona Lukánský's face and replied, "I can't." She was afraid their strangeness would slow her, and nothing, not even the pleasure of sailing down a mountain on her beautiful new skis, was worth jeopardizing her small chance of winning.

"Wise decision," said Olga, for once no hidden edge of disapproval in her voice.

"Very smart," agreed Ota.

Milena looked confused and Jirka explained the problem. "Oh, I see," she said, smiling at her daughter.

"You'll sharpen my old skis, *Tati*, won't you? And wax them?"

"I'll check the conditions first thing in the morning," promised Jirka. "And I'll wax your skis just right."

"Thank you," she said, relieved, certain Mr. Lukánský would not wax Ilona's skis nearly as well, if he bothered to wax them at all.

The next morning it was snowing, not heavily, just large soft flakes playing in the wind before floating lazily to the ground, laying a thin powder cover on the mountains.

Standing in front of the coal stove, Katrinka watched as Ilona dressed, at Mrs. Lukánský's insistence putting on layer after layer of clothing to protect her from the cold. "You better hurry," she said to Katrinka when she was finished. "You'll be late."

"I'm almost ready," said Katrinka, watching as Ilona and her mother and sister left the room. As soon as they were gone, Katrinka took off one of her sweaters.

"Katrinka, what are you doing?" demanded Milena sternly. "You put that sweater back on."

"I don't need it, *Mami*. Really."

"You'll freeze."

"No, I won't. It's not so cold. It's never cold when it's snowing."

"Why must you always argue, Katrinka? Do you want to get sick? Now, put that sweater back on."

"Please, *Mami*," begged Katrinka. "I hate it when I feel like a big fat pig and can't move." Milena hesitated. "Please," repeated Katrinka. "I *have* to go fast today."

"All right," said Milena, giving in. "It won't kill you to be cold, I suppose, for a little while."

"Oh, thank you," said Katrinka, throwing her arms around her mother, smothering her with kisses.

Milena laughed. "Enough. Enough," she said, hugging the child for a brief instant before letting her go. "The minute that race is over you come up here and put on another sweater. You understand me?"

"Oh, yes. I promise."

Katrinka found her father in the ski room, waiting for her. "Did you wax my skis, *Tati?*" she asked.

"Didn't I say I would?" he said, amused at how seriously she was taking this. Concealing a smile, he stooped to help her into her ski boots.

"The powder has slowed the course a little," said Ota, joining them. "I hope you took that into account when you waxed the little one's skis."

"I did," Jirka assured him, his smile broadening. Ota was taking this almost as seriously as Katrinka.

"How do you feel?" asked Ota.

"Fine," said Katrinka, forcing the word out. Her throat was so tight she could barely breathe.

"Nervous, eh?" said Ota, reaching out to pinch her cheek. "Good. Now, just concentrate and you'll do all right."

Outside the sky was still overcast and the snowflakes continued their graceful, easy fall. People in colored parkas and intricately patterned sweaters milled about, patches of brightness in the white landscape, those who were going to

80

race looking for their groups, spectators choosing their positions along each course. The mood was lighthearted. Laughter floated on the air. Voices issued amiable challenges and called out words of encouragement.

Jirka escorted Katrinka to where her group was assembling. He waved hello to Mr. Lukánský, a big, broad, somber man who acknowledged him with a slight inclination of his head without interrupting his conversation with Ilona. He stood with his hands on her shoulders, looking down at her, talking nonstop as she nodded her head at regular intervals in acceptance of whatever advice he was giving. He's pushing her too hard, thought Jirka, then wondered if perhaps he was not doing the same thing to his daughter, in another, more subtle way.

Like the other parents, Jirka helped Katrinka into her skis, checked her bindings one last time, and turned her over to Josef. "It doesn't matter if you don't win," he told her. "It's not important, as long as you try your best."

It *is* important, she thought, but didn't contradict her father. She wasn't sure he would understand how she felt.

"Good luck," he said, running his hand affectionately across the top of her blue wool hat. Katrinka nodded solemnly, then took her place in the line. He watched until she was on the lift, then went to find Milena.

"How is she?" asked Milena when he found her, standing near the end of the course with Olga, who was racing later in the day, as were Ota and Jirka.

"Nervous," said Jirka. "I had to laugh, she seemed so determined."

"I threw up before my first race," said Olga. "And I was much older than Katrinka."

"I just hope she's not too upset," said Milena, "when she doesn't win."

"She'll be heartbroken," said Jirka. He shrugged. "But what can you do?"

Riding up on the lift, Katrinka tried not to think about Ilona, or anyone. Instead, she pictured the ski trail in her mind, the places the run was straight, where it turned, where the mountain sometimes leveled out for a moment before it dropped steeply again. She had tried all week to memorize it, as Josef had suggested, so her body would know instinctively today just what to do and when. That was the way, Josef said, to avoid losing time making decisions. And mistakes.

As she neared the landing stage, Katrinka could feel her heart quicken and her throat grow dry, as they did every time now for fear that the hook again would not release. But it did, and Katrinka sighed, relieved. Letting go of the rope, she stepped away from the conveyor and made her way to the gate. Her starting position was six. Ilona's was two. There was a total of sixteen girls in the race, eight on each team.

Ilona was fidgeting edgily, her pinched face paler than usual in the thin light. When she saw Katrinka, she turned to the girl next to her and whispered something. The girl laughed. Katrinka turned away, ignoring them both, adjusting her scarf around her neck to keep the snow from blowing down the front of her parka.

Josef called to them and the first girl got into position, adjusted her goggles, waited for the signal, then pushed off down the slope. A few moments later Ilona followed her. Before long, Katrinka was in the gate, pulling her goggles down over her eyes, her hat over her ears, adjusting her scarf, her poles, waiting, waiting . . . And she was off, her waxed skis gliding over the powder, schussing straight down for a moment, then weighting her skis for the turn, left ski, right ski. Oh, it was wonderful. She bent forward, crouching low, making herself as heavy and fast as possible, her body remembering the way, her legs seemingly of their own accord traversing back and forth across the trail, beginning the difficult turn she always missed even before she was aware she had reached it. This was the best run she had ever had, the most effortless. Never in her life had she had so much fun.

One last turn and she could see the spectators at the bottom and hear them cheering the girl who had preceded her down. It was almost over, and for a moment she felt sad, wanting this moment to last forever. Then she crossed the finish line.

A moment later, she felt herself caught up in her father's arms. "Well done," she heard him saying, his voice seeming to come from far away.

"You looked as if you were flying," said Milena proudly, all her fears for the moment at rest.

"You were off balance on that last turn," said Ota. "Otherwise, you did very well indeed."

"Did I win?" asked Katrinka, returning to earth. "Did I?"

"We'll know soon," said Jirka, as he helped her off with her skis.

Katrinka turned back toward the course to watch the last girls cross the finish line and caught sight of Ilona frowning. She had forgotten even that. "Was I faster than Ilona Lukánský?" she asked.

"Unofficially," said Ota, "I think you were."

"But we still have to get the official times," cautioned Jirka.

I beat her, I beat her, thought Katrinka, hoping it was true. She stood facing the course, not really paying attention, waiting for the race to end. Someone fell on a turn and was carried off, though the word came back that she wasn't hurt. Finally, she saw the last girl glide to a neat stop just a few feet from her. She's good, thought Katrinka, a little worried. Very good. And fast. Then she heard her name being called. "And the winner . . . Katrinka Kovář."

"Katrinka, you won," said her father. "You won!"

Nine

This is not acceptable, Katrinka," said her father, "not acceptable at all." He put her report card down on the table and looked at her, his face uncharacteristically stern.

"I'm sorry, *Tati,*" she said.

"D in physics, C in everything else. You can do better than that."

Katrinka, close to tears, stared down at her shoes while Jirka studied her unhappy face and wondered what to do. His daughter was bright, he knew that, and she worked hard, or at least she always had until recently. She was up at five in the morning, spent an hour or so studying, bicycled to the sports complex for ice-skating practice, then attended school all day, followed by more sports or music lessons in the afternoon. When she got home, she studied a while longer, then helped to prepare the evening meal. By dinnertime she was exhausted and collapsed immediately afterward into bed. Weekends, of course, she skied, either racing or training. It was a daunting schedule for anyone, let alone a fifteen-year-old. But Jirka suspected that more than overwork was involved.

At fifteen, Katrinka was on the verge of womanhood. All her baby fat had gone. She was tall, already five feet seven, and slender, with just a hint of roundness to her shape. Her long dark braids had been sacrificed for a more fashionable short haircut, framing her face, emphasizing her clear skin, her pale blue eyes with their thick fringe of dark lashes and heavy arched brows, her high cheekbones, uptilted nose,

84

and full mouth. There was still something adolescently awkward about her, as if the pieces of her womanly puzzle were not yet fitting together, but, thought Jirka, someday quite soon, his daughter was going to be a beauty.

"Sit down, Katrinka."

She sat in the armchair opposite him, crossed her ankles, put her hands in her lap, and leaned forward anxiously. "I'll do better next year, *Tati*. I promise," she said, trying not to remember she had said the same thing after her last report, which had been no better.

"If you don't keep your grades up, you'll never be accepted by a university. And without a degree, what do you suppose will become of you? What sort of future do you think you'll have?"

"I'm doing well on the ski team," she said, having accepted that as the key to open all doors.

"Very well," agreed Jirka. Both were understating the case. Without doubt, Katrinka was the best female skier on the local team, which for three years in a row had been the provincial champion. That was, he supposed, part of the problem—the traveling she had to do for the races in Czechoslovakia and abroad. "But you have to be realistic, Katrinka. Now you receive money, equipment, clothing, food. Anything you need. Doors open to you that remain closed to others. But what will happen if for some reason you can't race anymore?"

"I'll always race," said Katrinka.

"Always," said Jirka with a shrug. "An athlete's career is good for as long as it's good, Katrinka, and, believe me, that's never for very long."

Everything that Ota Černý had predicted and Jirka Kovář had hoped had happened. Katrinka's natural ability, her competitive instinct, her relentless hard work had made her a champion; and, as a result of that, she was rewarded very handsomely by the system, so much so that Jirka sometimes wondered if perhaps he and Milena did not owe the apartment in which the family now lived to their daughter's success. Their name suddenly, one might even say miraculously, had reached the top of the housing list shortly after the local team had, thanks to Katrinka, won an important race. And afterward, when he had been granted a larger than usual pay raise, it had occurred to him that this too might be due to Katrinka, her contributions to the state, so to speak, compensating for his not being a member of the Communist Party. In either case there was no way to be sure. Trying to trace the course of a decision eventually reached in committee was, he imagined, like trying to find the source of some jungle river.

Now, in their kitchen, he heard Milena moving quietly about, preparing dinner, deliberately keeping out of the discussion with Katrinka, happy that for once she could rely on Jirka to take a firm stand with their daughter. That she frequently found him too easy on the child he knew and understood; but then, he often found her too hard.

"From the time school finishes until you start training, you'll work with me at the sports complex," Jirka said finally, his mind made up.

"But *Taři,*" said Katrinka, her voice filled with dismay, "I'm supposed to go to the farm." Not only did she love the farm and look forward every year to her time there, but this year it would be the only vacation she had. Dry training—calisthenics, jogging, and grass skiing—was as always starting early to get the teams into shape for the season.

"Not this year, Katrinka."

"But I always go."

"I don't want to argue about this. You're working at the complex this summer. It's just for a few weeks. Not such a long time." He tapped the report card which was lying face up on the table. "Don't you think you should do something to make up for this?"

Katrinka looked at the report with loathing and nodded. She had known such awful marks would merit some punishment, but she had never imagined anything so terrible as to be forbidden to go to the farm. What would František and Oldřich think? They probably wouldn't understand at all. They always got good grades. "Please, *Taři,*" she said.

Jirka shook his head firmly. "My mind is made up, Katrinka."

She could hardly believe it. Her father was always so reasonable, so understanding, so forgiving. Why was he doing this to her? Standing up, she excused herself quickly and ran from the room, not wanting him to see her cry.

Jirka looked after her, fighting the urge to follow and tell her he had changed his mind. Would it be so terrible, he asked himself, if he let her off with a reprimand? But that was what he had done the last time. He had considered putting a stop to her swimming, or to the music lessons, but she was doing so well in both. Katrinka did well in whatever she chose, that was the realization he had come to over the past few months. When she saw the point of working hard, she worked. When it was a question of winning a race, there was no stopping her. But studying to get good marks? The reason for that clearly eluded his daughter, and that was what he somehow had to demonstrate to her.

Jirka looked around the room. It had a new three-piece green velvet suite bought at a local furniture store; a small armchair transported by train from the farm, with a seat cover worked in needlepoint by Milena; a round table covered with a cloth that Dana had crocheted; and, on a stand made by Honza in his workshop, a television set, still a great luxury in Czechoslovakia in 1964. On the walls were framed family photographs. It was a comfortable room, Jirka thought, as he always did when sitting here waiting for his dinner.

A ten-minute walk from his parents', the apartment was on the upper floor of a two-story semidetached brick house in which there were four apartments in all. Similar houses, in brick or stucco, ran for several streets in either direction, terraced up and down the hillside until stopped by the business district of the city at one end and the forest at the other. Each apartment had its own private garden and a separate entrance, with an exterior staircase leading to the second level.

Like the others, except for the corner houses, which had more, the Kovářs' apartment had two bedrooms, a sitting room, and a kitchen large enough for a good-sized table. In their garden, Milena grew wildflowers, roses, and vegetables, not anywhere near yet the size and abundance of Jirka's parents' but improving every year. They had cupboards full of jarred fruits from the farm, canned vegetables, and homemade cheese. In front of the house was parked a two-year-old red Škoda. When Katrinka had started school, Milena had begun to work again as a librarian at the city's central library. Now, with two salaries, the Kovářs were able to afford many luxuries, not only a car and a television and yearly vacations in Yugoslavia or Hungary or Poland but, most important of all, at least one of them was able to accompany Katrinka when she traveled with the team to race.

They were very lucky, Jirka knew, to have so much. True, they all—Katrinka included—worked hard when so many others shirked responsibility or let the comfort of a secure job make them lazy. Without doubt, the Kovářs had earned whatever they had. But there was no discounting luck, or the fact that God had kept them well, and happy, and out of harm's way.

Jirka rose out of his armchair and went into the kitchen to find Milena. She was making potato pancakes; her hands were covered with flour and there was a streak of it on her cheek. The years, which had thickened his waist slightly and grayed his hair, had so far not done more to his wife than add a few lines to her face. Though she worked long hours at the library, did all the housekeeping, cooked the meals, and often made clothes for Katrinka and herself, she seemed to him as youthful, as graceful, as slender as ever. And as beautiful, he thought, though they had been married now for over seventeen years. Whatever their differences, he continued to want her.

"Well?" she said, looking up at him, her face wearing its usual worried look when Katrinka was the subject. "Did you tell her no farm this summer?"

He nodded and said, "She's very unhappy."

"She has to learn."

"Yes," agreed Jirka. What he wanted, more than anything in the world, was for Katrinka's life to be better than Milena's or his. "She has to learn."

The city of Svitov had wide boulevards lined with gray buildings, gems of baroque and art deco style masked by a bland Soviet monochrome. In the side streets, the three-story buildings were painted ochre and pink, as well as gray, and the charming town square, with its classic baroque buildings, was a palette of soft yellow and peach, pale green and creamy white. The city had large open areas of park; a red-brick technical college where Ota Černý taught physical training; a glass factory that was the area's major employer; a manor house, now a restaurant, in the style of a French château; and the movie studio, which occupied a commanding site on a hilltop adjacent to the city. It also had a cinema, a square, gray building with a low, flat roof, showing films from the USSR and other Eastern bloc countries to supplement the meager supply of native product; theaters, where mostly the classics were produced, as few modern plays ever earned official approval; a rococo central library with a basement full of banned books; restaurants specializing in native dishes with forays into Austrian cuisine; a large grocery store, its shelves stocked with milk, eggs, flour, and other staples; a street market; and the usual assortment of shops selling meat, clothing, cosmetics, furniture, and other household items, always too expensive despite the controlled prices.

To many people, more important than any of these, and the real heart of the city, was the sports complex, a large red-brick facility built in 1936. Here, the residents of Svitov and surrounding communities either participated in or observed sporting events. The complex had an Olympic-size pool, tracks for field events and running; tennis and handball courts; a hockey stadium; an ice-skating rink; rooms for gymnastics, weight training, physical therapy, and massages; a steambath; and a sauna.

Two years before, the man who had managed the facility from 1948 on had reached the age of sixty-five and retired. Jirka should have replaced him, but was passed over—his refusal to join the Party as always a stumbling block to advancement. The man who got the job was as lazy and inept as his predecessor, but amiable nonetheless, happy to leave Jirka alone to do as he saw fit. A wise decision. Jirka was hardworking and efficient. Since he was always willing to bend the rules a little in their behalf, the athletes were fond of him, and he had the respect of the staff. Most, knowing he was doing more than his share, were willing to work a little harder than they normally would have done, and the complex, in consequence, was maintained in excellent condition and at less cost than anyone expected.

The sports complex was as familiar to Katrinka as her school or her home. She was there most mornings for ice-skating practice, another sport in which she excelled, though she did not compete with the team since the events often conflicted with her skiing. She swam as well, did gymnastics, and played volleyball, which she hated. It was expertise in sports, not academic credentials, she believed, that would help her get admitted to university. If someone could ski and skate and swim the way she could, what difference did it make what mark she got in physics? It was beyond Katrinka why her father, normally so reasonable, did not understand that.

But once she got used to the idea of not going to the farm, Katrinka's usual optimism took hold and she began to think that perhaps working at the sports complex would not be so terrible. For one thing, it was full of old friends, people she had known all her life: she had been going there, at first with her father, then with her school, since she was a baby. For another, as she confided to her best friend, Tomáš, she was sure her father would give her interesting work to do, and when she wasn't busy, she could swim or skate or do gymnastics. In fact, Katrinka assured Tomáš the weekend before she was to begin, she was now certain her few weeks working at the complex would turn out to be a lot of fun.

The two friends were sitting on the bank of a stream, idly tossing handsful of pebbles into the clear water. They had raced their bicycles along the path into the woods to the pine tree that for years had marked the end of the course, Tomáš this time slightly in the lead. From there they had walked their bicycles along the familiar route through the tall trees to the stream.

Katrinka and Tomáš had been friends for almost five years now, since the Kovářs had moved into the apartment upstairs from Tomáš and his family. He was, in Katrinka's opinion, a vast improvement over Slávka. Though Tomáš was more studious than Katrinka, preferring books and films to sports, he was, when he made the effort, a good athlete, excellent at hockey and handball, a competent skier, fast on his feet, and agile climbing trees. Well matched intellectually and physically, they tended to treat each other as equals, from the beginning pretty much disregarding each other's sex, barring certain unspoken taboos like not removing their clothes to swim in the stream that was their favorite retreat.

As he leaned back against a tree, watching the clear, swift stream play with the reflection of the overhead clouds, Tomáš decided he was not so sure that Katrinka's reassessment of the summer was correct. Jirka Kovář, in his experience, was a nice man, and as reasonable as Katrinka claimed, but he had a very strict sense of right and wrong, of duty and fair play. If he meant this stint at the complex to be a punishment for Katrinka, then that was what it would turn out to be.

"What do you think he'll make you do?" asked Tomáš.

"Oh, I don't know," said Katrinka, tossing another pebble, making the clouds dance crazily on the surface of the water. "I could learn the switchboard, or help in the office. I guess I could even help the coaches with the younger kids. In swimming, or skating."

"If you want my opinion, you won't be doing anything that's fun."

"Why do you say that?" asked Katrinka, turning to look at him. He told her and she sat for a moment, regarding him silently. Tomáš was taller even than she, and thinner, with a thick mop of curly brown hair, a long, narrow gypsy's face, full lips, a large, straight nose, and deep-set, serious dark eyes. "I wouldn't be in this mess if it wasn't for you," she said finally.

"That's not fair."

"If I'd stayed home and studied instead of running off to see movies with you, I'd have gotten better grades."

"We didn't go that often," he said guiltily. Tomáš was movie mad. Every last cent he could lay his hands on, money he earned working part-time on his grandfather's construction sites, he spent on either books or films. When he could not talk Katrinka into disobeying her parents' rules to go with him, he went alone. He loved the dark theater, the flickering images that seemed to beckon to him, luring him into their world, capturing him with their wiles, replacing his life magically with their own.

"Often enough. If my father knew, I'd be dead," exaggerated Katrinka.

"Well, I won't tell," said Tomáš.

"We were lucky nobody ever saw us." She shuddered at the thought of what her parents would have said had she and Tomáš been discovered.

Tomáš's life was not happy, Katrinka knew, though he did not like to talk about it much. His father had left when Tomáš was two years old; his mother, who worked in the office at the glass factory, drank too much and on the weekends would stagger home late at night, singing loud enough to wake the neighborhood. The grandfather, with whom they both lived, was a mean-spirited man, quick-tempered and unyielding, a Party member who worked as an assistant foreman in a local construction business. The grandmother had died years before; some people said she had killed herself. Is it any wonder, Jirka often remarked, that Tomáš likes to keep his nose buried in a book or lose himself in dreams at the movies.

"I didn't *make* you come," said Tomáš. "You wanted to."

"Nobody can make me do anything I don't want to," said Katrinka inaccurately, with a teenager's arrogance.

"Well, I certainly can't," agreed Tomáš.

"Except my parents," conceded Katrinka, after a moment. "What do you think my father will make me do?"

"Something terrible," said Tomáš. "Something disgusting. You can depend on it."

"What could be that awful?"

"I don't know," said Tomáš. "But you'll soon find out." He looked at his watch. "It's almost time for lunch. You'd better get home." They got to their feet, picked their bicycles up from the forest floor, and began retracing their steps through the forest. It was Saturday and they had nothing to do all day but amuse themselves. "Want to go to a movie this afternoon?" he asked, and when Katrinka looked at him in exasperation, said defensively, "Exams are over. You don't have to study today."

"What's on?" said Katrinka, relenting.

"Lots of things. There's a Miloš Forman film, *Peter and Pavla,* that I want to see. And *Last Song,* by Mirek Bartoš. I suppose you'll want to see that one," he added. Tomáš always knew the names of the directors, and what other films they had made. He knew who the cameramen were too, and all the important crew members. He dreamed someday of attending FAMU, the film department of the Academy of Music and Arts, and of becoming a director himself.

Katrinka did not misinterpret the disapproval in Tomáš's voice as an unwillingness to go along with her choice. Though he had very high standards and was adamant about what constituted a good or a bad film, Tomáš would, she knew, sit through anything.

"All right," he agreed, with a disappointed sigh, when Katrinka had stated her choice.

"I have to ask my parents, though," she said. "I don't want to get into any more trouble."

Tomáš, who avoided going home as much as possible, was invited to have lunch with Katrinka, and afterward Milena and Jirka accompanied them both to see the Bartoš film, which all the Kovářs liked and Tomáš did not, or at least not much. "Predictable," he called it later in contemptuous tones, causing Jirka to smile. He himself had found the plot entertaining.

Katrinka could usually understand why Tomáš hated or loved a particular film, but often she found his opinions perverse, favoring some dull film for a subtlety of technique that eluded her, condemning an interesting one for a fault no more serious than being too popular—or at least so she thought. Her own taste was broader than his. She always enjoyed the movies that Mirek Bartoš made. "I liked it," said Katrinka. "It was very clever, right up to the end. That was a little phony," she admitted.

"A little!"

"And the photography was excellent."

"That," responded Tomáš, "I admit, happily. But . . ."

"Children," interrupted Milena. "For heaven's sake, it was only a movie."

Only! thought Tomáš, though he respectfully kept quiet. He was very fond of the Kovářs.

"To Tomáš," sniffed Katrinka, "movies are the most important thing in the world."

Katrinka accompanied her father to work on Monday morning, arriving at the sports complex with him at eight, which was the time Jirka usually began his day. She had asked him several times over the weekend what her job would be, but he had always answered vaguely, saying that he was waiting to see, telling her she would not get preferential treatment just because she was his daughter, but would be put to work where she was needed most. None of her childish pranks had ever upset him so much. Never before had he been this angry with her, and it made her extremely unhappy. She wanted her loving, understanding, agreeable father back, wanted their relationship restored to what it had been before this last marking period, and, to achieve that, Katrinka felt she would do anything in the world.

A few minutes later she had changed her mind. She was furious. Nothing she had imagined, nothing that Tomáš had suggested, was as awful as what Jirka had devised. He had assigned her to the janitorial department. "We're short-staffed there," he said coolly. "I don't expect you to like it, Katrinka, but I do expect you to do whatever job Ludwig gives you without complaining and to do it as well as you can. Is that understood?"

"Yes, *Tati,*" she said, trying not to let him see how angry she was. What a waste of all her abilities. He could at least have put her to work doing something useful.

But that was precisely what Jirka was trying to avoid: he did not want Katrinka coming away from this experience having enjoyed herself. He looked at his daughter with more admiration than annoyance. He knew how hot-tempered she was, how stubborn she could be, how right at this moment she longed to shout at him, something she had never attempted and he would not have allowed, no matter how indulgent a parent everyone thought him. The worst she had ever done was run out of the house and not return for hours. "All right," he said. "Now go and find Ludwig and tell him you'll be working for him."

Ludwig, a stoop-shouldered man with thin gray hair who had been there for as long as Katrinka could remember, greeted her arrival as an everyday occurrence, as if he had been forewarned, confirming Katrinka's opinion that his department was no more short-staffed than usual. She was correct. Jirka had stopped in to see Ludwig in the cubbyhole that passed for his office the preceding Friday and had asked him to put Katrinka to work. Ludwig had listened carefully to Jirka's repeated insistence that Katrinka not be given any special treatment, trying to figure out what it was the assistant manager really wanted. Did he actually mean what he was saying, or was he just saying it to keep up some pretense of fairness? Did he, no matter what he said, want Katrinka assigned only to the lightest work? Or was he perhaps suggesting the complete opposite, that Ludwig go out of his way to give Katrinka a hard time?

Ludwig liked Jirka Kovář and admired the way he did not let the inefficiency of the manager make life hell for the employees. He found him competent and fair, not usually subject to whims and the like. But this business of Katrinka, as Ludwig explained to his wife when he got home that night, was puzzling. And he did not like being in this position, uncertain of what to do, not knowing how he was expected to behave.

Finally, after a sleepless two nights, he decided to take Jirka at his word. When Katrinka reported for work, he assigned her a locker and a uniform and told her that one of his workers had called in sick and she was to replace her, cleaning the women's showers and lavatories on the second floor, as well as the adjacent pool area and corridors. He saw the anger flash like lightning in her face and considered for a moment changing his mind. Then he thought about Jirka and kept silent.

But as she scrubbed down the green tiles in the showers and wiped the chrome plumbing, Katrinka's anger dissipated. Soon she began to take pleasure in the way the tiles shone, the chrome sparkled, the basins and toilets gleamed when she had finished with them. The pleasure was short-lived, however. A class would finish and ten, fifteen, twenty dripping young women would enter from the pool and spoil the effect. "Still, it's not so terrible," she confided to Tomáš when she ran into him on the way home.

Tomáš, who was returning from a day spent on one of his grandfather's construction sites, nodded his dusty head in agreement. "Yes," he said. "Physical labor can be satisfying all right. I just don't want to spend my whole life doing it."

"Oh, no," said Katrinka, horrified at the thought.

Preoccupied with her thoughts, Katrinka was very silent at dinner that night. Neither of her parents pressed her to speak, though Milena cast worried glances in her direction and Jirka felt very pleased with himself, confident that all was going as he had planned.

"But why the janitorial department?" Milena asked him that night when they had gone to bed. She sat with her slight shoulders rising out of the sheets, her chestnut head propped against a pillow, her beautiful face serious as she turned to look at him. "When you said work at the sports complex, I thought you meant office work, or coaching."

"So did Katrinka, I'm sure," said Jirka with satisfaction. "This is better. Much better."

Milena thought of how hard she and Jirka worked to make sure that Katrinka had nothing but the best, and now, here she was, their daughter, light of their life, cleaning toilets. It was ridiculous. "Surely you can find her something else to do?"

Jirka's broad fingers moved slowly up his wife's bare arm and under the thin strap of her nightgown. "Can't you trust me?" he said.

"Of course I trust you," she said, not meaning it, as he very well knew. Where Katrinka was concerned, she trusted no one. "I don't understand you sometimes, that's all. I don't understand this."

"This?" he said, his hand moving lower to cup her breast.

Which reminded her of something else. "What do you think about Katrinka and Tomáš?" she asked.

"I think they're friends," he said, getting her point immediately.

"Well, don't you think they spend too much time alone together?"

"The thought of sex never enters their heads," he assured her.

Startled, she pulled away from him. "That isn't what I meant."

"Then what did you mean?"

Milena started to speak, and then kept quiet because of course he was right. "Are you sure?" she asked.

Laughing, he pulled her back into his arms. "Yes," he said. "They play with each other like children. You can see, when you watch them, how innocent they are."

"You watch them?" Sometimes Milena thought of herself as smarter than Jirka. And if intelligence could be measured in the number of books read, perhaps she was right. But in real life, to her surprise, he seemed always to be several steps ahead of her.

"She's my daughter. What do you think?" Then he sighed. "But we can't watch her forever. We can't protect her forever. We do the best we can. We teach her what we think she has to know. And then," he said, his arms tightening around his wife, "then we let her go and hold on to each other."

Every day for three weeks, Katrinka mopped the corridors and the tiles around the pool, cleaned the showers and the lavatories, swept the stairs and polished the handrails. Sometimes she wished she was in the pool swimming with the others, or in the gymnastics room running through routines, but mostly she was resigned to working. Boys her age passed by and smiled at her shyly, and occasionally she would stop what she was doing to talk with them. And while at first she was embarrassed when girlfriends saw her performing such menial tasks, she soon realized that, because her father had an important position, they were not contemptuous of the work she did, but envious of the opportunity she had to earn money over the summer.

Amazingly, they were jealous of her. If they had not liked Jirka Kovář so much, they would have accused him of abusing his position by employing his daughter. Katrinka found that interesting. Though someone else might be sneered at for cleaning lavatories, she, because of who she was, because she was thought to have some sort of power, was envied.

That was not the only lesson she learned. By the end of her first week at the sports complex, Katrinka had also grasped the point that Jirka was trying to make by insisting she work there: satisfying as it was to make a chrome faucet shine, it was also boring. And, as her father wanted her to do, she began to think about her future, about life without skiing.

So far, Katrinka had broken a leg skiing, and a hand. She had sprained ankles and wrenched muscles. Young and healthy, she had recovered quickly. But she had seen others hurt more seriously, hurt so badly they would never ski competitively again. The possibility of that happening to her now occurred to her for the first time. And the thought terrified her. What would become of all her wonderful plans then? With nothing to fall back on, no real education, no other skills, she would be condemned to a life of drudgery, a life like hers that summer, or worse. Though she accepted what Jirka had taught her—that all necessary work is valuable and that those doing it must be respected—Katrinka had no intention of wasting her time doing menial jobs. And not just because they paid so little, though the price of skis alone was enough to convince her of the value of money, but because she would go out of her mind with boredom. She promised herself she would never allow that to happen. Never. She would die first!

98

Ten

"Katrinka, over here!"

Standing just inside the door, Katrinka peered through the dim, smoke-filled interior, looking for Tomáš.

The Maxmilianka, a large, noisy café decorated in dark wood and brass, was a favorite with the film students at the nearby Academy of Music and Art. It served cheap, hearty meals and Czechoslovakian wine. The hours were long, the service lackadaisical, and the management not only did not mind wild behavior but seemed to cherish the café's reputation as a place where intense intellectual discussions frequently gave way to blows as students tried either to make a point or to keep a girlfriend. Love affairs often began and ended in the heat of passionate debate.

"Katrinka!"

She heard her name called again, saw a beckoning arm rising above the crowd, and turned to her friend Zuzka, saying, "There he is. Over there, in the corner. Come on." Plunging into the room, Katrinka headed through the dense crowd, unselfconsciously returning the smiles of the young men who made way for her and Zuzka as they passed.

Both Tomáš and Katrinka had got what they wanted. FAMU was the place to study to be a film director, and Tomáš had just completed his first term, as had Katrinka, who had started at Charles University in September of 1966.

For a Moravian athlete wishing to continue in sports *and* acquire a degree as a hedge against the future, there were two choices, the universities in Brno and Prague. But Prague was the capital city and its university was the oldest and the best, and that's where the Kovářs had wanted Katrinka to go. Thanks to her academic record (since her summer at the sports complex, it had remained excellent) she had been admitted to the language department, and, because of her skill on the ski slopes, she was one of only six women that year who, after rigorous trials, had made the city's ski team. Zuzka was another. They competed for Prague in national events and for Czechoslovakia in international competitions like the World Cup.

Tomáš pushed away from the crowded table and stood up as the two women approached. He enfolded Katrinka in a hug, bending his head to kiss her on both cheeks. As tall as she was, she still reached only to his chin. *"Zlatičko,"* he murmured. "I was beginning to think you weren't coming."

"We were late getting back," she said. "Snow." Then she turned and took Zuzka's arm. "This is my friend, Zuzka Pavlik. Zuzka, Tomáš Havlíček." She and Zuzka had met frequently over the years at various ski competitions, but only recently, since they had both made the national ski team, had they become friends. They made an attractive pair: both tall, Zuzka five feet seven, Katrinka close to five-nine; Katrinka with short hair so dark it was almost black and startling pale blue eyes; Zuzka with large, soft brown eyes and a cropped head of blond hair. She was not so beautiful as Katrinka, but her body had a hefty, attractive curve to it, and her face a sexy, feline look. She exuded an aura of womanliness, of warmth and good humor, that was very appealing.

"Dobrý den," Tomáš and Zuzka murmured to one another politely, shaking hands, quickly taking stock, Tomáš liking what he saw immediately, Zuzka not quite sure. Tomáš's features, taken individually, were not attractive. His face was too long, his skin too dark, his eyes too deep-set and serious, his nose too broad and lips too full. Nevertheless,

100

Zuzka found herself wondering what it would be like to kiss that mouth.

"Sit down, sit down," murmured Tomáš, rearranging the table, dispossessing friends of chairs for Katrinka and Zuzka. He tried, over the noise, to introduce them to the other young men and women at the table, all students at the film school. "They're on the ski team," explained Tomáš.

"Oh, skiing," said one of the young women dismissively, turning to her companion to resume the discussion that had been interrupted by Katrinka and Zuzka's arrival.

It was not that the national enthusiasm for sports had waned, or that the country had lost interest in its athletes. But something unexpected and exciting was happening in Czechoslovakia, and the students were caught up in it. The pall that had settled over the media and the arts with the communist takeover was finally lifting. The liberal weekly newspaper of the Writers' Union, *Literarni Novini,* now featured not only literary news but discussions of a reality people recognized as their own, as opposed to the airbrushed picture presented in the official press. Milan Kundera was teaching, writing, and being published. Václav Havel's plays *The Garden Party* and *The Memorandum* had been produced in Prague and in eighteen countries abroad. A talented generation of directors had graduated from FAMU, the film school, and were working at Barrandov Studios, drawn there by its adventurous head, Alois Pldenak. Films by Miloš Forman, Ivan Passer, Jan Němec, and Jiří Menzel could now be seen not only at home but in movie theaters in London and Paris and New York. So, to this one student at least, either Forman's recently released *Loves of a Blonde* was of far more interest than the results of a World Cup competition or she was simply jealous of the two beautiful young women who had invaded her territory.

"You're on the Prague ski team?" said one of the young men, smiling with open admiration at Zuzka and Katrinka.

Katrinka and Zuzka nodded. "*And* the national team," added Tomáš.

"Were you in Val-d'Isère?" asked Jan, a tall, too-thin young man with an intense face and serious eyes behind wire-rimmed spectacles. He was one of Tomáš's best friends, and, although he had known Katrinka for some months, he still felt so shy around her that he had to force himself to speak in her presence.

Katrinka nodded again. "We just got back," she said.

"What were you doing there?" asked a plump young woman as she filched a cigarette from a pack on the table.

"The World Cup," said someone, sounding disgusted with her ignorance.

"Oh, yes, of course. I forgot. How did we do?"

"Don't you ever read the papers?" asked another exasperated voice. The speaker was a small dark-haired woman with beautiful fair skin and a large hooked nose. "We won. At least, the women's downhill team won. Katrinka Kovář came in first." When Tomáš and Zuzka laughed, the young woman turned to them. "What's wrong? Didn't the paper get even that right?" Usually, the official newspaper, *Rudé právo*, could at least be counted on to report athletic victories with reasonable accuracy.

"She's Katrinka Kovář," said Tomáš, waving his cigarette at Katrinka.

The young woman with the large nose smiled and extended a hand. "Oh. I didn't hear your names, there was so much noise. I'm very pleased to meet you."

"Dobrý den," said Katrinka with a friendly, unassuming smile as she shook her hand. An only child, used to constant attention, Katrinka did not crave the spotlight so much as assume that it was naturally hers and, when she found herself in it, she accepted the position with a naturalness that was disarming. Outgoing and warm, she liked people and, in return, most people instinctively liked her.

"Tell us about the race," said the woman with the big nose, eager to hear.

"How did you do, Zuzka?" asked Tomáš, giving her a lazy, seductive smile, not so much to distribute the attention fairly as to make an impression.

"She was right behind me," said Katrinka quickly, eager to give Zuzka a share of the credit. "One wrong move and I would have been dead."

"Only Katrinka never makes a wrong move," said Zuzka, laughing, without a trace of jealousy.

Conversation about skiing gave way quickly to talk about tennis and other sports, and, of course, about the latest films. Nobody talked about politics. Years of caution had made that subject a taboo few were ready yet to break, despite the gradual easing of government restrictions.

As the night grew later, the restaurant grew more crowded, the smoke thicker, the talk rowdier. Snatches of song could be heard over the noise, renditions in Czech of popular Beatles' songs vying with traditional waltzes and polkas.

"Let's go dancing," said Katrinka.

"I'm exhausted," said Zuzka.

"It's early." She was still high from the race, she realized, her energy up and needing release. When it dissipated, she would collapse, perhaps sleep the whole of the next day. But right now, she wanted to dance.

"My head is splitting," said Tomáš.

"Don't drink so much," replied Katrinka pragmatically.

Finally, she succeeded in coaxing Tomáš and Zuzka and a few of the others into accompanying her. They slipped into their heavy wool jackets and out into the cold night. The moon was up and bright, illuminating the wide boulevard that ran parallel to the Vltava River. Across the expanse of gray water lay the Malá Strana, the Lesser Town, which had sprung up centuries before outside the old city's walls. Above it, rising out of the hillside like a castle in a fairy tale, were the turrets and towers of the Hradčany.

Tomáš, Zuzka, and Jan piled into Katrinka's little blue Fiat 600 and the others into a Škoda parked a short distance away. With the stipend she received from the government for skiing, the sale of her used equipment, summers spent working in a hotel in Munich, and the modeling she had begun to do soon after she had arrived in Prague, Katrinka had enough money for luxuries like a small car and the expensive gas to run it. Ota Černý's predictions and Jirka Kovář's hopes were coming true.

"Katrinka, you have too much energy," complained

Tomáš, not unkindly, since he was squeezing himself happily into the back seat next to Zuzka.

"Nonsense," said Katrinka. "It's just that you're so lazy." She smiled engagingly at Jan, who was settling himself in the front seat next to her. Too frail to play sports himself, he had an unbridled admiration for people like Tomáš and Katrinka, who could. And when they were female and beautiful as well, the temptation to adoration was too strong to be resisted. Now he stared at her, trying to think of something to say, but could not and only nodded, summoning up a faint, nervous grin.

"Lazy!" said Zuzka in tones of mock outrage as Katrinka started the motor and shifted neatly into gear. "Do you know how hard I work trying to keep up with her? I collapse, and she never gets tired." She was always amazed that Katrinka, who was so much slighter in build than she, should have so much more energy.

"I do," protested Katrinka. "Sometimes I fall apart, whoosh, just like that." She snapped her fingers and offered Jan another smile.

"Yes, she does," seconded Tomáš, "but unfortunately not until after she's run the rest of us into the ground."

Katrinka drove across the Most 1 Máje, one of the several bridges spanning the Vltava, into the Malá Strana and its maze of narrow cobbled streets to Maltese Square, where the Moskva, an old wine cellar with vaulted Gothic ceilings and walls lined with aged oak casks, was located. They danced to a Czech band trying to imitate the Rolling Stones. The music was loud and frantic and woke everyone up, injecting them with the same fierce energy that was keeping Katrinka on her feet.

"I'll drive you back to your dormitory," said Katrinka to the two young men when finally the Moskva closed and the group straggled out again into the picturesque square. A short distance away, the lighted dome of the Church of the Infant of Prague cast a soft glow in the night sky, and, beyond it, a two-hundred-foot copy of the Eiffel Tower rose darkly out of the Petřín Gardens, Prague's equivalent of the Bois de Boulogne.

"No, no, no," insisted Tomáš. "I want to clear my head." He kissed both young women on their cheeks. "It's not such a long walk. Be seeing you," he said to no one in particular.

"Good night," said Jan, formally shaking their hands before following Tomáš off down the street.

Katrinka and Zuzka got into the Fiat, and as Katrinka turned it to point toward home, a large dormitory in the mountains above the castle, Zuzka asked her about Tomáš.

"What about Tomáš?" He and Zuzka had behaved so politely to one another all night that there was no way Katrinka could know there was romance in the air.

"How long have you known him?"

"Oh," said Katrinka. "Forever. Since I was ten."

"That long," said Zuzka, considering the possibilities. "Are you in love with him?"

"With Tomáš? No, of course not."

"He's very attractive," said Zuzka, bridling a little, as if Katrinka had just questioned her romantic judgment.

"Tomáš?" repeated Katrinka. "I mean, of course he is." She was just not used to thinking about him in that way.

"You've never noticed?"

"Yes. Certainly. He's my friend, after all. I love him."

"Oh?"

"Not *that* way," corrected Katrinka firmly.

"Good," said Zuzka, satisfied. "So, you're not lovers." Though there was a great deal of sexual freedom in Czechoslovakia by that January of 1967, people generally were quite reserved about discussing it. Not Zuzka, however. It was one of the things that Katrinka found so likable about her, how direct and honest she was.

"No," said Katrinka. "We're not."

"Have you ever had a lover?" asked Zuzka, staring straight ahead out the windshield of the car, pretending to be absorbed in the intricate beauty of the narrow Prague streets, the tiny houses in a mix of architectural styles and periods, now barely visible since the moon had set. Though she prided herself on being outspoken, Zuzka was afraid that perhaps this time she had gone too far, that she might have offended Katrinka, whom she liked very much. But she did want to know. The subject of lovers, who had them and who did not, the whole subject of sex was of increasing concern to her. Lately, she rarely thought of anything else.

"No," said Katrinka, a little uneasily, not used to this sort of intimate conversation. She had been traveling since she was a young child, had been exposed to all sorts of romantic situations, observed them, but not been involved. Consequently, she was both knowing and pure, wary and curious. "Have you?" she asked.

"No, but I would like one." Turning her attention from the street to Katrinka, she asked, "Wouldn't you?"

"I don't know," said Katrinka, still under the influence of years of cautionary tales, psychological pressures, physical restrictions. She thought about it a moment longer. "Yes," she said finally, stopping the car in its parking place near the fourteenth-century building that was their dormitory. "I would."

"And the sooner the better for me," said Zuzka.

Up until the age of eight, boys and girls were on the same ski team. After that, they raced separately, though they still trained and traveled together, competing in the same places. So much proximity should have given rise to rampant sexual activity, and, in other countries, like England or Germany, Sweden or the United States, certainly did in the late fifties and early sixties. But not only was Czechoslovakia, despite the veneer of communism, a very Catholic country, the predominantly male coaches who traveled with the girls' teams were far more effective than a convent of nuns in curbing their charges' sexual urges. They watched them with alert and knowing eyes, worked them to the point of exhaustion, enforced strict curfews, supervised what they ate, what they drank, what they thought. And they did it usually not out of any profound moral commitment but pragmatically, not wanting their best women skiers to squander their energy on romance, not wanting to lose them to pregnancy. They warned their girls ceaselessly of the consequences of sex: not the fires of hell, but the loss of an athletic career with all its attendant luxuries—the financial stipends, the educational opportunities, the extra rations of food, the best skiing equipment, the choicest places to live, and, above all, the freedom to travel. With knowledge of contraception at best sketchy, the pill unavailable, and diaphragms, like condoms, not easily obtainable, the girls by and large heeded their coaches' warnings. Though women throughout Czechoslovakia may, in general, have been experimenting more, sexual activity, while not unknown, was rare among young female athletes. Fear and strenuous physical activity kept their raging hormones in check.

Did Tomáš have a lover? wondered Katrinka, now that Zuzka had raised the question. She thought of the women she had seen with him and thought it possible. There had been one in particular he had seemed to like, a plump blond girl who had worked in a restaurant. But Katrinka had not seen her with Tomáš in quite a while now.

It seemed strange to her that Tomáš and she, who had shared so much over the years, fears and longings, failures and achievements, should not have shared this experience. She considered whether or not she would like to have Tomáš as a lover. She thought of his face, which she knew as well as her own—the face that Zuzka found so handsome—and of his body, tall and very lean, though he consumed amazing quantities of food. She pictured him in various familiar attitudes, climbing the pear tree in a neighbor's garden, playing hockey, bicycling along the narrow road leading to the forest. She imagined him reading by the side of the stream in Svitov, putting his book aside and leaning forward slowly to kiss her. It was all right, she decided, this imaginary kiss, quite friendly, but not much more interesting than those he usually bestowed on both her cheeks when they met or said good-bye.

No, she decided finally, Tomáš would not do. He was too familiar, too much like a brother, too comfortable for a lover. Though she had no experience of love, of sexual, romantic love, she imagined it must feel altogether different from the way she felt for Tomáš.

Curiosity drove her. Always outgoing and friendly, with a manner more open and warm than flirtatious, Katrinka now, during practice, observed the young men on the team with appraising eyes; and, feeling her attention, they responded with eager smiles and long questioning looks. On the train to Badgastein, as it hurtled into the dark tunnel through the pass, she let a grand-slalom champion named Vladislav Elias kiss her.

She was not the only one. Blending with the sound of harmonicas and guitars and the voices singing, Katrinka heard the low indistinct murmur of men pleading, young women giggling, a slap, a whispered no. There was a tale told of a girl, more than one most likely, who had lost her virginity a year or two before on this same train in one of the WCs.

Vladislav murmured her name over and over, the sound muffled against her skin as his lips traced the contours of her face. It was not Katrinka's first kiss, far from it, but the others had been tentative, experimental, playful, eager, and brief. This was different. He took her bottom lip between his teeth, bit down gently, then slipped his tongue into her mouth. His hand moved slowly down her arm, to her waist, and up again to her breast. When she didn't protest, he began to fondle it gently. She felt breathless, she felt like a candle growing hot and soft. So this is what it's like, she thought.

Then, in the distance, she heard Ota Černý's voice, bellowing out over the others, singing a Beatles' song. Abruptly, she pulled away from Vladislav.

"What's the matter?" he said, dazed from both the kiss and its abrupt ending.

"We should stop," she said, a little surprised at the tremor in her voice when she spoke. The train raced out of the tunnel into the sunshine and she blinked. Sitting back, she smiled at Vladislav. "I liked that," she said.

"Will you meet me tonight?"

Katrinka considered it for a moment, then shook her head. "I can't," she said. She tried to think of a good reason, one he would find acceptable. "It's too difficult," she added, though even she was not quite sure what she meant by that.

The teams did not travel light. There were the athletes and their support personnel—technicians to sharpen and wax skis, maintain boots and bindings, keep all the various paraphernalia of skiing in good repair. Then, in addition to the coaches like Ota Černý who were primarily responsible for the team's performance, there were supposed trainers who were trusted members of the Communist party, secret police there to build morale with nationalistic slogans (a function fulfilled for noncommunist countries by the head coach), to make sure the team members held to the party line, and—most importantly—to prevent defections. It wasn't easy to escape everyone's notice.

"After the race?" said Vladislav, taking her hand. Usually, they were allowed a little more freedom then, win or lose, time to unwind and celebrate.

Katrinka studied Vladislav for a moment. It was true, she had enjoyed kissing him; but now that her curiosity was satisfied, she didn't feel eager to repeat the experience. It occurred to her that, though she thought him good-looking and had always found him pleasant enough, she didn't like him even as much as Tomáš, let alone more, and certainly not enough to consider him a potential lover. "I like it best when we all go out in a group," she said. "It's more fun."

"That depends," he said, smiling, "on what kind of fun you want to have."

Exactly, thought Katrinka, who stood up, pulling Vladislav by his hand. "Right now," she said, "I want to sing."

They walked down the swaying corridor to the dining car where Ota Černý sat surrounded by a group of tall, lean, good-looking and cheerful athletes, boys and girls. One played guitar, another a harmonica, the others sang. If they were anxious about racing the next day, it didn't show. The nerves would come later.

Ota looked up as Katrinka and Vladislav entered. What have they been up to? he wondered, noticing that Katrinka looked a little flushed. He would have to keep an eye on them, he decided. Katrinka was too good a skier to be allowed to get into trouble, not to mention the fact that she was the daughter of his best friend.

Ota made room for her on the seat next to him and motioned her over. The music had changed from the Beatles to a polka, and Katrinka had already started to sing, joining in the familiar tune, clapping her hands and swaying in time to the music. She smiled at him happily and sank into the space at his side, leaving Vladislav to watch her with admiring and hungry eyes.

She grew lovelier every day, Ota thought. The bright beautiful child he had adored had turned into a remarkably beautiful young woman, beautiful not just because of the perfection of her features, but because she was so full of life and energy. She was like a magnet that drew all eyes. Aware sometimes of staring at her, he had to force himself to look away. She was the daughter he had always wanted, he told himself, and, not wanting to show favoritism, was careful to treat her just as he treated all the other young women on the team. Often, he was even harder on her than the others, because she had so much potential, he told himself, because she could really make something of herself if she tried.

Ota Černý's career had sometimes run parallel to Katrinka's and sometimes intersected it. Over the years he had, from time to time, coached the particular local or provincial team that Katrinka happened to be on. Observing her closely one year, from a distance the next few, then closely again, he felt he was able to assess her abilities coolly and accurately. With her skill and strength, her energy and determination, Katrinka could, he became more and more certain, one day be an Olympic champion.

By the time Katrinka started at Charles University, Ota's team had done so well at the local and provincial levels that he had been promoted to coach of the national women's team. Seeing in Katrinka a potential star, it was he who had trained her, encouraged her, and supported her through the ordeal of tryouts for the Prague team. And when her success on that team had made her eligible for national competitions he was elated. "I knew it," he said to his wife, "the first time I ever saw her on skis. I knew she was good."

"Before you crow too loud," said Olga, "wait and see how she does when she's with first-class skiers. She hasn't had so much competition until now." Olga knew she was being unfair: Katrinka had many times, in many competitions, out-skied some superb athletes. But sometimes when she thought of the girl, such bitterness welled up in her heart she could not control either the black thoughts or the harsh words.

Though Olga had loved the child almost as much as Ota, her feelings had changed as Katrinka grew into a lovely young woman and Olga declined into—as she saw it—a barren old one. Tormented by guilt at the thought of the child she had aborted, at the irreparable harm she had done to her body, at the loss she had made Ota share, Olga gradually came to see Katrinka as a living reproach, a judgment from God, a constant reminder of what she, too, could have had were it not for her unpardonable sin. To escape from her guilt, Olga drank, not the way Ota did, in a crowd, with friends, for the pleasure of the taste and the soaring mood, but in secret and alone, to ease her anguish.

Ota watched her helplessly. He had thought that he understood and shared Olga's pain, but soon realized that it was something separate from his, more terrible and destructive. He gave her what sympathy he could, and looked for happiness elsewhere. He skied and played chess, drank and smoked and told stories with Jirka Kovář and his other male friends, he indulged in occasional brief affairs with women, but never with the girls he coached. That would have offended his sense of decency and honor. To him, those girls were not only a sacred trust, but the daughters he had never had. They were his greatest comfort. And when Olga saw that Ota was actually happy at work, she began to resent the ski team, and the girls on it, and especially to resent Katrinka, the source of her husband's greatest pleasure.

Badgastein is an old Austrian spa town nestled in a warm valley beneath the Tauern Mountains. It has radon waters supposedly good for the endocrine system, a charming fifteenth-century church, a scenic walk called the Kaiser Wilhelm Promenade, and a waterfall that cascades down from the mountain into a pool in the center of town. In spring and summer, its predominant color is the green of its building facades, ornate roof tiles, lush spreading shrubs, towering conifers. In winter, this green gives way to white, as snow covers everything with its deep rich mantle, making for excellent skiing on the east slopes of the valley.

The International Ski Federation championships were scheduled to begin the next day, so no sooner did the teams

111

arrive at the hotel than Ota Černý and the other coaches had them out on the trails, looking over the terrain so they could plan their runs, programming a response to the slope and curve of the mountain into their muscles' memory. During a race, the fewer the surprises the better.

Afterward, in the hotel dining room, they had dinner, good Austrian Wiener schnitzel with mashed potatoes and gravy, a subdued meal since everyone was by then preoccupied with thoughts of the race the next day. When they finished, they were advised to go to bed early and get a good night's sleep.

Four girls were assigned to each room in the hotel, a comfortable old inn on the outskirts of town. Sharing with Katrinka and Zuzka were two students from Brno University, one of them Ilona Lukánský, Katrinka's nemesis from the Svitov ski club.

Ilona had started university two years before Katrinka, and during that time they had skied separately, Ilona for Brno and then the national team, while Katrinka still remained with the Svitov ski club. Those years were a relief to Katrinka, who enjoyed competition but not the naked, aggressive sort that Ilona inspired. But once Katrinka made the national team, they were thrown again into each other's company.

Whatever her other faults, Ilona was a good skier. Katrinka was willing to admit that. But her efforts to ignore Ilona's needles and barbs failed again as they had when they were children. Though she managed to control her temper and not resort to verbal abuse in return, while skiing with Ilona, Katrinka felt not the generalized desire to win that characterized her at other times, but an intense need to beat her rival if she killed herself doing it.

"What were you and Vladislav up to, alone in that compartment?" asked Ilona that night when the girls were in their room preparing for bed. Someone seeing her for the first time would have found her pretty, with the curls of her soft white-gold hair framing her pale, flat face like a halo. But her expression was one of chronic discontent and her gray eyes seemed always sly, and those who knew her, after a while, saw only that.

112

"With Vladislav?" echoed Katrinka, surprised.

"You were with him a long time."

"What does it matter to you?" asked Zuzka belligerently.

"I'm just curious," said Ilona, her voice arch. She was not ever prepared to back down.

"We were not doing very much," said Katrinka.

"Are you jealous?" asked Zuzka. She did not like Ilona at all and was always eager for a fight, which Katrinka was equally eager to prevent.

"Don't be stupid," said Ilona.

"I've seen you looking at him."

"He's so handsome," said the fourth roommate.

"We all look," said Katrinka. "And wonder."

"Look but don't touch," said Zuzka, joining in Katrinka's laughter.

Ilona looked at them as if they were crazy. "What are you laughing about?"

"Do you want to bet she's not a virgin?" whispered Zuzka to Katrinka.

"You're impossible," said Ilona. "Both of you."

To Katrinka's surprise, Tomáš was at the station to meet them on their return to Prague. He stood on the platform waving his hat. "Katrinka! Zuzka!" he shouted, trying to get their attention. "Over here!"

"There's Tomáš," said Zuzka. She seemed very pleased to see him, but not at all surprised.

Katrinka looked at her friend suspiciously. "Did you know he would be here?"

Zuzka smiled. "I did hope," she said.

Tomáš, too, was beaming. His hair was wet as if he had just showered. His face looked newly shaven, and his cheek when he kissed her felt smooth and smelled of some scent Katrinka did not recognize. That, too, surprised her. Tomáš usually spent his extra money only on books.

"We lost," said Zuzka. Katrinka had hit a mogul too fast and had fallen, pulling a muscle in her leg. She had skied the rest of the day bandaged and injected with painkillers, but did not do well, placing eighth. Ilona had come in third, Zuzka fifth. The French women's team had won.

Tomáš wrapped an arm around each and said, "Then you really do need some cheering up. Come on, we're going to the Maxmilianka. Everyone's there already. We'll have something to eat, and afterward go to a film."

"I can't," said Katrinka. "I'm exhausted."

Tomáš and Zuzka both looked at her as if she had gone suddenly and completely mad. "You? Tired?" said Zuzka.

"I'm dead," insisted Katrinka. "My leg hurts."

"It's a good film," coaxed Tomáš.

"I'll see it some other time," said Katrinka. "Tonight I'm going right to my room to sleep."

"Oh," said Zuzka.

She sounded so disappointed that Katrinka realized she was about to be noble and offer to accompany her back to the dormitory. "But you two go enjoy yourselves. Don't worry about me. I'm fine. I just need to rest."

"You're sure?" said Zuzka.

"Certainly she's sure. She doesn't need you to put her to bed," said Tomáš, kissing Katrinka on both cheeks. "Relax," he ordered. "I'll see you tomorrow." Tomáš put an arm around Zuzka and steered her away through the crowd. She turned around once, shrugged as if wondering what on earth she was letting herself in for, then waved and turned away to keep up with Tomáš.

Katrinka watched them for a moment. Tomáš and Zuzka. She was both so unused to thinking of people in romantic terms and so obsessed lately with her own sexual drives that she had not realized until just then how interested her two friends were in each other.

"Katrinka!" She heard her name called and turned to see Ota Černý beckoning to her. He was standing by the bus, waiting for the last of the straggling team to board. "Are you coming with us?"

"Yes," she called and hobbled toward him.

"How's your leg?" he asked when she reached him.

"Fine."

"Don't forget, tonight, ice packs."

Katrinka was dreaming that she and Vladislav were on a train and he was kissing her, only suddenly it was a chair lift and he was making it rock dangerously and she was terrified, either that she would fall off or that Ota Černý would see them.

"Katrinka." A voice whispered her name. At first, she thought it was Vladislav while he kissed her. But then she realized it was not his voice at all, but a woman's. "Katrinka."

Her eyes opened and she saw Zuzka sitting at the edge of her bed. The room was gray, that dismal first light before the sun rises. "What's the matter?" she said. "Are you all right?" The terror of the dream persisted. Something must be terribly wrong for Zuzka to awaken her.

"Yes," she said. "Yes. I'm fine. I'm wonderful. I just wanted to tell you, I love Tomáš. Do you mind?"

"No. I knew it."

"That's why you didn't come with us tonight."

"I knew you two wanted to be alone, even if you didn't."

"Thank you," she said. In the dim light, Katrinka could just make out Zuzka's face. She was crying. "Oh, Katrinka. It was wonderful."

"What?"

"Making love, of course, you idiot." She sobbed. "It was absolutely wonderful."

Eleven

When Katrinka wasn't skiing, she was training, and when she wasn't doing that, she was attending class at the university, studying English, German, Russian, the histories of those countries, their society and culture, their art, literature, and music. She was in class as much as eight hours a day, enrolled in a six-year course for a master's degree in languages, which would qualify her for a job in teaching or journalism (someone, after all, had to adapt the news from the foreign press deemed suitable for publication in Czechoslovakia). The idea of being a translator in the diplomatic service especially appealed to her. She saw it as a way to keep her freedom of movement when she was no longer able to ski competitively.

Because of the amount they had to travel for competitions, both in Czechoslovakia and abroad, athletes were given some leeway but in general were expected to make up the work they missed and to perform well in exams. Those who did not were expelled from the university, and from their teams, losing all the privileges to which their status as star athletes had entitled them.

Deciding their fate, supervising every aspect of their lives—academic and personal—was the all-powerful sports committee. Individually, the members of the committee seemed jovial enough, men and women liking a glass of pilsen and a good laugh, standing on the sidelines cheering during a hockey match or ice-skating event or ski race. As a group, they were terrifying, holding court in a thoroughly modern room which everyone nonetheless persisted in seeing as a medieval torture chamber. Katrinka knew personally two people who had been called before them: one had been put on probation for failing a course; the other, a young girl, had been expelled from the university and dropped from the ice-skating team because she was pregnant. There was no appeal from committee decisions, and avoiding a summons to appear before them was every athlete's ambition. To that, even winning came second.

Katrinka knew the committee members by sight, smiled politely when she saw them during training or at races, exchanged a few friendly remarks with them at social gatherings, but, thanks to her straight-A average, had so far avoided any official contact. Which was why she was surprised when one day in early February, as she came out of the ancient stone building where her English class met into the cobbled street, one of them approached her, wearing an all too obvious frown. Katrinka felt an unfamiliar nervous flutter in her stomach, and she smiled anxiously. *"Dobrý den,"* she said. "How are you, Mrs. Hoch?"

A broad handsome woman in her late fifties, Mrs. Hoch did not smile or return the greeting. Instead, she waved a magazine under Katrinka's nose. "Katrinka, is this you?"

Katrinka looked at the magazine and saw her own unmistakable pale blue eyes looking back at her. "Yes," she said. The magazine was just out and it was the first time she had seen the cover. She looked fat, she thought.

"You're modeling?"

She nodded. "To earn extra money," she explained.

"You find your stipend insufficient?"

"Oh, no," said Katrinka, growing more nervous by the minute. Mrs. Hoch had a reputation, quite justified, for being hard on the girls, especially the pretty ones. With the boys, she was more sympathetic, even flirtatious. "I manage very well on it. But . . ." She hesitated.

"But?" pressed Mrs. Hoch, still frowning.

"With what I make modeling, I can afford a few luxuries." She pointed toward the blue Fiat 600, which was parked a short distance away. "Like my car. It's very useful to have a car," she added, thinking quickly, searching for a way to appease Mrs. Hoch. "Sometimes, after a race, I can get back to Prague much faster than if I have to wait for a train. That way, I don't miss so many classes."

"You don't find that this"—she gestured with the magazine again—"takes too much time? Interferes with your studies?"

"No. Not at all."

"How long have you been doing it?"

"Since last October," said Katrinka. Shortly after her arrival in Prague, one night at the Maxmilianka, she had met a young actress who modeled to make extra money. Lured by the prospect of doing the same, Katrinka had asked Tomáš to photograph her, had sent the pictures to the girl's agency, and, after an interview, had begun modeling shoes. Since then, she had modeled hats, gloves, makeup, and fashion. This was her first cover, but really it was amazing that no one from the committee had spotted her sooner. Or perhaps they only read sports news.

"Hmmm." Mrs. Hoch's face remained serious. "And what grades are you getting?" she asked, though she knew perfectly well. Katrinka told her and Mrs. Hoch nodded. "And you don't miss practice." It was not phrased as a question, since she already knew the answer to that, too.

"Never," said Katrinka firmly.

"See that you don't," said Mrs. Hoch. She snapped the magazine against the palm of her hand. "I'll not have this kind of nonsense ruining an athlete's chances."

"No, Mrs. Hoch," said Katrinka as the woman spun around and walked briskly away. "Jealous cow," muttered Katrinka, taking a long, deep breath, trying to ease the knot that had formed in her stomach. Though she knew that she had done nothing wrong and that some people—her parents, for example—might think she had been enterprising and ambitious, still she felt as if she had just come very close to trouble.

"Is this you?"

It was two nights later and Katrinka was with Tomáš and Zuzka at a table full of friends having dinner at the Maxmilianka. Again she regarded the broad face with its high cheekbones and blue eyes looking out from the cover of the magazine that had been thrust under her nose, then tilted her head up to see the man who had asked the question. When she saw who it was, her breath caught in her throat and for a moment she couldn't speak.

"It is you, isn't it?"

Katrinka nodded. "Of course it is," said Tomáš. "Who could mistake those eyes?"

Zuzka smiled at Tomáš and snuggled closer, linking her arm through his. She was not jealous, just inclined to make clear occasionally who belonged to whom.

"You're even more beautiful in person."

Katrinka felt herself blush, which she did not usually do, and hoped no one noticed. "Thank you, Mr. Bartoš," she said.

"You know who I am?" he asked, as pleased by this nod to his fame as he was by the notice of a beautiful girl.

"Oh, yes." Though she had thought she had forgotten what he looked like long ago, in fact she had recognized Mirek Bartoš instantly. She realized suddenly that she had always carried a vivid picture of him in her memory.

Bartoš pulled a pen out of his pocket and a crumpled piece of paper, scribbled a few lines, and handed it to her. "Will you call me?" he said. His long hair was graying, but he was as big and bold as ever, as commanding a presence. Katrinka hesitated, and he laughed. "Don't worry. I'm an old married man. It's for a part in my new film." He studied her for a moment, a quizzical look on his face. "You look just right," he said finally. "Have you ever acted?"

"Once," she said, smiling, not able to resist. "But it was a very small part." If she ever saw him again, she would remind him of the film he made one summer in Svitov and the little girl in the classroom scene who had one line to say.

"Call me," he repeated, and turned away, gesturing to the group of students accompanying him to follow.

"Who was he?" asked Zuzka.

"Mirek Bartoš," said Tomáš and, when he saw that name meant nothing to her, added, "a famous film director." The slight emphasis on the word "famous" indicated his disapproval. Both Bartoš and the group with him were too conservative for Tomáš's taste. "An old married man," he repeated, his disapproval growing more pronounced. "Do you know who his wife is?"

"Of course," said Katrinka. "Vlasta Mach."

"She's not a movie star," said Zuzka. "I know all the movie stars."

"No," said Tomáš, smiling again. At this point in their relationship, the first heady days of complete sexual rapture, he found Zuzka's absolute ignorance about anything other than sports totally charming. "She's not a movie star."

"Felix Mach's daughter," explained Katrinka.

"Exactly," said Tomáš, sounding very satisfied as he took another cigarette from the pack of Spartas on the table and lit it.

"Oh," said Zuzka. Even she recognized that name. Felix Mach was a high-ranking official in Czechoslovakia's secret police.

"Which may account for his success," said Tomáš, low enough so that only Zuzka, Katrinka, and Jan, who was sitting next to her, could hear.

"Nonsense," said Katrinka, leaping instantly to Bartoš's defense as she always did when Tomáš questioned his ability. "He's very talented."

"What did Bartoš want?" called someone from the other end of the table.

"To make Katrinka a film star," replied Tomáš cheerfully.

"Why not?" said Zuzka.

"Why not indeed?" said Tomáš, lifting his wineglass in salute.

"Are you going to call him?" asked Jan, his eyes soft and curious behind their spectacles. He did not seem the least bit surprised, or impressed, with Mirek Bartoš's interest in Katrinka. He considered it her due.

Katrinka turned and saw the adoring expression on Jan's face and wished again that she was able to return his feelings. He was such a good man, intelligent, hardworking, even attractive in a studious way. Would she ever fall in love? she wondered. "I suppose so," she said.

"Of course you're going to call him," said Tomáš.

"You know everything, don't you?" said Katrinka, irritated finally by Tomáš's teasing.

"Not everything, but this much I know: nothing would keep you from phoning him." He turned to the others at the table. "They're old friends," he announced.

"Don't exaggerate, Tomáš," said Katrinka.

"What do you mean?" asked Zuzka. "He didn't act as if he knew her."

"That's because she's changed so much he didn't recognize her," said Tomáš, who then proceeded to tell the story of Katrinka's film debut, turning to her from time to time, saying, "Right? Right?" Katrinka would agree that he was right and Tomáš would continue, exaggerating the details, acting out the plot of the film, imitating Katrinka's performance, reducing the table to laughter so loud everyone in the room turned to see what was happening.

"You make a much better schoolgirl than I did," said Katrinka, tears of laughter streaming down her face, no longer in the least bit annoyed. Then she saw Bartoš watching her from across the room, the look on his face so intent it was disturbing. He raised his glass to her as Tomáš had a few moments before. Katrinka nodded in acknowledgment, then turned her attention back to her friends.

"He recognized your face?" asked her mother, sounding doubtful when Katrinka phoned the next day to report her meeting with Mirek Bartoš. "But you were only five the last time he saw you."

"I don't think he *recognized* me, *Mami*," said Katrinka. "I think I must just have a certain type of look he needs for his film."

"Well, he's certainly consistent," said Milena. "You had that look last time, too."

"You're not to do anything that interferes with your schoolwork, Katrinka," said her father when he got on the line. He did not sound worried, merely responsible: it was his duty to give his daughter good advice.

Katrinka laughed. "You sound just like Mrs. Hoch."

"Who's she?"

"One of the sports committee," said Katrinka, describing her run-in with the woman.

"Why is she worried?" said Jirka, when Katrinka finished the story, coming immediately to his daughter's defense. "Your grades are good. You've been skiing well all season."

"I mentioned that. But very politely."

"They like to run your whole life, those people."

Katrinka could hear her mother in the background warning him not to talk too much. Caution was a way of life, people taking care not to have private conversations overheard for fear that they would be reported to the wrong people and trouble result. Before her retirement, Dana, Katrinka's grandmother, had spent enough time working as a telephone operator for the family to know just how possible, and frequent, eavesdropping was.

"Everything is fine, *Tati.* There's nothing to worry about."

"You'll phone Bartoš?" he asked.

"I think so. Why not? Wouldn't you like your daughter to be a film star?" she said, her voice teasing.

"I like my daughter well enough just as she is," he replied, his voice gruff with emotion.

Even through the telephone lines, Katrinka could feel the power of his love for her and was suddenly overwhelmed with longing to see him and her mother, her grandparents, the apartment in Svitov, everything and everyone that made her feel safe, secure. "Oh, *Tati,* I miss you. When will I see you?" Because of her heavy racing schedule, Katrinka had had little time to visit home that winter; and, for a family as close as the Kovářs, adjusting to the long separations was difficult. When Katrinka raced in Czechoslovakia, Jirka and Milena often made the trip together to see her; but for competitions abroad, only one parent was allowed to go and that required a visa, which was sometimes denied. Milena had attended a race in St. Anton in January, but Katrinka had not seen her father in the six weeks since Christmas.

"I'll be at your next race, I hope," said her father, "in St. Moritz. I'm trying to get a visa."

"I'll call you in a few days," said Katrinka. "After I've seen Mirek Bartoš."

"Don't say yes to anything," Jirka cautioned, "until you've had time to think about it."

"I won't," she promised. *"Dobrou noc, Tati."*

"Dobrou noc, miláčku," he said. He hung up the telephone and turned to Milena.

"I don't like it," she said, dropping the sock she had just finished darning into the basket at her side. She took a cigarette from the pack in her pocket, lit it, and looked up at her husband. "School, skiing, modeling, now this. She tries to do too much."

"Worry, worry, worry," said Jirka lightly, teasing her.

"You're worried too, for once. I can tell."

"It won't come to anything," he said, not wanting to admit even to himself that he *was* worried. He lit a cigarette and inhaled deeply. "She'll go talk to Bartoš. Maybe he'll let her audition for some part or other. There must be thousands of young girls who audition for parts and don't get them."

"If Katrinka wants it, she'll get it," said Milena pessimistically. "You know how determined she is."

"She's just curious about this film business," said Jirka. "That's all." He walked over and turned on the television, adjusting the dials to get the fuzzy gray picture as clear as possible. It was time for the news, not that he believed much of what he saw and heard on the state-run channel, but with no foreign newspapers or magazines permitted in the country, it was the only access people had to the world. When he turned, he saw Milena staring into space, frowning as she sat silently smoking her cigarette, the basket of darning forgotten. Settling into his armchair, he said, as much to himself as to her, "It's a waste of time to worry before there's something worth worrying about."

She looked at him and smiled. "So you always say."

But for once Jirka was totally unable to follow his own good advice. He was uneasy without quite knowing about what and wished that he had forbidden Katrinka to pursue this business with Mirek Bartoš. Only that was not how he was used to dealing with his daughter. After pointing out the advantages and disadvantages of any course of action, he had always, as far as possible, let her make her own decisions. That was the way to build character, he believed. But, even had he wanted to, it was too late now to change his behavior. Katrinka was eighteen years old, a young woman, resourceful and independent. It was unlikely that she would respond well, or obediently, to a doting father suddenly displaying dictatorial impulses. Finally, he shrugged. "We've always trusted Katrinka to make the right decision," he said. "And she always has."

Milena thought of all the decisions over the years of which she had not approved, starting with the very first to join the ski club. She thought of all the sleepless nights she had endured, worrying about her daughter. She thought of the broken arms and legs, the sprained muscles, the cracked ribs, of Katrinka's face deathly pale after an accident. Milena loved her daughter and was proud of her, but no, she could not in all honesty say she believed Katrinka's decisions had always been "right." "Well," she said to Jirka, the words out of her mouth before she could stop them, "she hasn't killed herself, so far, if that's what you mean," and then turned pale herself at the idea. She never allowed herself even to think that Katrinka might be in that kind of danger.

Jirka smiled wryly. "That's one thing we don't have to worry about with this," he said. "At least it isn't dangerous making a movie."

Later that week, as arranged with a secretary who answered the phones and set meetings, Katrinka got into her Fiat as soon as her last class of the day was over and drove the fifteen kilometers along the nondescript highway from Prague to Barrandov.

The studio was the usual large complex of soundstages and office buildings, editing rooms and dubbing stages. Mirek Bartoš's office was off a long, dim corridor in the four-story concrete-and-glass office block. The anteroom, where a secretary sat, was small and dark, with shabby furniture, reminding Katrinka of the offices in the sports complex in Svitov. Bartoš's own office was far more luxurious, as befitted one of Czechoslovakia's most successful old-guard directors. It boasted a reasonably new suite of upholstered furniture, sleek modern cabinets in blond wood, several floor lamps, a large desk piled with scripts and books, and an art nouveau lamp, its base a naked woman cast in bronze.

Bartoš, who was lying on the sofa making notes on a script, leapt to his feet as his secretary showed Katrinka into the room, pushed his glasses back onto his head, extended a hand, and greeted her warmly. "How good to see you. Come in, come in. Have a seat. Would you like some tea? Coffee?" He settled her in the sofa he had just vacated, arranged for the coffee, and dropped into an armchair opposite her, sitting silently for several moments, studying her face. "I know you," he said. "I'm sure I've seen you somewhere before."

"On the cover of a magazine?" she said.

He laughed. "Yes, of course. And in other ads, as well, no doubt. You've been modeling for a while?" Katrinka nodded. "But that's not what I meant," he continued. "There's something about your face." He shrugged. "Of course, you're very beautiful," he said dispassionately. "It could just be that."

Again, Katrinka felt herself blushing, something she was not at all used to, and hoped he had not noticed. "Do you remember a film called *Blood and Lilies?*" she said.

"Remember it?" His laugh was big and boisterous. "Do you think I ever forget one of my films? Even when I want to?"

"I was one of the little girls in the schoolroom scene, the one in the pigtails."

"Didn't all the little girls have pigtails?" he teased.

"You gave me a line to say." She repeated the line, not certain anymore whether she was performing it accurately or merely giving Tomáš's version.

He sat back in his chair, smiling. "It seems we both have good memories," he said.

His secretary brought in the coffee, and they drank it while Bartoš interviewed Katrinka, insisting she tell him everything that had happened to her since the filming of *Blood and Lilies.* He was a big man, with a powerful presence and an easy, seductive manner that totally charmed her: she felt as if she could tell him everything. "On the ski team," he said, when she had finished. "It seems I should know your name, too. I'm ashamed of myself."

"There are so many of us," she said, a pert smile relieving her words of any coyness, "and only one of you."

"Thank God," he said, his laugh booming out again. "Do you follow sports?"

"I don't have time. I ski a little. But . . ." He shrugged, then stood, went to his desk, picked up the script he had dropped there when she entered, and began riffling through it. When he found the page he wanted, he handed her the open script, and began pacing around the office, explaining the story of the film, slowly, with great attention to detail. It was another mystery, called *The House on Chotkova Street*, with a dark, complicated plot. "Are you following me?" he would ask from time to time. Katrinka would nod, and he would proceed, arms waving, voice changing as he enacted the parts of the different characters.

The idea that Mirek Bartoš was old enough to be her father never entered Katrinka's head as she watched him performing for her benefit, doing his best to interest and charm her. Yet it was his age, more than her lack of experience, that prevented her from realizing immediately, as she might have done with a peer, that her response to him was sexual. She thought it was admiration she felt, not desire.

When he finished, he said, "Well, what do you think?"

"It sounds terrifying." It was the only word that came immediately to mind.

"Good," said Bartoš, satisfied. "I hope it will be. Now I'm going to leave you alone for a few moments." He sat beside her on the sofa, leaning over to point at the open script on her lap. His nearness was disconcerting, and Katrinka wanted to move away but did not dare. She was afraid it would seem rude. "I want you to study this scene for a few minutes. And when I come back, we'll read it aloud together." He smiled. "All right?"

Katrinka nodded. "All right," she said.

He left and she sat studying the scene. She did not feel in

the least bit nervous. Probably because she did not care what happened, she told herself. It meant nothing to her, really. She remembered how bored she had been during the filming of *Blood and Lilies*. Perhaps she should just tell him as soon as he returned that she wasn't interested? But that too seemed a very impolite thing to do when he had shown so much interest in her. In any case, she probably would not get the part. And if she did, she could always say no.

Bartoš returned at last, holding another script, and sat again in the armchair opposite her. They read the scene together four times, each time with variations he suggested. Finally, he seemed satisfied. "That will do," he said. "You take direction well." It was his highest compliment.

"I have the part?" asked Katrinka, surprised that it had been so easy.

"Not quite yet," he said. "I want to see you on film. What you did when you were five doesn't count," he added, smiling. He knew the camera would capture her beauty. That he could tell from the magazine cover. But what he wanted on film was her incredible vitality, the energy coming from deep inside her that seemed to draw every eye. "Don't get your hopes up," he warned her. "The camera doesn't like everyone. And it's just a small part." Small, but crucial, he thought. But then he believed every part was crucial.

Again Katrinka was tempted to tell him she really wasn't interested, but something stopped her: an unwillingness to displease him perhaps, or an inclination to test herself meeting a new challenge, a desire for adventure, or simple curiosity about how much it was possible to earn acting. The previous June and July, for extra money, she had worked in a hotel in Munich before summer training began. That had been very hard work. If she could earn more acting, why not try? Katrinka was not mercenary by any means, but in a country where all but the basic necessities were rare and everything was costly, she had from an early age learned the value of money. It seemed to her foolish to turn down an opportunity to make more.

So she thanked Mirek Bartoš for the interview, scheduled an appointment with the secretary for a film test, got back in her Fiat, and drove to the Maxmilianka to tell Zuzka and Tomáš of the afternoon's events.

Tomáš bought her a beer to celebrate. "I thought you'd sneer," she said, pleased at his reaction.

He put an arm around her shoulder and squeezed. "I glory in your success," he said grandly. "I always do."

"This isn't success. Not real success. But someday," she said, lifting her beer to return the toast, "I'll glory in yours."

He put his other arm around Zuzka and held on to both of them. There was an intensity in his look, a passion, that he did not often let show. "You certainly will," he said. "I'll be better than Forman," he said. "Better than Menzel. Better than any of them."

The film test was even more successful than Mirek Bartoš had hoped, and the next hurdle, scheduling, which Katrinka had expected to be a major difficulty, turned out to be no problem at all. Shooting was not to start in any case until late spring, and Katrinka's part could easily be filmed, Bartoš insisted, between the end of the school year and the beginning of summer ski practice. He made it impossible for her to refuse, a technique (as anyone who knew him would testify) that Bartoš used to get anything he wanted. And he had decided that he did indeed want Katrinka.

He attended one of her races in early March and cheered her from the sidelines as Katrinka went full out to impress him, finishing first and giving Ilona Lukánský a double reason to sulk as she always did when Katrinka won. Afterward Bartoš went out of his way to reassure Ota Černý, who had reservations of his own about Katrinka's latest adventure, swearing that her scenes would be completed in time for her to join the team in August for practice. Olga Černý, when she heard about the film part, dismissed Katrinka as a butterfly, unable to stick to just one thing and make a success of it, a charge Ota denied as patently untrue. And Katrinka's parents, impressed not so much by Bartoš's charm as by his common sense, created no obstacles once he assured them that his film would not interfere with Katrinka's life, but in fact would help, giving her not only extra money but more freedom, the real wages of success in communist countries.

Since the part for which Bartoš wanted Katrinka was not large, someone should perhaps have thought it strange that he took so much trouble to secure her for the role. But no one did. The fact that he was married to Felix Mach's daughter put him, in their eyes, above suspicion. Who could believe that, with such a father-in-law, Bartoš would have the balls to be unfaithful?

extra money but more freedom, ... chances of success in
communist count...
Since the part ... K... attracts was not
huge, someone should perhaps have thought it strange that
he took so much trouble ... out of the role. But no
one did. The fact that he ... married to Felix Mads ...
daughter put him, in their eyes, above suspicion. Who could
believe that, with such a father-in-law, Bartoš would have
the balls to be unfaithful?

hen summer came, Tomáš and Zuzka, who could
not bear the thought of being separated for months, paid
flying visits to their families, then went hiking together
through Slovakia into Hungary. Katrinka, who had two
weeks free, returned to Svitov, gardened with her grandparents, stopped in occasionally to have coffee with Tomáš's
mother, then went with her parents to visit Aunt Zdeňka
and her cousins. Since the grandparents had died and her
husband had left to work in a factory in Brno, Zdeňka,
looking much older and plumper than Milena, who was only
two years her junior, ran the farm with her sons.

Despite all the changes, it remained a magical place to
Katrinka. No matter how busy her cousins were, they still
found time to go fishing with her, the dogs (Bruni and Babar
had replaced Rosa and Rudolph) still followed her everywhere, the chickens pecked at her legs as she helped Milena
to feed them, she and her father swam every day in the
pond, and at night the insects hummed and the stars
glittered overhead as brightly as ever. Every year, when it
was time to go, she was sad, but this time, the feeling of loss
was particularly strong, as if she were leaving her childhood
behind her forever.

The House on Chotkova Street was being filmed at
Barrandov, and when Katrinka returned to Prague, because
the dormitory was closed for the summer, she moved into a
small, inexpensive hotel in a side street off Václav Square—

which was not a square at all, but a long rectangle lined with hotels and shops—not far from the National Theater and FAMU. Since most of the cast and crew lived in the city, and those who did not had moved in with friends, Katrinka was the only one staying there. One of the women in charge of wardrobe had offered her a bed in her apartment, but Katrinka had politely refused. Being on her own seemed to her part of the adventure, not that she was there very often. Days on the set were long, and the hours of enforced togetherness, as well as the intensity of the work, quickly forged all the film's various personalities into a mock family—difficult, quarrelsome, helpful, and affectionate. There was always someone to talk to between scenes, to hang out with on free days, to grab a quick meal with at night.

Bartoš had Katrinka called to the set for two days when she was not needed, "to get the feel of things," he explained briefly, then deliberately ignored her. He was careful not to be caught looking at her, though he was aware every moment of where she was, what she was doing, to whom she was speaking. As always, he commanded the set, but he did it this time for Katrinka's benefit, to impress her, to make her feel his power. And she did. Whether she sat in a corner quietly trying to read, or stood at the buffet table drinking coffee and joking with the crew, she found her eyes straying always in his direction, hoping to find him looking at her, wanting to see him smile, feeling strangely lonely now that his attention was not focused on her. She wondered about his wife, Vlasta Mach, and listened eagerly for gossip during meals with the cast and crew, only by a great effort of will keeping herself from pumping them for information. What she learned was not much: Mirek and Vlasta both were rumored to have had lovers, though no one could name names, and everyone had to admit that people in their position always attracted that sort of speculation. Certainly, when seen together in public, they appeared to be a contented married couple.

For reasons she did not fully understand, Katrinka soon was not feeling as cheerful and energetic as usual. Something was undermining her normal good spirits. She came to the conclusion that it was boredom, and swore to herself in future to have nothing to do with making films.

As she had when she was five, Katrinka found the work itself dull. For someone with her restless energy, the endless waiting was a torment. And there was always something to wait for: lights to be rigged, cameras to be reloaded with film, sets to be dressed, actors to appear from makeup. It seemed to her that the only one busy all the time was Mirek Bartoš, and for that reason she assumed that he was the only one really enjoying himself. When Vendulka Gabriel, the lead actress, told her that nothing, absolutely nothing—not sex, not money, not drink, not even her child—gave her as much pleasure as performing in front of a camera, Katrinka wrote her off as neurotic.

Mirek Bartoš had once had an affair with Vendulka Gabriel but it was long over and the actress now was married, happily, with a two-year-old son whom, despite her casual words, she adored. When she saw how Mirek watched Katrinka, she considered warning the girl, then decided against it. We all have to grow up sometime, she thought. To her, Katrinka's innocence was not only astounding, but doomed. Someone would do something about it soon, she was sure, and there were many worse bastards in the world than Bartoš.

Midafternoon on the third day, when Katrinka was standing at the buffet table talking to one of the actors, a handsome young man named Ludă who played her boyfriend in the film, Mirek Bartoš came up to them and put an arm affectionately around her shoulders. "Well," he said. "Ready for your big scene?"

She felt as if an electric current were running through his arm into her body. Could he feel her trembling? she wondered. She did not want him to think she was nervous. "Yes," she said.

Ludă hoped he wasn't frowning. He had been trying for the past two days to attract Katrinka's attention and, now that he finally had, trust Bartoš to come along and interrupt.

"We'll rehearse it first, mark the set, rig the lights, then shoot."

She nodded.

"Cat got your tongue?" he teased.

"No," she said nervously. After days of being ignored, she now found his presence suffocating.

"Stage fright," said Ludă sympathetically. "Don't let it worry you. We all get it."

"Go easy on her, Mirek," said Vendulka, stopping to pour herself a cup of tea from the large samovar on the table. "She's new at this."

"Nonsense," said Bartoš, who understood perfectly what Vendulka meant. He gave Katrinka an apparently friendly hug. "She's an old hand. She made her debut in a film of mine at age . . ." He looked at Katrinka and smiled. "How old were you?" he asked.

They were almost the same height and, with his face turned toward her like that, their lips were only inches apart. She swallowed. "Five," she said.

"Five," he repeated.

"And how old were you?" asked Vendulka sweetly.

"Old enough to know better," said Bartoš with a laugh. "But I never do."

Vendulka smiled, shrugged, and walked away sipping her cup of tea.

"If you still had a pigtail," said Bartoš, his voice tender, "I'd pull it for luck, the way I used to. Let's get started," he called, summoning the crew to action as he removed his arm from Katrinka's shoulders and started back toward the set.

His arm draped so casually around her had made Katrinka feel uncomfortable. But now that it was gone, she missed it. She hurried after Bartoš, not wanting to delay the scene, not wanting to be out of his presence for a moment longer than necessary.

Katrinka's first scene was with Vendulka and Ludă. It was full of exposition and, as they rehearsed, Bartoš kept changing the lines, trying to put some life into it. Though Katrinka found it hard to keep up with the constant revisions, she found that finally, challenged by the need to remember the endless variations on what to say, where to stand, what to do, she was enjoying herself. But by the time the scene was working to Bartoš's satisfaction, it was too late to light and shoot it and he called a wrap for the day. As the crew and cast drifted away from the set, Ludă fell into step with Katrinka. "Mirek was right. You're very professional. It's hard to believe this is your first real part. I'm impressed," he said.

"Thank you," said Katrinka, pleased with the compliment.

"Do you have plans now?" he asked. "Would you like to have some dinner?"

"Katrinka!" Bartoš's voice interrupted before she could reply. She turned and saw him watching her. "Could I have a word with you, please?" Although phrased as a question, the request was clearly an order.

Katrinka felt her stomach knot with anxiety, which surprised her. Though always tense before a race, she was not at other times troubled by nerves, and authority figures, except perhaps the dreaded members of the sports committee, too easily succumbed to her charm for her to fear them. She turned to Ludă. "Maybe another time would be better?"

He nodded. "Don't look so frightened," he said encouragingly. "Directors do this to everyone. They love to have private little chats about scenes."

Katrinka smiled wanly, then turned and moved back to Bartoš, who was sitting in his high director's chair at the edge of the set, his script open in his lap. "Sit down," he said gently, gesturing to the chair next to his.

"Was I terrible?"

"Not at all. You were quite good." He smiled. "Frankly, you were much better than I expected. You learn quickly."

"I try." She could not understand why she felt so nervous around him. It was not like her at all.

"You mustn't be afraid of me."

"I'm not," she said firmly.

"Good. There are just a few things I want to go over before we start shooting in the morning, so we don't waste any time. All right?"

"Yes."

"Dobrou noc," called Vendulka loudly as she left the sound stage.

"Dobrou noc," responded Bartoš, not looking in her direction. As one after another of the cast and crew left, he remained oblivious to everything but the script in his lap and Katrinka sitting opposite him. He discussed the scene with her, its purpose and intention, suggested various approaches to her character, made her run lines with him trying first one interpretation then another. Finally, close to two hours later, he closed the script, stretched, checked his watch and said, "Oh, my God, look at the time. Come, I'll buy you dinner, then send you straight home to bed. There's an early call in the morning."

Mirek Bartoš did not, as a general rule, issue direct orders. He got people to do what he wanted simply by assuming they would. And because of his determined air and easy charm, everyone always found it easier to say yes to him than no. Katrinka, in that respect at least, was like all the others. It did not even occur to her that she might refuse to dine with him. But then she did not really want to refuse.

He took her to a small, expensive restaurant in the Old Town Square where he was well known and the waiters fussed over him. It had antique Meissen candelabra and excellent Czech food. Katrinka ordered the *svíčková,* beef in sour cream sauce, with dumplings and cranberries on the side. Bartoš watched her admiringly as she ate. "You like your food, don't you? Good," he said approvingly, as his eyes appraised her body. "And yet you stay so slender." Again, Katrinka felt herself blushing and hoped it was not going to be a habit when she was with him.

Talking to him was easy, she found. She told him about summers on the farm, about the chickens and the fruit trees, about František and Oldřich. She listened while he told her about the films he had made, the people he had known, about the film festival at Cannes and the Venice Biennale, about his *chata* in Bohemia where he spent long weeks walking in the surrounding woods thinking up new plots for his films. His wife was there now, he confided, for the summer. They had been married a long time and had developed many separate interests, he told Katrinka, not elaborating on what those were, adding only that they were both content to go their different ways.

As promised, as soon as the meal was finished he drove her the few blocks back to the hotel where she had earlier left her little Fiat. He leaned across her to open the door, kissed her affectionately on the cheek, and told her to sleep well. "I expect you to be very good tomorrow," he said.

Reluctantly, Katrinka got out of the car. She did not want the evening to end, she realized. *"Dobrou noc,"* she said. *"Děkuji."*

He smiled. "You're very welcome. Run along now. Before I change my mind," he added, softly, as she started inside. It was not conscience that was restraining him, but experience. If he moved too quickly, he knew, he would ruin everything.

Katrinka did not sleep at all that night. Instead, she replayed the evening over and over again in her mind. She could not remember ever having enjoyed herself more, with a man, that is. Mirek Bartoš was interesting, exciting, like no one she had ever known. She could not wait to see him again and the next morning got up eagerly, looking refreshed and full of energy. Searching through her meager wardrobe for something to please him, she chose a skirt and a ruffled blouse that showed off her neck and shoulders, climbed into the Fiat, and drove quickly to Barrandov. What the consequences of all these new and unexpected feelings would be it did not occur to her even to wonder.

But at the studio that morning, there was a problem with the lights. Preoccupied with technical matters, Bartoš ignored his cast. Looking around for the chief engineer, his eyes grazed Katrinka but did not see her. Again she felt strangely lonely.

"Now we're even more behind schedule," said Ludă. "He'll be in a foul mood all day."

Katrinka tried to keep herself occupied. She read, chatted with the crew, polished her nails, ran her lines trying to incorporate all Bartoš's suggestions from the night before, but always she felt restless, distracted. An annoying lethargy enveloped her. Boredom, she thought. Vendulka Gabriel, with a total lack of temperament, sat in her chair patiently doing needlepoint and, for once, Katrinka wished she had followed her mother's lead. Needlepoint seemed suddenly the perfect way to relieve tension.

Finally, the problem with the lights was solved, and

Katrinka found herself again on the set with Vendulka and Ludă, this time with the camera rolling. Contrary to Ludă's prediction, Bartoš was not difficult at all, but merry. Katrinka found herself beginning to relax, to enjoy herself.

That night Bartoš dismissed her with a wave of his hand, settling in his chair to talk to Vendulka. Again Ludă asked her to join him for dinner. She accepted and they drove separately back to Prague, meeting at the U Zlaté Hrušky, a pretty little restaurant in an eighteenth-century house not far from the castle. But though she found Ludă amazingly handsome, and though he flirted with her outrageously, she could not concentrate. She kept thinking about Mirek Bartoš and Vendulka Gabriel as she had last seen them, huddling together in the dark studio. What she was feeling was sexual jealousy, though of course she did not recognize it. She had never felt it before in her life.

Ludă walked her back to her car, put his arms around her, and kissed her on both cheeks. With a little encouragement, he would have kissed her properly, but Katrinka pulled away, and giving him the bright, friendly smile he found completely captivating, wished him good night.

"Do you have a boyfriend?" he asked, taking hold of her hand to stop her from moving too quickly away.

"No," she said, startled by the question. "Why?"

"I just wondered. *Dobrou noc,* Katrinka," he said, letting go of her hand.

Bartoš asked her to stay the next night, and the one after, and again two nights later, running through her scenes with her in the strange intimacy of a deserted sound stage, two people alone in a vast space, the only two people in the world. Afterward, he took her to dinner, a different restaurant each night, but always small and romantic, with the best food that Prague had to offer. He ordered the most expensive items on the menu, the best wines, and on their fourth evening together Russian caviar and champagne.

"You're drunk," he said approvingly as they left the restaurant, slipping an arm around her for support.

"Just a little," she admitted. She felt wonderful, lightheaded but completely alert, totally alive.

"I'll take you home," he said.

When they got to her hotel, instead of leaning over her to open the car door as he usually did, he got out and went around to the passenger side. He helped her out, escorted her into the lobby, past the conveniently sleeping porter, and up the stairs to her room. At various stages, it occurred to her that perhaps she ought to say something, to tell him that she could manage perfectly well on her own, to suggest that he had better go. But she didn't. Once again, his complete assurance made it difficult, if not impossible, for her to tell him he could not have whatever it was he wanted. But what did he want? She felt breathless, excited. But it wasn't the champagne. Her mind was absolutely, totally clear.

She could feel his hand on the small of her back as she turned the key in the lock of her door. "I should have brought the champagne," he said.

"Are you coming in?" she asked, not knowing what else to say.

"If you'll let me," he replied.

She opened the door and stepped inside, turning on the light, looking around quickly to see if all was neat and tidy. The room was newly painted, cheerful but small, without even a closet. It had a flowered chintz curtain concealing the clothes rack and tired furniture from the fifties—a worn armchair, a round table with a single chair, a chest of drawers, a night table, and a narrow bed covered with a chintz spread.

"Not bad," said Bartoš, completing his survey of the room and turning his attention back to her. "And now that you've got me here," he said, "just what do you plan to do with me?"

He was so large a presence, he seemed to her to fill the whole room. "I'm not sure," she said in all honesty.

"No?" It took him forever to close the distance between them, and, when he finally put his arms around her, she realized she had been holding her breath. His mouth covered hers and soon she felt his tongue, flicking here, there, eliciting small explosions of feeling. His hands stroked her body at first through its thin layer of clothing and then, miraculously, they found their way underneath and caressed her skin. He touched her where no one had ever touched her before, and instead of stopping him she wrapped her arms around him and ground herself into him, wanting to be closer, as close as it was possible to be.

Finally, he pulled back from her and said, "Would you like me to go?" But he was smiling, knowing he had just asked a supremely silly question.

Her hair was awry, her blouse was undone, she felt as if she were on fire. "No," she said. She would die if he left her now, she thought. If he stopped touching her, the fire inside her would go out and she would freeze to death.

He removed her blouse and skirt, undid her bra and slipped it off. He caressed her breasts first with his fingers, then with his mouth. Taking her hands, he put them on his belt. "Help me," he whispered, his breath warm against her ear. Awkwardly, she unbuckled his belt and unzipped the fly of his trousers, while he stood with his arms loosely around her, caressing her buttocks through the thin cotton of her panties.

He stripped off his clothes, then removed her panties, tracing their descent down her legs with his hands. "Turn around," he said when she was naked. "Completely around. I want to see you."

It was as if she had no will of her own, only his. She turned slowly, without embarrassment. "You're so beautiful," he said. "Your body is perfect." He wrapped his arms around her again and moved with her to the bed. "You've never done this before, have you?" She shook her head. "Don't worry," he said. "You'll like it."

Thirteen

You are crazy. Completely crazy," said Zuzka, the ball of wool on top of her red cap seeming to bob with outrage. She turned away from Katrinka, put her skis in the rack on the side of the bus and climbed in.

The sky was cloudless and blue as a sparrow's egg. The air was like crystal shimmering in the brilliant light and the snow-covered mountains paraded grandly to the horizon. It was a scene of overwhelming beauty, to which Katrinka was oblivious. Was Zuzka right? she wondered. Had she gone completely mad? And, if she had, was it any wonder? Placing her skis next to Zuzka's, Katrinka followed her friend into the bus.

"That was some fall," said Ilona Lukánský, pretending concern as Katrinka, walking down the aisle, moved past her. "You're lucky you didn't break anything."

Katrinka shrugged. "It wasn't so bad," she said. "Congratulations." Ilona's flat face lit with a sly, triumphant smile. It was December of 1967; they were in St. Moritz for a race; and, perhaps thanks to Katrinka's fall, Ilona had placed first.

"Bitch," whispered Zuzka, as Katrinka sat in the seat next to her. "But she's right. You could have broken your neck. The chances you take!"

The bus was full of teammates, most of whom avoided looking at Katrinka, trying to pretend that they had neither seen nor heard of her fall. She must be devastated, they thought. Why add to her embarrassment? All, including

140

Zuzka, assumed Katrinka had taken the turn too close on purpose, to increase her speed and give herself the advantage in the final lap of the race. But they were wrong. Katrinka had simply lost concentration. Her mind had wandered. Although she had studied the trail the day before, the map of it that she carried in her brain had been blotted out for a moment by the face of Mirek Bartoš. Before she realized she was anywhere near it, she had missed the turn and was hurtling straight for the edge of the cliff and a sheer drop into the canyon below. Panic had gripped her, and, for another split second, her mind frozen with fear, she had continued her mad dash toward eternity. But her young, healthy body seemed to have a will of its own, an instinct for self-preservation, and, without her consciously issuing any motor commands, the powerful muscles of her stomach and legs flipped her body around and across the fall line. Forcing herself to think again, she had turned in traverse and quickly tried to position herself for the next sharp twist in the trail. It was too late. Off balance, she had tumbled into the deep snow. Ilona and Zuzka were right, thought Katrinka, she could have hurt herself. Perhaps she had meant to. A bad fall might have solved all her problems.

"You lost concentration," said Ota Černý accusingly later that evening. He knew better than to believe that Katrinka had done anything so stupid as to take that dangerous turn too close on purpose.

"I'm sorry," said Katrinka.

"Sorry!" He banged down his glass and the beer sloshed over the rim and made a small puddle on the dark wood table. "A lot of good feeling sorry would do if you had killed yourself!" There were spotters all along the trail and they had provided him with a detailed report of Katrinka's fall. When the races had ended, he had gone himself to look at the site of the accident. He was not sure why. By the time his team raced in St. Moritz again the terrain would have altered, however subtly, making anything he could learn that day of little value. Nevertheless, in the rapidly fading light, he had skied to the place and stood for a long time peering over the edge of the cliff into the rocky gorge below, and the image of Katrinka lying there in a crumpled heap had filled him first with terror, then with rage. He began to tremble. It's because I've known her since she was a baby, he told himself, because her father is my best friend. Of course I love her, he admitted, Olga's accusations ringing in his ears. But even then he could not, would not, acknowledge that he loved Katrinka not as one loves a child, but as a man loves a woman.

"You must pay attention every moment," he insisted. "You can't let your mind wander. You can't daydream. Not if you want to win." He paused, then added more quietly, "You could have killed yourself today."

They were in the bar of the hotel. Upstairs, in the rooms, her teammates were partying with the members of the men's team, coaches and secret police turning a blind eye to the drink and the noise, to the high spirits that ended sometimes with complaints from hotel guests and threats of immediate eviction. A few months ago, Katrinka would have been at the center of the fun, singing, dancing, flirting, stealing kisses in dark corners. But tonight she was grateful to Ota Černý for insisting she accompany him to the bar for a drink and the inevitable lecture. It saved her the trouble of pretending to enjoy herself.

Katrinka looked up, saw the concern on Ota's face, and felt embarrassed. "It won't happen again," she promised.

"I hope not. You might not be so lucky another time."

"It wasn't luck." Katrinka forced a smile, hoping to wipe the worried look from his face. After all, he was not merely her coach, but her "Uncle" Ota. "I'm strong, and I'm good. As soon as I saw the mess I was in," she said, throwing her hands into the air like a magician demanding acknowledgment of a particularly masterful trick, "I saved myself."

Reluctantly, Ota smiled. "Sometimes I think your head is as big as your courage."

"Is it?" she said, her smile fading. "Do you think I'm conceited? I know Auntie Olga does."

"No," said Ota immediately. "Not conceited. Self-assured, which is good. And brave. Sometimes to the point of being foolhardy, perhaps."

"Isn't it worth taking risks, to get what you want?"

"That depends, I suppose, on what it is you want. And how big the risk is." He finished his beer and signaled to the waiter. "Anything else?"

"No, thank you," said Katrinka.

Ota asked for the check, paid it when it came, then walked with Katrinka to the elevator. From the shaft came the muffled sounds of a party in progress. "No one in the hotel will get any sleep tonight," Ota said. When they reached the third floor, they both got out, but instead of heading in the direction of the noise, to Ota's surprise Katrinka turned the opposite way. "Everyone seems to be in Ilona's room," he said.

"I'm a little tired tonight."

No wonder, thought Ota. A close encounter with death was always exhausting. Yet it was more than that, he suspected. But what? Katrinka had not seemed herself to him for weeks now. Her eyes, usually as pale as the sky on a clear winter's morning, had seemed dark with worry. There were faint shadows underneath, and her full mouth, always ready to smile, had unaccustomed lines of tension at its corners. "Katrinka, is anything troubling you?"

A look of sudden dismay crossed her face. "No, of course not," she said, in his opinion too vehemently. "Why do you ask?"

"You're sure?"

She took a deep breath, as if to calm herself. "I ache a little bit, from the fall," she said evasively. "That's all. It's nothing serious. I'll take a hot bath and be fine in the morning." They had reached her bedroom door. Katrinka opened it with her key, then turned again to Ota.

"If Olga seems hard on you sometimes," he said, "it's only because she expects so much of you. As do I. We're both very fond of you."

"I know," said Katrinka.

"If you ever have a problem, any kind of problem, you know you can come to me. You know you can rely on me to help you."

"Thank you," she said. "I'll remember that." She forced another smile, as brilliant as she could manage, hoping to

143

calm his fears. There was only one person in the world who could help her now, she thought, and she did not even have much confidence in him.

Zuzka, too, was concerned about Katrinka. She could not put her finger on when she had first noticed, but lately it seemed to her that her friend was much less exuberant than usual, much more preoccupied, even worried, and it was not at all like Katrinka to worry. "Something's wrong," she confided to Tomáš when she got back to Prague.

"Mirek Bartoš is what's wrong," said Tomáš, his voice sharp with disapproval. He lay on the bed, propped against the headboard, smoking, watching Zuzka as she unpacked her knapsack, admiring the curve of her breast, the roundness of her arm as she stretched to put a sweater on a shelf. They had moved in together at the beginning of the semester, three months before, and Tomáš was still intrigued and often aroused by the casual intimacy of their living arrangements.

"But why? They've been so happy. What could have happened?"

"What? Any number of things. His wife, for example."

"His wife? Pooh. What does she matter?"

Tomáš shook his head and laughed. "Do you think you'll feel the same someday when you're a wife?" he teased.

Zuzka looked at him suspiciously. Whose wife? she wanted to ask him. As much as he professed to love her, Tomáš never mentioned marriage. But, of course, it was out of the question now while they were both still students. "I wouldn't want a marriage without love," said Zuzka earnestly. "And you only have to see Mirek with Katrinka to know he loves her."

Tomáš ran an impatient hand through his thick curly hair and said, "Why shouldn't he love her? She's young, she's beautiful, full of energy and life." He sat up and dropped the butt of his cigarette into the dregs in the coffee cup on the bedside table. "He's like Dracula, feeding off her." To Tomáš, at twenty, Mirek Bartoš in his mid-fifties seemed an old man, but his disapproval of Bartoš's relationship with Katrinka went beyond the question of age. The style and charm of Bartoš's work, its wit and expert craftsmanship, were totally lost on Tomáš, in whose worldview a film director, no matter how successful, if lacking in new and exciting ideas, an original approach to the art of cinema, a sharp visual and profound human sensibility, was nothing more than a hack. Despising Bartoš's work as he did, Tomáš could not think of him as an acceptable lover for his friend. It seemed certain to him that Bartoš's sexuality must be as flat as his creativity, and that the man was using the vital and lovely Katrinka to jump-start a stalled libido.

Zuzka pulled the curtain closed around the clothes rack and turned to stare at Tomáš. "What a disgusting thing to say."

He shrugged. "We shouldn't worry so much. Katrinka can take care of herself." He reached out, grabbed Zuzka by the wrist, and pulled her toward him. He had not made love in three days, an eternity. "I missed you," he said.

"Did you?" She smiled with pleasure.

Tomáš pulled her down on top of him and let his lips travel up the smooth column of her throat to her ear. "Did you miss me?"

She had not, really. The train rides to and from St. Moritz had been fun, as always, and before a race she could not think of anything else, not even Tomáš. But now that she was with him and could feel the bulge in his trousers throbbing against her right thigh, the delicious wet slide of his tongue in her ear, the light flick of his thumb across the nipple of her breast, it seemed to her that she had been longing for this moment for days. "Oh yes," she said. "So much."

Sitting opposite Mirek Bartoš in the little restaurant in the Old Town Square, Katrinka tried to find the words to tell him what was troubling her, but could not. He was being so attentive, so charming, so loving, so delighted to be with her again, filling her glass with champagne, feeding her tidbits from his plate, stroking her thigh beneath the cover of the white tablecloth. Reluctant to shatter his mood, she pretended to enjoy her food and his stories, laughing appreciatively in all the right places, responding when necessary with appropriate comments. He looked at her adoringly and told her that Prague had been terrible without her, as if she had been away for months instead of just three days.

They were in the fifth month of their affair and Katrinka was more in love with Mirek Bartoš than ever. He was everything she had ever imagined in a lover: handsome, intelligent, charming, successful, attentive, and—contrary to Tomáš's prejudiced opinion—virile. When they were together, Bartoš was insatiable, wanting to make love two and three times a night. And because she was young and healthy and madly in love, Katrinka thought she could never get enough of him.

Because of his marriage, they were necessarily discreet, though not clandestine. They would sit for hours talking in the city's sidewalk cafés or wander along the intricately cobbled walks of the broad boulevards and narrow side streets, Bartoš pointing out the amazing jumble of architectural styles—Romanesque churches, Italianate palaces, Gothic towers, baroque and rococo buildings—coexisting in amazing harmony, their decorative facades and soft colors, the deep ochres and lustrous whites, the pale peaches and light greens, giving Prague the sheen of rich porcelain. He showed her where, during the Second World War, a German bomb had destroyed a section of the Old Town Hall, missing the fifteenth-century clock tower with its parading figures of Christ and the Apostles, and Death tolling the hour. Arm in arm, they would stroll past the Tyl Theater, where Mozart's *Don Giovanni* premiered in 1787, along Karlova, through the tower gate, and across the Charles Bridge, pausing to admire one or another of its thirty baroque statues. They would explore the winding cobbled streets of the Malá Strana, visit the art galleries in the Sternberk Palace or the castle, then recross the river to visit the old synagogue and Jewish cemetery in the Josefov. They would see plays at the nineteenth-century National Theater, go dancing in a fourteenth-century beer hall, dine in expensive restaurants. Although he chose places where it was unlikely that he might run into his father-in-law, or indeed his wife when she was in Prague, the possibility of meeting anyone else did not seem to worry him. People would gossip, he knew, but, after all, he and his wife had an understanding.

Since he had finished filming *The House on Chotkova Street*, Bartoš had been busy editing the movie for release while at the same time preparing his next script. But these activities, though demanding, were not nearly so time-consuming as directing. His days started later and ended earlier, his weekends were free, and so he had much more time and energy to devote to Katrinka. It surprised him frequently how often he did want to be with her, how much he enjoyed her company. Usually, he spent the minimum time required to coax a woman to bed, grew bored easily, and was eager to get away to resume the activities he found more interesting than romance: holding court for a group of admiring students, for example. But Katrinka never bored him. He found her beauty intoxicating, her interest and enthusiasm delightful, her zest for life contagious. Sexually, he was addicted to her. He had never felt like that about any woman before in his life.

Weekends, instead of seeking relief from her, he begged her to accompany him into the country, not to his *chata* of course, where Vlasta was usually staying, but to the wooden chalets of the mountain resorts in Valašsko, or the stucco-and-timbered inns of Slovakia. With practice in late summer and autumn and races all winter long, Katrinka could rarely join him, and none of his entreaties could ever shake her resolve. Her commitment to skiing surprised and infuriated him—and filled him with a reluctant admiration. No woman had ever before said no to him with such consistency, not even the willful Vlasta, whom he could still, when he made the effort, seduce into doing whatever he wanted. And each time Katrinka refused him, though irate, he found that his fury soon gave way to lust. And to that she never said no.

At the beginning of the school year, Bartoš had arranged for Katrinka to have a room in a small, charming house with flower boxes beneath the windows and a typical red-tiled roof in the Malá Strana, just below the castle. It was owned by the mother of a school friend of Bartoš's who had been killed in the war. Over the years, he had often given the woman money to supplement her meager income. This was the first time he had ever asked a favor in return. Happy to have the few extra crowns each month, she agreed, accepting without challenge his vague story of a passing acquaintance, a student in need of a place to stay.

With the excuse that Zuzka was moving in with Tomáš, Katrinka informed her parents that she wanted to move out of the university dormitory and into a room of her own; and since the landlady, Mrs. Kolchík, was obviously of good family and character, Jirka and Milena didn't object. Though she did not exactly lie, it troubled Katrinka not to tell her parents the whole truth, but she knew she had no choice. While they liked Mirek Bartoš, they would never accept him as their daughter's lover. Even if Katrinka could convince them that Mirek's age was irrelevant, still they would consider his wife an insurmountable obstacle. And no talk of modern marriages or of "understandings" would sway them. In that sense, they were old-fashioned and religious. They believed that marriage bonds held until death, no matter what the problems.

"Another coffee?" asked Mirek. "More wine?"

Katrinka shook her head. "No, nothing," she said.

He smiled. "Good. I want to take you home."

For once, she could not quite meet his eyes and looked away as if searching for the waiter, who hurried to them when he saw Mirek signal. She could not put it off any longer, she decided. As soon as they got home, she would tell him.

They left the restaurant and walked to where his car was parked. It was a cold night, the air crisp and clear, "Golden Prague's" thousand lighted church spires standing out in sharp relief against the cloudless backdrop of the star-laden sky. Katrinka felt her eyes fill with tears and was not certain whether it was the wind, or the sublime beauty of the night, or the ordeal awaiting her that made her want to weep. She trembled and Mirek put an arm around her. "You're cold," he said. "Oh, my poor darling, your coat is so thin. I must buy you a fur. For Christmas. Yes. It will be your Christmas present. A sable coat from Russia."

"No, no, I'm fine," protested Katrinka. "I'm not cold. It's a beautiful night." He had given her so many presents in the past five months, leather handbags from Italy, dresses from France, bottles of Chanel No. 5, a German record player, American blue jeans, luxuries to which only a few in the country had access. Mirek's films continued to earn hard currency in Germany, Switzerland, and Scandinavia—a recent one had even enjoyed a small success in Italy—and when he traveled abroad he was able to bring back what he liked without problems from customs.

So as to keep up the pretense of not knowing what was going on under her nose, by the time they arrived at the house, Mrs. Kolchík had retired to her room to avoid encountering, and possibly embarrassing, Bartoš. He and Katrinka could have raged through the dimly lit interior like storm troopers and still not brought her out to investigate, but still they moved quietly, hoping not to disturb her.

As soon as they entered Katrinka's room, Mirek pulled her into his arms and buried his face in her neck. "Oh, God," he groaned. "How I've missed you."

Instead of responding as she usually did, Katrinka pulled away. "Would you like something to drink?" she asked.

Surprised, Mirek let his arms drop limply to his sides and looked at Katrinka quizzically. What was going on here? he wondered. A knot of apprehension began to form in his gut. Surely his Katrinka, his resourceful, independent, loving, sexually uninhibited Katrinka, was not about to make a scene? Above all, Mirek Bartoš detested scenes—unless of course they took place on a soundstage. "Yes," he said. "All right. A cognac."

Katrinka's room, like the rest of the house, was cozy, and she was pleased to have it. It was furnished in a blend of inexpensive blond wood furniture and the few antiques the Kolchíks had rescued from the Nazis. In a corner was a side table where she kept the supply of liquor that Mirek had given her. She went to it and poured the cognac into an exquisite glass of hand-blown Czech crystal, also a gift from him, handed it to him, then poured one for herself. Smiling wanly, she took a sip, choking slightly as the liquid burned its way down her throat to her stomach. Her eyes filled with tears.

He lifted his glass to her in salute. Then, sitting on the bed, he took a sip of the cognac, savored its taste, lit a French cigarette, and waited. He was determined not to ask what was wrong. After all, she might just lose courage and the evening could then proceed without the detour Katrinka had in mind, exactly as mapped out by him earlier in the day when the image of Katrinka's naked body, in various intriguing positions, superimposed itself seductively on the pages of the script he was reading. A sudden panic seized him, momentarily displacing his annoyance. Surely she was not going to refuse to see him again? But of course not. He smiled. If that was it, he knew how to change her mind.

Seeing his smile, Katrinka gathered courage. He looked so big, so strong, so completely dependable, so reassuringly in love. "I'm pregnant," she said.

It took a moment for what she had said to register. "Oh, my God," murmured Mirek finally. "You're sure?"

He had never expected this. But then men never expected this, he reminded himself, however regularly it seemed to happen. He took a large gulp of cognac, and then, to his surprise, a wave of pleasure washed over him. Putting the crystal glass down on the bedside table, he stubbed out his cigarette, got up, went to Katrinka, and enveloped her in his arms. *"Miláčku,"* he murmured against her hair. "How pregnant?"

"Two months."

She pulled away from him so she could see his face, searching it for signs of anger, but all she could see was tenderness. He sat again on the bed and pulled her down across his lap, holding her as he stroked her hair. He had a son almost thirty whose wife was pregnant with their second child and a daughter a few years older than Katrinka who was expecting her first. It pleased him that he would have a child younger than his grandchildren. It made him feel more youthful than he had in years. "I thought you'd be upset," she said.

150

"It won't be easy." His hand slid from her hair down her arm and settled on the breast that would one day give sustenance to his child. He fondled it gently.

"What are we going to do?"

"I'm not sure. I have to think."

"The sports committee," she began, wanting to confide in him her fears of that all-powerful body.

"Leave everything to me," he said, interrupting her. "You trust me, don't you?"

"Yes," she said, wanting desperately to believe that somehow he was going to make everything all right.

He began to unbutton her blouse, holding her still as she shifted in his arms as if to stop him. "I want to see your breasts," he said, removing her blouse, sliding her slip and bra down to her waist. "They're so beautiful." Despite Katrinka's slenderness, her breasts had always been large and full. Now they seemed even more so to him. He cupped his hand around first one, then the other, reveling in the silky feel of them against his palm. "So beautiful," he murmured. Sliding her over onto the bed next to him, he bent his head and took her right breast in his mouth and sucked it gently, his hand resting lightly on her belly where his child was growing.

Katrinka tried to resist the sensations of her body, to prevent the meltdown that occurred whenever Mirek touched her. There were so many questions she wanted to ask, so many things they had to discuss. She wanted to know what he intended to do.

She touched his hair. "Mirek, tell me . . ."

His mouth released her breast and closed over hers as his hand left her stomach, reached under her skirt, traveled up the inside of her leg and pushed her panties aside. She cried out as his fingers entered her.

He lifted his head to watch her face now filled with passion. She was past caring about anything but making love, he knew. Reaching out blindly, she grabbed his head and pulled it back down to hers. "Don't worry," he said, resisting for a moment. "I'll take care of you. I love you." He could not believe just how much he loved her. He adored her. Surely he had never felt this way about any woman before? He could not give her up. He would marry her. That was it. Suddenly, everything was very clear. He would divorce Vlasta and marry her. "I love you," he murmured against her mouth, elation flooding him like a white light. "God, how I love you."

Fourteen

Katrinka, please, try to understand. There's nothing I can do."

"I do understand," she said, her voice flat, empty of all emotion. It had been a week since she had told Mirek that she was pregnant, a week without hearing from him, until today when she had found him waiting after her last class. She had seen his car parked next to hers and had run to it, a sudden rush of joy breaking like sunshine through the clouds that had overshadowed her all week. And then she saw his face.

"Get in," he said, leaning across and opening the door for her. He kissed her briefly, started the car, and headed across the Mánesův Bridge out of the city. "Sorry I haven't phoned," he said curtly. "I've been busy."

In the past week, hope and despair had seesawed wildly in her, trust in Mirek's love alternating with doubts about his courage. He would have to give up so much to be with her. Would he be brave enough to do that? Did she have any right to expect him to?

Yes, of course, she did, she assured herself, lying sleepless alone in her small brass bed at night. He was as much to blame for this child as she was. More so. He was the one who had flattered her, courted her, turned her head, made her fall in love. He should not have seduced her. He was older and theoretically wiser. He should have known better.

No, of course not, she argued at other times. She was no

fool. She had given herself to him freely, because she loved him. Why talk of blame? No one was to blame for falling in love.

Mirek, too, had spent a sleepless week, torn between the power of his feelings for Katrinka and his sense of self-preservation. He loved her now, wanted her now, but what of later? How many times before had he thought love would last forever, only to find that it barely endured a few months? What if he was to give everything up for her, and for their child (he, who was not very fond of children), to discover next year or the year after that he no longer cared about her at all? As unlikely as that seemed to him now, he knew it was possible, more than possible.

Some men would take the chance. Some men would think the world well lost for Katrinka. He certainly thought so at moments, in the dead of the night when he longed for her, during the day when the memory of her laughter distracted him from his work. But then common sense would intervene. Other men were not married to Vlasta Mach. As casual as she was about their relationship, as uninterested in his affairs as he was in hers, she had made it clear over the years that she would not consider a divorce, if only because her father would not approve. And her father was not a man to cross. Like it or not, Mirek was forced to admit that, despite his talent and careful apolitical stance, his film career would not have proceeded quite so smoothly without his father-in-law's assistance. Neither the opportunities nor his resulting success would have come so quickly, if Mach had not thrown the power of his position behind him. And should Mirek act against Vlasta's wishes, should he make her unhappy, not only would that helpful presence be removed but Mach might—with or without Vlasta's approval—seek revenge. Mirek Bartoš would not be the first Czech citizen to end his years in a Soviet labor camp on charges trumped up by the secret police.

All week he had walked through his and Vlasta's luxurious apartment in Prague's New Town, the Nové Město, looked at its sumptuous furnishings, the treasures he had brought back from abroad. He considered the comfort of his life, its security, and weighed it against the minimal existence in a labor camp. At the thought of it, his flesh grew cold and his breath came in anxious gasps. He scolded himself for being a coward, or a hysteric. This was not the sixteenth century, after all: hearts were no longer ripped out of living bodies, men were not castrated for love, or banished.

Then, with Vlasta and his children, Mirek had attended a dinner in honor of his father-in-law's birthday. He studied the faces of the Communist Party officials who were Mach's friends, noted the stern eyes belying the jovial smiles. "We have a good life," Vlasta said when they returned home.

"Yes," he agreed.

"It would be so stupid to spoil it."

Had someone been talking to her, he wondered, or had she noticed the change in him? "Yes," he said again.

She kissed him lightly on the mouth and, turning away, lifted her carefully manicured hands to her head and began removing the pins holding her lacquered hair in place. "I'm exhausted," she said. "It's been a long evening."

The next day he drove to the familiar rendezvous point and waited for Katrinka.

"What will you do?" he asked when he had finished explaining how impossible it was for him to leave Vlasta.

They were parked at the side of a narrow road on a hill overlooking the valleys of Bohemia. In daylight, below them, low green hills could be seen rolling sedately toward the mountains in the distance. But now it was night and all that was visible were the lights of a few farms scattered like stars on the dark landscape. Determined not to cry, Katrinka stared out the car window at nothing. "I don't know," she said.

"You can't keep the child."

"No. I don't know. I have to think." She was overwhelmed suddenly with fatigue. All she wanted was to sleep for a hundred years, to wake up when none of this mattered anymore.

Mirek was grateful he could not see her face. "I'll help. Whatever I can do . . ."

"Yes," she said dully.

He reached for her suddenly and turned her body toward

his, putting his arms around her, and hugging her with all his strength. "Oh, God, Katrinka. I love you. I do love you."

She pulled away from him abruptly. "Don't say that," she said. "I don't want to hear it."

He sat back against the door of the car. His face was bleak and he felt suddenly very old. "Yes, of course. You're right."

That night, all Katrinka could do was weep, sobbing into a pillow so that Mrs. Kolchík would not hear. She had never felt so alone in all her life, so frightened, so miserable and uncertain.

Even if Mirek had been willing to marry her, to take care of her and the child, the difficulties for Katrinka would still have seemed enormous: breaking the news to her parents, witnessing their heartbreak, their loss of faith in her; facing the sports committee, withdrawing from the university and the ski team, abandoning a promising athletic career, the hope of an Olympic medal, losing all her hard-won privileges. It was a lot to give up, but she would have done it happily for Mirek, handing over her life to him, trusting that he would provide the same safety and security, the same comfortable, loving home that she had always known.

Katrinka had imagined the position that Mirek Bartoš occupied as secure, his years of success guaranteeing it. That her love could threaten him was a wholly new idea to her. That his fears about labor camps might be farfetched, melodramatic, or merely an excuse he was using to push her as gently as possible out of his life did occur to her as she lay there in the dark, going over and over his words, trying to find some measure of hope in them. She found none, but dismissed immediately the idea that he might be conning her. He loved her. If it were possible, he would marry her, she was sure of it. But it was not possible, and that created a problem she alone could solve.

In the morning, she dragged herself to class, sat dully through the hours of instruction, refused Zuzka's invitation to dinner with her and Tomáš. "Tell me what's wrong," insisted Zuzka. "Tell me. You look terrible."

"Mirek and I had a quarrel," admitted Katrinka, unwilling to confide more.

"Bastard," muttered Zuzka when Katrinka was out of earshot, her affection for Mirek disappearing before Katrinka's obvious pain.

Again that night Katrinka lay sleepless in her bed, listening to the tick of the clock on the bedside table, weighing the alternatives. She had to make a decision, and quickly, about what to do, for if the sports committee were to suspect that she was pregnant, the choice would be taken from her. They would either insist she have the child and strip her of all her prerogatives; or, if they decided—for whatever reasons— that she would make an unfit mother, demand that she have an abortion. Neither was an alternative Katrinka was yet willing to accept, which was why she could not confess her problem to Ota Černý, who would be required to report her to the committee; why she was reluctant to discuss it with Tomáš and Zuzka, not that they would ever deliberately betray her, but who knew what they might let slip in an unguarded moment? As for her parents, the thought of telling them filled her with dread. How could she face their disillusionment and pain? Hers alone were hard enough to bear.

A race that weekend took Katrinka's mind briefly off her problems. Standing at the gate, waiting to start, she could think, as always, only of winning. And though she did not win, those moments of freedom, when she felt no fear, no pain, but only the rush and swoop of her skis on the snow, the exhilaration of her glide down the mountain, were a sign to her that there was life beyond Mirek Bartoš. The anguish came quickly flooding back, but that brief glimpse of salvation was enough to kindle a small spark of hope and to keep its flame flaring, however unsteadily, through the next dark weeks.

By the time she went home for the brief Christmas holiday, Katrinka had made a decision, which was just as well since her pale face and shadowed eyes could never have gone unnoticed by the always watchful, ever-worried Milena.

When they returned from dinner with Honza and Dana her first night in Svitov, Milena suggested they all have some

157

tea before retiring to bed. Jirka was about to excuse himself, since he had to be at the complex early the next morning, but a warning look from Milena stopped him, and he settled into his armchair.

"I'll help," said Katrinka.

"No, no, no," said Milena. "Talk to your father. I'll be right back."

Jirka lit a cigarette and smiled at his daughter. "It's good to have you home."

"It's good to be home," said Katrinka, sitting on the green sofa, hoping the cigarette smoke would not make her ill. Her stomach had been behaving very strangely of late.

Studying his daughter, Jirka wondered how he could not have noticed earlier how tired she looked. As always, she was trying to do too much, he decided. School, sports, modeling, probably out to all hours with her friends. He would have to have a word with her before she left at the end of the week. Again he regretted how brief her vacations always were, this one cut short by a race in Innsbruck. Katrinka clearly needed to rest.

Milena returned with the tea tray, poured them each a cup, and offered around a plate of small homemade pastries. Then she took her seat and looked at her daughter. "Well?" she asked.

For weeks Katrinka had rehearsed in her mind what to tell her parents, and how, trying first one approach, then another. No one way had seemed easier than the rest. She hesitated and then finally said, "I'm pregnant."

There was silence for a moment, as if Katrinka's words hung suspended, unheard, in the air, before falling like blows.

"My God!" whispered Jirka.

"I didn't want to tell you. I didn't know what else to do."

"Do? You should have done nothing, or at least been more careful," said Milena angrily.

Seeing the look on her parents' faces, as bad, no, worse than anything she had imagined, Katrinka began to cry, the first time since that terrible night when Mirek had told her he could not marry her. "I'm sorry," she said. "I didn't mean to hurt you."

158

Even Milena had not expected anything so terrible, not in her wildest imaginings, though, now that she knew, it seemed inevitable. Her beautiful, adventurous, brave daughter: of course she would fall in love and give herself without reservation or thought, of course she would get pregnant. Quickly, Milena was across the room and next to Katrinka on the couch, her arms wrapped around her weeping daughter. "It's all right, *miláčku*. It's all right. Don't cry. We're just surprised, that's all."

"Who?" asked Jirka, forcing the sound past the constriction in his throat.

As Katrinka told them about Mirek Bartoš, Milena felt waves of disbelief, anger, understanding wash over her in quick succession at the thought of the big handsome man who had flirted with her so many years before. Jirka felt only rage. Bartoš was his age, old enough to be Katrinka's father. For the first time in his life, Jirka felt as if he could kill. He got to his feet, uttering curses he had never before used in his home.

Startled, Milena looked at him. "Jirka, please . . ."

"It's not his fault, *Tati*," said Katrinka. "I knew what I was doing."

"You're a child. A child."

"I'm not. I'm a woman."

A woman. He looked at Katrinka again. "Oh, God," he said.

Katrinka wrenched herself away from her mother, got up from the couch, and went to him, throwing her arms around him. "*Tati*, please, forgive me. Please."

He held her for a moment. "I love you," he said finally. "More than my life."

Milena lit a cigarette and took a puff, hoping it would calm her. "You've decided what you want to do?" she said, certain that Katrinka had arrived home with her mind made up.

"Yes. I want to keep the baby."

"Katrinka, no! Think what you are doing!" She was crazy, thought Jirka, to throw away everything. How could she even think of it?

"I *have* thought. For weeks." Having an abortion certainly

159

made more sense, Katrinka knew that, but it was an option she had quickly discarded. And not simply for religious reasons. Her exposure to the rules of Catholicism, in communist Czechoslovakia, had been too haphazard for deeply held convictions to take root. She had not decided against abortion because she believed it a sin, but because she was afraid it would be an act she would regret all her life. Milena's grief over her miscarriages, Olga Černý's endless sorrow at being childless, these were the influences of Katrinka's youth, and they had instilled in her both a respect for the miracle of childbearing and a fear of being barren herself. "I'm going to keep the baby," she repeated, knowing it was a decision she would never regret.

The plan that Katrinka had devised was complicated, even baroque, but she was convinced that it would work. The crucial part, and the most difficult, was keeping her pregnancy secret until the end of the spring semester, by which time she would be in her eighth month. Tall, with a slender, well-muscled athlete's body, Katrinka was convinced she could, with careful dressing, deceive everyone, which was essential if she wanted both to avoid coming to the attention of the sports committee and to protect her freedom to travel.

At the end of the school year, she would go to Munich, supposedly to work at a hotel there, as she had in previous summers before the start of training on the Italian glaciers in August. Getting a visa for this was never a problem, since Katrinka was a trusted member of the ski team and had been traveling abroad, without incident, for years. Her parents would join her in Munich as soon as they could, though to avoid suspicion they would take a roundabout route to Germany. There they would stay until the baby was born.

Before leaving to see her parents, after weeks of refusing to see him Katrinka had agreed to meet Mirek again, but only to ask for his help. His connections were needed to get the necessary travel documents for Jirka and Milena, since, to avoid mass defections, government regulations did not allow whole families to travel abroad at the same time.

Mirek thought her plan crazy but agreed to do what he could. What would it cost him, a few bottles of French wine and some American blue jeans, bribes to the right people? It was getting off cheaply, he knew, though his relief was mixed with regret. He would have liked to keep Katrinka in his life. And the baby, too, strangely enough, though he had never thought of himself as particularly paternal. Certainly, his son and daughter had nothing but complaints about him as a father. Selfish, they called him. Obsessed with his films. Living in a world of fantasy. Yes. And Katrinka with her raven hair and exquisite blue eyes, her infectious smile and strong athlete's body that seemed to melt beneath him when he made love to her, she was his fantasy come true.

Mirek would help in another way, Katrinka told her parents. He had offered to pay for her care at a private clinic owned by a doctor whom he had met several times when visiting Munich at parties thrown by the city's political and intellectual elite for foreign artists. This doctor, Klaus Zimmerman, could be counted on to be discreet, Mirek assured her, though by that time discretion would matter only to him, as Katrinka would have no further use for it.

"And then what?" asked Milena. "After the child is born, what do we do?"

Katrinka hesitated a moment, then said, "I stay in the West, with the baby." Seeing the horror on her parents' faces, she added quickly, "What else can I do? Here, I'll have lost everything. In the West, I'll still have a chance to make something of myself."

"We'd never see you again," said Jirka. "Doesn't that matter to you?" Once a family member had defected, the others were never granted visas to travel abroad. That was all Jirka could think of now, though more than travel was in jeopardy. His job was at risk, as was Milena's. At the very least, they would lose all future pay raises and promotions. They had given birth to a traitor and would be punished for it.

"Of course it matters," said Katrinka, her voice full of anguish. "But what can I do? What choice do I have?" She took a deep breath. "Anyway, things are changing here. The rules are not as strict as they used to be. We'll see each other.

I know it." She was trying to convince herself as much as them.

Milena stubbed out her cigarette, stood and gathered up the teacups. "Let's go to bed now," she said. "It's late. And we're tired. Too tired to think. We'll talk more about this tomorrow." She picked up the tray and headed for the kitchen as Jirka and Katrinka, not daring to meet each other's eyes, said good night. In the kitchen, as she washed and dried the cups, Milena thought about the painted clock they had brought back from Poland one year, and the brightly patterned yellow pottery that had been a wedding present from her parents. She thought about the farm and Zdeňka and her sons, about Dana and her rose garden, about Honza, about this apartment where she had lived so happily with her husband and child. How could she bear to leave it all? she wondered.

When she had put everything neatly away, she went into the small bathroom and changed into her nightgown. She stared at her face in the mirror. There were deep lines now in her forehead and around her mouth. Her red hair was dulled with gray and her eyes, so like Katrinka's, were shadowed with pain.

For years, all she had done was work so that Katrinka could have the best of everything. She had cooked for her, cleaned for her, scrimped to buy her treats, sewn her fashionable clothes, worn herself out traveling to watch Katrinka ski, spent sleepless nights worrying about crushed ribs and broken spines. After all that, after the deprivation of the war years, the terrors of the communist coup, didn't she have a right to a comfortable and serene old age?

She wondered why she was not furious with Katrinka. Oh, she was angry enough, disappointed and hurt, but not enraged. What she felt at the moment, more powerfully than any other emotion, was pity for her daughter, imagining what the past few weeks had been like for her as she had contemplated the devastation of her life and tried all alone to salvage something from the ruins.

Milena thought about the babies she had lost, how she had wept for them, and still doubted if, in Katrinka's place, she would have had the courage to keep the child. Her daughter was stubborn, without doubt, and often foolhardy, but she was brave.

When she climbed into bed beside Jirka, she could feel him lying tense and awake beside her. She slipped her arms around him and cradled herself against his back. "We'll have to stay with her," she said softly. "In Munich. We can't leave her and the baby alone."

"I know." He turned to face her. "We'll have to leave everything behind."

"Yes. But we'll have each other." She kissed him. "We'll work hard," she said. "We'll build a new life."

Jirka, knowing how everything worried her, understood how terrified Milena must be at the prospect of starting over, at their age, in an unfamiliar country. "We'll go to England," he said, "or Australia." They had friends in both places, people who had left Czechoslovakia years before, at the time of the coup.

"It will be an adventure," said Milena.

"You're the brave one," said Jirka, realizing only as he spoke how true it was. All those years, she had lived with fear and not succumbed to it, allowing Katrinka and him the freedom to live as they liked.

"I wish I was," she said, sighing.

Neither of them mentioned Honza and Dana, or Zdeňka and her sons, or how painful was the thought of leaving them. Katrinka is right, thought Jirka, trying to comfort himself. The world is changing so quickly. Someday, we'll be able to see them again.

Fifteen

ell, my dear, I am happy to tell you the reports are all excellent. You are an extraordinarily healthy young woman. There is no reason why you should not have a completely normal childbirth."

Katrinka relaxed back into the Biedermeier chair and smiled at the doctor. Though she had all along believed herself to be physically fit, still it was reassuring to have it confirmed.

Klaus Zimmerman looked up from his reports and across the desk to where Katrinka sat facing him. Eight months pregnant and she barely showed, a phenomenon not unknown in his experience, but rare. If his examination had not shown her to be completely healthy, he might have been worried about the effects of lack of nourishment on the fetus, but he had seen nothing to cause him concern. "It is amazing, though, how slender you have managed to keep."

"I eat like crazy," said Katrinka, replying in German, a language she had studied in school and practiced during her summer trips to Munich. "But good foods." Determined to keep her weight down, she had, in fact, over the months watched her diet carefully. "And, of course, I exercise all the time."

Zimmerman looked down again at his notes. "You're a skier?"

"Yes," said Katrinka.

There was not much point now worrying her about the harm a fall could have done her and the child, so Zimmer-

164

man merely nodded and said, "I wish more of my patients would consider exercising."

He was tall and very thin, with strongly chiseled features, pale blond hair, and a slightly darker moustache. He looked like a film actor, Katrinka thought, and wished she could like him more. There was something about him that put her off, a coldness she sensed without being consciously aware of it, because with Katrinka as with all his patients—most of whom were wealthy women and a little in love with him—Dr. Klaus Zimmerman was all practiced charm. Now he smiled at her confidentially and said, "You have thought about what you intend to do after the child is born?"

His smile, Katrinka noticed, did not reach his eyes, which were gray and reminded her of how dull and cold the Baltic was one summer long ago when it had rained the entire time she and her parents were in Poland on holiday. "Yes," she said, nodding. He looked at her questioningly, waiting for her to explain. But in a police state, betrayal is common, discretion essential. Katrinka had been raised to keep her mouth shut. Even Mirek had been told only what he needed to know to help. "All the arrangements are made," she added, looking at Zimmerman coolly.

She's going to be difficult, thought Zimmerman, torn between admiration and impatience. Only nineteen years old, pregnant out of wedlock, and she handled herself like an aristocrat, dismissing him as if he were a nosy interloper instead of an experienced and successful doctor. He controlled the irritation he felt, mustered a sympathetic look, and said, "Mirek tells me you plan to keep the child."

"Yes," replied Katrinka curtly, startled that Mirek should have been discussing her in such an intimate way with this man.

"Are you sure that is wise?"

"Did Mirek tell you he disagreed with my decision?" asked Katrinka suspiciously.

Weighing the best way to reply to that, Zimmerman hesitated long enough for Katrinka to doubt him no matter what he said. "No. No, he didn't." In fact, Mirek had told him that he thought the girl mad to keep the child, but that he would do what he could to help her. "But when I offered to make arrangements for the child's future, he of course told me what you hoped to do."

"Hoped?" said Katrinka, catching the doubt in the doctor's voice.

"It is not so easy, you know, for an unwed mother to raise a child on her own."

"I'll manage."

Katrinka's knowledge of German was remarkably good, a credit to the Czech educational system in fact, but perhaps not fluent enough to appreciate the nuances of the language, thought Zimmerman. He spoke slowly, choosing his words with care, and tried to explain to her the difficulties of being an unwed mother, the stigma attached, the impossibility of providing adequate care for a child while trying to earn a living. He painted a bleak future, where a minimal existence was all Katrinka had to look forward to, where opportunities were nonexistent and drudgery the only way of life. "Is that what you want for yourself? For your child?"

Katrinka felt a sliver of fear, cold as ice, in her breast. She would rather die than live like that. "No," she said quickly. "No." She shuddered, then took a deep breath and continued. "But that's not how it will be," she said.

"Are you so sure?"

"Yes. Absolutely."

"Katrinka, my dear, you must be reasonable. You must consider your decision carefully. It affects not only your future, but your child's."

"I have considered it. I have thought about nothing else for months. I'm going to keep my baby."

Her voice was calm, firm. She was clearly not a young woman prone to hysterics, thought Zimmerman, with increasing admiration. He let the argument go, and spread his hands, palms up, in a gesture of entreaty. "Please understand," he said. "I want only to help you."

"Yes. I know." If Mirek trusted this doctor, then Katrinka felt she had no choice but to do the same, though she didn't like him.

Zimmerman got to his feet, saying as he did, "I want to see you again at the end of the month. Make an appointment with Mrs. Braun on the way out." He came around to the other side of the desk and escorted Katrinka across the luxurious carpet to the door. "Are you pleased with your accommodations?"

"Oh, yes," said Katrinka. "Mrs. Braun has been so kind. And everything is most comfortable." Mirek and Dr. Zimmerman had arranged that, too, between them, a room for Katrinka in an apartment in the Neuhausen section of Munich, not far from the Nymphenburg Palace and the clinic. The apartment was owned by Erica Braun, Dr. Zimmerman's private secretary.

"Good. Good. I'm pleased to hear it." He took her hand, held it for a moment, and looked deep into her eyes. "You are a very brave young woman." Again, he smiled, but this time Katrinka could see something like appreciation in his eyes. She returned the smile shyly, then extricated her hand as he opened the door for her and stepped back, allowing her to pass into the empty outer office. Katrinka had been the last appointment of the day.

Erica Braun looked up from the papers on her desk and watched them curiously for a moment. It's not gone as he planned, thought Erica, as Zimmerman's eyes briefly met hers. "When does the doctor want to see you again?" she asked as Katrinka approached her desk. A voluptuous woman in her late thirties, she had strong, handsome features, hair bleached to the shade of flax, a wide sensual mouth, and heavy-lidded brown eyes with which she now studied Katrinka carefully. She knew it was disloyal, but she was pleased that Katrinka had not given in to the doctor. Women too often did, herself included.

"At the end of the month, he said."

Klaus Zimmerman closed the door and returned to his desk. Sitting, he let his eyes wander lovingly around the room, admiring its silk-covered walls hung with gilt-framed seventeenth-century etchings, its elegant Biedermeier furniture, antique brass lamps, and collection of carved Chinese jade figurines, all designed to reassure and impress his growing roster of wealthy patients. Undeniably, he had achieved much in the ten years since he had started this clinic. No longer was he merely a moderately successful obstetrician and gynecologist, but one of the city's preeminent physicians, noted for his treatment of difficult cases, from infertility to problem childbirths. Reason told him he ought to be satisfied with what he had accomplished, but satisfaction escaped him. There was not yet enough money between him and the poverty of his youth. Would there ever be enough, he sometimes wondered, to block out the awful, degrading memory of himself at the age of twelve, at the height of the war, stealing from garbage pails to feed himself and his mother?

He thought about Katrinka Kovář, beautiful and headstrong Katrinka, about to condemn herself to a life of needless poverty. He thought about another of his patients, a spoiled little fool, distraught because she could not present her husband with an heir. Surely these two women were destined to be of help to one another, with himself acting as the hand of Fate, of course for a lucrative fee?

He thought about Katrinka's baby, whom he envisioned as possessing Katrinka's radiant beauty and vibrant good health combined with Mirek's talent and charm, a child worth a princely sum. He sighed. He had not expected Katrinka to be so stubborn. Few young girls were. Perhaps nearer the time, when the reality of her situation became more threatening, she would be willing to listen to reason. He hoped so. It was unlikely he would get his hands on another such baby in the near future, perhaps not soon enough to keep his willful, erratic patient from changing her mind or going elsewhere to seek a solution to her problem. And, in this particular instance, it was not just the money she would be prepared to pay that was so appealing, but what he knew would be her enduring gratitude, and that of her husband, a man with significant political influence. Klaus Zimmerman wanted someone like this man firmly in his debt. One never knew when a string would need to be pulled.

Katrinka left the clinic and took the U-bahn back to the center of the city, to the Maximilianstrasse. In Munich for just three days, not only had she filled her pretty yellow bedroom at Erica Braun's with fresh flowers and family photographs in an attempt to make herself feel at home, Katrinka had already found a job.

To earn some extra money while waiting for her baby to be born, the day after her arrival she had applied for work as a chambermaid at the Four Seasons, Munich's best hotel. It was the first week of June, the start of the tourist season, and extra help was always needed. Even without experience, Katrinka would have been taken on.

Compared to previous summers, the work on the evening shift seemed light, which was just as well. One of those rare women who stayed slender and lithe until the very end of pregnancy, still she did tire more easily these days. Katrinka turned down the beds, left chocolates on pillows, changed the towels, emptied the wastepaper baskets, and tidied the rooms. That done, she returned her cart to the housekeeping department and spent the remaining hours responding to requests for more glasses, more towels, another hanger, a laundry bag, providing the endless small services required in a deluxe hotel.

She was glad to be working, not only for the money but because it helped to make her forget that all she was doing was waiting: waiting for her parents to arrive, waiting for her child to be born, waiting for her new life to begin. Never a patient person, inactivity now would have driven her mad.

All the previous winter she had kept busy, traveling to races, attending classes, studying hard though she knew she would not be returning to complete her degree, taking her exams early (a concession made to athletes because of their sports schedule) so that she could leave Prague before her stomach grew too round. Ota Černý had watched her unusually frenzied activity with worried eyes, even going so far as to mention his concern to her father, who had looked slightly embarrassed but had dismissed the worry, assuring him that Katrinka was fine. Zuzka held Mirek Bartoš responsible for Katrinka's mood, but could get her to admit only that their affair was over. Tomáš noticed nothing at all. In January, Alexander Dubček had been elected head of the government and the heavy hand of the communist dictatorship was slowly being lifted. In that winter of 1968, there was something resembling freedom of the press in Czechoslovakia for the first time in twenty years. There was increased freedom of movement, freedom of thought and conversation. There was an excitement in the air, a hunger for change. But it was coming too slowly for some. Protest marches took place in Prague and throughout the country, demonstrations demanding immediate democratization. The students, as always, were the most radical element, and Tomáš, for whom artistic and political freedom were two sides of the same coin, was heavily involved in the protest movement.

Though she could hardly help noticing the new mood of exhilaration in the country, Katrinka was not only fully absorbed in her own problems but traveled abroad too frequently to stay in touch with the shifting political currents. Zuzka, too, for the same reason, felt removed from events and, even more disturbing, from Tomáš, bewildered by his new preoccupation with government and often frightened by it. As far as she was concerned, political involvement led inevitably to prison, never to change, or at least not change for the good.

At the end of the semester, Tomáš—not wanting to be away from the center of action—had decided to stay on in Prague, finding work there for the summer. Zuzka, after a few weeks' visit with her family, intended to return to be with him. Katrinka had said good-bye to them over dinner at the Maxmilianka. Feeling very sad, but determined not to let it show, she had dragged them from one disco to another, making them dance until exhausted, then had kissed them good night and returned for the last time to her room at Mrs. Kolchík's.

Another difficult farewell was to Ota and Olga Černý, with whom she and her parents had dinner at a small restaurant in the hills above the city when she returned to Svitov for a few days to collect her things. She was unnaturally gay that night, too, causing Olga later to insist that she had been drunk. But Katrinka got through the evening without tears, promising Ota at the end of it to be on time for summer practice in Cervinia. She was expected to meet him there in August.

The next day she said a tearful good-bye to her grandparents and, carrying a picnic lunch packed for her by Dana, left for Munich, driving her blue Fiat across the green Moravian countryside to the border for one last time. Her parents were to join her by the end of June, a month before the baby was due to be born.

The days in Munich passed quite pleasantly for Katrinka. The weather was sunny and warm, though not so humid as it would be later in the summer. Since she worked until after midnight, she slept late, for as long as nine and ten hours—she had never slept that much before in her life—rising just before noon. After breakfasting alone in Erica's large, old-fashioned kitchen, she would go out, spending a few hours visiting the sights of the city, the art and furniture collections in the Residenzmuseum, the smart shops in the pedestrian precinct leading to the Marienplatz, buying baby clothes in the Kaufhof department store, stopping for a pastry in the Café Glockenspiel, where she could watch the hours strike on the clock on the new Gothic facade of the Rathaus. Though not nearly so beautiful in her opinion, it reminded her of the clock tower in Prague's Old Town Square, and inevitably of Mirek Bartoš and the many times they had stood there to watch the hours strike.

One night during the first week of her stay, Erica Braun took Katrinka to see a production of *Tosca*. His plans for the evening disrupted by an inconvenient birth, Klaus Zimmerman had turned his tickets over to his secretary with instructions, no, *orders,* that she not only invite Katrinka but make clear that he was the source of the invitation. It was less a gesture of kindness toward a young girl alone in a foreign city than an attempt to ingratiate himself further into Katrinka's confidence. While she seemed to like Erica well enough, he could sense her coldness toward him, and he wanted, *needed,* Katrinka to regard him kindly, to think of him as her protector whose only concern was for her welfare.

While the evening did not achieve the desired result, it did succeed in turning Katrinka into a fan. The splendor of the opera house with its tiers of rococo box seats, the stylishness of the ladies' gowns, the elegance of the gentlemen, the soaring beauty of the music, all threads were woven together to make a night of seamless brilliance. Katrinka was captivated. When the tenor, of whom she had never before heard and who was not even particularly good, began to sing "E Lucevan Le Stelle," tears began to stream down her cheeks.

After that, Katrinka took every opportunity to go to the opera on her own. Lost in the music of Puccini or Verdi, Bizet or Mozart, it was possible for her to forget her own problems. Grieving for *Madama Butterfly* was much more acceptable to her as a pastime than feeling sorry for herself.

It was after a matinee performance of the latter, from which she emerged red-eyed and late for work, that she made her first friend a week or so after her arrival in Munich. Hurrying along the Maximilianstrasse toward the Four Seasons, weaving through the crowd, she went hurtling headlong into a young man. The paper bag he was carrying tore. New socks, undershirts, packages of boxer shorts went spilling to the ground. *"Do prdele,"* he swore in Czech as he bent down to pick them up.

Stooping to help him, Katrinka replied in the same language, apologizing while she gathered up the spilled packages, thrusting them back into his hands, anxious to be on her way. She hated to be late. Suddenly, she felt him go very still beside her. Standing, she looked down at him and said, "Are you all right?"

"You're Czech," he said.

"Yes," she replied, wondering how he knew. Then she started to laugh. "I didn't even realize I was speaking it."

He got to his feet and extended his hand. "Franta Dohnal," he said. He was, Katrinka guessed, somewhere in his late twenties. Perhaps an inch shorter than she, he was small-boned and slender, almost delicate, though not in an effeminate way. His coloring was dramatic, dark hair, fair skin, and eyes the color of jade. His smile was open and friendly. He was the sort of person it was easy to trust.

"Katrinka Kovář," she said, shaking his hand, then, as she started away, added, "Well, it was nice meeting you. *Dobrý den.*"

He fell into step beside her. "Have coffee with me?"

"I'm sorry. I'm late for work."

"After work?"

She shook her head. "I don't finish till after midnight. And then I'm always so tired."

"Tomorrow then?"

Under her loose-fitting cotton dress, the roundness of her stomach was barely noticeable, and she wore no wedding ring. She hesitated, afraid that, if she said yes, he would misunderstand.

"Just to help me brush up my Czech?" he coaxed. In fact, there was a large émigré Czech community in Munich and he had many Czech friends, though none quite so beautiful as this stunning dark-haired girl who had quite literally knocked the wind out of him this afternoon.

Katrinka laughed again, and, like every other man, Franta Dohnal found the sound of it completely captivating. "Yes," she said. "All right."

"Where?"

"The Café Glockenspiel. Do you know it? I sometimes stop there in the afternoon. Now I must go, really." And she sped away from him down the side of the hotel, toward the service entrance.

From their first cup of coffee, Katrinka made it clear to Franta that she was not interested in romance, implying that her heart was otherwise engaged, which, though she was trying hard to forget Mirek Bartoš, was unfortunately still true. She was in Munich, she told him, just to work for a while before joining the ski team in Cervinia for practice, a story that *would* have been true except for her pregnancy. That she never mentioned to him and he never noticed.

Fearing discovery, Katrinka refused to meet Franta's other Czech friends, afraid someone in his group would be more observant than he. What difference would it make? Katrinka sometimes asked herself, and though the answer always came back none at all, still she was unable to break the habit of discretion.

Franta had long since lost his. Most of his life he had been in love with cars, he confided to Katrinka, this time on her night off over dinner at Hirschgarten, a large open-air restaurant in the Nymphenburg Park. Since the time his father had taken him, when he was still a child, to the last Czech Grand Prix at Brno in 1949 and he had seen Peter Whitehead win in a wonderful red Ferrari, he had known that he wanted to be a race car driver. Finally, when he was fifteen, his father, realizing nothing would change his son's mind, allowed him to use his 1932 Aero to compete in small rallies run by the vintage car club to which he belonged, but with the stipulation that Franta agree to go to university and study mechanical engineering. That degree was Franta's passport into the Škoda technical department. From there, sheer determination and a few wins in the Aero got him on the Škoda rally team, which gave him the chance to travel to other European countries to compete. But soon, driving Škodas wasn't enough for him. He wanted to drive all the great cars. He wanted to race them, an impossibility while he remained in Czechoslovakia.

For a long time, he thought about how to make his escape. "Now, it's easy," he told her. "Since Dubček, the borders are open. But when I left . . ." He shook his head. "It was different then." If he had had relatives in the West, he might have been able to get a visa to visit them. If he had had money, he might have been able to buy one. People hid themselves in barrels or under trains to cross the border. Some merely walked.

Finally, he decided to apply for a job as a forest ranger at a site close to the Austrian border. Once he got it, he left Škoda and bided his time, learning the territory, the trails, the sentry positions, the routine for changing the guards. After about a year, one day while on duty, he picked up the backpack of supplies he had hidden in advance, walked deeper and deeper into the forest, waded through streams, and, terrified that at any moment he would be caught and brought back, crawled to freedom across two miles of the razed, featureless terrain that divided Czechoslovakia from its neighbor. That was two years ago. Now, thanks to a friend he had made on the Porsche team, he had a job testing cars for them. So far, he was still only competing in amateur races, but he had hopes, great hopes, for the future.

Since he was himself involved with someone at the time, Franta had no problem accepting the terms of a platonic relationship with Katrinka. She was beautiful and interesting, full of energy, eager to see and do everything, easy to talk to. He enjoyed her company and that was good enough for him. Romance was not essential. And Katrinka valued his friendship. He was considerate and interesting. She had never before met anyone so physically brave as he. And he was a link with home, keeping her from feeling lonely.

The night before her parents were to leave Svitov, Katrinka phoned them to make sure everything was going as planned. Not trusting the security of the phone, they kept the conversation general and vague, assuring each other that all was well, promising to see one another soon.

At the end of her eighth month, Katrinka was finally beginning to feel the effects of her pregnancy. She moved more slowly, tired more quickly, had trouble sleeping because the baby would not stop moving inside her. All she wanted was for her parents to arrive and for her ordeal to end. It would take Jirka and Milena, she estimated, no more than three days to reach Munich.

By the fourth day, Katrinka was frantic. She kept calling the apartment in Svitov, but received no reply. In desperation, she called her grandparents, who had not heard from them. Erica, trying to reassure her, suggested that perhaps they were merely enjoying themselves too much to hurry. But Katrinka knew better. Nothing would keep them from getting to her as quickly as possible.

Early in the morning of the fifth day, the phone rang in the apartment, waking Erica. She knocked on Katrinka's bedroom door and pushed it open. "Is it my parents?" asked Katrinka, who had not been asleep.

"No. It's someone called Tomáš."

"Tomáš?" Katrinka got up awkwardly from the bed, annoyed with Tomáš, whom she assumed was drunk and phoning to share some juvenile prank he considered hilarious. It did not occur to her then that Tomáš was not supposed to know where she was. "Tomáš? Do you know what time it is? What do you want?"

"Katrinka . . ." He sounded strained, hesitant, not like Tomáš at all.

175

"What is it?" Suddenly, she felt afraid.

"Katrinka, *zlatičko*, I'm sorry."

She could hear him weeping at the other end of the phone. "Tomáš, tell me what's happened."

"Your parents . . . Katrinka, there was an accident . . . the car . . ."

From what Tomáš told her and what she knew of her parents' plans, Katrinka guessed at what had happened.

Because the days were long at that time of year, Jirka had decided to keep driving as late as possible, hoping to make it to Munich even more quickly than promised. For once, impatient to see Katrinka, Milena had not argued with him. But sooner than they had expected, the day had dwindled to dusk and then to night, by which time they were deep in the mountains bordering Hungary, with no guest house or inn anywhere in the vicinity. Sometime around midnight, a convoy of Russian army trucks had come barreling around a curve toward them. Not expecting to meet a car on a remote stretch of mountain at that hour of night, the lead driver was probably not taking any particular trouble to keep to his side of the road. The two vehicles collided. The Škoda careened out of control and plunged over the side like a toy car thrown by a child, bouncing from ledge to ledge down the mountain, until it exploded in a bright ball of brilliant fire in the ravine below.

It took the army several days to recover the bodies, and more to identify the charred remains. They had informed Honza and Dana of the accident only hours after Katrinka had last phoned them. Not knowing how to reach her, they called Tomáš in Prague, hoping he would have a phone number for her in Munich. Of course he did not, but he got in touch with Mirek Bartoš, who did.

"What was the Red Army doing there? That's what I want to know," said Tomáš, his voice full of anguish. Katrinka, unable to believe what she had just heard, remained silent. "Katrinka! Katrinka, are you all right?" called Tomáš, cursing himself for having broken the news to her so badly, not knowing how else at that distance he could have done it.

"Yes, I'm all right. Thank you, Tomáš, for calling."

"Katrinka!" shouted Tomáš again, hoping to stop her from hanging up. But it was too late.

"What is it?" asked Erica, standing in the doorway, blond hair disheveled, a silk robe wrapped loosely around her. When Katrinka didn't reply, Erica went to her, and put her arms around the girl. She was trembling. *"Liebling,* tell me what's happened."

Katrinka tried to speak, but she couldn't. No sound came out of her mouth when she opened it. No matter how she tried, she could not say those awful words, could not say that her parents were dead. She felt suddenly dizzy. The room began to spin. And then everything went completely black.

Erica kept her from falling, supporting her weight easily, dragging her to a nearby sofa and laying her on it. Then she noticed that the bottom part of Katrinka's nightgown was wet. Water was gushing out of her. Quickly, she returned to the phone and called for an ambulance.

Katrinka's baby, a boy, was born at noon the next day, almost four weeks ahead of schedule. She held him in her arms, nursed him at her breast, but felt no pleasure in the sight of his little monkey face. Her pain was too great, and her guilt. If it had not been for her, for this child, her parents would still be alive.

She wept constantly. Not even the sedatives administered by Dr. Zimmerman gave her relief, only a few hours of tortured, dream-infested sleep before awakening again to the immediate, horrible knowledge of her parents' death. Each time, awareness hit her with the force of a Russian army truck barreling into a small red Škoda. She wished she had been with them in the car, and the baby too.

"What are you going to do, my dear?" asked Klaus Zimmerman when he stopped by to visit her.

"I don't know," said Katrinka dully, hardly listening to him.

"How will you manage?"

"Manage?"

"Surely you don't think you can take care of a child on your own, not in the condition you're in?"

"No," said Katrinka.

"Wouldn't it be best," he suggested, keeping his voice gentle, reassuring, "for both of you, if you were to give him up? If he were to be raised by a family able to give him all the luxuries such a beautiful child deserves to have, the luxuries you could never afford to give him?"

How *will* I manage? wondered Katrinka, whose plans had depended on her parents. Always independent, resourceful, now, without them, for the first time in her life she felt alone and frightened.

For two days she lay in her clinic bed, sedated, distraught with grief, her mind confused, while Klaus Zimmerman worried her with fake solicitude. Finally, she surrendered.

Magnanimously, he gave her until morning to think it over, to reconsider her decision, so that when she signed the papers she would be absolutely sure in her own mind that she was doing the right thing. In the morning, bright and early, he appeared with the papers in hand. "You're sure?" he asked her, as he handed her a pen and showed her where to sign.

"Yes," she said, signing her name. But as she handed him the papers, a moment of panic seized her, the only emotion other than grief she had felt for days. "Can I say good-bye to him?" she asked.

Zimmerman smoothed her lank hair back from her broad brow and shook his head sadly. "That would not be a good idea," he said. "It would be too painful for you. And right now, my dear, you don't need any more pain."

"No," said Katrinka.

"You did the right thing," he said, still stroking her hair with one hand while the other held the papers out of reach. "Now why don't you try to get some sleep. You know what Shakespeare says. You've studied Shakespeare, have you?"

Katrinka shook her head. "'Sleep that knits the raveled sleeve of care.' That's what you need. Sleep. Close your eyes." Katrinka did as told and heard Zimmerman's voice above her, whispering, "Good." A moment later, the papers grasped firmly in his hand, he went away, leaving Katrinka alone.

Sixteen

*Y*ou're not well enough to drive."

"Yes. Yes, I am," insisted Katrinka.

The sunlight streamed into Erica Braun's kitchen, giving the old-fashioned room a cheerful, cozy aspect while revealing in awful detail the pallor of Katrinka's skin and the shadows under her eyes, which seemed flat and dull, faded to the gray of an overcast day. Even her thick dark hair hung in lifeless strands to her shoulders. It was hard for Erica to believe that this was the same vibrant girl who had come to stay with her a little over a month before. "At least put off your departure for a few days," she suggested.

"I can't." Even the effort of picking up the cup of coffee seemed too much for Katrinka, but she forced herself, took a sip, and carefully replaced it in its saucer, noting as she did that her hand did not shake, a good sign. She took a forkful of egg from the plate in front of her. It was necessary to eat if she was to have the energy for the drive back to Svitov. The thought of driving terrified her: a car, to her, had become an instrument of death. But she had no choice. "I must be home for the funeral."

"My dear," said Erica softly, "if you phone your grandparents, they'll postpone everything until your arrival. Why do this to yourself?"

Katrinka shook her head stubbornly. "I'll leave this afternoon," she said.

Frowning, Erica stood up and began to clear the table. She was worried about Katrinka, very worried. The girl was in

179

no condition to make such a long drive, any length drive. But she knew of no way to stop her, short of jabbing another needle into her arm. And as far as she was concerned, Katrinka had had more than enough sedation. "Finish your breakfast," she snapped as Katrinka rose to help her, then, ashamed of herself, added more gently, "You need to build yourself up."

When Erica left for the clinic, Katrinka returned to her room. Here, too, the sun streamed in through the large windows, flooding the room with light, but she was oblivious to its unflagging cheerfulness. Moving slowly and with great care, as if afraid she might lose her balance, she began to pack her few things into the canvas duffel bag she had brought with her.

A week had passed since Tomáš's phone call and the birth of her child. Most of that time she had spent in the clinic. Two days before, she had returned to Erica's. She had wanted to leave immediately for home but it was obvious then, even to her, that she did not yet have the strength. She was feeling much better now, she assured herself. The first awful, agonizing rush of grief was over, and she believed herself calm, when in truth she was merely numb. To get through each day, she stopped every thought as it surfaced, cut off every feeling at its root. Afraid of the excruciating pain she would feel were she to remember, she remained in a daze behind the wall that sorrow had built.

But like all walls, it could be breached. Opening the bottom drawer of the rosewood dresser, Katrinka saw the neat pile of baby clothes, waiting as she had left them for the arrival of her child. A howl came ripping out of her throat, followed by a sob. Gathering up the clothes, she raced through the apartment and out its front door. She reached the incinerator at the end of the hall and, still sobbing, pulled it open. A blast of heat and the faint smell of burning refuse assailed her. Feverishly, she stuffed the clothes, some with their price tags still on, down the chute. A frail old man with a cane emerged cautiously from an apartment and walked by, eyeing Katrinka anxiously, wondering who this madwoman was, hair wild, tears streaming down her face, throwing away what looked like perfectly good clothes. *"Fräulein,"* he said gently, "do you need help?"

"Nein. Nein. Danke," sobbed Katrinka, closing the door to the incinerator and hurrying back to the safety of the apartment.

As soon as Dr. Zimmerman had left the room with the adoption papers, Katrinka had regretted signing them. She had shouted for him to return, but a nurse had come instead with something to make her sleep, assuring her that she would feel better tomorrow and could talk to the doctor then. When he returned the next day, Katrinka had begged him to tear up the papers, but he told her that she was still overwrought, that she did not know what she was saying, that she had made the correct decision, and that in any case it was too late. Her baby had already been given to his new parents. It was best, the doctor told her in his precise, reasonable voice, to do this as early as possible, to minimize the pain for the birth mother and to help the bonding between the child and the adoptive parents. "You'll see," he said, reaching out to touch her face. "This will all turn out for the best. Someday, you'll thank me."

May you burn in hell forever, Katrinka thought as she pushed his hand away and turned her face to the opposite wall.

Perhaps if she had said something to one of the nurses, asked to see an administrator of the clinic, threatened to consult a lawyer, Zimmerman would have relented for fear of scandal. But doing those things never occurred to Katrinka. Discretion was a hard habit to break. And if Erica Braun suspected what was happening, she pushed the thought away. She was too much in love with the doctor to allow herself to distrust him or take Katrinka's side no matter how her heart ached for the girl. To the divorced and childless Erica, Klaus Zimmerman was her whole life. His mistress since two years after his marriage to the shy, homely aristocrat who had provided him with the money to build his clinic, she was incapable of going against his wishes. And so the pressure brought to bear on Katrinka was known only by the doctor, who attributed to himself the best motives.

At noon, Erica returned from the clinic and found Katrinka still in her nightgown, lying on the bed in her room. But Erica's appearance was all Katrinka needed to snap out of her trance, get up, and prepare to leave, ignoring Erica's continued pleading that she remain another few days. Then, finally, when she could not change Katrinka's mind, Erica offered to drive her to Svitov. Hoping it would not come to that, but suspecting it might, Erica had already arranged for time off and the necessary visa, the latter acquired with the aid of a well-connected man only too eager to be of assistance since it was he who was in the process of adopting Katrinka's baby.

As soon as they set off, Katrinka knew she could never have managed the trip alone. She was too frightened to drive, too exhausted to stay awake even if she had mustered the courage. And Erica's presence was comforting, though she said little as she drove Katrinka's car across Germany and Austria into Czechoslovakia. They both sat for the most part in silence, lost in their own thoughts, oblivious to the beauty of the countryside—the blue lakes edged with granite mountains, the river valleys, pine forests, the onion domes of the churches. They stopped in Linz for a few hours' sleep at some nondescript modern motel, and set out again at dawn, arriving in Svitov early the next afternoon.

Erica stayed for the funeral, out of compassion and some vague sense of guilt, though she had thought she could not bear the sight of Katrinka another day, so pitiful it was to see her so changed from the sunny and hopeful young woman who had arrived in Munich. But even in her state of near-collapse, Katrinka did what she had to, tapping reserves of strength she had thought lost forever. When Mirek Bartoš phoned from Prague, she refused to speak to him, ordering Erica to tell him not to come to the funeral and not to call her again. "You've caused her enough trouble," Erica could not resist adding. "Just do as she says."

Katrinka planned the funeral, battled with the authorities to have everything as she wanted, as she believed Jirka and

Milena would have wanted. She comforted her distraught grandparents, standing between them at the graveside, her arms linked through theirs, looking regal and amazingly serene in the light that filtered through the dense branches of the pine trees.

Zuzka and Tomáš were there, with Mrs. Havlíček, Tomáš's mother; Ota and Olga Černý, their faces pale and sorrowful; Aunt Zdeňka, with tears streaming from her eyes; František with his new wife and his brother Oldřich. Even their father, Uncle Oldřich, had come, in tribute to the good times he and Jirka had had together; the employees of the sports complex and the library; old men and women whom Milena had never been too busy to help find books; athletes who had loved and respected Jirka; officials from the sports club and the city government, all came.

"May eternal light shine upon them," said the old priest, sprinkling the grave with holy water. "And may they rest in peace."

The day after the funeral, Katrinka opened the small trunk of her Fiat, put the leather suitcase inside, then went to join Erica, who had already settled herself in the car, ready for the trip to the train station and the return journey to Munich. Sliding behind the wheel, Katrinka put the key in the ignition. Suddenly, she began to tremble. She was terrified. For the first time since her parents' death she was behind the wheel of a car, and she was frozen with fear. "What is it? What's wrong?" asked Erica anxiously, worried about Katrinka's fragile emotional state.

"Nothing," said Katrinka after a moment. If she gave in to these terrors, her life would be hell. "Nothing. I'm all right now." She forced herself to turn the key in the ignition. The motor turned over, and she slid the car into gear.

"You're so pale," said Erica.

"I'm all right. Really." She made herself breathe regularly, trying to ease the tight knot in her chest. "I'm fine," she added a moment later as she steered the car down the hill toward the city and eased her way carefully around a stopped bus. She drove to the dull, featureless train station, an example of Soviet bloc construction at its worst, and waited with Erica until the train came. They had spoken little these past few days. Every serious topic of conversation had seemed too painful and all others too frivolous in the circumstances. Now, they stood on the platform, the tall, slender girl in a flowered skirt and white blouse mustering awkward words of gratitude for the statuesque woman in the smart navy traveling suit. "Nonsense," said Erica, as the train roared into the station, "I did what anyone would have done." *Perhaps I even wish I had done more,* she added silently to herself. She had agreed with Klaus Zimmerman that Katrinka's life would be ruined with an illegitimate child to care for, but now she wondered. The girl seemed so desperately lonely. In a sudden rush of feeling, she pulled Katrinka to her and hugged her. "Take care of yourself, *liebling,*" she murmured. "If you need anything let me know. Come to me whenever you want." She kissed Katrinka on both cheeks, released her, and, picking up her leather suitcase, boarded the train. "Write me," she called from the top step.

When Katrinka returned from the station, she found Tomáš and Zuzka waiting for her. They had offered to help clear out her parents' apartment, since it had to be made available for a family on the official list. She planned to sell or give away everything, except what was too precious, the framed photographs and albums chronicling the family history, afghans knitted by Milena, her needlepoint cushions, Jirka's fishing pole and skis. Those she would move back to her grandparents', where she was to have the same room as when she was a child.

"You should come with us," said Tomáš, "back to Prague." It was the middle of July and the political atmosphere was feverish. At the end of June, a manifesto called *Two Thousand Words* had been published by a reformist group of intellectuals, professionals, and workers, condemning the slow pace of government reforms and calling for civic protests. A few weeks later, a Warsaw Pact conference had condemned the declaration and insisted that censorship be reimposed. The government had rejected the ultimatum and called for meetings with the Soviet Union, which were going on at the moment in Slovakia. "We have to show them we're serious," said Tomáš as Zuzka watched him with obvious anxiety, knowing that a return to Prague meant more demonstrations and more danger. "That we mean business. There have been rumors for months that the Red Army is on the move. We have to show them that we can't be stopped."

At the mention of the Red Army, Katrinka grew pale. In Munich, absorbed by the life growing inside her, by the details of her own uncertain future, she had felt herself not only physically but emotionally removed from the turbulent events in Prague and throughout the country. Now she realized that Czechoslovakia's fight for freedom was not something separate from her own life. Without even realizing it, she had been involved. The convoy that her parents had met on that mountain in Hungary was moving toward the Czechoslovakian border. The mobilization of the Red Army had cost her, in a terrible twist of fate, her parents and her child. Seeing the look on her face, Tomáš stopped talking. He left the box he was packing and went to her, hugging her to him. "I was trying to distract you," he said. "I'm sorry."

She held on to him for a moment, comforted by his familiar strength. "It's all right," she said.

He pushed her away so that he could see her face. "You should come with us, you know. We'll keep you busy."

"Don't worry," she said. "I'll keep busy." She knew she would have to, or she would go completely mad.

Early the next morning, Katrinka, forcing herself again to get behind the wheel of her Fiat, drove to where the local ski team practiced in winter and dry-trained in summer, a small plateau from which two or three gentle hills extended upward to the forest line. At this time of year, the hills were covered with coarse green grass and weeds, with areas of sturdy wildflowers. The gates were in place, but the lifts, of course, were still, their wires, gears, and pulleys giving the place the feel of a derelict mining town.

Ota Černý was about to begin the practice when Katrinka arrived. Surprised, and a little alarmed by her pale face and gaunt figure, he went to greet her. "What are you doing here?"

"I must start getting into shape. Look at me." All her carefully made plans useless now, not knowing what else to do, automatically she had reverted to the normal routine of past summers.

"It's too soon, Katrinka," he said gently. "Give yourself a little time. A few days at least."

She shook her head. "I'll go crazy with nothing to do."

He hesitated a moment, considering. After all, he allowed his athletes to train, and sometimes even to race, with sprained ankles and pulled muscles, why not with a broken heart? "All right," he said finally. "But you must do exactly as I tell you."

"Haven't I always?" she replied, forcing a smile, a faded copy of her former brilliant smile, but a genuine one nonetheless.

He was so relieved to see it that he laughed. Putting an arm around her, he steered her toward the waiting group. "Not always, as you very well know. But this time you will follow my orders to the letter. Start when I say start. Stop when I say stop. Eat when I say eat." He regarded her critically. "We have to get some meat on you. Even a small wind would carry you away."

"I'm stronger than you think," she said, with another pale copy of a smile, hoping he would believe it because she certainly did not. She felt as frail and brittle as kindling, as if any new misfortune would snap her in two.

Over the next two weeks, Katrinka trained all day every day. Only by exhausting herself, she believed, would she be able to get her strength back. She bicycled and jogged; she did calisthenics, though no gymnastics or swimming because she could not bear yet to go near the sports complex, avoiding it even while driving, taking alternate routes, afraid of the painful rush of memories the sight of it would cause. With members of the local club getting into shape for the provincial competitions, she skied down the slopes on special grass skis. She jogged in the forest that climbed the mountainside, weaving in and out of the tall, slender trees masquerading as slalom gates, the cool scent of pine in the air, the twilight here and there broken by the sun penetrating the dense cover and catching her in its spotlight as she glided past. Though not hungry, she dutifully ate the beef and pork, the rich dumplings and homegrown vegetables prepared by Dana each night, then fell into bed and slept a sound, dreamless sleep while the old people sat in front of the television, watched one of the two channels, and tried not to think. Without Katrinka to fuss over, her grandmother would not have bothered to cook, nor Honza to tend the vegetables in his garden. Without her grandparents to comfort, Katrinka might often have given in to despair. As it was, they provided each other with a reason to carry on.

At the beginning of August, Katrinka went to Cervinia, where the members of the national team, who had been dry-training separately all over Czechoslovakia, gathered to practice on the Italian glaciers, the first official step in preparation for the racing season, which would begin in Europe in December. With both the men's and women's teams there were the inevitable new faces, but most were familiar, including Ilona Lukánský and the handsome Vladislav Elias, who had not yet completely given up hope of a romance with Katrinka. Zuzka came directly from Prague, where she had left Tomáš more deeply embroiled than ever in the freedom movement.

In the company once again of a high-spirited group of young people, Katrinka put up a good front. If she did not, as usual, organize the entertainment for the team's rare moments of leisure, she at least participated. If she did not tell the jokes, at least she laughed. If sometimes her mind seemed to wander, if she stopped singing for a moment in the middle of a song, everyone understood, or at least they thought they did. News of her parents' death had circulated quickly, and even Ilona Lukánský came to offer condolences. Despite her dislike of Katrinka, Ilona had always admired Milena, who never got bad-tempered and hysterical like her own mother. Milena had always been kind to her.

Gradually, through weeks that seemed to her like centuries, Katrinka's antidote for grief worked. Constant physical activity allowed her mind to rest and her body to gather strength. She gained weight, her skin lost its pallor, her dark hair regained some luster and her eyes their light. The pain of losing her parents and her child never went away, she did not think it ever would, but soon it was no longer an open wound, sapping her energy. And if at first she had gone on living only because she had to, eventually she came to realize how glad she was to be alive, and, far from feeling guilty about it, understood that her parents, now as always, would have approved and encouraged her strong will and stubborn refusal to fail. Zuzka was delighted to see the improvement in Katrinka's spirits; and Ota Černý felt his heart lift once again as he watched her gliding down the icy mountain trails, proud and free as an eagle. But even as they welcomed her return, they knew she had come back to them a different person, not precisely less radiant than before, but with a suggestion of unexpected depths, dark and troubling, like the swift currents in a lake whose still surface reflects only the sun.

Training that year, as every year, was intense, with the coaches driving the athletes until they dropped with exhaustion. Days began at dawn and ended at seven each evening when, aching and weary, the team members collapsed into their celibate beds and fell into a deep, dreamless sleep. No one thought about or talked about anything but skiing. It was the sole focus of their lives. Conversations introduced about anything else lasted for a few seconds before collapsing for want of interest. But in the third week of August, that single-minded focus, that isolation bubble created by a combination of obsession and fatigue, was shattered. All the ultimatums and rejections, the demands and the negotiations of the preceding months ended on August 20 when the armies of the Warsaw Pact marched into Czechoslovakia.

The newspapers carried news of troops invading cities throughout the country, and over the television in the hotel lounge came pictures of tanks rolling into Prague. Even the party members in the group watched with tears in their eyes. This went beyond politics, it went to the heart of patriotism. Training continued, but the obsession had shifted from sports to politics. In their free moments, the athletes now sat in front of the television and watched the Italian news, which, because it was uncensored, provided them with a more accurate picture of what was going on than people inside Czechoslovakia were able to get. Zuzka once thought she saw Tomáš in a crowd of protesters confronting some soldiers. According to the commentary, the protesters were arguing with the invaders, pleading with them to go home.

The demonstrations throughout the country were largely and incredibly nonviolent. The television showed pictures of graffiti denouncing the invasion on walls everywhere along with photographs of Chairman Dubček and President Svoboda. According to newspaper reports, all forms of assistance were being denied to the invading army, including food and water.

The mood of the team became anxious, even fearful. But had they been allowed the option of remaining in Italy, had the secret police for once decided to turn a blind eye, few would have taken it. Most, like Katrinka, were too worried about family and friends at home.

It was difficult getting telephone calls through, but Katrinka eventually reached her grandparents and was reassured that so far all was quiet in Svitov. For days, Zuzka could not find Tomáš anywhere and both she and Katrinka were frantic with worry. Finally, he answered the phone in the apartment he and Zuzka shared with other students. He had been arrested, questioned, but let go, not a big enough fish apparently for the communists to worry about. He sounded bitter and exhausted, and at one point in the conversation, he began to weep. "I never dreamed this would happen," he said. "I never thought it was possible."

Though Katrinka had taken no active part in the reform process, still, in the same way that—thanks to the happiness of her childhood, to the sense of security provided by her family—she had always expected life to go on being good to her, she had with equal optimism believed that Tomáš and all the others working for freedom in Czechoslovakia would succeed. Now she could see that she had been wrong on all counts, that she had in fact been not so much optimistic as incredibly stupid and naive.

Mirek Bartoš had taken Katrinka's virginity, not her innocence. That remained intact until the death of her parents, the loss of her child, until, finally, the invasion of Czechoslovakia shattered it completely. Only then did the carefree and openhearted girl who had believed that life would inevitably reward hard work and courage with success disappear completely, to be replaced by a woman who understood that life instead was uncertain and treacherous, a friend one moment offering gifts of amazing richness, an enemy the next providing only misery.

The knowledge did not make Katrinka bitter, only more determined. Life might try endlessly to defeat her, but, she promised herself, it would never succeed.

She pushed away regrets and tried not to wonder what would have happened if she had remained in the West, trying to build a new life for herself and her child. It was useless to dwell on that, she told herself. Instead, she concentrated on the future, reverting to the old, sensible plan formulated first by her parents, or by Jirka at any rate, to let athletic success provide her with the best that Czechoslovakia had to offer. Pregnant, she had lacked not only the skill but the strength to compete in the 1968 Olympics in Grenoble the previous February, but she made up her mind that, in 1972, she would not only make the team, she would win the gold.

Energy and enthusiasm came flooding back, and with them ambition. As Ilona Lukánský watched her with worried face and jealous eyes, Katrinka worked harder, took more chances, pushed herself to new levels of achievement. What she wanted, she knew, no one could give her. Love, happiness, success, even freedom, she must take herself from the hands of a reluctant and hostile life.

Seventeen

I sn't he beautiful? Isn't he precious?"

"She's like this all the time," said Tomáš, grinning. "I don't get any attention at all anymore." But the exasperation in his voice was feigned, and his face when he looked at his wife and son was full of love, and pride, as if, in having produced a child, he had accomplished something rare and wonderful.

"That's not true," said Zuzka, a little defensively, looking up from the baby. "For one thing, he sleeps all day." But when her eyes met Tomáš's, she too smiled.

Katrinka, watching them, felt suddenly lonely, pushed outside the tight circle of their love. "May I hold him?" she said.

"Oh, of course," said Zuzka. She leaned toward Katrinka who sat next to her on the sofa and transferred the snugly wrapped bundle into her arms. "Like this," she said, adjusting the baby's position slightly, "so his head is supported."

Katrinka cradled the child in her left arm and studied his face. Despite the cap of straight dark hair, the watery blue eyes, the mottled skin, she immediately caught the resemblance. "He looks like you," she said to Tomáš.

"Do you think so?" he said, pleased.

Katrinka nodded, looking at the baby's long face, the oval shape of his eyes, the miniature version of Tomáš's full, sensual mouth. "Your son," she said, "without a doubt."

"I should hope so," said Zuzka, laughing. "We're calling him Martin, after my father."

Who had her son looked like? wondered Katrinka. She had no memory at all of his face, which she had seen always through the haze of the various sedatives she had been given. But now, holding Martin, she suddenly recalled the feel of her own baby, the weight and length of him in her arms. He had been eighteen inches long at birth, she remembered. He had weighed six pounds and nine ounces. She ran a finger along the soft curve of Martin's cheek, and, all at once, she was fighting back tears. What would Zuzka and Tomáš think if she started to cry? How could she possibly explain? She had never confided her secret to them and had no intention of doing so now. "Here," she said, handing the baby back to Zuzka. "I think he's wet."

Startled, Zuzka said, "But I just changed him."

Tomáš laughed. "When you have a baby of your own," he said, "what will you do then?"

It was June of 1971, and in a few days her son would have his third birthday. Her son. Where was he now? she wondered as she often did, though she tried so hard not to. Were his parents good to him? Was he happy? The feel of Martin in her arms had broken through all her normal defenses and the endless, unanswerable questions came flooding into her mind. "That won't be for a long time," Katrinka said lightly, smiling at Tomáš, hoping he would not notice how upset she was. "Why worry about it now?"

When Zuzka had discovered she was pregnant, her immediate reaction had been panic. She and Tomáš had discussed marriage, but always as a distant event, something they might perhaps do when Tomáš got his film career launched. But although he had graduated from FAMU, he seemed little closer to accomplishing that, despite his obvious talent and the recommendations of his former professors, at least those who were still employed at the academy.

His involvement in the protest movement in 1968 was responsible for the trouble he had had finding work, Tomáš knew. Shortly after the invasion, Alois Pldenak had been removed from his post at Barrandov Studios and jailed on

charges of subversion; professors at FAMU were forced out
of their jobs; Miloš Forman, Jan Kadar, and Ivan Passer had
fled to the West; Jiří Menzel, who had remained behind, had
not yet been allowed to make another film. Censorship
returned in full force. And students like Tomáš, lucky to
have escaped with only a few broken ribs after three days of
questioning, to have been thought too unimportant for
prison, still remained suspect, not the sort of people for
whom nervous Party bureaucrats opened the door to success.

It was only thanks to Mirek Bartoš that Tomáš was
working at all, at Barrandov, as Bartoš's assistant. Tomáš
had not been fool enough to turn down the offer when it
came, despite the strings attached, most of which had to do
with Katrinka. He was required to keep the director supplied with news. And, though never stated aloud, it was
understood that he would intervene with Katrinka on
Bartoš's behalf and perhaps even negotiate a meeting. This
Tomáš did not do, although he sometimes wondered if he
would have gone even that far had Bartoš insisted, had it
been the only way possible for him to continue working in
film.

Without completely understanding the strength of
Tomáš's passion for his work, Zuzka—who was capable of
committing herself without reservation only to another
person—had sufficient insight to know he would not welcome another obstacle thrown in the path of his success.
And she had no doubt that an obstacle is exactly what he
would consider this child. She also suspected, though unable
to admit this even to herself, that what Tomáš loved about
her were the subtle curves of her healthy body, her total
availability for sex wherever and whenever he wanted, the
single-mindedness of her devotion to him—for which she
got very little in return but his offhand acceptance of her
when he was busy and his passion when he was not. Would
he be quite so in love should the equation change?

Afraid to tell Tomáš she was pregnant, Zuzka was equally
afraid to face the sports committee and put her fate in its
hands. Like Katrinka before her, she knew she had to lose
something—the man she loved, her child, her privileges as

an athlete, her guarantee of a secure future—and was terrified that somehow she would lose it all. Unable to decide what to do, she had finally confided in Katrinka.

"Tell Tomáš," Katrinka had advised quickly, not wanting Zuzka added to the list of women in the world mourning the loss of a child.

"I don't want to be a burden to him."

"What if he *wants* to marry you?"

"You think he does?" asked Zuzka hopefully.

"Why not? He says he loves you." Zuzka looked unconvinced and Katrinka continued, "You're not being noble, Zuzka, you're being crazy. *Andelíčku*, it's time enough to think about an abortion when there's no other alternative."

"I'd never forgive myself if I stopped Tomáš from becoming a director."

"What nonsense," said Katrinka, starting to laugh. "Believe me, nothing is going to stop Tomáš from becoming a director. Not you. Not your child. Nothing."

But even Katrinka had not expected Tomáš to be as pleased with the news as he was. The idea of being a father delighted him. Never having known his own, he was suddenly filled with the desire to make up to his child for everything he had missed himself. He and Zuzka were married immediately and, since her staying at the university was dependent on her continuing in sports, he insisted she leave for fear that she might hurt the baby skiing. Though Zuzka would have liked to remain for a while so as to hold on to her precious privileges for as long as possible, in that—as in everything—she deferred to Tomáš. She faced the committee and withdrew from the university, getting a temporary job as a clerk at Barrandov, that job too arranged with the help of Mirek Bartoš.

Even without Tomáš's intervention, in the three years since the birth of their son Katrinka had seen Bartoš any number of times, running into him at the Maxmilianka, at the theater, and once, when she was shopping in Václav Square, coming out of the Europa Hotel. But she had spoken to him only twice: when she had phoned his office, shortly after her return from Cervinia in 1968, to ask him again to find out what Klaus Zimmerman had done with their baby, and a few days later at the Maxmilianka, when she had let him draw her aside, away from the group of friends she was with, to a small booth in the back of the restaurant to learn what the doctor had told him.

Nothing, reported Bartoš. As before, Zimmerman had insisted he was unable both legally and morally to give Katrinka the information she wanted.

"Don't you want to know?" she had asked quietly, as if curiosity rather than outrage had prompted her question.

Bartoš had taken a deep breath and then said, "Zimmerman's right, Katrinka. You must forget what happened and get on with your life."

"I am getting on with my life. But forget? You don't know how sometimes I wish I could." She got up to leave the table, but as she started away he had reached for her hand and held her still for a moment.

"Do you hate me?"

The question had shocked her. "No," she said. "No, of course not."

"Then why won't you see me?" he asked, hope and self-pity blended in his voice.

"It would hurt too much," she had replied as if it were something he ought to have understood without being told.

He had let go of her hand and watched as she walked away, regretting not the loss of love, or even of sex, but the sense of excitement that Katrinka had brought into his life. Her energy and enthusiasm had infected him. She had made him feel not so much young as hopeful, as if he had not yet used up all his chances, as if new and golden opportunities awaited him, opportunities that this time he would have the courage to take. She had made him, for a while at least, believe that he could do anything: leave his wife, start over fresh, direct films as well as Forman or Menzel, neither of whom had the technical mastery of the medium that he did. Everyone said so, all his friends, and he himself was convinced of it.

Thank God, he had realized in time that what Katrinka offered was an illusion, or, perhaps, like many of his former colleagues at Barrandov he, too, would now be out of work or in prison. Thank God indeed. But mingled with the relief he felt was another, darker feeling, which he was sometimes tempted to name despair. His old pastimes brought him no pleasure. His new mistress, an actress just Katrinka's age, already bored him. And the thought of beginning another film caused no rush of excitement, but a sensation of incredible fatigue.

"Have you ever thought of leaving Czechoslovakia?" Katrinka asked Tomáš when Zuzka had taken Martin away, leaving her husband and Katrinka with an open bottle of Moravian wine and the luxury of an evening where neither of them was expected anywhere else. The room where they sat was small, like the rest of the apartment Zuzka and Tomáš had moved into a few weeks before. It had a faint musty smell, which all of Zuzka's cleaning and airing had not yet managed to subdue. The furniture was secondhand and homely, all that was available for what they could afford. Tomáš's collection of Hollywood film posters, brought from his mother's apartment in Svitov, covered the worn green wallpaper. The posters of *Loves of a Blonde* and *Closely Watched Trains* had been returned there, on the theory that no one likely to cause him trouble would ever manage to see the interior of that bedroom. His brush with the secret police had taught him to be cautious.

Tomáš took a long drag on his cigarette, then answered, "Of course, all the time. But . . ." he shrugged. "As hard as it is for me here, in the West it would be even worse. I have no credits, no reputation, nothing to use to convince people to employ me, only a diploma from a film school most of them won't even have heard of. I'd end up washing dishes or driving a cab. At least here, thanks to your friend, I'm working at a studio, not filming myself, but at least on a soundstage." Bartoš had begun filming another new movie, and Tomáš was his assistant on it, not a glamorous job perhaps, but in his opinion better than exile, which is what banishment from a studio would feel like to him. "At least I'm learning. Something new every day. You can't be on a film set and not learn."

"I managed," said Katrinka, laughing.

"You weren't interested," agreed Tomáš, pleased that she could now talk about those days without pain, none that he could see at any rate. "At least not in making films," he teased.

"But maybe it would not be so terrible in the West? Think of all the directors from Europe who went to Hollywood and were successful there."

"Korda, von Sternberg, Wilder?"

"Yes. Yes," said Katrinka eagerly, her voice coming out in a low, excited rush. "And all the others. You told me yourself how they got there and started over."

"They had established reputations. Like Forman and Passer now."

"You should not be so pessimistic," said Katrinka, sounding irritated. "You can't do anything if you don't try."

"I have a wife to take care of. And a baby. I can't go halfway around the world on some sort of fool's errand."

Katrinka sighed. "No, of course you can't," she said. "What was I thinking of?"

"Yourself, maybe?" replied Tomáš as he poured them each another glass of wine.

"Maybe," agreed Katrinka, after a moment.

"You have nothing to keep you here now."

"No. No, I don't." Her grandparents had died, Honza early in 1970, Dana a few months later. They were buried next to her parents in the cemetery in the forest, high in the hills above Svitov. Now when she went home it was just to lay flowers on the slab of black marble that covered the family grave. "Only the Olympics next winter," she added, after a moment. She had been training relentlessly for three years, building her strength, improving her technique, increasing her speed. No one on the Czech women's team was any competition for her, except Ilona Lukánský. Katrinka was certain that she would be among those chosen to compete—unless she did something stupid like break a leg in training this summer. Horrified at the thought, she leaned forward and knocked sharply three times on the wooden table in front of her.

"What?" said Tomáš.

"I want to win."

"You will." The odds were against her, he knew. Skiing was an expensive sport, and, short of money, Czechoslovakia did not compete in international championship races as regularly as other countries. That cost Czech athletes the competitive edge their rivals developed by constant honing of their skills. Still, once Katrinka set her mind on having something, she usually got it. If she was determined to win an Olympic medal, Tomáš for one was prepared to bet money, the little he had, that she would.

"A gold."

He whistled, then said, "Why not? Then you can support yourself in the West doing fancy ads for Bognor clothes, Rossignol skis, Nordica boots, and the rest."

Katrinka laughed. "Exactly," she agreed. Winning an Olympic gold had always in her mind been a passport to a better life, but this aspect of it had never occurred to her before. It certainly was something to think about.

"You're a complete capitalist," said Tomáš, smiling, with no hostility at all.

"I believe in hard work," said Katrinka. "Is that being a capitalist?"

"You want to make money. That is."

"Everyone wants to make money," said Katrinka. "Even you."

"I'd rather make art. But at the moment, I don't seem to be able to do either." They sat quietly for a moment, each thinking about the future and what it might possibly offer. Finally, Tomáš said, "You wouldn't have any problem. Even without a gold medal, you could still teach skiing."

"Or get a job in a hotel," added Katrinka, entering into the spirit of the fantasy.

"Or work as a translator. You'll get your degree next year."

"That's true."

Tomáš grinned. "Or become an actress."

Katrinka looked surprised. "Do you think I have talent?"

"No," replied Tomáš cheerfully. "But you're pretty. Often that's enough."

"I don't think I have the personality for it," said Katrinka with a sigh, remembering long, dull hours on a soundstage.

"And there's always modeling. Women in the West make a fortune doing that."

"Maybe," agreed Katrinka who was suddenly taking the discussion very seriously. "I've had plenty of experience here and a good portfolio to show." Though visas for work abroad were much harder to get under the new regime, Katrinka had continued to earn extra money by selling her used ski equipment for a small profit and by building her modeling career. She had become quite successful at it, doing designer showroom and catwalk fashion shows as well as photographic print work. "At least twelve covers," she added, including the one that had brought her to Mirek Bartoš's attention. "One way or another, I would manage."

As for most Europeans, for Katrinka intimacy was not measured by the ability to tell all. She did not feel the need to bare the secrets of her soul to her friends, or even to her lovers. For the most part, she kept her own counsel, out of a natural reticence, out of habit, because it was always the wisest thing to do. But her bond with Tomáš dated back to the forests of Svitov, to long afternoons by the river sharing childhood confidences. Since her parents had died, he was the only person with whom she felt free to speak, not to confide secrets necessarily, but to attempt to uncover by talking what had lain hidden in her mind for a long time.

When Katrinka had returned to Prague after the invasion of 1968, she found it a very different city from the one she had left in the spring. At first she had thought her response to it another symptom of the depression she had fought so hard against in Cervinia, but soon she knew it was more than that. The military presence was obvious everywhere; it had a stranglehold on the city, squeezing all the excitement and gaiety, all the life and hope of the preceding Prague Spring out of it. Fear had returned.

Katrinka had noted the changes with dismay. The decision to leave Czechoslovakia had not been made by herself and her parents out of any great sense of dissatisfaction with their lives, which had always been comfortable enough. What had convinced them ultimately to go was the realization that, despite all the liberalizing tendencies of the Dubček regime, success still could be achieved only within very narrow parameters and by strict adherence to the rules. By getting pregnant, Katrinka had jumped the line and broken those rules, and her fall from grace would not be seen so much as youthful folly as gross ingratitude to a state that had provided for her bountifully from her childhood. She would not get a second chance. And for people as hardworking, as ambitious, as the Kovářs, the idea of such a limited future for Katrinka had been intolerable.

But seeing the changes in Prague, in Svitov, throughout the country as she drove her Fiat back and forth across Czechoslovakia to various races, Katrinka began to think that life did not offer enough even to the people prepared to keep the rules. At the minimal level, they were housed and fed, they were educated, and their medical needs taken care of. If they were willing to work hard, they could afford luxuries like cars and televisions, winter weekends skiing in the mountains, summer vacations by the sea in Yugoslavia. Though it was difficult to credit some of the stories she read in the official press, Katrinka was sure that in other parts of the world life was far less good. Still, more and more it seemed to her that something was missing, something vital though less obvious than food or medicine. Tomáš certainly would have called it "freedom," a word he was very fond of, the freedom to travel, to do and say what you liked, to print known facts in newspapers, to make films reflecting rather than distorting life. He could go on about it for hours. But as valuable as Katrinka agreed freedom was, that still was not precisely what she meant, or at least not in the general sense of the word. What seemed to her to be missing in Czechoslovakia was the ability to live life to its full potential, to stretch to its limit, to follow where curiosity led, to accomplish something surprising and perhaps wonderful. People led narrow and circumscribed lives, for the most part not because their characters made them cautious, but because the state deprived them of the opportunity to do anything else. Only a few lucky ones like Katrinka were allowed adventure, risk, excitement, the sort of thrill she experienced on the ski slopes when, because of some combination of skill and judgment, of common sense and courage, she could either plunge headfirst into a drift or cross the finish line first. Only a few lucky ones were able to parlay that courage and skill into a better way of life. All the others plodded through to their graves hardly noticing they were alive.

"You really mean to go. You've been giving it a lot of thought," said Tomáš, surprised by the intensity in Katrinka's low voice, by the speculative look glinting behind the pale blue surface of her eyes.

"No," said Katrinka quickly. "Not really. I'm just as surprised as you are by what I'm saying." A wave of anxiety hit her and she looked anxiously around. "Do you think it's true, that there are listening devices planted in walls?"

Again Tomáš laughed. "Probably. But not in these walls."

"Still . . ."

Tomáš nodded. "You're right. Better to be safe." And until Zuzka returned a few minutes later bringing bulletins of Martin's latest feats, they talked about a film Tomáš hoped one day to make about Jan Hus, the religious reformer (or, depending on your point of view, heretic), to which he felt certain no one would object since it was set safely in the early fifteenth century and could not be suspected of having political significance, though of course it would. That was the whole point.

But later, in her room at Mrs. Kolchík's, where Katrinka continued to live despite its disturbing memories, she reviewed her conversation with Tomáš, working out its implications, wondering why the months she had spent reassessing life in Czechoslovakia should have culminated that night suddenly in the idea of leaving it.

Certainly, her going away permanently would not have been possible had her grandparents been alive and needing her. But now, Tomáš was right, there was nothing to keep her here, no family except for Aunt Zdeňka and her cousins who, however much they might love her, were not dependent on her presence, nor she on theirs; no lover because, though she had finally allowed herself to succumb to Vladislav Elias, the relationship was not serious, at least not to her, providing companionship and sex but little else; no one but Tomáš and Zuzka, her best friends, whom she would miss terribly if she could not see them again.

The thought of Zuzka and Tomáš reminded her of the feel of Martin in her arms, and again her eyes filled with tears, which this time she did not attempt to stop. That was what had made her think of leaving, she realized, not her growing dissatisfaction with life in Czechoslovakia, but holding Martin, who had reminded her of her son. What was his name, she wondered, this son whom she had always called "my baby"? Where was he? For years she had tried, if not to forget him, then at least to resign herself to his loss. Now she was certain that she would never do that. Tiny Martin had reminded her of how much she missed her child, how she lived constantly with the dull ache of his absence, how that ache provoked by a memory could turn to a pain so sharp, so brutal, it made her want to cry out. If she went to Munich could she find him, now, after all this time? she wondered—and knew that at least she had to try.

Eighteen

But how? That was the question that occupied Katrinka's mind relentlessly for the next several weeks. She knew that once she arrived in Munich, both Erica Braun and Franta Dohnal, with whom she had kept in touch, would help. But how was she to get there? Vacation visas to the West were no longer so easy to come by, not even for an admired member of the national ski team like herself. And when she traveled with the team, they were so closely watched escaping would be difficult, if not actually impossible.

Hiding under trains, crossing the border at night, like Franta, the idea of it terrified her. She was not physically brave, at least not in that way. There were some people she had heard of who had married Westerners to get a German or French or English passport, then emigrated legally. But how was she to find such a person? And even if Erica or Franta could help her with that, who knew how long it would take them to locate a person willing to put up with all the problems, all the paperwork involved? Now that she had made up her mind to go, impatient to begin the search for her son, the idea of delay was intolerable. Suddenly even the Olympics seemed a long way away.

But always she came back to the same problem. The important question was not when, but how.

Katrinka could think of almost nothing else. At the end of July, after finishing her last modeling assignment of the summer, she drove to Svitov before the start of summer training to lay a bouquet of daisies and bluebells on the black marble slab covering the graves of her parents and grandparents, and, as shafts of golden light filtered through the spread branches of the trees and birds sang cheerfully to one another, she sat on the soft carpet of pine needles, her head resting against the marble, trying to work out how it could be done. But Jirka and Milena for once failed her, offering no inspiration.

From Svitov she traveled to the farm, but the visit there did not relax her as it usually did. Though she fished and swam and helped with the chores as always, though she sat with Aunt Zdeňka and her cousins at night and joined them singing the old folk polkas they loved, the sight of František's pregnant wife reminded her constantly that she had a decision to make.

By the time she arrived in Cervinia to join the team, she had lost weight, not much but enough to cause Ota Černý to frown at her and ask what she had been up to the past few weeks. She assured him she had been leading an idle country life, then tried to turn her full attention to training. Over the next few months, the Olympic team would be chosen.

Ota's hair had by now turned completely gray, his face was marked deeply with lines, and the look of sorrow in his eyes never completely disappeared, not even when he laughed, which he did less and less often now. Jirka Kovář's death had not only cost him his best friend but, as a friend's death always does, forced him to confront all that he would never accomplish in his own life. It had made him lose hope, for himself and for Olga, who now smuggled a bottle of vodka to school in her briefcase and drank in her office between classes.

There was not much pleasure left for Ota. The act of sex, whether with Olga or others, filled him with such despair that he resorted to it rarely and regretted it afterward. He still enjoyed the taste of a pilsen beer and a cigarette, especially the Gauloises he was able to buy when abroad, but that was all, except for coaching. He took pleasure in that, bullying his team, coaxing them, trying to turn a group of mostly lighthearted young women into disciplined champions.

This year he had two potential gold medalists: Katrinka, of course, and Ilona Lukánský. There were one or two others on the team who by the next Olympics might be talents to reckon with, but no one else who had a chance to win in Sapporo in February. He often wished he could like Ilona better so that he could take more pleasure in her success, but there was something about her that defied affection, not just her sour face and sly, furtive air, but a vengeful, ruthless quality in her character. If she had to, and if she could, she would cheat to win.

His dislike of Ilona Lukánský made Ota careful. Having seen her, in the past, strike out viciously when hurt or threatened, he did not want to spark her resentment now and encourage her to do something she (and he) might regret. An Olympic medal was more important than indulging his personal feelings.

While Ota continued treating the others on the team with his usual blend of brusque criticism and teasing affection, on Ilona he lavished time and attention, leaving her in no doubt that he expected her to win at Sapporo. In that atmosphere, Ilona thrived. Her face lost some of its tight, worried look, her conversation its spiteful tone. She began to flirt with Vladislav Elias, with whom she had always been a little bit in love; and he, to make Katrinka jealous, responded.

Katrinka hardly noticed. She never doubted for a moment that Ota had complete confidence in her. Used to his criticism, his constant demands that she do better, she merely smiled in response and did as he asked. For his sake as well as her own, she wanted to win that medal. It was he who had seen her potential, who had encouraged her over the years, who had helped pull her through every tough spot. Now she wanted to reward him for his faith in her.

As for Vladislav, he was still so obviously in love with her that it was difficult for Katrinka to take seriously his attempts to prove that he was not, though in fact, once the first shock had passed, she might have been relieved. Sometime soon, before leaving Czechoslovakia, she would have to break with him. How much easier it would be for her, and for Vladislav too, if he were the one to end their relationship.

Though Katrinka tried to keep her mind free of thoughts about the future and stay completely focused on getting selected for the Olympic team—virtually an accomplished fact, in her opinion—and winning that gold medal, she could not. At night, sometimes, she dreamed about her son. In one dream, she would be looking for the baby in the rooms of a large, apparently empty house; in another, pushing him in a carriage along a sunny street in Prague or down a bleak, threatening alley. The locations varied, but the ending was always the same: filled with sudden terror, she would clutch the baby to her and begin to run while someone, a man, she assumed, though she could not see, chased her until she awoke.

During the day, at odd moments, she found herself often assessing the chances for escape. They did not seem good. In Cervinia, as everywhere, a bus collected the men's and women's teams at the hotel every morning, drove them to the ski lifts, then returned them to the hotel again in the evening. In the bus, on the slopes, even during shopping expeditions in town, they were accompanied by members of the secret police who could ski well enough to pass as assistant trainers but fooled no one as to the real nature of their jobs. Several were always on duty, guarding the athletes in the hotel, allowing a certain amount of partying and romance, but stopping anyone caught trying to leave the premises, no matter how innocent the motive. Escaping such vigilance might be possible, but it would not be easy, and it would have to succeed on the first try, because a second would never be allowed.

After days of useless speculation, one morning, standing at a gate at the top of one of the mountains, waiting to begin her run down, it occurred to Katrinka how she might do it. The idea hit her so suddenly it stunned her for a moment and she did not hear Ota's first order to start. He barked at her to pay attention, and she came to and pushed off. It was late in the morning and the sun had begun to melt the snow, leaving the trail sloppy and requiring Katrinka's full concentration. She tried to keep her mind on her skiing, but could not. The plan was absurd, she knew. Dangerous. Foolhardy. But it was possible. It certainly was possible, she thought, as her skis slid out from under her, tipping into the air while she fell painfully onto her butt.

Her opinion of the idea—it was too soon yet to call it a plan—did not change over the next several days. From no matter what angle she considered it, it remained foolhardy. And possible.

What appealed to her most about it was its speed. She would not have to wait hours or days or weeks to know if she had pulled it off. It would be obvious within minutes. To someone as impatient as Katrinka that aspect of the idea was irresistible.

The only problem with it was that same impatience. Having thought of the idea, she could not bear to put off trying it out. Though her good sense told her it was essential to wait until after the Olympics, until after she graduated from university, now she did not want to. Neither a degree nor a gold medal seemed so important to her when weighed against the opportunity to get away, to find her son, to begin a new life. Who knew if she would get another chance? It was easy to say wait until next year, but anything could happen between now and then. What if she did break a leg? What if she could no longer travel? What if she had a car accident? She leaned forward in her chair and hit the table in front of her three times. Since her parents' death, she was always a little nervous driving. Since their death, she knew that nothing in the future was certain.

Only Ota's reaction made her hesitate. How angry he would be. How disappointed. After all he had done for her, didn't she owe it to him to at least try to deliver him his gold medal?

But what if she waited and did not win? For the first time, she allowed the thought to enter her head. What if Ilona won instead? What if neither of them did? She knew the odds against them as well as anyone, but had simply until now refused to let that consideration enter her consciousness.

A week passed while Katrinka mulled the matter over in

her mind. Torn between impatience, anxiety, and guilt, she watched Ota and for the first time noticed how attentive he was being to Ilona. Though on some level she knew what he was doing, she nevertheless allowed herself to become convinced that he had decided Ilona was the skier with the best chance of winning in Sapporo. Normally, that would have made her eager to prove him wrong, but now it suited her instead to accept his judgment and believe that her departure would be no great loss to the team. Ilona saw her watching them and smirked with satisfaction. To have convinced Ota, whose preference for Katrinka had been obvious for years, that she was the better athlete was a triumph Ilona had never expected to taste.

Not content with one victory, at dinner two nights before they were scheduled to leave Cervinia, Ilona sat beside Vladislav and monopolized his attention throughout the meal. Flattered, and a bit attracted by the naked sexual aggression in her manner, he didn't resist, leaving Katrinka to talk to the others at the table, which, in other circumstances, she would not have minded in the least. But this night, she did mind, and, when the dinner had ended and they were on their way back to their separate rooms, she told Vladislav so.

"You're jealous," he said, not quite able to hide the pleasure in his voice.

"No. But you were rude, to me and everyone else at the table. I expect that from Ilona, we all do, but not from you."

"We were just talking."

"And the conversation was so interesting you couldn't spare one word, one look, for anyone else?"

"I did look. And you seemed happy enough to me."

"Well, I wasn't. I felt humiliated."

"That's ridiculous."

"You made such a *point* of not caring."

"You know what your problem is?" said Vladislav, tired of feeling guilty and deciding to go on the offensive.

"My problem?" Up until now, Katrinka had not really been angry. She had merely been trying to convince him that his manners could use some improving.

208

"Yes. Your problem. You can't take competition."

"Oh? And who told you that? Ilona?"

"You don't like her because she might just be a better skier than you are."

"You really believe that?" said Katrinka, outraged.

"Why not?"

"You're right," said Katrinka, finally losing her temper. "I don't like her. But not because she's a better skier than I am, though she may be. I don't like her because she's mean. Because she's selfish. Because she's been tormenting me since I was five years old. Because she's a bitch!" She turned away from him and headed back toward the hotel bar. Vladislav stood stunned for a moment, then hurried after her. He grabbed her by the arm and pulled her to a stop.

"Katrinka," he said. "*Zlatíčko,* I'm sorry. I don't know what got into me."

At the touch of his hand on her arm, all the anger left Katrinka. "It's all right," she said.

"You forgive me?"

"There's nothing to forgive." If she had cared for him more, she wondered, would he have tried so hard to make her jealous? "But I think, really, it's over between us."

He argued with her for a while. They went into the bar and sat, drinking fruit juices and mineral water, while he tried to change her mind. Half an hour later, one of the assistant coaches came over to the table, reminded them they were in training, and suggested they call it a night.

The men and women were on separate floors in the hotel, so they said good night in the elevator. Because he asked and because it seemed heartless not to, Katrinka agreed to discuss the matter further with him the next day, though she had no intention at all of keeping her word.

The next morning, Katrinka as usual rose first, showered, and then dressed quickly while her roommate was in the bathroom. Instead of the usual cotton vest she wore under her ski suit, she put on a jersey and into its pockets put all her extra money, her passport, the few pieces of Milena's jewelry, and the ring from Dana that she always carried with her. Everything else of importance was still in Svitov, in her grandparents' house, but she refused to think about that. What she wanted she would have to find a way to get later.

No one from the team was in the dining room when Katrinka arrived, for which she was grateful. Frightened that he would be able to read the signs of betrayal in her face, she had dreaded meeting Ota.

Knowing she would need the energy, Katrinka ordered a larger breakfast than usual and tried to eat it slowly, though her instinct was to gulp it down, so anxious was she to get on with the day. When finally she finished, the others were starting to arrive. She greeted them hurriedly, refusing a request from Vladislav to stay and have another cup of coffee, ignoring Ilona's smug greeting, rushing off instead to check on the condition of her equipment. What did it matter to her if they thought she was upset? Pride seemed irrelevant at the moment. She had other, more important things on her mind.

The technicians were already at work, tuning the skis, not paying much attention to what they were doing, the atmosphere in the room relaxed and easy, as it always was on the last day of training unless there was a big race to follow. Katrinka checked her three pairs of skis, decided the edges on one needed to be sharper, and coaxed a technician who was fond of her into doing it. The wax was another, more complex, problem since it was difficult to judge what the condition of the trails would be later in the day.

"What do you think?" she asked the technician.

"The blue paraffin will be fine," he replied. "See you through anything today." He began to rub the blue wax into the skis. "Why don't you ease up on yourself a little?" he said. "It's the last day. Have a little fun."

"Do you say that to all the girls?" she teased.

"Only to the ones who might listen. You do like a good time, I'll say that for you."

"Work hard. Play hard. That's my motto."

"You'll be at the party tonight?" he asked. Her smile was wonderful, he thought. It lit up her whole face and made her eyes shine like the sea in sunlight. He had already heard she had quarreled with Vladislav Elias.

"Have you ever known me to miss a party?" she replied,

laughing. She felt reluctant to add lying to the long list of sins she was sure to be blamed for.

Ota Černý and the other coaches chose the trails they were to ski according to some plan worked out among them the night before. The one she wanted was the third of the day, perfect timing as far as she was concerned, late enough for her to have warmed up, early enough for her to have plenty of speed and energy left.

On the first two trails Katrinka skied carefully, concentrating not on speed but on getting the feel of the terrain, the condition of the snow, warming up her muscles, and assessing the temper of her teammates and the trainers accompanying them. As it had been in the tech room, the mood on the slopes was lighthearted, careless. The strenuous weeks of training were almost over and there was a party to look forward to that night.

Before getting into the chair lift for the third trail, Katrinka complained about a loose binding, asked to change her skis, and put on the pair the technician had so diligently tuned for her that morning. When she reached the top of the lift, she found Ota waiting for her.

"You should have checked your bindings before you put the skis on," he said.

"I did. I guess I just didn't notice."

"Next time, pay more attention."

She smiled at him. "Yes," she said. "I will." What she was about to do was right, she was certain of that. She only wished that she could do it without hurting Ota Černý, without disappointing him. But with that instinct for self-preservation that is at its height in youth, it never occurred to Katrinka that she might change her mind, that she might sacrifice what she considered her own good just to please this man who had been like a second father to her. "Thank you," she said as he walked away, meaning, of course, for everything.

This time when Ota gave the signal for her to start, Katrinka was out of the gate like a shot. As her skis skimmed over the surface of the snow, all hesitation, all fear, all guilt, left her and she was filled with a wonderful sense of jubilation. Another skier was in front of her and Katrinka followed her down, careful neither to pass her nor to fall too far behind for fear of having Ilona Lukánský close on her tail. Then, at the bottom of the second slope, when her teammate headed to the right back toward Cervinia, Katrinka executed a neat parallel turn to the left, toward the border with Switzerland. Behind her she could hear Ilona, and someone else, shouting at her, telling her she was heading the wrong way. No, she thought, it's the right way. The right way! She felt free as a bird, as an eagle, soaring into the air over a rise, crouching low into the ground on traverse. She turned to look over her shoulder and saw a few scattered figures following her, some of whom she assumed were the secret police, who did not worry her at all since they were not nearly good enough to catch her. Could Ota, if he tried? Would he try? Looking again, she saw Ilona's black-and-white knit cap. Was it getting nearer?

"Katrinka, what the hell do you think you're doing?" shouted Ilona. "Come back."

Come and get me, she thought, though she kept her mouth shut and saved her energy for skiing.

From the gate, Ota Černý watched the pursuit, disappointment and anger raging in him as the last of his dreams fled with Katrinka toward the Swiss border. He felt stunned, betrayed. He had always, from her childhood, known she was capable of putting any mad scheme into action, but this was one he had never expected. And that she could do this to him (never mind to her country), run off without a word of explanation, he would never have believed.

He stayed where he was, knowing he was too old even to attempt to match Katrinka's speed. Nor could any of the party hacks who were attempting to now. Vladislav Elias possibly could have caught her, or one of the other members of the men's team, but they were skiing another trail. Only Ilona Lukánský had a chance. He looked around and saw that nobody else was even willing to try. Except for Ilona and the police, all, like him, were standing perfectly still, watching.

To his surprise, Ota felt a sudden surge of pride, and hope. Pride in Katrinka's daring, in her skill, certainly. But hope of what? For Ilona to catch Katrinka and hold her until the secret police caught up? Or for Katrinka's wild dash to freedom to succeed?

No, he realized, he did not want Katrinka dragged back against her will. He had thought her behavior strange for weeks now, subdued and abstracted, perhaps even for years, since Jirka and Milena had died. He had sensed her unhappiness and longed to comfort her without knowing how. What was she running away from? Or to? he wondered. Whatever it was, he hoped it would give her the kind of joy he had never found in his own life, except sometimes in her. Let her go, he thought suddenly, not certain whether it was a prayer to God or an order to himself. Let her go.

Katrinka thought, at times, that she could hear Ota's voice, and her father's, issuing instructions: how to position her body, where to put her skis, when to turn. As always, she obeyed, and felt herself increasing the distance between herself and her pursuers.

One figure was trying to cross the mountain in an attempt to cut her off, she noticed. Who was that? she wondered. Probably one of the secret police, since no one else would have tried anything so foolish. There was no way he could match her on the downhill. *"Ayiiiiiii,"* shouted Katrinka, terrified by the speed of her movement, terrified and exhilarated.

"Katrinka," shouted Ilona. "Stop!"

Again Katrinka looked over her shoulder and was reassured to see that Ilona was falling behind. Wax or skill? she wondered, and then laughed. It was all the same. What was speed without strategy? Courage without brains? I'm going to do it, thought Katrinka. I am really going to do it. Ahead was a sharp bend in the narrow trail, a wall of snow on one side, a sheer drop off the cliff on the other. Wait, she heard her father caution. Wait, she heard Ota's voice echo. Now! and she flipped her ski edges into traverse, then flipped again into the fall line and schussed straight down toward the rooftops of Zermatt, glinting in the sunlight. Behind her, she heard Ilona's shout as she fell going into the turn. *"Ayiiiiiii,"* shouted Katrinka again, "I did it. I did it!"

The
Past

---◆◆◆---

1971–1977

Nineteen

From the local police station where she went for help, Katrinka phoned Erica Braun, but there was no reply at the apartment and, when she called the clinic, the receptionist told her that Erica was away on holiday and not expected back in Munich until the next day. The thought that her friend might not be there had never entered Katrinka's mind while making her plans. Exhausted, frightened, for a moment she could not think what to do.

"Is there anyone else you know?" asked the elderly policeman, who seemed a little stunned to have found a defector on his doorstep.

"No. No," said Katrinka. A wave of despair hit her, followed almost immediately by one of relief. "That is, yes," she said quickly, as the image of Franta Dohnal's handsome face and smiling green eyes popped into her head. "Certainly, I do."

Information in Munich supplied the phone number, and Franta, when his phone rang, was obligingly at home. He answered in German and switched immediately to Czech when he heard Katrinka's voice. "Katrinka? Katrinka Kovář? What a surprise! Where are you?"

"Zermatt," said Katrinka.

"What are you doing there? Skiing?" he asked, his voice a mixture of pleasure in hearing from her and curiosity about why he had.

"No," said Katrinka, "not exactly," and in a quick rush of words she told him what she had done.

217

For a moment, there was a stunned silence on the other end of the phone, then Franta said, "I'll come get you." Katrinka tried to talk him out of it, explaining that she had called only to borrow enough money for the train fare to Munich, but Franta was insistent. "At a time like this, you need a friend around," he said. "Believe me. I know. I'll get there as fast as I can."

While waiting for Franta to arrive, Katrinka took care of the endless political formalities. She talked to all the necessary people and filled out all the necessary papers to secure both a temporary stay in Switzerland and the right to enter Germany. That process started, she checked into a small inn recommended—and paid for—by the police, converted her small amount of lire into Swiss francs, then went to the local post office and put in calls to Czechoslovakia, to Aunt Zdeňka at the farm, to Tomáš and Zuzka in Prague, to tell them what she had done and ask them to round up and keep safe the few treasured personal possessions she had left behind, both in her room in Prague and at her grandparents' house in Svitov. Aunt Zdeňka was worried and tearful, Zuzka worried and excited, Tomáš obviously jealous, but all wished her well and promised to look after her things.

"Tomáš!" she called quickly just as he was about to hang up the phone.

"What?"

"My car." She had almost forgotten about it. "It's yours," she said and told him where it was parked.

"But Katrinka, really, I couldn't . . ."

"Idiot," she said firmly, "what good is it to me? Use it. The key and papers are in the night-table drawer in my room at Mrs. Kolchík's."

"Katrinka, thank you . . . I'll pay you when I can."

"Sbohem, zlatíčko."

"No, no, not good-bye," he said. "Until next time."

Then she called Ota Černý in Cervinia.

"Prague is negotiating with the Swiss government for your return," he told her. The phone call had been put through to Ota's room in the hotel, but his voice sounded so strange, so guarded, that Katrinka suspected he was not

alone. Was there an extension in his room, she wondered?
Was someone listening? The secret police?

"I'm not important enough for anyone to care about."

"I care."

"Oh, Uncle Ota," she said, reverting to her childhood
name for him. "I'm so sorry. The *only* thing I am sorry
about is hurting you."

"Do you know what a chance you took? You could have
been hurt. Killed!" She could hear the frustration and rage,
the fear in his voice. "Ilona Lukánský broke her leg."

"Oh no!" Katrinka's distress was genuine, but not for
Ilona's sake. The girl could have let her go, said a happy
good-bye to her only real competition, but instead had
followed, not out of any political commitment, but as
always because she could not bear the thought that Katrinka
might get what she wanted. No, she was not sorry that Ilona
had hurt herself, only that Ota Černý had lost his chance to
win the Olympics that year. "That stupid, stupid girl," she
said.

"You're the stupid girl, throwing everything away. Everything you've worked so hard for since you were a child."

"I know you can't possibly understand why. And I can't
explain. But I had to do this."

"Come back, Katrinka. I can work something out. I can
make sure you'll be all right."

"I can't."

"Katrinka, please . . ."

"I love you," she said and replaced the receiver before he
could hear her crying.

Overwhelmed by an unexpected attack of homesickness,
by the enormity of what she had done in leaving everything
and everyone who mattered to her behind, Katrinka returned to the inn, hurried to her room, fell fully clothed
onto the bed, and cried herself to sleep. Exhausted, she slept
through to the next morning and woke to find a message
from Franta Dohnal. He had arrived late the preceding
night, but had not wanted to disturb her, knowing how
much she needed her rest. She called his room and, fifteen
minutes later, after showering and reluctantly dressing again

in her ski suit, the only clothes she had, met him in the lobby.

"Katrinka, Katrinka, what a girl you are!" he murmured as he hugged her with arms surprisingly strong for someone as slender as he.

"I'm so glad to see you," she said, comforted by the sound of Czech words. They made her feel less homesick.

"I told you," said Franta, slipping an arm around her waist. His head came just to the top of her ear. "Are you hungry?"

"Starving. I haven't eaten a thing except for some pastry the police gave me yesterday."

"Now," said Franta once they had ordered a huge breakfast from the dirndl-skirted waitress in the small café across the street from the inn, "tell me everything, every last detail. I still can't believe you're here."

Katrinka told him, the amazement and delight on Franta's face as she spoke helping to lift the cloud of melancholy that had enveloped her since her conversation with Ota Černý. When she finished, Franta reached across the table and clasped her hand. "I know you're wondering if you made a terrible mistake, but you didn't," he told her. "You did the right thing. As homesick as I get sometimes, I never regret leaving Czechoslovakia. Never!"

After breakfast, they hurried to the city hall, then waited until all the papers necessary for the journey had collected the required signatures and seals. By noon, they were in Franta's old Porsche en route to Munich.

"It was so good of you to do this," said Katrinka, when they had cleared customs at the border, grateful to have had Franta's reassuring presence beside her while the guards examined her papers.

"What are friends for?" he said smiling, his green eyes alight with admiration and pleasure.

She returned his smile, feeling so much less lonely now than she had before his arrival in Zermatt. Then the smile was wiped from her face, replaced instantly by terror. *"Do prdele!"* she swore, then cried, "Franta! Watch out!" He had pulled out into the opposing lane to pass a slow-moving truck as a car came hurling over the hill heading directly toward them.

"Relax," said Franta, laughing, flooring the accelerator. "There's plenty of time. See," he added, as he slid the Porsche back into the lane with seconds to spare.

"Please," said Katrinka, her voice breathless. "Don't take such chances."

He was about to protest, but when he saw how pale she was, he lifted his hand from the steering wheel and clasped hers, squeezing it lightly. "All right," he agreed. "I'll drive as carefully as an old lady on her way to church, if it will make you happy."

By the time they arrived in Munich, Erica had returned from holiday and was only too happy to take Katrinka in. *"Liebling, liebling,* how good to see you. My God, the things you get up to," she said as she hugged Katrinka, kissing her on both cheeks. She settled the exhausted young woman into the familiar yellow bedroom, lent her a nightgown to sleep in, reluctantly agreed to arrange an appointment for Katrinka to see Dr. Zimmerman as soon as he returned from his vacation, and the next day took her shopping for a change of clothes.

As soon as she had something other than a ski suit to wear, Katrinka set about regularizing her existence in Germany. She went from office to office, filling in the necessary forms, signing the required documents, making arrangements for the temporary papers she had been issued in Switzerland to become permanent as quickly as possible. When that was done she returned to the Four Seasons Hotel and asked for her old job back.

Working nights as before, Katrinka used her days to look for more lucrative work, making the rounds of the modeling agencies armed only with the magazine ads and covers that Erica and Franta—for their separate reasons—had managed to save over the years. Within a week, she had her first assignment, modeling designer clothes in a Munich showroom. It was only a day's work, but the fee allowed her to repay Erica and to buy some clothes, which she badly needed. She got one of the samples at cost, a cream-colored wool flannel pantsuit with a round-necked fitted jacket and bell-bottom trousers. Simple as the outfit was, it suited her, highlighting her creamy complexion, emphasizing her slenderness and height, giving her an air of elegance.

Her wardrobe was so meager she had very few choices, so it was that suit she wore for her meeting with Dr. Zimmerman. It made her feel mature, in control, light-years away from the frightened, pitiful young girl of their last encounter. She wanted to present herself to him as someone to reckon with, someone whose wishes had to be taken into account.

Her effort did not totally fail to impress him. He was willing to admit, to himself at least, that Katrinka had matured into a strikingly beautiful woman, her old vitality and youthful arrogance transformed into a compelling self-confidence; but to her all he said, rather coolly, was, "You're looking very well, my dear."

Katrinka did not waste time exchanging compliments across the neutral territory of his expensive antique desk, but immediately demanded the return of her son, to which Zimmerman replied that he had agreed to see her only as a favor to Erica and that it was absolutely the last time he would do so. He insisted he could tell her nothing about the boy, and would not even if he had the information she wanted. All he did know was that the child was gone, not even in Germany any longer. She would never find him and, if she had any sense, she would stop trying and get on with her life. "Why can't you be satisfied?" he demanded, his voice tinged with exasperation. "Your son has rich, loving parents. Do you think you could have provided him with so good a life? Never!" What he did not add, though he thought it, was that really she should have fallen on her knees to thank him for what he had done for herself and her child.

What he had done for himself, though, was something Dr. Zimmerman did not like to spend too much time thinking about, preferring to view his activities from the more attractive philanthropic angle. But in truth, the couple who had adopted the boy had been very generous, not only paying an enormous sum of money for the child but, over the years, the husband had provided favors of priceless worth: legal cover (exit visas, for example) for some of the doctor's more adventurous baby-selling activities, advance warning of impending changes in government economic policies (which took so much of the risk out of investing), applying pressure to ease restrictions on various real estate transactions involving the clinic, and once even clearing the way for the doctor's purchase of a schloss on the Rhine to which the title had not been clear. All in all, he had helped make Klaus Zimmerman an extremely wealthy man and the doctor had the good sense to be grateful. He looked at Katrinka with growing irritation. "You're young. You're very beautiful, Katrinka. I'm sure, if you made the least bit of an effort, you could find yourself a good man to marry. Do it, my dear. Marry and have a family. Forget the past."

What Klaus Zimmerman said, no matter how sensible it sounded, of course made no difference to Katrinka. He could not change her mind. She had made a terrible mistake in giving her son away and it was a mistake she was determined someday, somehow, to rectify. But she didn't threaten. She knew that would no more affect him than her pleading had. She had no power to make him tremble. Yet. She swore to herself that one day she would. "I never forget, Dr. Zimmerman. I won't say good-bye," she told him, her low voice steady and assured as she rose to her feet and headed for the door.

A finger brushing the tip of his neat blond moustache, Zimmerman watched her as she left, admiring her lean, strong body, the delicate curve of her hips. It was a pity, he thought with some regret, that he had made such an enemy of her: she was a very beautiful woman. He buzzed for Erica, who appeared immediately in the doorway. "In future, keep her away from me," he said.

"Yes, doctor," agreed Erica, her fondness for Katrinka in no way threatening her feelings for Klaus Zimmerman. She loved him and trusted him, believing that his only motive was to help the young girls who came to him in trouble.

"Don't you have any influence with her? Can't you make her see reason?"

"She's very stubborn."

"I won't have her making trouble."

223

"I'm sure she understands now that there is nothing she can do."

"I hope so. With women like her you never know." Which is why he preferred women like Erica, dependable, loyal, and so eager to please. He looked admiringly at her silky blond hair, her large mouth, the luxurious curves of her body, and remembered it had been weeks since they had made love, since before he had left on vacation. "How long is she staying with you? It's damned inconvenient, you know."

Erica smiled. "Only a few weeks more. Until she has enough money for a place of her own."

Zimmerman nodded, not listening to the answer but reviewing his plans for the evening in his head. "Is it possible for you to work late tonight?" he asked when she had finished speaking.

"Oh, yes."

"Good," he said and smiled in dismissal. Happily, he had had the foresight to furnish his office with a wide and comfortable couch.

Though Erica generously urged her to stay with her as long as she liked, Katrinka—as soon as she had saved a little money—began looking for an apartment and soon found one in Franz-Joseph-Strasse, in Schwabing, not far from where Franta lived, inexpensive enough for her to afford on her salary from the hotel plus what she made modeling. In an old building renovated after the war, the tiny two-room apartment was the first place of her own that Katrinka had ever had, and, though she borrowed some pots and pans and assorted china from Erica to get started and immediately bought a comfortable bed and standing lamp, she furnished the rest slowly, rummaging in secondhand stores in the Münchner Freiheit and Olympiapark flea markets, finding good, inexpensive pieces, polishing the faded woods to a bright sheen, reupholstering the chairs in silk remnants bought at bargain basement sales. Sometimes, as she was stretching the fabric over the frames, she would think of Milena's needlepoint, the stools and cushions abandoned in Svitov, and tears would fill her eyes.

Soon Katrinka's schedule was as hectic as any she had followed in Czechoslovakia. She worked nights at the hotel and modeled—when she got an assignment—during the day, in designer studios to start with, followed quickly by catwalk fashion shows, then print work. Some of her free hours she spent trying to get her apartment in order, but most of her time off Katrinka devoted to finding her son. In an attempt to get information, she cultivated relationships with people who worked at the clinic, but learned nothing, she supposed because they were too afraid of Zimmerman and worried about their jobs to talk. When that approach failed, she took trains to every city hall in the vicinity of Munich to search through files for some record of her child's adoption. Though she returned from these trips exhausted, her disappointment teetering on the brink of despair, she never quite gave up hope. There was always another city, another file, and the chance that one day she would find what she was looking for.

Her free evenings Katrinka spent with Erica, at the opera, usually, or with Franta and the group of friends he introduced her to—other Czech émigrés or coworkers from the Porsche factory—young men and women who liked to eat at Kay's Bistro or the Extrablatt and dance at Aquarius or Charly M.

Franta quickly became Katrinka's best friend, filling the void left in her life by Tomáš's absence. Linked by their backgrounds, their memories of home, their longing for the same rich Czech food, they also genuinely liked one another and had fun together. They loved to party, to dance. They loved Simon and Garfunkel, the Beatles, the Rolling Stones, whose songs they knew in Czech and would sing at the top of their lungs driving along country roads in Franta's old black Porsche. They loved to ski and, when they could, would take weekend trips—alone or with the group of friends—to Innsbruck and St. Anton, Lech and Kitzbühel. What they disagreed on were cars and opera. Franta, still employed as a test driver at Porsche, was determined to race, a desire that Katrinka viewed as suicidal; and her visits to the Opera House he, after accompanying her once, pronounced masochistic.

As the months passed, they became so close that both of them wondered from time to time why they were not lovers, and decided that the chemistry simply was not there. But it was more than that. Because she was so busy building a new life and trying to find her son, romance was of little interest to Katrinka just then. And Franta, who had no shortage of admiring women around him willing to provide all the sex he wanted, was reluctant to make a move where he sensed he might be rejected. Friendship, for the moment, was enough for both of them.

With the experience of her past summers at the Four Seasons, Katrinka, when she returned to work there on a permanent basis, advanced quickly from maid to floor supervisor. She kept track of the linens, the towels, checked the rooms to see that the maids were keeping them in good order, requisitioned needed repairs. Though the glamorous world of the front desk, smart boutiques, and elegant restaurants was far removed from her, nevertheless, on her way through the kitchens and laundries, the carpentry and electrical shops, the staff and supply rooms, the numerous and complex underground caverns that composed the building's nerve center, Katrinka began to get some real sense of the sort of service a deluxe hotel could and should provide. But as her modeling career became more successful, juggling the two jobs became difficult and Katrinka, fifteen months after her arrival in Munich, left the hotel. She could earn $100 a day as a house model, $200 an hour for runway shows. Even at management level—and Katrinka had no doubt that she would soon work her way up to that—hotel salaries were no match.

Life as a model was demanding, too, in a different but equally exhausting way from cleaning hotel rooms. To meet magazine deadlines, Katrinka sweltered modeling furs in summer and froze in bathing suits midwinter. For runway shows, she was up at six for fittings, rehearsals, and makeup. The clothes would be hung on a peg, hat and underwear on top, shoes and stockings underneath. With the aid of a dresser, Katrinka would put on outfit after outfit, changing from top to bottom, inside out, scarf over her head to keep her hair in place, using hairspray to remove accidental lipstick stains—when she was ready dancing out onto the runway to as many as sixteen choreographed routines learned on short notice. Even more exhausting was the showroom work, when Katrinka would model samples chosen from endless racks of clothing by buyers from all over Europe who were in Munich to look at new designer lines. There, added to the strain of changing every few minutes was the challenge of keeping her energy high all day, looking fresh and beautiful when fading, making clothes that did not fit look great. At the end of a session, she would not have the strength even to eat and would return home, drop her clothes in a heap on a chair, and collapse into bed, her makeup still on.

In March of 1973, out of the blue, early one morning, Mirek Bartoš phoned her. He was in Munich to promote the release of his latest film and suggested they meet at the Café Extrablatt for a drink. For a moment, Katrinka—still half asleep and thrown off balance by his sudden reappearance in her life—considered saying no, but only for a moment. Mirek was a tie to her home, to her youth, to a past she remembered now as idyllic and, though he certainly might be considered the instrument of its destruction, he was still a connection she was not prepared to cut completely. She had so few left.

Not only did Mirek arrive at the café with her portfolio of photographs, one of the things Tomáš had rescued from her room in Prague, but he had snapshots of the Havlíčeks, including little Martin, who had grown very tall in the eighteen months or so since she had last seen him, and a letter from Zuzka full of news, which Katrinka read eagerly as the sounds of Piaf filtered through the room.

"We could be in Paris," murmured Mirek, looking around the café. "Oh, how I'd love to be in Paris." With you, he thought but didn't say.

Though Katrinka had dreaded seeing him again, she was glad that she had and agreed to stay for dinner. She found him as merry and charming as ever, as knowledgeable and interesting. He had not changed at all since she had last seen him. But she had, she realized. She was no longer a young, impressionable girl and his egotism did not seem now like self-assurance to her; she no longer confused his success with talent. She still cared about him, she always would, but she was not in love with him, not even remotely, though she had been afraid she might be. When he asked her to spend the night with him at his hotel (not the Four Seasons, which his expense account would not cover), she refused.

"I won't ask you again," he said sadly. He put his arms around her, enveloping her in his big, comforting embrace. "Keep well," he murmured into her ear, then kissed her on both cheeks and let her go.

Two weeks later, Franta threw a party at his apartment. The guests included Franta's old crowd plus new friends Katrinka had made—supervisors and managers from the hotel, designers, agents, buyers, other young models. It was a wild night, reminding Katrinka of the times, after a race, when the Czech ski team would let loose and celebrate. Everyone ate mountains of the *goulâš* Franta had prepared and gobbled down Katrinka's *koláčky*. Endless bottles of beer and wine were drunk. Couples necked happily in corners. Katrinka played the guitar and Franta the balalaika while the others sang. Later, everyone danced to phonograph records of old polkas and new rock music.

It was dawn when the last of the guests set out drunkenly for home. Katrinka remained to help Franta, who was between girlfriends, clear up. Despite the hour, she felt clearheaded and happy, full of energy and hope in the future. And when Franta put his arms around her to thank her for her help with a kiss, she responded eagerly. Her meeting with Mirek may have set Katrinka free at last of her former lover, but it had also stirred up sleeping memories and feelings, had reawakened in her a desire for love, for *sex*, which her healthy young body had gone without for almost two years. And when she felt Franta's tongue slip gently into her mouth, his hand settle tentatively on her breast, Katrinka felt a spark flare and catch and blaze into the need to make love. It was a feeling different from the all-consuming fever of her relationship with Mirek Bartoš or the exuberant youthful lust she had experienced with Vladislav Elias. It was desire tinged with the tenderness of friendship. And when Franta pulled back for a moment and looked at her questioningly, Katrinka said nothing but just lowered her mouth again to his. Soon they were naked in Franta's large double bed—not in a sudden, wild blaze of overwhelming passion, not deeply in love, but lovers nonetheless because it felt so completely familiar and natural and good to be together, because they were, just then, the most important people in each other's world.

Twenty

The drive from Munich to Kitzbühel was only about 120 kilometers, most of it well-traveled autobahn and mountain roads certain to have been plowed after the last snow. But the January light was pale and murky, making visibility poor. Katrinka, always a careful driver, watched tensely for speed demons and stray patches of ice, pushing all thoughts of Franta Dohnal and their relationship temporarily from her mind, concentrating on getting herself and her new white 1977 Fiat Spyder safely to her destination. More than ever, driving terrified her.

She turned on the car radio and listened to the news, most of it about what it would mean for Europe when Jimmy Carter was inaugurated President of the United States in two weeks' time. The Associated Press had just voted Nadia Comaneci athlete of the year, reported the announcer. Athlete of the year. It sounded very good. What would have happened, Katrinka wondered, if she had stayed and competed and won the '72 Olympics? Did she regret leaving? she asked herself a moment later. No. Franta had been right. That was the one thing she never regretted.

In just under two hours, she reached the Golden Horn Gasthof, the small twenty-eight-room inn she had bought the year before. Not far from the cable car to the Kitzbühler Horn, set against a backdrop of pine trees and mountains, the inn was a pretty two-story chalet with a white-painted stucco base, an upper level of dark wood planks, a peaked roof, and decorative carved trim. In summer, the foreground of lush green, gently rising Alps contrasted sharply to its background of stark massifs, the Wilder Kaiser in the north and the High Tauern in the south, jagged granite peaks carved against an intense blue sky. Now everything was the uniform and brilliant white of deep powder snow.

Katrinka had discovered the inn shortly after her arrival in Munich, when she had gone skiing with Franta and a group of friends to Kitzbühel. She had fallen in love with the charming, inexpensive Hubner Gasthof—as it was then called—owned by a sweet old couple in their seventies who had inherited it from the wife's parents forty years before. As long as there was a room available she and Franta had always stayed there, and eventually Katrinka asked the Hubners if she could work weekend afternoons for room and board, not because she could not afford the cost but because she was trying to save money to make some sort of business investment as a hedge against the time she was too old to model. Short of help, the Hubners were delighted, and it was no hardship to Katrinka. In fact, she enjoyed it. Out on the slopes at nine, she skied until noon, then worked the rest of the day, making up rooms, settling new arrivals, confirming reservations, assisting guests with travel plans. Soon, Katrinka was even helping the Hubners with the accounts. Their two sons had been killed in the war and, with no children or grandchildren to interest them, they grew very fond of her, enjoying her company and the life and energy that seemed to infuse the inn when she was there. They came to depend on her, and Katrinka, in turn, came to love them.

Late in 1975, when Mr. Hubner suffered a slight stroke and the old couple had to consider putting the inn up for sale, Katrinka offered to buy it. Mrs. Hubner at first had seemed worried by the idea. "We would give it to you, *schatze*, if we could," she said, so much like a daughter had Katrinka become to her and her husband.

"Nonsense," said Katrinka. "You need the money, and I have it. I *want* to buy." The inn had seemed to her the perfect place to invest the small amount of capital she had saved. Familiar as she was with the place, there were unlikely to be any terrible surprises a few months down the road. She already knew its financial condition, the state of the roof and the furnace, what furniture could do with replacing. Aware of all its flaws, Katrinka had felt certain she would know how to make the most of its assets. She was convinced she could make it a success and, if not make her fortune, the inn would at least provide her with a reliable income not tied to the freshness of her face and the shape of her body.

Talking quickly and emphatically in an eager rush of words, Katrinka soon had the Hubners convinced. They in turn assured the bank manager of Katrinka's reliability. Reasonable terms were worked out, the down payment made, the mortgage loan arranged, and Katrinka became the inn's owner. And in the year since, thanks to judicious refurbishment, innovations like high tea in the late afternoon, clever advertising, and Katrinka's relentless courting of travel agents, the success of the inn had surpassed even her most extravagant expectations, though she was still too concerned about cash flow to give up modeling.

As Katrinka pulled into the drive leading to the Golden Horn, she noticed that Bruno had swept the walk and porch and cleared the parking area of snow. The lot was full, she was happy to see, a prosperous collection of Mercedes and BMWs, a Volkswagen and a Renault. From the chimney, a thin ribbon of pale gray smoke curled into the darkening sky. The lamps shone gaily behind the small-paned windows. The whole place looked idyllic, cozy, and inviting, even without the window boxes that in summer dripped brilliant red geraniums.

Katrinka took the canvas bag from the Spyder's trunk and entered the inn through the service door, deposited her things in the small room she kept for herself in the attic, and went back downstairs in search of Bruno and Hilde, her eyes on the alert for cobwebs, dust, a nick in the paint, a spot on the hall runner, a piece of furniture out of place. The Golden Horn had been in good condition when she had bought it, a simple, comfortable mountain inn, but now, after a year of hard work, if too small to be considered grand, it was nevertheless well on its way to being luxurious. She had cleaned it room by room, from ceiling to floor, attic to coal cellar. The paneling was varnished, the wooden trim painted, worn sheets and towels replaced with the best-quality linens Katrinka could afford. Local seamstresses had made new covers for chairs and beds, new curtains for the windows. The rooms were stocked with fragrant soaps, with small bottles of shampoo and body lotion, with boxes of tissue, cheap to buy but the kind of small service that impresses guests, makes them feel pampered, and brings them back on a regular basis. Each room was cleaned thoroughly twice a month, vacuumed and dusted every day, its sheets and towels changed, with more towels available on demand. The service was quick and courteous. Guests told Katrinka that they were not treated so well at hotels charging five times the price, then begged her to install a restaurant, which was out of the question. Breakfast was about all she and her staff could manage, plus the afternoon tea that had become so fashionable it attracted skiers from many of the neighboring hotels. In addition to tea, coffee was served, with rich local cream, homemade strawberry dumplings, scones, muffins, cakes, and jams, which Katrinka made herself from her grandmother's recipes and had recently begun to jar and sell with some success. When she had taken it over, the inn had barely been breaking even. This year, Katrinka expected to make a small profit.

Coming down the narrow staircase with its turned-wood banister into the lobby, Katrinka saw Bruno at the front desk, checking in a late arrival. Hilde was in the dining room, clearing the tables of the remnants of tea. Waving hello to Bruno, Katrinka went through the open French doors to give Hilde a hand.

"I was beginning to worry," said Hilde when she saw Katrinka. "Franta, is he all right?"

"Better. Much better. But it was a little hard for me to get away."

"Poor thing," she clucked, though it was not clear whether it was Franta or Katrinka whom she meant.

"How's it going? What's the occupancy today?"

The look of concern on Hilde's face was replaced immediately with a smile. "Only one room empty," she said

233

proudly. "Not counting Natalie's. And there's still tomorrow."

Bruno and Hilde were a married couple in their fifties, hardworking and responsible. Bruno was an Italian, a short, round, good-looking man with a weathered face and bright smile. Hilde was Austrian, blond, stout, a good two inches taller than her husband. They had answered the ad that Katrinka had placed in the local newspaper and, with two girls from the village, were the only help Katrinka had running the inn. Together, they kept track of reservations, handled arrivals and departures, cleaned and made up the rooms, did the laundry, prepared and served breakfast and tea. In addition, Bruno took care of the minor repairs and Katrinka all the accounts. It was a lot of work, but somehow they managed, and, for the most part, enjoyed it: the pay was good, the surroundings beautiful, and even the most difficult guests never stayed too long.

It was only when she retired to her room, after a late supper of cold meats and bread eaten with Bruno and Hilde in the kitchen, that Katrinka allowed herself to think again about Franta, to make some attempt to sort out the complex emotions that had assailed her earlier that day, in his hospital room.

"I hate to leave you again, so soon. I really do," she had told him. "But it's the height of the season. I'm not sure Bruno and Hilde can manage alone."

In an attempt to be reassuring, Franta had smiled, the effort merely emphasizing the gauntness of his face. "Don't worry so much," he said. "I'll be fine."

He was still so thin, his skin almost as pale as the white pillows supporting his head, but he was better. At first, Katrinka had not been able to believe that he would survive the accident, but now, even without the daily confirmation of the doctors, she could see that he was improving steadily. "Well, at least I know you won't be lonely," said Katrinka.

"No. Never lonely." His hospital room would be full of friends all weekend long, driving the nursing staff mad with their noise and practical jokes. He took her hand. "But I'll miss you just the same."

"I'll come back as soon as I can."

"Don't drive too fast," he said as she leaned down to kiss him good-bye.

She laughed. "You're a fine one to talk." Her lips brushed his cheek, then met his as he turned his face toward her.

"I wish you loved me," he had said.

"Oh, Franta. I do. I do." She must, she thought: he was her friend, her lover. But even as she thought it, she felt waves of dissatisfaction and restlessness wash over her, followed immediately by pity for him and guilt for her own disloyalty. "I wish you would believe me," she added, her voice low and quick and eager to convince.

"I try to," he said, letting go of her hand.

Within weeks of the start of their affair, Franta's dream had come true: he had become a race car driver. His success in amateur events had finally brought him to the attention of the March Formula 3 team and he was taken on by them. Though neither he nor Katrinka was aware of it then, or for a long time afterward, that had signaled the beginning of the end of their relationship.

Brave enough, and sufficiently practical, to make use of cars when she needed them, Katrinka still was terrified by them. They conjured awful memories. To her, they were a constant reminder of death. That Franta should willfully put his life at risk by racing them seemed to her to be madness. And because she was so afraid that he too might die, she did not allow herself to love him completely. She held something back as insurance against loss.

Despite her fears, Katrinka often accompanied Franta to races, indulging her passion for travel, covering Europe with him, stopping obsessively in local city halls on her journeys to check the records there for any sign of her child. Loyally, she cheered him on from Formula 3 to Formula 1 when March formed a new team. Soon after, he joined the Brabham team as their number two driver. Katrinka went with him to Monza and Estoril, to Hockenheim and Monte Carlo. But the crowds, the noise, the bright colors, the excitement, which in other circumstances she would have loved, horrified her. She was happy when either her schedule or the distance Franta had to travel prevented her going with him, though almost as terrible as watching him race was the tension of waiting to hear from him afterward.

It was driving back from the Golden Horn that the accident had happened, three months ago, and the irony of that never ceased to dismay Katrinka. Franta had not almost killed himself racing at Monte Carlo or Suzuka or Adelaide but on the drive back to Munich with her after a weekend in Kitzbühel.

As always, Katrinka had attempted to bury her worries in work, but the harder she tried, the further she and Franta had grown apart. That day, while she had been in her office doing the accounts, Franta was drinking, which he did when he was bored and unhappy. At the start of the drive, it was only his irritation she noticed, but thought it was due to his resentment at being ignored all afternoon while she had attended to business. But when she apologized, he launched into an attack, damning the inn and her, letting loose a volley of complaints: how little time and attention she had to spare for him, how she never really enjoyed watching him race, rarely went with him to parties, ran off instead to the opera when she had a free five minutes. When she stopped trying to defend herself, realizing it was useless, she became aware of the thickness in his speech. "You've been drinking," she said.

"That's right, don't try to defend yourself. Attack me instead."

"Franta, pull over, please. I want to drive."

"No."

"Please, Franta. You know how nervous it makes me."

"There's nothing wrong with my driving."

"Do it, please. A favor to me."

"A favor to you? Don't make me laugh! Why should I do you a favor? What do you do for me? You don't even love me anymore. If you ever did."

While he had been lying near death in his hospital room, and during the months of slow recovery afterward, Katrinka had pushed his accusation from her mind. In the first few weeks, she had stayed by his side night and day, returning home for just a few hours of restless sleep, a quick shower, and a change of clothes. Later, she had cut back on her modeling assignments, turned the running of the inn over as much as possible to Bruno and Hilde, and sat with Franta, quietly if he preferred, or talking, playing chess, reading to him: newspapers, car magazines, novels by Kundera, Hrabal, even Kafka, her mother's favorite. She did it without weighing her motives, because she had to, because he was all she had. How could she let herself doubt that she loved him?

But now that Franta was almost well again, due to be released from the hospital in a few days, the truth was screaming for attention.

In her room at the Golden Horn, getting ready for bed, Katrinka realized finally that Franta was both right and wrong, as was she. Climbing out of her clothes and into her pretty flannel nightgown, she understood that she did love him, but not in the way he wanted. If it had not been for the accident, their relationship would have ended by now. That was really what the quarrel, the last in a series of similar quarrels, had been leading to, and where it might have got if the car had not hit a patch of ice and spun out of control, leaving Franta with several broken ribs, a fractured collarbone, a damaged pancreas, and a concussion that had kept him unconscious for weeks. Katrinka, somewhat miraculously, had not been hurt badly, nothing more than a few bruises, thanks so they said to the seat belt she was wearing.

Katrinka stopped brushing her hair and stared at herself in the mirror of her dressing table. Her face, wiped free of makeup, seemed pale to her. There were shadows under her eyes and a few faint lines at their corners. She was twenty-eight years old and the idea of not loving Franta filled her with dismay. Though perhaps lacking in passion, her life with him had an emotionally stable quality that she enjoyed, a sense of belonging that she had missed since her parents, and then her grandparents, had died. She had grown up in a small but loving family and longed to be part of one again. In the general, rather hazy plan she had for her future, she and Franta one day would marry, have children, and her son—for whom she continued, haphazardly and relentlessly, to search—would one day be incorporated neatly into this happy group. Not that she had told Franta about him. It was not fear that kept her quiet now, nor shame, but that same lifetime's habit of discretion, which she found impossible to break even with a lover. And having to explain that she'd been pregnant when they met had seemed awkward, difficult, and really not necessary until she located the child.

In this case, Katrinka's habitual reticence was compounded by Franta's attitude toward children. Not only did he not like them particularly, he thought his life too unpredictable, too dangerous, for him to have a family. Katrinka agreed. But in this vague life plan of hers Franta would soon realize the folly of his ways, give up racing, marry her, and, like Tomáš, discover a latent paternal instinct.

As she moved from the dressing table to the bed, Katrinka wondered if this attitude of Franta's had created another insurmountable barrier between them, a hurdle she just could not jump? She wondered if, had he wanted children, she could have allowed herself to love him more?

But Katrinka did not allow her mind to travel too far along that line. What was the point? As much as she might want them to be stronger, her feelings for Franta were not enough to satisfy either him, or herself, now that she had realized the truth. Always more a pragmatist than a dreamer, used to setting goals she had a good chance of achieving, Katrinka thought it useless to try to back up and somehow put her relationship with Franta on the right track. For whatever reasons, they had arrived where neither of them really wanted to be, and had no choice now but to go forward, and in separate directions.

Tears welled in her eyes as she was overcome with nostalgia for the relationship that she and Franta would never have, where the affection they felt for one another would blaze into passion, then deepen into love, and end happily with marriage and children.

She would tell him as soon as possible, she decided, leaning back against the pillows of her bed, letting herself cry, needing to mourn the passing of Franta from her life. She would tell him as soon as he was out of the hospital and had his strength back. She dreaded doing it, hated the idea of hurting him, and herself. She would miss him terribly, his company, his encouragement, the sound of his voice singing Czech songs in the shower, his lean, pale body next to hers in bed. He had been the one steady, comforting feature of her life since she had left Czechoslovakia. She would be very lonely without him.

*K*atrinka? *Chérie,* are you awake? May I come in?"

The soft knock at the door and Natalie's voice calling brought a quick end to Katrinka's worrying about Franta and the future. Getting out of bed, she crossed the carpeted floor hurriedly on bare feet to open the door she had kept locked since the night a drunken male guest had decided to pay her a visit. She had eventually convinced him to leave but the experience had been frightening.

"You're late," Katrinka said as Natalie entered. The two women kissed, first one cheek, then the other. "I expected you hours ago."

Natalie shrugged. "There was a storm somewhere. All the planes were delayed. My God, look at what you are wearing."

Katrinka laughed. "You wear silk all the time, I suppose, even when you are alone in bed and cold?" Since Natalie understood little German and Katrinka less French, the women spoke using a cross-national vocabulary more or less in English, which both had studied in school.

"Of course, *chérie.* I have an image to preserve, even for myself." As Katrinka returned to the comfort of her bed, Natalie settled herself into an armchair and said accusingly, "You've been crying."

"About nothing important. Did you come alone?"

"Would I come all this way just to ski? Jean-Claude is at the Schloss. With his wife," she added bitterly.

Natalie Bovier was a buyer for Galleries Gillette, one of

the major Paris department stores, part of the Gillette chain, which included at that time other stores in Lyon and Marseilles as well as vineyards and specialty gourmet shops. She was also the mistress of Jean-Claude Gillette, the chain's owner, and had been since the age of seventeen, a year or so after she had gone to work at his vineyard in Chassagne, where she was born. Seeing Natalie one day helping with the grape harvest, he had decided she was meant for better things, himself for one. A collector of pretty girls, Jean-Claude had taken Natalie with him when he returned to Paris, installed her in an apartment near the Luxembourg Gardens, bought her clothes, taught her to speak properly, and employed her as a saleswoman in the Galleries Gillette. He had been married then, and was still married, though he and his wife had an "understanding," explained Natalie when she told Katrinka the story, reminding her instantly of Mirek and Vlasta Bartoš.

"Would you be so understanding if you were a wife?" Katrinka had asked later, when Natalie and she had become good friends.

"That depends."

"On what?"

Natalie's thin, straight nose wrinkled. *"Oh la la,* let me see. On whether or not I still loved him, I suppose. On whether or not I was amusing myself elsewhere." Then her mouth had curved into a sly grin. "Would you?"

"No, I don't think so," Katrinka had said. "I don't think I could stand it." Her affair with Mirek Bartoš had taught her a lesson that would last Katrinka a lifetime: infidelity was not romantic, it was destructive. Someone in the triangle eventually got hurt, very badly hurt.

That Natalie had risen so quickly through the ranks to her present glamorous position as the store's chief buyer for women's clothes was not due entirely to her relationship with Jean-Claude. She was intelligent, ambitious, a quick study with an innate sense of style and an almost uncanny ability to predict trends. Even had he not been sleeping with her, Jean-Claude would have been wise to promote her, and no doubt would have—eventually. There was simply no one better for the job, though others tended not to see it that way and credited Natalie's success, like a lot of women's, solely to her having fucked the boss, as if kissing his ass, as they did, was a more commendable way to get ahead.

Katrinka had met Natalie two years before when she was still a junior buyer flying into Munich to see the shows of some of the younger German designers. Talent was international, said Natalie, and one had to go everywhere and see everything to find "the jewel in the shit." When she could, she timed her scouting expeditions to coincide with Jean-Claude's business trips. Otherwise, she traveled alone, picking up company as she went since she could not bear solitude, usually men with whom she sometimes—though not always—slept, dining occasionally with women if they were intelligent enough to provide stimulating conversation. At a cocktail party after a show one night, she and Katrinka had fallen into casual conversation. They had ended up eating *Weisswurst* at the Franciskaner—courtesy of Natalie's expense account—and been friends ever since. Though in different ways, they were both adventurous and they shared an inclination to mischief and a keen sense of fun. Each thought she had found a soulmate and admired without reservation, or jealousy, the other's beauty, brains, skill in business, and success with men.

When Jean-Claude came to Kitzbühel to ski, if he was without his wife Natalie stayed with him at the Schloss Grunberg—Kitzbühel's most luxurious hotel—though, since he was known there, usually in a separate room. When Hélène accompanied him, Natalie preferred to stay at the Golden Horn, where at least she had the luxury of laughing with Katrinka. Though Jean-Claude complained bitterly of the inconvenience, he managed to spend part of every day there, and Natalie suspected that he liked it, or at least the novelty of having to expend a little effort to get what he wanted.

And no matter how often he allowed himself to be tempted by other women, he continued to want Natalie, a little to her surprise, since her mother, employed as a laundress at the vineyard's château, had warned her repeatedly, from a very early age, that rich men changed their women almost as often as their shirts. "I'm his little dog," said Natalie once to explain the endurance of her relationship with Jean-Claude, "his *chienne*, well-trained, obedient, affectionate, eager to please. Who could bear to part with such an adorable pet? Especially as I am always in heat."

The epitome of chic, Natalie gave the impression of beauty without being more than pretty. She was tall, though less so than Katrinka, and even thinner, a size four, with translucent skin, a thin, straight nose, firm chin, soft curly hair the color of sunlight, and large green eyes flecked with amber. What softness she might have had at seventeen was long gone. At twenty-seven, she herself was like a jewel, cut by Jean-Claude's master hand, polished to perfection, brilliant and hard, at least on the surface, though what attracted men to her was neither her looks nor her style, but a sort of erotic energy, troubling and very exciting.

"I'm getting fed up," said Natalie.

"With Jean-Claude?"

"With being treated like a picnic basket, carried here and there, dropped in a corner, ignored till he's hungry, and then a small piece of chicken breast, a glass of white wine, a bit of cheese and *ouff*, the meal is over." Katrinka laughed. "It's not funny, *chérie*."

Katrinka grew serious at once. "So I see. What happened?" she asked.

Natalie shrugged. "Nothing of any significance. I got my period this afternoon. A waste of time my being here: he won't come near me. And the trip was impossible." She kicked off her shoes and put her feet up on Katrinka's bed. "Some men don't mind, you know. Does Franta?"

"Oh, yes." But Mirek Bartoš had not minded at all, Katrinka remembered. It was like being massaged with hot oil, he had said, like entering a ripe sun-warmed plum, like coming in a bath. He had loved the sensation, and so had she.

"Big babies, afraid of a little blood."

"They don't know what they're missing."

"And they don't care, the fools. What are you doing tomorrow?"

"Skiing for a few hours in the morning. Working the rest of the day. We're full this weekend."

"Tomorrow night you're having dinner with me at the Schloss."

"Natalie, that's not a good idea."

"Don't worry. I won't make a scene."

"Why do that to yourself?"

"Do what? Go out in public instead of hiding away? Enjoy myself? Eat a decent meal?"

"There are many places we could go for a good meal."

"We're going to the Schloss. I'll make the reservation." She stood up, leaned over the bed, and kissed Katrinka on both cheeks. *"Bonne nuit,"* she said.

The worried look did not leave Katrinka's face as she watched Natalie amble to the door. "What's the use of embarrassing Hélène? Or Jean-Claude?"

"To amuse myself?" replied Natalie, turning to look at her.

"I don't like it."

"No one will be embarrassed. Hélène will pretend not to know me. And Jean-Claude will be annoyed, or enchanted. Who can tell? You'll come with me, won't you?" She sounded suddenly like a child about to be deprived of a promised outing.

Katrinka nodded. "Yes," she said. After all, what were friends for?

"Good," said Natalie. *"À demain.* Don't forget to lock the door."

In the morning, Katrinka was up at six to help Hilde prepare the breakfast, which was served in the dining room from seven-thirty to ten. After that, she helped make up the rooms so that the girl on morning duty could finish at a reasonable hour. At ten-thirty, she knocked at Natalie's door to ask if she planned to go skiing that morning, and was greeted with complaints about continuing cramps and a declaration that Natalie, with the French translation of *Looking for Mr. Goodbar* for company, would not move from bed until it was time for dinner. If it had been an executive meeting at the Galleries Gillette or a fashion show, nothing would have kept her away, but Natalie was not in the least athletic and put up only a minimal show to please Jean-Claude, who was.

By eleven, wearing her chic new star-studded ski suit (aside from the needed money, the ability to get clothes at reduced prices was one of the continuing attractions of modeling), Katrinka was standing in line waiting to take the cable car to the Horn. Being the first one out on the mountain in the morning had been one of the required sacrifices for buying the inn.

Although the line moved with reasonable speed, to Katrinka, who was always in a hurry, it seemed to creep along, though none of her irritation showed. Why make a fuss and spoil the morning for herself and everyone around when there was no hope of getting the cable cars to move faster? Instead she chatted to the others, guests at the Golden Horn, employees of other hotels, residents of Kitzbühel she had come to know over the years, her words tumbling out in a fluent rush of accented German, or English, a Czech word thrown in here and there, her laughter frequent and infectious. There was no visible trace of last night's unhappiness, no swollen eyes or haggard face. The wind had added a pink tip to her nose and a blush to her cheeks, and her eyes were as clear and bright as the sky. But then she spotted in the queue two couples she had sometimes seen in the company of Klaus Zimmerman and his wife on their visits to Kitzbühel and her fragile hold on good humor was shattered. Any reminder of the doctor inevitably awoke painful memories, and Katrinka felt a familiar stab of anguish as she thought of her continuing and futile search for her son.

The couples had a young, rather homely little girl with them and two boys. As she was in the habit of doing, Katrinka studied the boys for a moment, searching for some trace of Mirek and herself, certain she would know her son the moment she set eyes on him. They were about eight or nine years old, the right age. One of them was dark and looked sullen, the other had lighter hair and a charming grin. Both were extremely good-looking. But she saw nothing familiar in either, nothing that sparked her maternal

instinct or tugged at the psychic bond she was certain must
exist between herself and her son. It was difficult to tell to
which of the couples any of them belonged.

In the Hornbahn to the middle station, Katrinka rode
with three guests from the inn, and chatting to them helped
to restore her to a reasonable mood. But that was as high as
they were going and, when she transferred to the cable car to
the top and thought she would have to do the ride alone, she
felt the cloud of gloom returning. Even on a good day, no
place in the world seemed as desolate to her as a gondola
moving slowly in space high above a snow-covered mountain. But just as the car left the station, a man racked his skis
next to hers and jumped in quickly, taking the seat opposite.
He smiled. "Hello," he said.

Relieved to have his company, Katrinka smiled in return.

"You speak a hell of a lot of languages," he said, taking off
his black wool cap and running a hand through his thick
brown hair. It turned up a little at the ends, she noticed. "I
was listening to you down at the bottom of the lift," he
added, by way of explanation.

"Europeans always do speak a lot of languages," said
Katrinka.

"And Americans don't?"

"Do you?" she asked.

He laughed. "Only English," he said without the least
trace of embarrassment, without a hint that it might be
considered a failing. "Though I think it might be a good idea
to learn Japanese."

He was just over six feet, Katrinka estimated, with broad
shoulders, slender hips, and the physical assurance of an
athlete. She did not find him handsome, she thought, then
corrected herself: she did, though it was difficult at first to
pinpoint why. His brown eyes were set too close together,
his nose was too big for his long, narrow face, and, though
his teeth were not, his smile was crooked. But despite all its
imperfections, his face was appealing, his smile was wonderful, and there was about him a vitality, an aggressive
self-confidence, a suggestiveness that hinted subtly at sex, all
of which, decided Katrinka, was very attractive. "Why
Japanese?" she asked.

"Someday soon Japan is going to be the world's number one economic power."

Katrinka doubted this very much. "Bigger than the United States?"

He smiled crookedly and nodded. "Hard as that may be to believe."

"And Germany?"

"Much." She frowned, and he laughed. "You don't think I know what I'm talking about, do you?"

"You did clearly spend much time thinking about it all," she said politely.

"More than you can imagine," he said, finding both her and her accent adorable, and he spent the few remaining minutes of the ride explaining to her all the reasons why he believed as he did. Though he did not succeed in convincing her, Katrinka was suitably impressed with the extent of his knowledge and pleased that he had quickly moved the conversation beyond small talk to something of interest. He no more liked to waste time than she did.

As the gondola pulled into the station, he leaned over, opened the door, jumped out, and extended a hand to help her. Katrinka took it and could feel the strength in his arm, steadying her as she leapt out onto the platform. Quickly, they removed their skis from the rack and headed for the slope.

He pulled on his wool cap, stepped into his skis, and watched as she adjusted her equipment. God, she was gorgeous, he thought. The tight fit of her one-piece ski suit hid nothing, and he admired her long legs, narrow hips, high round ass, tiny waist, the full curve of her breasts. And her face: skin as smooth as a rose petal, eyes . . . he had never seen eyes quite that color before, so pale and brilliant a blue, like bits of colored glass, like perfect turquoise stones. When she pulled down her goggles to cover them, it was . . . well, like a cloud obscuring the sky. He laughed to himself. Waxing poetic, that was a little out of his line.

As she pulled on her mittens, she shivered slightly. "Cold?" he asked, surprised since the sun was shining and under his layers of clothing he felt quite comfortable.

"I do not wear much under my suit."

"I'll hold the thought," he said, smiling.

Though she did not quite get the idiom, she understood enough to blush and was irritated with herself. She had not blushed in years. "I do hate feeling so tied up I can't move. I'll be all right once I start to ski. See you . . . ," she said, pushing off so quickly it startled him.

"Wait . . ." he called. "Damnit," he muttered, annoyed with his stupidity. In that long gondola ride, instead of discussing economics, why had he not at least asked her name and where he could find her? He was not usually so slow to make a move. But then, he had not expected her to bolt for safety. Most girls would have waited. You're an arrogant sonovabitch, aren't you? he thought as he started off in pursuit, intending to follow her to the bottom and find out all he needed to know then.

Within minutes he knew he had no chance of doing that. He saw her confidence and speed schussing, watched the skill of her parallel turns, neat, controlled changes of position midair, and knew he would never catch her. The last he saw of her, she was sailing off the edge of the piste, over a large boulder, in a daring jump to the slope below. By the time he reached the edge and looked over, she had disappeared, down one of the mountain's three forking trails.

Instead of admiration, what he felt was annoyance, only a hint of it, but so unmistakable he could not kid himself it was anything else. He was a good skier, but she was better, much better, and while he might have accepted that with reasonable good grace in a trained athlete, a *male* athlete, it was damned irritating to be shown up by a woman of unknown credentials, and one, moreover, who had not had the good taste to wait until he had got around to asking her name and phone number.

Twenty-Two

The Schloss Grunberg was *the* place to stay in Kitzbühel. Formerly a mountain retreat of some wealthy but minor Hapsburgs, it had been sold after the First World War and converted into a hotel, which at first had catered to exactly the sort of people a Hapsburg prince might have invited home for the weekend. More recently, its guest list had been expanded to include important government figures, wealthy businessmen, and some film stars, though these were mostly European.

Set in extensive grounds ringed by a fringe of tall pines, the Schloss was a large white asymmetric structure with a gable roof and ornamental chimneys. Not particularly imposing from the outside, its interior, however, was pure baroque: coffered ceilings and painted paneled walls trimmed in gilt, porcelain stoves, Aubusson carpets, crystal chandeliers. The dining room was decorated with an eighteenth-century mural depicting an elegant party picnicking by a lake, its vignettes using food as a unifying device: a young woman offering an apple to her lover, a boy teasing a dog with a bone, a girl with bonnet askew, pink ribbons streaming in the wind, chased by two enraged siblings (judging from the similarity of their features) as she makes off with a bowl of cherries. Even midwinter, the mural, combined with the extensive use of potted plants, gave guests the effect of dining alfresco on a pleasant day in early June.

"It's charming, this room," said Natalie, whose eyes sparkled with the anticipation of coming combat. She had dressed carefully for the event in an Yves St. Laurent dress that did not so much flatter her as proclaim her importance. It was very new and very expensive.

"We have been sitting here for fifteen minutes," said Katrinka, who was in a much less expensive but stylish peasant-style dinner dress in embroidered ivory silk crepe de chine, "and no one has come near us to take our order."

Natalie, who could have picked out a faulty stitch in a couture gown at five hundred paces, was much less interested in service than Katrinka, whose business it was to care. She shrugged and said, "We're in no hurry."

"That's not the point." Katrinka looked around for a waiter, caught the eye of the maître d' and signaled him over. "We would like to order," she said firmly, in German.

The man gave a stiff bow, a mere jerk of the neck, and said, "Certainly, *Fräulein*. I'll send your waiter immediately."

As he walked away, Katrinka sniffed in disapproval. "We may not be as important or as rich as the guests at this hotel, but if we do pay the same price for dinner, I think we deserve the same service."

Natalie laughed. "Maybe we should suggest a discount instead?"

"A brilliant idea," said Katrinka. "What you say? Ten percent off for lousy service, twenty for terrible, thirty for the worst?"

The sommelier approached, interrupting their laughter. They ordered, in honor of the upcoming event, a Chassagne-Montrachet, though not a Château Gillette, which was not on the menu. "Jean-Claude spends enough money here," murmured Natalie when the sommelier had left. "They could at least lay in a supply of his wines."

"Whose fault, do you think?" said Katrinka, whose interest in business had grown steadily since her purchase of the inn. Someone in the Gillette corporation had clearly not done his job. "But Jean-Claude must read the wine list. He must know. I wonder why he doesn't do something about it?"

Natalie shrugged, but whatever insight she was about to provide was prevented by the waiter who had at last arrived to take their order and, by the time he had gone, something else had captured her attention. "Look," she said. "Look who's just come in." She had taken the seat that faced the entrance to the dining room.

Katrinka did not turn her head for fear of being obvious. "Jean-Claude?" she asked.

"No. It's Sabrina."

"Who?" It was a name Katrinka did not recognize.

"She's a columnist for *The Globe,* a London paper. Last summer she was in Paris for the couture collections. *Oh la la,* what she did to St. Laurent. Devastating, absolutely devastating. And his show was brilliant, really. Ahead of its time. Of course, Sabrina was not the only one," added Natalie, "but she was the worst."

Unable to resist, Katrinka turned her head and searched the room for this elegant arbiter of good taste. "Where?"

"There, moving past the woman with the apple," said Natalie, indicating the mural she meant with a barely perceptible movement of her head. "The one who looks like a sick mouse."

"She writes about fashion?" Katrinka had rarely felt so shocked. The woman's upswept hair was falling out of its clips in dull, lifeless strands, her makeup looked smudged, and, in a year when waistlines were definitely in, she was wearing a full, gathered blouse over a long straight skirt in what looked like a very cheap silk. "What is that thing she is wearing?"

"With Sabrina it is always difficult to tell."

Sabrina was with her husband, a slight, pale man, the sort who was never noticed. They were with a party of people Natalie did not recognize, though she assumed (from the appalling way they were dressed, she said) that they were English. But it was the group entering behind Sabrina that caught and held Katrinka's attention. Waiting for the maître d' to seat them, they stood in a loose circle, chatting together easily like people well known to each other. There were three couples: a beautiful petite brunette with wings of silver hair framing exquisitely chiseled features, accompanied by a tall, elegant man; a pretty young woman with short-cropped brown hair, very pregnant, holding hands with a man who had the rugged good looks of a Viking adventurer; and a gorgeous redhead with masses of thick, long hair and skin as fine as porcelain, escorted by the man Katrinka had met on the gondola that morning.

Afraid to be caught looking at him, she turned quickly back to Natalie. "The people behind Sabrina," she said, "you do know them?"

Natalie surveyed the group a moment, then turned her attention back to Katrinka. *"Le blond est américain,"* she said. "Mark van Hollen. He owns newspapers. He's gorgeous, yes? And very much in love with his wife, they say. Faithful, too, if you can believe such a thing."

"And the dark one, with the wavy hair?"

The group apparently was not dining together. When the maître d' returned, he escorted only the man from the gondola and his redhead to their table, while Mark van Hollen and the others awaited their turn.

Natalie studied the couple with narrowed eyes for a moment, then looked away, shaking her head. "No. Him I don't know, I'm sorry to say. He is quite something."

"You think he's handsome?" said Katrinka, who was not sure she did.

"Not pretty like an Alain Delon or Marcello Mastroianni, but handsome, yes. Very sexy." She turned for another quick glance. "Look at that mouth," she said.

Katrinka was trying not to look at him at all. But then, to her dismay, the maître d' seated him facing her, several tables away, but directly in her line of vision. *"Do prdele!"* she muttered.

Having learned enough Czech from Katrinka to know when she was swearing, Natalie looked at her and said, "What's wrong?" Katrinka told her, and Natalie smiled. "You discussed business?"

"It was interesting," said Katrinka defensively. "More interesting than flirting."

"Since when have you anything against flirting?"

"I don't. It can be amusing. But it is certainly not original."

252

"Ah, yes," said Natalie, "economics as a sexual ploy. Most original. You liked him."

Katrinka shrugged. "He's not available." The redhead was very beautiful, thought Katrinka. No wonder he had talked economics and not bothered to flirt. But he had flirted, she contradicted herself a moment later. He had just done it in a much less obvious way than she was used to.

"Was he wearing a wedding ring?"

"No, but that means nothing," said Katrinka. "Anyway, what it does matter? *I'm* not available."

Natalie was tempted to contradict this, but decided to hold her tongue. People never reacted well when you pointed out to them that their relationships were dead and rigor mortis about to set in. They much preferred to believe that some extraordinary lifesaving measures might yet intervene to revive them. Like herself, she admitted in a rare moment of honesty, preferring to believe that something might come of her affair with Jean-Claude. Was it because solitude was so much more terrifying than unhappiness? she wondered. Familiarity so much less threatening than change? Even Katrinka, who was by far the most courageous person Natalie knew, was unwilling to pronounce her relationship with Franta over, though everyone, even Franta, knew it was. "If you ask me," she said, ignoring Katrinka's preceding remark, "it was fate your running into him again tonight."

"Fate?" said Katrinka, giving a slight ladylike snort of derision. "In a place the size of Kitzbühel, how was I supposed to avoid meeting him again?" But still she would have preferred him to be alone, or at least not so obviously attached to a woman of such stunning good looks. Katrinka felt a slight tug of disappointment, then pushed it away as disloyal to Franta who, she remembered with a twinge of guilt, was lying in a hospital bed in Munich and, if not quite alone, still no doubt miserable and lonely.

The sommelier returned with the Chassagne-Montrachet, which Natalie pronounced acceptable, followed quickly by the waiter with their first course, a salad for Katrinka and salmon quenelles for Natalie, who was always hungry when

253

she had her period. They had just finished their main course and the busboy was clearing the flower-patterned Meissen china when Jean-Claude at last entered the dining room accompanied by his wife, Hélène, and three other couples.

Hélène was a small woman, dressed in what Natalie recognized instantly as an Ungaro. She had a large nose, skin concealed by dramatic makeup, and dark sloe eyes outlined heavily in black. Jean-Claude was just under six feet, slender, with perfect, almost delicate features, eyes like black onyx, a high brow, and dark hair which he wore longer than was fashionable. He was elegant and charming and irresistible to women.

"Jean-Claude's just come in," said Natalie, her gaze carefully averted from the progress of his party across the floor to its table. "Don't look," she hissed.

"I won't. Are they alone?"

"Of course not," sneered Natalie. "He'd die of boredom if he had to dine alone with Hélène. They're with the Agnellis and some other people." She looked up as she said that, her gaze met Jean-Claude's, and she smiled sweetly. If he was angry, he didn't let it show. He nodded in her direction. He even smiled politely, an acknowledgment of the presence in the restaurant of an employee, not a lover. It was hard to say who was fooled by the performance. Not his wife, certainly. Not Sabrina, who watched it with malicious enjoyment. She had observed their affair for some years and had even referred to it in her column, though obliquely enough not to cause Jean-Claude any distress. Natalie had been delighted with the publicity, though she had pretended otherwise. It annoyed her when Hélène got all the notice.

"Bâtard," she muttered, her eyes filling with tears.

"You want to leave?" asked Katrinka.

Natalie shook her head. "It would be too obvious."

"If you mind so much, why don't you end it?"

Natalie looked at her as if she were mad. "I love him," she said.

They ordered dessert, put on a good show of animated chatter while awaiting it, adequately concealing their discomfort at being in a room where both, for separate reasons, were afraid to let their eyes stray for fear of encountering an awkward, disconcerting glance. When the waiter finally arrived with the desserts, he was accompanied by a busboy with two crystal flutes and the sommelier bearing a bottle of Louis Roederer Cristal, which he presented to Katrinka.

"We did not order champagne," said Katrinka firmly, not prepared to let herself be coaxed into something she did not want.

"A gift, *Fräulein*," said the sommelier, handing her a note.

"Who sent it?" asked Natalie as the steward opened the bottle and poured them each a glass.

Katrinka tore open the envelope and scanned the card. It said, "You should not have run away," and was signed "Adam Graham." "The man from the gondola," she explained, handing Natalie the note, which was not a discreet or sophisticated thing to do, but she was not thinking clearly. She felt both pleased and annoyed, flattered at the attention and irritated (though not really surprised) that a man should treat a woman accompanying him with such flamboyant disregard. The redhead, she noticed, was not at the table, gone to the powder room, most likely. Had he planned even that with the sommelier? she wondered. "He has nerve," she said to Natalie, her annoyance finally defeating any pleasure she had taken in the gesture. She would hate to be treated like that.

"Very daring," agreed Natalie with admiration, if not quite approval. Not only did Natalie have a much more primitive sense of right and wrong than Katrinka, but she enjoyed the cut and thrust of complicated love affairs, except of course when the blows struck beneath her guard. She looked up from the note to Katrinka's disapproving face and said, "Smile, *chérie*."

"That poor girl," said Katrinka.

"*Ouff*," said Natalie with supreme Gallic indifference. "For all you know she's his sister." Picking up a champagne flute, she turned in her seat, smiled at Adam, and took a small sip of champagne.

From where she was sitting, Katrinka could see Jean-Claude observing the proceedings with great interest and a small frown etched into his brow. "Natalie, you make a spectacle of yourself," she said warningly.

"Not at all." Natalie faced Katrinka again, took another larger swallow of champagne and put the glass down. "I am being polite. You, on the other hand, are being a prude."

"Jean-Claude thinks you're flirting with him."

"With Adam Graham? *Vraiment?*" Natalie smiled, brilliantly this time, her pleasure unbounded. "How wonderful. Maybe he thinks this mysterious Mr. Graham sent *me* the champagne." Mischief crept into her smile. "If Jean-Claude asks, you mustn't say," she instructed Katrinka.

"And that Sabrina can't take her eyes off you."

"Better and better," said Natalie. She laughed. "Who would have thought the evening would turn out so well?"

Looking around, Katrinka noticed that the two couples who had entered the dining room with Adam Graham were also looking in their direction. Her eyes met those of the Viking, Mark van Hollen, and for the second time that day, she felt herself blush. It was all so embarrassing. "Finish your dessert," she said to Natalie as she signaled for the check. She tried to avoid looking at Adam Graham, but it was impossible. His stare was like the annoying buzz of a mosquito, constantly drawing her attention. Finally, she gave in and nodded coolly in his direction, hoping that brief acknowledgment of his existence, that slight gesture of thanks, would satisfy him.

It didn't. What the hell is the matter with her? he wondered, not understanding in the least why she looked as if she had just been insulted instead of sent a bottle of 1969 Cristal. He was tempted to go to her table to ask just what he had done to annoy her so badly when Alexandra returned from the powder room.

Politely, he stood while she seated herself, but she noted again that his attention was clearly focused elsewhere, as it had been since they had sat down to eat. "Adam, is something bothering you?" she asked.

"No. Why?" he asked.

"You've been preoccupied all evening."

"Sorry," he said, returning his attention to her. "My mind's still on business." He had known her for as long as he could remember, had taken her out off and on over the years, and even slept with her when, like now, he was not seriously involved elsewhere. But, though he had duly noted her blossoming into a beauty somewhere along the way, she was too familiar to him to inspire more than affection, and his passion, when roused, had less to do with her than a general need to get laid.

Alexandra, on the other hand, had believed herself in love with Adam from the age of six. And, after years of accepting humbly the casual and sporadic relationship that he offered her, she was determined that this time he would not get away from her as he had so often in the past. She was twenty-nine years old, Adam thirty-two. In her opinion, it was time for them both to settle down. She smiled reassuringly. "You're not worried?" she said. "I don't believe it. You know you always get what you want."

Adam's gaze strayed again to Katrinka, who was settling the bill, quickly and efficiently he noted, without a lot of puzzled study or confused conversation with her friend. "Do I?" he said.

"Always," repeated Alexandra, knowing she had said exactly the right thing to please him.

Twenty-Three

The following morning Katrinka skied the Ehrenbach and the Hahnenkamm, down the latter's Streif run from which, to her annoyance, women were banned from racing. Equally to her annoyance, she found herself looking for Adam Graham on the ski lines and the lifts, and was disappointed when she failed to catch sight of him either there or on the piste. She would have liked, overnight, to have forgotten all about him and his crooked smile and the bottle of champagne which at one moment she saw only as a gesture of gallantry, and at another as one of betrayal. Images of both Franta and the redhead superimposed themselves over the memory of Adam Graham's long, attractive face. Their conversation of the preceding day replayed itself in her mind, as did the scene in the restaurant. When she and Natalie were leaving, she had allowed herself one quick glance in his direction. How mystified he had seemed by her behavior, how disappointed, how totally uninterested in the woman with him.

That Adam Graham had made such a successful invasion of her thoughts surprised Katrinka. She was a beautiful woman, used to being pursued by men, and, though on a superficial level she found their interest flattering and enjoyable, it rarely caused havoc in her mind. She brushed their attentions off, until—like Mirek Bartoš or Franta Dohnal—they proved themselves serious.

Adam Graham did not seem at all a serious person to her, at least not about women. And while she was willing to admit that a little flirting on a ski lift and a single bottle of champagne did not make a Don Juan, she nevertheless, in view of the redhead, found it difficult to consider him trustworthy. She wanted to stop thinking about him, but could not. She wanted not to want to see him again, but clearly did. She wanted not to search the crowd for the sight of his athletic body and thick curly hair, but kept looking. She felt a little ashamed of herself for behaving like a schoolgirl and was suddenly anxious to leave Kitzbühel so that she could put the whole episode behind her. Once back in Munich, with Franta, she was certain that Adam Graham would retreat quickly to the safe distance of an amusing memory.

On her way to the last run of the day, Katrinka found herself sharing a lift with the man she called the Viking. Newspapers, she thought, prodding her memory for what Natalie had told her about him. Happily married. Mark van something or other. Her thoughts preoccupied by another man, she had paid little attention to Natalie's capsule biography.

He was much handsomer than Adam Graham, Katrinka thought, too handsome. His hair was the color of corn silk, as were his brows and lashes, his eyes the color of slate. He looked like an aristocrat, the rugged intelligent sort who turned adventurer. All he was missing was the bushy beard. It was difficult to imagine him confined in an office, running a newspaper empire.

When he said hello to her it was, to her surprise, in German, and in German she replied.

"You have a Czech accent," he said after he heard her speak. His manner was friendly, curious, but not in the least flirtatious.

"You have a very good ear."

He laughed. "For an American?"

"Are you American?"

"So," he teased, "your ear isn't as good as mine."

"You speak German very well."

"My parents were Dutch," he said. "I spoke it as a child. When you speak two languages, why not three?"

"Why not?" said Katrinka in English, showing off a little.

When they reached the top, they stood for a moment discussing the various descents while they adjusted their goggles and gloves and ski poles. They had decided on different trails, and Mark pushed off first. *"Dobrý den,"* he called in Czech, lifting his ski pole a moment in a polite farewell gesture.

Surprised, Katrinka laughed, and he turned around at the sound, obviously pleased with the reaction. *"Dobrý den,"* she called after him. A nice man, she thought, remembering him as she had first seen him, hand in hand with his pretty, pregnant wife. What a lucky woman, she thought, with a sudden surge of longing, to have a husband like him. A husband and a child.

On her return to the Golden Horn, Katrinka entered as usual by the back door and went immediately to her room to change. She was pinning her long dark hair up into a twist when Natalie knocked on the door. "Come in," she called, her mouth full of pins.

Natalie entered, a glass of wine in her hand, a smile on her face. She was wearing a cashmere jumpsuit in a shade of emerald green that complemented her eyes, made her skin glow, and brought out the gold in her hair. *"Bonjour, chérie,"* she said, her voice lilting and happy.

"What you have been up to?" said Katrinka, curious.

"Jean-Claude came by this morning." Natalie sprawled comfortably in Katrinka's armchair. "We had an awful fight."

"He was angry because we had dinner at the Schloss."

"Furious," agreed Natalie.

"Well, what you did expect?"

"I wanted to see him, and I got what I wanted," said Natalie with no guilt at all. "Do you think if I had behaved myself he would have come by this morning?"

"You should go back to Paris," said Katrinka.

"I should. But?" she shrugged. "My cramps are completely gone. I think I'll ski this afternoon."

"Of course. It is the deep powder snow that keeps you here." Katrinka put the last pin in her hair, smoothed a few stray strands into place, picked up her lipstick and began coloring her lips.

"You have a wonderful mouth," said Natalie dispassionately, assessing Katrinka's looks as coolly as she might a model's before a fashion show. "Very sexy."

"Thank you."

"He *was* jealous," continued Natalie, returning to her primary subject.

"Jean-Claude?"

"Certainly Jean-Claude. Of that American you met yesterday."

"He did believe you were sent the champagne?"

"Exactement. Apparently, the American is rich, not *very* rich—yet—but not to be dismissed. He's up to some very clever things, I think. I said I had found him charming. You did, didn't you?"

"Yes," said Katrinka reluctantly, refusing to elaborate.

"So, we fought, and then we reconciled. We did not make love, of course," she said, a note of disgust in her voice. "But," she added cheerfully, "he is taking me with him to New York next week."

It seemed a terrible kind of life to Katrinka, much worse than anything she had experienced with Mirek Bartoš. With Mirek, until the end, it had been possible to forget he was married, since he and his wife had led such separate lives. There had been little about their affair that was clandestine, or humiliating, both of which Natalie's relationship with Jean-Claude too often was. But Natalie, in a perverse sort of way, did not mind. In fact, she seemed to enjoy it—the secrecy, the scenes, the drama of threatened rupture and ecstatic reconciliation.

"New York," said Katrinka, trying to sound pleased for Natalie. "I would love to see New York."

"It is not the best time of year to go," said Natalie, shrugging, "but then, beggars cannot be choosers."

Exactly, thought Katrinka once her limited English had caught up with the meaning of the proverb. How she would hate to be a beggar.

* * *

Jean-Claude returned to the inn later that afternoon for tea, stopping off after his last run before returning to the Schloss. Racking his skis outside, he unzipped his down parka as he entered the lobby, went into the lounge to find Natalie, who had already returned from her brief foray to the slopes, and escorted her to the dining room. He looked flushed and exuberant, his eyes, normally dark and opaque, alight with satisfaction. His hair was damp from snow and with one hand he smoothed it straight back from his high forehead. When he saw Katrinka, he smiled. He's a rogue, she thought, but a charming one. She really could not help liking him. He kissed her on both cheeks, then put an arm familiarly around her shoulder. "A table for two," he said, "unless you would like to join us?" The question was neither casual nor friendly, but loaded with suggestion. Jean-Claude was a terrible flirt. No, more than a flirt. He was quite serious about his intentions. He would like to go to bed with her and made that plain one way or another whenever they met. The fact that Natalie was her good friend made no difference to him at all.

"I can't possibly, Jean-Claude. I'm working," said Katrinka with a polite smile. "But thank you."

"Another time," he said, not in the least daunted by her cool tone.

"Katrinka never has free time. She works harder than anyone I have ever known," said Natalie, who rather liked Jean-Claude to pursue other women, even her friends, since it made him seem even more unpredictable, dangerous, and exciting. Had Katrinka responded, however, that would have been another story. Natalie would have felt outraged, betrayed. The offense would have been unforgivable.

"You should come and work for me," said Jean-Claude to Katrinka as she led them to their table. "I'll make you rich."

"Ha!" said Natalie.

"What?"

"You haven't made me rich," said Natalie in French.

"If I made you rich," said Jean-Claude, also in French, "how would I ever control you?"

Katrinka returned to the entrance and stood surveying the

room with a feeling of intense satisfaction. Saturdays were usually the best days, but even this late on a Sunday afternoon it was almost full. She had considered for a while just serving drinks, but had ultimately decided that, with so many places already catering to the boozy crowd, it made more sense to be innovative. Her instinct had been correct, because afternoon tea at the Golden Horn Gasthof had become an instant Kitzbühel success, attracting even those who might actually prefer to drink, though never at the cost of being thought unfashionable.

Most of her own guests had stopped in, but the majority were from other hotels in the area who wanted a change from afternoon cocktails. There were a large number of children and, among them, Katrinka spotted the three she had noticed on the Hornbahn line the previous morning. Only one of the couples was present. The man was rather distinguished looking, admitted Katrinka grudgingly, and the woman attractive in a cool, stylish way. The children ate their tea without speaking. No one seemed to be having much fun. Frowning, Katrinka turned away from the memory of Klaus Zimmerman and immediately saw another couple she recognized, a brunette with wings of silver hair and her elegant husband. They had been talking to Adam Graham at the Schloss the night before. As she continued to seat new arrivals, supply fresh cream and new pots of jam, check bills and make change, Katrinka's eyes returned to them again and again: anyone who knew Adam Graham seemed suddenly to be of particular interest to her.

Their clothes were quiet but obviously expensive. Their manner was assured but not demanding, confident though not in the least arrogant, as if always getting exactly what they wanted without any noticeable difficulty had made them humble in the face of their good and others' bad fortune. They were about forty, Katrinka estimated, older than the van Hollens or Adam Graham and his redheaded friend, but like them indisputably American: healthy without being robust, athletic but slender, sleek, coiffed, and manicured.

When Hilde brought her their bill, covered with a pile of

colorful Austrian marks, Katrinka made the necessary change and took it herself to their table.

"Now I know where I've seen you," said the woman, breaking into a smile. Someone more familiar with American regional accents than Katrinka would have spotted a hint of New England in her speech. "You had dinner last night at the Schloss."

She had remembered the scene with the champagne, thought Katrinka, otherwise she would never have made the connection. "Yes. I do think the food there is very good."

"Excellent," said the man, bestowing a cautious but appreciative smile on Katrinka. She was wearing a long-sleeved white blouse with a ruffled neckline, a peasant skirt, a wide belt, and soft suede boots, a simple outfit but one that flattered her, emphasizing her height and flattering her figure.

"Adam Graham sent champagne to your table," said the woman, somehow managing to make this sound not nosy, but simply factual.

"We met yesterday on the Hahnenkamm," said Katrinka as if that explained everything.

Trust Adam, thought the man, not to let a good thing escape him.

"You work here?"

Katrinka smiled. "Actually, I do own it," she said.

"Why, how wonderful," said the woman, sounding truly pleased by the information. "It's a delightful place. And this tea! I can't tell you how much I enjoyed those scones. And the jam. Homemade, isn't it?"

"Yes," said Katrinka, debating whether or not to confide that she had made both the scones and the jam.

"It tastes just like my grandmother's."

"And mine," said Katrinka, deciding it was good business to sound domestic, even if she preferred for some reason that this woman think of her as elegant and sophisticated, a successful model, a *hôtelier*.

The woman laughed. "Don't tell me you made it?" and when Katrinka nodded, held out her hand and said, "I'm Daisy Elliott, by the way. And my husband, Steven."

"Katrinka Kovář," she said as she shook their hands.

"You must have dinner with us one night," said Daisy.

"That is kind of you, but I return to Munich tonight. I do hope to see you here again some time," she said as she turned to leave.

"I'm sure you will," said Steven politely.

As she walked away, Katrinka heard Daisy say, "We must buy some jam before we leave. The children will love it."

"The children," said Steven, "are all at school."

"For breakfast, when they visit. It really is lovely."

"What on earth did you mean," he said, as soon as Katrinka was out of earshot, "inviting her to dinner?"

"You're such a snob."

"I am nothing of the kind. I just hate being bored by strangers."

"It's so much more pleasant, I suppose, to be bored by people one has known all one's life?"

"At least then one knows how to take preventive action."

"She's lovely. And clever." Steven's look demanded that his wife prove her point. "Well, just look at this place." He looked around and grudgingly admitted that it was indeed attractive, comfortable, and well run, but he still did not see why that meant he should be forced to have dinner with the woman who owned it. "Steven, darling, do admit you thought she was gorgeous."

"Stunning," agreed Steven.

"You were practically drooling."

Steven Elliott was far from a snob. He was just a cautious man who preferred sticking to known quantities. Though he often admired his wife's propensity to dive off the deep end into friendships and sometimes wished he could follow her with equal abandon, some inherent restraint, perhaps some gene passed down through generations of proper Bostonians, kept him from it. "One can admire," said Steven, "without wanting a closer association."

Daisy, who came from an even more proper background, seemed to have missed out on that gene completely. "That's just it," she said, "I can't."

* * *

Tea was over and Katrinka back in her room resting before leaving for Munich when one of the maids knocked at her door and told her someone was asking to see her.

"Who?" asked Katrinka. "A guest? Not a complaint, I hope." She felt tired and not in the mood to smooth ruffled feathers.

"No, *Fräulein*. I've never seen him before. He's waiting in your office."

Reluctantly, Katrinka got up from the bed. "Next time, you should remember to ask the name."

"Yes, *Fräulein*," said the girl as she turned to leave. "Sorry." She was only seventeen and had been working at the inn for just a few weeks.

Katrinka smiled. "Tell him I'll be right down."

Though afterward it seemed perfectly obvious, at the time it was not Adam Graham she expected to find waiting for her in her office. In fact, Katrinka was so surprised when she entered and saw him sitting in the armchair near the desk that it was all she could do not to let her mouth drop open and exclaim, You! in high melodramatic fashion.

"Hello, Miss Kovář," he said. He was still in his ski pants and parka, both obviously expensive though worn from years of use, rather than ostentatiously new like most Americans' gear. They suited him, giving him a substantial, aristocratic quality, like the Elliotts'.

"It's pronounced Ko-vash," she corrected. Then she smiled. "Hello, Mr. Graham," she said.

"Adam."

"Katrinka. Would you like something to drink?" she asked and when he declined, sat, though she knew it was an unfriendly thing to do, behind her desk.

Adam settled himself again in the armchair. "The Elliotts told me where to find you, in case you're wondering."

Katrinka frowned. However nice her manners, that Daisy Elliott was an incredible busybody. "Yes?" she said as if surprised he should be interested.

"They also said you're heading back to Munich tonight."

She nodded. "In a little while. I have some business to take care of before I leave."

"Would you consider having dinner with me first?"

"What?"

"After you finish your work, I mean." He was smiling as if he had not just made an outrageous request, as if there was no redhead waiting for him back at the Schloss. It was a wide, innocent smile, full of charm and earnest entreaty.

"And your friend?" said Katrinka, trying not to sound disapproving, though she was, very.

"Friend?"

"The one with the red hair."

"Oh, Alexandra?" He had not really given that problem much thought, he had set out so quickly to track down Katrinka. "She won't mind."

"No?"

"She's used to me. I often have business meetings I can't get out of."

"How lucky for you. And sad for her."

"No," he said, realizing he was giving an extremely bad impression. "Real business meetings. I'm a genuinely busy man."

"I'm sorry," said Katrinka, "but I really can't tonight."

"She and I are just friends, you know, if that's what's bothering you. We've known each other since we were children."

Katrinka was tempted to point out that knowing someone for a long time was no reason to treat them rudely, but she only said, "My boyfriend is expecting me."

Adam was shocked, though of course it was only to be expected that someone as beautiful as Katrinka Kovash should have a boyfriend. But seeing her alone had convinced him, because he wanted it that way, that she was, so to speak, between engagements. "You could call him," suggested Adam. "Tell him you'll be late."

"I could," said Katrinka, smiling demurely. "But you understand after being away from him for a few days how anxious I am to see him." That will show the bastard, she thought.

Again Adam felt that slight sense of irritation this woman always seemed to arouse in him. What the hell was he doing here, anyway, he asked himself, begging, when he had Alexandra waiting? "Another time," he said as nonchalantly as he could manage, hoping as he stood up to leave that the poker face which served him so well in business had not failed him.

"You'll be returning to Kitzbühel?" asked Katrinka before she could stop herself.

"You never know," he replied, managing not to smile at the first chink in her armor that he had found.

She got up from her chair and joined him on the other side of the desk. "Well, perhaps the next time you're here, the four of us could have dinner," she said, pleased with herself for making such a quick recovery.

He laughed and said, "Stranger things have happened." He held out his hand and she took it, returning his handshake firmly. She's a strong woman, he thought, with some disapproval. But then his eyes strayed briefly to the thighs concealed by the soft fabric of her skirt and he remembered how firm and muscled they had looked in her ski pants. He wondered what it would feel like to have them wrapped around his waist. He looked up and met her eyes. "I'll be seeing you," he said.

"Auf Wiedersehen," she replied, but, as he walked out and closed the door firmly behind him, she was filled with immediate regret. Despite Franta and the redhead, she had wanted to have dinner with him. It was totally crazy, but she did. Returning to her chair, she sat down and from the desk drawer removed the ledger she had to complete before leaving. She had behaved exactly right, she told herself, as she opened it to the correct page and began entering the weekend's receipts from the list Bruno had put on her desk. Exactly right, she repeated, though her assurance did nothing to ease her regret.

Twenty-Four

*M*iss Ko-*vash?*"

For a moment, Katrinka thought she was hallucinating. What would Adam Graham be doing in Schwabing, or, to be more precise, on the exact street in Schwabing where she lived? Her hand still on the key in the lock of the building's front door, she turned. "Yes?"

But there he was, looking handsome and prosperous in a navy cashmere coat, his thick dark hair curling uncontrollably at the ends, his crooked smile warm and engaging. "Miss Ko-vash, would you like to have dinner tonight?" He was carrying a bottle of Veuve Clicquot and a large bouquet of pink roses.

"How you did find me?" she asked, grammar forgotten, as it often was when she was excited or surprised.

"Easy." He had phoned the Golden Horn and Hilde had given him Katrinka's address and phone number in Munich. When he had called her apartment that morning her cleaning lady had told him what time Katrinka was expected home. He looked very pleased with himself. "Don't you think my ingenuity should be rewarded?" he asked, adding as Katrinka hesitated, "I'm alone in Munich. You could save me from a very lonely dinner. I hate eating on my own, don't you?"

"No Alexandra?"

"No Alexandra."

There was no Franta anymore either, at least not in the same way as before, but Katrinka did not think it necessary

269

to mention that just yet. "I would love to have dinner," she said.

Unlocking the front door, she invited him in and led him up the three flights of stairs to her small apartment. She thought occasionally about moving to somewhere bigger, but when she had spent so much time at Franta's it had seemed foolish, and, even now, though both the Golden Horn and her modeling career were doing well, she still was hesitant to spend the extra money on rent when the lounge at the inn needed redecorating and the dining room could use a new set of china.

"Very cozy," said Adam as Katrinka turned on the light and invited him in.

"Tiny."

"But very nice."

Adam meant it, too. Most women, in his opinion, decorated in a fussy, cluttered way as if determined to make men feel uncomfortable. That was certainly the style of his family's home in Newport, which was crammed full of heirlooms collected over generations of cautious but luxurious living. Not a surface was free of some memento of the past, every wall hung with paintings acquired by some astute ancestor. Despite the size of the house, twenty-two principal rooms plus servants' quarters and carriage house, Adam frequently felt claustrophobic there.

In contrast, Katrinka's small apartment was airy and spacious, with light-colored walls, a Biedermeier sofa and armchair, a few other well-chosen antique pieces, some photographs on side tables, and an eclectic array of art, from small pencil sketches to watercolor drawings to a large silk screen print over the mantel. Though a far cry from his own stark apartment in Manhattan, it was both simple and appealing.

Katrinka brought out two crystal flutes and, while she went to put the roses in water, he opened the champagne and poured them each a glass, handing her one when she returned. "To us," he said.

Her cheeks, to her annoyance, were instantly flooded with pink. To hide her embarrassment, she laughed. "You go very fast."

"Fast? It's been over two months since we met."

"This is our first . . . ." she hesitated, then said, since no other neutral word came to mind, "dinner."

"And whose fault is that?"

"It's not a question of fault," she said, taking a sip of champagne, wondering if sufficient time had passed for her not to be considered as endorsing the toast. She did not want him to think that her agreeing to dinner was a blank check for anything else he might have in mind.

"Hurry and change," he said. "I've made a reservation at Aubergine for eight-thirty." It was arguably the best and most expensive restaurant not only in Munich, but in West Germany; its chef had studied with Paul Bocuse in Lyon and Katrinka had been wanting to dine there for years. Nevertheless, she hesitated: she hated being taken for granted. Adam noticed and said placatingly, "I was prepared to go alone if you'd said no. More than eating by myself, I hate mediocre food." It was another reaction to his mother, who considered making a fuss over food to be vulgar and had never employed more than just adequate cooks, a perverse streak of New England puritanism.

Katrinka wore her best dinner suit, a Chanel she had bought a few weeks before, with a fluttery pleated skirt and a coral crepe de chine jacket over a tank top in beige and gold lurex. Even at cost it had been a considerable extravagance, but when she saw the appreciative look on Adam's face any regrets Katrinka might have had about splurging fled. Around her neck she wore a rope of good-quality imitation pearls, and in her ears pearl drops.

"Beautiful," he murmured as he helped her into her coat, which was an attractive but far from warm black wool she had had for years. His breath on the back of her neck when he spoke made her shiver. "Are you cold? Don't you have anything warmer to wear?"

"This is fine," she said. Her only other coat was the heavy tweed she wore to work.

"I have a car waiting outside."

They drove to the restaurant in his hired black Mercedes sedan, driven by a uniformed chauffeur. It was a new

experience for Katrinka and she liked it, perhaps the
convenience more than anything, the car waiting at the
curb, the driver moving quickly to open the door, no waiting
for taxis, or walking to the U-bahn, shivering in the cold,
getting drenched by the rain.

Aubergine's maître d' seemed to know Adam, greeting
him with an expansive smile that included Katrinka, escort-
ing them to a table that Adam decreed perfect. He recommended the venison with berries, and, though Adam looked
uncertain, Katrinka thought it sounded wonderful and they
ordered it.

"Americans are . . ." She searched for the word. "Cautious eaters," she said finally.

"I had the sole last time," said Adam, a bit defensively.
"It was superb."

"I do believe everything here is wonderful."

Everything was, including the service. Katrinka wondered if Adam was an enormous tipper and looked to see if
others were receiving the same kind of attention. To her
trained eye, it looked as if they were.

The meal, starting with an appetizer and with sorbets
between courses, was long and leisurely. They had time to
tell each other the edited stories of their lives. Katrinka told
Adam about her childhood in Czechoslovakia, her training
as a skier, her early career racing, about her first love—
though of course she did not mention her child—the death
of her parents and grandparents, her decision to leave.

"You escaped on skis?" asked Adam, astonished and
impressed.

"I was terrified," said Katrinka, nodding.

"I'm not surprised."

She told him how Franta had come to Zermatt to get her
and brought her to a friend in Munich.

"He was the boyfriend you were having dinner with that
night?" Katrinka nodded again. "And now?"

"It's over." Her immediate sexual response to Adam had
reminded Katrinka of what her relationship with Franta had
always lacked—passion. If she had needed convincing that
they were at a dead end, that was it. Still, she had waited to
tell him that their affair was over until he was out of the

hospital and making plans to race again. Franta had not been surprised. For months, even before the accident, he had sensed her withdrawing from him.

"What if I said I would give up racing?" he had asked, though he was far from sure he was prepared to go that far.

"Do you want to?" Franta hadn't answered for a minute, and finally Katrinka had said, "I think it's too late. No matter what either of us do to try and patch things up, it's too late."

"We're still friends," Katrinka told Adam.

"Like Alexandra and me." It seemed to him as good a time as any to get that issue resolved.

They had known each other from childhood, Adam explained. Alexandra's parents were not close friends of the Grahams, but they knew enough of the same people, even claimed some family in common, to ensure their appearance at many of the same weddings, funerals, and assorted parties. One of Adam's cousins was the same age as Alexandra, and when the two attended Miss Porter's together . . .

"Miss Porter's?" asked Katrinka.

"A school for girls, young women, in Connecticut," explained Adam impatiently. Miss Porter's seemed to him to be irrelevant. But to Katrinka, who had a great desire to know everything, it was another bit of information to add to her rapidly expanding collection.

"It is a good school?"

"Excellent. My sister went there. And my mother."

Aware of Adam's impatience, and having learned all she needed to for the moment, Katrinka settled back demurely to listen.

"Anyway," continued Adam, "there was a time when Alexandra always seemed to be at the house. One night a crowd of us were going off to a party and I asked her to be my date." She had been fifteen then and he had noticed she was suddenly beautiful. For the rest of the summer, he had been wildly, possessively in love with her, but in the autumn when he returned to MIT there had been other beautiful women, who had had the added attraction of being willing to sleep with him. Three or four years later, he and Alexandra had made love, but it had been—for him at any

273

rate—a surprisingly tepid encounter. It was as if what passion he was capable of feeling for her had spent itself the summer she was fifteen while he sat alone in his bathroom masturbating. "We've dated on and off since then," he told Katrinka, "whenever we're between romances. We like each other. We enjoy each other's company. We keep each other from getting lonely."

Several months before, Adam had considered asking Alexandra to marry him. She was, he thought, exactly the sort of wife he ought to have: beautiful, intelligent, from a good family—though one without much money. With her background (her family, her upbringing, her art history major), she would create, he was sure, a showplace home. He was equally sure that she would be a gracious hostess, an excellent mother, and, if his luck held—and here he had some doubts—as undemanding (or as easily deceived) a wife as she had been a girlfriend. His parents would have been all for the marriage, since they liked Alexandra and had recently made it clear that they thought it time he settled down, if only to put a stop to the reputation of playboy that he was acquiring. They did not at all like how frequently his name cropped up in the gossip columns. They considered it vulgar.

While Adam was not prepared to sacrifice too much to make his parents happy, like all children, on some level, he craved their approval, especially his mother's, if only because she gave it so rarely. Since he was beginning to agree with them that he ought to marry soon, Alexandra had occurred to him as a way to please his parents without making himself miserable. None of the women he had felt more passionate about quite lived up to his idea of a good wife, and passion, his at any rate, did not seem to last. At least his feeling for Alexandra, whatever it might be called, had endured for a very long time.

But any idea of marrying her had receded to the back of Adam's mind once he had seen Katrinka at Kitzbühel. It had occurred to him that, if he could so eagerly set about the pursuit of another woman, it might yet be a little soon for him to think about settling down. While being faithful to Alexandra was not to him an expected, or even a desirable, aspect of his marriage, he did think he should at least be able to make it through his honeymoon without being tempted.

"Neither of us has any illusions," Adam told Katrinka, not quite honestly, since he had never asked Alexandra's opinion of their relationship. "We're just good friends. That's all we've ever been."

The busboy arrived to clear their plates, sparing Katrinka the trouble of having to comment, which was just as well since she did not know what to say: I'm so glad; It's really none of my business; Why are you telling me all this? And then the waiter came to take their order for dessert. "Just coffee, please," said Katrinka.

"We'll see the trolley," said Adam.

And Katrinka chose a piece of chocolate gateau because she had noticed that men, while they did not like fat women, perversely did like women who could eat. They seemed to find it sensual, erotic. Franta had always been irritated with her when she ordered salads or refused desserts.

"The apple tart," said Adam.

By the time the waiter had—with great flair—served their choices and delivered them cups of steaming dark coffee, Katrinka, looking to change the conversation, asked, "How many sisters and brothers you do have?"

"One," said Adam: Clementine, older and safely married. "She was never the handful I am."

"Handful?"

He smiled, delighted with her odd English and occasional gaps of knowledge. "Hard to handle. Difficult."

"Oh."

Both his parents were alive, Adam told her, and living in the house in Newport (in Rhode Island, one of the states, he explained), where he had been born. Clementine had been two when his parents had moved into it. His mother's father had died and they had inherited some money and could afford a grander place than the one they had been living in.

His father, Kenneth Graham, built yachts, wonderful old wooden sailing yachts. Once upon a time, the business, a family business dating back to the early eighteenth century, had been quite successful. But now, since the popularization of fiberglass in the late 1950s, what little money the company made came from refitting old wooden yachts, since only a few romantics persisted in having new ones designed and built for themselves. Fortunately, inherited money provided enough income to keep the family in luxury, so no one minded very much when the business barely broke even.

Judging from the indulgent but patronizing tone of his voice, Adam did not, Katrinka guessed, share his father's romantic view of commerce. She asked him what he did.

"I build yachts."

"You do?" she asked, obviously surprised.

He laughed. "Among other things. I own shipyards, three so far, and build racing yachts, cruising yachts. Not wooden ones, though. Motorboats, trawlers. Anything that floats."

After studying marine engineering at MIT, Adam still had not been sure that he wanted to get permanently involved in the family business. Instead of going to work with his father after graduation, as everyone but his mother had expected, he went instead to Harvard to get his master's in business. Then, for lack of a better idea, he got a job with a Wall Street brokerage house, hated it, quit and went to Florida to work in a shipyard there, then to England to do the same. By the time he was twenty-five, his parents had despaired of his ever being able to stick to anything. And so really had he. Then two factors coincided to change his life: he came into his inheritance from his grandfather and a small shipyard in Larchmont, New York, was put up for sale. Using the inheritance as collateral, Adam got a bank to put up most of the money for the purchase, his first real business coup given his lack of credentials. He bought the shipyard, hired a talented young designer, and built a number of successful small yachts. Two years later, he bought another yard in Miami and, a year after that, one in Bridgeport, Connecticut. Now, looking to expand still further, he was negotiating for one in Bremen.

That must be, thought Katrinka, what Natalie had meant by his being up to some very clever things. Jean-Claude must have heard about it somehow.

"I'm on my way back to Bremen to close the deal."

To Katrinka's surprise, the thought of his leaving made

her feel very sad. "When do you have to be there?" she asked before she could stop herself. I've had too much to drink, she thought. Champagne, wine. Much too much.

"Tomorrow." He smiled. "Though if all goes well, I may be able to stop in Munich on my return." What was not at all clear was whether he was referring to Katrinka or the business deal in Bremen.

One of the problems of dealing with someone as self-confident as Adam Graham, thought Katrinka, is that, like Mirek Bartoš, he made it seem so much more reasonable to fall in with his plans than to disagree. But, if the idea of Adam's going away made her feel so lonely after just one dinner, what would it be like when they had gone to bed together? *If,* she corrected herself, not when. It was obviously much better not to get involved with him at all.

"Would you like a brandy?" asked Adam.

"No," said Katrinka. "Absolutely not. Thank you," she added finally, aware that she had sounded a little abrupt.

Outside it had begun to rain and again Katrinka was aware of how wonderful a luxury it was to have a car and driver waiting at the curb, to be safely settled inside against the comfortable leather seats before the rain had ruined her shoes or spoiled her hair.

"Would you like to come back to my hotel for a night-cap?" asked Adam.

"Nightcap?" As far as she knew, it was something people in the last century used to wear on their heads while sleeping.

"A good-night drink."

"Oh. I did have enough, thank you," said Katrinka.

Adam gave the driver her address, then rolled up the dividing window and sat back, putting an arm around her.

"Where are you staying?"

"The Four Seasons."

"I did work there, as a chambermaid." He had let her know how rich he was; she might as well tell him just how poor she had been.

"When?" he asked, interested and not at all disapproving.

"Oh, summers. In the late sixties, when I was at university, to make some extra money. And when I did move to Munich in 1972, but just for a little while."

He laughed. "I've been staying there for years. You never made up my room. There's no way I would have forgotten you."

"Probably not," she said. "The world is not so small."

The closer they got to her apartment, the more anxious Katrinka became, which was not like her at all. Usually, she was clear about what she wanted, and decisive about how best to get it. With Adam she was ambivalent. Oh, she wanted him, she knew that. But not only did she sense that it would be a mistake to make his "conquest" of her too easy, she felt reluctant to become involved physically with a man who was leaving Munich in the morning, who might not be returning for months, who might not phone her again if he did—given the fast pace at which he lived and how quickly the circumstances of his life might change. It was not a question of underestimating her attractions. Men had always found her desirable, and she knew it. Many to whom she had given no encouragement beyond a friendly smile and a polite interest had even professed to being in love with her. But she also knew enough about human nature to understand that what men achieved easily they often did not value.

When the car had pulled to a stop in front of her building, the driver got out but for some reason did not immediately open the rear door. Adam, whose arm had rested lightly on her shoulders for all of the drive, now pulled her closer and buried his face against her throat. "Are you going to ask me in?" he said, his breath tickling the sensitive spot below her right ear.

"I have to be up at five in the morning." A decision had to be made and, again uncharacteristically, Katrinka decided in favor of caution.

"It's almost not worth going to sleep, is it?" He began to kiss her and Katrinka's resolution weakened as she felt his mouth on her throat, on her eyes, on her mouth. When his tongue darted between her lips, and her heart began to race and her bones to melt, she knew that if he asked again she would have to say yes. But what he said was, "I'm leaving in the morning. I don't have time to court you properly," and she remembered why it was that she had decided against going to bed with him.

Gently, she pulled away, easing herself out of his arms. "It is always sad to ruin a good thing by trying to hurry it," she said.

"I'm not sure when I'll be able to get back."

Was that a threat or a bribe? wondered Katrinka. Had he forgotten he had told her earlier that he might stop on his return from Bremen? Or did he mean now that he would not because "all" had not gone well? "You're a very busy man," she replied neutrally.

"I haven't been able to get you out of my mind. You know I stopped in Munich just to see you."

Pleased, she smiled though she knew it was probably not true. "I'm glad you did."

"You don't seem glad," he said, sounding sulky.

"I'm sorry you feel that way because I did enjoy myself tonight. You are very good company."

If you only knew *how* good, he thought, but decided against saying it. Asking for what he wanted, or on occasion taking it, that was all right. Begging for it was not. Neither was petulance, which showed a definite lack of style. "So are you," he said, with a sudden resurgence of charm. "We'll do this again sometime."

"I hope so." She leaned toward him and kissed him lightly on the mouth, then turned to the door and touched the handle. It opened immediately and the chauffeur extended a hand to help her out of the car. "Thank you," she said, smiling at him, wondering at his superb timing. How had he known when to spring into action?

Adam followed Katrinka out of the car to the building, waiting politely while she turned the key in the lock, then pushing the heavy door open for her. Katrinka wondered whether he would ask again to be allowed in. Most men would. But Adam did not. Instead, he put his arms around her and kissed her, this time a friendly, not a passionate kiss. "I'll phone you," he said.

When? she wondered, but did not ask. How long would it be before he returned to Munich? "I did have a lovely time."

"So did I," said Adam, realizing as he spoke the words that he meant them despite the evening not having gone exactly as he had planned. He watched until the door closed, then returned to the car and told the driver to take him back to the hotel. Like Katrinka, he had to be up early in the morning, at the airport by seven, though he was so wide awake he doubted he could sleep. Too bad, he thought, with both regret and irritation. Sex always relaxed him. His annoyance deepened as he realized that from each of his three encounters with Katrinka he had come away without getting what he wanted and that, instead of being sensible and refusing to waste any more of his valuable time on her, he was already beginning to think about when he could see her again.

What it was about Katrinka that intrigued him was no mystery to Adam, and it certainly was not only her looks. Alexandra was easily as beautiful as she, to some people perhaps even more so. But Katrinka had something more appealing to him than beauty: she had intelligence, exuberance, energy. That's what had interested him on the line to the gondola, once those startling blue eyes and that stunning body had caught his attention. She had seemed so curious about everything and everyone, so radiant, so full of life. Talking to her, he had not been disappointed. And when she had skied away from him, he had felt, then as now, torn between annoyance and admiration.

Katrinka was not an easy person to forget. She lingered in the mind, or certainly had in his over the past several months. In the press, he was often accused of having charisma, which he interpreted as the ability to make people sit up and take notice. Whatever it was, he suspected Katrinka might have it too. Without it being at all necessary, he had scheduled a stop in Munich just to see her again.

And now, after an evening spent in her company, his feelings were more confused than ever. The account she had given of her life, the rigor of her years of skiing, the bravery of her escape, the cleverness with which she had built a successful business, all increased his admiration. No woman he had ever met even remotely resembled her.

But he was not used to being rebuffed. He did not like it. And if he was willing to credit Katrinka with being unique, could she not at least have had the sense to understand that he was not like other men? That he had no intention of reducing their relationship to a one-night stand? He felt hurt that she did not trust him.

Convinced of his good intentions, nursing his grievance against Katrinka, Adam of course forgot the many times he had meant to call some woman again (some woman who clearly expected him to, hoped he would) and had not. Usually it was because whatever current he was riding at the moment had carried him too quickly away. His life was like that, fast-moving. An important business deal had intervened, an unexpected trip, a chance encounter with another woman, something to chase what was really not very important (good manners, a niggling sense of responsibility) from his mind. With Katrinka, he was certain it would have been otherwise.

Back in his hotel room, Adam pushed all thoughts of her from his mind and began reviewing the papers for his meeting the next day. He wanted the Bremen shipyard badly. The three he presently owned were doing well, extremely well: they had made him a wealthy man. But not wealthy enough. He looked around and saw people who had started with nothing, people like Mark van Hollen and Jean-Claude Gillette, coming from nowhere, making vast fortunes, elbowing the old-line aristocracy, like the Grahams, like Daisy and Steven Elliott, like poor Alexandra Ogelvy's family for God's sake, onto the sidelines. Well, others from his background (*class* was what he meant, but did not like to think, let alone say) might not mind retiring genteelly from the fray, living happily on their vast, and in his opinion endangered, capital, but no one was going to push Adam Graham off the playing field. Never content with being second best, not at school, not at sports, not with women, he had no intention now of letting a bunch of nouveau riche "entrepreneurs"—how respectable the word sounded, he thought contemptuously—walk away with the prizes. He was determined to be a player, a high-stakes player. His three shipyards were his ante and he was going for the pot.

Suddenly, amused by his own ambition, he laughed. His mother's maternal granddaddy had been a riverboat gambler, though no one in the family, except one of his mother's sisters, ever talked about him, and she only when feeling compelled to explain some of Adam's more disreputable behavior, his frequent appearances in the tabloid press with a starlet on his arm, for example, his lack of suitable caution negotiating business deals, his crazy idea of expanding into Europe in the middle of an economic slump.

Adam, however, did not put much stock in heredity, nor did he think of himself as a gambler. Though he could see that the sort of excitement he experienced when beginning to negotiate a deal might be very like what his great-grandfather had felt sitting down to a game of high-stakes poker, what drove Adam was not the desire for either thrills or money, but arrogance. It was not danger he wanted, but power. Thinking again about the meeting the next day, he felt a pleasurable tingle of anticipation, a slight anxiety, a surge of unbeatable self-confidence. Maybe I did inherit a few of the old guy's genes, thought Adam. Laughing, he put away the papers, turned out the light, and went to sleep.

Without a big business deal to distract her, Katrinka did not fare so well. She lay awake most of the night thinking about Adam, regretting that she had refused to spend the night with him, wondering if she would ever see him again.

Makeup skillfully applied concealed the paleness of Katrinka's skin, the faint shadows under her eyes the next morning. A cup of strong black coffee got her moving. Feeling the need to spoil herself, instead of the U-bahn she took a taxi to the showroom where she was working that day: a reminder that, however far a cry a taxi was from a chauffeured limousine, she did not need Adam Graham to provide luxuries for her. Looking out the taxi window, as always searching the faces of the passing schoolchildren, hoping to see her son, she managed to put Adam out of her mind. By the time she arrived at the showroom, she was feeling almost like her usual self. And once the lights were on and the music playing and she was dancing down the runway in a gown of brilliant red paper taffeta, she forgot completely about Adam Graham and began to enjoy herself.

When she returned home that afternoon, she took a nap and awoke feeling refreshed. She called the Golden Horn to talk to Bruno and Hilde, as she did every day, to discuss the occupancy figures (the inn did a good business in the spring and summer months with vacationers traveling through the Tyrol stopping in Kitzbühel to climb, play golf, ride horseback, or swim in the Schwarzee) and the progress of the off-season repairs. But that afternoon the discussion of the late delivery of a new kitchen oven was interrupted by the sound of the doorbell. Leaving Bruno hanging, Katrinka went to the door and opened it to find a young boy in jacket and cap holding an enormous basket of red roses, six dozen at least. *"Fräulein* Kovář?"

Stunned, Katrinka only nodded, then realized something more was expected of her. Quickly, she crossed to the coffee table, cleared a space, and asked the boy to put the roses down. Going to the phone, she told Bruno she would call him back, then found a mark for the boy, signed the receipt, and ushered him out. There was not a doubt in her mind who the roses were from; still she eagerly tore the white envelope open to read the message. "Wait for me," it said and was signed with love from Adam.

Wait for him? What did he mean? she wondered. And, more important, for how long?

But questions about Adam's motives were lost in the pleasure that filled her. She had been sent flowers before, many times, but never so many, arranged with such style and simplicity that, despite the abundance of roses, the basket did not seem extravagant or ostentatious. It was of course from the most expensive florist in Munich.

To celebrate Franta's departure for Phoenix for his first race since the accident, for dinner that evening Katrinka went with him and a group of friends to Kay's Bistro, whose

ever-changing decor that week was pure Hollywood. Afterward, Franta wanted to dance and they all went on to
Nachtcafé, so it was nearly three when Katrinka finally
returned to her apartment. As she entered the door the
phone began to ring, and, convinced it was Franta with
further instructions about what to do with his mail or how
to take care of his apartment while he was away (Katrinka
had volunteered to do both), she picked up the phone and
said, in Czech, "Franta, leave me alone, please. I'm exhausted. I must go to sleep."

"Katrinka, is that you? It's about time. Where have you
been?" The voice was tired, petulant, unmistakable.

"Adam?"

"I've been phoning you for hours."

The pulse in her throat began to throb. She felt suddenly
short of breath. "I did go out with friends. Dancing," she
said. "Thank you so much for the roses. They are beautiful."

"You like roses?" he asked, as if afraid to hear that she
might actually have preferred the white orchids he had
decided not to send.

"Oh, yes." She thought of her grandmother's garden in
Svitov and her voice caught. "They are my favorite flower.
And these are perfect, every one, so lovely."

"I couldn't sleep."

"Your meeting did not go well?"

Adam laughed and when he spoke again both the fatigue
and the peevishness were gone from his voice. "It went
about as well as I expected. But I got back from dinner and
phoned you and you weren't there. I've been going crazy
wondering where you were."

"I do often go out with friends," said Katrinka.

"And you always stay out so late?"

"Sometimes. You have another meeting tomorrow?" she
asked, changing the subject.

"Yes. You'd think," he said, his voice heavy with exasperation, "that if someone wants to sell something to someone
who wants to buy, the sale would be a piece of cake. But it's
not. One thing about business, it's never easy." He spent a
few minutes outlining some of the problems he was having,
the main ones being the amount of cash he was being asked

to put up and a contractual requirement to keep on some of the senior management.

"If they're good, that should be no problem."

"The company's been losing money for years."

"Then refuse."

"That's just what I've been doing. There were a lot of unhappy faces around the conference table."

"Do you think this is a . . . a . . ." She searched for the right English word.

"Deal-breaker?"

"Yes."

"No, I don't think so."

"Good luck."

"Thanks. Are you going out again tomorrow night?"

"It's possible. Sometimes we decide at the last minute."

"If I have time, I'll phone you. What time will you be in?"

Katrinka laughed. "Adam, if I do not know yet I am going out, how I can tell you what time I will come back?"

"Well, I'll try to phone you," he said, carefully not making a commitment. "Think of me."

"Good night, Adam."

"I'll be thinking of you," he said, then replaced the receiver, turned out the light, and went instantly to sleep.

But, again, Katrinka lay awake thinking of Adam Graham. He was difficult, demanding, unpredictable, and exciting—qualities he shared with Mirek Bartoš. But there, she realized, the resemblance ended. Not only was Adam free, he was so much younger than Mirek, he seemed so much more vital and aggressive. He had not yet compromised with life, perhaps never would. And unlike Mirek, who had, she realized in retrospect, loved her for her youth, for her face, for her body, but paid little attention to her mind, Adam seemed interested in all of her. It was a type of flattery she was completely unused to and liked very much.

More roses arrived the next day, champagne-colored, in another extravagant arrangement. That evening, with the excuse that she needed to get a good night's rest, Katrinka turned down an invitation to dinner from a friend, one of the models with whom she frequently worked, and then regretted it because she was afflicted with such anxiety waiting for Adam's phone call that she could not settle either to read or sleep. At midnight, when she had just made up her mind that he would not call, the phone rang and they spent an hour talking, recounting the details of the day to one another as if they had been friends, lovers, for years.

The pattern was repeated the next day and the next, Katrinka making sure to be home from wherever she had spent the evening no later than eleven so that she would not miss Adam's call, though by then she had little doubt that he would keep phoning until he found her in. She had learned that he was nothing if not persistent.

On the third night, he said, "I should have everything wrapped up late tomorrow afternoon, in time to make the six o'clock flight to Munich. Where would you like to have dinner?"

"I'm leaving for Kitzbühel in the afternoon," she said, without thinking.

"No, you're not. You're staying in Munich to have dinner with me."

Despite the flowers and the phone calls, Katrinka had scarcely dared to hope that Adam would stop in Munich before returning to New York. But now that he was, instead of pleasure, what she felt was annoyance at his assumption that she should change all her plans to suit his convenience. "You are not the only one with business to take care of," she said.

"We'll go to Kitzbühel together the next morning," he replied, sounding quite reasonable for a change, not the least bit irritated by her stubbornness, "if your business is that important. Just wait for me in Munich."

Is that what the note on the roses had meant? she wondered. "You can spend the weekend?" She made no attempt to conceal her delight.

"I shouldn't, but I will. Now, where do you want to eat?"

Never in her life had Katrinka felt such a sense of excitement, anticipation, not before exams at school, not before a race, not when waiting for Mirek Bartoš to turn away from the other actors and speak to her. She phoned

Natalie in Paris because she thought she would explode if she didn't tell someone how she felt. The next day she had lunch with Erica Braun, with whom she still kept in close touch, and afterward went shopping and bought herself a new Valentino evening dress, on sale, spending too much money, but wanting something elegant and pretty to wear for Adam. Returning home, she washed her hair, rinsing it with lemon to bring out its highlights, took a long, luxurious bubble bath, gave herself a facial, a manicure, a pedicure. I'm being ridiculous, she thought at one point. What if he doesn't come, she thought at another, panicking suddenly. What if he stands me up? I'll feel like such a fool.

But at eight-thirty the bell rang and, when Katrinka opened the door, there was Adam, exactly on time, his thick brown hair ruffled by the wind, his eyes shining, this time a bottle of Louis Roederer Cristal in his hand.

"You did get the shipyard," she said.

"I did get it," he replied teasingly. "We closed the deal at three."

As if they had been lovers for years, with a complete lack of self-consciousness, she threw herself into his arms. She could feel the bottle of champagne against her bottom as he kissed her. After a few minutes, he pulled away. "Wait," he said. He put down the champagne, began to take off his coat.

"I'll go get glasses."

"No, not yet." His coat off, he pulled her back into his arms. "What a lovely dress. Is it new?"

"Yes."

"I like it."

He began to kiss her again, his mouth moving up her throat to her ear, her cheek, her eyes, down her nose, to her mouth. His tongue slipped inside and met hers, and she thought she heard him groan. Or was it herself? If he took his arms away she would fall, she thought, she felt so weak with desire. His left hand stroked her throat, her shoulder, moved down and cupped her breast. His right hand moved from her hair to her back, found the zipper of her dress. Oh, yes, she thought, this is what making love should be like. She had almost forgotten. She could not wait to be naked in his arms. She could not wait to feel him inside her. Reaching for his tie, she began to undo it.

He moved away from her slightly and she felt suddenly worried. "Don't you want your dinner first?" he said.

For a moment, she did not understand what he was talking about. Finally, she said, "No. No, I don't."

"I'm so glad," he said and pulled her close again.

Twenty-Five

*A*dam, you do have to stop this. Really. It's too much."

"Don't you like it?"

"It's beautiful. But . . ."

"Try it on." As Katrinka hesitated, Adam stepped behind her, draped the coat around her shoulders, then turned her to face him. The dark, lustrous fur matched the color of her hair, made her skin seem pale and soft as a cream-colored rose. "You look wonderful in it," he said.

"All these gifts are not necessary," she said, knowing she sounded ungrateful, but worried that he might think her mercenary.

He kissed her lightly on the nose. "To me they are. I enjoy giving you things."

And what things! In the three months since they had become lovers, Adam had given Katrinka a pair of Cartier diamond-set tortoiseshell hair combs, a gold Bulgari bangle bracelet, a Van Cleef & Arpels ruby and diamond flower clip brooch, a natural pearl necklace, a cushion-shaped sapphire ring, a heart-shaped Lalique paperweight, a Louis XV gold-mounted porcelain snuffbox—an endless succession of gifts whose exact value Katrinka had no way of assessing, though she knew each was expensive as well as beautiful. He never returned to Munich, which was at least four times a month on his way to and from Bremen, without bringing her something. Once, he had taken her to the Grand Hotel du

Cap, at St.-Jean-Cap-Ferrat, for the weekend. When he was not with her, he sent flowers every day, enormous bouquets of roses, and every night he phoned.

His extravagance both delighted Katrinka and made her uneasy. Until Adam's appearance in her life, she had lived frugally, working hard for every necessity, and even harder for the luxuries. The gifts from her parents and grandparents had come as rewards for her achievements, or so it had seemed to her; even those from Mirek and Franta, though generous, had not shaken her belief that what she wanted she must earn, what she got she must pay for. But she had done nothing to earn this flood of presents from Adam, and their cost was so clearly colossal that the idea of repayment of any kind was ridiculous.

"I only want you," she said.

"You have me," he replied, laughing. "Why not take the mink as well? Come on, Katrinka," he coaxed, "don't spoil my fun."

She slipped her arms into the sleeves of the coat, turned again to look into the mirror, and thought how warm she would be in it next winter. "You are completely crazy," she said, "to buy me a mink coat in June."

"I didn't mean to buy it. I just happened to be walking past a store on Fifty-seventh Street, and there it was in the window. I couldn't resist."

"You do never resist."

"Not you," he said, turning her around to face him, slipping his arms under the coat and around her bare waist. Because he had just arrived in Munich after a two-week absence and was half-crazed with desire for her, he had waited until after they made love to give Katrinka the coat. Now he wanted her again. He always wanted her. When he was away from her, the idea of her tormented him, and he rearranged his work schedule relentlessly to accommodate stopovers in Munich to see her.

While he stroked her naked back with his hands, his mouth followed the line of the partially open coat to her breast. He took a nipple between his lips, flicked it with his tongue, and felt Katrinka's arms tighten around his neck, her body arch in pleasure. In a moment, they were on the floor, on top of the mink coat, Katrinka's legs gripping his waist as he moved deeper and deeper into her. Finally, after a long time, they finished and lay quiet, each one trying to come to terms with the depth of feeling the other inspired, so much stronger, more compelling than anything either had experienced with other lovers, sometimes bewildering in its intensity, producing alternately joy and terror.

As Adam pulled away from her, his cock fell for a moment into the valley between her legs, leaving a smear of semen on the dark silk. He smiled with satisfaction. "Now you have to keep the coat," he said.

When he came to Munich, Adam still took a suite at the Four Seasons and he and Katrinka stayed sometimes there, sometimes in her apartment in Franz-Joseph-Strasse, depending on where they had spent the evening and what the plans were for the next day. Because Katrinka had a modeling assignment in the morning, after the opera (*Aida* —and it was a measure of how deeply Adam felt for her that he consented to sit through it) and dinner at Aubergine, they returned to her place and, before falling asleep, made love once again, and again the next morning when barely awake. Afterward, as Katrinka tried to extricate herself from Adam's arms, he held on. "Don't go," he said. "Come with me to New York."

"I do have to earn a living."

"No, you don't. I have enough money for two."

She smiled, but still struggled to free herself. "Adam, let me go, please. I hate not to be on time."

"Marry me," he said.

Katrinka lay still, her head against Adam's bare chest. She could hear his heart beating. "I do love you," she said. She had told him that for the first time the month before at Cap Ferrat. They had gone sailing in a rented twelve-footer, and as the boat had dipped and rolled along the swells of white-capped indigo water, she had lain dreamily observing how the deep robin's-egg blue of the sky faded to gray where it met the water line, thinking about nothing in particular, feeling relaxed and contented. Then she had dropped her eyes to look at Adam at the tiller, his thick brown hair curled by spray and highlighted by the sun, his quirky, handsome face raised to estimate the effect of the wind on the mainsail, his muscular body poised to spring into action. Adam had returned her look and, without thinking, she had said, "I love you," realizing as she said it that it was true.

"Is that a yes?" he asked now.

"Yes," she replied.

"You'll marry me?"

"Yes."

"I love you," he said. "God, I love you."

Whenever she had thought about a future with Adam, Katrinka had not been able to see it clearly. They came from different countries, different worlds really, and she could not find a way to reconcile the two. Either because of these differences or because the relationship was as yet very new, marriage had not occurred to her as a serious possibility. When the idea had entered her mind, the problems were so obvious that she had quickly pushed it out again. She preferred to assume vaguely that Adam and she would continue their long-distance affair until . . . Until what? She could never get further in her thoughts than that.

So Adam's proposal surprised Katrinka and she said yes quickly because, loving him, there was no other possible response. But faced with the consequences of that yes, she was worried.

Though Adam clearly did not understand and was irritated by her decision, Katrinka refused to go with him to New York. As he reluctantly kissed her good-bye, Adam promised he would return before the end of the month and insisted that next time he would not leave Munich without her.

But how *could* she leave Munich? she asked herself over and over during the day at work as she went through the routine of dressing and undressing—for each dress, suit, and gown changing underwear, stockings, shoes, earrings, hat—forgetting to double-check the assistant, who, though every outfit was carefully arranged and numbered, often made mistakes. Usually Katrinka paid strict attention to

292

each detail, knowing how a sale could be jeopardized by something as seemingly insignificant as the wrong color stockings, but for once she was too preoccupied with her own future to feel concern for that of the young designer whose work she was modeling.

How could she leave Munich? she wondered as she lay awake that night after an hour-long phone call from Adam, now back in New York in the apartment Katrinka apparently was soon to see. Intent as usual on getting what he wanted, Adam foresaw no serious difficulties and was full of plans for their future: they would live in New York of course, but travel often to Europe, or anywhere else they wanted whenever they liked; they would create a financial empire unrivaled in the world; Katrinka would meet his family, who would love her; he would buy her a house, build her a yacht. He was in love for the first time in his life and wanted to give the object of that love everything. "We're going to be happy," he promised.

But life was not, she knew, as simple as Adam Graham insisted on believing, or as easy to control.

That weekend Katrinka went as usual to Kitzbühel, to the Golden Horn, helped in the kitchen and dining room, did the accounts, made lists of needed renovations, interviewed young women to replace one of the maids, who was leaving. The whole time she seesawed endlessly between ecstasy and despair, returning always to the same question: how could she leave Munich? At times she saw Hilde watching her with a look of mingled speculation and worry. "Is everything all right?" she asked finally. Katrinka assured her that everything was.

Fond as she was of Hilde, Katrinka could not confide in her. As always, she found it impossible to confide in anyone, not her best friends, not the man in her life. Her parents had been her only real confidants, the people to whom it was safe to confess anything, and now as she walked in the soft afternoon light across the green valley, through fields of daisies and buttercups and bluebells, picking a bouquet of wildflowers as she went, for once oblivious to the staggering beauty of the landscape, the grazing cows dotting the hills that rolled calmly toward the Kitzbüheler Horn, whose summit even in summer carried pockets of dazzling snow, Katrinka thought longingly of her father and mother, missing them as acutely as ever.

She felt so alone. For a moment, she wished she were back in the Maxmilianka with Tomáš and Zuzka, drinking beer, arguing about films, deciding where to go to dance. She still corresponded with them regularly. Tomáš had directed his first film the year before and it had been well received by both the authorities and the public. He was now preparing another—to his dismay, a mystery—but at least he was being allowed to direct. Zuzka was a contented wife and mother. Martin, whose birth had changed Katrinka's life, had just had his sixth birthday.

Life in Czechoslovakia had not been simple, or easy, but at least Katrinka had understood its rules. And in Munich and Kitzbühel, although those cities had offered her greater freedom and opportunities, still they were European cities and she had created a life there not so different from the one she had always known. But marriage to Adam Graham would introduce her into a world that was totally new—to a new continent, a different culture, to a life of strange customs and unfamiliar luxury. The idea of it excited her, and frightened her as well. Would she be able to be the kind of wife that Adam wanted, that he expected? She was willing to try, but always she came back to the same question: how could she leave Munich?

"Katrinka, are you sure you're all right?" asked Adam when he phoned. "You sound funny."

"I do sound like I'm in love," she said and spent another sleepless night.

When she returned to Munich, Katrinka phoned Erica Braun and asked her to dinner, but was invited instead to the apartment to see some redecorating Erica had done. The walls had been painted pale green trimmed with white, new carpets had been laid throughout, the furniture in the living room reupholstered in a flower-patterned silk with matching curtains hung at the windows there and in the adjoining dining room. The effect of the whole was soothing, peaceful.

It must have cost a fortune to do, thought Katrinka. "It's beautiful," she said. "It's like sitting in a garden."

"I got a large bonus at Christmas," explained Erica, "and thought this is what I would like most to spend it on. I'm at home so much."

By now in her late forties, Erica had aged hardly at all in the nine years since Katrinka had first met her. She remained an attractive, voluptuous woman, her skin taut, her hair colored a few shades lighter than its original blond, only a few more lines at the corners of her large brown eyes and full mouth to mark the passage of time. Men should have been beating down the door to get to her, thought Katrinka. "You should go out more," she said.

"Women my age don't have so many opportunities."

"Nonsense. You just don't see them."

Erica thought a moment. "Perhaps you're right," she said. Perhaps if she gave up waiting for Klaus Zimmerman's infrequent visits, she would begin to notice these other opportunities. She sighed. There was little likelihood of that. Though she did not wish to, she loved him. No, she was obsessed with him and had been since the day she had started working for him, over fifteen years before. Making love to her, which he had done a few months later, had increased his hold only slightly. And now, whether he did or not was irrelevant: made love to or ignored, she still thought only of him.

Seated at the kitchen table where they had once shared breakfast, Katrinka and Erica ate the Wiener schnitzel and mashed potatoes Erica had made because she knew how much Katrinka enjoyed them. They drank a nice hock and talked about the *Aida* which both had seen, though on different nights, about the Golden Horn, which Erica visited occasionally, about everything but Klaus Zimmerman, who Katrinka, usually so perceptive, did not realize was Erica's lover: it was inconceivable to her that an intimate relationship could exist between this woman she was so fond of and a man she detested. The amount of rage Zimmerman could still provoke, the sense of fear and frustration, the loathing, shocked even Katrinka when occasionally she ran into him in Munich or Kitzbühel. But perhaps even more shocking to her was her ability to nod and smile pleasantly in greeting, not wanting to alienate him further, still hopeful that someday, somehow, she would convince him to help her.

"And how are things going between you and Adam?" asked Erica finally, when she had cleared the last dish and they were settled comfortably again in the sitting room with a pot of coffee and two lovely new Villeroy and Boch china cups on the low antique table between them.

"He asked me to marry him."

"And?"

"I said yes."

Erica smiled. She had met Adam one weekend in Kitzbühel and liked him. *"Liebling,* what good news. I wish you happy." She leaned toward Katrinka and kissed her cheek. "Congratulations."

Katrinka looked back at her bleakly. "How can I leave Munich?" she asked.

"Bruno and Hilde can go on running the inn. Or you can sell it. There is nothing really to hold you here," replied Erica firmly, knowing exactly what Katrinka was getting at.

"My baby," said Katrinka. "How can I leave him?" Her eyes clouded with tears.

Erica made an impatient clucking sound. "Katrinka, *liebling,* you must forget the past."

"So everyone always says. But how do I do that?"

"Do you love Adam?" asked Erica, ignoring the question.

"Yes."

"Then you must marry him."

"I *want* to marry him. But . . . ."

Erica interrupted, asking "You've been here in Munich how long now? Six years? And if in all that time you haven't found your child, what makes you think you will in another year? or three? or ten?"

Katrinka had long ago realized she could not trace her child through the public records, though she continued to search wherever she traveled. Contacts at the clinic had revealed nothing, despite her few awkward attempts at bribery once her modeling career had provided the money. She had exhausted every avenue open to her and still she could neither stop trying nor give up hope. "I think someday

I might pass him in the street, meet him in a shop, see him playing in the English Garden. I never stop looking. I would know him if I saw him. I would."

Again Erica made an impatient sound. "You might just as easily pass him in the street in New York. What makes you think he is still in Germany?"

Her eyes clouded with sudden suspicion, Katrinka leaned toward Erica and said accusingly, "You know where he is. You do!"

"I have told you before, I do not," replied Erica coolly. "I am simply pointing out that these days people do not always stay in one place. Whoever adopted your son could live anywhere in the world."

"You've seen the file," persisted Katrinka.

Erica rose and began to place the coffee pot and cups on a silver tray. "Adoption files are not kept at the clinic. I have also told you that before." She did not look at Katrinka and her voice was full of reproach. For a moment, she remained motionless, then she put a hand on Katrinka's shoulder and said gently, "Don't be crazy, *liebling*. Life is offering you another chance at happiness. Take it."

What Erica said filled Katrinka with a great sense of elation. If her son was no longer in Munich, in Germany, in Europe, then marrying Adam did not mean that she was abandoning her search for him but rather multiplying her chances to find him. It was a liberating thought, freeing her of the sense of guilt that had plagued her since she had said yes to Adam's proposal.

In constant reassuring touch with Adam by phone, Katrinka began wrapping up her life in Munich: the day-to-day running of the Golden Horn was turned over to Bruno and Hilde; she advised her modeling agency that she would no longer be available for work; she shipped her favorite pieces of furniture and important mementos to the inn for storage, packed her clothes and photographs, sold everything else, moved out of the apartment and into a suite at the Four Seasons to await Adam's arrival.

Staying at the hotel without him made Katrinka feel odd. Her life took on an unreal, dreamlike quality. Awakening alone in the enormous bed, she could not remember where she was. And walking through the opulent rooms, she could hardly believe she was not there to dust the gilded furniture, vacuum the patterned carpets, to get down on her hands and knees to wash the bathroom's marble floor.

Katrinka spent two days alone at the Four Seasons before Adam arrived, bringing with him a battered canvas bag, not one of his usual suitcases, though it looked vaguely familiar to Katrinka. As soon as the bellman left, Adam wrapped his arms around her for a hello kiss but did not push it further when he sensed her distraction. "Aren't you glad to see me?" he asked a little petulantly, looking very pleased with himself despite the words.

"Of course," said Katrinka, trying to turn her attention from the bag to Adam, assuring him that she had missed him very much while he was gone, but finally she gave in and pointed. "What is that?"

"I was wondering how long it would take you to recognize it."

"Recognize it?"

"Don't you?"

Suddenly, she did. "It's my father's bag." She sat on the floor, pulled it toward her, and opened it. "Where you did get it?"

His mouth twitched into its crooked smile. "Where I did get it?" he teased. "From Tomáš, of course."

"Tomáš! You went to Prague!"

He nodded. "Yesterday. I left New York a day early."

"That's why no phone call last night," she said accusingly.

"I tried. Believe me. The Czech phone system leaves a lot to be desired."

From inside the bag Katrinka pulled out several small needlepoint cushions. "My mother did make these," she said to Adam, tears welling in her eyes.

Adam sat in an armchair and watched her, smiling, supremely pleased with his surprise and Katrinka's response. "Tomáš said to tell you he still has your father's skis. I refused to bring those."

"This is fantastic. Absolutely fantastic," said Katrinka,

poring over the hoard of treasures that Tomáš and Zuzka had kept safe for her. There was a small bag of jewelry, including a locket that had belonged to her grandmother and her grandfather's tie pin. There were packets of letters tied with string, some exchanged by Jirka and Milena when they were courting, others sent by Katrinka to her parents while she was abroad racing. Most precious of all were the photographs, albums of them. She sat in Adam's lap for hours, showing them to him: that's *Babi* and *Děda,* she would say, pointing to her grandparents; look at *Mami* and *Taťi;* how young Aunt Zdeňka looks. Wasn't she pretty? but *Mama* was beautiful. Her hair was so red, and her skin so white. She had beautiful hands. Can you see? And there's Tomáš and me. See how he's frowning? He hated to have his picture taken. The memories came flooding back and she began to weep as Adam held her and stroked her hair.

"Maybe this wasn't such a good idea," he said after a while.

"Oh, no. No, it was a fantastic idea. I was so afraid I did lose all these things forever. Thank you. *Miláčku,* thank you so much."

Katrinka got up to pour them each a fresh drink, Adam a whiskey and water, herself a glass of wine, then sat in an armchair opposite him and listened while he explained how clever he had been, copying Tomáš's address and phone number from Katrinka's book. He had called Tomáš from New York to let him know he was on the way, pulled a few strings to get a visa quickly, left New York a day early, and flew to Prague. "I stayed at the Palace," he told Katrinka. "That could be a terrific hotel if it was smartened up a little."

"Where's the money to come from?"

"You know the trouble with communism?" said Adam. "It doesn't work."

"You think the people who live in communist countries did not figure that out?" said Katrinka. "But what they can do about it?"

The food, however, was surprisingly good, admitted Adam, and plentiful. He had taken Tomáš and Zuzka to dinner at the Zlaté Hrušky, near the Castle, then stopped back at their apartment to see Martin and collect the bag for Katrinka.

"Martin? How is Martin?"

"He's a cute little kid," said Adam admiringly. "Smart, too. We got along great."

"Do you like children?" asked Katrinka, looking up from the snapshots that Zuzka had sent.

Adam grinned again. "Do you mean do I *want* children?"

"Yes."

"Sure. Aside from the fact that my mother keeps telling me it's my duty to carry on the family name. My mother is always full of helpful suggestions about what I should or should not do. Most of them I ignore. But I like the idea of children, of leaving a piece of myself behind when I go. Do you?"

"Oh, yes. Very much." She knew that it was a perfect moment to tell him about her son, but found that she could not. The habit of discretion was too difficult for her to break. Tell only those who absolutely need to know had been her rule from her childhood. And now it was not so much that she wished to conceal the truth from Adam as that she could think of no reason why he ought to be told. After all, what would telling him accomplish? Nothing. What difference would his knowing possibly make to their lives? None.

Adam's hair needed a trim and thick strands of it curled over the collar of his shirt and fell across his forehead. Katrinka got up from her armchair and went again to sit in his lap. She ran her fingers through the thick dark curls at his neck. "You did give me the best wedding present," she said.

"That's what I wanted to do," he murmured, his mouth against her throat. "Speaking of which. Where do you want to get married? Here? In New York? Newport?"

Katrinka thought for a moment. "If we marry in New York or Newport, it will be a big family wedding?"

"If my mother has her way. And she usually does."

How alone she would feel, thought Katrinka, with all of Adam's family around and none of her own. How much she would miss her Aunt Zdeňka, her cousins and their wives, Tomáš and Zuzka, Ota and Olga Černý, how much she would miss her parents and grandparents. Could she stand

300

it? "Here," said Katrinka. "Unless you do mind not having a big wedding."

"Mind?" He kissed her nose. "You must be joking. I'd be grateful to you for sparing me all the fuss."

Kitzbühel or Munich? That was the next decision. Katrinka pondered the question for a few hours before realizing that she wished to be married in neither place but in St.-Jean-Cap-Ferrat, in a small church which she and Adam had found when they had visited there. Because it was where she had first realized how much she loved Adam, Cap Ferrat was a place Katrinka felt very attached to. And because they had both gone there for the first time together, it was "their" place in a way that neither Kitzbühel nor Munich was. When she told Adam, he was delighted despite the extra trouble the decision would cause. While Katrinka went shopping for her trousseau, Adam phoned the embassy in Paris and spoke to Kenneth Rush, the new ambassador and an old family friend, to ask his help clearing the obstacles the French insist on putting between any person and his desired goal. There was the usual trouble about birth and baptismal certificates, but within days the arrangements were made.

Adam hired a private plane and he and Katrinka flew to Cap Ferrat by way of Bremen, where Adam had a meeting with Lucia di Campo, a designer, and Khalid ibn Hassan, the Saudi prince. The meeting, about a yacht Prince Khalid wanted to build, went so well that by takeoff the wedding party included Lucia, who was in any case a close friend of Adam's, and the prince, who insisted on giving the bride away.

The plane had been liberally stocked with magnums of Roederer Cristal and the small party had turned festive by the time they touched down in Nice, where a limousine was awaiting them with more champagne cooling in a bucket. When they arrived at the Grand Hotel du Cap, they found Natalie, who was to be Katrinka's maid of honor, already there. And when the wedding party assembled an hour later for dinner, it had increased yet again by one: Lucia's husband, Nick Cavalletti, had left their three-year-old daughter with her nanny in their house near Florence and had hopped the first plane he could get in order to join them. They made a striking couple, Nick very tall and dark and flamboyant, Lucia tiny and ladylike, with pale auburn hair and oval eyes the color of chestnuts. She clearly adored him. It was hard to tell what he felt about her, noted Katrinka. His manner with his wife was proprietary, possessive, affectionate, but there was a speculative gleam in Nick's eye when he looked at other women.

Adam introduced everyone, strangers embraced like old friends, and Nick put his arm around the tipsy Lucia and said, "Natalie and I obviously have some drinking to do to catch up," and led them into the bar for another round of champagne.

They drove to the hill village of Eze to dine at Château de la Chevre d'Or, though by then they were in no condition to appreciate the view of the Riviera spread out below them. Afterward, they continued on to Monaco to gamble at the Casino in Monte Carlo for a while, then, dragging Khalid away from the roulette table only with difficulty, on to Jimmy's for more champagne and dancing. By the time they returned to the hotel, it was three in the morning and it seemed hardly worth the trouble of going to sleep, or so Adam insisted. Whereupon Katrinka said he could continue partying with Nick and Khalid if he liked, but she would go to Natalie's room to get some sleep: she refused to show up at her own wedding looking like a hag.

"Now don't be like that," said Adam, putting his arms around her.

"I'm going to bed. I haven't seen my wife in over a week," said Nick, looking accusingly at Adam.

"You're not in any condition to do much about that tonight," said Adam.

"Wanna bet?"

"Boys, boys," said Lucia gently, "lower your voices, before you get us all thrown out." Katrinka had liked Lucia immediately. She was bright, talented, friendly, and amusing. Nick she was not so sure about. Adam had told her he was a well-known and very successful criminal lawyer, but he was a bit too slick for her tastes, everything about him a little too sharp. Adam, however, seemed to enjoy his company, though it was Lucia who was his friend.

Khalid glanced at Natalie, to whom he had been very attentive all evening. Aware of his interest, and admiring his handsome dark face and soft brown eyes, she was tempted. But not for long. Things were going too well between her and Jean-Claude at the moment. *"Bonne nuit,"* she said, smiling sweetly. *"À demain."*

They all said good night and retired to their beds, Adam with Katrinka, Nick with Lucia, Khalid and Natalie alone.

The Chapel of St. Hospice was on a small jut of land extending out from Cap Ferrat past Paloma Beach. Set on a promontory, the chapel had, on one side, an old graveled cemetery whose marble tombs were decorated with porcelain flowers and faded photographs of the dead, on the other, a view of the coast from Beaulieu to Cap Martin. It was a simple nineteenth-century building, with white plastered walls decorated with framed colored drawings, a statue of St. Anthony to the side of the main altar, another presumably of St. Hospice about to have his head cut off by a Saracen, and in the nave, behind the table which served as an altar, a painting of the Assumption.

Katrinka loved the simplicity of the chapel. What it lacked in marble and gold, it more than made up for in serenity and charm. As she walked up the narrow aisle arm in arm with Adam, flanked by Natalie and Khalid, Lucia and Nick, she was convinced of the rightness of her choice. She wore a short cream-colored suit and a small matching hat on her head. In her right hand she carried a bouquet of champagne-colored roses with baby's breath. From the back of the chapel came the sound of the *Ave Maria* played by two musicians from the village in an accordion and violin duet. On the altar, an aged priest in black robes and white cassock, with a stole around his neck and a faint stubble of gray beard shadowing his face, stood holding his prayer book, waiting for them to reach him and the ceremony to begin. His name was Père Boniface, Katrinka remembered being told. When they stopped in front of him, he made the sign of the cross over them, smiled, and began to speak.

Adam took her hand in his and Katrinka, looking up, met his eyes. The love she saw there took her breath away. What seemed an eternity later, she heard the priest ask, "Do you, Katrinka Milena Kovář, take this man . . ."

"Yes," said Katrinka, her voice clear and firm.

"Yes," she heard Adam say a moment later.

Natalie sniffed, Lucia dabbed at her eyes with a handkerchief, Khalid and Nick grinned as if they had just personally accomplished something wonderful. Adam slipped a wide band of braided gold on Katrinka's finger. The priest murmured something, and Katrinka felt Adam's arms close around her and his mouth touch hers. "I love you," she heard him whisper against her lips. It was her son's ninth birthday, and for the first time since he was born, Katrinka felt gloriously, supremely, ridiculously happy.

The

Past

❦

1977 – 1991

Twenty-Six

"*H*ow she can say these things?" Katrinka's voice was full of confusion, hurt, anger.

Adam looked up from the copy of *The Financial Times* he was reading and shifted his body in the wide airplane seat for a better view of his wife. Despite her distress, she looked, he thought, very beautiful in the three-piece Chanel suit he had bought her the day before. Its color was the same pale blue as her eyes. "What things?" he asked.

"Look!" She handed him the Xerox of Sabrina's *London Globe* column.

For two days after the wedding they had remained at the Grand Hotel du Cap in Cap Ferrat, then had flown to Paris for another few days at the Plaza Athénée. The package of newspaper clippings, sent by express mail from Adam's office in New York, had arrived only a short time before they were to leave for the airport and the trip home. Adam had scanned the clippings just long enough to determine what they were about, then had placed a call to his mother in Newport. He had hoped to break the news of his marriage to her in person, in retrospect an impossible plan: someone had been certain to talk.

His mother, however, had not been at home when Adam phoned, which meant that he would be several hours deeper into trouble before he could speak to her. Not that he was particularly upset by this. The territory was too familiar. Since the only possible way to avoid quarreling with Nina Graham was to do exactly as she wished—an option he refused to consider—Adam generally concealed his plans from her, which, if it did not prevent argument, at least had the benefit of its being too late, by the time she found out what he was up to, for her (always a resourceful woman) to do anything but disapprove. Only recently she had commented that were she to stop reading the papers she would have no idea what was going on in his life, adding that such ignorance would not be without its blessings. But of course a new daughter-in-law, unlike an unsavory girlfriend or risky business deal, could hardly escape her notice.

Adam read Sabrina's column quickly. It was in her usual style: rather breathless, rather bitchy, full of snide humor. Headlined "The Playboy and the Model," it referred to Katrinka as the "ex-girlfriend of Formula I star Franta Dohnal," and implied she had abandoned Franta after an accident that had almost ended his career, first having stolen Adam away from Alexandra Ogelvy, his "longtime girlfriend" who, heartbroken, had had to cancel her order for a Dior wedding dress, losing a hefty deposit, for which, Sabrina sincerely hoped, Adam would reimburse her since the whole world knew the Ogelvys didn't have a dollar left to their name. There was a photograph of Adam and Alexandra, but none of Katrinka.

When he had finished, Adam handed the Xerox back to her, saying, "It's not so bad."

"Not a word is true," said Katrinka, outraged.

"Some words are," said Adam, grinning. "The Ogelvys *are* broke."

"She makes me sound like a tart."

"And I certainly fell madly in love with you, practically at first sight."

"How you can laugh!" said Katrinka, her voice an equal mix of irritation and disgust.

"We're going to be in the papers a lot, Katrinka, and you have to learn not to take any of what's said seriously, or you'll be miserable. Columnists write whatever they like, true or untrue, fair or not fair."

"More champagne?" asked the flight attendant, a young woman with mouse-brown hair pulled back in a twist.

"Yes, please," said Adam.

Katrinka watched as the attendant refilled their glasses, then picked up hers and took a sip. She had never flown first class before and she liked it, though not so much as flying in the private plane that Adam had hired to take them from Munich to Bremen to Cap Ferrat and on to Paris. What a luxury it had been not to have to check in, or wait at the gate, or struggle to find an empty overhead rack to stow the carry-on luggage. She stretched comfortably in the wide first-class seat, then turned to Adam. "Why don't people sue?" she asked.

"It's not worth the time or the money, unless what's said is very damaging. Usually it's not. Usually it's just garbage. How about the other papers? What do they say?"

Katrinka shuffled through the pile of Xeroxes, scanning the columns in *The International Herald Tribune,* London's *Mail* and *Sun,* New York's *Post* and *Daily News.* "Nothing as bad as Sabrina's," she said. "A couple are even nice: Liz Smith in *The News,* Suzy in *The Post.*" She shook her head in bemusement. "This Rick Colins, in *The Chronicle,* he gives our whole itinerary the night before the wedding: dinner at the Château, gambling at the Casino, dancing at Jimmy's. And my wedding suit, he describes it exactly. How he can know?"

"They all bribe waiters, maître d's, friends."

"Friends?" The idea was distasteful.

"So-called. Some people even provide the details themselves," adding when he saw Katrinka's disbelieving look, "Publicity has its value, sweetheart. You'll see."

Katrinka gathered up the papers, put them back in the envelope, and into Adam's attaché case, which she then pushed under the seat out of the way. She did not want to think about newspapers anymore or the columnists who wrote for them. The idea of being subjected to their constant scrutiny made her uneasy. It was not that she was shy, or unused to attention. From the age of six, when she had won her first race, she had been more or less in the public eye, and her visibility had increased over the years as her success as a skier and a model, as well as her brief excursions into film, had made both her face and name familiar in Czechoslovakia and then Germany. She had frankly enjoyed the publicity. Outgoing and friendly, she had liked the kind, even affectionate greetings she had received whenever she was recognized. But that recognition had been for a very public part of her life and, she realized now, agreeably kind for the most part, critical only when she had skied a bad race, and accepted then with something approaching resignation because it had been expected and deserved.

Her wedding seemed to Katrinka to be a different thing entirely, not a public event but a quiet, private affair which she had not expected would be open to public comment. That it had been both upset and offended her. She sighed and looked at Adam, who sat with his eyes closed, breathing evenly, as if asleep. Suddenly, she smiled. She had married him for better or for worse and, if she was prepared to accept luxurious hotel suites and first-class travel, then Adam was right and she had better get used to bitchy columnists and, judging from his comments, an unpleasant mother-in-law.

The lights dimmed, the side windows came down, the cabin plunged into darkness, and the movie began. It was *Oh, God* with George Burns. Hoping to sleep for a few hours like Adam, she arranged the pillow beneath her head, readjusted the blanket, and closed her eyes. A moment later she felt his hand slide under the light wool cover and settle on her thigh. Opening her eyes, she turned to look at him, but he still seemed sound asleep. Again, her eyelids dropped, and again she felt Adam's hand move, down her leg, to the hem of the skirt. It stroked her knee for a moment, then tugged her legs apart, and began to inch upward slowly along the inside of her thigh. This time when she looked at him, his eyes were open and sleepy, and he was smiling. She opened her mouth as if to say something but he shook his head to discourage her. Removing his hand from her, he lifted the arm rest, moved closer to her on the seat, and turned her to face him. Over his shoulder, she searched the dim cabin, anxious about possible witnesses, but the seats across the aisle from them were empty, the high backs protected them from those in front or behind, and the flight attendants had retreated to the galley to tidy up and relax after the meal service. Reassured, she returned her attention to Adam as she felt his hands again on her thighs lifting her body slightly from the seat so that he could, still concealed by the blanket, raise her skirt and slip her panties and hose down past her knees. Reaching to take them off entirely, leaving them in a crumpled heap on the carpeted plane floor, she could feel Adam's hands stroking her bottom, her stomach, between her legs. She turned back to him and, as his mouth closed over hers, she opened the belt of his trousers and pulled down the zipper of his fly.

"You're crazy," she whispered, her hand fondling his cock, enjoying the swollen silky feel of it, running her fingers along its tender underside, around its mushroom tip. "Crazy."

"I love you," he said, stroking her until she was close to coming, keeping his mouth on hers so she would not cry out, then, finally, with one quick movement, entering her.

When they came it was with a huge silent shudder. Afterward, they lay quiet for a moment, mouth to mouth, arms and legs still entangled, waiting for their breathing to steady. Finally, Adam pulled away and began to reassemble himself under the cover of his blanket while Katrinka readjusted her skirt and tucked her panties and hose into her purse to be donned later in the toilet. When she looked at Adam, he was smiling, a smug satisfied smile. Katrinka felt herself blushing. He reached over and took her hand, kissed it, and, still holding it, closed his eyes and went to sleep.

When they left the customs' hall, Adam and Katrinka were met by a uniformed chauffeur, a short, stocky man somewhere in his mid-forties with sandy hair and freckles. "Katrinka, meet Dave," said Adam as Katrinka extended her hand to shake the driver's. "Dave, this is Mrs. Graham," continued Adam.

Either Dave had read the newspaper reports or someone in Adam's office had told him the news, because he showed no surprise at Adam's announcement but merely shook Katrinka's hand, murmuring that he was pleased to meet her, and that if he could be of any help to her she was to let him know. His English had an odd accent which Katrinka did not recognize.

"Dave's been my driver for . . . how long now, Dave?"

"Five years, sir. The car's right outside." He led them and their porter through the terminal to the black Mercedes sedan at the curb, and settled them inside.

Katrinka leaned back against Adam, looked out the tinted windows of the car, and regarded the expanse of steel and glass buildings, concrete ramps, traffic-jammed roads, parking lots, yellow cabs, Hertz minivans, and tried to believe she was in New York. "It looks like everywhere," she said.

"Airports do."

"Where is Dave from?"

"Where?" Adam sounded startled by the question. "The Bronx," adding when he saw Katrinka's puzzled expression, "It's a borough of New York City. I'll get you a map," he said, rolling down the window separating them from Dave, "Mrs. Graham needs a map of the city. Could you get her one, please, Dave? Maybe two. Something to give her the overall plan, and a pocket one she can carry with her when she's wandering around."

"Yes, sir," said Dave.

Katrinka sighed, not so much daunted by having to learn her way around a new city (after all, she had done it all before) as overwhelmed by the strangeness of her new life, by its luxuriousness and complexity. How odd it suddenly felt not only to have a husband, but to have been removed without any reasonable warning from everything familiar and dropped without preparation into the middle of Adam's cluttered world, to deal with his driver, secretary, housekeeper, his mother and father, the family and friends he referred to in a bewildering avalanche of names. Her old life, in comparison, had been very frugal and solitary.

"Tired?" asked Adam.

"No," said Katrinka. "Excited." And, as she said it, she realized it was true.

Most of the ride in from the airport Katrinka found uninteresting, the dull Queens landscape extending in the relentless tedium of bleak shops and filling stations, factories and apartment buildings, vacant lots and cemeteries for endless miles.

"It gets better," said Adam reassuringly.

And it did. As they approached the Fifty-ninth Street Bridge, she saw the steel-and-glass skyscrapers sparkling in the afternoon light, making New York appear a city set with jewels. Then came the streets jammed with traffic, the blare of the car horns, the pavements crowded with hot, tired people, the buildings towering up to unbelievable heights, an electric current in the air, and, as the black Mercedes turned into Sutton Place, home to the Vanderbilts and the Morgans, a sudden rush of elegance and comparative quiet.

Adam lived in one of the larger buildings, in a six-room apartment stripped of any connection to its original grandeur. It was decorated in a minimalist style, with gray lacquer walls, black leather sofas, chrome-and-glass furniture, and a black lacquer entertainment center gleaming with the latest in audio/visual equipment. The stereo speakers stood taller than a man and occupied positions of honor in the sitting room. There were no ivy plants, no ficus trees. Over the black granite mantel hung an Ed Ruscha Standard Oil painting. Other art in the room included a Twombly, a Serra, a Warhol lithograph of Mick Jagger, and a metal sculpture by John Chamberlain. The rest of the apartment, including the housekeeper's bedroom on the other side of the granite-and-chrome kitchen, was all in the same style, which was as different from the Graham family home in Newport as Adam's decorator had been able to make it.

Adam introduced her to Carter, a tall, slender man with a face like a greyhound, who, he explained, did everything: cooking, cleaning, laundry. Katrinka shook his hand and detected in his words of welcome a more familiar accent, one she had heard frequently in Kitzbühel: definitely British, she thought. Carter took the luggage from the driver and disappeared with it down a long corridor, as Adam spread his hands indicating the apartment, and said, "Home. What do you think?"

It was too stark for Katrinka's taste, yet it had style and even elegance. "I'm not sure," she said. She sank into one of the sofas. "It's comfortable." She looked around the room. "Peaceful." The Warhol lithograph reminded her of the parties the ski team used to have after the races when they would dance to music from the West, singing along with the Stones. "It is like nothing I have seen before, but I think I can like it."

"You better," he said, taking her hand and pulling her to her feet. "Come on. Let's go take a shower."

While Katrinka lay trying to nap in the king-size bed, amid the black-and-gray Bill Blass sheets, she could hear coming from the next room the low, indistinct murmur of Adam speaking on the phone with his mother. His voice had an edge to it she had never heard before: irritable, impatient, argumentative, though it was never raised above normal conversational level. Finally, she heard the receiver returned to its cradle and Adam enter the bedroom.

"Is she very angry?" asked Katrinka.

"Aren't you asleep yet?"

"I'm too excited to sleep. Is she?"

"No more than usual," said Adam, removing his paisley silk dressing gown and putting on a pair of jockey shorts he took from a drawer in a large black lacquer chest. "We'll go up for the weekend. She'll settle down once she meets you."

"What about your father?"

"He's a nice guy. You'll like him."

"And your sister?"

"Clementine will follow Mother's lead. I'm not sure she'll be there. Unless Mother summons her, of course."

"You know, Adam, you do make her sound very . . ." Katrinka searched for the word.

"Unpleasant?"

Katrinka shrugged. It was not quite the word she had been looking for, but it would do.

"She's really not. She's really very charming. She'll have you eating out of her hand in no time at all."

"Eating what?" It was an expression Katrinka had not heard before.

Adam laughed, amused as always by the gaps in Katrinka's knowledge of English, and opened his hand, palm up. "You know, like when you feed a favorite pet. You'll like her."

Katrinka was not so sure. "I am more happy all the time," she said, "that we did marry in Cap Ferrat."

"So am I." He had put on a Lanvin summer suit of lightweight striped wool, a white shirt, and polka-dot tie. He bent over her prone form and kissed her. "I have to go into the office for a while, to catch up on some paperwork, make a few phone calls. Try to sleep. We'll go out to dinner at about nine."

A rush of loneliness overwhelmed her as Adam left the room, and Katrinka realized that it was the first time in over a week that they had been separated. How would she spend her time with him gone? she wondered. How would she keep herself occupied? She was not in the least bit domestic. Did Adam know that? With Carter around, Adam would not, of course, expect her to cook or clean, which was just as well. Though she could do both when she had to, and very well in her opinion, she much preferred to pay someone else to do that work while she earned the money to pay for the service doing something she enjoyed more. But what could she do in New York to keep busy, at least until Adam and she had children? Her modeling portfolio was in a trunk she had shipped from Munich. Perhaps when it arrived, she would begin making the rounds of the agencies and try to start a new career. At twenty-eight, to get photographic assignments would be difficult, but showroom and runway work, with her experience, ought to be possible. Would Adam mind? wondered Katrinka as she drifted off to sleep.

That evening they had dinner at "21" with Lucia and Nick Cavalletti, who had returned to New York after spending a few days at their house in Florence. As she followed the maître d' to the table, Katrinka was aware of heads turning and sensed rather than heard the hum of conversation that followed their progress. For one uncomfortable moment, she thought that perhaps there was something wrong with the way she was dressed, then dismissed that idea as nonsense. She was wearing the short white Chanel cocktail dress that had been one of her Paris acquisitions, perfectly cut, perfectly simple, appropriate for dining out in any decent restaurant anywhere in the world. And Lucia, in a short dress of peach silk that highlighted her thick auburn hair and fair skin, was reassuringly in a similar style.

No, it definitely was not her wardrobe that was causing comment, realized Katrinka after a moment, but her marriage, or rather the suddenness of it, everyone's curiosity no doubt fueled by the speculation in the press.

Her back straight, her head held high, an easy smile on her face, Katrinka, who was used to running the gauntlet of buyers and press at runway fashion shows, seemed oblivious to the attention she and Adam were getting. But she didn't like it. When the maître d' stopped at a table near the bar and asked Adam if it would do, Katrinka looked longingly at the distant part of the room away from the door and all the turned heads and whispered conversation and suggested that perhaps it would be quieter there, but Adam said, "No, no, this will be fine. Thank you."

Once they were seated, Nick leaned toward her, smiling, and said, "Do you want everyone to think that Adam's gone broke?" Katrinka looked at him blankly and Nick gestured toward the area where Katrinka had suggested sitting. "It's like being exiled to Siberia," he explained.

"This is *the* place to sit," added Lucia, who seesawed between an aristocratic disdain for publicity and a businesswoman's appreciation of its uses. She shrugged and continued, "Though it is a bit like being an animal on display at the zoo. Upstairs is all right for business meetings."

It was Katrinka's first experience of the subtle rules that govern social life in New York. Apparently, comfort and privacy were irrelevant; being seen was what was important, and, once you had achieved a certain level of visibility, to lose it was not only humiliating but harmful. As long as people thought he was successful, explained Adam, business would continue to boom. If they began to doubt it, he would soon begin to lose money.

"But you are successful," said Katrinka.

"Very," assured Nick, who wished he was pulling in per

316

annum what Adam Graham was, though he had hopes that someday, perhaps soon, he might.

"Appearance is what counts," said Adam. "Not fact."

"I thought maybe all the talk would stop if we were out of sight."

Lucia smiled and shook her head. "You have no idea what a stunning couple you and Adam make." Tall, good-looking, elegant, above all rich, they carried themselves with such flamboyant assurance, thought Lucia admiringly, they could not escape notice. Nor could the circumstances of their marriage, its seeming haste and apparent unsuitability (it was, after all, the alliance of an American blue blood with a Czechoslovakian nobody) dropping like a heaven-sent bit of gossip to enliven a dull New York summer. "The talk isn't going to stop," added Lucia, who spoke from experience. Her own marriage to Nick, against her mother's wishes, had attracted its share of speculation. And continued to.

Katrinka sighed and Adam reached over and put his hand on top of hers. "For better or worse," he said.

Katrinka laughed. It was a deep, hearty, infectious laugh and the others soon joined her, accomplishing just what Katrinka had hoped to avoid: every head in the room turned toward them. "Exactly what I have been telling myself all day," she said.

Lucia quietly pointed out to Katrinka some of the celebrities present whom she, of course, would not have recognized: Daniel Moynihan, recently appointed ambassador to the United Nations; Rick Colins, the columnist who so had impressed Katrinka with his detailed knowledge of her wedding; Michael Bennett, the director. Others came over to offer congratulations and be introduced to the bride: John Gutfreund, the man to watch at Salomon Brothers, and Neil Goodman, his counterpart at Knapp Manning, both of whom had had business dealings with Adam; Philip Johnson, the architect, who was a friend both of Lucia's mother and Adam's parents; Mark van Hollen, the handsome Viking from the ski lift and his no longer pregnant wife, who announced happily that they had just had another son; and Daisy and Steven Elliott, who remembered meeting Katrinka in Kitzbühel.

317

"That lovely inn," said Daisy. "And that jam." She licked her perfect lips. "I had it finished before any of the children got a chance to taste it." She turned to Adam. "You have married a very enterprising woman."

"Don't I know it."

"I hope you'll be very happy, my dear," said Steven, his long body seeming to collapse rather than bend toward her as he gallantly kissed Katrinka's cheek.

"Can you have lunch with me tomorrow?" Daisy asked Katrinka.

"Why, uh, yes, of course." She turned to Adam. "Unless you did plan something."

"Not a thing," said Adam.

"Good. One o'clock. Le Cirque." She turned to Lucia, whom she had known forever. "Can you join us, darling?"

"I'd love to."

"We'll map out a campaign," said Daisy cryptically as she started toward her table, her small body moving with extraordinary determination, as if she were on her way to conquer a kingdom, not order a meal.

"Campaign?" asked Katrinka, who found the constant stream of well-wishers a little dizzying.

Lucia laughed. "Daisy loves to organize. We call her 'the little general.'"

"I need organizing?"

"Well, you don't know anyone in New York, except us, do you?" asked Adam, who had not previously considered how difficult it might be for his new wife to make friends in a foreign city. Had he thought of it, he would have asked Daisy as well as Lucia to help, to introduce Katrinka around. He was delighted she had volunteered. "And Daisy knows everyone."

"This jam of yours must be something," said Nick, a hint of envy in his voice. He had thought when he married the well-connected Lucia di Campo that his place in society was fixed, but he had long since realized that he was merely tolerated for his wife's sake, not liked, despite his looks and charm, or admired for the legal coups he more and more regularly pulled off. Of all Lucia's friends, only Adam and Daisy seemed to have any real affection for him, and he

318

sometimes suspected that was merely because he (and perhaps the Mafia dons on his client list) intrigued and somehow amused them. "Daisy's a sweetheart, but she doesn't often go out of her way for a stranger. Steven won't let her."

"I will make you some sometime," offered Katrinka, wondering where in New York it was possible to buy red currants and raspberries and whether Carter would mind if she messed up his perfect kitchen. What a lot there was she had to learn.

The next day Katrinka accompanied her husband to his New York office, a suite of rooms in the Seagram Building whose main attraction for Adam was its proximity to the Racquet and Tennis Club across the street where he regularly worked out. She met his personal secretary, Debbie Ingersoll, a leggy blonde who seemed efficient enough to have been hired for her skills rather than her obvious good looks; John MacIntyre, known as Mac, a few years older than Adam and his right-hand man; and a bewildering number of others—the heads of the design team, advertising, marketing, and public relations, assorted lawyers, draftsmen, junior executives, receptionists, file clerks, secretaries, runners—about eighty people (the shipyards had their own staffs), all of whom were eager to be introduced and to offer congratulations. Mac produced a bottle of champagne, there were toasts all around, and Debbie presented Adam and Katrinka with their wedding gift. The mood was festive as Katrinka quickly removed the white ribbon and silver paper, lifted off the top of the box, felt her way through the mound of shredded paper, and extracted a tall vase of Baccarat crystal. Tears welled in her eyes. "Oh, it is beautiful. So beautiful." She shook hands, kissed cheeks, thanked them all so sincerely, was so warm and friendly, so unlike the rather cool, haughty beauties everyone in the office was used to seeing with Adam Graham that Katrinka instantly won hearts, except perhaps for Mac's, which was said not to exist.

"Now, can we do a little work around here?" asked Adam genially, putting an end to the party if not to everyone's good mood. He walked Katrinka to the elevator and kissed her good-bye. "Have a nice lunch," he said. "I'll be home about seven."

It was a hot, humid New York summer's day, and in the few seconds it took Katrinka to get down the steps of the Seagram Building and into the waiting car at the curb her sleeveless linen dress was already sticking uncomfortably to her body. Gratefully, she sank into the Mercedes' air-conditioned interior and cool leather seats.

Dave closed the door and went around to the front of the car and got in. "It's a stinker today, all right," he said. "Where to now, Mrs. Graham?"

"Le Cirque. You know where it is?"

"Yes, ma'am."

Daisy and Lucia had already arrived and Katrinka was shown to their banquette, which was immediately to the left of the front door. Was this *the* place to sit? wondered Katrinka as she kissed her new friends hello and settled herself in the chair held for her by the attentive maître d'. "Katrinka, this is Sirio," said Daisy. "He owns this wonderful place. Sirio, the new Mrs. Adam Graham."

As they sampled the Brie twists and picked delicately at their salads, the introductions continued as people stopped by to say hello to Daisy or Lucia, who, between them, seemed to know everyone: Eleanor Lambert, who compiled the list of the world's best-dressed women (of which Daisy was frequently one); Mikhail Baryshnikov, the new star of American Ballet Theater; Mario Buatta, the interior designer; and Margo Jensen, a good friend of Daisy's. Margo, the fashion editor of *Chic*, with her frizz of charcoal hair, pale white skin, and brilliantly colored mouth, was the most interesting-looking woman Katrinka had ever seen—dramatic, original, almost beautiful. She regarded Katrinka carefully with appraising eyes. "Well, you've certainly caused a sensation," she said, her bright red mouth curving in an attractive smile, "coming out of nowhere and making off with one of our most eligible bachelors." Her manner was so open and friendly that it was difficult to take offense at what she said.

320

FOR LOVE ALONE

"The bachelor I'm glad to have," replied Katrinka, returning Margo's smile. "The sensation I could live without."

Margo laughed. "Not me," she said. "My life depends on finding new faces, new personalities, to please the crowd. You model?"

"How you did know that?" asked a startled Katrinka.

Margo's smile grew wider. "I have my ways," she said. "May I call you? Shall we have lunch one day?" She foresaw many business as well as personal advantages to pursuing the new Mrs. Graham, with her stunning good looks and charming accent. All those misplaced verbs, the substitution of *v* for *w*, *z* for *th*, it would all make such good copy.

"I would enjoy that," said Katrinka, who had liked Margo instantly.

"You're a hit," said Daisy, watching Margo walk away, then added, "Have you two met?" as Rick Colins paused for a moment en route to his table.

"Yes, last night," he replied. Extremely tall, about six feet five inches, slender to the point of gangling, Rick Colins in his late twenties still had an awkward adolescent air about him. It was an endearing quality which, combined with his good looks—light brown hair, hazel eyes, a strong nose, dimpled chin—and exquisite manners, made people both like and trust him, unusual for a gossip columnist, and extremely useful. He was wearing a large bow tie, his trademark.

Katrinka, against her better judgment, found that she liked him. "It's nice to see you again," she said.

"His parents are heartbroken about him," confided Daisy once Rick had moved away. Like Daisy, Rick Colins came from old New England money, but his family was merely comfortable, not rich. A product of Choate and Princeton, he had been expected to do something respectable, like become a banker or corporate executive or university professor, but instead had dabbled in theater for a while, and then begun to write. Witty magazine pieces on the foibles of the wealthy had earned him a sizable reputation and that, plus knowing or at least having entrée to all the right people, eventually got him a column at *The Chronicle*. "And writing nonsense does, I suppose, seem a terrible waste when he is

321

so very intelligent. On the other hand, he is perfectly happy, and that's all that counts, isn't it? You'll be in his column tomorrow, my dear. 'Lunching at Le Cirque with Daisy Elliott, of the Boston Elliotts, and Lucia di Campo, talented yacht designer, the divinely beautiful Katrinka Graham, bride of entrepreneur Adam Graham.'" When Katrinka did not look particularly pleased at the prospect, Daisy added, "If you want to have an interesting life in New York, you have to make people want to know you. And someone like Rick Colins can help."

Since in Katrinka's limited experience what gossip the newspapers printed was largely untrue, it was difficult for her to understand why people who presumably knew much better than she how untrustworthy such accounts were should have any interest whatsoever in meeting her. But when Katrinka expressed this thought, Daisy merely smiled at her indulgently. "What the papers say doesn't matter in the least, as long as they say something. You see, here people aren't talked about because they're interesting. It's the other way round. They're interesting because they're talked about."

"Daisy's exaggerating a little," said Lucia, whose mother came from a prominent New York family with an almost paranoid aversion to publicity. Her father, a successful painter who had emigrated from Rome just before the beginning of the Second World War, had driven his proper in-laws wild with one mad attention-grabbing stunt after another. As a result, he had lost a wife, and more or less a daughter, but had become a far more successful artist than his talent alone deserved. "Old money tends to avoid the limelight. It's new money that revels in it. The free publicity is good for business."

"Old money is so stuffy," said Daisy, whose wealth, as well as her husband's, dated back to fortunes made in merchant trading in colonial America. "It's not the publicity I like, it's the fun."

Even living in a communist country, the division between rich and poor had always been apparent to Katrinka, and the study of history made obvious that some people had had money for much longer, even hundreds of years longer, than others; but never before had she realized that a circumstance as incidental as time might actually divide the wealthy themselves into separate classes. "The Grahams, Adam's family, are they old money or new?"

"Old," said Lucia.

"Very old," added Daisy. "On the Graham side at least. The Grahams have been building ships of one kind or another since 1760. Adam's mother, Nina, was a Landor. Railroad money. Old enough."

"But Adam does not hate publicity."

"No," said Lucia dryly.

"Lucia's right," added Daisy. "In addition to everything else, it's good for business." She could have commented a bit more on the subject of Adam Graham, but did not think she was yet on good enough terms with his new wife to treat Katrinka to a little amateur psychologizing. But Daisy did find Adam an interesting case. At first she had thought he courted the press just to irritate his parents. Then she had thought it was because he had as a child been given too much money and no responsibility. Then she had realized his motivation was something more complicated than either of those. An only son, indulged, even spoiled, he had been raised, by his mother at least, with an inflated sense of his own and his family's worth in both social and financial terms. Proud, even arrogant, Adam must have been very shocked when he had realized that his illustrious family's fortunes were in fact in decline, that for generations the Grahams, and the Landors for that matter, had been living on rapidly depleting capital, and that the power and prestige of the name were disappearing even more swiftly than the money. And while the Graham family star was sinking into oblivion, whose was rising? Pop singers and television actors, film directors and computer designers, real estate developers and advertising executives, salesmen and hustlers, the sorts of people he had been raised to consider somehow inferior. Not that he did, of course. He had too much respect for success to discount those who had achieved it. But he was not about to take second place to them, to relinquish what he considered his rightful place, to give up one inch of social position or one ray of limelight. If

Adam had his way, and Daisy thought that he might, the Graham fortune would be repaired with a vengeance. But she said none of this to Katrinka, asking instead, "Have you met the Grahams yet?"

"We are going to Newport this weekend."

"Kenneth, Adam's father, is a sweetheart. You'll adore him. But Nina is a bit of a dragon."

"I expect she'll be angry because we did marry without her consent."

"She'll get over it," said Lucia kindly, though she knew Nina Graham too well to think her surrender would be quick or easy. "Once she meets you and sees how perfect you are for Adam." It would not, thought Lucia, be easy for any woman to live with Adam Graham and not be devastated by the power of his personality or the demands of his ego, but Katrinka seemed to her to have the sort of self-confidence, the levelheadedness, the inner strength to pull it off.

Katrinka smiled at Lucia gratefully. "Have you known Adam a long time?" she asked.

"We were at MIT together," said Lucia. They had briefly and unhappily been lovers—Adam had liked then to run a number of women simultaneously. If business interests had not made it necessary, they might never have become friends. "And when he bought his first shipyard, I began designing yachts for him."

"She's very talented," said Daisy.

"I know," said Katrinka. "I saw her drawings for Khalid ibn Hassan's yacht."

"Are you doing that?" asked Daisy, clearly impressed. The yacht was to be the biggest—and most expensive—ever built. "How lovely. Well, this has been a most productive lunch," she said, sounding very satisfied as she gathered up her purse and prepared to leave.

"Thank you," said Katrinka with genuine gratitude, touched by the older woman's friendliness and generosity. "I did enjoy myself."

"So did I. We'll do it again next week. Perhaps at La Grenouille? It's good to cover all bases. And of course I'll start arranging a dinner for you, to introduce you around a bit more formally."

"Really, I don't want you to go to so much trouble for me."

"Don't be silly, my dear. I enjoy it. It's not often I meet someone I genuinely like. And I did like you, from the moment I set eyes on you." She stood up, as did Lucia, and both women started to move away from the table, then stopped as Katrinka remained firmly seated.

"The check," said Katrinka softly. "It did not come yet."

Daisy smiled. "Oh, they send a bill sooner or later. Don't worry," she said breezily. "It was a lovely lunch, Sirio. See you soon," she added as she led the others from the restaurant, apparently oblivious to the heads turning to watch their exit.

Nothing worked here the way it did in Europe, thought Katrinka, who was overwhelmed by how much she had to learn about the customs of this strange country.

"Lucia, I'll drop you at your place, if you're going home," said Daisy as soon as they got outside, then turned to Katrinka and added, "Would you like a ride, my dear? Or have you got a car?" Katrinka declined when she saw Dave waiting a few feet away. "I'll phone you on Monday," continued Daisy gliding past her chauffeur, following Lucia into the car's dim interior, "to find out how the weekend went. Remember, don't let Nina bully you. Too many people do."

"I won't," said Katrinka, hoping it was a promise she could keep.

Twenty-Seven

After a childhood spent amid the hills and forests of Svitov, after skiing the Krkonoše, the Carpathians, and the Alps, the drive along I-95 from New York to Rhode Island seemed very flat and dull to Katrinka. Even after turning off the thruway onto the two-lane road that would take them to Newport, the landscape did not in her opinion improve significantly. Thin patches of trees alternating with stubbled fields, charming antiques stores, bleak gas stations, and worn frame houses hardly compared to Czechoslovakia's dense forests edged with wildflowers or its tiny villages with their red-tiled roofs and slender church steeples set in the distant hills.

The top of Adam's Porsche Carrera was down and Katrinka wore a scarf around her head to keep her hair from blowing wild. A Barbra Streisand tape was playing and she swayed in time to the beat and sang along in Czech. From time to time Adam would look at her and smile, not just because he thought she was beautiful with her eyes closed, her long neck fully extended, her face raised to the sky, caught up in the music and completely oblivious to him, but because he was still intrigued by the apparent inconsistencies in her background. Though Western newspapers and magazines were not available in Czechoslovakia, Katrinka had told him, American and English pop, as sung by local groups, was standard fare on the radio. There were waiting lists for houses and apartments, people were forced to share, divorced couples having no alternative had to go on living together, but an ordinary family could afford a small summer cottage in the mountains. The state controlled production and distribution, private enterprise was forbidden, promotions were hard to get unless you were a Communist Party member, but energetic people worked two or three jobs and could afford a car, the old lived comfortably on pensions, the government took care of the sick, and there was plenty of food in the shops.

What Katrinka told him of her childhood and adolescence did not conform to Adam's preconceived ideas of the sterility of life in a communist country but, though it did not make the system any less horrible to as confirmed a capitalist as he, to someone who believed as completely as he did in free expression and free enterprise, who would fight for a market economy with the fervor his revolutionary forebears had displayed at Bunker Hill and Valley Forge, at least Katrinka's stories made him realize what a narrow experience he had of the world, what an edited view, a blinkered perception of life in other countries, which was not, he realized, a good way to continue if he hoped to realize his ambitions of a global financial empire. (The shipyards in Bremen had been just the first step.) Katrinka had made him think, a novel experience for him in a relationship.

Adam was not looking forward to the visit with his parents: he knew the opening moves, at least, would be difficult. But he did not doubt for a moment that Katrinka would win them over quickly. How could they fail to see what an extraordinary find she was? How lucky he had been to meet her? Be as completely charmed as he by her foreignness, her accent, the odd manner in which she occasionally strung a sentence together, the way she combined beauty with intelligence and courage, femininity with self-reliance and ambition? When he thought about how close he had come to deciding to return immediately to New York rather than go to Kitzbühel that weekend he was overwhelmed with a sense of gratitude, thanking his lucky stars, his good fortune, his fate, whatever it was that made him feel now so much like destiny's darling. He reached over and put his hand on Katrinka's thigh. Immediately her eyes opened and she gave him a look of such complete love

327

and trust he felt a moment's panic. How could he possibly keep from disappointing her? Or she him? came the second unwelcome thought, even more disturbing than the first. "Here it is," he said, "Newport," his smile dispatching the unpleasant notions to some remote dungeon in his mind where he kept all such worrying ideas under heavy guard.

Katrinka surveyed the pretty town, its red-brick and colonial-white frame structures, its clock tower and main square. It could not, of course, compare even to Kitzbühel for beauty, let alone Prague, but it had a simple charm that appealed to her, and a connection to the past, a sense of history, which even the oldest buildings in New York seemed to lack, so caught up was the city in the new, the modern, the happening. "I do like it," said Katrinka. "It is lovely. Really lovely."

"I grew up here," he said, pointing the Carrera toward Bellevue Avenue, driving past all the grand mansions, their manicured lawns, impressive shrubbery, and stone facades visible behind the tall iron fences, showing Katrinka where the Astors had lived, the Whitneys, the Morgans, indicating which houses still remained in private hands and which now were owned by the Historical Society and open for viewing by the public.

"Your family does live in one of these?" asked Katrinka who, though she knew the Grahams were wealthy, had not expected anything quite so grand.

"Oh, no," said Adam. "Mother likes her privacy. And you don't get much here."

To show Katrinka some of the sights, he had detoured through the town, but now it was getting close to lunchtime and they were expected, so Adam headed his car for what he still sometimes thought of as home.

"It's called The Poplars," said Adam as the Carrera turned into a graveled road bordered with tall, graceful trees meticulously spaced at regular intervals, "for obvious reasons."

They had entered through the side gate, the main ones being closed except when the family was entertaining formally, so the approach was not as impressive as it might have been along the other longer, wider, poplar-lined drive. Still, when the trees came to an end and the service road broadened into a courtyard and Katrinka caught her first glimpse of the house, she let out a small gasp. "My God, it's enormous."

Designed by Horace Trumbauer, the architect of many of the Newport mansions, the house was a long, rectangular building of gray stone with a pitched slate roof, turrets, gables, and French doors opening onto stone terraces at the sides and back of the house. It was set in twenty-five acres landscaped by Frederick Law Olmsted, who had designed Central Park in New York. Each room of the house had a view of either the ocean or the gardens or both.

"I'm not sure how many rooms it has exactly," said Adam. "My sister and I used to try counting them, but we always forgot one, or counted the same room twice. Over twenty anyway. And there's a carriage house, there, beyond that grove of trees, which we use as a sort of cabana for the swimming pool. We used to have great parties there when I was a kid." He got out of the car and came around to open Katrinka's door. "Come on. No point putting off the inevitable."

"I feel like wreck."

"You look great. Beautiful. Don't worry. Everyone will be as crazy about you as I am."

Adam put a comforting arm around his bride and led the way up the three wide stone steps to the massive front door, which was flanked by urns dripping ivy. He rang the bell and they waited what seemed only an instant before the door was swung open by an elderly man in dark pants and a white jacket. "Mr. Adam," he said, smiling with genuine pleasure.

"Hello, Edward. Nice to see you again. This is my wife, Katrinka. Sweetheart, this is Edward, our butler." There were several servants, Adam had warned her: a butler, a footman, a cook, a kitchen maid, a laundress, two house-maids, and a chauffeur. Extra help was brought in as needed.

As Katrinka, murmuring a few words of greeting, extended her hand to shake Edward's, she thought she detected a quick worried look flit across the butler's face before he smiled pleasantly, told her how pleased he was to meet her, and that Mr. and Mrs. Graham were awaiting them in the garden room.

They passed through the large center hall, its paneled walls covered with paintings and lined with antique benches and tables, through a large sitting room, its paneling painted a pale green and hung with landscape oils, its gilt-trimmed Louis Seize furniture upholstered in silk, to a large room with stone walls and floor, filled with wicker furniture, plants and cut flowers everywhere, a Huysmans painting over the mantel. In the far wall was a series of French doors opening out onto a flagstone terrace. Beyond that was a stretch of unblemished lawn dropping down to the public Cliff Walk and the ocean.

But Katrinka noticed neither the terrace nor the view, since her eyes were firmly fixed on Adam's parents. His father, Kenneth Graham, looked like an older, paler version of Adam, with the same long narrow face, pronounced nose, and close-set eyes, but without his son's vitality and sex appeal, or the attractiveness that was a product of both. He was seated in a wicker chair, studying a drawing, a glass of what looked like gin and tonic on a table next to him.

Nina Graham was seated on the wicker sofa, a matching gin and tonic in one delicate pink-tipped hand, the other flicking through the pages of *Town and Country,* which she was regarding without much real interest. In her early sixties, she was beautiful, slender, small, with perfectly sculpted features, a wide sensuous mouth, cool gray eyes, and tinted blond hair pouffed and sprayed. She wore a simple Halston sheath, a pearl choker and earrings, making Katrinka feel fussy and overdressed in the fashionable "wrap look," a print shawl draped and tied around a Calvin Klein blouse and skirt.

"Hello, you two," said Adam, his arm still firmly around Katrinka. He was prepared if necessary to propel her resistant form deeper into the room. "Meet Katrinka."

But if she felt a bit as if she were walking into the lion's den, Katrinka did not look it. She looked completely at ease, assured, even regal, her smile warm and gracious enough to avoid arrogance. I do want you to like me, she seemed to be saying, and am prepared to go out of my way to see that you do; but if you refuse, I can manage perfectly well without you.

At the sound of Adam's voice, his parents looked up. His father smiled and got instantly to his feet, intercepting Adam, shaking his hand, kissing Katrinka's cheek. "Well, well, well," he said, "what a surprise you two sprang on us."

"We did surprise ourselves a little," said Katrinka. "I hope you do forgive us?"

"There's nothing to forgive," said Kenneth Graham. "Nothing. As long as you two are happy, that's all that matters."

"Oh, my darling," said Nina Graham, getting to her feet and embracing Adam, who stooped to kiss her. "I was never more shocked in my life." Her eyes welled with tears.

Adam, who seemed totally unmoved by her emotion, nevertheless said with a great deal of practiced charm, "I'm sorry about that. I got so carried away, I didn't think. But you can see why." Now, he put his arm around his mother and propelled her toward Katrinka, who stood waiting with her smile still firmly fixed.

"Yes, I can see. You're lovely," said Nina, taking Katrinka's hand. "Welcome to The Poplars, my dear. I'm so pleased you could find the time to come finally. I have been longing to meet you. My son's wife. I still can't believe it."

"Neither can I," said Katrinka. "It all did happen very fast."

"Very," agreed her mother-in-law dryly.

"You just can't get over the shock of my taking your advice for once," said Adam, his tone light and teasing, though no one believed for a moment he was anything but serious. He turned to Katrinka. "She's been after me to get married for years. And as soon as I found the right girl, I did."

"An elopement was not exactly what I had in mind."

"It was hardly an elopement," said Adam. "Just a quiet wedding."

"Drinks?" asked Kenneth Graham. He took everyone's

331

order, crossed to the fully stocked trolley, freshened his wife's drink, made a Cinzano for Katrinka and a gin and tonic for Adam.

"Come sit by me, my dear," said Nina, seating herself again on the sofa, crossing one leg over the other. She was wearing neat navy and white pumps.

She resembled Daisy Elliott, thought Katrinka. Though Nina Graham was years older, they were, at least superficially, the same type. Both were small, elegant, aristocratic, and beautiful. Both were full of energy and obviously determined to have their way. But while Daisy was full of warmth and humor and offered easy affection, Nina was cool, reserved, and always implicitly disapproving. "I am sorry if it did make you unhappy," said Katrinka, going in her usual forthright way to the heart of the matter. "But we both did want a small wedding."

"Did you? And your family approved?"

"I have very little family left," said Katrinka. "My parents did die a long time ago."

"Yes," said Nina, with no trace of sympathy in her voice, "well I can see in that case it might not have mattered to you, though I have always thought that all women dreamed of beautiful white weddings. I certainly did. And my daughter. But perhaps it is simply not the custom in *communist* countries," she added, with a slight but unmistakable edge.

"All I can remember is Clementine in tears before *her* wedding," said Adam, leaping in before Katrinka could answer, taking the opportunity to turn the spotlight from his wife to his sister.

"Oh, Clementine," said his mother dismissively. "Clementine always does as she's told."

"As a good child should, or so you've always told me," said Clementine from the doorway. A small smile fixed on her face, she crossed the room toward them, her husband, Wilson Benning, following close behind. As Adam had predicted might happen, his sister had been summoned home to meet his bride. "Really, Adam," she said, "can't you ever do what's expected of you?" She kissed him rather reluctantly on the cheek, then turned to Katrinka, extending her hand politely. "You must be Katrinka. How do you do?"

Embarrassed by his wife's coldness, a faint red flush invaded Wilson's face as he shook Adam's hand and then Katrinka's, murmuring vague, polite phrases which were interrupted by Kenneth Graham's again offering drinks, his way of dealing with awkward situations, Katrinka had already noted.

Clementine, who resembled her father and brother, was in fact completely her mother's daughter: cool, aloof, constantly appraising and slyly critical. Her husband, Wilson, was just under six feet, with thinning fair hair and the beginnings of a paunch. Even in khaki pants and a sports jacket he looked like a banker. They lived just outside of Providence, close enough for Wilson's commute into the bank every day not to be too taxing, and had a summer place in Hyannisport on Cape Cod. Clementine did not work at all, preferring to stay at home and raise her two sons (ordered by their grandmother to remain at home for the day with their nanny) and sit on the board of various local charities. She did not look in the least bit charitable to Katrinka.

Lunch was difficult, but not deadly. No matter whether they presented it as outright curiosity or polite interest, the family was keen to know not only how and when Adam had met Katrinka and all about their marriage, but also the background of this woman with her odd accent and regal manner. It was an unusual situation for the Grahams. Normally the people they met socially were already connected to them in some way and their stories either known or familiar. The others—the servants, the tradesmen, the general run of acquaintances casually met in the course of living—they did not bother about beyond polite exchanges of information given and taken with minimal interest. But Katrinka was unknown territory, which, like reluctant travelers forced by circumstance (an earthquake, perhaps, or a famine) to leave the comfort of their homes, the Grahams set out to explore and, if found suitable, colonize.

Once seated around the dining room table, formally set with linen placemats, silver flatware, Wedgwood china, and Venetian crystal, waited on by Edward, the butler, and a young footman who served the stringy chicken and overdone vegetables, the family took to grilling Katrinka. Prodded by their questions when she hesitated, she gave them an account of her life, of a warm and loving family, a hard but rewarding childhood, a successful academic and sports career, the heartbreak of her parents' death, and her subsequent decision to leave Czechoslovakia, all as concisely as she could manage, while Adam looked on proudly waiting for them all to be as bowled over by her story as he had been. But while his father certainly looked impressed, and Wilson seemed inclined to be wowed if only he dared, Nina Graham and Clementine managed to convey interest and even, at times, surprise, but garnished always with their specialty, a slight dash of disapproval.

Lack of interest she could have understood, perhaps even boredom, though she would happily have stopped talking if only they would let her, but disapproval? Of what? wondered Katrinka as she watched their faces. It was disconcerting. Looking back on her life, she was in general proud of what she had achieved. Her only source of regret, a constant nagging ache, was the memory of the child she had given up, and the Grahams, of course, knew nothing of him. Nor would they ever, she decided at that moment, unless somehow, miraculously, she managed to find him. For that, she was willing to earn their criticism. For that, she would put up with anything.

When Katrinka had finished, Nina Graham looked at her, smiled rather thinly, and said, "What a remarkable story," the tone of her voice conveying that she did not believe most of it and considered her son a fool for having been taken in. But the suggestion of disbelief was so faint it was unchallengeable.

There was a brief, embarrassed silence and then Kenneth Graham jumped into the void, saying sympathetically, "When you left Czechoslovakia, you left everything behind? How awful for you."

"Not everything," corrected Katrinka. "I did take with me a few pieces of my mother's jewelry, nothing valuable, except to me. And Adam"—she looked across the table to her husband and for the first time since she had arrived at

The Poplars smiled a totally unselfconscious and loving smile—"did go to Prague to get photographs, old letters, and some other small things. He knew how much they did mean to me."

"Why, Adam," said Clementine, sounding genuinely surprised. "I've never known you to be thoughtful."

"Oh, he is," said Katrinka, not certain whether or not Clementine was serious. "To me. He is wonderful."

Adam laughed. "You see. How could I resist her?"

"Why would you want to?" said his father gallantly.

"No one ever said you were completely crazy," said Wilson, prepared to risk Clementine's anger just this once to side with his brother-in-law, whom he did not much like, and his new sister-in-law, who, he was prepared to admit at least to himself, was a knockout.

"Indeed," said Nina Graham with the peculiar edge that gave everything she said a double meaning.

"It's not a big yard by any means," explained Kenneth Graham to Katrinka when she asked him about his work, his eyes bright and his face a little flushed with drink, sounding more proud than humble, "but it's been in the family, on the same site, not too far from here, since 1765. We've built some fine yachts in that time."

"The company's designed and built some America's Cup contenders," said Adam. "If you're nice to him, Father will show you the models."

Katrinka knew just enough about yachting to know that the America's Cup was one of the most important of the international sailing competitions. "I would love to see them," said Katrinka.

"Not many," said Kenneth Graham, "but some of the best. We've had a few winners."

"Not in your time of course," said his wife. She was smiling and could just have been stating a fact.

Disapproval was not a value judgment Nina Graham arrived at after serious thought; dissatisfaction was not an emotion resulting from genuine disappointment. Both were simply techniques her unconscious had learned to use to her advantage at a very early age. Her refusal to be satisfied, she had discovered somewhere along the way, encouraged people to try harder to please her. They focused their attention on her, spent their time searching for new and innovative ways to make her happy and, when they failed—as inevitably they did—simply started all over again.

Had Nina been a less adorable child, a less beautiful and engaging woman, she never would have got away with it. Her perpetual air of discontent would have driven people off in droves. She would have been accused of whining, though of course she never did: she would have considered that a sign of weak character. But since she had been always both lovely and clever, had an ample supply of wit and charm, could be warm when she made the effort, and had cultivated the appearance of stoically enduring life's more unpleasant aspects, her many admirers rarely defected.

Of course her ploy had its serious drawbacks. For one thing, Nina could never allow herself to be approving or contented or happy for fear of having the endless supply of attention withdrawn. To ease the inevitable pain this caused, she often drank too much. And within the family circle, among the people who felt most powerfully the force of her constant disdain, only her husband and Clementine were still willing to make the always futile effort to please her. Adam seemed long ago to have given up.

Not that the Grahams were any more aware of the dynamic that drove them than most families. They simply played the game, not knowing it was one, unaware of the rules that over the years had been established.

And the rules dictated that at this point Adam should get angry because, although he pretended (most of all to himself) that he did not care a damn about his mother's opinion of his actions and had agreed to marrying Katrinka in the first place, and in the chapel at Cap Ferrat in the second, to demonstrate exactly that point, of course he cared. While he pretended to take no notice of her reactions, always, on some primal level, he was hoping to get that nod of approval, that smile of satisfaction, that spontaneous joyful hug that would tell him that at last he had succeeded in making his mother happy. Of course he had wanted her to approve of his choice, to like, even to love Katrinka. But once again he felt like the little boy who had bought his mother a pin for her birthday with his pocket money only to be told when she opened the present that, while she appreciated the thought, she felt it her duty to tell him it was never a good idea to buy cheap jewelry for a woman he professed to care about. And he never had since.

Of course Adam's anger was always primarily with himself for having been sucked again into Nina's game, but he insisted on believing that it was directed at his mother for reasons having nothing to do with him: the way she subtly belittled her husband, for example. Although her contempt had early on determined his own attitude toward his father, he felt on principle bound to defend him, and sometimes even to love him.

"The modern yachts use fiberglass, aluminum, all sorts of lightweight alloys which make them faster," explained Adam quickly, his annoyance showing, although his father seemed oblivious to his wife's implied criticism. "Father works almost exclusively in wood."

"These days, refitting older yachts mostly, since few people are mad enough to commission a new wooden yacht. But I enjoy my work. And I do all right."

"Well enough to keep a roof over the family head," said Adam, indicating the dining room with its silk-lined walls hung with priceless oil paintings, its large cabinets displaying Sevres porcelain, Wedgwood china, Baccarat and Waterford crystal.

"Don't be vulgar, Adam," snapped Clementine, cued to speak by Nina's frown.

"There's nothing like wood, if you ask me," said Kenneth, as usual heading off the quarrel, as aware as any of them—and completely unconcerned—that inherited money kept the family, not his income. "I leave all the innovative materials to my son, with my blessing."

"And I intend to use every last one of them," said Adam, following his father's lead, letting the argument go for Katrinka's sake, "and all the new ones as they come along."

"Your Bremen shipyard got the commission on the Hassan yacht, I heard," said Kenneth.

"Yes."

"Hassan?" asked Clementine.

"Prince Khalid ibn Hassan. A Saudi. Oil money," explained Wilson.

"Oh."

"Well, you're off and running. Congratulations," said Kenneth.

"Yes," agreed Adam. "It was quite a coup."

"Now, don't let's start talking shop," interrupted Nina. "Or we really will bore Katrinka to death."

"Not at all," said Katrinka. "Business interests me very much."

"Oh, yes," said Nina coldly. "That inn of yours. I had almost forgotten."

Whatever hopes Katrinka may have cherished of finding in Adam's mother someone to replace her own were gone. Instead, into Katrinka's mind suddenly came the image of Ilona Lukánský and the memory of the deep satisfaction she had felt that day at the *chata* when she had finally given in and hit back. But of course she could not strike this awful woman who happened to be Adam's mother, she could not beat her in a race, could not do anything but learn to tolerate her. But it was not, Katrinka realized, going to be easy.

Twenty-Eight

Nina Graham insisted on a small wedding reception to introduce "Adam's bride" to family and friends, so most of Katrinka's time in those first few weeks following her arrival in the United States was spent either with Daisy Elliott at fashionable restaurants collecting introductions, or commuting between New York and Newport, helping her difficult mother-in-law plan a party that neither of them particularly wanted and each would have been happier to arrange without interference from the other. But if Nina could not exactly order Katrinka out of the proceedings, Katrinka on her part was not prepared to let Nina Graham bully her into the background of her own marriage. For one thing, she wanted to learn what her mother-in-law had to teach; for another, she hoped to prove that she had something of value to contribute. After all, while she might be inexperienced in the ways of Newport and New York, she had worked at one of Europe's grandest hotels and run her own inn successfully for years: she did know a thing or two about planning and management, about catering and pleasing the customers.

The reception was held at The Poplars under a striped marquee erected in the garden, with catering by local companies, flowers from New York, a giant wedding cake from Quincy, Massachusetts, and music by two groups, one classical and one pop. Aside from members of the immediate family, guests included other Grahams and Landors;

339

friends such as Lucia di Campo and Nick Cavalletti, Alexandra Ogelvy and her parents, Steven and Daisy Elliott; various other Boston Elliotts, Auchinclosses, Morgans, Vanderbilts, Astors; assorted Episcopalian clergymen, including one bishop who was distantly related; the presidents of Harvard, MIT, Tiffany's, IBM, Lazard Frères, Kidder Peabody, and Chase Manhattan. Everyone drank too much, danced too hard, laughed a lot, and agreed both that Adam and Katrinka made a stunning couple and that this was the best party they had been to in a long time. Its success left both Nina and Katrinka with, if not a greater liking for one another, at least a grudging respect, though the only words Nina could muster to express this were, "I don't think it went too badly, do you? Of course the flower arrangements could have been a bit more subtle and the music at times was quite . . . loud."

"Anything excessive gives Mother the most awful headache," said Clementine.

It was during their week cruising the Mediterranean in a yacht hired for what Adam referred to as their "second honeymoon" (during which he left her once to fly to Bremen for a meeting and spent much of the rest of the time on the phone) that Adam suggested to Katrinka they move. The Sutton Place apartment, he said, might have been fine for his bachelor days but was not right for the kind of life he planned to lead in the future. Though he liked the decor himself, he could see that it was perhaps too stark for most people's taste and not the right environment for either impressing or relaxing business associates into giving him the best of a deal. It was also too small for the kind of entertaining he would in future need to do, not to mention the size family he wanted to have.

"How big is this family you plan?" Katrinka asked, sitting up to apply some suntan lotion. They had taken the yacht's Zodiac to one of the islands dotting the sea to picnic and sunbathe. After swimming, they had eaten the lunch of cold chicken, cheeses, pâtés, fresh fruit, and bread packed for them by the chef, and now were lying on a large quilted blanket turning a deeper shade of tan.

"I don't know," Adam replied. "Three children, maybe four." His eyes opened and looked at her. "What do you think?"

"Oh, I'm to be consulted? I thought you did work everything out already."

His lips curved in the crooked smile she found irresistible. "I do get a bit bossy, don't I?"

"A bit?"

"Somewhat, a little," he continued, misunderstanding, his smile broadening as always at what he considered the delightful gaps in his wife's grasp of English, defining the phrase as he had become used to doing for her.

"I know what it does mean," she replied, more irritated than she meant him to see.

Sitting up, he took the bottle of suntan lotion from her. "Let me do that," he said. Starting with her feet, he began to rub the oil into her skin, working his way slowly up her legs. "I've worked alone for so long, Katrinka," he explained. "And lived alone. I haven't consulted anybody about anything since I was in my teens. I'm out of the habit. You have to give me a chance. I'm not used to the idea yet of being married."

"It did happen so fast," she agreed, prepared to see his side of things. And she could understand how adjusting to this marriage might be easier for herself than for Adam. Even if she had grown out of the habit over the years, she at least knew what it was to trust, to confide. She and her parents had discussed everything, relied on each other's advice, made decisions together. But of course that would not have been possible for Adam with his. "You must have been so lonely," she said, her heart suddenly breaking for the solitary little boy she imagined him to have been. Surprised, not quite understanding what she meant, he looked at her, his hand suddenly still on her leg. "When you were a child," she added.

"Not really." He thought of the crowds of friends, the parties, the wild times, the *fun* he had had growing up—which, of course, was not at all what Katrinka had in mind. "But being married to you is much nicer than I ever thought being married could be," he had said.

Extending a suntanned arm, she touched his face. "It is for me, too."

"Well, how many children do you want?"

"Four. Five," she said, feeling the familiar stab of pain. "As many as possible." She still searched the faces of children in the streets, in hotels and restaurants, in department stores. Sometimes she wandered through FAO Schwarz, hoping to recognize him among the boys playing with the train sets and the model cars. She didn't know what else she could do to find her son, not even with Adam's money at her disposal. "I do love children very much," she added, hoping Adam had not noticed her sudden distress.

He hadn't. He poured a small amount of oil into his hand, put the bottle down, rubbed his palms together, and began again to stroke her legs, moving upward, over her knees, gently prying her legs apart. "Don't you think we should get started?" he had said, his fingers straying under the thin protective strip of her bikini.

What was the point of brooding when nothing good could come of it? Katrinka asked herself, then pushed the sad thoughts away. "Can they see us from the boat?" she asked before giving herself up entirely to the pleasure of the moment. There was a telescope on the deck and a crew left behind with nothing much to do.

"Not if they don't look."

When they returned to New York, Adam plunged back into business, to which, since his courtship of Katrinka had begun, he had paid less attention than usual. The preceding year, Graham Marine in Larchmont had launched an innovative twenty-nine-foot sailboat of fiberglass construction which, because of its speed, ease of handling, and affordable cost, had taken the small boat market by storm. Its success had been followed up with what had turned out to be an equally good seller, a thirty-three-foot boat of similar design, which had the effect of boosting sales of the larger yachts so that the yard had turned a healthy profit the past two years. Graham Marine Bridgeport had had almost as big a success, with a series of trawlers, sportfishers, and small motorboats, while the Miami yard had continued to attract commissions for luxury motor yachts. Adam now wanted to use the publicity being generated by the upcoming launch of Khalid ibn Hassan's yacht to boost business even further in the luxury field while working with a team of designers on a new sailboat of under twenty feet, hoping to lure first-time buyers into the market with a craft that combined as many of the features of the successful twenty-nine footer with an even more affordable price tag. In addition, he was designing a new racing yacht for himself.

With Adam constantly on the move between Bridgeport, Larchmont, Miami, and Bremen, spending as many as ten or twelve hours a day at his office even when in New York, Katrinka, though she accompanied him when she could, often was left alone in Manhattan. Missing the familiar comfort of her former life and her old friends, sometimes she would phone Natalie in Paris, or Erica in Munich. She would write to Tomáš and Zuzka, to her aunt, her cousins, and sometimes even to Ota Černý. But though she kept in touch with her past, she refused to yield to the waves of loneliness which often threatened to overwhelm her and set about building a new life for herself in New York.

Carter took care of the housework and cooking, so after consulting with him about particular chores she might want him to do, letting him know who would be in and out for what meals, whether or not guests were expected, and discussing the menu, Katrinka's domestic duties were done for the day. She would then put in a call to Hilde and Bruno in Kitzbühel to keep up with business at the Golden Horn, finish reading the newspapers, take care of correspondence, write whatever thank-you notes she owed for Dave to hand-deliver in the afternoon, then dress for lunch at Le Cirque or La Grenouille or any one of the fashionable restaurants where she met Daisy or Lucia or Margo Jensen of *Chic* or Rick Colins of *The Chronicle* or some of the other people to whom Daisy had introduced her and who now were beginning to extend invitations, either curious about or wanting to be seen with the beautiful new wife of New York's former most desirable bachelor. Some mornings she went with Lucia di Campo (who was tiny and needed, literally, to work her butt off to keep in shape) to exercise class at Lotte Berk's and quickly got into the habit of going even when Lucia was out of town. Twice weekly she would have her hair done at Kenneth's or her nails at Dinmar, with touch-ups in between for gala events.

Invitations to these galas increased rapidly, as Daisy and Steven Elliott seemed to be on every committee for every charity in New York. Adam, who saw these events—as did everyone else—as a way to extend his list of business contacts, insisted they go as often as his travel schedule permitted, buying either tickets or tables, not the best tables, since his income did not yet permit that kind of extravagance, but good enough so that the Grahams would be noticed.

Compared to what she was used to achieving in a day, this was not for Katrinka a particularly demanding schedule and she found that she had more than enough time to spend on the only job Adam had specifically asked her to do—looking for a new home for them. Though at first rather daunted by the prospect of having to search the whole of Manhattan Island, which she did not yet know well, for the perfect place, Katrinka was relieved when Alexandra Ogelvy told her that there were really only a few acceptable areas in which to live, certain parts of Fifth and Park avenues, certain East Side cross streets in the Sixties and Seventies. Though Daisy pooh-poohed that notion, citing Mrs. Vanderbilt's daring colonization of Sutton Place in the twenties, Katrinka suspected that, given Adam's grand plans for their new apartment, the right neighborhood would be number one on his list of priorities.

Because of their long-standing relationship with the Grahams, the Ogelvys, of course, had been invited to Adam and Katrinka's reception and one or two other gatherings at The Poplars over the summer, but Katrinka managed for a long time to evade Alexandra's attempts at friendship, one way or another wriggling out of suggested lunches in the city. Though their conversations at the various parties had been cordial enough, still Katrinka had sensed hostility in Alexandra, and resentment. While she did not go so far as to think that Adam had lied about his relationship with the beautiful redhead, Katrinka did suspect that he might have misjudged the depth of her feeling for him. So while Katrinka sympathized a little with Alexandra's viewing her as the predatory "other woman," however untrue it happened to be, she nevertheless preferred not to become more involved with her socially than necessary and was surprised that Alexandra pursued the matter. But pursue it Alexandra did, until, finally, Katrinka had no choice but to say yes.

One Thursday in early September they met at the Plaza's Edwardian Room for lunch. With its paneled walls and luxurious silk curtains, its spacious and quiet elegance, its beamed ceiling and chandeliers styled like old-fashioned gas lamps, it was one of Katrinka's favorite places, reminding her of some of her favorite European restaurants.

Seated at a window overlooking Central Park, they ordered salads and half a bottle of white wine. At a nearby table, Katrinka noticed, Mark van Hollen was having lunch with a woman much shorter and squarer than his wife. He looked up suddenly, caught her eye, and smiled. The woman with him turned to see who or what had attracted his interest and Katrinka recognized her as Sabrina, the columnist. Though Sabrina smiled as well and nodded her head in acknowledgment, there was nothing friendly in her gaze. It was coldly assessing and unaccountably hostile.

"What I did do to make her so angry?" murmured Katrinka, adding quickly as a startled Alexandra began to turn to see who on earth Katrinka was talking about, "Don't look. It's Sabrina." The name clearly meant nothing to Alexandra and Katrinka explained. "She's a newspaper columnist. In England. She writes for *The Globe*." She suddenly remembered that someone, Daisy probably, had told her that *The Globe* was one of Mark van Hollen's papers.

"Gossip?"

"Yes."

Alexandra made a face. "Vile work."

"Rick Colins seems very sweet," said Katrinka, not so much giving her own opinion as soliciting Alexandra's. It was the way she added to her store of knowledge, no matter what the subject.

"Oh, yes," agreed Alexandra. "Everyone likes Rick."

They passed the first part of the lunch discussing how Katrinka was settling into life in the United States. Finally, Alexandra asked Katrinka if she would mind if she smoked, reached into her purse to extract a handsome gold cigarette case, and, before the headwaiter could produce a match, lit her own cigarette with a gold lighter. Both case and lighter had been Christmas presents from Adam. "I keep trying to give it up, but I can't," she said.

Katrinka nodded sympathetically. "I'm lucky. I never did start." It was one of the practices the various ski-team coaches had actively discouraged.

"Adam and I have been friends for so long, since we were children." Katrinka nodded, acknowledging the fact, and Alexandra continued. "So I thought it might be nice if you and I got to know one another." She pushed her red hair back from her exquisitely pale face with an impatient hand. "Frankly, I'd hate to lose Adam's friendship. It means a lot to me. And I don't see how I can keep it if you and I don't get along." That was true as far as it went. What Alexandra saw no point in explaining was *why* she wanted to keep Adam's friendship: not, as Katrinka suspected, because she had once been, or still was, in love with him, but because Adam and his family provided her with access to a world to which she was entitled by birth but excluded from by poverty—if poverty in Alexandra's case could be defined as a lack of serious money.

Not that Alexandra did not care about Adam. She did. But a lingering affection was certainly not her primary reason for wanting to keep him in her life: it was her desire to remain on New York's A-list. Without the Grahams, Alexandra's invitations to the parties that counted, by the people who mattered, would be seriously reduced, possibly to none at all. So while Alexandra could understand Katrinka's reluctance to be friends, a reluctance she mistakenly attributed to Katrinka's jealousy of her (in Alexandra's opinion, at any rate) superior looks and former relationship with Adam, she was determined to overcome it.

Admiring Alexandra's apparent honesty, Katrinka was determined to equal it. "I did think you would resent me for marrying him," she said.

346

Alexandra flicked the ash from her cigarette into the ashtray on the table. "Oh, I was angry at first. I mean, put yourself in my place. You would have been, too. But it didn't take me long to realize that Adam would never have married me. He never loved me, not enough anyway. And of course now I understand that I never really loved him, not seriously. What I felt for him was always a sort of schoolgirl crush." Katrinka could not help a skeptical look, which Alexandra caught. "Not that Adam's not wonderful," she added diplomatically. "But now that I am in love, really in love, I know the difference."

"You're in love?" said Katrinka, relieved of the slight burden of guilt she could not help feeling, though Adam's behavior was hardly her fault. "How wonderful."

To Katrinka's surprise, Alexandra's eyes welled with tears. She shrugged. "It won't work out."

How could someone as beautiful as Alexandra have so little self-confidence? wondered Katrinka. "Why say such a thing? Why think it? You must be optimistic." Set your goal, she had been taught, work like hell to achieve it, believe always that you will.

While the waiter poured them more coffee, Alexandra took another cigarette from the case, lit it, inhaled deeply, and, releasing a cloud of pale gray smoke, said as soon as they were alone again, "He's married." Both of them were a little taken aback at her words, Katrinka because she was so reserved herself about her personal life, and Alexandra because she had not meant to go so far in her attempt to disarm Katrinka and win her sympathy. But faced with someone she instinctively felt could be trusted, and who might understand, Alexandra could not resist the temptation to talk about her new love affair.

His name was Neil Goodman, she told Katrinka, who repressed a start of surprise. After only three months in New York, even she recognized the name. He had just got himself appointed CEO of Knapp Manning, one of the country's biggest brokerage houses.

Alexandra's family had scraped together enough money to send her to the best schools, perhaps in order to keep up appearances or, more practically, in the hope of marrying her off well. And if Adam Graham had not always been lurking in the background of her life, she might have taken some interest in one or another of the eligible young men who were always somewhere in her vicinity.

After leaving Miss Porter's, Alexandra had gone on to Bennington, earned a B.A. in art history, and then, with no clear idea of what to do with herself beyond trying to marry Adam Graham, had worked in a number of art galleries in New York while waiting for him to propose, an expectation that never quite died because, no matter how many girls he dated in between, he always came back to her. Even when the proposal failed to materialize in Kitzbühel, Alexandra did not give up hope. Nevertheless, as given to fantasy as she was concerning Adam, she tried to be pragmatic about the rest of her life. When in early February she had heard about a job at Sotheby's that paid better than the one she currently held, she had applied, and because of some excellent recommendations had been hired: her personal life aside, Alexandra was far from stupid and she did know her subject, which was seventeenth-century Dutch art, a category that included Franz Hals, Jan Vermeer, and Rembrandt von Rijn, among others.

Apparently, Neil Goodman's family, on his mother's side, had been Dutch Jews, and that slender connection fostered an interest in the art of the Netherlands. As soon as he had some money, he began collecting, not Rembrandts or Vermeers of course ("yet" he often said) but landscapes, seascapes, and genre paintings. In April, during a preview of a scheduled sale of Dutch art, he had met Alexandra and been impressed that someone as beautiful as she could know so much about what, next to making money, was his favorite subject. She had handled his bidding for the sale; he had come away with a very nice Jan Steen and had taken her to lunch in gratitude. When he suggested dinner, she said yes. And why not? she thought, since Adam was spending more and more time in Europe (courting Katrinka, though Alexandra did not know it then) and her social calendar showed a depressing number of free evenings. It was good for business, she told herself. Neil Goodman was wealthy, and he bought art. If a dinner or two encouraged him to buy more and saved her from being bored, what was the harm?

What she had not counted on was falling in love. "He's not handsome," she told Katrinka, "at least not in the way that Adam is. He's about an inch shorter than I am, and balding, but he has the sweetest face, dark eyes, the shortest, straightest nose, and a sort of bushy moustache. Normally I hate men with moustaches, don't you? But his just emphasizes how full and sexy his mouth is. He's the sexiest man I've ever known. Well, one of them anyway," she corrected herself instantly, not wanting Katrinka to think she was in any way attacking Adam. Neil Goodman was also married, if not happily, at least contentedly enough he had always thought, to his high-school sweetheart. They had four children, the youngest of whom, a daughter, was sixteen. "He says he loves me, but that he can't leave his wife. That it wouldn't be fair to her, or the children. But is it fair for him to stay? That's what I want to know. He's fifty-four years old. How many more chances will he get to be happy? Really happy?"

Katrinka thought of Mirek Bartoš, of the way she had fallen, without realizing it, into love with him, of the times she had asked herself the same questions about him and Vlasta. The circumstances had been so different, she knew: Alexandra was not so young or so naive as she had been and the consequences of her affair were not so potentially dangerous, but the emotions were the same—the longing, the confusion, the horrible loneliness, the pain. And if it crossed Katrinka's mind that Neil Goodman's money was even more powerful an aphrodisiac than Mirek's glamour and sophistication had been, she generously pushed the thought away. Who was she to judge? Instead Katrinka made soothing and sympathetic noises, said she was sure that Neil loved her (what else could she say?), pointed out that happiness was not everyone's priority, that duty for some people came first, hinted that, however incredible now, Alexandra might actually survive the end of the affair, in the (of course) unlikely event it should come to that.

Katrinka paid the check and, still preoccupied with

memories of Mirek and where they inevitably led, to their missing son, nodded absentmindedly to Mark van Hollen and Sabrina and followed Alexandra from the restaurant.

"She doesn't look very happy, does she?" said Sabrina, her small calculating eyes following Katrinka's progress toward the door. "For a bride?"

"Haven't you ever heard of a lover's quarrel?" asked Mark, his handsome suntanned face crinkling in a smile that did not reach his eyes, which remained as cool and calculating as his star columnist's. What a bitch, he thought, though no sign of his opinion showed in his manner. Sabrina was one of *The London Globe*'s great assets and he had no intention of losing her. In fact, he had summoned her to New York in an attempt to find ways to increase her value to him.

"Do you have them?" she asked. It was the sort of question she prided herself on putting to people she ought to have been afraid of.

"All the time," replied Mark, laughing aloud this time. He couldn't help admiring her guts. "But that's not for publication."

"Of course not," said Sabrina, an eyebrow lifting slightly. "I do know on which side my bread is buttered."

When Katrinka told him how successful the lunch had been, Adam was delighted. He had encouraged a relationship between Alexandra and his wife, not because he particularly liked to keep old girlfriends around but because he made it a practice never to let potentially useful people get away. And Alexandra, operating on the same principle, having accomplished her mission, felt a great sense of satisfaction and fully enjoyed the fruits of her success. From then on, she not only met Katrinka often for lunch but joined her and Daisy, Lucia and Margo, for long gossipy sessions at the latest "in" places and, though she often made an effort to pay, was always defeated by the quickness of the others, who, knowing she did not have the money, would not allow it. In return, she did small favors for them, presented them with little gifts, kept them informed of what was happening at Sotheby's, gave advance warning of interesting pieces of jewelry coming up for auction: if you had an eye, that's where the best bargains were always to be had, perfect birthday or Christmas presents for close friends, or for yourself—the Queen of Romania's pearl-and-diamond choker, the Duchess of Windsor's flamingo pin, all for much less than jewels of similar size or quality would have cost at Winston's or Buccellati. And not only did Alexandra help Katrinka, always the eager student, develop *her* eye for painting and jewelry, she steered Katrinka to the sections of the city where Adam would find it acceptable to live, and introduced her to the head of the real estate division at Sotheby's, ensuring that Katrinka got first pick of what came up on the market.

It was through this Sotheby's connection that Katrinka found the perfect apartment—a sixteen-room duplex completely surrounded by a wide terrace, at the very top of a prewar building at Sixty-fourth Street and Fifth Avenue, overlooking Central Park. As soon as she saw it, Katrinka knew this was it, the place she wanted to spend the rest of her life with Adam.

Twenty-Nine

Daisy, who had been with Katrinka for the first viewing of the Fifth Avenue apartment, had approved. For the second, Lucia had accompanied her, since Katrinka wanted the benefit of her designer's eye. Then, convinced her first instinctive reaction to the place had been correct, she showed it to Adam, who fell in love at first sight. He made what seemed to Katrinka an exorbitant offer, a price of three hundred thousand dollars was eventually agreed upon, and when escrow closed the Grahams were invited from Newport to view the fait accompli. Kenneth in his gentle, courtly way appeared to like it without reservation, but Nina smiled her usual doubtful smile and said it was lovely, though the dining room was a bit small and really it was hard to believe it was worth the money when one considered what one could buy in Newport for the same amount.

After that, Katrinka no longer had to wonder how to fill her days. With decorating and furnishing the apartment added to her more and more demanding social schedule, her frequent trips abroad with Adam, the time still needed to oversee the running of the Golden Horn, she had to learn to manage on six hours or less of sleep a night.

The decorator Katrinka chose, after interviewing those recommended by friends or whose work she had seen and admired, was one with little experience and no reputation —Carlos Medina, who had once worked as Lucia's assistant. Looking at his few completed assignments, Katrinka was impressed with their quality; she viewed his sketches and found his work beautiful as well as original. Most of all she liked his attitude: he was easy to talk to, eager to listen, firm in his convictions but not arrogant. He was twenty-five years old. Son of an Acapulco shop owner and a tourist from San Francisco who had fallen in love and stayed, Carlos was small and dark, with straight black hair and soft dark eyes. His movements were quick and precise, his voice a rush of interwoven Spanish and English, each completely without accent. Adam thought she was mad to trust him, but Katrinka, as usual, decided to follow her instincts.

Carlos's sketches for the renovated apartment struck the balance between Adam's taste for the austere and Katrinka's desire to create a comfortable, homey environment. He inundated Katrinka with swatches of fabric, with color charts and carpet samples. He showed her pictures of kitchen cabinets and shower stalls. He dragged her to showrooms to view furniture and appliances, to antique sales for important accessories. The choices available seemed to be limited only by the amount of time she was willing to spend exhausting them and by the size of her budget. Adam had said the sky was the limit, but the more cost-conscious Katrinka was always willing to take an extra few hours to find the thing of comparable value at a lesser price.

On the theory that since they were going to live in the apartment together they should be equally involved in making choices, Katrinka had at first consulted Adam about almost every aspect of the redecoration but, when that did not provoke boredom in her husband, it resulted in quarrels that left both of them surprised by their ferocity. Two independent people, used to having their own way, in no circumstances would it have been easy to reconcile their differing tastes without making one or the other feel like a loser in a battle of wills. But added to this was the complication of Adam's relationship with his mother. Every disagreement with Katrinka struck some primal chord in him, and he fought her as if he were fighting for his life. These quarrels were never really resolved. They simply ended in exhaustion with both of them falling into bed and having sex with a feverish intensity that was an attempt to translate their anger back into love.

Soon Katrinka learned to narrow the selections down to two or three that she liked, and to show those to Adam so that together, peaceably, they could make the final decision.

The walls of the sitting room and dining room were lacquered and sanded again and again until just the right color and texture were achieved. The banquettes in the library were installed and removed and installed again until the fit was perfect. The hallway carpet was ripped up and returned because of a defect only Carlos and Katrinka could see. The marble in the hallway was flawed and had to be replaced, while one of the sitting-room chairs had to be reupholstered because its Scalamandre fabric was deemed imperfect. Workmen refused to appear, antiques arrived scratched or broken, incorrect orders were delivered and no one seemed interested in retrieving them.

It took almost a year but finally the apartment was done. The new kitchen was painted terra-cotta and had sleek brown-tone Bosch cabinets, a tile floor, a glass table, and a large picture window with a triangular pediment overlooking the terrace. Adam's bath had a series of windows with interior blinds that curved from the floor into the ceiling. It was done in lustrous gray granite with a sunken spa tub and stall shower, while Katrinka's, complete with bidet, was in white-veined gray marble. The guest bathrooms were simpler but still luxurious, all done in white onyx with cabinets in a variety of pale earth colors, their long vertical shapes echoed in the narrow windows which extended from ceiling to floor and gave a view of the terrace from the bath. The library was paneled in pale limed oak with a wide banquette in a quilted beige Clarence House fabric occupying most of two walls, the others taken up with a window overlooking Central Park and fitted cabinets concealing the sophisticated sound system, the top-of-the-line television, and new Sony Betamax. Furniture in the adjoining living room was large and overstuffed, covered in cream-on-cream striped Scalamandre silk, with cream lacquered walls and Oriental carpets scattered over a parquet floor, the simplicity of the decor highlighted by the beautiful woods of the carefully chosen antiques, by the sculptures and paintings. Adam's collection in this context did not seem so much stark as striking.

By the time the last piece of furniture was in place and the final painting hung, it was the spring of 1979—a perfect time for a party to celebrate, decided Katrinka. With the help of Adam's secretary, she drew up a list and sent out invitations, sixty for cocktails, twenty-four to stay on for dinner. She had had small dinner parties before in Sutton Place, but this was the largest entertainment she had yet attempted on her own in New York, and the prospect made Katrinka a little nervous. Though every day she was becoming more and more familiar with the many subtle rules of the city's social life, she was aware that there was much she had yet to learn and, while she sided with Daisy in thinking it was all at bottom nonsense, still Katrinka did not want to do anything that might embarrass Adam. She loved him completely, more every day, and the sole object of her life, without her even realizing it, had become to please him.

With the new chef, Katrinka planned the menu for the party. With Carter and Anna Bubeník, the Czech housekeeper hired to help Carter with the increased pressure of running the larger Fifth Avenue establishment, Katrinka cleaned the apartment and organized the terrace, sorted the linen and chose the dinner service and cutlery. The night of the party everything sparkled, the chandeliers, the crystal, the gold flatware and side dishes burnished to a high sheen. Vases of exotic flowers, orchids and calla lilies and birds of paradise, arranged that afternoon by Salou, were everywhere. Cases of Louis Roederer Cristal lay chilled and waiting to have their corks popped. A young pianist Katrinka and Adam had heard play in a supper club one night sat at the cream-colored grand piano and played requests, Gershwin and Sondheim, Arlen and Porter.

Adam's parents had been invited, and his sister Clementine with her husband. Daisy and Steven Elliott came; Lucia di Campo and Nick Cavalletti; Alexandra Ogelvy with her escort, an associate from Sotheby's; Margo Jensen with her husband Ted, an attractive man with grizzled hair and horn-rim glasses who was a successful Seventh Avenue manufacturer; Natalie Bovier with Jean-Claude Gillette, in town to sell Bloomingdale's some of his specialty gourmet items; Walter Hoving; Estée Lauder; Carlos Medina; John Fairchild; Malcolm Forbes; Liz Smith; Rick Colins; the executive staff of Adam's New York office; Ronald Perelman, Claudia Cohen, Ted Turner, assorted spouses and dates, and—to Alexandra's dismay—Neil Goodman and his wife, a pleasant-looking woman with gray hair and a plump, matronly figure.

"Oh la la," said Natalie to Adam, as they kissed each other's cheeks. *"Ça c'est magnifique."*

"Does that mean you like it?" he asked, smiling his crooked grin, admiring the slim body barely concealed by the slight black cocktail dress.

"How did I ever let you get away from me, *chérie?"* said Jean-Claude to Katrinka. They stood talking in the center of the sitting room, drawing every eye, their relaxed stance and easy laughs making people wonder how long they had known each other, and how well. Katrinka was wearing a Givenchy, which Jean-Claude recognized from the Paris prêt-à-porter collection earlier in the year, a short, fitted strapless dress, with sleeves and bodice of rhinestone-studded sheer black silk crepe georgette. In her ears were diamond clips and in her dark hair diamond-studded combs sparkled like stardust. She looked magnificent, he thought. "I must have been out of my mind."

"No," said Katrinka, laughing. "Just very busy."

"If only you had not been friends," he said, with a mock rueful look at Natalie.

"That would have mattered?"

He shrugged. "Perhaps you would not have noticed then how busy I was."

"Nice place," said Ted Turner in his flat voice with its pronounced Southern drawl.

"Indeed," said Nina Graham. From inside the apartment came the sounds of Cole Porter, and across Central Park, past the darkening pond and the soft shapes of the newly leafed trees, the last traces of pink in the sky above the West Side buildings could be seen. How clever of Katrinka, she thought, to have found an apartment with such a lovely terrace. "It could do with a bit more color, I suppose, but on the whole they've made a nice job of it."

"I hear you're racing in the Fastnet this year," said Kenneth to change the subject. The Fastnet was the culmination of the Cowes Week regatta and one of the most challenging of the ocean races.

"You bet," said Turner.

"So's Adam."

"This is the first I've heard of it," said Nina, who did not at all sound as if she liked the idea.

"They tell me you designed this," said Rick Colins, the hand holding the champagne flute gesturing vaguely behind him to indicate the room as he backed Carlos Medina into a corner near an Italian chrome-and-glass pedestal on which sat a large vase containing an arrangement of rare orchids.

"Yes," said Carlos, a little belligerently, always on the alert for criticism, though so far he had received only praise.

"It's fabulous."

"Thank you," said Carlos, softening. He had always been drawn to tall, fair young men. "I think your bow tie is delicious."

"Do you? I'm tired of them myself, but they've become a bit of a trademark. I don't think I'd dare to be seen in public without one." Rick was famous for his ties, small neat ones or large flamboyant bows, as the mood struck him, always in wild patterns and colors.

"Marketing," said Carlos, nodding, a hint of bitterness in his voice.

"The most important business tool. I'm a writer," he added, introducing himself. "You know," he said after the small talk was out of the way, "I'm thinking of redoing my place. If you wouldn't mind, I'd love you to take a look, though I don't think even you could transform the little rat hole."

"You'd be surprised what I can do," said Carlos, his smile knowing and infinitely agreeable.

"What are you doing later?" asked Rick, when he got his breathing back under control.

"Rick," called Margo Jensen, a gleam of speculation in the depths of her smoke-colored eyes, "what do you think about doing a piece on this place?"

As Margo paused for a moment to pick up a glass of champagne from the tray of a passing waiter, Rick surveyed her brilliant red dress and startling makeup and wondered how he could best convey the impact of her presence to his eager readers. Like looking into a kaleidoscope? Seeing a Chinese circus? She was all light and color, absolutely dazzling. Next to her, Ted Jensen always seemed rather pale and insignificant, despite the good physique and Italian suits. But he was neither, Rick knew.

Ted had grown up on Manhattan's Lower East Side. His father was a cutter in a dress factory and his mother did hand finishing. Working his way through NYU, majoring in business, in his sophomore year, he had met Margo, another student, at a party thrown by mutual friends. There had been no hint then of the stunning woman she would later transform herself into, yet he had been as attracted to her humor, her style, her clear-eyed view of the world as she had been to his intelligence, his quiet strength, his unexpected appreciation of her virtues. As soon as they had graduated from college, they married.

After several years working as an accountant, Ted had taken on a new client, a young designer whose work he thought showed promise. When Margo agreed, Ted borrowed the money from an uncle and went into business. That business had made him a wealthy man. Ted now owned several lines of name-brand clothes that sold well in upmarket stores. But, of course, thought Rick, it hadn't hurt him to have a wife as influential in fashion as Margo. "For *Chic?*" he asked, after introducing her to Carlos.

"Of course, for *Chic,*" replied Margo. "If your contract permits, my darling." A fashion layout of Katrinka photographed in Manhattan's latest showplace, the Graham apartment, would sell magazines, Margo was sure.

"It permits," said Rick, who considered it not worth the paper it was written on. Sabrina's column had begun appearing in *The Chronicle,* significantly cutting into his space and prestige, making Rick's New York insider information seem limited and rather dull when compared to Sabrina's relentless tracking of the international jet set from her London base. He was looking for a way to give his employer, Mark van Hollen, the finger.

As Katrinka walked by on her way to rescue Adam from the wife of a client for whom the Miami yard was building a new yacht, Margo extended a hand tipped with long red nails and placed it lightly on Katrinka's arm. "Rick has agreed to do a piece about the apartment for the magazine."

"This apartment?" asked Katrinka, sounding surprised. Though pleased with what she had achieved, even proud of it, she had not considered it grand enough to attract the attention of the press.

Margo nodded. "It's a visual delight, my darling. Simple, elegant, yet luxurious and dramatic," she said, sounding like copy. She favored Carlos with a wide red-lipped smile. "You two have done wonders. It will photograph like a dream. Six pages, I think, at least."

"If Adam agrees," said Katrinka, "I would love it." To her an appearance in *Chic* seemed a seal of approval, a sign that she had done Adam proud, a small shield against Nina's constant and annoying barbs.

"He'll agree," said Margo, her full red mouth curving in a dry smile. She understood very well how much Adam Graham valued publicity.

"You've been avoiding me all night," said Neil, trapping Alexandra in the long hallway on her return from the powder room.

"I was being discreet."

"I think you should meet my wife."

"No," said Alexandra, horrified.

"She'll think it strange. She knows you've helped with some of my recent buys."

"Don't make me do this, Neil."

"Just say hello to her," he coaxed, leaning toward her, letting his mouth brush against her ear. She trembled slightly as she felt the combination of soft breath and bristling moustache that she found somehow so erotic. "Talk to her for a minute. That's all." He took her arm and steered her across to where his wife stood chatting to Daisy and Steven Elliott.

"Alexandra, hello," said Daisy, looking as always poised and alert and ready for action. "Haven't Katrinka and Carlos done an amazing job?"

Both of them had seen the apartment from time to time during the various stages of its redecoration and had at times been doubtful and at others approving of Katrinka's choices. Neither had expected it to turn out quite so well. "Amazing," echoed Alexandra, who would have sounded more sincere had her attention not been focused on Mrs. Goodman.

What on earth is wrong with Alexandra? wondered Daisy.

"You look stunning," said Steven, bending his long graceful frame to kiss Alexandra's cheek. "As usual."

They made an odd-looking group: Steven tall and fair; Daisy petite and dark; Alexandra long-legged and slender with a flamboyant head of flaming hair; Neil an inch shorter than she, but trim, with dark brown receding hair and soft brown eyes; and his wife, Susan, plump, graying, with a pretty face and gracious manner.

"Susan, I want you to meet Alexandra. She's the woman I've been telling you about, from Sotheby's."

"Oh, you're the one responsible for that wonderful Kalf still life that Neil just bought. I'm so pleased to meet you."

I'm a bitch, thought Alexandra. A bitch. I have to stop seeing him. "Hello, Mrs. Goodman," she said pleasantly, aware of Daisy's concerned and curious look, hoping her own thoughts did not show so clearly on her face. "A lovely party, isn't it?"

Katrinka made a quick foray into the kitchen to see that all was on time, then passed into the dining room to survey the laid table to make sure all was in order. She eyed approvingly the gold-rimmed Picard dinner service, the gold-plated Buccellati flatware, the fine Czechoslovakian crystal. Instead of one large table, there were four small ones set with pale gold linen cloths, tiny tasseled lamps, and six places each, the perfect size to encourage dinner conversation. It all looked beautiful, thought Katrinka, opulent despite the simple lines and lack of decorative detail.

Returning to the party, Katrinka studied it with the same approval she had just accorded the dining room. It was a success, she thought. The hors d'oeuvres had been delicious, the champagne excellent, the music first rate. People, in fluid groups that changed shape easily and often, seemed relaxed and happy. Some had gathered around the piano and were singing the familiar tunes. For a while her eyes followed Adam—smiling, gracious, charming, and oh so handsome—working the room. She noted the way heads turned to look at him as he passed. She could see the eagerness with which everyone, men and women, greeted him, how they liked to be near him, touch him, talk to him, wanting to be connected to the surge of energy, the vitality, emanating from him. From Adam, her eyes drifted to Malcolm Forbes, seated on the silk sofa, deep in conversation with Lucia—about designing him a new yacht, hoped Katrinka. Nick, her husband, was talking to Jean-Claude Gillette, about race horses, was Katrinka's guess, since Jean-Claude owned them and Nick liked to bet. Rick Colins and Carlos Medina had eyes only for each other. Natalie was chatting with a woman, much to Katrinka's surprise, until she remembered having been introduced to her by her escort, one of Adam's executives, as a buyer at Saks. Daisy was deep in conversation with Iris Love, the archaeologist, and the usually sedate Steven was unabashedly eyeing the date of some Wall Street financier, a woman with long honey-colored hair in a tight blue taffeta dress with a high bodice and plunging back. Sugar Benson. Katrinka remembered the name because it had struck her as odd. In the whole room the only false note was struck by Alexandra, who seemed almost feverishly gay.

Gradually the crowd thinned as those invited only for cocktails began to take their leave. They shook hands with Adam, kissed Katrinka, issued invitations which they promised to follow up more formally soon. "See you at Cowes," said Ted Turner as he left, not noticing the blank look in Katrinka's eyes. *Cows?* What was that?

Nina Graham, who missed nothing, came up to Katrinka and said, "Hasn't Adam told you he's racing in the Fastnet? How like him! I had hoped that now he'd at least keep *you* informed of his plans."

The Fastnet? thought Katrinka, who was saved from having to reply to her mother-in-law by Liz Smith saying good-bye.

The dinner, too, passed without a hitch. Katrinka had minimized the possibilities for friction by seating Nina at Adam's table, Kenneth beside herself, and Clementine at a third table with Alexandra who, now that the Goodmans had left, was able to enjoy herself a little. The soft strains of piano music drifted in from the sitting room, the wine and conversation flowed happily, the food was delicious, and when the chef came in at the end of the meal he was greeted with a round of applause.

"That went well," said Adam later, as they ushered the last guest out the door.

"I did think so," said Katrinka, smiling happily. "God, I'm tired." She turned to Carter and Anna and the maid who had started to clear up. "Thank you all, very much. You did do a fantastic job."

"Leave what you can till the morning," said Adam.

"It won't take us long, sir," said Carter, knowing no one, including himself, would be pleased to wake and find the debris of the party in evidence.

They all wished one another a good night and, arms around each other, Adam and Katrinka walked down the long carpeted hallway to their bedroom. "You did a great job," said Adam, "with the party, with the apartment, with everything."

"You mean it?"

"Even Mother approved," said Adam with a tired grin, as he and Katrinka began to undress, crossing in and out of their separate bathrooms, getting ready for bed. "Couldn't you tell?"

"Not really," said Katrinka, "to tell the truth. It was Carlos mostly," she added, wanting to give credit where it was due.

"Bullshit. That little faggot would have had gold-frilled curtains in the living room if you hadn't watched him every minute."

"How you can say that?" said Katrinka, surprised and a little annoyed at Adam's dismissal of Carlos and his work. She admired both enormously. "Carlos is very talented. He does have very good taste."

"So do you. So do I for that matter," said Adam, as he regarded her graceful figure disappearing under a fall of turquoise silk.

"What is Cows?" she asked as her face emerged from the folds of fabric.

"A port on the Isle of Wight, off the coast of England. There's been a regatta there each year more or less since 1776. You know that new sailboat I'm building at Larchmont?" Katrinka nodded and pulled the diamond combs from her hair, letting it drop softly to her shoulders. "It's for a race there in August. The Fastnet."

"Oh," said Katrinka. Of course Adam had not meant to keep it from her, he had just not got around to telling her yet. "I did wonder what Ted Turner was talking about."

Adam got into bed and lay, his arms beneath his head, watching his wife. "He's racing as well. You'll like Cowes Week. Everyone will be there. It's a lot of fun."

"Hmmm," said Katrinka.

"What's the matter?"

She wasn't sure. "Nothing," she said. Adam had so much to occupy his mind, all the pressures of business, plus his family: he worried about his father, she knew, and tried to throw business Wilson's way to help Clementine and the boys. It was no wonder that he sometimes forgot to let her know what he was planning. "I'm just tired."

"Then hurry and come to bed," he said with a deliberately comical leer. She finished putting her jewelry away and got into the king-size bed beside him. Instantly, he slipped his arms around her and she felt his lips moving slowly up her neck to her ear. "Too tired for this?"

"Never," she said. She wanted him always as much as he wanted her, more, she sometimes suspected. She loved him so much, wanted only to please him. But what was she to do now that the apartment was finished? How was she to spend her days while Adam buried himself in businesses, designed his yachts, planned his races at this strange place called Cows? After a lifetime of strenuous activity, it was hard to resign herself to idleness for long. She had too much energy to do nothing. She needed something to occupy her mind, to keep her from dwelling too much on the only flaw in her perfect life. If she were to get pregnant, she thought, not for the first time. But she and Adam had been married now for almost two years and there was still no sign of a child. It had been so easy with Mirek, so very easy. Why did life insist on playing such cruel games? But she would never let it get the best of her. "Never," she said again. "I do love you so much."

Thirty

es, yes, send him up," said Katrinka urgently into the phone. She replaced the receiver, put the papers she had been studying back into their folder, laid it on the table beside the banquette, and waited anxiously for the doorbell to ring. As soon as it did, she leapt to her feet and raced to answer it. With Anna, who had trailed her by seconds, looking on in surprise, Katrinka threw open the door and flung herself into the arms of the man on the threshold. "Tomáš! Tomáš! I can't believe it's really you."

He was wearing a pair of jeans and a leather jacket, with a red canvas bag slung across his shoulder. His hair was as thick and curly as ever, with no trace of gray. There was still no fat on his long, lean body. Except for some new lines at the corners of his eyes and mouth, he looked exactly the same. *"Zlatíčko!"* he said. They stood embracing for a moment, then stepped back for a better look at one another. "Look at you!" said Tomáš. "What an elegant lady you've become."

"And you, a successful film director at last. Oh, Tomáš," she murmured, hugging him again, "I am so happy to see you." Tears streamed down Katrinka's cheeks while Tomáš blinked rapidly to keep from crying. "Come in, come in." She stepped back, took his arm, and pulled him into the apartment. "Do you want something to eat? Something to drink?"

"Coffee. Coffee will be fine."

"Anna, this is Tomáš Havlíček. I've been telling her all about you for days," she said to Tomáš. "Anna Bubeník, our housekeeper." Though Tomáš had become over the years reasonably fluent in English, the three spoke, without thinking, in Czech.

"Dobrý den," said Anna, shaking his hand. "I am looking forward to seeing your film."

The pleasure in Tomáš's face dimmed slightly. "Ah, you're coming to see it?" he asked. Tomáš was with a delegation from Czechoslovakia for the screening of one of his films at the New York Film Festival the following week.

"Anna and her whole family," said Katrinka. "We already arranged the tickets."

"I'll bring coffee," said Anna, as Katrinka, her arm still linked with Tomáš's, led him through the apartment back to the library where she had been sitting when the doorbell rang.

Tomáš looked around and whistled. "What a place!"

"Do you like it?" she said eagerly. A lot of hard work had gone into the creation of the apartment and she never really tired of showing it off.

"It's beautiful."

"Thank you," said Katrinka, feeling a warm rush of pleasure at his praise. In the five months that had passed since the Grahams' "housewarming" party, the apartment had appeared in *Chic* and *Vogue,* and *Architectural Digest* had just scheduled a session to photograph it for an article on Carlos Medina, now one of New York's hottest interior designers, so Katrinka hardly needed more confirmation of her taste. Still she had worried a little about what Tomáš's response to her home would be. He was her oldest and best friend, but she had feared that the difficulties of his life might have turned him bitter or cynical or, worse, envious of her success. She should have known better. Tomáš would never resent her wealth. He had never cared about money. "It's been so long," she said, as she pulled him down onto the banquette beside her. "So long." Though they had exchanged letters often over the years, this was the first time she had seen him since her departure from Czechoslovakia eight years before. "How is Zuzka? Martin? Have you brought pictures? Tell me everything." The words tumbled out of her in a low, excited rush, her Czech as fluent as ever, thanks to Anna with whom she constantly lapsed into conversations in that language, to Carter's annoyance. One of them inevitably would have to translate.

Katrinka looked wonderful, thought Tomáš. He noticed the faint shadows under her eyes and dismissed them. From the time she was a small child, twenty-four hours had never been enough for Katrinka to accomplish all she planned for the day.

Anna entered with a tray laden with coffee, cups, and a plate of chocolate chip cookies, saying apologetically, "I wanted to make some Czech pastries, but Mrs. Graham said you would prefer these."

"He eats Czech pastries all the time at home. Here, he should have something different. Chocolate chip," she said, laughing. "Very American."

Tomáš unzipped his canvas bag and pulled out an envelope of photographs, handed it to Katrinka, picked up a cookie, took a bite, and pronounced it excellent. Pleased, Anna retreated, and Tomáš shifted his attention to his friend, explaining the photographs as she sifted through them: a visit to Zuzka's parents, Zuzka a few pounds heavier but as beautiful as ever; a summer holiday in Svitov with Tomáš's mother, grown very frail; Martin, a lean, dark, pint-sized version of his father, bicycling down the familiar path in the woods nearby; Martin's eighth birthday party; Martin and Tomáš skiing; Katrinka's grandparents' house, appropriated by the state, now rented to some executive from the glass factory, but still in good condition. Tears again welled in Katrinka's eyes as the memories came flooding back. *"Babi's* roses," she said, "how wild they've grown." It still pained her that, because of her illegal exit, she could not go back.

"Nothing's changed," he said. The political regime was as repressive as when she left, he told her, 1968's brief flurry of freedom and hope not only over but, in the intervening eleven years, almost forgotten. Because of his involvement in the student protests, Tomáš never would have had a chance to direct a film had it not been for Mirek Bartoš, for

whose help he was, despite his continuing low opinion of
Bartoš's work, sincerely grateful. "Though it's really you I
have to thank, Katrinka," he said. "Bartoš never would have
lifted a finger, if it hadn't been for you." Tomáš had
remained Bartoš's assistant until, with a film set to begin
principal photography, the director had been struck with a
case of acute appendicitis. The studio had wanted someone
on their approved list to take over, but Bartoš had insisted
on Tomáš's replacing him and, though his father-in-law had
died some time before, the Mach connection still counted
for something, and Bartoš was given his way. That film,
according to Tomáš's disdainful opinion, was bland enough
to meet with critical and political approval, so he was
allowed to direct another. His third had been chosen as an
entry for the New York Film Festival. It was historical,
about Jan Hus, not quite the one Tomáš had once planned to
make because the script had had to be watered down to meet
censorship requirements and some of the best scenes had
been cut for the same reason. "It has moments," said
Tomáš, "which make me almost proud." He shrugged. "But
over all it is not so good, not what I intended. I wish you
didn't have to see it."

"Try and keep me away."

It so depressed Tomáš to talk about the film that the
conversation quickly reverted to family matters. As soon as
Martin had started school, Zuzka had begun to work as a
secretary to someone in the Ministry of Culture. She
enjoyed it well enough and the extra money came in handy.
The family had replaced Katrinka's old Fiat with a new
Škoda and lived in a two-bedroom apartment in the Nové
Město, the New Town. Sometimes they thought about
having another child, but always decided to wait until their
circumstances were even more secure.

"Better not to wait too long," said Katrinka.

Tomáš was surprised by a sudden bleak look in her eyes,
but it was gone so quickly that he thought he must have been
mistaken. He shrugged. "If Martin is the only child we ever
have, we're blessed." All in all, life was not bad, he admitted. He adored his son, loved his wife. His marriage was a
happy one.

"Never tempted by actresses?" Katrinka teased, hoping to cover her momentary lapse.

"Tempted," said Tomáš. "But no more." All his passion was spent making films.

"And how is Mirek?"

"Older, but still handsome, still charming. He's directing a film right now, and having an affair with his star. He still has a way with the ladies. And his wife still turns a blind eye."

Katrinka laughed. "They're almost sixty now. You would think they'd be tired of the game."

"It makes them believe they're still young. He always asks about you," added Tomáš after a minute. "He's never forgotten you."

"I haven't forgotten him," said Katrinka.

Tomáš had news, too, of Ota Černý. Olga's drinking had become such a problem that she had been pressured to stop teaching, and Ota spent so much time and energy caring for her that he had little left for the responsibilities of coaching a team for international competitions. He was working again on the provincial level.

"My defecting hurt him," said Katrinka sadly.

"Perhaps," responded Tomáš. "Who can tell? But your first responsibility was to yourself. You have nothing to reproach yourself for."

"I wish I could do something for him."

"You write him. You send gifts. That's enough. It makes him very happy."

Katrinka had decided that Tomáš and she would dine alone, at the apartment. Adam was away overnight. He had flown to Miami for discussion about a design problem in the new motor launch and, convinced that Ronald Reagan was going to be elected President in November and that the new administration would increase defense spending, on his way back he was stopping in Washington for meetings with some Republican senators. By putting his bid in early, he was trying to pave the way for a contract for the Bridgeport yard to build medium-sized navy patrol boats.

"Is Adam away often?" asked Tomáš at one point, trying

369

to determine the cause of the troubled expressions he sometimes caught flitting across Katrinka's face.

"All the time," she said, laughing. "So much that a few months ago we bought a plane. Wait until you see it! It's enormous." It had a gray leather and chrome sitting room, a teak-paneled conference room with a table large enough to accommodate twelve, an office, a master bedroom cabin with private bath, a guest cabin and shower, and quarters for the crew. "Usually, I go with him. But this time I wanted to stay in New York to see you."

When dinner was ready, Katrinka and Tomáš moved their conversation from the library to the dining room where Carter, his greyhound's face impassive, waited on them with quiet efficiency, always ready with what was required not only before it was requested but before it was even thought of. Finally, he left them alone over coffee and Tomáš shook his head in bemusement. "Is it like this every night?"

"When we have dinner at home."

"You really landed in the lap of luxury," said Tomáš.

"Oh, yes," agreed Katrinka with a laugh.

They talked until two in the morning, when Katrinka offered Tomáš a guest bedroom for the night, but he shook his head, saying it would make his security guards too nervous and he did not want to have to deal with the consequences of that. "But I've sent Adam's driver home," said Katrinka.

"It's not far. I'll walk." He was staying at the Algonquin, on Forty-fourth Street, which pleased him because he knew its associations with people like Ben Hecht and Nunnally Johnson whose screenplays he admired.

"This is New York," said Katrinka, "you are not walking, not alone, at this hour."

"I won't be alone," said Tomáš with a smile. "I have no doubt my guard is downstairs waiting for me."

"Then you can both take a cab," said Katrinka, phoning down to the lobby to ask the doorman to call a taxi. They fixed a time to meet the next day and kissed good night, each leaving the other with mixed emotions, not only the ones they had expected—the happiness at seeing one another again mixed with regret that their reunion would be so short—but concern, Katrinka's for Tomáš because his career was clearly not going the way he wanted, and Tomáš's for Katrinka because no matter in what glowing terms she spoke about Adam and her marriage he knew something was wrong.

With the car and driver at her complete disposal until Adam's return, Katrinka the next day took Tomáš sightseeing. They went to the Statue of Liberty and Bloomingdale's, the Empire State Building and the Museum of Modern Art. They drove down Wall Street ("So this is the granite heart of capitalism," said Tomáš with something akin to wonder when he saw it), through SoHo and Chinatown, Little Italy and Washington Square, and uptown to the theater district, the West Side, and Harlem. Tomáš loved it, and hated it. "It's so seedy," he said, "so filthy. And yet so alive, with such a cold beauty. What a terrible place it must be to live. Terrible and wonderful."

"Yes," agreed Katrinka. "Both."

Adam arrived back from Washington in a good mood, pleased with the reception given him by the senators, one of whom was a key figure on the Appropriations Committee. He took them all to dinner at Elaine's, which catered to the kind of showbiz crowd he thought Tomáš might enjoy seeing at play. With the spotlight definitely off him and little chance to talk business, it was the sort of evening Adam might well have hated. But the glow of his successful day carried him through, and in any case he liked Tomáš: the time they had spent together in Prague, when Adam had gone to collect Katrinka's things, had forged a bond between them. Rather than bored, he found himself sitting with his arm draped across the banquette behind Katrinka, his fingers just barely touching her shoulder, enjoying the stories, the humor, the easy camaraderie which somehow, though he had shared none of their history, included him. He wondered why he did not have this sort of relationship with any of his friends—until he realized that, no matter how many times they crewed on each other's boats or stood as godparents for each other's children, the competition between them was just too keen.

At the thought of children, he frowned. His mother was beginning to be particularly irritating on the subject, carrying on as if he wasn't even trying. God, if she only knew. And if only she would let him run his life without trying to meddle. He saw Katrinka's questioning look and replaced his frown quickly with a smile in anticipation of trying again that night, as soon as they could decently return Tomáš to his hotel. He had missed Katrinka, he always did when they were apart. They had been married for over two years and still he wanted her, all the time. He had not been unfaithful once, despite the many temptations, not even last night in Miami with a very pretty secretary who had been eager to work late. He never would have believed it. Never in his life had he confined himself to one woman for so long.

Tomáš's film was screened the next night, and despite his own reservations about it, the critics and audience were impressed, recognizing his talent, attributing the film's flaws to the Czech government's heavy hand. Afterward, Adam and Katrinka threw a small party for Tomáš at their apartment. In addition to their usual circle of friends, the Grahams had invited a number of people they thought Tomáš might enjoy meeting: the reclusive Woody Allen put in an appearance, and Diane Keaton, both of whom had won Oscars the preceding year for *Annie Hall*. William Goldman came, and Joseph Papp, David Mamet, Robert de Niro, Mayor Koch, Martina Navratilova, and Miloš Forman. As if the film were going to be a great commercial success instead of disappearing the next day without a trace, the mood was festive, the evening ending with Katrinka, Miloš, Martina, Tomáš, and a security guard, who was posing as a member of the film delegation, singing Czech folk songs to Katrinka's accompaniment on the guitar. Adam's mother would not have approved had she been there, but she was not, and everyone else had a grand time. When Rick Colins wrote about it in his column he described it as a most unusual party for New York: innocent and fun.

When the time came for Tomáš to leave, Katrinka did not

accompany him to the airport, but said good-bye to him at the Algonquin, where she had arrived with bags full of presents for him to take home to Zuzka and Martin and the Černýs, clothes, makeup, stockings, toys, food, liquor, cigarettes, as much as he could carry. "I hope customs lets me keep some of this," he muttered.

"The liquor is for them," said Katrinka, smiling.

"You think of everything, *andeličku*, don't you?"

"Sometimes I think too much," she said.

Tomáš put his arms around her. "Why won't you tell me what's wrong?" he asked, sorry he had put the question off until now when it was far too late for her to answer in any depth. But he had been reluctant to pry, knowing that they had stopped confiding everything to each other the day she had gone to bed with Mirek Bartoš.

"Nothing," she said. "Nothing important. You see how my life is. It's wonderful. But there are some things I want that I can't seem to get, and sometimes that makes me unhappy."

"Like what?"

"A child."

"You've been married such a short time, Katrinka."

But with Mirek she had become pregnant right away, she thought sadly. Why now, when she wanted a baby so desperately, couldn't she conceive? She shrugged, adding, "And I want Adam to give up sailing."

"He loves sailing. I hardly know him, and I know that."

"It makes me so afraid." She had not thought seriously about Adam's hobby until the Fastnet race that August. Until then, a little more than a month ago, it had seemed, in her ignorance, to be a safe enough pastime. But while she had waited on the Isle of Wight for four dreadful days as the fleet of 306 yachts tried to make the 606-mile run from Cowes to Fastnet Rock off the Irish coast and back to Plymouth in a gale with top winds of 75 miles per hour, she had learned otherwise. The waves were as high as houses, one survivor had reported. Another had said that sailing in the storm was like riding a roller coaster nonstop for days. Helicopters, tugs, trawlers, frigates, and Royal Navy jets were called to the rescue. At the end, fifteen men were dead, including one of Adam's crew, struck by the falling mast that had kept the sixty-five-foot yacht from finishing. Adam was shaken but determined to try again: Ted Turner's yacht, *Tenacious*, had won in record time. "I've lost so many people, Tomáš, so suddenly, so violently, I couldn't stand it if I lost Adam, too."

"Zlatičko, it's not like you to worry like this."

"About the people I love, yes, yes I do. Sometimes I worry until I think I'll die of it."

"You must stop," he said sternly, "because it does no good at all."

"I know."

When, a few days later, she had tried to tell Adam how she felt, he had been at first irritated, then angry. "I have enough trouble with my goddamn mother," he had shouted, seeing Katrinka's fear as only another and more terrible form of Nina Graham's disapproval. "Don't you start." Katrinka, who saw no similarity at all between herself and her mother-in-law, had protested, but since she would not give up trying to make Adam at least see her point of view, the quarrel grew more and more heated and, for the first time, did not end with them in bed, making love. Instead, the next morning, Adam had left for Bremen without her and it was two days before they got the chance to make up, with nothing really resolved.

Since then they had not discussed the matter at all, and when Adam went out sailing, Katrinka tried not to let him see how frightened she was. Sometimes, in an effort to conquer her fear, as she had to some extent with cars, she went with him, but more than once they had been caught in a sudden squall on the sound, which ended with her being more terrified than before.

"Think how you would feel if Adam tried to make you give up skiing."

"If he asked me, I would do it, because I love him."

"Forgive me," said Tomáš with a smile, "but I doubt it. You would think he was a fool for asking you, and maybe even a bit of a coward."

"I'm not a coward!"

"Nor a fool. Try and see his side of it."

374

"I do, Tomáš. Believe me, I do."

They embraced one last time and, amid a flurry of last-minute messages, wishes for the future, unspoken fears about further meetings, Katrinka watched as Tomáš joined the other members of the committee in the limousine that was to take them to the airport. She waved until it was out of sight and then got back into her own car and told Dave to take her home. Sadness overwhelmed her as she sank into its soft seat, but she knew that it, like her fears, like the longing for the child she had lost and the one she wanted to have, might lessen her happiness at times but could never destroy it. Only Adam could do that. Losing him, she was sure, would be the one thing in life she could never survive.

*T*think I'm too comfortable here to bother going to Paris," said Daisy, her petite body oiled, her eyes closed, her classically beautiful face, amply protected, she hoped, by sunblock, turned to the sun.

"We did promise Margo we would meet her," said Katrinka, who was lying on the chaise next to Daisy on the tiled patio overlooking the pool.

"She'd understand."

"And Natalie," persisted Katrinka.

"She would much rather join us here."

"And Alexandra."

Daisy groaned. "It will be so hot in Paris," she said, reluctant but surrendering.

As much as Katrinka enjoyed spending time at the villa, she would not be sorry to leave, at least not for a few days. She was feeling unusually restless, both because Adam was away and because of the intriguing ad she had noticed in *The International Herald Tribune* a few weeks ago. In Paris, once she managed to escape from her gang of girlfriends, she intended to follow it up.

Adam had been gone for over a week, flying to meetings in Bremen, Miami, New York, and to Scotland, where he had recently acquired a shipyard on the Clyde. Buying it had seemed a foolhardy gesture since it had been close to bankruptcy with little hope of a turnaround in a depressed economy. But a classic yacht Adam admired had been built there at the turn of the century and, not wanting to see that piece of sailing history lost forever, he had bought the yard, yanking it back from oblivion, had streamlined its management, and now was trying to revive its fortunes with defense contracts from the Third World.

From Scotland, Adam would return briefly to St.-Jean-Cap-Ferrat and then fly on to Athens, where he was negotiating for the purchase of a tanker fleet. That, too, seemed a foolhardy move, since the collapse of the oil market in 1973 had devastated the tanker business, which had not improved in the eight years since. But not only did Adam like a bargain—and tankers in the summer of 1981 were cheap—but he predicted that when world shipping picked up, as it was bound to do soon, there would be a demand for old tankers as long as new ones remained prohibitively expensive to build. Everyone had grown so used to his making a fortune in nearly impossible circumstances that even his closest business advisers no longer bothered to argue when he announced a new and apparently harebrained scheme. "He must smell money," they said consolingly to each other, pushing away fears for his welfare and their job security.

Katrinka hoped to accompany Adam to Athens, which she had never seen. Though she traveled with him as much as she could, he seemed to her these days to be away too often, and his schedule made her own seem empty, though she tried to keep herself busy not only with the usual round of exercise class and luncheon dates, but by continuing to manage the Golden Horn as well as sit on numerous committees for the charities that occupied so much of Daisy's time. But it was not really enough, which is why she had convinced Adam to buy this villa in Cap Ferrat.

Once the New York apartment was finished, Katrinka and Adam had begun discussing the purchase of a country home. They had considered Newport (which was immediately rejected by both as too close for comfort to the elder Grahams), the Hamptons, Martha's Vineyard, any number of places within a reasonable distance of New York. Katrinka had hired a helicopter and searched by air, getting a sense of the size, seclusion, and security of the various properties before investigating on foot. There had been many places she had liked, but none she had fallen in love with until, during a weekend with Adam at the Grand Hotel du Cap, she had found, quite by accident, a ruin in the hills above St.-Jean-Cap-Ferrat.

The villa had been built in the 1920s by a wealthy English aristocrat, Lady Marina Granville, an intrepid traveler who, on one of her journeys to North Africa, had fallen in love not only with the culture but, some said, with a Bedouin sheik. To commemorate what must have been the high point of her erotic life, Lady Marina bought two acres in Cap Ferrat, employed an architect from Marrakech, a local builder, and artisans from surrounding villages to construct for her a fantasy three-story Moroccan villa. It had ceilings and panels of carved and inlaid wood, walls and floors of mosaic tile, and an Islamic tower with a charming wooden balcony. Carved tables and chairs, leather poufs, woven rugs, and Oriental couches, new and antique, were imported from Morocco and combined with surprisingly harmonious effect with family pieces from the Granville estate in Yorkshire. Glass doors framed by delicate ironwork opened from the house onto courtyards of marble tile and splashing fountains, or terraces of sand-colored brick laid in herringbone patterns. Wide stone steps led down to a tiled swimming pool. From the changing rooms at the far end extended a sweeping semicircle of steps that met at a patio of intricate stonework, beyond which was a long galleried walk overlooking the sea.

The villa had been passed down through several generations, while the Granvilles' failing fortune had made maintenance at first difficult and then impossible. The family had allowed it to fall into such a state of decay that the cost of restoration had put off most potential buyers. But not Katrinka. She loved the house, loved the romance behind its construction. Adam was at first resistant but he quickly saw her point. The villa could be had cheaply, it was in a convenient location for most of his European businesses (Nice airport was about twenty minutes away), and he trusted Katrinka, who had not exceeded her budget on the Fifth Avenue apartment, to keep the restoration costs to a reasonable amount. All in all, Adam figured that the Villa

Mahmed (its name, people suggested, was a contraction of those of Marina and her lover) would end up costing less than a house in any of the other locations they had considered, and be far more impressive.

Again, Katrinka summoned Carlos Medina to her aid. They unearthed the original plans, scoured North Africa as well as Europe from Spain to Turkey for duplicates of what had been lost or destroyed, had recreated what could not be replaced, and, like Lady Marina, used local artisans to do the work. When they had finished, those who had not liked the Villa Mahmed to start with pronounced it a folly, others admired it. Rick Colins, who was living with Carlos and admittedly might have been prejudiced, described it in an article for *Architectural Digest* as "a work of genius," without specifying whether it was Lady Marina, Carlos, or Katrinka to whom he referred. Rick had finally quit *The Chronicle* to free-lance, leaving the field to Sabrina, who had replaced him. Sabrina described the villa as a joke. As far as anyone knew, she had never seen it.

Either way, Katrinka did not care. Adam, whom she most wanted to please, was satisfied. Despite the Oriental opulence of its decor, the villa was spacious and uncluttered, cool, serene, and, above all, comfortable, with secluded areas perfect for thinking, reading, or—inevitably in Adam's case—work.

To the loud and unusually direct disapproval of Nina Graham, who blamed it for their continuing childless state, Katrinka and Adam led an increasingly active life, moving regularly between New York and Cap Ferrat, with frequent side trips to London and Paris, winter holidays in Aspen or Kitzbühel or St. Moritz, traveling when possible in the Boeing 727, usually with an entourage that consisted of Mac and Debbie, Adam's assistant and his personal secretary, as well as Carter, whose responsibility it was to see that they were all comfortable at every hour of the day or night, no matter where they were.

Except for the staff, Katrinka and Daisy were alone at the villa. Steven Elliott had left the day after Adam for a business meeting in London with Lord Crighton, head of a large merchant bank, who was trying to arrange joint financing with Boston Federal, the bank founded by the Elliott family in 1867 and still controlled by them, for the purchase of one of New York's larger office buildings. He had not said when he was returning and had not been heard from since, unlike Adam, who called Katrinka at least once, sometimes twice a day from wherever he was.

With the departure of the men, the frantic round of socializing had stopped. There were no more dinners at the Grand Hotel du Cap or the Château de la Chevre d'Or in Eze, no jazz evenings in Juan les Pins, gambling in the Grand Casino in Monte Carlo, or dancing at Jimmy's until dawn. Katrinka and Daisy, tired from the weeks of nonstop activity with their husbands, lay on the blue-and-white tiled patio, by the blue-and-white tiled pool, and basked in the brilliant sun, lulled by the heavy scent of pine in the air and the hum of invisible insects. They had stirred from the villa only for a short cruise on Malcolm Forbes's yacht as far as San Remo to buy, so it was said, the best pesto sauce in the world, and again for a party for the Aga Khan thrown by Prince Khalid ibn Hassan at his villa in Cap Martin, for which Adam had meant to return. However, weighing a possible defense contract against an order for a bigger and better yacht, he had finally decided that it was more important to accept the invitation to a casual Saturday lunch with Margaret Thatcher at Chequers.

"It does seem a pity to leave," said Daisy the next morning, looking regretfully at the villa and the lush scarlet bougainvillea climbing its sand-colored walls. A light mistral had come up and the air was clear and the temperature perfect, somewhere in the mid-seventies. "Don't you think we're mad?" she said to Carter, who had remained behind, when Adam left, to supervise the local staff.

"You'll be back soon, I'm sure, Mrs. Elliott," replied Carter diplomatically.

"In about five days," said Katrinka. "I will phone from Paris with details." Carter nodded and helped them into the car as the driver loaded their bags into the back of the white Rolls. "Oh," continued Katrinka, "and I do think that Mr.

and Mrs. Goodman will be with us, and that Mr. Graham and Mr. Elliott will return by then."

"Yes, Mrs. Graham," said Carter, who could have coped with twice that number without blinking an eye.

"The things you make me do," said Daisy, still grumbling, as the car set off for Nice.

"My revenge," said Katrinka, laughing, "for the way you make me run around New York until I'm ready to drop."

"You love it," said Daisy.

"Oh, I do. I do. Most of the time," she added with an odd note in her voice.

Daisy looked fondly at Katrinka and smiled. "Perhaps Nina is right," she said gently, "and you ought to stop driving yourself so hard." She knew how much Katrinka, and Adam for that matter, wanted a child.

"Nonsense," said Katrinka emphatically. "I go crazy when I have nothing to do."

As Daisy had feared, Paris was hot and steamy, with a thick heat haze hovering over the city. But once she was in the cool and luxurious Plaza Athénée having lunch in the Relais Plaza with Katrinka, Natalie, Margo, and Alexandra, her good humor returned. "This is delicious," she said, not referring to the kir royale she was sipping but the fact of being in Paris with her friends. "Shall we go over the schedule, make sure we've got everything organized?" The little general was back in action.

The women were in Paris for the summer haute-couture collections. Lucia di Campo, who did not see the point in spending vast amounts on clothes, had said no to Katrinka's invitation to join them, and instead had remained at her house in Florence to work on the designs for a yacht that Adam had decided to build for himself and Katrinka, agreeing only that she and Nick and their daughter would visit the villa sometime before the end of the summer. But Margo, as fashion editor of *Chic,* and Natalie, as head buyer for Galleries Gillette, were required to be there and had exhausting schedules, with as many as seven shows in a day to attend, requiring a mad dash between each in a tangle of people and cars. The others, who were on the most expen-

sive shopping spree in the world, could be more selective,
limiting themselves to two, or perhaps three each day: Yves
St. Laurent, of course, Dior, Givenchy, Chanel, Ungaro, a
look in at Patou to see what Christian Lacroix was up to.
They would take chauffeur-driven cars to the Grand Hotel,
the George V, the Intercontinental, the Theatre National de
Chaillot, and the other venues, arriving in a crush of traffic,
moving hurriedly through the warm wet air of Paris to, if
they were lucky, air-conditioned interiors. Some, like the
Ecole des Beaux Arts, were not. But, within a few minutes,
no matter how cool to start, even the grandest of baroque
ballrooms was uncomfortably hot, the narrow gilt-trimmed
chairs placed too close together, every inch of space
crowded with aides trying to replace chaos with order,
arriving guests kissing old friends hello, photographers
jockeying for place, reporters looking for an angle, the floors
strewn with camera tracks and cables requiring elegant
ladies in sleeveless, and sometimes strapless, summer
dresses to clamber inelegantly over them, straining the
fabric of their skirts as they scampered up and across the
runways and climbed over chairs to find the ribboned name
tags marking their places, even the thinnest finding themselves uncomfortably squashed when they sat, and not able
to use their programs as fans because careful notes had to be
made in the margins as the music blared, the lights glared,
and the models began their stunning progress down the
ramp.

Most of the men present were with the press corps, quiet
print journalists making notes and rowdy photographers
calling instructions to the models from their vantage points
at the rear. Some lovers and fewer husbands accompanied
their women—rich Hong Kong businessmen, Australian
moguls, American film stars—sitting behind them, putting
a possessive hand from time to time on their shoulders,
leaning forward to whisper when there was something they
particularly liked, or decidedly hated. The women were
more varied: the designer's chic aides, the casual photographers, the rumpled newspaper reporters, the stylish columnists, the elegant magazine editors, and the exquisite rich
who occupied the best seats, those who were most likely to

buy (and only about twenty-five hundred women in the world ever do buy couture) or who would bring the most publicity occupying the prized front row. Working out the seating plan was every designer's nightmare.

Natalie was with the contingent from Galleries Gillette, but Margo, as fashion editor of the influential *Chic,* was in one of the best seats, near John Fairchild of *Women's Wear Daily* and Sabrina of the van Hollen chain. Katrinka, who had been attending the collections since her marriage, buying enough to supplement her wardrobe and please her favorite designers, and who last year for the first time had made Eleanor Lambert's International Best-Dressed list, was in the front row, along with Daisy, who had made it every year for the past ten. Behind them sat Alexandra, at the collections for the first time. After years of to-ing and fro-ing, passion and guilt, Neil Goodman had finally left his wife and married Alexandra the preceding March. He had instructed her not to be intimidated by the prices, but this early in her marriage, Alexandra was determined to take his instructions with a dash of discretion and had set her budget at a hundred thousand dollars, for which, she estimated, she could get three dresses, two suits, and a ball gown.

After each show, most of the audience traipsed backstage, filing past the designer in a straggly line to offer congratulations. While the ensembles were returned to their numbered clothes racks and draped with sheets, the models struggled into their clothes and the press interviewed the celebrities in the crowd. Wonderful, original, terribly exciting, they said, no one wanting to be the one to announce a disaster, happy to leave that to John Fairchild or Suzy or Sabrina in the pages of their publications the following day.

Between the shows, Katrinka and her friends would return to the hotel to rest, have lunch, and, later in the day, meet in the bar to sip champagne and compare notes on what they had seen, taking care not to have their choices overlap, since they so often attended the same events. Only when all the shows were over would they decide finally what to buy, stopping by the couture houses to try on the samples, or sending requests to the designers for sketches and fabric samples and price quotes before placing an order. Those

383

who bought frequently from a particular house had their measurements on file and mannequins built to size to be used for all but the final fitting.

In the evening, they would go out to dinner, Daisy, the organizer, rustling up enough men to make up the numbers. Neil Goodman, who spent his days visiting museums, was always in attendance; Jean-Claude Gillette could be relied on for an evening or two; Rick Colins, there to cover the collection, and Carlos Medina, who had accompanied him, could be drafted to serve, as could any number of business associates of Adam's or Steven's, the former husbands of old friends, married men in Paris without their wives, rich men and playboys who liked to be seen with beautiful women. They would dine at famous restaurants like Tour d'Argent, or the latest trendy *boîte* that would be out again before their next visit to Paris. Afterward they would go to Régine's, occupying a table in the corner nearest the dance floor, the section from which all but the rich or famous were barred by burly waiters, dancing under the faceted mirrored ceiling which gave the room, down so many flights of mirrored stairs, the feeling of a cavern roofed with stalactites. Sometimes they would attend parties thrown by friends or hosted by designers, each of whom would select a particular woman, usually someone with a celebrity status of her own, to honor with a dinner—a way of showing gratitude for past purchases and attracting publicity for the new collection, a friendly bit of business with advantages for both. Wherever they went, they rarely got to bed before two or three, and were up again by at least eight to prepare for the first collection of the morning.

With virtually every moment of the day and night planned, it was not easy to escape the others, but on the last afternoon, when Katrinka was supposed to be in her suite resting, she left the hotel and, instead of taking the car which she had hired for her entire stay in Paris, got into a taxi and instructed the driver to take her to a street not far from the Beaubourg. From there, she walked to the address on the ad she had clipped from *The International Herald Tribune*.

The office of Zeiss Associates was on the top floor. It was

not at all the small, seedy suite of rooms Katrinka had anticipated, but something altogether more familiar and comforting, carpeted in deep pile, with leather furniture, and lithographs hanging on walls covered in seagrass paper. Behind the neat glass-and-chrome desk sat an attractive young woman in a smart linen dress. She looked up as Katrinka entered and smiled. *"Bonjour, Madame."*

"Bonjour. Monsieur Zeiss, s'il vous plaît."

"Est-ce-qu'il vous attend?"

Katrinka nodded, and the young woman asked her name. "Madame Novotna," she said, using her mother's maiden name.

The receptionist picked up the phone, spoke into it, and a few moments later one of the double doors leading from the interior offices opened and a man came into the reception area. "Madame Novotna?" he asked as he came forward to greet her.

"Yes," she said, extending a hand to shake his.

"I'm Paul Zeiss," he said in an accentless English that seemed somehow foreign. He was a slight, gray man, with a pale attractive face, longish gray hair, and horn-rimmed glasses over blue-gray eyes. Even his suit was a light gray woven silk. It was impossible to tell what his nationality might be. "If you'll come this way, please." He led her through the door and along a corridor lined with offices on one side and lithograph-covered walls on the other, to a large square room at the end furnished in the same expensive modern style as the reception area, with large windows giving a view of one colorful corner of the Beaubourg and a number of traditional green mansard roofs. "Please," he said, "be seated. Would you like some coffee?"

"I would," said Katrinka gratefully, "if it is not too much trouble."

It wasn't, he assured her, and buzzed his secretary with the request. Until the coffee appeared, they contented themselves with small talk, the weather in Paris, why Katrinka was in the city, where she normally lived, none of which information she had given on the phone when she had called to make the appointment.

"How did you find out about us, Mrs. Graham?" he asked, when the coffee had arrived. Startled, Katrinka stopped stirring the packet of sweetener into the thick dark brew and looked up. "It is my business to know who people are as well as where. You and your husband are often in the papers."

She smiled ruefully. "I did intend to tell you my name once . . . once we did come to an understanding." She took a sip of coffee, then said, "I saw an ad in the *Herald Tribune*. It said you traced missing persons." After seeing the ad, she had, of course, made a few discreet inquiries. What she had discovered was that Zeiss Associates was an investigative agency with a reputation for being reliable, trustworthy, and extremely successful.

"Yes," he nodded. "Lost heirs usually. Kidnapped children. And adults," he added, almost as an afterthought, though in a Europe rife with radical political groups, finding political hostages had become Zeiss Associates' most lucrative form of employment.

"There is someone I do want you to find." She hesitated. For weeks she had thought about almost nothing but this and had made up her mind to do it. But now, confronted with the reality of her decision, it was difficult to take the first step. What she was about to do could jeopardize her entire life, deprive her of the respect she had worked so hard to win, her social position, her good name, and perhaps even Adam's love and trust, a thought she found unbearably painful.

"Yes?" prompted Paul Zeiss.

"My son," said Katrinka finally.

Katrinka's search for her child may have been haphazard and amateurish, but she had tirelessly explored every possibility that occurred to her until she had run out of ideas. Then she had consoled herself with the hope of running into the boy somewhere, sometime. She often thought that she traveled so much only to increase her chances of finding him. And when Adam went anywhere without her, she suspected that it was not just missing him that made her feel

386

so anxious while he was gone but her sense of having lost an opportunity. So, when Katrinka saw the Zeiss ad in the *Herald Tribune*, she was flooded with relief as well as excitement. Here, at last, was something real, something practical she could do to find her son.

Katrinka told Paul Zeiss the story of her love affair with Mirek Bartoš, the birth of her child, the death of her parents, her signing of the adoption release, and subsequent futile attempts to recover the boy. Reticent as always, she told him as little as possible, only what he needed to know to do the job. But even confiding that much she found hard, especially to this odd gray man, a total stranger.

Zeiss listened imperturbably, betraying no emotion. If his heart was wrung at the thought of a beautiful young girl, alone and helpless, tormented by grief and guilt, it did not show. It was as if he had heard it all before, which indeed he had in one form or another. When she finished, he said merely, "You know, giving up your son may indeed have been the best thing you could have done for him. Not that I approve of Klaus Zimmerman's methods, you understand," he added quickly. "But the boy could be happy, living a good life with devoted parents."

"I would do nothing to harm him," said Katrinka firmly. "But I need to know where he is, how he is." She choked back a sob. "I do need to know." Katrinka supplied Zeiss with the dates, the names, the addresses. "You will handle this yourself?" she asked.

"Of course, Mrs. Graham. Though not without help, you understand."

"And it will be entirely confidential?"

"Entirely."

"Not even my husband is to know." It was an admission she was reluctant to make, but it was necessary. If her son was found, if he was unhappy, if he needed her, then she would tell Adam. She would not risk her relationship with her husband before there was a point to it.

"I understand."

They worked out the details of the arrangement, reports to be sent to Katrinka in plain envelopes, payments to be made through her Austrian bank so that she could conceal the transactions in the Golden Horn's books. "How soon will I hear from you?" she asked as she stood to leave.

"I will send you a report every month. You'll hear from me sooner only if I have something significant to report. But, Mrs. Graham, I advise you not to get your hopes too high. I am very good at what I do, I assure you. There's no one better. But even I am not always successful."

"I can live with disappointment," she assured him. "It is doing nothing I cannot stand."

By the time Katrinka returned to her white-and-gold suite at the Plaza Athénée, she was exhausted, drained by the effort of her appointment with Zeiss. She put the Do Not Disturb sign on the door, took off her clothes, turned down the bed's quilted satin cover and got in, hoping to sleep for a few hours before meeting the others in the bar at eight as planned. But she was too wound up to sleep. She called room service and ordered tea and the afternoon papers, then took a brief shower while she waited for them to arrive. When they did, she stretched out again on the bed and began to thumb through them, skimming the world news, the financial reports, the reviews of the various collections, paying little attention to anything until an item in Sabrina's column in *The Globe* made her breath catch in her throat. The vicious bitch, she thought, more lies! Why does she never stop? Quickly, Katrinka threw on some clothes, picked up the newspaper and her key, left her suite, went next door to Daisy's, and rang the doorbell. For a long moment there was silence and Katrinka was afraid that perhaps Daisy had gone out, but finally the door opened slightly. "Who is it?" said Daisy, sounding sleepy and annoyed.

"Katrinka. Can I come in?"

"Oh, yes. Of course, darling. Just a minute." The door closed again and Katrinka heard the sound of the safety bar being released before Daisy threw the door wide open and said, "You sound upset. What is it?"

"Something in the papers." She brushed past Daisy, went

into the luxurious sitting room, and sat on the tapestry couch. "May I have a drink?"

"Certainly. What would you like?"

"Brandy, please."

"Hmmm," said Daisy. She poured the brandy and put the glass on the ornate table in front of Katrinka, then sat next to her on the sofa, glancing at the copy of *The Globe* that Katrinka was clutching. "It's Sabrina again, I suppose."

"Yes."

"It's not something about Adam?" said Daisy, sounding horrified.

Katrinka shook her head. "It's about Steven," she said finally.

"Steven!" Daisy sounded absolutely incredulous. "What on earth could Sabrina write about Steven?"

"It's awful, and probably a pack of lies as usual. But someone is sure to say something. I thought you should see." She handed Daisy the paper. "Page seven," she said.

Daisy opened the paper, found the page. "Oh, my God," she murmured, shock and disbelief mingled in her voice. The headline, in large black type, said, "Naughty Steven Caught with His Hand in the Sugar Bowl." Below it was a large photo of Steven Elliott, his arm around a woman's shoulder, four of his fingers disappearing under the thin strap and draped bodice of her dress.

The photograph, Sabrina explained, had been snapped in Steven Elliott's limo, outside Annabel's, the trendy London disco where the couple had been seen dancing several nights in a row. In case anyone should happen to think that they might have met there by chance, Sabrina went on to point out that the two had been staying together at the Savoy since Mr. Elliott's arrival in London, the week before. Mr. Elliott, confided Sabrina to those who did not know, was from a prominent Boston family, president of one of the largest banks in the United States, married to a socialite related on her mother's side to Franklin Delano Roosevelt, and father of two sons and a daughter, all older than Ms. Benson, former star of such pornographic favorites as *The Naughty Schoolgirl* and *Isabelle at Night*. Still only twenty-three, she had once vacationed in the Greek Isles with Prince Andrew, accompanied Rod Stewart on a world tour, been kept by an Australian entrepreneur, been seen at Aspen with an American film star and Palm Beach with a Wall Street tycoon. Since Mr. Elliott had not taken any pains to conceal his affair with the notorious Sugar, wondered Sabrina, was divorce in the air?

"The old fool," said Daisy, but there were tears in her eyes.

Katrinka picked up the glass of brandy from the table and offered it to Daisy. "Here, take some of this."

Daisy took a sip, choked a little, and put the glass down. "I'm all right," she said. But she wasn't. Her skin had turned yellow under the tan and her eyes had the glazed look of a stunned animal.

"It may not be true," said Katrinka cautiously.

"He was fondling her breast in public," said Daisy, who would not have sounded more outraged if Steven had been caught exposing himself.

Katrinka made a case for Steven: he had perhaps run into Sugar at Annabel's, drunk a little too much, made a fool of himself. But that did not necessarily mean that he had Sugar with him at the Savoy, or that they had been seeing each other regularly either in London, or anywhere else. "You know how Sabrina does love to twist the truth."

But, for once, Sabrina had been absolutely accurate, as Steven himself confirmed when Daisy finally reached him an hour later at the Savoy. "I'm sorry, Daisy," he said. "Really so very sorry. I didn't mean you to find out this way. I was going to tell you myself when I got back to the villa. I love her, Daisy. I want to marry her."

Never one for hysterical scenes, Daisy repressed a shout of mingled rage and pain and tried to be reasonable. The phone call went on for hours as she pleaded with her husband not to do anything foolish. She could understand, she told him, if after almost thirty years of marriage he wanted a fling, but surely he could not be so crazy as to throw away their marriage, his relationship with Daisy and the children, for (she was tempted to say a whore, but didn't) someone young enough to be his daughter. But Steven's

mind could not be changed. To him, Sugar Benson was the
Fountain of Youth. When he touched her smooth flesh,
smelled her fresh scent, felt his prick spring to life under her
hand, he felt young again. And that to him was worth more
than all the familiar comforts of his once respectable and
even happy life.

Steven and Sugar had met for the first time at Katrinka
and Adam's, at the party they had thrown to show off the
Fifth Avenue apartment when it was completed. She had
come with the Wall Street broker she was then dating, who
happened also to handle some of Steven's investments. He
had noticed her immediately. It was hard not to notice
Sugar. Just twenty-one then, she had seemed somehow
older, with long honey-colored hair, creamy skin, cat's eyes,
a short, straight nose, a poutingly seductive mouth, and a
rounded body, which she took no trouble to conceal. That
night it was draped in blue, with a back that plunged to the
crack in her bottom. When they were introduced, Steven,
who had always before been reluctant to admit a stranger
into his life, found it hard to resist touching her.

The next winter they met again at St. Moritz and in the
summer on Sardinia. The following year they ran into each
other several times in several other places. They never did
more than exchange a few words, dance a few times, but
Sugar's face and body, her soft Southern drawl, began to
make frequent appearances in Steven's daydreams. The
pout of her mouth, the expression in her eyes, promised
something exciting, dangerous. Then one night in London,
earlier in the year, they had both turned up at the same
party. He was on his own, she was with an escort. He asked
her to dinner the following night and she accepted. They
had dined at the Connaught, gone to Annabel's to dance,
and when Steven, always the perfect New England gentlemen, offered to take her home, she had looked at him with
what seemed genuine surprise and drawled, "But, honey,
don't you want to make love to me?"

Her frank sexuality instead of disgusting him as he once
might have supposed it would, excited him terribly. He had
not been so eager to have a girl since he was sixteen years
old. He took her back to his hotel and did indeed make love

to her, not once but—and he would not have believed it possible—three times that night. What her eyes and mouth promised, Sugar Benson delivered, in spades. Steven Elliott was hooked.

While Daisy spoke to Steven and afterward to her children, hoping to break the news to them before they read it in the papers or heard it from someone else, Katrinka returned to her suite to rearrange the evening's dinner plans, returning later to help Daisy into bed and sit with her until the sleeping pill she had taken helped her to a restless sleep. Then she went down to join the others in the bar.

"Where could he have met a woman like her?" asked Alexandra, lighting a cigarette, her eyes clouded with troubled thoughts, wanting to put as much distance as possible between herself and Sugar Benson. The former Mrs. Neil Goodman, she knew, would consider them only too alike.

"Everywhere," said Natalie, with a shrug. She had streaked her hair even blonder and it suited her, making her skin shine and her large green eyes glitter. "She was at the Schloss at Kitzbühel the last time we were there. *C'est vrais, chérie?*" She turned to Katrinka for confirmation. "She was with that very horrible German count. But I remember that she and Steven danced."

Katrinka only vaguely recalled seeing them together. Klaus Zimmerman had also been staying at the Schloss Grunberg then and, ever since Katrinka had married a wealthy American, he was quick to acknowledge her, making it difficult for Katrinka to dismiss him with a curt nod as she previously had. Once, at the opera in Vienna, he had brought his wife over to her to be introduced and Katrinka, startled and angry, but not wanting to embarrass the shy, timid woman, had elected to be polite. And on that last visit to Kitzbühel, Zimmerman had insisted that Katrinka meet some friends of his, two couples she had seen him with from time to time over the years. Adam quite liked one couple. The husband was the German ambassador to Uruguay, and Adam always liked people who might one day be useful. Katrinka had detested them all. Sugar might have appeared naked in the dining room that night and Katrinka would not have noticed, so upset was she and so determined not to let Adam know. "I think Steven did meet her at one of my parties," she said regretfully.

"What does she see in him? That's what I don't understand," said Margo with a shake of her wild frizzed head.

"Steven is a very handsome man," said Alexandra. "Courtly, elegant, with exquisite manners."

"I know, I know," said Margo impatiently. "But, I mean, really, compared to Prince Andrew?"

"Prince Andrew would not marry her," said Natalie. "Steven Elliott will."

"He wouldn't!" said Margo, outraged.

Alexandra said nothing, knowing that Steven very well might. After all, hadn't Neil left his wife to marry her? Not that the two cases were similar. She and Neil had been in love, very much in love. Nor was she a tramp.

Katrinka shook her head sadly. Until a few hours ago she had thought Daisy and Steven Elliott the happiest married couple she knew. "I think he does want to," said Katrinka, "and Daisy does have too much pride to stop him."

They sat there silently for a moment, four women dressed in their designer clothes, every strand of their hair perfectly in place, their nails long and polished, sipping their Campari and sodas and their kir royales, looking rich, successful, secure, each feeling suddenly threatened. Steven had been the most steadfast, loyal, devoted husband they knew, and Daisy, the most secure of wives. If he was capable of leaving her, just like that, without warning, tossing close to thirty apparently happy years into the trash can, what of their men? Would Alexandra be abandoned someday for someone younger by the sexually aggressive Neil? Would Ted decide after a few more years of marriage that Margo, his college sweetheart, his shrewd adviser and steadfast supporter, was a bit of a nag? Would Jean-Claude, who had not even bothered to marry Natalie, drop her in favor of a nubile young thing discovered in the corridors of one of his châteaux? Would Adam decide Katrinka was not so unusual after all and leave her for someone he found more exotic?

"Pauvre petite," said Natalie.

"Poor *Steven*," said Margo, correcting her, charcoal eyes flashing with anger. "He's the fool, trading in a class act for a tramp."

No, they each reassured themselves. It will never happen to me.

Thirty-Two

It's not like you to be timid."

"Not timid, careful. This is a big step," said Katrinka.

"No bigger than a lot you've taken before," said Adam. "Think about it this way," he added encouragingly. "What have you got to lose?"

Katrinka smiled. "Millions?"

"True," agreed Adam, "but that's what you stand to make, too. That's the fun of it. Not knowing how any deal is going to turn out. Not knowing whether you're going to win or lose."

"You always think you're going to win."

"But I don't *know*. What I do is estimate whether or not the odds are all on my side. In this case, I'd say, they're all on yours. And even if you did lose everything," he said, his brown eyes glinting with laughter, his mouth curved in the crooked smile that could get Katrinka to do anything at all, "you'd still have me. And I'm rich."

They were in the Graham jet returning to New York from Bremen, where Adam had had a series of strategy meetings designed to increase the yard's production. It was the autumn of 1982, Ronald Reagan had been president for twenty-two months, and Adam was convinced that the world's economy was starting to pick up and that the demand for luxury items would soon follow. He wanted to take advantage of the Bremen yard's success building yachts for people like Adnan Khashoggi and John Kluge, for Prince Khalid ibn Hassan and Alan Bond, to try to corner the market on luxury boats by guaranteeing not only superior workmanship but, in an era that increasingly demanded immediate gratification of every whim, quick delivery.

As usual, Katrinka had used Adam's trip to Bremen as an opportunity to take care of her own business.

First, she had stopped in Munich, as she frequently did on trips to Europe, to visit Erica Braun, with whom she had kept in touch, primarily because she was genuinely fond of the woman who had been so kind to her, but also because Erica remained her strongest link to Klaus Zimmerman, supplying Katrinka with a more detailed view of his life than the brief, factual reports from Zeiss Associates.

"Liebling," Erica had said as they sat at the familiar kitchen table drinking tea, "you should go see him." In the fourteen years since the birth of Katrinka's son, Zimmerman had amassed a considerable fortune, thanks—it was assumed—to the success of his clinic, which had become one of the most advanced centers in the world for the treatment of infertility. In truth, it was selling babies that had made him rich. "It's foolish of you not to. He might be able to help."

Knowing how devoted Erica was to the doctor, Katrinka normally tried to control her hatred of the man when his name came up in conversation. But this time she could not repress a shudder. She shook her head vehemently.

Erica frowned, started to speak, then restrained herself. Though once she had found Katrinka's dislike of the doctor both unreasonable and irritating, over the years she had begun to suspect that it might be justified. But the suspicion remained vague, confused, suppressed. Still in love with Zimmerman, she was convinced, justifiably, that, whatever the flaws in his character, his reputation as a fertility specialist was deserved. So, finally she just shook her head sadly and said, "I think you're making a mistake, *liebling,* a big mistake."

"Never. I could never let him touch me again." It was the one thing Katrinka would not do to have a child.

* * *

396

From Munich, Katrinka had gone on to Kitzbühel to consult with Hilde and Bruno about replacing the Golden Horn's central heating system before the start of the ski season. While there, she had received an offer for the inn from Heinrich Ausberg, a local hotel owner who was looking to expand his holdings and saw the Golden Horn as a good investment.

Three months before, Katrinka would not have considered selling it. But recently she had heard through a contact in Sotheby's business real estate division that the Cabot, a sixty-room hotel on Madison Avenue between Sixty-sixth and Sixty-seventh Streets, was for sale. Curious, she had stopped by to have a look one day on her way back from lunch at Le Cirque. Despite its rundown appearance, the elegance of the hotel's architecture had appealed to her. Though built only in 1922, there was something about it that reminded her of hotels in Prague. And, when she saw the interior, she was convinced that she could make something special of the Cabot, turn it into a small jewel like Anoushka Hempel's Blake's Hotel in London.

The cost had put her off initially. The asking price had seemed to her astronomical for a building in need of so much renovation. But then, even if she had considered the price of the hotel fair, there was also the problem of where she was to find the money to buy it. True, she could have asked Adam and he would most likely have said yes, but this was something she wanted to do completely on her own. Though Adam had always, right from the beginning, discussed business with her, taking it for granted that she was smart enough to follow him through the maze of his various interconnecting deals, she had found that he was not really interested in hearing her opinions about any of them. Years of constant carping from Nina Graham had made him wary. Anything beyond an encouraging "How brilliant!" or "You're absolutely right, darling" from his wife inevitably put him in a bad temper. Question a decision and a fight was certain. Though she could hardly keep from pointing out potential pitfalls when she spotted them, and though Adam was always quick to apologize when she had been right,

Katrinka thought it best for their marriage to keep as much as possible out of Adam's business affairs. And to involve him in hers seemed to her to be crazy.

While she was trying to decide what to do, someone had made an offer for the Cabot and was accepted. That was that, thought Katrinka, until she had heard, the day before Adam and she were to leave for Europe, that the financing could not be arranged and the deal had fallen through. When she received the offer for the Golden Horn, it had seemed as if the hand of fate was busily weaving.

"More wine, Mrs. Graham?" asked Carter, who as usual was flying with them.

"Yes, please, Carter," she said. He refilled her glass and went to replenish Adam's scotch and water, while Katrinka, comfortable in the Yves St. Laurent black leather pants suit she liked to wear traveling, sat with her legs tucked up under her on the plane's gray leather couch and studied the offer. Adam, stretched out on the adjoining couch, shoes off, the trousers of his pin-striped custom-made Fioravanti suit slightly rumpled, his pale blue Turnbull & Asser shirtsleeves rolled up, studied her. He dropped the sketches he had been looking at back into their folder, put it on the glass-topped table beside him, and extended a hand to Katrinka. "Let me see those," he said. She handed him the papers. He glanced at them quickly, then said, "How much is the asking price for the Cabot?" She told him. "You'll get it for at least five hundred thousand less," he remarked absently as he began making notations on a yellow pad. When he finished, he looked up at her and said, "If it was me, I'd do it."

She took a sip of wine, looked at the sheet of yellow paper Adam passed to her, then looked at him. He was still tanned from his summer of sailing. In August he had finally won the Fastnet Race in a sixty-foot yacht that he had helped design. Though scared out of her wits during the entire four days, not able to eat or sleep, when she had greeted him at the quay in Plymouth she had felt enormously proud to be his wife. His body looked trim and gracefully muscled under the khaki pants and anorak, his skin was a deep honey color, his brown hair rumpled by the wind, his eyes glowing with satisfaction. Ruthless some people thought him, but not Katrinka. She saw only that he was determined, intelligent, shrewd, courageous, and so very attractive. "I will do it," she said finally.

"That's my girl," he said, sitting up and reaching for her. He pulled her into his arms and kissed her. "One smart lady." He always thought her intelligent, but never more so than when she was doing as he said.

Katrinka needed the Cabot. With the Fifth Avenue apartment and Cap Ferrat house finished, with Adam's attention absorbed not only in building business for the shipyards and the tanker fleet he had finally purchased the year before but in planning his next business coup, Katrinka needed some new project to stop her thinking about the son whom Zeiss Associates seemed to have made little progress in finding or the child she was as yet unable to conceive. She needed something to keep her busy.

"What you need," suggested Nina Graham whenever she was with Adam and Katrinka, "is a child. You and Adam have been married over five years now. Don't you think you should follow the example of Alexandra and that dreadful Neil Goodman, stop jet-setting around, and start a family?" While she disapproved in general of people like Neil Goodman, whatever doubts she may have had about Alexandra's suitability as a daughter-in-law had vanished with the announcement of her pregnancy. If only Adam had had the good sense to marry her, Nina Graham's manner conveyed all too clearly, the Graham family would have had its heir. "It is, after all, a perfectly ordinary and relatively simple thing to accomplish."

Even had she known how much her words hurt, the elder Mrs. Graham would not have hesitated to say them. She was not one to proceed delicately when she believed plain speaking was required to get what she wanted. And what she wanted was a grandson. Clementine's boys were all well and good, but they were not Grahams. However little respect she might have for her husband, Nina Graham had plenty for family and tradition. The Grahams had helped settle Massachusetts Colony; they had been among the first to make their fortune there as shipbuilders and Yankee traders. They had supported independence and republicanism; they had fought for both in the Revolutionary War, the Civil War, the First and Second World Wars. Kenneth Graham's older brother, a captain in the navy, had been killed during the Normandy landing, leaving no children. Adam was the last of the line, and if all families consider the possibility of extinction with great sadness, the proud Grahams viewed it as nothing short of tragic.

But for almost a year Katrinka had been consulting fertility specialists, a humiliating, inconclusive process. Some found nothing wrong with her. Others suggested theories, each a different one. None found the fact of a previous child worth much discussion. All proposed treatments. Katrinka took pills, made charts, kept track of her temperature, tried to get Adam to make love when the signs indicated she was at her most fertile, not an easy task given how often they were traveling, how frequently they were separated. And Adam, though as desperate as Katrinka for a child, hated the whole process, refused to go for an examination, and took the position that he was not going to be bullied by either his mother or Katrinka into fucking to order.

Katrinka pleaded, then raged, then—knowing she could not change Adam's mind, at least not then—decided to put the matter on hold for a while. Soon, she realized she was slipping into a depression. Neither her busy social schedule nor the time she devoted to sitting on the committees of various charities was able to use up her massive energy or stop her active mind from straying into painful areas. Then she saw the Cabot.

From the plane, Katrinka called Herr Ausberg in Kitzbühel and informed him that he would be hearing from her lawyers with a counter-offer. The next day she made a bid on the Cabot. Within three weeks, she had sold one property and bought another, having negotiated one price up, the other down, protecting Hilde and Bruno in the process, keeping Adam out of the proceedings until she needed his guarantee to get a mortgage, the banks having refused to give her one without it. Furious, she swore it would be the last time: on her next deal, she raged, they would come to her, begging to lend her money. Adam tried to calm her down, but his pointing out that she was an unknown business entity in New York did little to help. "If I was the man," she raged at him, "and you the woman, you think they would ask you for guarantees? No!" Unreasonable as she knew she was being (she did, after all, understand how business worked), Katrinka still felt that there was something humiliating about needing Adam's signature on her loan papers when she was bringing to the table the millions she had made on the sale of the Golden Horn.

But once the deal was done and the papers signed, Katrinka put her anger aside and turned her energies instead to the Cabot. Again she called in Carlos Medina, and together they walked the hotel room by room, deciding on an approach to the renovation. Eventually they decided that, in order to achieve Katrinka's ambition to have the Cabot resemble one of the small, charming baroque hotels of Prague, it would be necessary to close it while the work was being done. Since that meant money would be flowing out with none coming in and Katrinka's resources were not unlimited, it was important to reopen the hotel as quickly as possible. They drew up a schedule that most builders told them would be impossible to meet, and the few who conceded that it might could clearly be seen to be lying. Finally, they found one they trusted, and Katrinka hired him on the spot.

Work began and Katrinka's sleep again was reduced to five or six hours a night when in New York. From early morning to late into the evening, she was preoccupied with the Cabot. She spent hours each day at the site, making sure the workmen did not slacken their pace. When she was not there, she was with Carlos reviewing fabric swatches and paint samples, trying out different types of gilt for effect, selecting marble for the decorative columns in the lobby and for the floors of the bathrooms, traipsing through furniture showrooms, previewing sales at Christie's and Sotheby's, buying antiques and paintings at auction. When she could, she lunched with friends, went to exercise class, had her hair and nails done, and attended meetings of the two committees she was still on. Her days were full and soon her high spirits and rampant optimism were back in full force.

"I think I do need to hire a driver of my own," said Katrinka one morning at breakfast as she ran down her schedule for the day. Her first stop of the morning was at the hotel site, to which she could walk, but after that her appointments were scattered all over town. It was a particularly horrible January day, teeming with rain, and taxis would be impossible to get and, since Dave was set to drive Adam to Bridgeport, there was no help from that quarter.

"Sure," said Adam, his concentration divided between Katrinka and the copy of *The New York Times* he was reading. "Call Debbie. She'll arrange everything. Do you want a car like mine?" He always had a recent vintage four-seater Mercedes sedan for business use and either a Ferrari or a Porsche for driving himself.

"Yes. Only gray, I think. And soon I must hire a secretary, too. I could use some help."

"I don't know why you've waited this . . ." He stopped speaking suddenly as he scanned an article quickly and then handed the paper to Katrinka. He was frowning. "Look at this," he said.

She took the paper from him and glanced at the article he had indicated. It was short and its contents terrible. "Oh, no," she gasped, her eyes filling with tears. Mark van Hollen's wife, two sons, and the family's housekeeper had been killed in a fire in their home in Greenwich. Mr. van Hollen, it said, had been traveling on business when the fire occurred. The cause was unknown, but it was suspected that faulty wiring in the recently restored house was to blame. The article went on to detail Mark's life, how after an impoverished childhood in Pittsburgh he got a part-time job in a local printer's shop, worked his way through Carnegie Tech, graduated, and quickly built an international publishing empire, with printing plants, binderies, magazines, books, and newspapers, including both influential journals like *The Washington Dispatch* and tabloids like *The New York Chronicle* and *The London Globe*.

Katrinka picked up *The Chronicle* and scanned its pages for more information, but it contained even less. Mark van Hollen had a reputation for being publicity shy and the editors of his own papers knew better than to give any news concerning him too much play. It added only that, since he had bought it, *The Chronicle* had been transformed from an inconsequential tabloid to a respected newspaper while retaining its broad popular appeal.

Katrinka handed *The Chronicle* to Adam, whose only comment when he had read the piece was, "Respected newspaper? It's still a scandal sheet, pure and simple." Mark van Hollen's rags-to-riches fame always irritated Adam, as if it somehow minimized his own riches to mega-riches climb.

"The first time I did meet him was in Kitzbühel," said Katrinka, "the same day I met you. He was so handsome. Like a Viking."

"You thought he was better looking than I was?" It was hard to tell whether Adam was merely curious or plain annoyed.

"Yes, but not so attractive. You had something . . . ."

"Sex appeal?"

"Yes," laughed Katrinka. But then she grew somber again. "They came into the dining room that night at the Schloss. Do you remember? You stopped to talk to them. I did think then how pretty his wife was, and how much in love they seemed." She began to weep.

"Katrinka," said Adam, more surprised than sympathetic, "you hardly knew them."

"To lose your family like that, you can't know. It is the most awful thing in the world. Poor man."

The image of Mark and Lisa van Hollen lingered in Katrinka's mind all morning, depriving her of the pleasure she usually felt while hunting treasures for her hotel or watching her dream being slowly transformed into reality by workmen who, though they sometimes resented her attention to what in their opinion were petty details, admired her nonetheless for her determination, her good taste, and her sense of fair play.

When she arrived at La Grenouille for lunch, Katrinka found the others waiting for her, their mood almost as subdued as her own. In fact, the whole restaurant's mood seemed somber to her: Rupert Murdoch grim and unsmiling as he sat talking to a couple of men in Italian suits; Cindy Adams distracted and not paying much attention to the starlet she was lunching with; the Baronessa di Portanova and Joan Schnitzer, in from Houston, listlessly pushing food around on their plates, while Barbara Walters and Shirley Lord of *Vogue* made halfhearted efforts at conversation; even Rick Colins's brightness seemed dimmer as he greeted her. Of course, it all could have had something to do with the weather, since it certainly, for once, was not the economy, but Katrinka doubted it. Mark van Hollen had his enemies of course, but in general he was liked and admired. He had a self-assurance that fell far short of arrogance and a reputation for being a shrewd but fair dealer, while his avoidance of the limelight gave those predisposed to envy him little to feed on. Everyone was feeling very sorry for him, and for themselves, the morning's news a reminder that neither success nor wealth was a guarantee against disaster.

"It's so sad about Mark van Hollen's wife and children, isn't it?" said Alexandra, who had given birth in December to her first child, not the son Nina Graham had expected, but a beautiful girl with a down of soft red hair covering her head, whom Katrinka nonetheless coveted, though she tried very hard not to let her longing show. "I couldn't stop crying all morning," added Alexandra, who was still in a highly emotional postpartum state.

"A nightmare," agreed Katrinka, kissing her hello.

When their salads were placed in front of them, they tasted no more than a few forksful.

"Pretty little thing, Lisa," said Margo, her charcoal eyes sad. "And so sweet."

"She led a magic life, I always thought," said Alexandra who had once envied the rich and pretty Lisa. "It just goes to show you."

"We were in ballet class together," said Lucia, "when we were children. At the School of American Ballet. She was

404

very talented, but of course not nearly tough enough to make a career of it. Not that her parents would have let her, I suppose. They didn't approve of her marrying Mark either. Not 'our kind,' they told her." The contempt was obvious in Lucia's voice, not—her friends understood—just for Lisa's parents, but for her own mother, who had said much the same about Nick, and for Nina Graham, who had delivered a similar verdict concerning Katrinka.

In Nick's case, though, thought Daisy, there was more than enough reason for disapproval, even if Lucia refused to see it. But all she said was, "Terrible snobs, the Sandfords. And with so little reason. They made their money in meat-packing in the twenties in Chicago. I mean, really. How dare they look down their noses at anyone, especially someone as special as Mark van Hollen? Dangerous pastime anyway," she added, trying to lighten the mood. "It's bad for the eyes." Daisy certainly refused to look down her nose at anyone, including the notorious Sugar Benson, who had married Steven as soon as his divorce from Daisy was final. Even her best friends never heard Daisy say anything more than she hoped they would be very happy.

But Daisy's attempt to relieve the gloom failed. The photographs from the morning's papers were too vivid in everyone's mind: the smiling dark-haired woman and the two adorable blond boys, looking the image of their handsome father. "The Sandfords must be heartbroken," she added after a moment. "Lisa was their only child. And Mark must be suicidal. He adored her and the boys."

"I must write him," said Katrinka. "But, oh God. What is to say?"

After lunch, Katrinka rode with Daisy in her car back to the Cabot and found that for once it was not just generosity that had prompted Daisy's offer of a ride. She had an ulterior motive. "I wanted to talk to you alone," she said as soon as they were settled and the window between passenger and driver closed.

"Why?" asked Katrinka, suddenly apprehensive. "Something is wrong?"

"No," said Daisy reassuringly. "Nothing's wrong. It's just

that I'm going to move from New York. It's too full of memories." Her voice was calm, even cheerful, with no hint of the pain that making the decision must have cost her. Steven had married Sugar Benson the month before, in December, in a much publicized event in Palm Beach. Most of his and Daisy's mutual friends had attended the wedding. Though Steven had resigned his position at Boston Federal, taking early retirement and a large cash settlement, he was still after all one of the wealthiest men in America.

Daisy had loved Steven, perhaps not passionately even as a young girl, but she had been comfortable with him and contented. She had believed them to have a good marriage, the best of anyone they knew—easy, companionable, sharing an interest in sports, liberal politics, and other worthy causes. They had produced three children together and had devoted themselves tirelessly to helping their youngest overcome her drug problem. By the time they succeeded, the family had seemed welded into such a tight unit that Daisy had felt nothing but death could ever divide them again.

When Sabrina broke the news of the affair, and Steven announced his decision to divorce her and marry Sugar, Daisy had fallen apart. She had felt not only shocked, but humiliated and heartbroken. Seeing how distraught she was, Katrinka had sent out an immediate SOS to Adam, who stopped in Paris on his way back to Cap Ferrat in the Graham jet to pick up Katrinka, Daisy, and the Goodmans. They had stayed at the villa virtually incommunicado for a week, Carter fending off calls from the press, an extra security guard hired to cope with any potentially pushy reporters (the Elliotts were not particularly big news but Sugar Benson was), Katrinka acting as liaison between Daisy and Steven and the children. When she was not hysterical, Daisy spoke to her husband and children herself. No matter what she said, Steven's mind could not be changed. The two Elliott sons and one daughter were furious enough with their father to discuss having him declared mentally incompetent and wresting control of his fortune away so that *that* woman would not get her hands on it. But Daisy soon calmed down, calmed her offspring down, returned to New York, and made arrangements for the divorce with the cool efficiency and ladylike demeanor with which she managed most things. Her friends admired her courage, but nevertheless waited for another collapse, for the scenes, the self-pity, the outbursts of rage, but none came. Sometimes she wept, but she recovered quickly. If she was angry, or bitter, she did not allow anyone to see it. She was too proud to perform for the public, to turn her life into a cheap drama for everyone to watch. That she left to Steven and Sugar, who seemed never to be out of the pages of the tabloids.

"The children are all settled and happy. They don't really need me at their beck and call every moment. And I'm restless," continued Daisy. "I think a change will do me good."

"Where will you go?" asked Katrinka.

"I don't know. London, perhaps. I like London. I have friends there. Perhaps Paris. I'm going to try them both for a while before making up my mind."

Katrinka felt a pang of dismay. Daisy had been her first real friend in New York. Katrinka would miss her terribly when she left. "I wish you would reconsider," said Katrinka sadly.

"You and Adam spend so much of your time now in Europe. We'll see each other as much as ever, my dear. You'll hardly notice me missing. But I have a favor to ask of you."

"A favor? What favor?"

"Now that I've made up my mind, I really want to leave quickly. Which means that I need someone to replace me as chair of the Children of the Streets fund-raising gala."

"Oh, Daisy, how can I? Getting the hotel ready to open takes up all my time."

"It's not really all that time-consuming," said Daisy inaccurately.

But Katrinka had been vice-chair of another of Daisy's committees the year before and knew better. "I would not want to do a bad job."

"Think about it, darling. I know you'd be marvelous. And I could leave with an easy conscience." It was a new charity,

407

one that Daisy had been instrumental in founding, and she knew it needed someone with Katrinka's energy and flair to replace her.

Though Katrinka promised to think about it and let Daisy have her decision in a day or so, she had already made up her mind not to do it. She did not see how she could possibly oversee the renovation of the hotel and plan a gala fund-raiser simultaneously.

"A pity," said Adam when she told him about Daisy's suggestion that night.

"Yes," agreed Katrinka.

"It would be a lot of good publicity for us," he added, looking up to watch Katrinka brush her hair, a sight he never failed to enjoy.

The bedcovers had been turned back by one of the staff and Adam was lying on top of the crisp Frette sheet, clad in a pair of paisley silk pajamas, sheafs of paper surrounding him, a folder on his lap.

"Don't we get enough publicity?" Katrinka asked, directing her question to the reflection of his face in the mirror of her black-lacquer dressing table.

"That's the age-old unanswerable question," said Adam, "how much is enough? Speaking of which, you better do something soon about hiring a publicist for the hotel. You don't want its opening to go by unnoticed."

"I think I change its name to Praha," said Katrinka, putting down the brush, adding as she disappeared into the adjoining bathroom, "That's Czech for Prague."

Adam thought about it a moment, then called, "I like it. It's unusual. The publicists will love it. You can use some of the staff from Graham Marine if you like."

A moment later Katrinka reemerged from her bathroom looking like the proverbial cat who had swallowed the cream.

Adam took one look at her face and said, "You didn't happen to sniff some happy powder in there, did you?"

"I did have the most wonderful idea," said Katrinka.

"Would it have anything to do with coming to bed and making love to me?" he said as he gathered up his papers

408

and threw them into the briefcase on the floor beside the bed.

Katrinka crawled into bed and knelt, one knee on either side of Adam. He put his hands on her silk-covered hips and let them slide slowly down her legs. "I will do them both together."

"Both?" His hands reached the edge of her gown and began to retrace their path, this time along the bare length of her legs, firmly muscled from the skiing she did each winter and the hours at Lotte Berk's exercise class, as silky to the touch as the fragile fabric that had covered them.

Katrinka's head dropped forward until her mouth was just inches away from his. "The fund-raiser and the hotel."

"I thought you said you didn't have time?" The fingers of his right hand came to rest for a moment in the valley between her cheeks, stroking her there.

Her thick dark hair fell forward and caressed his face as she brushed her lips slowly back and forth across his mouth. "I will . . . if the fund-raising gala is the opening-night party for the hotel."

Adam laughed. "Oh, that's brilliant!" His fingers resumed their forward movement and found the spot they were looking for. "Brilliant!"

Katrinka gasped. "I did think so," she said, pleased, and knelt back a little on his fingers, taking the weight off her hands so she could undo the buttons of his pajamas. His chest was sculpted with muscles, matted with a soft cover of dark hair. She leaned forward again to kiss him. "I love you," she said. "So much."

In the morning Katrinka called Daisy and said she would be delighted to chair the Children of the Streets fund-raiser, on certain conditions. Those were quickly agreed to by the people who needed to be consulted, and Katrinka set to work. She hired one of New York's best publicists to handle the Praha, settled an assistant, Robin Dougherty, a bright, pretty freckle-faced eighteen-year-old from Brooklyn, in the room in the apartment she used for an office, had a third phone line installed, and, at Robin's recommendation, purchased an Apple computer, which was the latest thing in home and small-office equipment. Katrinka bought herself a new gray Mercedes sedan and employed a driver, Luther Drake, a tall good-looking black man with a schoolteacher wife and a son in Queens. "The hours will be terrible," she warned him, thinking about his wife and child.

"But the pay is good," he replied, apparently not bothered by the hectic schedule she outlined for him. The work was steady, the income guaranteed, and when she was out of town, which was often, he would make up for the lost hours with his family.

Before leaving for London, Daisy turned over all her records to Katrinka. A tireless Robin checked names and addresses, drew up lists, revised them again and again as Katrinka dropped and added names. Katrinka planned the event, consulted with her committee, drafted a letter of invitation. Life got so hectic, Katrinka took to driving from the apartment to the hotel so that she could work in the car and not lose time walking. She quarreled with Carlos Medina about delays in deliveries, and made up with him again when work was completed on time. She bullied the electricians, the plasterers, the plumbers, the painters, the men who laid the carpets and tiles, all of whom complained bitterly about her behind her back but worked harder nonetheless and felt a keen sense of satisfaction when the job was completed and she complimented them for work well done. Anyone caught loafing or drinking, anyone who would not work, she fired. When she lost her temper, which was rare, she apologized sincerely. She swore she would never work so hard again.

Her schedule was impossible. She gave up her exercise class at Lotte Berk's and instead had a trainer come to the apartment at six-thirty every morning. Except for a lunch every two weeks with her friends, and the social engagements she could not cancel, she went nowhere and would have stopped eating when Adam was away if her housekeeper, Anna, had not insisted on bringing her trays of food and standing over her while she sampled them. Katrinka canceled trips with Adam so often that he began to complain he never saw her and she took a few days off to accompany him to Miami. The break did her good. Refreshed and invigorated, Katrinka went back to work with a vengeance. When not at the apartment planning the fund-raiser or at the hotel checking on the renovations, she was making discreet inquiries and compiling names for a possible hotel staff. As the work on the hotel neared completion, she hired Michael Ferrante away from the Carlyle to be the Praha's general manager and consulted with him about heads of department for the front desk, housekeeping, personnel, marketing, food and beverages, guest services—all the numerous divisions it takes to keep even the smallest hotel operating. Her greatest coup, though, was hiring the sous chef from Le Cirque, for which Sirio would never forgive her but which guaranteed the quality of the Praha's restaurants. His first assignment was to help Katrinka plan the food for the gala.

The week before the April opening was a nightmare. The hotel's new ovens refused to work, the carpet for the lobby, which was being flown in from France, was lost in transit, deliverymen dropped a heavy piece of furniture in the foyer, breaking its leg and shattering the marble. An astronomical number of things, petty and great, seemed to go wrong and hours were lost putting them right again. But the day finally arrived and everything, miraculously, was ready except for the paintings that had yet to be hung in some of the bedrooms.

Since the public rooms of the Praha were not so large as those of New York's grand hotels, Katrinka had designed the gala as a movable feast. In the main dining room, first floor restaurant, and small ballroom, booths had been set up behind which celebrity chefs like Oprah Winfrey and Sylvester Stallone, Roger Moore and Elizabeth Taylor, Sugar Ray Leonard and Joan Collins prepared and served their favorite recipes as Bryan Miller of *The New York Times* good-humoredly tasted everything and compiled a one-, two-, three-, and four-star list to be announced at the end of the evening. Tables were set up in each room where guests could stop to eat before moving on to sample what was being served elsewhere. Bands of strolling musicians played requests. In the ballroom a rock group played and those who wanted to danced. Everyone, it seemed, wanted to.

Daisy had not returned from England for the event, as she had bought a country house in Surrey and was in the middle of decorating it. But the Goodmans were there and the Jensens, and Natalie had flown in from Paris both for the party and for some meeting, about which she had been very evasive on the phone.

Margo sighed and said, shaking her frizzed head with mock sadness, "You would do us all a big favor if you would just get something wrong once in a while." Then she smiled. "You've done a great job."

"C'est vrai. Ça c'est formidable," said Natalie, as she hugged her. She looked as if she had gained a little weight, which suited her, but there was a strained look on her face which Katrinka did not then have time to question.

"You've got quite an eye, honey," said Neil Goodman, from whom that was a great compliment. He prided himself even more on his taste than on his business skill.

Katrinka moved away from the protective circle of her friends and mingled with her guests. "I hope you do enjoy yourself, Sabrina," she said, forcing herself to be cordial.

"These parties are always such a bore," replied Sabrina, "don't you think?" She had tried to do something with her mouse-colored hair and failed, and had already dropped some spaghetti sauce on the white bodice of her Givenchy gown. It looked as if someone had tried to stab her in the heart, which Katrinka for one would have been tempted to do, if she thought for a moment that Sabrina had one.

"No," said Katrinka brightly, "I do like a party."

"Cow," muttered Rick Colins in Katrinka's ear a few minutes later. "Not you. Sabrina. You look stunning." She was wearing a long Yves St. Laurent gown with an all-over embroidered design by Lesage in silver, brown, turquoise, and gold to resemble the scales of a fish. The turquoise brought out the pale blue of her eyes and her cheeks were flushed with excitement. On her finger was the thirty-two-carat yellow diamond Adam had given her last year for her birthday. "Will you dance with me later?" asked Rick.

Katrinka nodded and, turning, could see her mother- and father-in-law talking to Bill and Pat Buckley, went over to say hello, and got out of the way quickly before Nina

412

Graham could say something to annoy her. It was her night and she wanted to enjoy it.

"Great party, Katrinka," said Sugar Ray.

"I don't know when I enjoyed myself so much," said Carol Sulzberger, her arm linked through that of her smiling husband, Arthur. Did that mean *The New York Times* would give the hotel a good review? wondered Katrinka, as she thanked them, smiling broadly, pleased at how well everything was going. She saw Robin gazing around her in amazement and said to her, "You did work hard enough, now go enjoy yourself."

"It's all so wonderful."

Katrinka looked around at the beautiful people in her beautiful new hotel and agreed that indeed it was. She found Carlos, looking small and dapper and exquisitely handsome, and took him away from John Richardson, with whom he'd been discussing Picasso. "We did do it," she said and kissed him. "Thank you."

But it was Adam and she who were the sensations of the evening, not the fun of the gala or the elegance of the new hotel. He was wearing an Armani tux and looked exactly what he was—young, rich, handsome, unbelievably successful. He had the Midas touch: where others might make an occasional mistake, buy into a dud business, misjudge the right time to acquire or divest, everything Adam got his hands on turned to gold. Including his wife. Not only did men find her sexy and intelligent, but women actually *liked* her. It was unheard of.

As Adam put an arm around her and led her into the ballroom to dance, people stared. "Everyone's looking at us," he whispered. "You're the most beautiful woman here."

"And you are the handsomest man. And the smartest," she added.

With the exception of Sabrina in *The Chronicle*, who concentrated on the celebrities who had *not* put in an appearance because a new charity in an unfamiliar location could not tempt them from grander activities, the papers the next day were full of praise for the gala, which had managed to raise over one and a half million dollars for Children of the Streets. They were no less effusive about the Praha, at least the look of the place, which they pronounced variously elegant, rich, stylish, sumptuous, fine, tasteful, and exquisite. The phone rang with people congratulating her on her success. Adam's sister, Clementine, called to say how much she and her husband had enjoyed themselves, and, a few minutes later, Nina Graham said the same, her only "but" that Sylvester Stallone was a much better actor than chef.

When Adam left for his office, Katrinka delayed her own departure for the Praha a few minutes to take a beautifully arranged tray from Anna and carry it herself to the guest room where Natalie was sleeping. *"Bonjour,"* she called cheerily as she entered.

Natalie groaned. "Go away, Katrinka," she said. "I am so tired."

"You do have a meeting at eleven," reminded Katrinka. "Here are coffee and croissants." She put the tray down on the vanity table and turned to go.

"No, wait," said Natalie, sitting up. "Pour me a cup of coffee, *chérie*, will you?" she asked. Katrinka poured a cup and handed it to Natalie, who gulped it as if she were dying of thirst. *"Oh la la,* that was wonderful." She handed Katrinka a cup for a refill.

She looked so pale and haggard, thought Katrinka. "Are you drinking too much caffeine?" she asked.

"I look awful," said Natalie.

"No, no," said Katrinka quickly. "Just a little pale."

"Je suis enceinte." Katrinka's French did not go that far and she looked at Natalie blankly. "I'm pregnant," translated Natalie.

"What? Oh! How wonderful!" said Katrinka, repressing a surge of envy.

"It is not wonderful," corrected Natalie. "Why should it be wonderful? Do you think Jean-Claude will divorce Hélène and marry me?"

"Won't he?"

"No."

"You did tell him."

Natalie nodded. "And do you think I want *ce petit bâtard* to raise all on my own?"

414

"It is all the fashion now," said Katrinka, who did not quite know how to deal with Natalie's obvious anger.

"Not for me," she said violently. "I have been offered a job by Saks Fifth Avenue. That is my meeting this morning. I am going to get rid of the baby and take it."

Katrinka moved from the chair and sat beside Natalie on the bed. "Natalie, wait," she said as soothingly as she could manage. "How can you make a decision when you are so upset? Wait until you are a little bit more calm."

"*Ouff,* when I am rid of it, I'll be calm. Not before." She began to cry, murmuring "bastard" over and over again in French, referring either to Jean-Claude or her unborn child, Katrinka was not sure which.

Katrinka put her arms around Natalie, holding her while she sobbed, her mind filled suddenly with images of her infant son's sleeping face, and, strangely, the newspaper photo of Mark van Hollen's two boys. Did Natalie know what she was giving up? wondered Katrinka. Did she have any idea how much she might regret this later? "What if something happened," said Katrinka, "and you could never have a child?"

"Nothing will happen," said Natalie, unable to stop her tears. "It's a simple procedure. Very safe."

"But . . ." persisted Katrinka.

"Nothing will happen," said Natalie, pulling away from Katrinka. "I should not have told you. I thought you would understand."

"I'm sorry," said Katrinka, after a minute, her eyes filling with tears. "It is that I do want so much to have a child."

Again Natalie flung herself into Katrinka's arms. "I know, I know," she wept. "Life is so terrible. So completely terrible."

The tears crept down Katrinka's cheeks. No, she thought. Not completely. Not always. But sometimes, like now, unbearably painful.

Thirty-Three

How that does compare to the forecast?" asked Katrinka, her usual quick speech slowed to accommodate long distance and a portable phone. "Good. And reservations?" She was sitting cross-legged in a lounge chair on the deck of the *Lady Katrinka*, the Graham yacht, wearing a white Gottex bikini and a large straw hat with pink cabbage roses pinned to the brim, making notes with a ballpoint pen on the pad in her lap. "Robin? Robin? Can you hear me?" she called loudly. "Yes. Now is all right. Repeat the figure, please."

In the distance, the city of Venice shimmered like a rose-and-gold mirage in the haze of afternoon heat. On the dock a slender man in khaki shorts and striped shirt, his longish dark hair slicked back from his high forehead, sauntered past, caught sight of Katrinka, and stopped for a moment to watch her. Behind his dark glasses, his look was speculative, amused, as if his mind was toying with an entertaining idea. Retracing his steps, he climbed the metal gangplank linking the yacht to the shore and went aboard, smiling confidently at the deckhand who, though meant to keep intruders off, recognized him and let him pass.

"You did FedEx me the new brochures?" said Katrinka into the phone. "Good. I will phone with changes before it goes to the printer." She issued a few other instructions, replaced the receiver, and looked up as a shadow fell across the bottom half of her lounge.

416

"You have been avoiding me, Katrinka," said Jean-Claude Gillette, smiling down at her.

"How nice to see you, Jean-Claude," she said cordially, but he was quite right: she had been avoiding him, and for over two years, since the morning Natalie had told her she was pregnant.

Katrinka had known she ought to mind her business. Nevertheless, she had phoned Jean-Claude as soon as she got to her office at the Praha. Even as she dialed she had not been sure what she was going to say to him and, when she heard his initially warm voice turn cold at her intrusion into his personal life, she had almost given up. But she thought of Natalie's face, its sophisticated mask blurred by tears, and continued. She suggested that if he was not prepared to live with the consequences of the relationship, perhaps he ought to stop stringing Natalie along. And, when he was really furious, she had asked him to try at least to calm her down so that she would not, while she was so upset, make decisions she might later regret.

In his reply, Katrinka heard not the practiced charmer who had more than halfheartedly been trying to seduce her for as long as she had known him, but the legendary Jean-Claude Gillette of the boardroom, the man whose keen wit and sharp tongue, it was reported, could disembowel an unwary competitor quicker than a samurai can lop off an enemy's head. He could not divorce his wife, he told Katrinka—who had not suggested it—if only because she would not at all like the idea (as if that mattered to him). And Natalie's getting pregnant was hardly his fault since contraception was her business, not his. In any event, she seemed not to want the child, much preferring to take the job in New York, and that of course was entirely up to her. Women, despite all the propaganda about maternal instincts, in his experience frequently did not want children: herself, for example, married for years and no sign of a child. If she preferred to run her hotels, playing businesswoman rather than mother, why should Natalie not be allowed to do the same?

The conversation had ended with them shouting at each

other so angrily that Robin had come running into the room
to see if Katrinka was all right. Trembling with rage,
embarrassment, and, most of all, pain, she had replaced the
receiver and insisted she was fine, though she was fighting to
keep back tears. Jean-Claude had been trying to hurt and
had succeeded, touching the one subject on which Katrinka
was infinitely vulnerable. Not that she regretted making the
call: she had had to do what she could for Natalie.

When Jean-Claude and Katrinka had run into each other
a few months later at a party in Cannes (by which time
Natalie was already living in New York) and again in St.
Moritz the following year, they had spoken civilly to one
another but had not indulged in the usual light flirtation that
had characterized their friendship. But recently Jean-
Claude had reverted to his former style and seemed surprised when Katrinka still remained distant.

"Natalie has forgiven me," said Jean-Claude, dropping
onto the lounge next to her, extending his legs, crossing his
sandaled feet, making himself comfortable. "Long ago. Why
can't you?"

Katrinka smiled and, though it was far from her usual
beaming smile, Jean-Claude seemed pleased at the prospect
of a thaw. "You did do something you think you should be
forgiven *for?*" asked Katrinka. "That's news to me."

He reached over and took her hand. "It is what *you* think
that matters. I don't like having beautiful women angry with
me."

"I'm not angry with you, Jean-Claude." The anger was
long gone. Only sympathy for Natalie remained, and a
continuing dislike of Jean-Claude's behavior. Mirek Bartoš
had at the very least *cared*.

"Good," he said, smiling, releasing her hand. "Then may
I have a drink?"

Katrinka signaled a steward, who took Jean-Claude's
order and returned quickly with two large iced and minted
glasses of tea.

"Wonderful invention," said Jean-Claude, sipping the
drink appreciatively. He looked as if he planned to stay a
long time, which was ridiculous since his own yacht was

moored only a few berths away. It was not so big as the *Lady Katrinka,* but that was hardly surprising. When the Grahams had launched the motor yacht from the Bremen yard the year before it had been the largest in the world, a feat that Adam had gone (as he himself punned) to great lengths to achieve. It had a cruising range of three thousand miles, a top speed of thirty knots, totally silent and vibration-free motion due to the machinery placed in the stern, with jets and no propellers for a shallow draft that allowed it to enter waters impossible for other yachts of its size. Jon Bannenberg had designed the body and Lucia its interior. It had accommodation for over fifty crew members and thirty guests, three dining areas, an exercise room and sauna, a game room, and a helicopter pad. Everything was in the restrained luxurious style favored by Adam, each cabin in paneled wood with built-in furniture, carpets and curtains in soft neutral colors, cream leather sofas and chairs, mirror accents, and a galley of stainless steel with wood trim. *"C'est beau,"* said Jean-Claude, looking around appreciatively. "I must discuss with Adam his building me a new yacht. I am quite bored with mine."

"I'm sure he would love to," said Katrinka.

"Where is he?"

"Making phone calls."

"You two, nothing but business, business, business all the time."

"And you?"

His gourmet boutique at Bloomingdale's had been such a success that Jean-Claude now had them in Neiman-Marcus and Marshall Field. He had acquired a department store chain in England and another in Canada, where a Galleries Gillette had opened in Montreal. The rumor on the street was that Gillette CIE was planning an expansion into the United States. He owned stud farms in France, Ireland, and Kentucky. But Jean-Claude shrugged, picked up Katrinka's hand again and kissed it. "I leave time for my hobbies." And he did. He was an expert horseman and skier. And he was never without a woman at his side, sometimes even his wife. "And I certainly would not spend all my time on the phone if you were nearby to distract me." Katrinka laughed and Jean-Claude turned to her, smiling a little ruefully. "Are you ever going to let me seduce you?"

"I do doubt it," said Katrinka who, however much she disapproved of him, found his charm very potent. "Even though I find you very attractive," she added with a reassuring smile.

"Well, that's something," he said, then continued in a voice that did not sound terribly interested, "Where is Natalie?"

"Oh," replied Katrinka vaguely, "I think maybe she did go to Torcello."

"With Prince Khalid?"

"Yes," admitted Katrinka. And, when he frowned, she said irritably, "Jean-Claude, really. You're not jealous?"

"Perhaps," he admitted. "A little," he qualified. Though he saw Natalie rarely now that she had left him to work in New York, their affair continued out of force of habit, if for no other reason, and he could not quite rid himself of the idea that she was his. "But mostly I am worried. Khalid has a wife."

"He is allowed four, which is three more than you."

"It is a different thing entirely."

She did not want to quarrel with Jean-Claude, decided Katrinka, and certainly did not want to admit to him that she was worried herself. "We should not discuss Natalie," said Katrinka, "or we will end up shouting at each other again."

That would indeed be terrible, agreed Jean-Claude, who got to his feet, leaned over to kiss her good-bye, said he looked forward to seeing her that night, and disappeared down into the cabin, reappearing on the lower deck, making his way down the ramp to the dock.

"Was that Jean-Claude I saw?" asked Daisy, emerging moments later from the yacht's dim interior into the hazy sunlight, looking exotic with her small tanned body swathed in a silk sari, her newly acquired blond hair concealed by a turban.

"Mmmm," murmured Katrinka. "He is worried about Natalie."

"Aren't we all?" said Daisy, unwrapping herself and sinking into the lounge Jean-Claude had recently vacated.

Katrinka sighed but did not reply. So many of her friends needed worrying about at the moment, not only Natalie, who, having failed to break Jean-Claude's hold on her by moving to New York, seemed determined to do it by involving herself with Prince Khalid. There were Margo and Ted Jensen, who had planned to come with the others to Venice but had canceled when a fire in Ted's factory had completely destroyed the building and its machines as well as his entire line of fall clothes. And Lucia, whose brilliant design career was increasingly overshadowed by the notoriety Nick was attracting by defending some of New York's best-known mobsters. And even Daisy herself, involved with beautiful, blond Bjorn Lindstrom, twenty years her junior.

Everyone had been more than a little shocked but inclined to be indulgent when the dignified Daisy began to appear everywhere with "that boy" in tow. But when she moved him into her house in Surrey, her children stopped speaking to her as well as their father, and her friends began to be afraid that she was getting herself involved too deeply with someone bound to hurt her. Daisy laughed at the idea. After Steven, she claimed, no one could hurt her again. Bjorn was amusing, handsome, charming, a good lover, rather sweet, and could be relied on to behave, as long as she controlled the purse strings. Why shouldn't she enjoy herself?

Why indeed? conceded her friends when Steven and Sugar seemed to be having a whale of a time, following the social calendar around the world, living up to his income, which, with the economy beginning to soar, was considerable. In every newspaper photo, Sugar seemed to be wearing a new designer dress, another piece of incredible jewelry: a thirty-three-point-seven-carat sapphire pendant with a circular-cut diamond surround reportedly worth over a million dollars, an emerald-and-diamond necklace worth two, diamond bracelets, strands of pearls, ruby rings. They traveled first class, stayed at the best hotels, had homes in Palm Beach and Paris. Daisy could never reconcile this Steven Elliott of the tabloids with the fiscally responsible, socially aware, committed husband and father to whom she had been married for so many years. At least she had no illusions about Bjorn, she explained to her friends, and surely there had to be some emotional safety in that. And he was so much cheaper to maintain than Sugar: an occasional Piaget watch, diamond tie pin, or leather jacket was all he needed to make him happy.

Daisy sounded so confident and in control, Katrinka sometimes thought she was foolish to be concerned about her. And Natalie as well. After all, Khalid was intelligent, rich, cosmopolitan, charming—an endless list of attractive qualities, the best of them that he was obviously mad about her. If Natalie was not worried about his being a Muslim and married, with four daughters, why should her friends be? Again, why indeed? But they were. Even Lucia managed to brush off Nick's problems by saying notoriety was the price of success, attributing any attack on her husband to either upper-class snobbery or anti-Italian prejudice.

Only the usually cool, chic Margo acknowledged that she was in trouble: the fire had wiped the Jensens out. Not only was Ted depressed, he was drinking, she suspected; and Margo was struggling to manage him, the children, their finances, and her demanding job at *Chic*. It was almost a relief to have someone who was confused and unhappy admit it, and Katrinka called her every day to listen, which she supposed did some good, giving advice when asked, offering money which was always refused.

At least she did not have to worry about Alexandra and Neil Goodman, thought Katrinka. The booming American economy and Knapp Manning's success putting together leveraged buyouts was making Neil richer by the minute, and he happily indulged his beautiful second wife in her every whim, allowing her to reclaim the social territory her parents had lost along with their money, his former quiet, suburban life (work all week, golf and a dance at the club on weekends) replaced by an endless round of parties, which he had to admit he enjoyed for their own sake as well as for the stream of new business contacts they provided. He loved Alexandra and their life together, and was—to his first wife's disgust—a doting father to their children. In return, Alexandra adored him.

The Goodmans, their two children, and a nanny were guests on board the *Lady Katrinka*, as were Natalie, Nick and Lucia, their twelve-year-old daughter Pia, Daisy and Bjorn, and, best of all, Tomáš Havlíček. In Venice for the Biennale, where he had had a film showing, Tomáš had stayed on for the gala with the permission of the Czech government, which was certain that, since his wife and child remained in Prague, Tomáš would return home on schedule.

All the passengers on the *Lady Katrinka*, plus Jean-Claude and Hélène Gillette, Prince Khalid and an entourage that did not include his wife and children, who were at home in Riyadh, Mary McCarthy, Gore Vidal, Gianni Agnelli, scores of international industrialists, European royalty, and jet-setting aristocracy, were in Venice for the week of festivities that would climax with the 1985 ball sponsored by the Save Venice Foundation.

"Let's go for a cruise," said Adam, coming up on deck. His dark hair had highlights from the sun and his skin was tanned a deep honey. He was wearing a pair of red swimming trunks, Topsiders, and large dark Ray-bans.

"Do we have time?" asked Katrinka.

"Just a short one. I'm feeling restless." He always did when not in motion, but they had only arrived from St.-Jean-Cap-Ferrat the night before and had agreed to spend the day in port. They had made it through until just after lunch.

"I bet you don't even exercise to stay in shape," said Daisy glumly as she surveyed Adam's broad shoulders and chest, the flat stomach, the muscled arms and legs.

Smiling, he leaned over Daisy and kissed her forehead. "Does that mean you'd rather have me than your handsome young Swede?"

She touched his cheek fondly. "How can you possibly expect me to answer that with your wife present?"

"It will teach her to appreciate me more," said Adam without looking at Katrinka.

"More?" said Katrinka, laughing. "When I do worship you now?"

"That's what I like to hear," said Adam, turning to smile at her. She was so beautiful, he thought, so intelligent, and so *nice*. Why then had he felt so irritated with her lately? "We'll go just to Bibione," he said, and picked up the phone to notify the captain.

Everyone was present and accounted for except Natalie, who was not expected to return until late, and all were in favor of a cruise, especially Pia and the two Goodman children, so the gangplank was raised and the yacht slowly backed out of its berth.

It was much cooler on the open sea. The guests meandered from deck to deck engaging in aimless conversations, watching the changing scenery, admiring the view, the children wanting to know when they could swim.

"What do you think of Khalid?" Daisy asked Lucia, who, having designed his yacht's interior, was presumed to know him well.

"I like him," replied Lucia.

"Will he ask Natalie to marry him?"

Lucia shrugged.

"And if he does, will she say yes?"

"She wouldn't," said Alexandra, to whom the unthinkable was always that until it happened. "She'd never settle for being someone's *second* wife. I mean, simultaneously."

"Why not?" said Daisy. "She settled for being Jean-Claude's mistress, for how long? Fifteen years? That's longer than a lot of marriages last these days."

"You don't suppose Daisy would actually marry Bjorn, do you?" Lucia asked Katrinka a little later on.

"Why you ask? She did say something to you?"

"No, but she obviously has marriage on the mind."

"She is just worried about Natalie," said Katrinka.

The boat cruised past Lido di Jesolo, Eraclea-Mare, Caorle.

"Are you happy?" Daisy asked Bjorn as he settled his long beautiful body on the chaise next to her. He had hair the color of corn silk and eyes as blue as the Adriatic sky. He was an actor, he had told her when they met on a ski slope in

Switzerland, and had appeared in several Bergman films. Did she recognize him from *Fanny and Alexander?* She did not: she never went to foreign films. At least she hadn't until she met him. It was one of the many pleasures to which he had introduced her.

Bjorn picked up her hand and kissed it. "I am always happy when I'm with you," he said like the perfect pet he was. Daisy smiled contentedly and he thought, really, how fond he was of her, though the rest of her friends, however polite they tried to be (and he was willing to concede that they did try) were so obviously suspicious of him they left him feeling always a little uncomfortable. He did not, after all, want that much from Daisy: a trip to Hollywood, perhaps, and a chance at a career in American movies. But whenever he suggested it, she said no. He was confident, though, that one day she would give in; and, in the meantime, while he built a comfortable little nest egg from the small amounts of money she regularly gave him, he practiced his English.

"Now look at that," said Nick, indicating Daisy and Bjorn with a slight movement of his head. "A real killer."

"No shortage of them," said Neil. "They seem to be wherever you look."

Nick looked at the short plump Neil with his balding head and bristling moustache, considered whether or not to feel insulted, decided in favor of a noncommittal laugh, and began to pump him on the current behavior of Wall Street, which was running mad with money lust. When there was that much money changing hands, said Nick, there was corruption, and where there was corruption, there would be—sooner or later—the need for a good criminal lawyer, like himself.

"That's a very puritan attitude," said Neil. He had never liked Nick, who was, for his taste, a little too smooth with his slick dark hair and Italian silk suits, a little too handsome and sinister in those newspaper photos of him standing, smiling, behind some notorious mobster. It was a pity Alexandra and Lucia were so friendly. "You don't have to be crooked to make money."

"It usually helps," replied Nick, who had, by necessity,

become something of an expert in financial matters since the government always tried to nab his clients for tax evasion when they failed to do so for murder.

Pinning her long red hair haphazardly up on top of her head, Alexandra for a moment watched her husband deep in conversation with Nick, then turned back to Katrinka. "Neil's enjoying himself," she said happily. "He wanted to go to Maine. Can you imagine? And miss this. And I'm sure it was just because Maine is so much closer to New York, and the business. You're so lucky that Adam likes to travel."

"I think sometimes too much," said Katrinka. "He works too hard."

"So do you."

"I need something to keep me occupied when he's busy."

"You know," said Alexandra, lighting a cigarette, "I've been thinking that I do, too, now that the children are getting older. I want to start a gallery. Dutch art, old masters, my specialty. What do you think?" She had stopped smoking, and drinking, each time she was pregnant, but started again immediately after. No matter how hard she tried, she could not seem to break the habit.

Katrinka considered the possibility and said, "Now is a good time. People are making money and, when they make it, they do want to spend it."

"That's what Neil says."

When they reached Bibione, they dropped anchor and went swimming. The crew launched a couple of Sunfishes from the hold and, with Lucia watching anxiously, the twelve-year-old Pia got one to herself while Adam took the oldest Goodman child, a daughter, wrapped safely in her life jacket, for a sail as the two-year-old wailed that he wanted to go, too, and Adam promised him, dismissing Alexandra's terror, that he could have a turn later if he promised to be good.

From the deck, Katrinka watched Adam holding the girl in his arms as he maneuvered the small sailboat in the light wind. What little envy she had felt had long since been replaced by genuine affection for her friends' children, but sometimes she could not help wondering if Adam ever regretted not having married Alexandra. "Look at him. He is so good with children," she said to Tomáš, lapsing easily into Czech as he came up next to her and slipped an arm around her bare brown waist. "He really does enjoy them."

"You have a good life, Katrinka," he said, not meaning her obvious wealth, which was of much less significance to him (and he was sure to Katrinka as well) than that she was busy, productive, successful, and married to a man she respected and loved.

Katrinka thought of the weeks she would be spending soon with Nina and Kenneth, Clementine and Wilson, who were to join Adam and her for a cruise of the Greek Islands to celebrate the Grahams' forty-fifth wedding anniversary, weeks of Kenneth Graham's vague alcoholic disappointment, of Nina's constant disapproval, free-floating before, focused now on the single issue of her nonexistent grandchild. She thought of the endless stream of reports from Zeiss Associates full of details of tedious checking and double-checking of leads that led nowhere when followed. She thought of the fertility clinics where, from time to time, she was poked and prodded, measured and analyzed, X-rayed and laparoscoped. She thought of Adam, who sometimes now seemed distant even when he was with her, distant and dissatisfied. "Would you give up Martin for all of this?" she asked.

"You can't make bargains with life, Katrinka, trading this for that, making exchanges when you don't like what you've been given."

"Are you happy?"

"Yes. No. It depends on the day. I have a good wife, a beautiful son, a place to live, a job, food on the table. If I don't have the freedom to make the kinds of films I want to make, well, who in this world gets everything he wants?"

"It never makes you miserable?"

He smiled. "Often. But I get over it."

"So do I," said Katrinka, laughing. The sky overhead was the intense blue of a painted ceramic dome, the gaily striped sails of the Sunfishes bobbed on small foam-capped rushes of water. She could see her husband relaxed and happy, laughing as he turned the small boat into the wind. She was surrounded by people she loved, in a setting of great beauty. "I'm a very lucky woman, Tomáš, and I know it."

Thirty-Four

That night, the Grahams and their guests were invited to a party hosted by Kurt and Luisa Heller at their palazzo on the Grand Canal, one of the stellar events in the Save Venice calendar. Heller was a German diplomat, his wife the daughter of a leading German industrialist, and, though Katrinka found them both rather cold and dull, Adam had insisted they attend. He always made it a point to cultivate people with influence in a country where he had significant business interests, in this case the shipyard in Bremen.

After a light supper, Adam and Katrinka and the others climbed into the yacht's Cigarettes and were transported along the dark canals, past the softly lit palaces with their intricately carved balconies and crumbling facades, gliding by gondolas filled with men and women in evening dress, some in costume. Except for the hum of the Cigarettes' motors or the occasional passing vaporetto crammed with noisy Venetians and curious tourists out for the evening, it might have been the fifteenth century.

By the time they arrived, the party was in full swing, the sound of the rock music blaring from the ballroom a strange counterpoint to the faint light of the crystal chandeliers, the flickering of tapers in silver sconces, the heavy scent of flowers, the staff in embroidered livery, and the guests moving slowly from room to room in elaborate evening dress. The palazzo, which had once been the home of Lord Byron, had been purchased three years before by the Hellers. The couple had shored its sagging foundation and sinking walls and restored its cracked and peeling interior at a cost, or so Sabrina had reported in her column, of three million dollars.

"I don't believe it," whispered Daisy as they entered the crowded ballroom.

"What?" asked Katrinka absentmindedly as she admired the carved and gilded ceilings, the muraled walls, the marble floors, reminders of how worthwhile it was to save Venice. The foundation was the only charity of that sort the Grahams supported outside the United States. Let the French save Versailles was their motto.

"Mark van Hollen."

As soon as Daisy said his name, Katrinka turned her attention to the crowd and spotted him in a group several feet away. His hair, bleached by the sun, was almost white, and he was thinner and had grown a beard, but there was no mistaking him.

Seeing them, Mark excused himself and came over to say hello. "My dear, it is so good to see you," said Daisy as he kissed her cheek.

Murmuring *"Dobrý den"* with an unexpected, teasing smile on his face, he shook Katrinka's hand, then Adam's, then the four of them stood talking for a moment, awkwardly, no one quite certain what subject to tackle, until Mark broke the deadlock by asking Daisy to dance, leaving the others to wonder if his appearance at the party signaled his return to the social world from which he had been absent since the death of his wife and children. In two and a half years, he had not dined at the fashionable restaurants or attended the expected charity balls and dinner parties. If he skied, it was on remote mountains where the glitterati did not go. He traveled extensively, either alone or with hired guides—photographic safaris in Africa, explorations of the disappearing rain forests of Borneo and Brazil, mountain climbing in Wales, trekking in Thailand. He returned for important board meetings and handled all other business by phone. Contrary to all predictions, his long-distance management had not hurt his business: stocks of the various van Hollen enterprises were trading at higher prices than ever.

When Katrinka danced with him later, to a nice old-fashioned fox-trot, she found herself uncharacteristically tongue-tied. Though she had written him at the time of Lisa's death, she felt now that some further words of sympathy were in order. But what was there to say? And would he mind her bringing it up?

He did so himself. "What is there about me that makes everyone tongue-tied?" he asked.

"We are surprised to see you, that's all."

"I had to return to all this someday, and I thought saving Venice seemed a better excuse than most."

"I was so sorry," she said. "It was so terrible."

"Yes," he agreed. It had been hell. It still was often, but not all the time anymore. He smiled, a surprisingly natural, easy smile. "But life goes on."

"Yes," she said, her head full of her own memories, "and sometimes it is even fantastic."

"It has its moments," he said, swinging her into a turn. "Like now."

As she stepped back to him, she smiled. "Are you flirting with me?"

He nodded. "Practicing," he said.

"Good." Flirting was harmless, amusing, a form of social currency like friendly kisses delivered to the air above someone's cheek and promises to meet for lunch or dinner soon. It was something that everyone did.

But later, dancing with Jean-Claude, Katrinka revised her opinion of the pastime. Not that she minded Jean-Claude's flirting, which she knew would become a serious attempt at seduction only if she gave the right signals. What bothered her was his pointing out how much Adam seemed to be enjoying himself with some woman Katrinka did not know at first but then recognized as the star of that summer's hit movie, a tall, leggy blonde wearing a long clinging dress that plunged to her middle both back and front. She felt a sudden unexpected pang of jealousy. "If you think I sleep with you because my husband talks to a pretty girl," she said, "you are crazy, Jean-Claude." As soon as the words were out of her mouth, she regretted them. The satisfied smile on Jean-Claude's face told her that he thought he had breached

431

one of her best defenses, her complete faith in Adam's fidelity. Which was nonsense of course. She trusted Adam absolutely. And if lately their lovemaking had become less frequent and less intense, well, after eight years of marriage that was only to be expected.

The evening went downhill from there. Having scored a small victory with Katrinka, Jean-Claude went on to try his luck with Natalie, attempting to distract her from Prince Khalid. But he managed only to provoke a quarrel and make Khalid, brown eyes flickering with sudden hatred, more determined than ever to have her.

Then, while Katrinka was talking to Princess Caroline of Monaco, she felt a hand on her arm and, turning, saw Klaus Zimmerman, his mouth, defined by its thin blond moustache, curved in a smile.

The situation was impossible. She could not be rude to Zimmerman without being rude to the princess and so was forced to introduce him, which was exactly what the social-climbing doctor had intended. Katrinka managed it graciously, but was beginning to feel the strain of the conversation when someone claimed the princess's attention and she excused herself.

"The Hellers have restored the house beautifully, haven't they?" said the doctor in German, his voice easy and assured as if they were indeed old friends.

"Yes," agreed Katrinka, her eyes straying across the room to where Kurt Heller was talking to Gloria Thurn und Taxis. It was Zimmerman who had introduced the Grahams and Hellers at St. Moritz, though Katrinka had remembered them and their friends, the Brandts, from Kitzbühel. Both couples had visited the resort often, with their children, whom Katrinka now noticed in a group of young people negotiating with the band about what to play next. The Hellers' dark-haired son had his arm around the waist of the Brandts' homely daughter, while her handsome brother leafed through a wad of lire for an appropriate tip. It had always struck Katrinka as odd that people of such obvious respectability would have anything to do with Zimmerman. But then, she had a tendency to forget that most of the world considered him respectable as well. She started to turn away. "If you'll excuse me . . ."

He put a restraining hand on her arm. "You're looking more beautiful than ever, Katrinka."

"Please let me go," she said coolly.

"Do you ever think that perhaps I am the one who made this all possible for you?" Zimmerman knew it would be wiser to keep out of Katrinka's way, to avoid tempting her to do something rash. But as often as he resolved to do just that, he saw her and changed his mind. The truth was, he enjoyed their encounters. He liked tormenting her. And, in any case, rich Americans were not to be ignored. No matter how many wealthy, influential people Zimmerman added to his list, he was never satisfied, and the Grahams had access to many.

"Never," said Katrinka.

"Not only a rich husband," Zimmerman went on calmly, "but a rich woman in your own right. How many hotels do you own now? Two?" Katrinka had bought a second in New York, the Graham, as soon as the Praha had begun to make money. "And I read in the papers recently that you are thinking about buying a third. Would any of that have been possible if you'd had a squalling brat to look after?"

"Where is he?" asked Katrinka, unable to help herself. "Tell me!" But when Zimmerman only shrugged, her slanted eyes narrowed and she said, her voice ice cold, "If you don't let me go, I'll slap you. And don't think I'm afraid to make a scene."

"Why are you always so unreasonable, Katrinka?" he asked as he released her. But before she could leave him, Adam, who had been so happily occupied elsewhere all evening, appeared suddenly at her side with Barbara Walters. "You always know the most interesting people," murmured Zimmerman before greeting Adam and the television star in English.

Katrinka introduced him to Barbara Walters and reminded Adam that he had met the doctor at St. Moritz. "Oh, yes, of course," said Adam, as he shook Zimmerman's hand, his voice polite, not associating him with the Hellers, remembering only vaguely that this was someone Katrinka seemed to dislike.

Katrinka restrained a sigh of relief. If Zimmerman suspected for a moment that Adam knew nothing of her past relationship with him, he would certainly try to blackmail her into helping enlarge his social circle instead of merely trying to embarrass her into it. But she was sure that Zimmerman would again misunderstand Adam's coolness, thinking it stemmed from complete knowledge when actually it was a result of his total ignorance—and lack of interest in someone whose usefulness was uncertain.

"If you'll excuse us," said Adam. "There were some people asking about Katrinka."

"Of course," said Zimmerman with a slight bow. "Until next time."

"I was telling Adam I want to do a piece on you both, for my show," said Barbara Walters as soon as the doctor was out of earshot.

"Both of us?" said Katrinka, surprised and a little flattered.

"You've both had quite a year."

They had indeed. Not only were Katrinka's two hotels running smoothly and successfully, but she had succeeded in raising over three million dollars for the Children of the Streets Foundation, having built the charity up from an unknown entity to one of the most successful in the world, funding programs for destitute children in Africa, South America, Europe, and Asia as well as the United States. And Adam had added a cruise ship line to the roster of Graham companies and made the cover of *Time* when his sleek sixty-foot sloop, *Vengeance*, built at the yard in Scotland, came in first in the Whitbread Round-the-World race. It seemed as if everything either one of the Grahams touched turned to gold.

"I've told Barbara we'd be delighted," said Adam in a voice that announced the matter settled.

"Certainly," said Katrinka. "It would be fun. When we do it?"

They were discussing dates when Daisy came up, and, after spending a moment or two in polite conversation, said she absolutely had to introduce Katrinka to some darling person or other and whisked her away.

"Who you do want me to meet?" asked Katrinka as Daisy led her through the dense crowd.

"No one. Steven's here. With Sugar. What on earth am I going to do?" She sounded almost frantic. Though Steven and she spoke to each other often on the phone, discussing business and the children, they took care to deliver enough clues about their social schedules to make certain that, without making an issue of it, their paths never had to cross.

"He did know you would be here?"

"Certainly, he knew. I suppose this was just too big an event for Sugar to miss. Perhaps I should leave? Bjorn and I can take a gondola back to the yacht."

"Daisy, really, how you can run away? Just go over and say hello. Then it's done, and you do never have to worry again."

Daisy hesitated a second and then laughed. "Of course. You're absolutely right. What was I thinking of?" With a sudden onslaught of courage, she turned around, marched over to Bjorn, who was an uncomfortable member of a group that included John and Susan Gutfreund, Neil and Alexandra Goodman, and the starlet who had been dancing earlier with Adam, linked her arm through his, murmured a few polite words, and led him off to meet her ex-husband and his current wife.

"He looks quite ill, don't you think?"

Katrinka, turning, controlled an expression of dismay when she recognized Sabrina, lipstick smudged, mousy hair tumbling in an untidy mess from the knot on top of her head.

"Steven Elliott, I mean. The Swedish boy looks as if he's never been sick a day in his life. Quite delightful."

"Hello, Sabrina," said Katrinka noncommittally. "What a beautiful gown." And it would have been had anyone else been wearing it.

"I have not made up my mind yet," continued Sabrina, unwilling to let herself be sidetracked by Katrinka, "if his paleness is due to summer flu or all those exhausting sexual pranks Sugar enjoys so much."

Katrinka had heard several rumors lately, unpleasant rumors, about Sugar's sexual inclinations. Apparently, she liked games, sometimes brutal games, and what someone had described as "Benetton sex," simultaneous partners in a variety of sexes and colors. It was hard to imagine the proper, gentlemanly Steven participating.

"Or perhaps it is just the presence of Paolo di Cortina," continued Sabrina when Katrinka failed to respond.

"Paolo di Cortina?" asked Katrinka before she could stop herself.

"Standing next to Sugar," said Sabrina, referring to a man whose adoring regard for the elaborately gowned Sugar could be seen even at a distance. He looked somewhere in his early seventies, short and slender, clean-shaven, with a thick head of obviously fake hair, and delicate white hands he fluttered about him when he spoke. *"Count* Paolo di Cortina," she expanded helpfully, "old Italian family. Very wealthy. Sugar seems to be fond of him."

"Then certainly he must be wonderful company," said Katrinka dryly. Why was Sabrina telling her all this? she wondered.

"This isn't the first time Daisy has actually met the stunning Sugar, is it?" said Sabrina, more or less answering Katrinka's unspoken question. She wanted to trade the information she had for some she did not yet know, barter being the primary exchange mechanism for gossip.

Katrinka quickly ran through the possible answers and found none that Sabrina would not be able to twist to suit her purposes. Even keeping quiet had its risks. "Yes, it is," said Katrinka finally, deciding on the truth. "Daisy and Steven phone each other all the time, but this is the first chance they did have to meet. They all travel so much."

"So do you and your husband," said Sabrina, going after other fish.

"Yes." Katrinka forced a bright smile. "And always together when we can. Where is your husband tonight?" she asked to change the subject, and knew instantly she had made a mistake.

"We've separated," said Sabrina coolly, all pretense of cordiality gone from her voice.

"Oh, I am sorry," said Katrinka.

Sabrina looked at her with eyes full of envy and hatred. What would you know? her look seemed to say. What would someone as beautiful as you, as rich, as desirable, know about how much it hurts to lose a man?

"It is always difficult," continued Katrinka, "even when it is the best thing for everyone."

"We really had nothing in common anymore," said Sabrina truthfully. Elbowing anyone in her path to the sidelines, she had risen speedily through the ranks at a London tabloid, dropped her surname, and become a columnist of such international power that to be ignored by her was the equivalent of living in exile in Gorky, while her meek and placid husband had remained in his minor press position at Downing Street with no ambitions to go further. Sabrina had been bored with him for years and had felt, no matter how little he intruded, that he was somehow in her way and should be disposed of. Still, she liked having a husband to produce when the occasion demanded one, and when he left her for a pretty young aide in the Foreign Office, she had not liked it at all. "But, as you say, these things are always difficult. If you'll excuse me," she said, hurrying off.

Eventually the awful evening came to an end and the Grahams and their guests returned to the *Lady Katrinka* as they had come, traveling along the dark canals by Cigarette while the sky gradually lightened in the east. It would be like this all week, thought Katrinka, never getting to bed before dawn, and she was already exhausted.

For once she did not mind when Adam dropped off to sleep without even a kiss. How long had it been since they had made love? she wondered as she lay next to him, trying to stop her mind from counting the weeks so that perhaps she too could get some rest. But just as she slipped over the border into oblivion, she was hauled back again by knocking at the door. "Katrinka, Adam, are you asleep yet?"

It was Tomáš. As Adam sat up groggily wondering what the hell was going on, Katrinka leapt out of bed, pulled a silk wrap over her teddy and raced to the door. "What is it?"

"It's Martin. He's ill." Tomáš stumbled into the room, looking dazed. "Zuzka called, while we were out. I called her back. It took me hours to reach her," he said, his voice sounding panicked.

Katrinka took his arm and led him to one of the leather armchairs, murmuring, "Come in, sit down," adding over her shoulder to Adam, "Get some cognac."

Adam, already out of bed, went quickly to the liquor cabinet and splashed some Courvoisier into a glass. "Here," he said, handing it to Tomáš. "Drink it down."

Tomáš gulped it, then choked a little.

"Tell us what happened," said Adam.

It had taken him over an hour, he explained, to get through to Prague, to a number he did not recognize but which turned out to be the hospital where Martin had been taken. When he was finally put through to Zuzka, she told him that soon after he had left for Venice Martin had begun to complain of headaches and dizziness. She hadn't thought much of it, thinking perhaps it was just the flu, until he began to lose his balance and fall. Then she had rushed him to the hospital. An X-ray had revealed a brain tumor, but whether benign or malignant they did not know. And the doctors refused to operate, insisting they had neither the equipment nor the experience for such delicate surgery.

Nothing could be done until morning. Katrinka convinced Tomáš to try to get some rest, and she did the same, but sleep eluded her and by nine she and Tomáš were on the phone with Prague, finding out what arrangements had to be made to move Martin from there to the United States. As soon as it was a decent hour in New York, Katrinka woke Robin and asked her to put together a list of the best surgeons and of the hospitals where neurosurgery was routinely done while Adam began calling various senators in Washington asking their help to cut through the red tape.

With their guests fending for themselves and the social life of Venice carrying on for the most part without them, within forty-eight hours Adam and Katrinka had organized everything. An experienced surgeon at Massachusetts General in Boston, one of the best neurosurgical hospitals in the country, had agreed to perform the operation as soon as Martin got there. Adam and Katrinka had provided the Czechoslovakian government with a written commitment

FOR LOVE ALONE

to pay all of the Havlíčeks' travel and medical expenses. Exit visas had been issued, and entry visas to the United States were waiting at the embassy in Prague. The Graham jet was on its way from New York to pick up Zuzka and Martin; Katrinka and Tomáš were to fly to Paris and take the Concorde from there to New York, then a shuttle to Boston to meet them.

"If I don't get back before you leave," said Katrinka, as she hugged Adam good-bye at the Venice airport, "I'll meet you in Athens."

"Don't worry about it," he said in a reassuring voice that did not reassure her at all. Didn't he want her on the family trip? "Martin's the only one who's important now. Just take care of him, and Tomáš and Zuzka. They need you right now, even more than I do." He grinned. "I can handle Mother and Clementine alone, if I have to." Of course he wanted her there, she comforted herself. He was just being considerate.

"Sorry to leave you with a boatload of guests," she said.

"Don't worry," he repeated. "We'll all manage fine without you."

"That's what I do worry about," she said with a wry smile, "most of all."

He kissed her again. "I'll miss you."

"Thank you," said Tomáš, shaking his hand. His deep-set dark eyes were red from worry and lack of sleep. Despite his tan, he seemed pale. "I am so grateful to you, to Katrinka . . ."

"I . . . I hope everything goes well. Martin's a great kid."

"You wouldn't recognize him now," said Tomáš, his eyes brimming with tears. "He's almost as tall as I am."

Then Adam grinned suddenly and said, "You know, it just occurred to me that there's been one glorious bureaucratic fuck-up."

"What?" said Tomáš nervously, wondering what the hell Adam was smiling about.

"Someone forgot you weren't in Czechoslovakia."

"Oh, my God," said Katrinka, laughing. "Adam is right. Someone did or the government never would let Zuzka leave. You are all free."

Even Tomáš started to laugh.

"Everything's going to be fine," said Adam. "Count on it. Absolutely fine."

For hours, Katrinka sat with Tomáš and Zuzka in the hospital in Boston waiting while the fourteen-year-old Martin suffered through brain surgery. How could they bear it if he should die? she thought, remembering her own loss, her own pain. But of course he would not die, she assured herself, her normal optimism flooding back. He would be fine.

Zuzka, so big and blond, usually as boisterous as a Valkyrie, was faded and quiet. Tomáš sat with his long body curved into what seemed a giant cosmic question mark. Why? he seemed to be asking silently, hour after hour. Why my son? Why me? Why anyone? What is the point of all this suffering?

Katrinka did not try uselessly to cheer them up, but brought cups of coffee and insisted that they eat something, if only sandwiches from the hospital cafeteria. When she returned to the Four Seasons Hotel, where Robin had booked rooms for herself and the Havlíčeks, it was only to make phone calls: to check in with Robin in New York, with Adam in Venice, with Zuzka's mother, waiting anxiously by her phone in the small village where she lived for news of her grandson.

Ten hours after its start, the operation was finished and the surgeon, a sandy-haired, heavyset man in his late thirties, took long comforting drags from a cigarette and told them that the tumor had been a hemangioblastoma, and benign. It would be twenty-four hours before they could be certain of how well Martin had tolerated the surgery, and longer before they knew if there would be any permanent side effects, but so far, so good. Though they found the surgeon's words reassuring, it was only when they saw Martin, an hour later in intensive care, looking pale but alert, smiling cockily, as if he had just pulled off an amazing feat, that they really believed he would be well.

"Děkuji," he whispered to Katrinka in Czech, at Zuzka's insistence.

"*Andeličku*, you're welcome," she replied, almost giddy with relief. "But you must start learning English now."

While waiting for the decisive twenty-four hours to pass, Katrinka found an apartment for the Havlíčeks to stay in until Martin was completely recovered. She insisted Zuzka go shopping with her for food and groceries, hoping to introduce her friend gently into the foreign world she was about to inhabit. She lured Tomáš from the hospital long enough to open a bank account, then called New York and instructed Robin to deposit money in it. Then, as soon as she was certain that all was going well, she left to join Adam in Athens as she had promised, taking the Graham jet, which had waited for her at Logan. Lulled by the hum of the plane's motors and the comfort of the double bed in the master cabin, she got her first good night's sleep since her arrival in Venice.

Rested and happy, she greeted Nina and Kenneth, Clementine and Wilson, with a show of affection that surprised even her: with Martin safe, she felt as if she could forgive anyone anything. In truth, she was fond of Kenneth, understanding that the alcoholic haze in which he shrouded himself constantly was the only shield he had from Nina's quiet but obvious contempt. Sitting next to him at dinner, Katrinka listened as he pointed out the many fine qualities of the *Lady Katrinka*, obviously proud of how rich and successful his son had become, his ego not in the least troubled to have been surpassed in spades. As he talked contentedly, happy to have someone paying attention to him for a change, it seemed so unfair to Katrinka that Kenneth's approval should not count for something, should not somehow balance for his children the weight of their mother's scorn. But it didn't comfort them in the least. Like their mother, they had got into the habit of dismissing his opinions.

"Thank God you're back," said Adam when they were alone later in their cabin. He pulled off his tie and unbuttoned his shirt. "It's been hell. I must have been out of my mind to suggest it. Two weeks. Christ!" He took off his trousers, folded them neatly and hung them over the press.

"It was very nice of you," said Katrinka, hanging her dress in the closet. "You thought your mother might enjoy it and you were trying to make her happy."

"Why? When I know it's impossible."

Katrinka had wondered the same thing herself, but just said, "You know, I do believe sometimes she is enjoying herself and just hates to admit it."

"I wouldn't put it past her," said Adam. "What an impossible woman." He grabbed hold of Katrinka's arms as she walked past and pulled her to him. He slid his hands down her body, enjoying the silky feel of her slip against her skin, all his former irritation with her forgotten. Everything seemed always to go more smoothly when she was around. Burying his face in her neck, he said, "I've missed you."

"Good," she said.

"Did you miss me?"

"Always."

He looked up at her. "You're sure Martin is going to be all right?"

"Yes. Oh, God . . ." Suddenly the fear and loneliness of the past week came flooding back and she clutched Adam to her. "Make love to me, Adam. *Miláčku,* please. Make love to me." She felt his lips closing over hers, then the thrust of his tongue in her mouth. It's been so long, she thought. So long. His hands were under her slip, moving up her body, hooking into the elastic of her panties, tugging them gently down. Into her mind came the image of Martin as she had last seen him, his head swathed in bandages, lying in his hospital bed. And superimposed over that was the image of him as a baby sucking at his bottle as she held him in her arms. Maybe tonight, she thought. Maybe tonight.

Thirty-Five

There was a sharp knock on the door, but before Katrinka could respond it opened and Nina Graham, blond hair in a neat teased pouf, dressed for the city in a smart Galanos suit a few seasons old, swept into the office, calling to Robin, "I'll have coffee, thank you," before shutting the door behind her.

Katrinka closed the folder on the pile of papers she had been trying, unsuccessfully, to concentrate on for hours and, hoping her dismay did not show, rose to greet her.

"Really, Katrinka," said Nina as Katrinka's lips grazed her cheek, "must you and Adam live your entire lives in the pages of the tabloids?" She moved to the sofa and sat, dropping the offending newspaper—*The Chronicle*, of course—onto the coffee table. "It's in such poor taste."

"We do not hand out press releases about these things, you know," said Katrinka, regretfully leaving the sanctuary of her desk to sit opposite Nina, one of whose perfectly arched eyebrows lifted incredulously.

"I'm delighted to hear it, though it would not surprise me in the least if you did. It seems I never open a newspaper without finding a photograph of one or both of you."

"We both do have publicity departments to promote our businesses. That's all," said Katrinka, holding to the position Adam had taken with his mother over the years. "Or is making money in bad taste too?" she added, her irritation beginning to poke through the guard of polite affection she usually wore with her mother-in-law.

It had been an awful morning, starting with Sabrina's column, the resulting quarrel with Adam, the endless phone calls and faxes from concerned and curious friends, climaxed by Nina Graham's appearance, uninvited, at Katrinka's Praha office. Nina was in town for her usual monthly afternoon of shopping at Bergdorf's, an early dinner with friends at the Four Seasons, an evening at the theater, and an overnight stay with Adam and Katrinka before returning to Newport the following morning. Today, she had decided to forgo the shopping for a heart-to-heart with her daughter-in-law.

"All I know is that generations of Grahams have done quite well financially without having their names in the headlines of these disgusting papers."

"The times were different," said Katrinka. "It is not possible anymore to control what the press reports."

"Excuse me," said Robin, entering with a tray of coffee and miniature pastries from the Praha's restaurant.

It was a ridiculous argument to be having, thought Katrinka as Robin served the pastries and poured the coffee. She was no happier than Nina Graham about Sabrina's most recent column, and Adam was furious. No sooner had he seen it than he had revised his schedule, ordered the Graham jet, and taken off for Europe, leaving Katrinka in New York to face the embarrassment alone.

As soon as Robin left, Nina said, "At least Kenneth has been spared," without a trace of irony that now, too late, she was willing to consider her husband's feelings. "He loathed seeing the Graham name exploited."

In March of 1986, Kenneth Graham had died suddenly of a heart attack. Of all the family, Katrinka was perhaps the most saddened by his death. Having grown up without the cushion of wealth that permitted Kenneth Graham to be so casual about his finances, Katrinka had a keen sense of the value of money, but she nevertheless admired her father-in-law's refusal to be concerned about increasing the family fortune, contenting himself instead with a quiet pride in his work. She had become very fond of him. Because he was neither her husband nor her father, she had been more tolerant of his weaknesses and better able to appreciate his gentle manner, his unfailing courtesy, shy affection, his attempts to provide an antidote for his wife's venom.

But in the six months since his death, Kenneth's position in his family had shifted. Without the reality of his presence to distract her, he became for Nina the arbiter of all things Graham, the standard against which behavior was either acceptable or not. And his children, who had paid little enough attention to him when he was there, guiltily tried to make up for it now that he had gone. Clementine and Wilson endowed a scholarship in marine engineering in Kenneth Graham's name at MIT. And Adam not only refused to sell his father's shipyard but made few changes in its management. "Not everything has to be a gold mine," he replied when a reporter from *The Wall Street Journal* asked him why. "It's keeping beautiful old yachts afloat, bits of American naval history, and as long as the yard pays its way doing it, that's good enough for me."

One of the few not surprised by his decision was Katrinka. She had always been aware of Adam's affection for his father, had known how much Adam cared about history, about tradition, how proud he was of the role the Graham family had played in the development of naval design from colonial days to the present. And after years of watching him set sail in all kinds of weather, ignoring her silent protests, her unspoken terror that he would never come back, she knew that, like his father, he loved boats and wanted to preserve them.

What *had* surprised her was Adam's sudden about-face, his agreement to see a fertility specialist after refusing for so long. Until his father's death, whenever she had asked him to go for testing, he had insisted it was not necessary. He had made a girl pregnant once in college and that, he seemed to think, gave him a clean bill of health. From her hours spent consulting doctors, from all the reading she had done on the subject, Katrinka knew that the matter was not as simple as that. Age caused havoc in the body, stress affected sperm as well as ovulation, there were symptomless diseases and hidden infections that damaged reproductive organs. Her own experience indicated that a prior pregnancy might not be relevant, though unless Zeiss Associates should succeed in reuniting her with her son, she was not prepared to go into that with Adam, no matter how difficult telling him later might be. But when she did point out to her husband the many factors that could have affected his fertility, they quarreled, and so Katrinka stopped insisting he be tested. Then Kenneth Graham had died and when another bit of minor surgery on Katrinka in early September had not resulted in the desired pregnancy, Adam broached the subject himself.

Not inclined to amateur psychologizing, neither Katrinka nor Adam delved too deeply into the reasons for his change. To Adam it suddenly seemed the least he could do after all the pills Katrinka had taken, the procedures she had undergone, the crazy hormone-induced surges of hope and despair she had endured, that he go and get himself checked out. To Katrinka, nothing seemed more normal than that Adam, approaching his mid-forties, should finally have reached the point where, like her, he was willing to do anything possible to have a child.

It was more complicated than that, of course. Like most children, Adam wanted to please his parents and, perversely, prove his independence by ignoring their wishes. And because his mother was the dominant figure, it was with her he acted out his show of rebellion, going out of his way to earn the disapproval she was quick to show, doing what he knew she would dislike, taking a position opposite to any she held. When having a child became an issue instead of an event that Adam had expected to occur without any undue effort on his part, once Nina Graham began to demand a grandchild, Adam naturally felt forced to resist. But just as his desire to build a business empire and amass a fortune sprang not only from his own pride and innate ambition but from an unconscious need to earn from her the respect his father never got, so there was the desire to produce a son to satisfy his mother's dynastic ambitions as well as his own.

Kenneth Graham's death tipped the balance. It made pleasing his dead father suddenly more important to Adam than defying his live mother, brought to the surface paternal instincts he had tried to ignore. Losing a father made Adam want to have a son.

What was splashed across the front page of *The Chronicle* and detailed in Sabrina's column inside were the results of Adam's physical. "Graham Counts His Billions" ran the headline in large type over a photograph of Adam in a hospital gown carrying a glass jar which might or might not have been empty. "Tycoon Adam Graham Last Week at Miracle Clinic" ran the caption underneath. Inside the paper, Sabrina's column was headed, "What Money Can't Buy, or Can It?" In it, she detailed what she described as "the Golden Couple's heartbreaking attempts to have a child, the only thing so far their vast fortune has not been able to buy them." She gave a rundown of their assets that would have put *Forbes* to shame, listed the doctors Katrinka had seen over the years, the courses of treatment, the surgical procedures. She told of Adam's initial reluctance to consult a specialist and how, finally, he had agreed to his wife's demands. The previous week, she reported, he had been examined by one of the preeminent fertility doctors in the country and given a clean bill of health. His sperm were healthy, his count was normal, up there in the billions where it ought to be. So, what was on the Grahams' busy schedule now? she wondered. Would Adam and his "Katrinket" (as she had started, annoyingly, to call Katrinka) arrange a private adoption? Or pay a surrogate mother to bear their child?

"How do they get pictures like that?" asked Nina, looking with enormous distaste at *The Chronicle*'s cover.

"A concealed camera. The paper did bribe someone at the clinic."

"Disgusting," murmured Nina as she picked up a cup of lustrous Sevres porcelain. "Lovely china. My mother had a set exactly like this." At least I did do one thing right, thought Katrinka as Nina settled back again in her seat and fixed her with a look that was trying hard to seem sympathetic rather than crafty. "Then I assume the details I read in that rag are correct?"

"More or less," conceded Katrinka.

"And may I ask what you and my son intend to do now?"

447

"Do?"

"You are not considering adoption?" Her voice said plainly that she would not approve.

"We did not discuss it," said Katrinka truthfully, searching for a polite way to tell her mother-in-law to mind her own business. "Yet. We still hope to have a child of our own."

"And how do you propose to manage that?"

"The usual way," said Katrinka shortly.

"You're how old now?"

"Almost thirty-eight."

"Hmmm," said Nina, taking another sip of coffee.

Katrinka resisted the urge to defend herself, to say she was still young, healthy, in perfect physical condition, with no terrible diseases ravaging her insides, no blocked tubes or defective ovaries. While everyone had a theory, why she was unable to conceive was a mystery as yet unsolved. But that was not a conversation she wanted to have with this woman who was no friend of hers. Instead, she remained silent until Nina leaned toward her confidentially and said, "It would be so sad for my son not to have a child."

"And for me?"

"Oh, of course for you, too," she said, sounding startled.

"What you want we should do?" said Katrinka. The words came in a characteristic rush, her voice as low and soft as always but cold and angry. "You think I should divorce Adam? You think then he would have children with someone else?"

"Katrinka, I really did not mean to upset you."

"Yes, you did. What I don't understand is why. You do think Adam and I are not upset enough?"

"You have completely misunderstood my meaning."

"I hope so," said Katrinka.

Nina Graham stood, preparing to go. "Adam has left for Europe, I understand?" Katrinka nodded. "Then perhaps it's best if I return home this evening after the theater."

"That is up to you," said Katrinka. "But you are welcome to stay. Even if we have disagreements, you are still Adam's mother."

Nina nodded her small neat head graciously. "Thank you.

Perhaps next month." Katrinka escorted Nina to the door of her office, but for once the women did not go through the charade of exchanging kisses. "Will you tell Adam about our conversation?" asked Nina, less concerned than curious.

Katrinka shook her head. "Adam and I, we do love each other, you know."

"Love," said Nina as she went out the door, "is all very well, but it is far from everything."

One of the secretaries cleared away the coffee tray and, feeling even more restless and unhappy, Katrinka settled herself behind her desk and again tried to concentrate on the pile of papers requiring her attention. There were requests for her to lecture, invitations to conferences, announcements of awards for the Praha or the Graham, or herself as their owner. There were solicitations for money, appeals for her to serve as chair of various charity committees. She had to draft a Christmas letter on behalf of the Children of the Streets Foundation, review the overnight and weekly figures for the two hotels, make a decision about firing the personnel director at the Graham, reply to a fax from Carlos about the renovation of the hotel in London she had purchased earlier in the year, an endless list of things to do, decisions to make, no matter how much she tried to delegate. Normally, she enjoyed the pressure. The quick pace that being busy made necessary was the speed at which she moved most comfortably. But that day what Katrinka wanted was to be at the villa in Cap Ferrat with a truckload of plants from the nursery to set into beds and long hours of physical activity ahead of her, leaving her no time to think until she collapsed at night into an exhausted and dreamless sleep.

The phone rang and Katrinka spoke briefly to one of the secretaries at the Graham, setting the time of the next executive meeting. Michael Ferrante, the Praha's general manager, stuck his head in the door, then came in and sprawled in an armchair while they discussed a proposed package deal Katrinka was organizing with the head of Adam's new cruise ship line. When Michael left, she returned her attention to the pile of papers and succeeded so well in losing herself in them that she was surprised when

Robin entered, saying, "You'd better go if you want to get to the opera on time."

"It is six already?" said Katrinka with a surprised look at her watch. She had just enough time to get home to change.

With Adam in Europe she had considered not going to the opera that night for fear of running into someone she knew, but not only would her pride not allow her to keep away, Placido Domingo was singing in *Tosca* and she did not see why Sabrina should deprive her of that pleasure. She had phoned Rick Colins, who had happily agreed to escort her. She knew from experience there was no one better at running interference than he. "You did give Luther the schedule for the evening?" she asked Robin.

"Uh-huh. He's waiting for you outside." She handed Katrinka a large brown envelope. "This came FedEx a few minutes ago," she said, then went over to the coffee table and picked up *The Chronicle*. Her snub nose wrinkled with distaste. "You want me to get rid of this for you?"

"Please," said Katrinka as she tore open the envelope. At the moment *The Chronicle* was not even of minor interest to her. All her attention was focused on the envelope. Though it was unmarked, she knew it was the monthly report from Zeiss Associates. As always, she could feel her lungs fighting for air, her heart beating frantically in her chest. Like the many others she had received over the years, this report would most likely contain nothing of importance. Still she could never control the wild surges of hope and alternating panic that afflicted her each time she received one.

"You want me to tell Luther you'll be right down?" asked Robin, hinting politely that Katrinka ought to get a move on.

"Yes," said Katrinka, not paying attention, scanning the contents of the ten-page report. In a moment her breathing steadied and her heart regained its normal rhythm. As she had expected, her son still had not been found.

Zeiss Associates were most methodical and diligent. After retracing all the obvious steps Katrinka had taken to try and find her son (and, like her, getting nowhere), they had become more adventurous. Refused access to the records of the Zimmerman Clinic for lack of "proper authorization," they had bribed one of the staff and had a good look around. In Katrinka's file, which still existed, they found nothing but her medical charts, copies of the adoption release papers she had signed, nothing that wasn't perfectly legal or that provided any clue to what had happened to her son. They looked for additional files, in the baby's name and in the father's name, but again found nothing. Only when they decided to check the clinic's catchall chronological file, meticulously searching through papers dating from Katrinka's arrival in Munich to a year after the baby's disappearance, did they come across their first lead, a letter from a lawyer requesting a copy of "Baby Kovář's" birth certificate, which was needed for filing with the adoption papers.

When Katrinka had received that report from Zeiss, for the first time in a long while she had felt optimistic, as if finding her son was a real possibility instead of only a fantasy she stubbornly refused to let die. But the lawyer who had sent the letter had relocated not once but several times, and when the Zeiss detective had finally succeeded in tracking him down he had been dead for more than two years. His successor had either returned the files to the clients who wanted them or destroyed those of the ones who didn't, leaving nothing but a copy of the letter he had written to each, providing the detective with only a list of names and addresses, in all parts of the world, every one of which had to be tediously and individually investigated. After three years of searching, the paper trail had still led nowhere. As always, at the end of the cover letter, Paul Zeiss had asked politely whether or not she wished them to proceed.

Robin stuck her head in the door. "Katrinka, you're going to be real late if you don't get out of here."

"Phone Paul Zeiss," said Katrinka as she put the envelope into the file drawer in her desk and locked it. "Tell him to proceed. I go, I go," she added quickly to Robin as she got to her feet and hurried from the traditional comfort of her own office into the high-tech secretarial area. "See you in the morning," she called, going through the door, past reception, and out of the executive suite.

Robin didn't know what was in those envelopes that always had such a peculiar effect on her employer. She was curious, of course, and more than once had been tempted to try to have a look when Katrinka was away, but she was far too honorable to act on that impulse. Katrinka trusted her, she knew, and Robin didn't want to betray that trust. Besides which, her boss was surprisingly reserved, even shy, despite the broad smile she mustered for the cameras, and Robin was willing to respect that.

She went into her office, a smaller room but furnished in the same style as Katrinka's, and looked up Zeiss Associates on her Rolodex. It was a detective agency, that much Robin knew. And her instructions were to talk to no one but Paul Zeiss himself. She dialed the number, waited, asked for *Monsieur Zeiss, s'il vous plaît,* and wondered what it was all about.

Lincoln Center was planned as the cultural heart of New York City, including theaters, concert halls, a library, an open-air band shell, and the Juilliard School. Its buildings were classically inspired (which meant that they looked modern without resembling either giant colored boxes or prisons), were decorated with serious art, and had seats especially designed to fit the average American hip size. Whatever the quibbles about its architecture or the quality of the art presented, to Katrinka, as Luther opened the door of the Mercedes and Rick Colins climbed out and extended a hand to help her, it seemed a haven of sanity in New York's mad world. Walking up Lincoln Center's broad steps from Columbus Avenue into its large flagged plaza, seeing its three main buildings all alight, the dancing colors of the Chagall murals visible behind the glass facade of the Metropolitan Opera House, the play of the black marble fountain, the hawkers selling tickets, street artists performing, people strolling to waste time or hurrying to meet friends, was for Katrinka one of the great pleasures of life in that city.

Dressed quietly in a short black Donna Karan dinner suit with silk lapels and a sheer georgette blouse, her dark hair pulled back in a French twist, her only jewelry a yellow diamond pin set with white diamonds and matching ear clips, Katrinka still caused heads to turn as she crossed the plaza with Rick at her side. Some people recognized her of course: she had been on the cover of *Chic*, after all, was regularly featured in *Architectural Digest*, *Vogue*, *W*, as well as the other fashionable magazines and (at least in Nina Graham's opinion) had appeared far too frequently in the pages of *The Chronicle* and *The Daily News* for her to be anonymous. But most people had no idea who she was, and turned to look only because she was tall, regal, beautiful, and had that compelling radiance created by the combination of energy and self-assurance. "Who is she?" people whispered, knowing she must be "someone."

"So far so good," said Rick as he ushered her across the grand lobby lit softly by chandeliers of Austrian crystal and up the wide red carpeted staircase to her box in the center of the parterre.

Katrinka looked at Rick's boyish face and smiled. "I did forget. No one will be here," she said. "It's not a gala." Only an event brought the people in her circle and their attendant press to the opera.

Rick opened the door into the box and Katrinka entered, passing through the small foyer and down the step to where Margo and Ted Jensen were already seated on the upholstered chairs. Ted got immediately to his feet as Margo turned to greet them. "Hello, darling," she said, looking, with her rail-thin body, white skin, bold nose, deep-set eyes, and vermilion mouth, as if she had sprung from a German expressionist painting. "Why Rick, how nice to see you. Adam away?" she asked, turning her attention back to Katrinka.

"In Europe," said Katrinka, kissing them both hello. "He did change his plans this morning and go." And he had not phoned her all day as he usually did after a quarrel, to make contact if not exactly to apologize.

Margo frowned. How like Adam, she thought, to leave Katrinka to face the heat alone. But she knew better than to criticize him to his wife and so, instead, asked when she expected the London Graham to open.

"Soon," said Katrinka, "December first." She grimaced. "I'm terrified."

"Nonsense," said Margo, "it will be fabulous."

"Problems with the rebuilding?" asked Ted, who did not glide over problems as easily as Margo.

"Only the usual ones," she admitted. "But the casino? It's a whole new world for me."

As usual, she had fallen in love with the hotel (then called the Royal) at first sight. It was on a small street, off St. James's, not far from Piccadilly, an excellent location near all the smart men's clubs. The former townhouse of an English duke, its paneled walls, Grinling Gibbons carving, painted ceilings, and Robert Adam library had survived its conversion to a hotel after the Second World War. But in the early sixties the entire upper floor had been turned into a gambling casino, reducing the number of rooms while increasing the hotel's profitability. It was the casino that had made Katrinka hesitate.

Finally, however, she had decided to go ahead with the purchase, cheered on by Adam, who, after buying the cruise ship line, had converted two of the ships into floating gambling palaces. Now, in addition to running the two New York hotels, the Fifth Avenue apartment, and the Cap Ferrat house, supervising the renovation of the London Graham, chairing the Children of the Streets Foundation, sitting on the committees of five other charities and on the board of the Metropolitan Opera and New York City Ballet, Katrinka was also spending as much as one week a month on those ships learning the business of gambling from Adam's managers. But still it was a foreign world to her, one very dangerous for a novice, and she could not help worrying.

"Carlos says it's looking fabulous," said Rick. He and Carlos had been living together for over five years and were, in Rick's opinion, as much in love as ever. Not a day went by that they did not spend at least an hour talking long-distance at great expense. When not discussing how much they missed one another, Carlos told endless funny stories about the difficulties of working with the English, their constant tea breaks, their refusal to deviate from custom ("We don't do it that way here, guv"), none of which Rick thought it wise to repeat to Katrinka, who did not find what she considered slipshod work or indifferent attitudes amusing.

"We should fly over for the opening," said Ted, pushing his horn-rimmed glasses back on his nose with his index finger, "and help you celebrate."

"I would love that," said Katrinka.

Ted had just returned from a few months at the Betty Ford Clinic. His curly hair was grayer, and he looked very thin and completely colorless next to his vivid wife. But Margo looked at him and smiled as if relieved at what she saw. He wasn't drinking, and that was good. If only he would regain his confidence. She missed his jaunty self-assurance. Reaching across, she put a loving hand on his arm. "Better yet," she said, "why don't we wait and take the children for the holidays? It would be wonderful to be all together in London."

"Sure, if you like," he said, a barely perceptible frown flickering across his face.

Margo realized instantly what she had done wrong, overruled his suggestion, and here she was determined to build up his sagging ego again. When the business had been lost in the fire and Ted, to fight depression, had begun to drink, it seemed for a while, a long while, as if their life was falling apart. But Margo had held it together, quitting her job at *Chic,* taking over the business, renting new space, making deals with the banks, with the designers, the factory workers, the retailers, getting a new line of clothes cut and sewn and into the shops, all the while reassuring her son and daughter, paying their college fees, and encouraging Ted to dry out. Now, finally, she was beginning to see an end to the trouble. When Ted left the Betty Ford Clinic, he had joined AA and was sticking to the program. The business, while not yet in the black, was starting to do well. Soon, she hoped to be able to turn it completely over to Ted and withdraw, picking up the pieces of her own career. She loved her husband and was certain that he loved her, but she doubted that they would work well together as partners in business. Their egos required separate domains. "No," she said, "I think you're right. The opening would be more fun. We can take the kids to Aspen for the holidays. Or just stay home if you like."

Ted's pale face creased in a smile, giving a hint of the competent man he used to be. "It would be nice to be home this year," he said. He had been away from his family too much the past several months, and the thought of spending the holidays peacefully in Scarsdale was very appealing.

Watching the exchange between the two, Rick envied them despite their troubles and hoped that the bond between him and Carlos would prove to be as strong and as long-lasting. And Katrinka, who in truth had not expected the Jensens' marriage to survive the trouble, was filled as always with admiration for the caring wife and devoted mother who hid behind the colorful mask that Margo wore for the world. She had fought to save what she loved, and she had won. At least for the moment. The memory of Steven and Daisy and how totally secure they had once seemed to her made Katrinka wary. Was it ever possible to judge the state of another's marriage? Was it even possible to judge the state of her own? Why had Adam been so angry with her that morning? she wondered, not for the first time that day, feeling her irritation with him come suddenly rolling back. It was hardly her fault that Sabrina had got hold of that story.

The conductor came out into the pit to a round of applause, the overture began, and Katrinka forgot everything, losing herself as always completely in the music. But all too soon she heard the closing bars of the first act and saw the giant velvet curtain begin to fall as the audience shouted its approval. "Shall I go rustle us up something to drink?" asked Rick. "Some champagne?"

"Why don't we all go?" suggested Ted.

While the men dealt with the crowd at the bar, Katrinka and Margo waited out on the balcony overlooking the plaza. "Have you heard from Natalie?" asked Margo as she pulled her jewel-studded gold compact from the Judith Lieber purse and began to refinish her face.

Katrinka nodded. "We talk on the phone two or three times a week. She's lonely, I think."

"Why on earth do you suppose she did it?"

Katrinka shrugged. "She does love him."

"Him or his money?"

"Him, his money, and the fact that he does love her so much," said Katrinka, smiling. "He adores her."

"And to get even with Jean-Claude, I suppose," said Margo, closing the compact and returning it to the purse.

"That, too," agreed Katrinka.

As soon as she had returned from Venice, Natalie had quit her job at Saks, left New York, and moved into Prince Khalid's London house. A few months later they were married. Only Adam and Katrinka had gone to Riyadh to the wedding. The Jensens were Jewish, as was Neil Goodman, and so were not welcome in Saudi Arabia; Alexandra would not go without her husband; Daisy had come down with the flu; and Jean-Claude of course had not been invited. Despite Khalid's obvious love for Natalie, the splendor of his palace, the ropes of pearls, the diamond chokers, the Van Cleef & Arpels ruby-and-diamond cluster brooch, the Chaumet coral-and-diamond necklace that Khalid had given his bride, when it was time to go, leaving Natalie behind made Katrinka uneasy.

"People are always worried by what they don't understand," Adam had said as the Graham jet climbed into the cloudless blue sky above the Gulf. "And that's a culture we really don't know much about."

"Neither does Natalie," said Katrinka, looking dismally at the small crystal dish that had been the wedding favor. She had not been allowed to view the wedding ceremony, nor had any other woman. "That is what frightens me."

With the bombing of Libya in May and the possibility of escalating violence, her anxiety had increased. But Natalie seemed unfazed by it all. Her only complaint was that she had no friends in Riyadh, no one to gossip and laugh with. But that, she was sure, would come in time.

"What does she do all day?" asked Margo.

"Shops, I suppose. And she does travel with Khalid. She says they are as much in love as ever and very happy. Maybe it will work," added Katrinka optimistically.

Margo shook her halo of frizzed hair, but said nothing. It was not that she was anti-Arab, she assured herself, just practical. When people married out of their own religion, their own culture, all the problems of marriage were bound to be exaggerated. How was Natalie going to cope with that other wife and four daughters once the honeymoon was over?

The men returned with a Perrier for Ted and a bottle of Dom Perignon for the others and they remained on the balcony drinking, Rick regaling them with stories about Nancy Reagan, on whom he had just done a feature for *Chic*, enjoying the splash of the fountain and the play of light in the plaza until, suddenly, the easy atmosphere was interrupted by the appearance of the model whose face that month was on the cover of *Vogue* escorted by none other than Mark van Hollen. His sun-bleached hair was a few inches longer than fashion dictated. He still had his tan but not his beard and, if he did not look exactly happy, at least the lines of misery were gone from his face and the shuttered look from his eyes. "God, he's gorgeous," murmured Rick, not even aware that he had spoken aloud.

Margo called hello but, as Mark approached, Katrinka found her surge of instinctive pleasure at seeing him fade when she remembered that he was the owner and publisher of *The Chronicle*. As she greeted him she saw a flicker of surprise in his eyes and realized that her social mask must have slipped, allowing him to catch sight of her anger. She made no attempt to remedy the situation, letting Margo lead the conversation, responding politely when she had to, keeping quiet otherwise. Soon, to Katrinka's relief, the warning bell sounded, and she excused herself, expecting Rick to fall into step beside her. But it was Mark who did that, with Margo and the model gossiping about a mutual friend, and Rick and Ted bringing up the rear as they headed back to their seats.

"You're angry with me," said Mark.

"Why I should be angry with you?" said Katrinka, her voice as cool and polite as she could make it.

"What Sabrina writes is her business," replied Mark, who didn't like to play games. "I have no control over her."

"I understand. Freedom of the press."

"Exactly."

"Then why I do never read about you and . . . uh, your friends in Sabrina's column?"

"For one very simple reason. I am of no interest to the public. I make it my business not to be." He looked at her as coldly as she had looked at him earlier. "People who court the press, Katrinka, shouldn't be surprised when they end up in the papers."

"We 'court' the press, as you say, for business. We advertise. We publicize. Our private life is nobody's business."

"Unfortunately, newspapers don't make such subtle distinctions."

They had reached Katrinka's box and she opened the door. *"Good* newspapers do," she said.

The others were right behind them. Everyone said their good-byes, but before Katrinka could disappear into her box, Mark said, "Katrinka, that friend of yours I met in Venice. Tomáš? I heard his son was ill."

Surprised, Katrinka turned. "Martin. Yes. But he is all right now, thank God." The slight dizziness the boy had experienced for a while after the operation had lessened over time, and now it seemed he was completely well. The family had moved to Los Angeles and Tomáš, miraculously, had found an agent, though as yet no film to direct. Martin was in school, Zuzka had conquered her initial culture shock and was working at a sporting-goods store as a saleswoman and Tomáš as a ticket taker in a local movie theater. It was a way for him to see movies free.

"I'm glad to hear it," said Mark. "Well, good night."

The question about Martin had made a dent in Katrinka's anger. "Good night," she said, a grudging smile warming her face. What an unpredictable and infuriating, stubborn and kind man, she thought.

The applause signaling the conductor's entrance into the pit began. He raised his baton, the music swelled, and the curtain was slowly raised. Again, Katrinka forgot everything.

Afterward, Margo and Ted refused an invitation to dinner, collected their car from the parking lot, and drove home to Scarsdale, while Katrinka and Rick went backstage to see Placido Domingo and then went with him and his wife, Marta, to dine at the Russian Tea Room. Then, Katrinka and Rick went on to Le Club to dance: she didn't want to get home until it was a reasonable hour to phone London, which was five hours ahead.

It was just after two when Katrinka let herself into the apartment, checked her messages, and found that Adam still had not called. She tried him at Claridge's, where he was staying, but he was out, at an early breakfast meeting, she guessed. She left a message and began to get ready for bed, thinking—to her surprise—not of Adam but of Mark van Hollen. Here was a man who had lost his wife and children, the greatest horror Katrinka could imagine, but he had not allowed it to ruin his life. He had withdrawn; he had traveled, as far as he could, trying to forget his grief in the upper reaches of the Amazon and in the Himalayas. But he had come back, if not completely healed, at least whole enough to run his businesses successfully, to take a healthy interest in women, and to continue caring about people in general, whether it was by supporting welfare programs in his newspapers or by remembering that Tomáš Havlíček's son had been ill. Mark van Hollen was living proof, thought Katrinka, that grief did not have to make you bitter, or deprive you of pleasure in what was good in your life.

The phone rang and she quickly tissued the cream from her face and ran to answer it, sitting on the bed as she picked up the receiver.

"Katrinka, it's me, did I wake you?"

"No, no. I just got in a while ago."

"Did you enjoy the opera?"

"It was fantastic. Just what I did need tonight."

"Yes. Look, about that column, I'm sorry. I don't know what got into me."

"Sabrina affects people that way," said Katrinka dryly.

"I guess I overreacted."

"No. It was horrible. But it was not my fault."

"I know."

Suddenly, without having planned it, she said, "Adam, listen, we can't let this ruin our lives. Even if we can't have a baby, we do have so much else that's good. We have each other."

"You're the one who's been pushing for a baby," said Adam, sounding suddenly irritated, "not me."

"I know that. But I do think now is time to stop."

"If that's what you want."

"I want what's best for *us*," said Katrinka.

"I don't understand you sometimes, Katrinka. Why this sudden change of heart?"

Why indeed? she wondered. She was not completely sure herself of all the reasons, but knew at least one important one. "Because fighting with you does hurt too much. It hurts our marriage. I love you, Adam. I don't want to lose you, not for anything, not even for a baby."

"Just try and lose me," he said, the laughter coming back into his voice.

No, she thought, that is just what I will *not* try. "When you will be home?" she said.

"Tuesday, I think. I have to spend a few days more in London, and then fly up to Scotland and have a look at things there."

"What if I take the Concorde tomorrow and meet you?"

He hesitated a moment, then said, "Do it."

"I will. See you tomorrow. Good night, *miláčku*," she said, replacing the receiver on its cradle and settling back against the pillows of the bed which Anna had turned down for her before retiring for the night. The relief she felt was enormous, as if a burden she had been carrying for years had suddenly been taken from her. No one has everything, she told herself.

Thirty-Six

Katrinka was up at six as usual. Her personal trainer arrived at six-thirty, and, after a forty-minute exercise session, she showered and dressed. Adam had already left for Miami, so Katrinka breakfasted alone, as she did most mornings of late, on black coffee and newspapers, then discussed the luncheon menu with John, the chef. Natalie was in New York with Prince Khalid and Aziz, their nine-month-old son, Zuzka was visiting from Los Angeles, and Daisy from London, so to celebrate all her friends being in the same city at the same time—a rare occurrence of late—Katrinka had invited them all to the apartment for a quiet lunch and a good gossip.

The menu decided, she browsed through the photograph album of Polaroid snapshots—a catalog of all the Grahams' china, linen, crystal, and side pieces arranged in twenty-two possible combinations—considered the possibilities for a few moments, then instructed Carter to use arrangement number four, the antique Franciscan Flower luncheon set she had bought at Christie's with the apple blossom crystal glasses and the flowered Porthault place mats. Katrinka had made the same sort of album for the Villa Mahmed and the *Lady Katrinka:* it saved so much time to be able to point to a photograph rather than have to explain exactly what it was she wanted every time guests were expected.

By nine she was at her desk at the hotel, where she stayed until it was time to meet her friends at the Plaza for the Scaasi show. Katrinka always made it a point to go to the ready-to-wear collections in New York, not only because she liked to support American industry, but because she admired the designs of people like Scaasi and Bill Blass, Calvin Klein and Oscar de la Renta, Donna Karan and Carolyne Roehm, as well as the chutzpah of Victor Costa, who could knock off a Paris fashion with flair and sell it to his home-side customers for a fraction of the cost of the haute-couture original.

After the show, the friends returned to the Graham apartment, Natalie in her hired Rolls with Aziz and his nurse, the rest in Katrinka's Mercedes. Anna took their coats, Aziz was banished to one of the guest bedrooms for a nap, and Carter served aperitifs in the sitting room. At one promptly, lunch was served.

A little while later, Zuzka looked around Katrinka's dining table at the exquisitely groomed, exquisitely wealthy women gathered there for lunch and thought, completely without bitterness, how nice it would be to be rich. For her and Tomáš the streets of America had not been paved with gold. "It is crazy business," she said. Fed up with the film industry in general and her husband in particular, she had jumped at the chance to spend a few days in New York with Katrinka. Going with her to the collections was fun, even though she could not afford to buy anything. Tomáš's first film had been released to disastrous notices, the one he had been preparing was canceled, another job did not seem to be on the horizon, and money was becoming a serious problem in the Havlíček household. Zuzka's salary (she had been promoted to manager of the sporting-goods store where she worked) barely covered the family's living expenses. Still, however fed up—and homesick—she sometimes got, she consoled herself with the knowledge that life was definitely better in Los Angeles than it had been in Prague. Picking at the fillet of perfectly prepared sole on her plate, she added, "Completely crazy."

"No crazier than any other," said Alexandra, whose new gallery, thanks to the booming 1987 economy and the skyrocketing prices of art, had repaid her husband's initial loan and was making significant profits each month, while Knapp Manning, Neil's company, had figured out new and innovative and pretty much inexplicable ways of raking in money.

"I hear Aziz," said Natalie, getting to her feet and rushing from the room.

"Banking is not in the least bit crazy," said Daisy, who had not been paying much attention to the economy, her mind fully occupied of late with wondering how to divest herself of Bjorn Lindstrom, sweet as he continued to be, without hurting his feelings and what, if anything, to do about Steven, whose life seemed to be falling apart.

"Not crazy?" said Katrinka, signaling Carter to refill the wineglasses. "It is the craziest of all."

"Is it?"

"Don't tell me that Bjorn keeps you so busy you don't have time even to read the papers?" said Margo, laughing. Now that she had, against the odds, taken her husband's floundering clothes-manufacturing company and pushed it firmly back up into the black, she considered herself quite the financial expert.

"I must say I do spend quite a lot of time thinking about him."

"*Thinking,*" said Margo, adding as Carter left the room, "What a waste."

"Not as big a waste as reading the papers," said Lucia, her voice full of disgust. Nick was handling the trial of Santo Zuccarelli, who had recently been indicted on twenty-two felony counts, including three charges of first-degree murder, and while, once upon a time, the press had been willing to accept that even the most hardened criminal deserved a good lawyer, lately they had taken to calling Nick *consigliere*.

"They have been hard on Nick lately, haven't they?" said Alexandra, without too much sympathy in her voice. Though she was fond of Lucia and adored Pia, she did not care for Nick at all and would not be in the least surprised if everything the papers hinted about him was true. She took a cigarette from the gold-plated case in her purse and lit it.

"You really should give that up," said Daisy.

"I've tried," said Alexandra with a shrug. "And failed."

"I did believe here everyone is innocent until proved guilty," said Katrinka.

"That's the theory," said Margo.

"Propaganda," said Zuzka. "Bullshit. Same here as everywhere."

"It's so hard on Pia," said Lucia. A delicate, shy fourteen-year-old, Pia had inherited her mother's talent and her father's looks, but none of his brashness. "Every time she picks up a newspaper or turns on the television, there's her father. And those rich brats at her school, they're making her life a nightmare."

"Poor sweetheart," said Alexandra, trying to imagine her own daughter in a similar situation.

"You must get her out of there," said Katrinka.

"I know," said Lucia. "Right after Easter we're sending her to school in Florence. We spend so much time there anyway."

"Le voilà," said Natalie, reentering the dining room.

"Oh, how gorgeous," said Margo, and though Natalie did indeed look fabulous in a brilliant leather and wool Lacroix minidress with large amethyst earrings set in solid gold and a bracelet to match, it was not to her Margo was referring but to the boy she had in her arms. He was nine months old, chubby, with creamy café-au-lait skin and brown almond-shaped eyes outlined with a thick fringe of dark lashes.

"Isn't he adorable," said Natalie, her voice full of pride. The little boy looked around him at all the strange smiling women and yawned, not yet fully recovered from his nap.

"Andeličku," murmured Katrinka, extending her arms. Aziz smiled and went to her immediately. They were old friends. They had met at St. Moritz at Christmas and had seen a lot of each other since his arrival in New York the week before.

Though Natalie got to London, Paris, and St. Moritz quite often, this was her first trip to New York since her marriage. Khalid had taken the Presidential Suite at the Plaza and then left her there with Aziz and a contingent of maids and guards and drivers while he went off to Kentucky to visit a stud farm owned by someone he had met at the last

465

Newmarket horse sales in England. Natalie was reveling in her freedom, going everywhere, seeing everything, catching up with the world of American fashion by accompanying Katrinka and the others to the collections to see what Bill Blass, Donna Karan, Bob Mackie, and the rest of the New York designers were up to. She loved showing off her clothes and her jewels and her child. She looked stunning and seemed happy. Only once did an odd remark make the others think that perhaps all was not so glorious as she said.

They had been barraging her with questions, displaying their awful ignorance of life in Saudi Arabia, and had got around to discussing the weather there—an innocuous enough subject—when Natalie began to describe how "amusing" it was when a group of women swathed in their black chadors came in out of the heat and threw off their long robes to reveal the very latest in haute-couture mini sundresses. There was a moment of stunned silence. Then Zuzka, who was not quite sure she had understood, said, *"You* wear veil?"

"Certainly," said Natalie, sounding defiant, "in public."

"You don't!" said Margo, whose feminist sensibilities were outraged equally by Muslim women in chadors, Hassidic women concealing their shaved heads under wigs, and any other religious (or political) practice she considered sexist.

"But you're not Muslim," said Lucia.

"My husband is."

"My husband is Jewish," said Alexandra, "but he doesn't expect me to observe the rules of his religion, and to tell you the truth, I don't think I would, even if he asked."

"And if you lived in a country where it was the law?"

"I'd leave him," said Alexandra who believed it was the truth, though she could no longer even imagine a life without Neil Goodman.

Keeping Aziz amused by letting him try to catch her dangling earrings, Katrinka said nothing. At St. Moritz, at Christmas, Natalie had told her that in Riyadh she could not drive a car herself, or go out alone, and that if she appeared in public with too much bare skin she might be struck in the street by the slender sticks of the religious police. Katrinka

466

had been as horrified then as her friends were now, but in the intervening months had decided that if Natalie was content it was pointless for her to worry.

"How can I do that?" said Natalie. "I love him. And you know," she added brightly, "we have a house in London, a chalet in St. Moritz, an apartment in Paris. We are almost never in Saudi. And for the little bit of time we are, it is not terrible. It is like dressing up for a costume party. *C'est vrai.* It is like living in the *Thousand and One Nights.*"

No one found the idea appealing, however romantic Natalie tried to make it sound. Katrinka and Zuzka, who had lived a large part of their lives under a repressive political system, were unable to think of any restrictions on freedom as "amusing." And the others, who had suffered only the limitations of insufficient money or parental consent or the subtle sexism that pervades American society, could not bear the idea of losing any of their hard-won liberties. However, they all realized it was not possible to continue arguing the subject with Natalie as if it were an abstract problem of women's rights as opposed to the reality of her life. If she was happy with her husband and son, who were they to tell her that she shouldn't be?

"Yes," said Daisy, wanting to restore the equilibrium of the room, "I can see you might enjoy that. The customs of other countries are always so fascinating."

"When in Rome . . ." said Margo graciously, agreeing that the conversation should end.

Katrinka waited for Margo to finish the sentence and when she didn't asked, "When in Rome what?"

"Do as the Romans do," finished Margo, laughing.

"Ah," said Zuzka, who also had not understood the expression, "a proverb."

Katrinka laughed. "I think I know this language, and all of a sudden you say something and I do have no idea what you mean."

"What you don't know isn't much," said Margo.

"And it certainly hasn't held you back any," said Lucia.

"I would give anything," said Daisy, who was still trying to master Italian, "to speak as many languages as you do, as well as you do. Americans are hopeless."

"That is because," said Katrinka, "you think the United States is the center of the universe."

"When everyone else knows it is really France," said Natalie.

They all laughed and, to everyone's relief, the tension suddenly was gone. Then Aziz began to fuss, Natalie declared him hungry, called for the nurse, someone noticed the time, and the women abandoned the dining room for the various guest bathrooms in order to prepare themselves for the afternoon's activities.

After attending two more shows with her friends, Katrinka left them for an executive committee meeting at the New York Graham, going from there to the Praha to deal with whatever paperwork and phone calls had piled up in her absence. She called the London Graham, where occupancy was slightly down though the casino was doing well, reviewed with Robin the details of the following week's Metropolitan Opera fund-raising gala, which Katrinka was chairing, then returned home to shower for the second time that day before dinner at Mortimer's with Natalie and Prince Khalid, who had returned from Kentucky.

"Are you and Adam always like this?" asked Zuzka, lapsing into Czech as she and Katrinka sat in the apartment's cozy, softly lit library, drinking Campari and sodas, waiting for Adam to finish dressing. He had returned late from the day in Miami, which he had spent with his head designer from New York, the Miami design team, and a crew of accountants, reviewing the details of a proposal for a multimillion-dollar contract for a new, fast, electronically sophisticated, heavily armed Coast Guard patrol boat.

"Like what?"

"Never still for a minute."

Katrinka shook her head. "Sometimes we collapse. We go to Cap Ferrat and sleep for a week, or take the *Lady Katrinka* for a cruise. I go to the Canyon Spa Ranch or Saturnia Doral to get back into shape, and Adam goes sailing. But we like to work. We get bored when we have nothing to do."

"I love it. I must force myself to work. But Martin, he's that way. He must always be busy, playing football, basketball, like a real American kid, jogging, working out. And Tomáš, he goes out of his mind when he's not directing." She picked up her glass and took a sip of her drink, a way to make herself stop talking. But when she put the glass down again, she continued, "Katrinka, I'm worried about Tomáš. Very worried. Something terrible is happening to him. He's so depressed all the time, and when he's not depressed, he's angry. He's awful to Martin, and to me. And now that I'm finally used to living in Los Angeles, finally *like* it, he hates it. He says coming to America was a terrible mistake. Martin feels so guilty. He's beginning to believe he ruined his father's life by being sick."

"That's crazy," said Katrinka.

"I know, I know, but you try talking sense to a sixteen-year-old boy."

"Tomáš is so talented," said Katrinka reassuringly. "He's sure to find work soon."

"I used to think so. Now I don't know."

"Does he need a new agent?"

"He's tried. No one's interested in him. Katrinka, you should see what he's like. You'd hardly recognize him. He's rude, surly, to everyone. He's a monster."

"Is he drinking?"

"No, not in the way you mean, not like a real alcoholic. But there are women. I can smell them on him when he comes home." Zuzka's eyes filled with tears and she opened her purse to rummage for a handkerchief. "I don't know what I'm going to do."

"Zuzka, *zlatíčko*, it doesn't mean anything," said Katrinka. She got up to sit beside Zuzka on the banquette. "His ego is wounded, that's all. And making love to a pretty young girl makes him believe for a little while that he's not such a failure."

"Sometimes I think I hate him."

"*Zlatíčko, zlatíčko,* he'll come to his senses," said Katrinka soothingly, not because she believed it, but because it was the only thing to say in the circumstances. She put her arms around Zuzka. "He'll stop being such a fool. He loves you, and Martin. And he *is* talented. Someone will realize it sooner or later."

Zuzka wept against Katrinka's shoulder for a moment, then suddenly pulled her head back and laughed, embarrassed. "That dress cost a fortune, and look at me, I'm ruining it."

"You're not," said Katrinka. "Anyway, it doesn't matter."

"Ready?" said Adam, stepping into the doorway, looking fit and handsome and not in the least tired from his round-trip to Miami and the long day of intense meetings. He noticed Zuzka's red eyes, smiled sympathetically, and said, "Would you like me to leave and come back again in ten minutes?"

Zuzka laughed. "No, no. I did cry enough. Now I want to eat."

Katrinka stood, went to Adam, slid her arms around his waist and kissed him lightly on the lips. "You look very handsome tonight," she said. "A new suit?"

"No. A new dress?" There was just a hint of disapproval in his voice.

"No," she replied, trying not to frown, letting her arms drop to her side. "It's the Carolina Herrera you did buy me for my birthday two years ago. Remember?" Lately, it seemed to her that Adam, whom she had relied on so long for sympathy and support, took whatever opportunity he could to criticize her, subtly as now, or much more openly, alone and in company. He had, for example, begun to follow Nina Graham's line that Katrinka spent too much money on clothes. Well, she did spend a lot, but it was *her* money. She had earned it. And did she try to stop his spending a fortune on new sailboats? Or kick up a fuss when he went out in them, risking his life?

"Oh, yes," said Adam, lying, "I thought it looked familiar. Well," he said, "let's get this show on the road. Where are we having dinner?" he asked as he escorted them toward the door, helped them into their wraps, and out the front door to the elevator.

"Mortimer's," said Katrinka. Adam frowned. He had

decided to dislike Mortimer's for no other reason than to be difficult, Katrinka thought, but before he could complain, she added quickly, "Khalid did want to go there."

He shrugged. "Can't be helped, I suppose." His official position was that they dined out too often, but most of the dinners were business—his business—even that night's, when the purpose was not really for Katrinka to see Natalie, but for Adam to seduce Khalid into ordering another yacht.

"It did seem rude to refuse," agreed Katrinka, eager to avoid even a minor disagreement.

At Mortimer's, Glenn Birnbaum greeted them at the door and ushered them to their table, in the front room of course. It was just the five of them for dinner, Natalie and Khalid, Katrinka, Zuzka, and Adam. Superficially it was a pleasant evening. Khalid, even in Western dress, was incredibly good to look at in his dark and soulful way, enormously considerate, and very charming. Natalie looked splendid in a gold lamé dress by Scherer, her emerald necklace and earrings (though probably not nearly as expensive) outdazzling Katrinka's twenty-carat yellow diamond pin and making Zuzka's fake pearls fade to insignificance, not that she cared. Dressing to compete with her friends was the last thing on Zuzka's mind.

The conversation was light. They talked about horses, skiing, yachting, who had run into whom where, the Aga Khan and his kidnapped racehorse, Alan Bond and the America's Cup. Katrinka laughed and joked, contributed her share of gossip, and wondered why she was not enjoying herself, then realized it was because of the way Adam's eyes had clouded briefly when Natalie and Khalid began to play the proud parents and rave about Aziz. He was Khalid's only son.

The peace Adam and Katrinka thought they had made with themselves and life about not having a child had turned out to be only a cease-fire, broken from time to time by uncontrollable surges of longing; and while once it had been Katrinka who most desperately wanted a baby, now their positions had reversed and it was Adam who bitterly regretted their childlessness. Not that he understood this. His sense of deprivation was vague and unspecified, expressing itself in a general irritability, a free-floating discontent that focused from time to time on incidental details, causing him to overreact to a typographical error in a letter typed by his secretary, to a steak not the precise shade of pink he liked, to a host of small inconveniences. But it was Katrinka who caught the brunt of his anger. It was as if, in failing to produce a child, she had shown herself to be inadequate in every other area. In his opinion, she could do nothing right anymore: she talked when he needed to be quiet, was silent when he wanted her to speak; she was always free to travel with him when her presence would be inconvenient, and never when he would have liked her company; she accepted invitations to events when he would have preferred to stay home, and turned them down when he thought it would be good for business to attend; when what she wore attracted the attention of the press, he accused her of being extravagant and, when it did not, of turning into a frump. The result was, they were both miserable.

To hide the black mood that had overtaken him, Adam flirted with Zuzka and Natalie, not enough to annoy Khalid, who tended to be jealous, but sufficient to let everyone know all was not well between him and his wife. Katrinka pretended not to notice and talked with Khalid until she was genuinely distracted from her own problems by the entrance of Sugar Benson Elliott, though without Steven, whom she had divorced at the beginning of the year. Her escort was Count Paolo di Cortina, with his small frail body, taut lifted face, and thick mop of fake hair looking for all the world like a cuckolded husband from an Italian farce.

"Oh la la," murmured Natalie who spotted them a moment after Katrinka did.

"Oh, Christ," muttered Adam.

"Oh no," said Katrinka, "they are coming this way."

"Why, hello, you all," drawled Sugar, smiling as if certain they were delighted to see her. "How nice to run into you. You know Paolo, don't you? Count Paolo di Cortina, my fiancé?"

"We did meet, I think," said Katrinka, "in Venice a few years ago."

"Hello, Sugar," said Adam, kissing her cheek gallantly. "Looking gorgeous as ever." Her honey-colored hair was hanging loose in soft waves. Her eyes were heavily made up and her lips were full, pouting, and wet with gloss. She was wearing a Bob Mackie dress that draped her body like a second skin, a heavy gold necklace and bracelet from JAR in Paris, and a cushion-shaped diamond engagement ring that was well over twenty carats. The overall effect should have been cheap, but wasn't. The twenty-nine-year-old Sugar carried herself like a queen.

"Piacere," murmured the count as Adam introduced him and Sugar to Zuzka. Sugar barely paid her any attention, writing her off as insignificant.

"Remember to give my love to Daisy," said Sugar, as she and the count moved off, following the maître d' to their table.

"An interesting woman," said Khalid speculatively as he watched her undulate away.

"Chienne," muttered Natalie, making Khalid and Adam laugh.

"Who are they?" asked Zuzka. Katrinka explained quickly, and Zuzka's eyes grew wide. "Some man was stupid enough to leave Daisy for that whore?" she asked.

"That mouth could make a man think of doing some very strange things," said Adam.

"Not only *think,"* said Katrinka in Czech, repeating the rumors she had heard about Sugar and Steven's sex life.

"Does Daisy know?" asked Zuzka.

"She must," said Katrinka, "but we never talk about it."

"What are you saying?" asked Natalie.

"This is what I live with all the time," said Adam lightly, "Katrinka babbling nonstop in some language I don't understand."

"You could try to learn," said Katrinka in English before she could stop herself. Adam had not even bothered to learn Japanese, though his prediction had come true: Japan had become the United States' chief economic rival. She turned to Natalie. "I was explaining about Sugar and Steven."

Natalie's straight nose wrinkled in distaste. *"Ouff,* that poor fool. Maybe now that she's left him, he can get his life together."

Khalid shook his head and the others turned to him, demanding to know what he had heard. He shrugged, as if what he was about to say was commonplace. "Only that Steven has acquired some very odd tastes, which he continues to satisfy one way or another."

"He was the most perfect gentleman," said Katrinka to Zuzka. "A good husband, father. It's so hard to believe someone did change that much."

"If he's happy," said Adam with a shrug.

"He looked ill," said Khalid, "when I saw him in Paris."

"He has looked that way a long time," said Natalie.

"Daisy did see him, too," said Katrinka, "and is very worried."

"The mess people do make of their lives," said Zuzka, careful not to look at anyone as she said it.

Getting ready for bed that night, Katrinka and Adam wondered about the probability of Khalid's buying a new yacht and what had become of Khalid's first wife since no one ever mentioned her, and if Count Paolo di Cortina would live long enough to marry Sugar. If she was working him as hard as she had Steven, said Adam, he for one wouldn't bet on it.

What they did not discuss was anything that was really on their minds, above all, the state of their marriage. Adam changed into silk paisley pajamas, Katrinka into a black teddy. They got into bed, turned out the light, and made love. It was the way they convinced themselves that everything was all right.

Thirty-Seven

The next morning Adam left for Europe. Katrinka would have liked to go with him. She wanted to check on the hotel and casino in London and see Paul Zeiss in Paris, and though she had far too much to do in New York right then to leave, she would have had Adam suggested it. But he didn't, and she felt reluctant to ask. So once he had gone, and Zuzka had returned to Los Angeles, Katrinka buried her worries, as she always did, by keeping busy. She slept little, spent at least ten hours a day attending to business, and the rest of the time socializing with friends. Daisy had a dinner for sixteen at the apartment she kept in New York for her occasional use. Another night John and Susan Gutfreund hosted a party for twenty-four. Katrinka spent the weekend with the Goodmans at the estate in Pound Ridge that they had just bought. Otherwise, she dined at the usual restaurants and went dancing afterward at Le Club. Always good-natured and optimistic, she let her troubled ego be soothed by a stream of dinner partners, a retinue of international businessmen—successful, rich, often handsome, all flatteringly attentive—who were either business associates of her own or provided for her by her hosts. She laughed and flirted, but kept her escorts at arm's length. Whatever her problems with Adam, Katrinka had no sexual interest in anyone but him, and never doubted that he felt the same.

As he had promised, Adam returned in time for the Metropolitan Opera gala. As chairperson, Katrinka had spent months organizing the event, pulling off a major coup when, accompanied by a member of the board with business contacts in Japan, she had flown to Tokyo and convinced the government there to underwrite it as a public-relations venture.

This time, Katrinka had decided to forgo Carlos Medina's help and use a Japanese designer to achieve an authentic environment. It was a nightmare to plan and organize, but she had surrounded herself with reliable people, and, by the day of the gala, with the usual number of last-minute crises, all was done. The huge tent erected next to the Opera House had been divided into dining and display areas, each decorated in a distinctly Japanese motif, with rock gardens, bamboo fountains, and carp ponds as well as a teahouse with rice-paper walls and tatami floors. There were displays of Japanese textiles, antique kimonos, modern fashions; exhibitions of Nintendo games and Sony's new digital tape; demonstrations of the latest computer technology; an abbreviated Kabuki performance, and another by Kodo, the drummers; food of incomparable delicacy prepared by master chefs; a Japanese rock band for those who wanted to dance; and a top-of-the-line Toyota (for use as a second car, of course) as a door prize.

Everyone came, international jet-setters, politicians, the heads of multinational corporations, stars of stage and screen, New York socialites, Hollywood moguls, and, of course, the press, mixing and matching with one another, delighted at the chance to rub shoulders with celebrities from other realms, film stars trying to corner politicians, politicians to court business executives, business executives to cozy up to film stars.

"How you think it's going?" Katrinka asked Daisy as they moved through the crowd, her observant eyes assessing every detail, prepared to spring into action should anything be wrong. She could see Robin talking to one of the caterers. Her sister-in-law Clementine and her husband, Wilson, were with the Bill Buckleys, singing hymns, she imagined, to Ronald Reagan. Ted stood admiring the Japanese garden with Carroll Petrie while Margo chatted to Princess Yasmin

Khan and Beverly Sills to the Gutfreunds. Having coaxed Ed Koch out from under the earphones of the Sony demonstration, Nick was lecturing him, presumably about the flaws in the city's crime-enforcement program, while Lucia tried to ignore what her husband was up to and pay attention to Richard Gere, who was flirting with her. Bjorn Lindstrom was playing electronic basketball with a beautiful long-legged woman in a black balloon-skirted minidress, whom Katrinka recognized as the star of a recent teenybopper film. Alexandra, giving Akio Morita the benefit of her best smile, was probably trying to interest him in the Rembrandt she had heard was coming up for sale, while her husband stood with Ace Greenberg and Prince Khalid, each no doubt trying to maneuver some piece of valuable financial information out of the other. Natalie was dancing with Adam, flashing like a Roman candle as her jewels caught the light when she moved.

"Everyone's having a marvelous time. Relax," said Daisy, who, at fifty, and thanks to the skilled fingers of Stephen Hoefflin, the Los Angeles plastic surgeon, looked a good ten years younger than she was in a new short-length evening dress of chocolate-brown silk and ostrich feathers.

Katrinka was also in a short evening gown—a turquoise embroidered Japanese silk designed by Kenzo. Around her neck and woven in her hair, she wore ropes of Japanese pearls. "Do me a favor," she ordered as her eyes suddenly hit on something that required fixing. "Go rescue Placido from Sabrina. He does look desperate."

"Certainly," said Daisy, going to do as instructed. "Greater love than this hath no woman," she muttered to herself, taking a glass of champagne from a passing tray. "Hello, Sabrina," she said, moving between the two. "How lovely to see you. Placido, darling, I do think Zubin was looking for you. He wanted to introduce you to someone or other."

Trying not to appear too grateful for the interruption, Placido excused himself and hurried off, as Sabrina, surprised to be greeted so cordially, said, "Why, Daisy, don't you look stunning. St. Laurent?"

477

"Hmmm," acknowledged Daisy, "and you're wearing . . . That is a Galanos?" As usual, with Sabrina, it was difficult to tell: her lumpy body did the oddest things with clothes.

Sabrina nodded, then peered curiously around the room. "And where is the beautiful Bjorn?"

"Oh, around," replied Daisy, waving a hand, "flirting with a starlet no doubt, or trying to convince a Hollywood agent he has talent."

"Does he?"

"An absolutely breathtaking amount, and you can quote me."

Sabrina laughed but her eyes stayed cold and inquisitive. "So does Sugar Benson, I hear."

"I don't doubt it for a minute," replied Daisy who had expected an attack from Sabrina and refused to be rattled by it. "I only hope Paolo di Cortina can fully appreciate it."

"Sugar told me their wedding is scheduled for as soon as the divorce is final, at the family palazzo."

"How lovely for them," said Daisy, smiling. "I do hope they'll be happy. Such a well-matched couple, don't you think? Now, if you'll excuse me. I see friends I must say hello to."

"See you soon again, I hope," said Sabrina. "Perhaps next time with Steven?"

The audacity of that almost took Daisy's breath away, but she recovered quickly. "Oh, I shouldn't think so," she said cheerfully, moving quickly away before she was tempted to hit the woman. In Daisy's opinion the world would be a much better place without either Sabrina or Sugar Benson. Poor Steven, she thought. Now that her anger was spent, the strongest emotion she ever felt for her former husband was pity. He had looked so thin and tired when she had seen him in Paris, but he claimed to be well and not in the least sorry either to have married Sugar or to have been left by her. She had opened up a new world to him, he had told Daisy, removed him from his stuffy, predictable life and introduced him to adventure. For that he was grateful. But he had no illusions about her character: she was mercenary and manipulative, and he was happy that she had left before running through all his money, leaving him free to pursue his own interests without fear of imminent bankruptcy. What those interests were, he did not elaborate on, though Daisy had a good idea, having heard enough gossip over the years.

"You look so sad," said Bjorn, as he came up to her and slipped an arm around her waist. "Were you missing me?"

"Yes," said Daisy, forcing a smile. He was so sweet, almost thirty now. Though she had not yet marshaled the determination to do anything about it, she had been thinking for some time that he ought to leave the nest and get on with his own life. Her motive was not purely unselfish. If she was to be perfectly honest, she was a little bored by him. As much as she appreciated his attentiveness, and his very great skill in bed, they did not after all have much in common. Was he faithful? she wondered. Was he brave enough not to be? "Who were you talking to?"

"An actress. She was telling me about Hollywood. Daisy, it sounds awful, and wonderful, like the most interesting place in the world. We really should go there, you know."

"Well," said Daisy, "certainly you should, since you want to so much."

Bjorn's smooth pale face wrinkled in dismay, his blue eyes turned smoky. "Are you trying to get rid of me?"

Daisy lost her courage and laughed. "Of course not. What in the world would I do without you?"

Watching Daisy as she turned to Bjorn and kissed him lightly on the mouth, Nina Graham frowned in disapproval. "Really, whoever would have thought Daisy would turn into such an old fool?" she said to Katrinka.

"She is only fifty."

"He's still young enough to be her son."

Katrinka's blue eyes glittered with anger but she controlled it and said, "They make each other happy."

"For such a hardheaded businesswoman, you are a terrible romantic," said Nina, downing her champagne and quickly replacing her empty glass with a full one from a passing waiter's tray. Though she meant her remark to be critical, she could not quite keep the admiration from her voice. Looking around, she added, "You're having quite a success tonight." Sometimes it astounded her what her daughter-in-law was able to achieve.

"I hope so," said Katrinka. "It is for a good cause."

"You genuinely like opera, don't you?"

"Yes."

"That's so surprising, isn't it, for someone coming from your background?"

"Maybe," said Katrinka, smiling, having grown over the years to expect an endless stream of barbed comments from Nina. "But not as surprising as Adam hating it. With all the advantages he did have."

"Oh, yes," agreed Nina with easy disapproval, "he's quite the Philistine, my son."

Malcolm Forbes interrupted them, his face flushed with champagne, his hair falling forward onto his forehead. He complimented Katrinka on her gown, on her pearls, on the success of the gala, on her business expertise, and Adam's knack for making money. He hinted he might be ordering a yacht from Adam, so impressed was he with the design of the *Lady Katrinka* and a subsequent one Adam had built for Prince Bandar of Saudi Arabia. When he had finished heaping praise, he asked Nina Graham to dance, leaving Katrinka to Rick Colins, who claimed her as soon as she was free.

"Great band," he said, as he led her onto the floor. He looked like an English schoolboy in evening dress, with dark trousers, a cutaway coat, and a black silk scarf tied in an elegantly drooping bow.

Katrinka nodded. "I did hear them when I was in Tokyo." She caught sight of Adam dancing with the actress with whom Bjorn had been playing electronic games earlier in the evening. Every eye on the floor seemed to focus on them, she noticed.

What she did not notice was that everyone not watching Adam was watching her. In a room full of stars, they still commanded attention—because they were young and attractive, because the aura of success surrounding them drew people as powerfully as a magnet, because (with the possible exception of Akio Morita and Prince Khalid, about whom no one particularly cared) they were thought to be the richest people there.

"You are all right?" Katrinka asked Rick when they paused to catch their breath. Instead of brimming over with his usual boyish enthusiasm, he seemed a little subdued to Katrinka, even worried. "You did tangle with Sabrina," she added, suddenly concerned that her beautifully planned gala was going to be pulled to shreds by dueling columnists.

"Not yet," he said, with a spark of sudden enthusiasm. He and Sabrina loathed each other, not only because they were rivals for the same limited and trivial information about who was where with whom wearing what, but because each was what the other most despised. To Sabrina, Rick was a privileged elitist writing puff pieces about other privileged elitists, while, to Rick, Sabrina was a lower-class snob (the worst kind) determined to trash the people she envied even if she had to lie to do it. When Mark van Hollen had decided to run her column in *The Chronicle*, Rick had had no choice but to quit, and for a brief moment Sabrina believed she had won. But, since then, Rick's career had expanded into magazines and television with a syndicated interview show on Channel 11 in New York. And though Sabrina never stopped trying to get a program of her own, no television executive had yet been adventurous enough to give even a half-hour chat show to someone who always looked as if she had not changed her clothes in a week. Worse, Sabrina suspected that people actually liked Rick while they only pretended to care for her. That suspicion made her vindictive and she was inevitably harshest in her column to the people, like Katrinka, to whom Rick was closest.

"No argument here, please," said Katrinka. "I do want this to be a perfect night."

"I wouldn't do that to you," said Rick. "God, I need a cigarette. I wish I hadn't given up smoking." He gestured with his champagne glass to where Carlos was talking to a tall, fair man, who looked very distinguished and rather foreign and asked in as neutral a voice as he could manage, "Do you know who that is with Carlos?"

So that's it, thought Katrinka, relieved. He's jealous. She looked where Rick had pointed and said, "Yes. Carlos and I did meet him when we were working on the London Graham. He's Sir Alex Holden-White. A curator at the Victoria and Albert museum."

"I see," said Rick.

"He has a lover," added Katrinka. "Someone famous, whose name I forget. He writes biographies."

"Oh," said Rick, sounding relieved. "I should go over and say hello."

Rick and Carlos were another of those couples Katrinka considered so stable that nothing could come between them, but the look on Rick's face reminded her that she had been wrong in the past. "You should," she agreed. "Let's go, I'll introduce you."

When she had done that, she returned to the disco to dance with Khalid, with Placido Domingo, with Ted Jensen, then excused herself to begin another survey, moving from group to group, making sure that Akio Morita was still enjoying himself, that no one looked lost or lonely because such a person might never again be coaxed into giving a vast sum of money to a cause, no matter how worthy. It was growing late, and she was starting to feel tired, wishing that everyone would stop having quite so much fun and begin to go home.

Governor Cuomo was the first to oblige her, leaving with his wife, Matilda. Katrinka looked around briefly for Adam, wanting him to say good-bye to the governor, but he was nowhere in sight. Half an hour later, when the crowd had significantly thinned, she still had not found him. She was just beginning to wonder if he had perhaps gone home without her, and even to worry that he had been taken ill, when she was waylaid by Sabrina, smiling coquettishly, her little ferret's eyes glinting with curiosity. "What *do* you suppose Adam and Mike Ovitz have been talking about for the past hour?"

Katrinka smiled politely and said, "Sailing, probably. Nothing else interests Adam that much."

"Not even money?"

Katrinka laughed. "Especially not money," she said, and continued chatting with Sabrina for a few moments, trying to keep the conversation light and friendly, not that she had much hope of wringing a word of anything but the faintest praise from the woman, but why offend anyone deliberately? As soon as she could, Katrinka made her escape, and, seeing Alexandra, stopped her. "Who Mike Ovitz is?" she asked.

"He runs one of the big agencies out on the West Coast. A major Hollywood power broker. Why?"

"Someone mentioned his name, that's all."

"I saw him talking to Adam a little while ago," said Alexandra. "Near the teahouse."

Curious, Katrinka headed for the teahouse but, when she got there, Adam had already left. She found him finally, dancing again with the actress in the minidress.

It was not until the gala ended and they were home getting ready for bed that Katrinka learned what had kept Adam talking to a Hollywood agent for so long. He had told Ovitz he was in the market for a film studio.

"You are serious?" said Katrinka, pulling a robe on over her transparent teddy. She knew she was about to break her own rule not to interfere in Adam's business plans, and knew that by doing it she ran the risk of forcing him to proceed. But for once she could not keep her mouth shut.

"Very," said Adam. "It's an interesting business, expanding all the time. Cable and video are breaking it wide open."

"It's a crazy business. Completely crazy," she said, echoing Zuzka.

"What do you know about it?" he asked as he folded his evening clothes neatly and hung them up. He was beginning to sound irritated, as he always did when someone challenged a decision he was determined to make.

"As much as you. Maybe more." Because of Mirek and Tomáš she had followed the entertainment industry, not closely but with interest, in the financial pages of the papers she read. "It's not like other businesses. It's much, much riskier. There are no rules, no formulas for success." Her voice was low-pitched and steady, but the words tumbled out of her mouth in a rapid flow. She was not sure of all the reasons why she felt so strongly that Adam's buying a studio was a bad idea, but she did know that, in addition to the film industry being too unpredictable, for people with major business interests in Europe, Los Angeles was three thousand miles in the wrong direction. "People guess, and if they do guess right, they win. Mostly they lose. Like roulette."

"So far you and I have done all right with gambling." The cruise ships he had converted to casinos had made him another fortune, and the casino in the London Graham had become one of London's "in" spots. "I don't see any reason to stop now."

Katrinka sat on the turned-down bed, her legs crossed under her, watching him get into his pajamas. "It's not the same. In gambling the odds are with the house."

"You think I don't know what I'm doing?" he asked, his voice angry, his eyes alight with rage.

She avoided answering directly. "You know I do never interfere . . ."

"Then, goddamnit, don't start . . ."

"You will make a terrible mistake," she said, her voice rising to match his.

"Because you fucked a film director once you think you're an expert?"

"No! Because I read *The New York Times* and *The Wall Street Journal,* like you. Why you do say such terrible things to me?"

"Why *do* you say," he corrected angrily, adding, "Because I want you to keep the hell out of my business."

"Your business *is* my business. We're married, remember?"

"If you only knew how much sometimes I'd like to forget," he said, turning barefooted and stalking out of the room, slamming the door shut behind him.

Uncrossing her legs, Katrinka stretched out on the bed, staring at the closed door. Her pleasure in the evening's success had evaporated with Adam's anger. Tears welled in her eyes but she felt too tired, too disheartened, even to cry. It was not just that his words had hurt her or that she was upset about his plans. In other marriages, she knew, people had disagreements which they argued out, sometimes one partner conceding, sometimes the other. People compromised. But her own marriage was not like that. Not only would Adam not even listen to an opinion contrary to his own, but he always did exactly what he wanted, no matter whom he inconvenienced or hurt in the process. In business, he got away with it because of his success; in his personal relationships because, when getting his way, he was extremely supportive in helping others get theirs.

Katrinka had learned early that for the sake of peace she had to let Adam go his own way, and for the most part, she didn't mind. His sailing continued to terrify her, but once she had understood how much he loved the sport, she had stopped pestering him about it. If he asked her advice she gave it; if she saw a potential problem in a business deal, she pointed it out, but always tried not to challenge him. Watching Nina Graham, she had learned that confronting Adam head-on only made him more determined to follow whatever course he had set.

Reaching up, Katrinka turned out the light and lay with her eyes open, staring into the dark. There was no point even attempting to make things up with Adam now. He was too angry. He would sit in the library for a while watching television and either fall asleep there or go to bed in one of the guest rooms. Over the next few days, they might continue to argue, but neither one's position would shift. Eventually, one or the other would call a truce, Katrinka most likely, and they would apologize for having lost their tempers, pick up the pieces, and get on with their lives. But Adam would have his film studio.

Thirty-Eight

*T*he brochure did not do the hotel justice. It did not at
all capture the beauty of its landscaped park, the elegance of
the public rooms, the luxury and charm of the guest
accommodations. Even the splendid art nouveau casino was
made to look dull and uninteresting. Whoever had hired the
photographer ought to be fired, thought Katrinka, and the
photographer banned from taking pictures.

In reality, the hotel was enchanting. It had been built in
the last quarter of the nineteenth century, renovated extensively at the height of Deauville's popularity as a resort, and
modernized from time to time since then. Making it even
more attractive, the twenty-five acres of property on which
the hotel was set could be subdivided and sold as individual
building sites.

Her real estate contact at Sotheby's had advised Katrinka
that the hotel was for sale, and on their return from a trip
that included stops in Athens, Bremen, and Cap Ferrat,
Adam and she had stopped off in Deauville to see it. His
immediate advice had been to buy. Not only was the price
good, but an instant profit could be made subdividing and
selling the property. Katrinka was tempted. The hotel's Old
World charm had appealed to her at once and she could see
vividly what she would make of it with Carlos's help. Still,
she hesitated.

"What you think?" she said to Carlos, handing him the
brochure to look at.

They were in her office at the London Graham, seated

facing each other on chintz-covered sofas, a tray of tea with scones and cream on the antique table between them. On the windows were matching chintz curtains, the side tables and armchairs as well as Katrinka's desk had the delicately bowed legs of Queen Anne furniture, and on the yellow-painted walls below the dentillated cornices hung engravings and aquatints of picnic scenes, boating parties, tranquil landscapes, and Palladian mansions. It might have been the sitting room of an English country house.

"The hotel must have been a grand old place in its heyday," said Carlos, leafing through the brochure, trying to gauge its potential from the inadequate photographs he was looking at.

"You would love it."

Carlos smiled, his large spaniel's eyes alight with amusement. "When have I ever disagreed with you?"

Katrinka laughed. "All the time," she said, observing him fondly, admiring the way the cream linen Ralph Lauren suit and rust T-shirt set off his striking Latin looks. "The headaches you give me!"

"You know your every wish is my command."

"Ha!"

For over ten years they had worked together, successfully creating the three Graham hotels as well as the New York apartment and the Villa Mahmed. In that time, they had developed enormous respect and affection for one another, and had learned to understand each other's moods. "Usually when you've found a new place you go off like a cannon," said Carlos. "Nothing holds you back. This time you seem hesitant. What's wrong?"

Katrinka shrugged. "Maybe I get lazy."

"I think it's my turn to say 'ha'!"

"No, I'm serious. Why give myself more work? more trouble? And with the economy the way it is . . ." The bull market had ended in October of 1987, taking a steep dive, wiping out fortunes. Eight months later, the Grahams were still holding on, but if there wasn't a turnaround soon, Katrinka was not sure what would happen. "The trouble is I hate to pass up a bargain. And Adam thinks I should buy."

Carlos resisted the temptation to point out that Adam

always wanted to buy, that he was one of the most acquisitive men in the world, and said only, "Well, there can't be any hurry. Nothing's selling fast these days. Let me know if you want me to go take a look at it."

"I will."

They both stood and Katrinka walked with him to the door. "Have you seen Rick lately?" asked Carlos, not quite able to disguise the strain in his voice. Rick and he had separated a year before and Carlos was now living in London with Alex Holden-White, the museum curator. Rick had taken the breakup badly. From a social butterfly, he had turned into a worker ant, performing all necessary tasks diligently, methodically, but with none of his former gusto. He made his magazine deadlines on time, but the spark had gone; his writing commissions declined steadily, his television show began to sink in the ratings, he slept only with the aid of Halcion, and his love life came to a dead stop. Heartbroken over Carlos, he claimed he wasn't interested in sex; but there was more to it than that: the AIDS epidemic was decimating the ranks of his homosexual friends and he was terrified. But in the last month or so, Rick had seemed to be making a comeback. If he wasn't yet ready to plunge into a new affair, at least his sense of humor had returned. He was turning up at parties, looking as boyishly handsome as ever. A few people claimed to have seen him laughing.

"I did see him at a party just before I left New York," said Katrinka, who was fond of both men, but whose sympathies in this case lay very much with Rick.

"And?" prompted Carlos.

"He was fine," said Katrinka.

"I'm glad to hear it." Carlos was fond of Rick, too fond, in Alex Holden-White's opinion. There were times when he missed him very much. He could never laugh with Alex as he had with Rick. But then, with Rick, he could not have had the sort of satisfying intellectual discussions he and Alex shared, or had entrée to Alex's world, where conversations about art and music, economics and politics were considered more interesting than gossip. Was there any such thing as the perfect mate? wondered Carlos, as he leaned forward and kissed Katrinka's cheek. "It was great seeing you," he said. "If you have time while you're here, let's have lunch."

When Carlos had gone, Katrinka returned to the sofa, picked up the brochure from the table, and looked at it again. With the world economy in such bad shape, and with no recovery on the horizon, the hotel was being offered at much less than its real value. It was a good deal, but . . . No matter what Adam said, this was not the time to expand. The hotels were still making a profit, though if the economy continued to get worse, there was no way to avoid a sharp decline and Katrinka was already cost-cutting to stave off sinking too far into the red. The Graham small-boat sales were holding steady and its naval defense contracts on the rise because of the recently declared "war on drugs" and the increased commitment throughout most of the world to greater military spending. However, tanker and cruise ship revenues were down, as well as the revenue from luxury yacht sales, and the newly acquired Olympic Pictures Corporation was still operating at a loss. To Katrinka, 1988 seemed a good year to be prudent.

That, however, was not the real reason for her reluctance to buy the hotel in Deauville. No matter how good the teams she assembled to staff her properties, or her homes, overseeing them still took a great deal of time, as did her commitment to Children of the Streets and the other organizations whose boards she was on. To add another business to her hectic schedule would be madness when Adam and she already saw too little of each other. Sometimes it seemed to her that the only time they actually talked was aboard the Graham jet, and then only when one or the other of them was not on the phone. The days when they had made love surreptitiously on airplanes were a distant, happy, rather unreal memory. Now, even with a cabin containing a queen-sized bed, they never did, falling into it instead determined to sleep so as to be clearheaded for negotiating whatever business deal lay at the end of the journey. After eleven years of marriage, reasoned Katrinka, that was only to be expected. At least they still made love, unlike Tomáš and Zuzka, unlike a great many people Katrinka knew who seemed to have eliminated sex from their married lives; and if Katrinka and Adam's lovemaking lacked the enthusiasm and fire and frequency of their early days together, when it happened it was still satisfying. Their time apart made their reunions exciting. It kept their sex life from growing dull.

But it also kept their emotional life from becoming deeper, or more intimate. When Adam and Katrinka did talk, if not about friends or family, their conversation concerned business. They never discussed themselves, their marriage, their continuing childlessness, what pain they felt because of it, glossing over their hopes as well as their fears. And if in business they gave each other valuable advice and emotional support, backing each other all the way even when the decision, as with the film studio, was a disputed one, in every other area they had little understanding of one another and nothing in common except for skiing, which they both enjoyed. Katrinka loathed sailing, Adam only tolerated the opera. Adam loved contemporary art, Katrinka had more traditional tastes. Though Katrinka was hardworking and ambitious, she was not aggressive. Adam was all three: it was he who had the killer instinct. Even their attitudes toward their social life reflected this difference—Katrinka enjoying it because she was by nature gregarious and liked to mingle with interesting, successful people, Adam cultivating it resentfully because it might help him make his next deal.

What Adam and Katrinka had, rather than a marriage, was a business partnership with sex thrown in. And on those terms the relationship was a success. Katrinka, however, wanted more. Despite her habitual reticence, her tendency to play her emotional cards very close to her chest, she craved the sort of intimacy her parents had had with each other, that she had had with them, where anger and resentment flared and receded, where disagreements were fought over and resolved without the threat of love's withdrawal.

Adam, too, wanted more, though far from sure what that might be. All he knew was that he felt perpetually restless, and that each successful coup he pulled off failed to ease his dissatisfaction. Nothing ever lived up to his expectations. Life, he felt, was constantly shortchanging him.

There was, of course, no way they could give each other what they wanted. Adam was incapable of the sort of intimacy, the kind of all-accepting love, that Katrinka longed for. He could deal with her as an intelligent equal, as he had from their first meeting, but the barrier he had erected against his mother kept every other woman from getting close.

And nothing Katrinka could do, no way that she could be, would ever satisfy her husband. Even had she produced the child that he wanted, Adam, like his mother, would have found some other lack to feed his chronic discontent. But as Nina Graham's husband and children never stopped hoping that someday, somehow, they would manage to please her, Katrinka could not stop trying to make Adam happy. That had been the underlying motive of everything she had attempted and achieved since meeting him: she had wanted to be worthy of her husband, to make him proud of her; she had wanted to earn his admiration and keep his love. But despite all her efforts, he looked at her more and more often with a coldly critical eye and was increasingly harsh in his judgment of her—what she wore, what she did, what she said, how she said it. Her sometimes fractured English, which he used to think adorable, now only irritated him.

They said "I love you," and believed they meant it, though they never stopped to think whether or not the words remained true. Compared to other couples they knew, their problems seemed minimal, the result of stress, fatigue, the pressure of business, their hectic schedules. Work, they believed, was the culprit. And if neither could see a way to remedy the situation, Katrinka at least was determined not to make it worse. She tossed the prospectus for the Deauville hotel into the wastepaper basket beside her desk.

Later, as they were dressing for dinner, Katrinka told Adam of her decision, and he, of course, disagreed. His was the Wall Street philosophy of buying low, selling high, and not only did he think she was stupid to pass up such a bargain, he considered her refusal to take his advice a criticism of his business judgment. His irritation with her was obvious, but Katrinka was determined not to argue. She merely shrugged and said that she had more than enough work to keep her busy at the moment and in fact was looking for ways to lighten her load. What she would like, she told him, was to take a long vacation that summer, just the two of them, cruising on the *Lady Katrinka* to somewhere they had never been before.

Usually, the prospect of spending time on water was enough at least to tempt Adam, and Katrinka expected him to say it was a great idea and he'd try to arrange it. But instead he raised his eyes from the knot he was adjusting in his tie and looked at her in the mirror. Though his thick hair was flecked with white and his face had acquired a network of lines, still the image reflected back at her was of a youthful, handsome man, his arrogance and energy as powerful an aphrodisiac as ever. He flashed her a crooked smile and said, "Sorry, sweetheart, no can do. Business is too unstable right now for me to be out of touch."

Out of touch, thought Katrinka, with telephones, faxes, and a helicopter pad on the yacht? But again she didn't argue because she knew, though he would not admit to it, at least not to her, that he was particularly worried about Olympic Pictures. Though two of the summer releases were performing well at the box office, neither of them had been the needed blockbuster, and, while Adam and his executives in public professed great confidence, in private there was still a lot of nail-biting going on. The studio was a bottomless pit, requiring endless infusions of cash to keep it going. Without a big hit, in a tottering economy coming up with the capital was not easy. All hopes now were pinned on the films scheduled for a Christmas release, and it was his desire to oversee their production that made Adam reluctant to travel for any length of time.

"Maybe next year," said Katrinka.

Adam nodded. "This year, all I'll have time for is the Fastnet race in July. Will you come with me to Cowes or would you rather stay in Cap Ferrat?"

Either way she would worry, but at least at Cap Ferrat she

would not have to pretend to be enjoying herself as she always did at Cowes, surrounded by all those yachting enthusiasts. "I stay at Cap Ferrat, I think."

"Whatever you like," said Adam, turning to look at her. Although it was June, the weather was cool, and Katrinka was wearing a turquoise satin minidress and a long-sleeved short double-breasted yellow jacket by Jasper Conran, her only jewelry diamond ear clips, her wedding ring, and a large, cushion-shaped aquamarine ring set with diamonds. "You look lovely," he said without enthusiasm.

The Grahams were dining with Prince Khalid and Natalie at their house in Cheyne Walk, on that stretch of the Chelsea embankment overlooking the Thames where Mick Jagger had once owned a house and Paul Getty Jr. still did. It was a large, gracious red-brick Georgian house with nine-paned windows and a pedimented door, but its interior lacked the cozy, and frequently shabby, clutter of the typical English home. It was decorated monochromatically in pale, creamy whites, against which unusual pieces of furniture—Indian silver armchairs, Portuguese inlaid ebony-and-ivory chests —stood out in sharp relief. The surfaces of the furniture were kept clear of all but one or two carefully chosen objects, a Chinese bronze, a Persian vase. The overall effect was of lightness and space. The house had a lovely, serene quality that was totally at odds with Natalie's high-strung personality.

There were eighteen guests for dinner, including the Aga Khan and his wife, the Saudi ambassador to London, several of Khalid's business associates, as well as Daisy and Bjorn Lindstrom, Alexandra and Neil, Lucia and Nick, and the Grahams. With the exception of the ambassador and his wife, everyone was in London for Royal Ascot, the five days of horse racing which, with the Chelsea Flower Show, Wimbledon, the Henley Regatta, and Cowes, numbered among the prime social events of the English summer.

Daisy did not look well, thought Katrinka as she chatted absentmindedly with the Aga Khan. She had just returned from a trip to New York to see Steven, who a few months before had been diagnosed as having AIDS, not contracted from Sugar as it happened (according to Steven she had been tested and found negative) but from either one of the many sexual partners to whom his association with Sugar Benson had led him, or from his experiments with drugs. He was living alone in the small apartment on East Seventy-first Street he had kept for himself and Sugar to use on their infrequent trips, cared for by a network of AIDS "buddies," visited frequently by his children, who amazingly had rallied around when they heard of his illness, and by Daisy. Katrinka, too, stopped in to see him from time to time. She found him thin and pale, as good-mannered and gracious as ever, but so incredibly sad, not because he was sick and dying, but because he had made so little of his life and hurt so many people in the process.

Dinner was served by a number of unobtrusive Arab servants who shuttled quickly and silently between the dining room and kitchen, bearing gold trays full of lamb and rice and Arabian-style vegetables. There was no alcohol, and, since she had seen Khalid drink in the past, Katrinka wondered if this was in deference to the Aga Khan, who was after all the spiritual leader of the Ismaili Muslims—though seeing him in top hat and tails often made that difficult to keep in mind. It was an odd, eclectic group, but all had at least one thing in common, an interest in making money, so the conversation avoided the danger areas of religion and politics, and stayed firmly centered on business. By the time Natalie stood, signaling, in traditional English fashion, the withdrawal of the women to leave the men to their brandy and cigars (though in this case it was more likely to be thick Turkish coffee and cigarettes), the mood—despite the absence of liquor—was jovial: friendships had been formed, and the possibility for future deals created.

The tradition of withdrawal had had a very practical motive: it left the men free to relieve themselves out the dining room windows into the shrubbery, and the women to find whatever indoor conveniences were in existence. Since these were modern times, Khalid and his guests took turns in the bathroom nearest the dining room while Natalie led the women upstairs to the guest bedrooms and their adjoining loos. Katrinka she pulled into her own room, sent a waiting maid off to fetch some totally unnecessary towels, and closed the door firmly behind her. *"Chérie, you must help me,"* she said, as soon as she and Katrinka were alone.

"What you want me to do now?" said Katrinka, smiling in exasperation, wondering what mischief Natalie was hoping to drag her into.

"I want to leave Khalid."

Startled, Katrinka sank into one of the white bergère chairs and stared at Natalie. *"Ay yi yi yi,"* she said softly, more in astonishment than disapproval. Until that moment, Natalie had seemed aglow not only with the jewels she wore around her neck, in her hair, on her arms and fingers, but with happiness.

"You don't know what it's like, *chérie."* Natalie sat on the edge of the bed, clasped her hands in her lap, and leaned toward Katrinka, pleading for understanding. "If we could live all the time here in London, or in Paris, it would be different. But Khalid has business in Saudi and lately he is spending more and more time there. This time I can't go back. I *won't* go back." Tears began to seep from her eyes and run down her cheeks. She brushed them away impatiently.

"You did tell Khalid?"

Natalie shook her head. "I asked to stay here in London, with Aziz, when he goes back, but he said no. We argued. For months we've been arguing, but nothing I say matters. Nothing I say ever matters."

What had seemed exotic and interesting to Natalie during the first few years of her marriage now seemed unbearable, even for the few months a year she normally spent in Riyadh: the confinement to the harem, the wearing of the chador in public, the inability to go out alone, drive a car, run an errand. All the freedoms to which she had been accustomed her whole life were denied her in Saudi Arabia. And added to that was not only the indignity of being Khalid's second wife, but the insult of being expected to deal politely, even pleasantly, with his first, whom he had never divorced, when they found themselves together at family birthdays or the weddings of friends. To Khalid, all this seemed unimportant, a few months of restricted living a small price for Natalie to pay for the love and luxury he lavished upon her. At first, Natalie had felt the same. While she had perhaps never loved Khalid deeply, she had loved him sincerely. And still did. She simply could no longer live with him.

"Meet me tomorrow for lunch," pleaded Natalie. "You must help me work out a plan."

"Tell Khalid you do want to leave him. Arrange a settlement. Get a divorce."

"I can't."

"If you run away, you'll have nothing. How will you support yourself?"

"If I tell him, he'll never let me keep Aziz," said Natalie. "He'll take him back to Riyadh and I'll never see him again."

"Khalid would never do that," said Katrinka, who had always liked him. He was an intelligent man, a civilized man. It was hard to imagine him behaving like a medieval tyrant. "Certainly he doesn't want to lose his son. No man does. But he won't take him from you. You'll share him."

"He's told me," said Natalie, "and I believe him. I can't give up Aziz, Katrinka. I gave up a child once. I can't do it again." She meant, Katrinka knew, the abortion she had been so determined to have years before. While never quite regretting her decision, which she had considered necessary at the time, Natalie afterward could never completely reconcile herself to her loss. "You understand that."

"Yes," said Katrinka.

"You'll help?"

"Of course." Natalie had made it impossible for her to refuse.

There was a knock at the door and, when it opened, the maid entered with her arms full of towels, followed a moment later by Daisy, who looked, Katrinka thought, tired and very worried. "How you doing?" asked Katrinka.

Daisy shrugged. "One thing you learn about life," she said, "you just have to get on with it."

Steven's illness had affected Daisy deeply, worrying and depressing her, making her unable to give up her relationship with Bjorn, though she was long past getting any real pleasure from it. She could not bear to lose both men at the same time, she had told Katrinka, admitting the hold Steven continued to have on her. No matter who or what had come between them, they were bound by history, by children, and by continuing affection.

Would it be like that for Natalie and Khalid? wondered Katrinka. Somehow, she doubted it.

Soon the women had all reassembled, and Natalie, her streaked makeup hastily repaired, returned them to the drawing room on the first floor, where they were joined shortly afterward by the men. She suggested a game of charades and Katrinka quickly seconded her, anything not to have to make conversation. They played until the Aga Khan announced it was time for him to go, and soon after that the party broke up.

It was still only midnight and Katrinka suggested going on to Annabel's. Nick, whose defense of one of his Mafia clients had ended three days before in a hung jury, was on a high and could not sleep anyway. Neil, proud of his expertise on the dance (as well as the trading) floor, agreed. The group piled into the Grahams' limo and Adam directed the driver to take them to Berkeley Square.

It was after two by the time Katrinka and Adam finally returned to the hotel, but instead of going directly to their suite, they detoured to the casino so that Katrinka could check on business there as she liked to do each night, if possible, while she was in London. They rode in the small antique elevator with its etched glass and decorative brass up to the top floor where the doors opened into a large space resembling a private ballroom in an eighteenth-century London mansion with paneled walls set with mirrors, ornamental moldings painted in contrasting shades of pale blue, Corinthian columns, gilt trim, swagged and tasseled curtains at the windows and, suspended from the gilded ceiling, dimly lit crystal chandeliers. Over the wood floor, a rich Wilton carpet had been laid, and tables set out for blackjack, roulette, *chemin de fer,* and craps. The guests were dressed variously in formal and informal evening attire and waiters in black tie circulated among them offering coffee, tea, and soft drinks on the house since liquor was forbidden by law in gaming establishments in London. Voices were hushed and indistinct, the sound of the croupiers occasionally rising above them, calling *"Mesdames et messieurs, faites vos jeux.* Place your bets, please." It could not have been more different from a Las Vegas casino, or, for that matter, from the rowdier casinos on Adam's ships.

Their entrance caused a small stir, as it had earlier at Annabel's, since their faces were familiar from the pages of London's tabloids, the tales of the Grahams' incredible financial success, combined with exaggerated reports of their global holdings, making good copy everywhere in the world. But the lure of gambling proved stronger even than Adam and Katrinka's considerable appeal, and the attention of the gamblers returned quickly to the tables.

The recession, which no one wanted to admit was happening, appeared to have passed the London Graham by. At first glance, business seemed to be good, an assessment confirmed by the manager, Alistair Codron, a slender, dark-haired man with a smooth manner and an acquired upper-class accent, who came hurrying to greet the Grahams as soon as he was informed of their arrival. "Well, Alistair, how we doing tonight?" said Katrinka, smiling as she extended a hand to him.

"Remarkably well," said the manager, beaming at her, taking her hand as if about to kiss it, contenting himself with shaking it instead. "Splendidly, in fact."

"My wife is fluent in several languages, including English," said Adam with an indulgent smile as he shook Codron's hand, "but somehow she can't seem to get the verbs right."

"Mrs. Graham's English is charming," said Alistair gallantly.

Katrinka resisted the urge to point out that Adam still could speak no language other than English and contented herself with saying, "I do speak Czech with perfect grammar."

"Well, that's not how you speak English," he said with the

498

same indulgent, even affectionate smile as he put an arm around her waist and pulled her close to him.

That was what Katrinka found so confusing about Adam's behavior, the way he seemed to be trying to push her away and draw her near at the same time. And what kept her from resenting him was her belief that his hostility was fleeting and due to stress, while his affection was deeply rooted and constant. It never occurred to her that what passed for love might simply be pride of possession.

Adam launched into a conversation with Alistair, asking questions, exchanging stories, comparing notes on the hotel's gambling action and operations versus those of the floating casinos, all as if Katrinka were not directly involved, or even present, which was annoying though not perhaps as infuriating as it might have been had all the information not been familiar to her after hours spent seated at her desk poring over the London Graham's financial reports. Alistair, to his credit, never replied to Adam without at least a referential look toward Katrinka, which she noted with approval and some pleasure. He at least remembered who was paying him.

When his curiosity was satisfied, Adam ended his conversation with Alistair and spent a few minutes with Katrinka playing goodwill ambassador, mingling with the guests, hoping to lure the tourists back to stay at the Graham and to encourage the others to continue visiting the casino. Then, just as they were about to leave, the elevator doors opened and in swept Sugar Benson Elliott with a tall, distinguished-looking, gray-haired man in his early fifties. He was wearing a dinner jacket and black tie, and Sugar looked amazingly sedate and rather elegant in a black Armani gown that only hinted at the lush curves of her body, honey-colored hair swept up on her head, with becoming wisps falling across her forehead and emphasizing the sunken planes of her cheeks. Only her full mouth, carefully outlined and lipsticked in a brilliant, lustrous red, hinted at the sexual athlete she was reputed to be.

"Oh, no," groaned Adam softly. Though he had wondered more than once what she would be like in bed, Sugar was too obviously a golddigger to attract him. Showering a lover, even a wife, with gifts was one thing, paying for sex entirely another. To him, the difference between them was vast.

"Thank God Daisy didn't come with us," whispered Katrinka, as she tried to arrange a smile on her face.

"Why, Katrinka, Adam, how lovely to see you," said Sugar in her soft Southern lilt, altering her course and steering her escort toward them. She kissed them hello, then said, "I want you all to meet my friend, Nigel Bevenden, the Duke of Cumber."

Katrinka could see Alistair watching them from across the room with something close to amazement on his face as she shook the duke's hand and wondered what to call him. They stood chatting for a few minutes, Sugar quite relaxed and happy to be recounting details of her travels over the past several months, everyone else anxious to get away. Finally, Adam, saying he had an early meeting the next day, made their excuses, and amid blatantly fake wishes to see each other soon again, they all said good night.

"What you call a duke?" Katrinka asked Adam as they headed for the elevator.

"Asshole," said Adam. "At least that's what I'd call one who's with Sugar."

Katrinka laughed and repeated the question to Alistair, who had intercepted them at the elevator.

"Your grace," said Alistair, who still wore a very odd expression.

"There is something fishy about this duke?" asked Katrinka.

"No. Not at all," said Alistair quickly. "He's quite normal. For a duke," he added, which made Adam laugh.

"I never took you for a socialist."

Alistair looked horrified. "I'm not. Far from it."

"There is something fishy then about Sugar Benson?" asked Katrinka, determined to find out what was bothering Alistair.

"Is she a friend of yours?"

"No."

"An acquaintance," added Adam.

"Why?" asked Katrinka.

Knowing that she was not going to let him off the hook until he told her what was on his mind, Alistair said reluctantly, "Well, it's only rumor, of course, Mrs. Graham, but you do know how rumors so often turn out to be true? Well, the thing of it is, I have heard that Sugar Benson is running a brothel."

"What?" said Katrinka, who really could not believe her ears. She knew, as did everyone, thanks to Sabrina's acid pen, that Count Paolo di Cortina had died before marrying Sugar, leaving her with nothing but a few expensive pieces of jewelry, which his children were trying to reclaim, but she still had her alimony from Steven and, with her looks and sexual skill, the chance to marry any number of wealthy men, young or old. Why would she set up in business running a bordello?

"A very high-class sort of brothel. No cheap tarts out of Shepherd's Market, nothing like that."

"I suppose that explains the gown," said Adam. "Now that she really is a whore she doesn't have to dress like one."

"This is nonsense. There is no way it could be true," but even as she protested, Katrinka began to suspect it was.

"As I said, Mrs. Graham, it is only a rumor."

"You keep the streetwalkers out," said Adam, turning to survey the elegant women in the room, "but not the high-class hookers."

"Streetwalkers," said Alistair wryly, "can't afford the membership fee."

"Do you believe it?" Katrinka asked Adam as soon as the elevator door had closed and they were alone.

"Don't you?"

She nodded. "Why she would do something like that?"

"Would she do," corrected Adam automatically. "Knowing Sugar, just for the fun of it. And for the money."

"You think she's attractive?"

"I see her appeal, but I don't want to go to bed with her, if that's what you mean." He stepped closer to Katrinka and put his arms around her. "I never want to go to bed with anyone but you," he said, kissing her neck. The idea of Sugar and her brothel had excited him.

"The elevator is glass," said Katrinka, shivering under the touch of his lips, reminding herself as well as Adam that they were on public display.

"You like doing it in public," said Adam. "You're an exhibitionist. Remember those plane trips we took?"

The elevator door opened at their floor, saving Katrinka from having to reply. But she was smiling. It was almost three o'clock in the morning and she was about to make love with her husband.

Compared to Natalie and Daisy, she didn't have a care in the world.

Thirty-Nine

"You complain that in Riyadh you can't drive," said a smiling Katrinka the next day when she saw Natalie emerge from the interior of a chauffeured Rolls outside Le Caprice where they were having lunch, "and here you go everywhere with a car and driver." It was such a beautiful early summer day, with no sign of rain, just wisps of white clouds skimming across a pale blue sky, that Katrinka had walked the short distance from the Graham to Arlington Street.

"It's not the same," said Natalie as she kissed Katrinka hello. "Here I feel like a spoiled wife. There I feel like a prisoner."

The restaurant was modern and bright with plate-glass windows looking out onto the street, a long bar, white tablecloths, simple flower arrangements, and neutral walls hung with black and white photographs of famous people. The maître d' greeted Katrinka by name and, as curious eyes discreetly noted the high style of the two women—most of the diners were soberly dressed for boozy business lunches —escorted her and Natalie to the table against the wall that was preferred by the Duchess of York when she dined there with friends.

They ordered the grilled chicken, without the *pommes frites,* had a green salad instead and a side order of asparagus. Jeffrey Archer, lunching at a table across the room, sent over a bottle of wine. Katrinka, who had met him several times at a number of social events, flashed him a grateful smile and asked the sommelier to thank him. To their relief, there was no one else in the restaurant they knew.

As the women ate, they discussed quietly, so as not to be overheard, what Natalie was to do. Their mood seesawed. At one moment they were mature women with a difficult, even heartrending problem to solve; at another, they were schoolgirls planning an adventure, or thieves a caper, for an instant losing sight of the seriousness of what they were doing, caught up totally in its excitement.

By the time they finished lunch, they had made a rough plan of how to proceed.

Unwilling to give up the entire work week for Ascot, Katrinka and Adam were scheduled to attend only twice. On Opening Day, they and the Goodmans, as well as Daisy Elliott and Bjorn Lindstrom, would be joining Natalie and Prince Khalid in their box. On Ladies Day, they were to be the guests of Lord Crighton, head of Somerhill Rice, the merchant bank, in White's tent. The Cavallettis would be with Natalie and Khalid for the entire time. Untroubled by the rumors surrounding Nick, Khalid found him amusing, and he was fond of Lucia, who had designed the yacht Adam was currently building for him.

Natalie and Katrinka debated for a while whether or not to take Lucia into their confidence and decided against it. It didn't seem to either of them fair to involve her. They also agreed not to tell Adam, who might think it in his best interests to let Khalid know what his wife was up to. After much discussion, Ladies Day was designated "D" Day.

When she returned to her office, Katrinka placed a call to Jean-Claude Gillette in Paris. His secretary told her he was traveling and was reluctant to give the details of his itinerary. Not one to take no for an answer, Katrinka persisted, and by the end of the day had succeeded in reaching Jean-Claude in Toronto. Quickly, she explained what was happening and he listened, not interrupting, only muttering in French from time to time. When Katrinka asked him to make his private plane available to take Natalie to Los

Angeles, he agreed instantly. He remained fond of Natalie, but, even more important, he was delighted to be proved right. From the beginning, he had believed her marriage a mistake.

"And when will you leave that terrible husband of yours, *chérie?*" he asked when they had concluded their arrangements.

"Jean-Claude, really, I don't have time for this nonsense right now," said Katrinka. "Please, just be sure your plane is at Heathrow on Thursday."

Jean-Claude laughed and promised there would be no mistakes on his end.

Robin had accompanied the Grahams on the trip as she sometimes did when Katrinka needed additional help in Europe, and Katrinka turned the remaining details over to her to handle. It was she who hired the "getaway" car, and, on the pretext of returning something to Harrods as a favor to Natalie, managed to smuggle a selection of clothes and jewels as well as Natalie's passport out of the Cheyne Walk house.

On Ladies Day, Katrinka awoke even earlier than usual, lay in bed so as not to disturb Adam, who was sleeping beside her, and ran through the plan again, looking for its flaws. She found none. Only if luck should go against them would there be trouble.

When Adam was in the shower she phoned Robin to confirm the details for the last time and Natalie to reassure her. As usual, Katrinka had only black coffee for breakfast, but even that managed to make her feel a little queasy, and she realized she was very nervous about what she was about to do. Suddenly, the whole escapade struck her as crazy, and she was tempted to phone Natalie again and call the whole thing off. But she stopped herself. It was not her life that was at stake, but Natalie's, and only Natalie had the right to decide what to do with it. As a friend, her best friend, Katrinka felt she had no option but to help.

"Are you all right?" asked Adam as Katrinka fumbled awkwardly with the catch of her pearls. "Here, let me do that." He took the perfectly matched strand from her, fastened it around her neck, then stepped back to look. She was wearing a new Valentino pink linen suit with a fitted jacket and flower-patterned lapels whose design was echoed in her shoes and the trim of her pink straw boater. "You look beautiful," he said, but he searched her face anxiously as if he sensed something was not quite right.

"And you look very handsome," said Katrinka, admiring his black tails and dove-gray waistcoat. Reaching out, she straightened the knot of his red silk tie. She hoped he would not be too angry when he found out what she had done. "We make a good couple."

"The best," he agreed quickly, picking up his top hat and popping it open. He put the hat on his head and surveyed himself in the mirror. "I still feel ridiculous in this thing."

"But you do look so distinguished."

"Successful and rich?" Katrinka nodded and Adam laughed. "Good. Come on, let's go. I don't want to keep Lord Crighton waiting. I have to borrow some money from him."

As frequently happens in London in June, heavy dark clouds threatening rain moved slowly across the blue sky alternately concealing and revealing the sun, which shone brilliantly when allowed. At Ascot, lines of cars proceeded past the entrance to the track and into the various parking lots, some stopping first to allow passengers to emerge, men in top hat and tails, ladies in silk dresses and summer suits, odd hats perched atop their heads, raincoats thrown over their arms, umbrellas in their hands.

The graveled courtyard inside the main gates teemed with people, some entering and leaving the green booth to the left of the entrance where invitations were checked, fees paid, and entry permits issued, others stopping to buy racing forms at the kiosks, still more having their purses and pockets checked by security guards, round little men in black bowlers and elderly ladies in silk dresses wearing pretty straw hats.

Inside the park, crowds of people, parading their finery, strolled across the green lawn toward their boxes, their seats in the stands, toward the refreshment booths selling strawberries and champagne.

"Oh, God," murmured Alexandra, "there's Sabrina."

506

The Goodmans had accompanied the Grahams in their limousine. Daisy and Bjorn had taken a separate car while Nick and Lucia had ridden with Natalie and Khalid. They would all meet in Khalid's box immediately after lunch.

"Where?" said Katrinka, looking around warily. Sabrina was the last person she wanted to have to deal with that day. "Oh, no," she murmured when she saw the pudgy figure in a lime green suit that did terrible things to her complexion. "Why she does always wear what will look worst on her?"

"For God's sake, keep Daisy away from her," said Adam. Daisy had been very upset about a piece Sabrina had written recently about Steven.

"Daisy can handle Sabrina," said Alexandra.

"The only way to handle her is by strangling," muttered Neil, glaring at the lime green figure talking to Jane Seymour, who looked beautiful in a simple beige suit and straw boater. Neil had found himself cropping up in her column from time to time, accompanied by snide innuendos about his business dealings.

From White's tent, viewing a race was impossible but it was only a short walk from it to the Royal Box, to the paddock where the horses paraded before each race, and to the track beyond. Properly speaking, it was not a tent at all, but a bright rectangular glass enclosure with a canopied roof which sheltered the members of White's, the fashionable men's club, and their guests from the uncertain English weather. Headquartered in St. James's Street in London, it was an old club with old rules, which were followed diligently. Only members were allowed to sign the tab, and women were not permitted to join. At the door of the tent, officials checked credentials and allowed only those with the proper badges to enter. There was a coat check for umbrellas and top hats, a bar, and a tote for placing bets. Beyond these, long tables were set with linen, china, and crystal for members to lunch on cold salmon or lamb chops in green aspic. Dress was, for the most part, subdued, no outlandish hats or miniskirts, which would have breached the code. Decorum had to be maintained. Members of the royal family often stopped in later in the day for tea.

By the time the Grahams and the Goodmans entered,

Daisy and Bjorn had already arrived and were seated in the bar with Lord Crighton, his wife, and several others, having drinks. Lord Crighton was a dapper, portly man, and his equally round wife had flawless, virtually unlined skin despite her sixty-something years. Standing next to them was a man Katrinka immediately recognized. She nudged Adam, who restrained a smile. It was Sugar's friend, the Duke of Cumber, looking uncomfortable as he introduced them to his wife, a tall, horsey woman. As soon as he politely could, the duke led her away to join their own group. To his intense relief, they were not that day with Lord Crighton's party.

Daisy was so deeply engrossed in conversation with a large, broad-shouldered bearlike man with salt-and-pepper hair and beard that she seemed not to have noticed her friends' arrival. She looked much better than she had a few nights before, more rested, as if finally she had been able to sleep. "Who is that Daisy is talking to?" she asked Bjorn.

"Some sculptor," said Bjorn dismissively. "Italian. His name is Riccardo Donati. I've never heard of him, have you?"

Katrinka admitted that she had not, but when Alexandra heard the name, she said, "Oh, my God, is that Donati? I must go say hello." Although her specialty was seventeenth-century Dutch art, she tried to keep abreast of what was happening in the world of modern art, and in Italy Donati was definitely happening. Daisy, however, did not look at all pleased with Alexandra's interruption, noted Katrinka with amusement, and Bjorn unhappily turned his attention to one of Lord Crighton's homely but extremely rich daughters.

Katrinka always enjoyed Ascot, its pageantry and quaint rules, the formality that the English not only accepted but seemed to cherish. And though at first she had to make an effort to appear normal, soon, despite her worries, she managed to get some real pleasure from the event. She chatted with friends and acquaintances in the bar, studied the race form, listened to tips, placed her bets at the tote and, when she sat next to Lord Crighton at the lunch table, was as charming to him as she would have been even had Adam not wanted to borrow a fortune from his bank. Accompanying the others after the first course to watch the procession of landaus and outriders bringing the royal family and their guests across the park from Windsor Castle, she smiled at the restrained smattering of applause from the ladies as the Queen rode past, and the polite tipping of top hats by the men. It was all so very English.

As soon as lunch was over and Lord Crighton's guests scattered temporarily to find loos, watch a few races from the rail, or visit friends, Katrinka and Adam set off in the fine misting rain with the others in their party to visit Natalie and Khalid in their box. With them, to Bjorn's disgust, was Riccardo Donati, who, it turned out, knew Lucia and Nick from Florence where he had a house in Fiesole not far from theirs.

Khalid's box was crowded with guests he had invited for the day and others who had stopped by just to say hello. The Grahams had met almost everyone before, and what was meant as a short visit started to stretch to a lengthy one as they reviewed prior meetings, compared notes on the races, and had their glasses constantly refilled with Khalid's private supply of Cristal. Aware of Natalie's anxiety, Katrinka tried to hurry her group with little success, unable to pry Daisy and Riccardo loose from Nick and Lucia, or Adam from a Saudi who was interested in tankers. Only Bjorn seemed as eager as she to get away. Finally, Katrinka suggested viewing the horses in the paddock before the next race, and Natalie quickly agreed, while Adam and the others fell in more reluctantly with the idea. Very slowly, the Graham party started to leave. As everyone remembered later, Natalie went over to kiss Khalid good-bye, but preoccupied with a discussion of the chances of his horse later in the Gold Cup, he seemed almost irritated when she interrupted and said quickly, "Yes, yes, that's fine. Hurry back."

Oblivious to the odd dresses, the extravagant hats—the towers and birdcages, the flowers and feathers—trying not to let their nervousness show, Katrinka and Natalie accompanied the others to the paddock where the Queen, who had a horse running, was viewing the parade with the Duke of Edinburgh and the Queen Mother. The rain had stopped again and they climbed into the packed stands and watched for a moment until Natalie leaned forward, whispered to Katrinka, and began to work her way down through the dense crowd toward the exit. Katrinka, in turn, whispered to Daisy, then followed Natalie. Daisy explained briefly to the rest that Natalie was feeling unwell and Katrinka was returning with her to her box. No one seemed to think that in the least bit strange.

As soon as they were clear of the paddock, Katrinka and Natalie, praying they would not run into anyone they knew, hurried back across the lawn toward the main gates, and came face to face with Mark van Hollen.

At least it's not Sabrina, thought Katrinka with what little gratitude she could muster.

"How nice to see you," said Mark.

Katrinka introduced him to Natalie, who looked sick with anxiety and, as soon as she reasonably could, started making excuses to get away.

"Is something wrong?" asked Mark, who could not help noticing their agitation.

"Well," said Katrinka, "Natalie is really not feeling well."

"And I've been keeping you standing here, talking. I am sorry. I was just so pleased to see you. Is there anything I can do to help?" he asked kindly.

"No, nothing. Thank you," said Natalie, looking back over her shoulder as if afraid of being pursued.

"You just want me to get out of your way, right?" said Mark, stepping aside with a rueful smile.

"I will see you later, I hope," said Katrinka gratefully.

Natalie said a curt good-bye and resumed her dash for the gates, Katrinka following after her as Mark stood watching them, wondering what in hell was going on. Natalie had not looked so much ill to him as worried. Finally, he shrugged and turned away, heading back toward the box where the remainder of his party waited.

"Good afternoon, Mr. van Hollen," said Sabrina as she fell into step beside him.

"Hello, Sabrina. Having a nice day, I hope? Not losing too much money?"

She nodded absently, told him she had one winner so far, and got straight to the point. "Wasn't that Mrs. Graham I saw you talking to?"

"Yes," said Mark curtly.

"And Prince Khalid's wife?"

"Yes." Though he understood the importance of Sabrina to his newspaper chain, and paid her a fortune to prove he knew her worth, he didn't like her and discouraged the attempts she made to pump him for information.

"They seemed to be in a great hurry."

"Did they?" said Mark. "I didn't notice. If you'll excuse me, I have to get back to my friends. Enjoy yourself, Sabrina."

"I always do," she said. Sabrina stood looking after him a moment, then changed directions, waddling on her too-high heels toward the gate, reaching it in time to see a black limo pull away from the curb and Katrinka starting back across the graveled courtyard.

"Leaving so early?" asked Katrinka pleasantly. She had known she would not be able to escape Sabrina's eagle eye for long.

"Oh, no," said Sabrina. "I wouldn't dream of leaving before the end of the day. Who knows what I would miss? Was that Princess Khalid in the limousine?"

"Yes. She was feeling a little ill. Too bad she did have to miss the Gold Cup. Prince Khalid has a horse running, you know. But I am sure he will forgive her. You must not tell a soul," said Katrinka in a low, confidential rush, "but I do think she might be pregnant again."

Sabrina's small eyes lit with pleasure. It was not much of a story, but it was something. "Really? How lovely for her and the prince. And her little boy is how old now?"

"Almost two. Now, I must hurry. I do want to see the next race. Bye, Sabrina." She dreaded to think what Sabrina would do to her in print, what awful stories she would contrive, when she found out that Katrinka had lied to her. But perhaps she never would find out, thought Katrinka

511

optimistically. And in the meantime she had bought Natalie some time.

Robin had ridden in the limo to Ascot to make sure the driver did not miss his passenger. She had brought with her the suitcases packed with clothes for Natalie and Aziz, the jewels, and the passport. So far, there had been no mistakes and she was feeling pleased with herself, though there was plenty of room yet for something to go wrong and Natalie herself didn't seem to be in great shape. She was looking out the rear window at the receding racetrack and murmuring, *"Qu'est-ce que je fais, je suis folle, qu'est-ce que je fais?"* over and over.

Though she did not understand the exact meaning of the words, Robin got the general sense. She leaned forward reassuringly, her red hair spilling over Natalie's suit, clashing with its bright pattern. "If you've changed your mind," she said reassuringly, "that's okay. We'll figure something out."

"No, no," said Natalie. "No, I have not changed my mind."

Opening the bottle of champagne, Robin poured a glass and offered it to Natalie, who swallowed the chilled drink gratefully and returned the glass to its holder. She took off her hat, ran a hand through her blond curls and, leaning back against the leather seat, closed her eyes. She began to cry softly, murmuring in French, unaware that she was speaking aloud. Robin took her hand and held it.

His nurse had been instructed to take Aziz to Battersea Park, directly across the river from Cheyne Walk, and to be certain to get him home by three-thirty. It was three o'clock when the limo approached the park and Robin told the driver to stop.

Natalie was no longer crying. Leaning forward, she peered anxiously from the window. This was the point at which the whole plan could fall apart. Robin asked the driver for the car phone and handed it to Natalie, who called her house and asked to speak to the nurse. "She's not home yet," she said, handing the phone back to Robin. "For once she's doing as she was told, thank God." Trying to kidnap Aziz in

512

front of the prince's entire household had been more than she could face.

Natalie reached into her purse, pulled out her jeweled compact, opened it, and repaired the damage crying had done to her face. A few minutes later the nurse, pushing Aziz in a stroller, walked out of the park. With her was a security guard. Her red eyes screened by dark sunglasses, her lips curved in a smile, Natalie got out of the car and approached the pair. She spoke to them a moment in Arabic, managed somehow to reassure them, picked up Aziz, and carried him back to the car. The chauffeur closed the door after her and, as he crossed into the road to return to the driver's seat, she rolled down the window, called something to the nurse and guard, waved and turned back to the driver. "Hurry," she said urgently.

"Take us to Heathrow," said Robin.

The driver could not resist a quick, curious look at Natalie before starting the car and driving off. Whatever was up, he decided, was none of his business.

The rest of the afternoon passed in a blur for Katrinka. Returning to White's, she found the others just beginning to have tea and told them that Natalie had not been well and had decided to return home. When Khalid sent one of his retainers to ask what had happened to his wife, Katrinka repeated the story. Eventually, of course, Khalid himself came and asked *how* she had returned home and Katrinka, looking blank, said that she had seen her leave in a limo. Wasn't it one of his? Confronted by Khalid's concern, Katrinka had an almost overwhelming desire to blurt out the truth. But she didn't, saying only that she was sure Natalie would be all right. The letter Robin would send by messenger to him as soon as Natalie was safely on her way to Los Angeles would tell Khalid all his wife wanted him to know.

The matter did not end there, of course. As soon as Khalid returned home and found no trace of Natalie or Aziz, he was on the phone to Katrinka demanding to know what was going on. And later, when he received Natalie's letter, he called again.

Adam was in the sitting room, going through some papers when the phone rang. He answered it, talked a moment to Khalid, then called to Katrinka, who was trying to take a nap before joining the Goodmans for the theater, to pick up the extension. Reluctantly, she did.

Confronted by Khalid's panic, torn between pity for him and fear for Natalie, for a moment Katrinka was silent. What if Natalie was mistaken and Khalid would let her keep Aziz? But even as the thought crossed her mind, Katrinka knew how unlikely that possibility was. "I'm sorry, Khalid," she said, "there's nothing I can tell you." As difficult as this might be for him, Katrinka could imagine nothing worse in the world for a woman than losing a child. She could not allow that to happen to Natalie if there was anything she could do to prevent it.

"You must tell me," he pleaded.

"If I hear anything, I'll let you know," she promised, intending to keep her word. She could at least let him know they were well.

"If you hear from her, tell her to call me."

"I will."

"I have to talk to her."

"I will tell her, I promise."

She hung up the phone and saw Adam standing in the bedroom doorway, watching her. From that morning he had known she was up to something. "You masterminded the whole thing, didn't you?" he said. "Don't bother to deny it," he went on before she could say a word. "It's written all over your face."

"I did not plan to lie. To you," she added.

"But you didn't plan to tell me, either."

"It did have nothing to do with you."

"Nothing! I'm in the middle of building that man a yacht," he said angrily. "Do you know what this stunt could cost me?"

"And that is all you care about? What it will cost you?"

"What else am I supposed to care about?"

"Natalie? Maybe Khalid?"

"If their marriage is on the rocks, that's their problem. Mine is trying to keep my businesses afloat."

514

"And our marriage? What about that?"

"What has that got to do with anything?"

"We never talk, Adam."

"Obviously. Or you would have told me what you were up to."

"About things that matter, to us."

"Bullshit. Didn't I go to Deauville with you? Didn't we spend hours discussing whether or not you should buy that goddamn hotel? And every other hotel you own?"

"Business!" said Katrinka, unable to keep the disgust out of her voice.

"Do you know how many wives right now, everywhere in the world, are pleading with their husbands to talk business with them? How many husbands treat their wives like dimwits? What the fuck do you have to complain about? At least I give you credit for having some brains. I did until today, that is. What the hell were you thinking of?"

"Khalid would have taken the baby away from her if Natalie had told him she was leaving."

"So?"

"How could I let that happen?"

"It was none of your goddamn business."

"Natalie is my friend."

"And I'm your husband. Your first loyalty is to me. And if you've lost me Khalid's commission, Katrinka, I swear to God, I'll make you pay."

What was the use, she thought. He would never understand. An enormous wave of fatigue washed over her. "You do have nothing to worry about," she said wearily. "Natalie left in Jean-Claude's plane. Khalid will blame him for everything."

Adam was silent for a moment. Then he smiled. "Was that your idea too?" Katrinka nodded, and he laughed aloud. Now that he was out of danger, Adam's anger had given way to amusement. Having Jean-Claude take the blame for Katrinka's actions felt somehow satisfying. He moved across to the bed and sat on the edge next to her. "I said you had brains, didn't I?" Leaning forward, he put an arm on either side of her. "You really are something."

Lying motionless, she let him nuzzle her neck but when he

515

moved his mouth to her lips, she raised her hands to his shoulder and held him off. Mingled with the love she felt for him, for the first time, for reasons she did not entirely understand, was a hint of dislike. "It has been a terrible day," she said. "I'm so tired. I must get rest before we meet the Goodmans."

Forty

How you doing?" asked Katrinka, dropping into the lounge chair next to Alexandra.

Looking up from the copy of *Art Forum* she was reading, Alexandra groaned. "I'm starving, and exhausted." Except for a peaked cap concealing her red hair, the large designer glasses hiding her eyes, and two thin strips of leopard-skin-printed bikini, her body—with not an ounce of unnecessary flesh on it—lay bare to the sun. "And I want a cigarette," she added. "How about you?"

"Dead," said Katrinka, unscrewing a bottle of suntan oil and applying it to her smooth golden skin.

On the other side of the pool, Zuzka was talking to Carla Webb, the petite, pretty, dark-haired golfer who had won the LPGA championship that year and the British Open the year before. After a moment, they got to their feet, wrapped pareos around themselves, and headed back inside. Natalie had not been seen for some time and was presumed to be in her room, since the spa's strenuous morning activities inevitably wore her out.

After flying to Los Angeles in the Graham jet, Katrinka and Alexandra had dropped Adam at the offices of Olympic Pictures, picked up Zuzka and Natalie, and driven by limo to the Golden Door for a week of diet, exercise, and relaxation which Katrinka, at least, felt she needed badly. The strain of the last several months had left her exhausted. Though her debt burden was small enough and her hotels of

517

a size and in a price range to weather the recession which no one was yet willing to admit the country was in, still it took a great deal of management, of planning publicity and marketing strategy, to keep the three of them above the sixty-four percent break-even figure.

Adam, too, was working harder than ever, traveling farther and faster, trying to keep his business empire from falling apart. When she could, Katrinka as always went with him, though he seemed often not to care whether or not she did, and sometimes came right out and refused her company. "I've got enough on my hands right now," he had snapped when she suggested accompanying him to Los Angeles. "I don't need you to deal with."

"I go to the Golden Door," she said, determined not to let him leave without her. Lately, he had spent so much time on the West Coast that once or twice she had caught herself wondering whether it was his involvement with films or with starlets that made these trips necessary. She had immediately pushed the thought aside as ridiculous. Anyone with half a brain could see the studio was hemorrhaging money. Of course he was concerned. And of course he would not want to admit the seriousness of the problem to her since she had been so set against his buying Olympic in the first place. "I call my girlfriends," she said, "and we all go. You should go too," she added.

"Who's got the time to go to a goddamn spa?"

"You need to rest," she said stubbornly. "When we do get back from Los Angeles, why we not take the *Lady Katrinka* and sail to Mustique?"

"Why *don't* we take," he repeated. "When in God's name are you going to learn how to speak?"

"I speak well enough for everyone but you," she pointed out calmly. "And your mother." From Nina Graham's point of view, Katrinka still could do little right. "And your sister," she added as an afterthought. "Only the Grahams seem to mind how I talk and dress. Where I go, what I do."

Adam and Katrinka's smiling faces were appearing with increasing frequency in newspapers and magazines, from *The Wall Street Journal* to *Vogue* in the United States, from *Paris Match* to *Osservatore Romano* in Europe. The articles

reported how rich and famous and very much in love the
Grahams were. And sometimes Katrinka believed them.
And sometimes she felt as if the ground were shifting
beneath her feet, as if the earth might open at any moment
and swallow everything that mattered to her, Adam and
their life together.

Katrinka sighed and Alexandra turned to look at her.
"Why do we do this to ourselves?" she asked.

Katrinka looked at the pool and the beautifully landscaped gardens and laughed. "Because it's good for us. And
we can afford it."

Working as hard as she did, Katrinka looked forward to a
few days at a spa once or twice a year, usually after planning
a big charity gala or when back from a round of exhausting
business trips. She went with Adam if she could talk him
into it, or whichever of her friends could spare the time, to
the Bonaventure or Saturnia Doral in Florida, the Canyon
Spa Ranch in Arizona, La Costa or the Golden Door in
California. For Katrinka, the purpose was not so much to
lose weight, as she rarely gained more than a pound or so, as
to cleanse her system, tone her body, and rest.

Wherever she went, her days followed more or less the
same spa pattern, an early morning walk, followed by a light
breakfast, then exercise with a trainer, group aerobics,
another exercise class, and a lunch consisting of a few
tomatoes and lettuce leaves. Her afternoon's activities were
much less strenuous: an hour or so of lazing around the
pool, a facial, mud bath, salt scrub, herbal wrap, manicure,
pedicure, collagen mask, a shower, a massage, then a light
dinner, and bed. After a few days of such pampering, she felt
ready again to take on the world.

Katrinka finished oiling her body and dropped the bottle
back into the basket. She picked up the latest Barbara Taylor
Bradford novel and sighed contentedly. One of the great
pleasures of coming to a spa was having time to read
something other than newspapers. But she had no sooner
opened it than she heard her name being called and, looking
up, saw Zuzka, racing back toward her, shouting in Czech.

"What is it?" asked Alexandra, startled. "What's happened?"

"She is saying something about the Berlin Wall," said Katrinka, getting to her feet.

Since the point of going to the Golden Door was to rest, no one had read a newspaper or watched television in days. But Zuzka's attention had been caught by a news bulletin as she walked past the lounge and she had stopped to listen.

"They do tear down the Wall," said Katrinka, translating Zuzka's excited babble for Alexandra. "It's on television." She picked up her white cotton cover-up and slipped into it, following Zuzka back toward the lounge, meeting Natalie, who was on her way out.

"Oh la la," said Natalie, surprised at the sudden explosion of energy. "What's going on?"

"Where were you?" said Alexandra. "You missed lunch."

"On the phone," replied Natalie with an edge of guilt they were all too excited to notice. As it was, the answer surprised no one. Natalie was always on the phone. For a few months after she had left Khalid, she had been in a terrible state of depression, but, eventually, through lawyers, she had worked out a reasonably amicable divorce settlement, which allowed the prince to see Aziz, though only in Los Angeles. That done, she began to build a new life, using her exquisite collection of jewels as collateral to raise financing for a boutique on Melrose Avenue in West Hollywood. The boutique had prospered, to everyone's surprise, primarily because Natalie, her ability to spot a trend still active despite years out of the business, had specialized in finding talented young designers whose work she sold at reasonable prices, drawing buyers who were no longer willing, or able, to spend vast sums on clothes by name designers. Recently, she had opened branches in Costa Mesa and Palm Springs, and was considering others in New York and Palm Beach. Natalie's success had been quick and she had thrived on it, while the men clustered around her as thick as ever, drawn by her neurotic energy, her soft blond curls, and her mysterious green eyes.

"What has happened?" she asked, falling into step beside Katrinka.

Katrinka told her what Zuzka had reported, and they hurried into the lounge, joining the growing crowd in front

520

of the television screen. For Alexandra and Natalie and the other guests at the spa, all mesmerized by the news, the collapse of communism in East Germany was both incredible and exciting. It filled them with wonder and satisfaction. Their capitalist way of life had been vindicated, and the archenemy was going down to defeat. But Katrinka and Zuzka felt not so much satisfied as joyful and full of hope. They wanted the democratic movement to spread eastward to Czechoslovakia. Mikhail Gorbachev had promised that this time Soviet troops would not intervene.

"Maybe we can go home," said Zuzka in Czech, tears welling in her eyes. "Katrinka, think, if this happens in Czechoslovakia, we can go home. I can see my parents again before they die." She turned to Carla Webb, who was sitting beside her, and repeated, in English, "Maybe I go home soon."

Carla, who had been spending a lot of time with Zuzka since her arrival at the spa, smiled sympathetically and said, "After this, anything seems possible."

Tears streamed down Katrinka's cheeks and she stood up, murmuring, "I must call Adam." It was a moment she wanted to share with him.

"He is in a meeting now," said Natalie, her eyes still glued to the television screen. "You won't be able to reach him." Then, realizing what she had said, she turned to Katrinka and added. *"Ouff,* I forgot to tell you, he phoned, and when he couldn't get you, he tried me. He had heard about the Wall and wanted to talk to you. He said to call him later."

"Oh," said Katrinka, feeling somehow deflated. Why would Adam have asked to talk to Natalie? she wondered, then decided it must have had something to do with Khalid, with whom Adam had remained friendly, though Khalid's relationship with Katrinka was strained. Despite Jean-Claude's having taken all the blame, the prince still suspected her involvement in Natalie's leaving him. Katrinka sat back down again and returned her attention to the screen.

For the remainder of their stay, the television in the lounge, broadcasting CNN all day long, drew the women like a magnet between exercise classes and facials, herbal wraps and massages. They pored over newspaper accounts and talked about nothing else over their lemon water and vegetables. So involved were they in world events that they failed for a long time to notice what was happening right under their noses.

"Where is Zuzka?" asked Katrinka impatiently a few days later as the driver loaded their bags into the limousine. The Graham jet was scheduled to leave for New York at eight and she did not want to quarrel with Adam about a delay.

"Saying good-bye to Carla Webb," said Alexandra.

"Oh la la," murmured Natalie, and when the others turned to look at her, added, her voice loaded with speculation, "They have been spending a lot of time together this week."

Katrinka's own eyes widened as she took in Natalie's meaning, but she shook her head, saying, "Nonsense. They're friends. Nothing more." Though the fact was seldom alluded to by a press corps that liked and admired her, it was general knowledge that Carla was a lesbian.

"Ouff," these friendships between women," said Natalie, "I have seen them happen when husbands pay too little attention to their wives. It is not at all uncommon."

"Maybe not in Riyadh," snapped Katrinka. Her short temper had less to do with Natalie's innuendos about Zuzka than her growing anxiety about the state of her own marriage. Somehow, every phone conversation she had had with Adam during the week had ended in an argument.

"Zuzka's not gay," said Alexandra, sounding shocked.

The idea shocked them all a little. Though they had a number of lesbian friends whom they accepted without question, it was still a jolt when someone long considered heterosexual was suddenly suspected not to be. And not only had Katrinka known Zuzka since they were teenagers, she was married to one of her best friends. "Of course she's not. Natalie is being ridiculous."

Natalie shrugged. *"On verra,"* she said.

Looking flushed and happy, Zuzka approached the car, murmuring apologies for being late. She had been with Carla and completely lost track of the time, she explained.

"She did promise to teach me golf," said Zuzka, as she settled herself beside the others in the car. "Maybe that will take my mind off Tomáš and what the bastard's up to."

The others carefully refrained from exchanging knowing looks.

The petite, quiet Carla found the large and hearty Zuzka irresistible. From wherever she was playing a tournament, she telephoned several times a day. When in Los Angeles, she kept her promise to teach Zuzka to play golf. She moved slowly, but relentlessly. Zuzka, who had not been courted so devotedly in her whole life, who was starved for love, who resented her husband's neglect, was hurt by his constant infidelities, who had not had sex with him in over a year, was as shocked as her friends when she realized what was going on. But she felt more flattered than outraged, and did not stop the lunches at Michael's or Morton's, or refuse the invitations to dine alone with Carla in her Benedict Canyon house. When she finally succumbed it was to curiosity rather than lust, though the lust soon followed. No one in all her life, certainly not her husband, had ever paid so much attention to learning her body, knowing its needs, satisfying her totally.

Gradually it occurred to Tomáš that Zuzka had changed, and at first he was relieved. She had stopped questioning him about his activities, stopped sulking at his absences, stopped making jealous scenes. He could come and go as he pleased without a word from her. But when more and more often he returned to the apartment in Los Feliz where they still lived and she was not there, it was he who questioned and sulked, Zuzka who reminded distant and vague.

Tomáš called Katrinka in New York, asked how soon she was returning to Los Angeles, was relieved to hear she was accompanying Adam again on his next trip, and suggested they have dinner. Since they spoke often on the phone and always made time to see each other alone, Katrinka did not find either the phone call or the suggestion odd, though there was something in Tomáš's voice that made her wonder. He sounded worried and, for the first time in a long while, as far as she knew, he had no need to be. After years of earning money doing odd jobs, he was finally, thanks to Adam's okay on a project, going to direct a film.

They agreed to meet at Spago, Wolfgang Puck's trendy restaurant perched above the Sunset Strip, only a short drive from the Beverly Wilshire Hotel where Katrinka and Adam always stayed when in Los Angeles. Reaching the parking valets within seconds of each other, they left their cars to the attendants, and kissed hello as the photographers, who always lay in wait for arriving celebrities, snapped their picture. Tomáš looked embarrassed. But Katrinka smiled and posed patiently. She was too polite not to cooperate and she sympathized with the photographers, who were just doing their job. "Who's your date, Katrinka?" one of them asked.

"My friend," said Katrinka. "Tomáš Havlíček. He is directing new film for Olympic Pictures," she explained helpfully, wanting both Adam and Tomáš to profit from the publicity.

"I hate this shit," muttered Tomáš as he hurried Katrinka inside.

"Be nice to them," she said, "and they will be nice to you," which had been her experience—with the exception of Sabrina, of course.

It was late and the restaurant was crowded, the noise level high and cheerful as Katrinka and Tomáš, stopping en route to say a brief hello to acquaintances, followed the maître d' down the steps and across the floor to their table by the window overlooking the Strip.

"Where's Adam tonight?" asked Tomáš, once they were seated and the drinks had been ordered. As always when they were alone together, they spoke in Czech.

"Business meeting. And Zuzka?"

"I have no idea," said Tomáš. "She never tells me where she goes anymore."

Katrinka studied his face. Tomáš's curly hair was completely gray, his large deep-set eyes were ringed with lines, and there were deep furrows on either side of his full mouth. "Adam said the revised script is much better," she said.

Tomáš shrugged. "It still needs work." He was grateful for the job and would do it as well as he could, but it was hack work, the sort of work he had always despised. Sometimes he was filled with despair, not sure where his life had taken the turn that had brought him to this, instead of to the great and important films he had wanted to make.

The waiter brought their drinks and they ordered. Then Katrinka asked a few more questions about the movie he was scheduled to direct, but Tomáš did not want to talk about the film. Neither did he seem interested in discussing how Martin was doing in college, nor even the incredible changes in Eastern Europe, the wave of democracy that had swept eastward over the past month, Czechoslovakia's "Velvet Revolution," nor the country's new leader, Václav Havel. "Everything you wanted in sixty-eight," she said to him, "it's happening now, Tomáš." Again, he only shrugged.

The waiter brought their food and, as Katrinka cut into her roasted Chinese duck, she said, "I'm going to go back, after Christmas."

"Yes. Zuzka wants to go too, but I'll be filming." His mother had died the year before and he had no other family there, no compelling reason to go back, and in fact dreaded the idea of returning. There, he was certain he would feel even more strongly the loss of all he had hoped and dreamed.

"I want to see Ota Černý," said Katrinka. "And my aunt and cousins." She sighed. "Everything will have changed so much."

"I am worried about Zuzka," said Tomáš, changing the subject abruptly.

So was Katrinka, though she was not prepared to admit that to Tomáš. In their frequent phone conversations, the usually forthright Zuzka had recently been evasive and moody, happy one moment, depressed the next, refusing to admit, when asked, that she was upset about anything at all. "Why?" asked Katrinka.

"She is out all the time and, when I ask where she goes, she refuses to say."

"And you tell her where you go, I suppose."

"I tell her something at least."

Katrinka shook her head in despair. "Men!"

"What?"

525

"You are complaining that Zuzka refuses to lie to you the way you do to her."

"You think she's having an affair," said Tomáš bleakly. He put his knife and fork down on the plate, his grilled veal chop barely touched.

"And if she is, do you blame her, after the way you've been acting?"

"I love her," he said. "The other women have nothing to do with my feelings for her. They are something I need, that my *ego* needs. I never meant to hurt her." He shook his head. "If only Zuzka was as blind as other wives."

Katrinka felt a stab of fear, like a jab from a cold dull blade. Though Adam had always traveled a great deal, recently his trips alone had begun to worry her. She could not quite put her finger on why this should be, could find no rational justification for it, and usually dismissed her worries as foolish. But the suspicion she could not rid herself of entirely, no matter how she tried, made her ask, "What other wives?"

"No one in particular," responded Tomáš evasively.

"Do you mean me?"

He forced himself to look directly into her eyes. "No," he said, "of course not."

Though she wanted to believe him, Katrinka was not certain she could. Tomáš was about to direct a major motion picture for Olympic Pictures. She knew that whatever love and loyalty he felt for her came second to that. He would do nothing to jeopardize his relationship with Adam.

Tomáš reached across the table and took her hand. "If I had meant you, *zlatíčko*, would I have been stupid enough to say anything?"

No, of course he would not have, Katrinka assured herself. "No," she said.

Wolfgang Puck, making the rounds of the room, stopped by for a moment to chat. Katrinka introduced him to Tomáš and complimented him on the meal. After some small talk, the popular restaurateur, smiling broadly, moved on to Joan Collins.

As soon as he had gone, Tomáš said, "What am I going to do?"

"Talk to Zuzka," responded Katrinka after a moment, sounding more confident than she felt. "You love each other. You'll be able to work everything out."

"I don't need this kind of shit when I have a movie to plan."

"I said talk," cautioned Katrinka. "Not shout."

Unfortunately, Katrinka was less and less able to follow her own advice.

The Grahams returned to New York in time for Christmas, and they got through that smoothly enough. Though Adam probably would have leapt at the chance to spend the holiday anywhere but with his mother, Katrinka's sense of family always prevented her from suggesting they make other plans. So, as was customary on Christmas Eve, they drove in Adam's Ferrari, loaded with gifts, from New York to the family home in Newport, which Nina refused to sell, though it was a monstrous drain on her income, reduced, like almost everyone else's, because of the slump. Once there, they admired the Douglas fir decorated with ornaments passed down from generation to generation of Grahams, ate too much, drank even more, endured Nina's barbs, put up with Clementine's complaints, Wilson's pomposity, the arrogance of their two sons, the dullness of the assorted relatives invited for Christmas lunch. As soon as possible, they fled back to Manhattan.

They didn't start fighting until they were getting ready for bed, when Adam announced that instead of leaving for St. Moritz in the morning, as planned, he would be flying to Los Angeles for a few days.

Recently there were few decisions made by either that did not provoke a quarrel. Usually it was Adam who pounced. If Katrinka wore a blue dress, he was annoyed because it wasn't pink; if short, because it wasn't long; if she wore her hair up, he wanted it down; if she arranged to go out, he wanted to stay in, and if they stayed in too often, he accused her of turning into a bore. When he attacked, she countered. Resenting his constant criticism, his permanent air of disapproval, she said things she later regretted, questioning his business judgment, the money he was throwing away on

Olympic Pictures, the enormous burden of debt he was finding it harder and harder to service. As does everyone who falls in love, they had revealed to each other their weak points, their vulnerable areas; and like any couple with problems, they attacked them constantly and with unerring accuracy.

Perhaps foolishly, Katrinka had seen the trip to St. Moritz as a chance to put things right. Always concerned about how little time they spent together, she had looked forward to an entire week in Adam's company, hoping that, despite the phone calls and faxes that followed them everywhere, without the day-to-day stress of business, some of the strain on their marriage would be relieved and they could relax, enjoy themselves, and stop the endless petty squabbles that were making them both miserable.

When Adam told her he would not be going with her, Katrinka's disappointment turned instantly to anger. That his company had a film starting to shoot in three weeks with an inexperienced director (that is, Tomáš) about whom everyone was nervous was not, in her opinion, a good enough reason to break a promise to her, especially since she considered Adam's staff at the studio more experienced about film and probably better able to make decisions than he.

They went to bed still angry and, the next morning, when Adam promised to meet her in St. Moritz at least in time for her birthday, Katrinka only shrugged and told him to suit himself.

Forty-One

S ince Adam was not accompanying her, Katrinka decided to take the Concorde to Paris and, instead of making a direct connection to St. Moritz, to spend the night at the Plaza Athénée and see Paul Zeiss before continuing on.

When she arrived at his office the next morning, she found little changed from her last visit, or, for that matter, from her first, nine years before. No doubt the paint had been freshened and the carpet replaced several times, but anything new blended so comfortably with the old as to be unnoticeable. Even Zeiss himself appeared always the same—a placid, gray man, looking more like an accountant behind his horn-rimmed glasses than the detective she had hired to find her son. And this time, he was, as always, quite unperturbed at not having done so.

"Finding a needle in a haystack always takes time," he replied in his oddly perfect English when she pointed out the enormous sums of money she had spent to accomplish nothing. "If you wish to stop," he added, shrugging, "that is, of course, entirely your decision."

"But are you any closer?" she asked, always reluctant to make that decision.

"Who knows? The paper trail so far has taken us nowhere, but that is not to say it goes only to a dead end. Sometime soon, perhaps, one of the names on Herr Kleiser's list will lead us to your son." Herr Kleiser was the lawyer, now deceased, who had handled the child's adoption, and most

529

of Zeiss's time and Katrinka's money had been spent tracking down his former clients in the hope of finding the one who had Katrinka's son.

"Soon," murmured Katrinka, her voice impatient and despairing.

"Before you make up your mind, there is one matter I do want to discuss with you." Zeiss took a swallow of the coffee his secretary had brought them a short time before, then said, "Over the years, we have compiled quite a case against Dr. Zimmerman, all circumstantial as yet, but there is evidence not only of his having sold babies illegally but of his having arranged for fake documents to transport them out of Germany. All we are missing is the one person willing to confirm what we know to be true."

"I suppose you have offered people money to talk."

Again Zeiss shrugged. "Of course. For one reason or another, everyone has thought it in their best interests to remain silent. But now, I think, someone *will* talk, to you if to no one else."

Katrinka understood him immediately. "You mean Erica Braun? She knows nothing, or she would have told me years ago."

"Perhaps if she cared for you more than for Zimmerman. Do you believe that to have been the case?"

"No," said Katrinka. The realization that Erica was in love with the doctor had not come to her in a sudden flash but gradually as the only explanation for Erica's blindness concerning him. "But even if you're right—and I still can't believe she knew what he was up to—she'll never do or say anything to hurt him."

"Did you know his wife died?"

"Yes. Erica told me the last time I saw her."

"And that he remarried six weeks ago?"

"No," said Katrinka, surprised. She had been so busy, she had not phoned Erica in over two months.

"As you can imagine, Mrs. Braun is distraught. If you have a word with her . . ."

"And then?"

"When we have our witness, we will turn the evidence over to the police."

530

A weapon, thought Katrinka, as she stared out the window at the one visible corner of the Beaubourg. Finally, a weapon to use against him. She turned back to Zeiss. "I will let you know," she said. Rising, she extended a hand and as he shook it, she added, "Keep looking for my son."

Again Katrinka changed her plans. Returning to the hotel, she asked the concierge to book her on the next flight to Munich and from there to Zurich and on to St. Moritz. Then she put in a call to Daisy, with whom she was staying, to tell her she would not be arriving until late, warning her, if Adam should call, only to say that she was en route.

"You don't have a lover, do you?" asked Daisy, who had paid Bjorn Lindstrom's fare to Los Angeles and was currently involved with Riccardo Donati, the sculptor. It was his chalet in St. Moritz to which Daisy had invited Katrinka, Adam, and a small group of friends.

"God forbid," said Katrinka, laughing. "Adam is all I can handle."

It was only when the plane touched down in Munich that Katrinka realized she had no idea whether or not Erica Braun was at home. But luck was with her and, when she phoned from the airport, Erica answered and immediately invited her to the apartment. Katrinka hailed a cab and soon was sitting opposite her old friend at the table in the large kitchen where they had spent so many hours talking to one another over the years. Erica had lost weight and with it her voluptuous beauty. She had allowed her pale blond hair to go gray, and her face was lined with pain. "Ah, *liebling, liebling,*" she said as she served Katrinka the luncheon of cold meat and potato salad that she had prepared, "it is so good to see you."

The ulterior motive for her visit momentarily forgotten, Katrinka listened while Erica told of her wasted years waiting for a man who did not love her, who had used her as he used everyone who crossed his path. She had quit her job at the clinic and was living on her savings, spending too much time alone drinking. "Why was I such a fool?" she said, rocking back and forth in her straight-backed chair.

"How could I have believed that one day he would leave that foolish wife of his and marry me?"

"You're a beautiful, kind, fantastic woman," said Katrinka, her voice tender, full of concern. "So many men would want to marry you. Only you chose the wrong one to love."

Erica poured herself another glass of the Rhine wine she preferred and swallowed it. "His new wife is very rich. I think he must have been sleeping with her even before the other one died."

"You have to forget now. Start to make a new life for yourself."

"You can say that," said Erica, "you're still young. For me, it's different."

"You're not old. You're not even fifty-five yet," said Katrinka impatiently. "Oh, I hate to see you making yourself so unhappy over that rat. When I think of what he did to you, to me, to so many people . . ."

"You were so young, so confused. He acted in your best interests," said Erica, who had not yet lost the habit of defending him.

"What he did was wrong. It was immoral *and* illegal. He took advantage of my weakness. He sold my baby, he sold other babies, he transported them out of Germany with fake papers, and he made himself a fortune doing it. He should be punished."

Erica put down her wineglass and stared at Katrinka. "That's why you came," she said.

"Yes," said Katrinka softly. "I heard only today he had remarried. I came without thinking really how upset you must be. I'm sorry."

Erica shrugged. "I should have realized."

"Erica, you know how much I care about you. How grateful I am to you."

"Why be grateful to me?" asked Erica bitterly. "I suspected what he was doing, but I couldn't make myself believe it. Not at first. And when, later, I was sure, I didn't try to stop him." She began to cry. "But, *liebling,* I didn't know then, I promise you. I did what I thought was best for you."

"I know. I know," said Katrinka soothingly. She felt no resentment at all toward this woman. All her anger, all her hatred was for Zimmerman alone.

After a few moments, Erica wiped her eyes, took another sip of wine, and said, "What do you want me to do?" And when Katrinka looked at her blankly, for the moment not quite understanding what she meant, she continued impatiently, "What is it you came here to ask me?"

Katrinka hesitated. Did she have the right to make this poor woman suffer even more? But the desire to find her child finally overwhelmed even her pity. She told Erica about Zeiss and the evidence he had gathered against Zimmerman. "We need you to confirm what we already know," she said when she had finished. "If you do that, I can force him to tell me where my son is."

Erica rose from the table, opened another bottle of wine, and poured them each a glass, remaining silent as she thought. Finally, she said, "I'll give you a statement, but you have to swear to me you'll never use it in court."

Katrinka hesitated. That was not her intention now, but she hated to make promises she might not be able to keep.

"Swear to me," insisted Erica.

"I swear," said Katrinka finally.

Before leaving, Katrinka wrung from Erica a promise that she would begin to look for a job as soon as the holidays were over, and that she would spend Easter with Adam and Katrinka at the Villa Mahmed. Erica had visited the villa several times before and had cruised with the Grahams on the *Lady Katrinka,* so it was not shyness that made her hesitate. She did not feel like doing anything, she insisted. "That will change as soon as you find a job," said Katrinka, who had an unfailing belief in the healing power of work.

From the airport, she called Paul Zeiss and told him that Erica had agreed to sign a sworn statement, but that he was to do nothing with it without Katrinka's approval. Then she phoned the head of the modeling agency for which she had once worked and recommended Erica for a job as receptionist.

* * *

A car met Katrinka at the small St. Moritz airport and she collapsed gratefully into its luxurious leather seat. She roused herself sufficiently to greet Daisy and Riccardo, Riccardo's two sons, their wives and children, Lucia, her daughter Pia, and the Jensens, all of whom were staying at the chalet. Curiosity was evident on all their faces, but Katrinka was too tired to offer any explanations and asked to be shown to her room. She showered quickly, collapsed into the luxurious feather mattress on the old-fashioned carved-wood bedstead, and fell instantly asleep.

She thought she would sleep for days, but was awake at seven, before anyone but Riccardo, who did not know her well enough to ask why she had arrived so late, though he, like the others, wondered. Instead, they talked about Daisy, who had been upset the preceding day by a phone call from her daughter to tell her that Steven had been hospitalized with pneumonia, always a bad, if not immediately fatal, sign with AIDS victims.

"She will go to New York as soon as the holidays are over," said Riccardo.

"You'll go with her?" asked Katrinka.

"For part of the time, at least. I have work to do and," he added, smiling, "it is not so easy for sculptors to move their studios."

Riccardo was in so many ways Daisy's opposite. A year or so older than she, he was as large and untidy as Daisy was small and precise, as shy as she was gregarious, as tied to his studio in Fiesole as Daisy was free to travel the world. But in the eighteen months since they had met, they seemed to have learned how to accommodate those differences. Though Daisy had kept her apartments in New York and London, she had sold her house in Surrey and bought a fifteenth-century farmhouse outside Florence, not far from Lucia's, where she now spent most of her time so as to be near Riccardo. And Riccardo tore himself away from his work several times a year not only to go skiing, but to keep Daisy company on some of her travels. They had evolved a life-style that seemed to keep them both happy.

But it was always easy in the beginning, reflected Katrinka, when people first fell in love. Then they were willing to do anything to please the other. It was later, much later, that the problems started.

The first run down the mountain, and Katrinka felt her spirits soar. The sun shone brilliantly and the light was crystal clear. Everything stood out in sharp relief, the aquamarine sky, the snow-covered mountains, the lift cables, the pine trees, the brightly colored bodies hurtling along the piste. Her body flew through space, and she gloried in the speed and excitement of it, the freshness of the air, the rush of the wind, the straining of her muscles as she made long, fast turns. For the moment, everything was forgotten but her pleasure in the sport.

From time to time she caught sight of Riccardo and his sons or Ted Jensen, looking fit and happy now that he had been sober for three years and his business was clearing a healthy profit again. She returned their waves and continued without stopping to speak, reluctant to have her tranquil mood shattered. When she stopped for lunch and saw that Lucia had preceded her into the restaurant, she was tempted for a moment to leave and return later. The peacefulness of the morning seemed very precious to her and she was reluctant to let it go. But Lucia saw her and smiled and Katrinka resigned herself to the inevitable and joined her.

"How you doing?" said Katrinka, sitting down.

Lucia smiled, for a moment relieving the bleak look in her chestnut-colored eyes. "You sneaked out this morning before any of us could find out what you've been up to," she said.

"Nothing very interesting," replied Katrinka. "I heard Erica Braun was not feeling so good. I went to see her for a few hours."

Lucia had met Erica a few times at the Villa Mahmed. "It's nothing serious, I hope," she said, sounding concerned.

"Man trouble," said Katrinka. "But I think she will get over it, the way we all do, sooner or later."

"Yes," agreed Lucia, looking miserable. They ordered a light lunch of grilled veal and vegetables and when the waiter left Katrinka asked if Lucia had heard from Nick. "He calls every day," she said bleakly.

535

"And?"

"I'm not going back to him."

"Ay yi yi yi," murmured Katrinka sympathetically. Lucia had certainly made the right decision, but it was a painful one for her.

"I can't believe what a fool I've been," said Lucia, echoing Erica Braun's words. "What a complete idiot."

At about the same time that rumors had started to circulate about the possibility of Nick's being hauled before a grand jury on a number of felony charges, snide pieces about Lucia's work began appearing regularly, not only in Sabrina's column, but in *The Daily News, The Post, New York Magazine, Vanity Fair,* in articles written by substantial journalists. At first, Lucia had been more worried about Nick's trouble than from her own bad press. For years, she had accepted his explanation that he defended mobsters because somebody had to, because that was the American way. She had, in truth, admired him for his courage. And she was so in the habit of defending him, starting with their first date and her mother's pronouncement of Nick as "unsuitable," so used to dismissing attacks against him as blind prejudice, that she continued to take his part without much real thought when others grew increasingly skeptical. Even the need to send their daughter out of the country to get her away from the publicity had not weakened Lucia's faith. The press attacks against Nick she considered harassment and the charges of felony a direct result of New York's ambitious attorney general trying to make a name for himself combating the Mafia. And when the press started taking potshots at her, that had only confirmed, not changed, her opinion.

But then Carlos Medina, who had been her protégé and longtime friend, insinuated that she had stolen a commission from him. Furious, Lucia had accused him of jealousy, and Carlos had countered by saying that Nick was strongarming people into hiring her. At first she thought the whole idea crazy. With her excellent reputation and long list of pleased clients, why would Nick have to intimidate anyone into giving her work? But Carlos's words continued to rankle, the press attacks continued, and so Lucia went to

Adam to ask him to try and find out if there was any truth to what Carlos had said. Adam made a few phone calls and discovered that quite a few of the builders he knew, as well as some of the boat owners, confirmed Carlos's story: Nick had "encouraged" people to hire his wife by hinting at the problems they might encounter if they failed to do him the favor.

When Adam told her that, Lucia, of course, was furious. Savvy enough to understand the importance of connections in business, she knew that few people got far without favors. But what Nick had done went beyond, far beyond, the accepted code of one hand washing the other. He had blackmailed people into using her, and for no reason. That was the insanity of it. Though far from arrogant, Lucia did have a healthy respect for her own talent, and was convinced that any job Nick had "helped" her to she could have got for herself on her own merits.

Nick was only too happy to admit what he had done when Lucia confronted him. In fact, like the secret sender of a Valentine's Day card, he had hoped he would be discovered so that his thoughtfulness might be appreciated. He had helped his wife and was proud of it. What, after all, were husbands for? That she considered his help insulting, degrading, demeaning, he could not understand. The reasons for her fury were a mystery for him. He thought she was overreacting and would calm down. She didn't. If Nick could stoop to blackmail when it wasn't necessary, what was he capable of doing when it might really be useful? Her faith in him was totally shattered. His motives for defending his Mafia clients might once have been as pure as he had always claimed, but no longer. Somewhere along the way, he had been corrupted. If he was not guilty of all the felony charges being leveled against him, she was certain he was guilty of some. Early in December, Lucia moved out of their apartment and went to the house in Fiesole to be near Pia, who was in school in Florence, then brought her daughter to St. Moritz to join Daisy and Riccardo for Christmas.

"All those years, I trusted him," said Lucia. "I must have been out of my mind."

"No crazier than any other woman in love."

"He ruined everything between us. He took away all my pride in having made it on my own."

"You did make it on your own," insisted Katrinka. "What Nick did was stupid. It hurt you. But how can it take away your pride in all your beautiful work?"

"I'll never forgive him," said Lucia. "Never."

As Katrinka had feared, the encounter completely shattered the morning's tranquillity and with it her pleasure in skiing. Then, on her third descent, it began to snow hard, the wind blowing the icy flakes into her nose, her ears, down the collar of her turquoise ski jacket. With only a pair of panty hose under her ski pants and a thin silk shell under her parka, she was soon freezing and decided to call it a day, returning to the chalet for a hot shower and a nap before the night's festivities.

They dined at the chalet, Riccardo's grandchildren with their nannies in the nursery suite, the others in the paneled dining room with its coffered ceiling and walls hung with old tapestries, a corner occupied by one of Riccardo's monumentally playful tin sculptures. The mood was so festive that even Lucia was caught up in it.

"We have great news," said Margo.

"I'm glad somebody has," said Daisy cheerfully.

Margo leaned her elbows on the table, put the tips of her long red-painted fingernails together, and said to Ted, "You tell them."

Ted grinned. "We've had an offer for the business. A good offer."

"You mean someone still has money to invest?" asked Lucia.

"Not the banks," said Katrinka.

"We're selling," said Ted, his eyes shining behind his horn-rimmed glasses. "Packing up. Getting out of New York."

"Going where?" asked Riccardo.

"Palm Beach," said one of Riccardo's sons. "I love Palm Beach."

"Florence," said Daisy. "You'd love living there. It's perfect."

"I would like very much to live in California," said the second of Riccardo's sons.

"We thought," said Margo, "maybe the south of France. We always love staying at the Villa Mahmed so much."

"That would be fabulous," said Katrinka.

"Maybe Monte Carlo," said Ted. "Great tax breaks there."

"We're having such a great time trying to decide," said Margo, "we'll never make up our minds."

After dinner, they went to a party at a neighboring chalet and did not return home until three. But again the next morning, Katrinka was up early and out on the slopes by eight. She skied until the lifts stopped in the afternoon, partied again that night, and the next day won two of the races in the St. Moritz/Gstaad competition. Adam always seemed to phone when she was out and, when she returned his call, he was in a meeting, out to dinner, somewhere as unavailable as a ski slope. He left a message finally that he was arriving late on her birthday.

The Prince and Princess of Thurn und Taxis were throwing a costume ball at the Palace Hotel that night, and when Adam had not yet arrived by the time the others were ready to leave, Katrinka decided to go along with them rather than to wait, not knowing how long he would be delayed.

It was a decision she lived to regret.

The theme of the ball was "Celebrities," and costumes ranged from the elaborate to the casual: Charlie Chaplin, W.C. Fields, Marilyn Monroe, Shirley Temple, Will Rogers, Dolly Parton. Riccardo went as Prince Albert and Daisy as Queen Victoria, Margo and Ted as Ginger Rogers and Fred Astaire. Lucia, dressed as a nun, insisted she was Mother Theresa, and Katrinka, in a red wig and slinky Bob Mackie dress, Rita Hayworth playing Sadie Thompson.

Entering the ballroom, the first person Katrinka saw was Prince Khalid in his white robes and checked keffiyeh. Lucia laughed for the first time in weeks and said, "Who does he think he is, Rudolph Valentino?" and then went over to say hello to him and his new wife. She and Adam had managed to stay close to the prince, but he and Katrinka still avoided one another when possible. Natalie remained a sore point between them, even though this wife (one of three) was younger, blonder, more beautiful, and had just given birth to a son.

"My God," said Daisy loudly over the blare of the rock music, pointing to a young woman with dark upswept hair, high cheekbones, pale blue eyes obviously the effect of contact lenses, in a copy of an Ungaro gown Katrinka had worn to a recent gala in New York, "she's come as you."

"You've become very famous, my dear," said a familiar voice in German.

Turning, Katrinka saw Klaus Zimmerman in a raincoat and soft hat, looking like Max von Sydow in *Three Days of the Condor*. Her usual anger flared briefly to be replaced immediately by relief. Now that he had found her, she did not have to seek him out. "Hello, Dr. Zimmerman," she said pleasantly as her friends drifted off to greet people they knew, leaving her to talk to him alone. "How convenient to find you here."

"Convenient?" he echoed, confused by her unexpected cordiality.

"Yes, I was hoping to be able to speak to you. And now you've saved me a trip to Munich."

He bowed slightly. "Always happy to be of service to you, my dear."

"Dr. Zimmerman," said a young man in German as he touched the doctor lightly on the arm. "So sorry to interrupt, but my parents and Mrs. Zimmerman are wanting to leave."

"Ah, yes, Christian. Do you remember Mrs. Graham? You've met her, I think."

The young man clicked his heels together and bowed slightly. "A pleasure to see you again, Mrs. Graham," he said politely, though it was clear he did not remember her.

He was a handsome young man, in his early twenties, with

540

dark hair, beautiful fair skin unmarred by any shadow of a beard, high cheekbones, and dark brown, slanted eyes. So preoccupied was she with Zimmerman that it took Katrinka a moment to place him. "Christian Heller," she said. "Is that right?" He was the son of the diplomat with whom Katrinka and Adam sometimes socialized.

"Yes. How kind of you to remember me."

"You have changed since the last time I saw you."

"For the better I hope?" He smiled at her, fully aware of the effect his looks had on women.

"I do hope so," said Katrinka, returning his smile.

"Tell your parents I will be with them immediately," said Zimmerman, dismissing him.

Again, Christian Heller gave a click of his heels and slight bow. "Good-bye, Mrs. Graham," he said.

"Thinks he's quite a charmer, that boy," said Zimmerman disapprovingly.

"But he is," said Katrinka.

Zimmerman smiled, "Do you think so?" he said, no longer sounding annoyed. "And what did you want to see me about?"

"To tell you that now I have enough evidence against you to convict you of any number of crimes, from baby-selling to using forged documents."

"Ridiculous," said the doctor angrily. "You don't know what you're talking about."

"If you tell me where my son is, then maybe I forget what I have learned. Otherwise . . ." she shrugged.

"You're bluffing," he said.

"You'll receive proof soon. Think about it," replied Katrinka. "And let me know. Only, if I were you, I would not take too long. I have wasted so much time already."

Zimmerman turned abruptly and walked away, his face pale, his eyes angry. Katrinka watched him as he joined the Hellers and a tall voluptuous woman in a flesh-colored dress and short blond wig, whom she assumed was his wife. She looked, thought Katrinka with irritation, as Erica might have twenty years before.

"Who on earth was that?" asked Lucia breathlessly,

winded from a brief turn on the dance floor with one of Riccardo's sons.

"The man who broke Erica Braun's heart," said Katrinka. And mine, she added silently.

"He looked furious when he walked away," said Lucia. "You must really have let him have it."

"Not yet," said Katrinka, "but I will."

Katrinka danced with Riccardo and his sons, with Ted, and her host, the portly Johannes, who was known as the Prince of After-Darkness, with Gianni Agnelli, with a number of younger sons of deposed heads of state, and was just about to call it a night and return to the chalet to see if Adam had yet arrived when Jean-Claude Gillette grabbed her by the arm and led her out onto the floor. She repressed a groan. Jean-Claude could be very amusing, but, just as often, he could be difficult, and Katrinka did not feel up to coping with him now with the inevitable scene with Adam still to come.

They danced silently, the music making it impossible to speak. When Katrinka finally pleaded exhaustion, Jean-Claude put an arm around her waist as if to prevent her escape and escorted her from the floor, taking a glass of champagne from the tray of a passing waiter and handing it to her to drink. He took another for himself and lifted it in a toast. "Happy birthday," he said.

As always, he surprised her. "Jean-Claude, how sweet you are to remember."

"I thought women preferred men to forget," he said, leaning forward to kiss her lightly on the mouth. "You get more beautiful every year."

She laughed. "What a terrible flirt you are, Jean-Claude. How your wife does put up with you?" He had not bothered to come in costume but wore a dinner suit. His long dark hair had streaks of bright silver and the furrows in his high forehead were deeper, but otherwise he had not changed.

"The same way you put up with your husband, I expect."

She laughed. "You and Adam are nothing alike," she said, though it was not quite accurate. They were both ambitious and cunning, ruthless and charming. It was their styles that differed. Jean-Claude's was suave and sophisticated in the

European manner, while Adam's was direct and as American as a Cadillac.

"Not true. For one thing, we have exactly the same taste in women." He shrugged. "But unfortunately he has been more successful with mine than I with his."

He was implying something unpleasant. Katrinka understood that much, but somehow she could not quite get his meaning. I have had too much champagne, she thought. "If you think Adam is sleeping with your wife, you're wrong."

"Oh no," said Jean-Claude cheerfully. "Certainly not with my wife."

"You do talk such nonsense, Jean-Claude," said Katrinka irritably.

"Katrinka, what an innocent you are," he said, drawing her closer. He kissed her neck. "And I must say I wish you weren't."

She pulled away and said, "Why I do feel you're talking in code tonight?"

"Shall I translate?" He ran his hand gently up her bare arm to her shoulder. "Sleep with me."

"A tempting offer," she replied with a smile, trying to lighten a moment that had suddenly become too intense. "But unfortunately I do love my husband."

"The more fool you," said Jean-Claude, his hand dropping to his side.

Too many women had used the word "fool" to her in the past few days for it not to register with Katrinka. "Why am I a fool?"

"What keeps your dear husband in California when you are here?"

"How do you know where he is?"

"How? Because Natalie told me, of course."

"Natalie?" And suddenly she knew. "Oh, my God," she said. "Natalie."

"Yes," said Jean-Claude, "Natalie."

"Katrinka, my dear, are you ready to go?" asked Daisy. "We're all ready to drop. Oh, hello, Jean-Claude. What a poor sport you are not to wear a costume."

"You look lovely, *chérie*," he said, kissing her on both cheeks. "As always. May I stop in tomorrow to see you?"

543

"Certainly. Come to lunch if you like. Is your wife with you?"

He waved a hand. "Over there somewhere."

Daisy hooked her arm through Katrinka's. "Come along. You look absolutely bushed." She turned to Jean-Claude. "She's up at the crack of dawn every day skiing. It can't be good for her. See you tomorrow," she said, leading a dazed Katrinka toward the door.

Adam was in bed, asleep, when Katrinka and the others arrived back at the chalet. Still too numb to feel angry, she turned on the light and sat in the pretty printed armchair, staring at him, waiting for him to wake up and face her, wondering what she was going to say to him. Finally, he turned over, threw an arm across his eyes and groaned. "Katrinka, for christsake, turn off the goddamn light. I'm beat." When nothing happened, he removed his arm, opened his eyes, and looked at her. For a moment, he almost didn't recognize her, and then remembered she had been to a costume ball. "Happy birthday," he mumbled. "Your present is on the dresser. Hope you like it."

"Natalie did help you pick it out?"

He sat up and said, "I've never needed help to choose gifts for you." His salt-and-pepper hair was all awry. His face was pale and tired, but his eyes were suddenly alert and wary.

"Is it true?"

He looked at the clock on the bedside table and said, "Katrinka, it's three-thirty in the morning. I've been traveling for over fifteen hours. Can we please discuss whatever is bothering you tomorrow?"

She pulled the red wig off her head and ran a hand through her dark hair. Her head was beginning to ache. "I want to know. Are you sleeping with Natalie?"

"What gave you that crazy idea?"

"Are you?"

"Look, it's not what you think . . ."

"You are!" The words were almost a wail.

Adam pushed back the covers, swung his legs over the side of the bed, rested his feet on the floor, but did not get up. "Katrinka, we didn't mean it to happen. We went out to

544

dinner. And I suppose we both had a little too much to drink. One thing just sort of led to another."

"How long?"

"I don't know. Six months maybe. Nine months."

"How could you? The two of you? Natalie is my best friend!"

"I told you," said Adam, beginning to sound irritated, as if he were being forced to repeat an instruction to a particularly dim subordinate, "we didn't mean it to happen."

"Fine," snapped Katrinka, the anger beginning to melt away the ice that had formed inside her. "And that does mean I should forgive you?"

"I didn't ask you to forgive me."

"Do you love her?" Adam sat silently, as if weighing his answer. "Do you?"

"I don't know. Maybe. Yes," he said finally, though not even sure he meant it. The relief he felt was enormous, as if he had been in prison and was suddenly free.

A low cry escaped Katrinka. The tears welled in her eyes and flowed down her cheeks. He got up and went to her. "Don't touch me," she said. He stepped back, not certain what to do. "I want you to leave. Go to the hotel. Go anywhere. I don't want you here."

"Katrinka, be reasonable . . ." Why was he arguing, he wondered, when all he wanted was to go?

"Take one of the cars. I'll send someone to get it in the morning. Just go away."

"Katrinka . . ."

"Go away!"

Silently, Adam went to the closet, took out his clothes, and began to dress. Katrinka sat in the armchair, her eyes closed, tears streaking her makeup, refusing to watch him. When he was ready, he said, "I'll call you in the morning."

"Don't bother. I'll send your clothes with the driver."

Staring helplessly at her, Adam felt as if he had waited for this moment for years and, now that it had come, he regretted it. He didn't want to go. He didn't want to leave her. Was it possible, he wondered, that he still loved his wife? "Katrinka . . ." he said again, softly.

IVANA TRUMP

"Just go," she shouted. "Go!"

He left, and she got up from the chair and flung herself on the bed. She could smell him on the pillow, on the sheets. How could this be happening to her? she wondered. Adam and Natalie. Why had she never suspected? Her husband and her best friend. A joke. "Oh, God, what a fool. What a fool."

546

Forty-Two

By the time Adam phoned the next morning, Katrinka had already left to ski. After a sleepless night, she had dragged herself from the bed, taken a shower, put on some makeup which did not quite conceal her swollen eyes, donned her ski clothes, and ridden the lifts to the top of Piz Nair. Action, as always, was her instinctive reaction to pain; keeping busy was the way she kept from falling apart.

Losing Adam would be awful. But, she reminded herself, she had been through worse and survived.

Katrinka kept out of the way of everyone she knew, waved and pushed off down the piste when anyone approached her. Not hungry, she ignored lunch and stopped only occasionally for a cup of black coffee. Late in the afternoon she realized she was so completely exhausted that, if she returned to the chalet, she would finally be able to sleep. One more run, she told herself, and that's it. But as she readied herself to hop onto the chair lift to Corvigila, Adam, ignoring the others waiting patiently in the line, came up beside her and got on as well. "I've been searching for you for hours," he said.

A red ski cap partially covered his thick hair. Lines of fatigue and worry were deeply etched around his eyes. He looked pale, as if he too had spent a sleepless night. What she wanted him to tell her was that none of it was true, that he loved her, and no one but her. But from the solemn expression on his face and the guilt in his eyes, she knew there was not much chance of that. Suddenly she laughed.

When he had considered all of Katrinka's possible reactions to his sudden appearance, Adam had not listed laughter as one of them. He looked completely startled.

"This is how we did meet," she said.

For a moment, Adam seemed at a loss as he searched his memory, then his mouth curved in the crooked smile that, angry as she was, Katrinka could still grudgingly admit was attractive. "I remember," he said.

The brilliant blue of the sky had faded to gray, and a fog had blown in, obscuring the upper part of the mountains, enveloping the chairs in front and behind them in mist. A few snowflakes began to drift past, carried on the wind. The world seemed eerily quiet. Gently, they rocked back and forth on the chair lift, for the moment silent and awkward as strangers looking for an excuse to speak.

"I'm going to rent a house in Beverly Hills," Adam said finally. "I think we should try living apart for a while."

"You want a divorce?"

"I don't think we should do anything while we're both so upset," he replied.

"And you do think I'll get less upset if you go on sleeping with Natalie?"

"We had problems long before Natalie."

"Well, screwing my best friend was no way to solve them."

"I don't want to talk about Natalie. Natalie is not the issue."

"She is for me." If Adam had done what men of his age often do, if he had found a girl unsophisticated enough not to notice his feet of clay, naive enough to be impressed with him, someone without an ounce of cellulite to make himself feel young again, Katrinka thought she might have understood. But to betray her with a woman of her own age, with one of her best friends, seemed to her to be a malicious act. Even if she believed their love genuine, which she did not, how could she ever forgive them? "If you do want this marriage to last, stop seeing her," she said because she had to.

"No," said Adam. "Not yet."

The chair lift reached the station and she leaped off, coming to a stop a few feet away, adjusting her goggles and gloves while waiting for Adam to join her. "You did hurt me so much," she said when he came up beside her.

"You think any of this has been easy for me?" he shot back, as usual concerned primarily with himself.

Rage wiped out any inclination to be reasonable. "Fuck you," she said, pushing off down the slope.

He took off after her. "Katrinka, wait! We have to talk."

"I want a divorce," she shouted over a shoulder.

"Don't be stupid!"

"I want a divorce!" She crouched low into her skis, minimizing the wind resistance.

"Katrinka!"

She knew that Adam, a much less experienced and more careful skier, could never catch her. He would find her at the chalet later, if he wanted to. He would phone her. There would be lawyers and papers and endless conversations. But, for now, skiing out of his clutches was a small satisfaction, the only one she was going to have for a long while.

For once Katrinka overcame her usual reserve, and told her curious friends (who had not failed to notice Adam's arrival and sudden departure as well as his repeated phone calls during the morning) that he was having an affair and that she was filing for divorce. To Katrinka's dismay, neither Daisy, nor Margo, nor Lucia seemed particularly surprised at Adam's behavior, though they denied vehemently having known when Katrinka asked them. They had just assumed that Adam, like most men, needed an occasional fling, and begged Katrinka not to be hasty, insisting a brief sexual interlude was nothing to wreck a marriage over. They were trying to give sensible advice, but it rang false. Margo did not believe Ted capable of being unfaithful to her, and Lucia would have left Nick even sooner had she caught him in one of his many affairs. Only Daisy, given the opportunity, might have treated infidelity with a ladylike disregard, but Steven, of course, had not given her the chance and she was hoping Riccardo would never put her to the test.

When they heard the woman involved was Natalie, their

positions shifted, but only slightly. They were shocked, outraged, understood Katrinka's humiliation and pain, but still advised her to wait. Adam would grow tired of Natalie, they assured her, and return home. If she loved him, why not give her marriage a chance to survive?

But the marriage was over. Katrinka knew it. There was nothing to wait for. When Adam left Natalie, and she was sure he would sooner or later, he would not go back to her but move on to someone new. "He's never satisfied," said Katrinka to her friends. "He always wants more than he has. He wants a child and I can't give him one." She began to weep and Lucia, moving to the sofa beside her, put her arms around her and began to cry, too, though more for herself and Nick than for Adam and Katrinka. Soon, Daisy and Margo were aware of tears streaming down their cheeks as each remembered Adam and Katrinka at the beginning of their marriage when they had seemed so young and beautiful and so very much in love.

The next day the house party ended. Riccardo's sons and their families left for their homes near Milan; Lucia for Fiesole to return Pia to school before going on to Bremen for consultations with the engineers on a yacht she was designing; Margo and Ted, Daisy and Riccardo for New York. Katrinka had also intended to fly to New York, via London where she had meetings scheduled with the management of the Graham, but the thought of returning to the Fifth Avenue apartment she had decorated so carefully to please Adam was unbearable. So, once she had spoken to Anna, her housekeeper, and to Robin, to the managers of the two New York hotels, had taken care of business and confirmed that all was under control, she faxed Robin a list of the clothes she would need and asked her to FedEx them to her immediately. Then she booked herself on a flight to Prague.

Walking down Pařížská from the Intercontinental Hotel, where she was staying, through the old Jewish quarter, past the crumbling synagogue, along the wide avenue lined with art nouveau apartment buildings, airline offices, book and clothing stores, toward the Old Town Square, what Katrinka noticed first was how much shabbier everything looked after seventeen more years of neglect. Then she saw all the signs of the city's coming back to life. A few newly painted shopfronts brightened the general seediness; there were attempts at attractive window displays; people smiled; the general mood was cheerful, optimistic. It was possible to see how the street might one day soon come to look again like the Parisian boulevard it had once tried to copy. And the Old Town Square with its fifteenth-century clock tower and fairy-tale facades needed only some plaster and paint to resemble a set in a Disney film. The whole city was like Rip Van Winkle awakening from a long sleep troubled by nightmares.

Katrinka walked for hours, the sights of Prague bringing memories rushing back to her as she strolled along the banks of the Vltava, past FAMU where Tomáš had gone to school, the Maxmilianka café, scene of all their revels, across the Charles Bridge, through the winding streets of the Malá Strana lined with charming tile-roofed houses, in one of whose small bedrooms she and Mirek Bartoš had once been lovers, and up the Old Steps to Hradčany. Entering the castle's inner courtyard, she caught sight of the cathedral, went in, and sat quietly for a long time under its soaring Gothic arches, bathed in the golden light that filtered in through the yellow clerestory windows, trying not so much to pray as to rid herself of the confused and angry thoughts tormenting her. Then, by an alternate route, past the Loretto shrine and the scattered buildings of Charles University, she made her way back to the hotel.

In the morning, Katrinka rented a car, a Škoda, put her suitcases in the back, and drove the two hours to Svitov. The familiar snow-covered countryside with its gentle hills and dark pine forests calmed her as Prague had not. She felt the comforting presence of Jirka and Milena everywhere.

When she reached the street market in Svitov, Katrinka parked the car and got out. As she walked along the stalls filled with fruits and vegetables, flowers and clothes, people who had worked with her father or mother, neighbors, friends, old schoolmates, recognized her and stopped to say hello. Their names came to her with amazing speed and accuracy. *"Dobrý den,"* she murmured over and over again, smiling and shaking hands. They wanted news of her life and she gave it to them in a nutshell. Your parents would be proud of you, they told her, beaming with pride at her success. Amazingly, there was no resentment. Life was suddenly too full of possibilities for them to be jealous of another's good fortune. When they asked if she was married, she told them she was. Children? She told them no, and their smiles faded slightly. There's time, they murmured and began to speak of their own.

She bought two large bouquets of flowers and drove out of the city and into the hills to the cemetery where her parents and grandparents were buried. Steering the car carefully along the rutted road between the pine trees and gravestones, she searched for the familiar markers, found them, and stopped the car a few feet from the family tomb. It was a gray day, with snow threatening and a faint mist veiling the tall trees and silent graves, carrying faint sounds like coded messages from a distant world. Her eyes filling with tears, Katrinka brushed the cover of snow from the tomb's black marble surface, laid the flowers across it and sat, waiting for the message she was sure would come. None did, and after an hour, numb with cold, she rose and returned to the car. Only as she was driving the familiar route to the city did she realize that for the first time in days she felt at peace.

Back in Svitov, Katrinka toured the sites of her childhood: her schools, the sports complex where Jirka had worked, the technical college where Ota had taught. She drove up into the hills above the city to find the apartments where Tomáš and she had lived, and on to her grandparents' house. There she knocked on the door and asked if she might be allowed to see it; but the stocky middle-aged husband and wife looked at her suspiciously and, afraid she meant to dispossess them, refused. Many people whose property had been nationalized by communist regimes were filing repossession claims with the government, one of the many problems caused by the return of democracy and capitalism to Eastern Europe, but Katrinka had no intention of doing so. Now that it was possible, she hoped to return to Czechoslovakia often, but thought that an apartment in Prague or a house in the country would suit her better. She apologized to the people for disturbing them and returned to her car, disappointed. She had wanted to see her grandmother's rose garden.

The next door she knocked on was Ota Černý's. For a moment, he seemed not to recognize her, though in fact it was simply that he had been asleep and thought he was still dreaming. "Katrinka, *zlatíčko*," he murmured finally as he hugged her. "I can't believe it. Come in. Come in."

His hair was almost completely gone and his face was lined with age and weather, but he had kept his height and his firm athlete's body. He still skied, he told her, though he had turned sixty-nine on his last birthday and had retired from coaching four years before. "And I still drink too much beer. Would you like one?"

"Please," she said, as he escorted her into the small sitting room with a green three-piece suite that was almost identical to the one her parents had owned.

Olga had died six years before of cirrhosis of the liver and Ota had remarried, a pretty plump woman, a widow, with three children, so now he had the family he had always wanted. "Seven grandchildren," he told Katrinka proudly.

His wife, Maria, insisted that Katrinka stay for dinner, and then for the night. She had vaguely planned to stay at Svitov's one hotel but had made no reservation and happily agreed. "I've made goulash," said Maria. "I hope you like it. And *palačinky*."

"*Ay yi yi yi*," said Katrinka, "how wonderful that sounds. I haven't had a good home-cooked Czech meal in years."

They dined at a table in the kitchen, and Katrinka gave them the heavily edited version of her life, then listened contentedly to their stories of their children and grandchildren. At about ten, Maria excused herself and went to bed, less because she was tired than because she understood that Ota wanted some time with Katrinka alone.

"She's a good woman," said Ota when she had left.

"You deserve one."

"And do you have a good man?" asked Ota, taking a Sparta cigarette from its soft package and lighting it.

"You still smoke?" said Katrinka disapprovingly.

"Not much anymore. Maria nags. Though at my age, what difference can it make?" Then he fell silent.

"I'm getting divorced," said Katrinka finally. The words sounded strange to her, and untrue.

But Ota had no difficulty believing them. He had known something was troubling her. "There's nothing else to do?"

Katrinka shook her head. "I don't think so."

"I know you'll make the right decision for yourself. You always do."

"Not always."

"Ah, well," he said sadly. "Who does?" He took a long drag on his cigarette, and then added, "The important thing is to have no regrets." He was riddled with them.

"I'm sorry I disappointed you."

"You must forget all that. It was a long time ago. And all I remember now is the pleasure you brought me, *zlatíčko.*"

They sat up reminiscing for a few hours more, then Ota showed Katrinka the room where she was to sleep, kissed her good night, and went to bed. It was a small room, very like the one she had had as a child, filled with the heavy blond-wood furniture that had been, if not popular, at least available in Czechoslovakia in the 1950s. Katrinka changed, went down the hall to the bathroom, washed her face, brushed her teeth, then returned to her room, turned down the printed comforter on the single bed and got in. The scent of lavender assailed her, the years disappeared, and she felt like a teenager again. For the first time in almost a week, Katrinka fell quickly into a deep, dreamless sleep from which she did not awake until she heard Maria in the kitchen the next morning and smelled the strong scent of coffee filling the house.

From Svitov, Katrinka drove to the farm to see her Aunt Zdeňka. Here, too, everything was older and shabbier than she remembered, the fences sagging even lower, the frame buildings desperately in need of paint, though her aunt assured her that they had managed very well over the years, using the money Katrinka sent regularly not only to repair the farm machinery but to buy clothes and some luxuries like a new car or refrigerator or pay for family vacations.

Not nearly the adventurous travelers that Jirka and Milena had been, they had gone only as far as Yugoslavia and the sea.

At seventy, Aunt Zdeňka was still spry and energetic. František, who was two years older than Katrinka, was a handsome, vigorous man, as full of mischief as ever. His wife, Olinka, was sturdy and reliable, managing him affectionately and sharing his work running the farm with steady good humor. They had three teenage children, two strapping sons and a lovely girl, also named Milena, who had her great-aunt's red hair and deceptive air of fragility. She watched Katrinka with longing eyes and listened hungrily to tales of life in the United States. "Oh, I would love to see it," she sighed.

"Well, you'll come to visit me one day," said Katrinka. "You'll all come. Soon. What a time we'll have!"

Katrinka's cousin Oldřich and his family had moved to Brno, where he was teaching agricultural studies at the university.

She stayed at the farm for three days, tramping through the snow-covered fields with her cousin's teenage sons, skating on the frozen pond where Jirka had once taught her to swim, sitting around the fire at night, playing the guitar that Oldřich had left behind, singing the same polkas she had sung as a child.

Before leaving Czechoslovakia, there was one other person Katrinka felt compelled to see, and how strong the impulse was troubled her a little. Nevertheless, when she returned to Prague, she called Mirek Bartoš. A woman answered, a young woman, who asked who was calling and heard the name without recognition. She put down the phone, and, in the distance, Katrinka could hear her calling, *"Tati,* telephone." His daughter, thought Katrinka.

Mirek's voice was thinner than she remembered it. He sounded both surprised and pleased to hear from her and agreed happily to meeting her for lunch, though when he suggested the Maxmilianka for old times' sake, Katrinka suggested instead the small café in the Europa Hotel in Václav Square.

Katrinka arrived early, sat in one of the bentwood chairs and studied the room. The Europa's deco interior was desperately in need of refurbishment and Katrinka played briefly with the idea of buying it, imagining how wonderful she and Carlos could make it with a little effort. But then she remembered how much she had to deal with at the moment and her sudden surge of energy receded, leaving her feeling sadder and more forlorn than she had in days. Her eyes filled with tears and she reached into her purse for a handkerchief, muttering to herself in English, as a familiar voice said cheerfully, "Don't tell me I've made you cry already?"

Looking up, Katrinka saw an old man, still big and broad, but with a slight stoop, thinning gray hair, and wrinkled skin. About the same age as Ota Černý, Mirek Bartoš looked years older. Only his dark brown eyes recalled the vigorous, sexy man she had known. Katrinka was both horrified and relieved. Whatever remnants of romantic feeling she had still retained for him withered instantly and all her reservations about seeing him dropped away. She stood up to hug him. *"Miláčku,"* he said softly, "what a wonderful surprise it was to hear your voice. How good it is to see you."

They ordered a wine from Moravia and small open-faced sandwiches of cold meats and fish. As they ate and drank, they filled each other in on the essentials of their lives. Mirek had retired, Vlasta had had a stroke and was in a nursing home since help at home was impossible to get. He lived now with his son and daughter-in-law in the same apartment.

"So that was who answered the phone," said Katrinka. "I thought it was your daughter."

"Ah, no. She lives with her husband and children, not too far away. She's a film director, you know. A much better one than her father, much more adventurous, like your friend Tomáš."

Katrinka told him about Tomáš's new film and then about her own divorce.

"You've had no children?" he asked. She shook her head. *"Miláčku,* I'm sorry," he said.

Katrinka looked at him. "Do you know where he is?" she

asked and understood then why she had needed so desperately to see him. She had never been able to rid herself completely of the suspicion that Mirek might know what had become of their son.

"No, no, I don't. Zimmerman wouldn't tell me. I would have told you, you know. You were so unhappy you broke my heart."

He began to weep, the tears coursing down his withered cheeks, and Katrinka was overwhelmed with pity for him. It wiped out any lingering trace of anger. She reached across the table and stroked his hand. "It's all right," she said. "It wasn't your fault. You did what you had to. We all did."

The next morning, Katrinka flew from Prague to Frankfurt and from there to New York. Normally an excellent traveler, this time she found the flight unbearably long and grueling. Filled with dread at what she had to face on her return, she was unable to sleep and—completely exhausted—greeted Luther, her driver, with relief as well as affection when she saw him waiting for her outside the customs hall. As usual, heads turned as people recognized her and Katrinka made an effort to appear relaxed and happy, returning the smiles of those who greeted her while Luther ran interference, taking care that no one came too close. When they reached the parked Mercedes, Luther opened the door for her, and she saw Daisy sitting inside. "I thought you might like to see a friendly face," she said.

"I'll just be a moment," said Luther, closing the door, going to the trunk to help the porter load the luggage, as Katrinka collapsed gratefully into Daisy's arms.

"Are you all right?" asked Daisy, noticing with dismay how pale and tired Katrinka looked.

"Yes. Much better. Ready for anything now. I was right to go home," she said.

"You look so tired, poor dear."

"There was no way I could sleep on the plane, with so much on my mind. But how is Steven?"

Daisy hesitated a moment, then said, "He died last week."

"Oh, Daisy, I am so sorry."

"We were all there with him. The children and me." She shrugged. "It was time."

"Yes." She shook her head, as if trying to clear it. "Poor Steven."

"I keep remembering him the way he was when I first met him."

Katrinka smiled. "He would like that."

"Yes," agreed Daisy. "He would."

It was not the time of day when Adam normally would have been at home and yet the apartment seemed to shout his absence. Daisy accompanied Katrinka inside so she would not have to enter alone, and remained with her while she tried to eat some of the lunch that a worried Anna had prepared.

"Where's Carter?" asked Katrinka.

"In Los Angeles, with Mr. Graham," replied Anna.

"Yes. Of course." Katrinka lay the fork down on the plate, the tuna salad virtually untouched. She had no appetite and could hardly keep her eyes open.

"Time for a nap," conceded Daisy, who escorted her down the long corridor to the master bedroom, then left her standing in the doorway while she went to the closets and threw open their doors. "The son of a bitch has left his clothes," she announced.

"I think he did go right to California," said Katrinka, her voice weary. She felt too tired to be upset. Or perhaps she just didn't care?

"Well, I didn't want you to be alone when you saw them. I can remember when Steven left what a nasty shock it was to go home and find his clothes still hanging there."

"An empty closet might be worse."

"Yes," agreed Daisy, "I thought of that, too." She drew the curtains, then stayed until Katrinka changed and got into bed.

"You're a good friend, Daisy," said Katrinka.

"So are you," replied Daisy, smiling as she opened the bedroom door. "Try to sleep," she said as she left.

To her surprise, Katrinka slept soundly, through the

remainder of the afternoon and the entire night, not awakening until nine the next morning. Rising, she showered and shampooed her hair, put on a comfortable jumpsuit, and, armed with a pot of black coffee, retreated to her office to make phone calls. She spoke to Robin and to the general managers of all three Graham hotels, scheduled meetings for later in the afternoon, phoned the lawyer who had handled Daisy's divorce and made an appointment to see him the following day. As she was talking to him, a call came in on the house line, and a moment later Anna stuck her head in the door and mouthed that it was Adam.

"Where the hell have you been?" he asked as soon as she had said hello.

"None of your goddamn business," she replied, all desire to be civil gone once she had heard the irritation in his voice.

The conversation deteriorated from there, until Katrinka, trembling with rage, hung up on him. She might not want a divorce, she might love Adam and be heartbroken at the prospect, but an unexpected thought flashed into her mind: if he went, he would take with him the heavy weight of his constant disapproval. She felt a rush of relief, like someone pulled from in front of an oncoming train. But it was gone in an instant, and all the humiliation and pain, the rage and grief came flooding back.

The phone rang again and, fearing it was Adam, Katrinka waited for Anna to pick it up. But it was Robin calling from the Praha. "Paul Zeiss is trying to reach you. He says it's important. Do you want me to patch through a call?"

"Please. And hurry." A wave of excitement caught Katrinka, leaving her breathless. Zeiss had never phoned before. Surely he would not do so now only to tell her that he had still been unable to locate her son? Replacing the receiver, she began to look through the folder of mail that Robin had left for her to review, but she couldn't concentrate and instead sat staring at the phone, waiting for the flashing light that signaled a call a split second before the ring. What was taking Robin so long? she wondered.

"More coffee, Mrs. Graham?" asked Anna from the doorway, her face full of worry.

"No, no more coffee. Some chamomile tea, please, Anna. I did have too much caffeine, I think."

The phone rang again and Katrinka started a little, then picked up the receiver. "Yes?"

"Paul Zeiss," said Robin.

"Mrs. Graham?"

Katrinka recognized the soft, precise voice of Paul Zeiss. "You did find something out?" she asked excitedly.

"Not exactly," he said.

An unfamiliar edge of concern colored his voice. "What is it?" she asked.

"We did as you instructed. We got a signed statement from Erica Braun." He hesitated.

"Yes?" she prompted.

He continued with his story, slowly, as if choosing his words with great care, as if English was an unfamiliar language to him. He told Katrinka that he, personally, had called on Dr. Zimmerman and presented him with copies of Erica Braun's sworn statement, the statements of two other people who had succumbed to bribes once they learned that Erica had talked, as well as the other evidence gathered by the Zeiss detectives over the years. Zimmerman had been shocked by the extent of the documentation, and shaken. He had wanted to know how he could be certain that, if he told Katrinka where to find her son, she would not use what she had discovered against him for revenge.

"I told him he would just have to rely on your good nature."

Katrinka laughed. "Where he's concerned, I have none. But I did promise Erica."

"Yes, well, he seemed to understand how deeply you disliked him."

"Hate him," corrected Katrinka.

"Yes."

Anna entered with the tray of chamomile tea, put it down on the desk in front of Katrinka, and left.

"He was very afraid that you would use what you had learned to ruin him."

"How I would love to."

"And rather than face the shame, well, that is . . ."

Uncharacteristically, Zeiss was stumbling over his words. "I believe that is why he killed himself."

It was not what she had expected to hear. "What?" she said, certain she had misunderstood.

"He shot himself, this morning. In his office, in Munich."

"No," whispered Katrinka, horrified.

"He left no note, no explanation."

"Shot himself?" she repeated. "But why? All he had to do was tell me where to find my son."

"I suppose he didn't trust you not to prosecute, Mrs. Graham. I suppose he couldn't believe you wouldn't want revenge. Death must have seemed preferable to losing his good name, losing everything." He was silent for a moment, then said, as if forcing himself to continue, "There's one other thing." Katrinka waited, knowing that this, too, would not be good news. "He shredded his files. If there was anything in them that might have led us to your boy, it's gone."

Despair overwhelmed her. Zimmerman had been her only link to her child, and now he had escaped her by taking his own life, taking all the hope she had ever had.

"I will of course send you a written report," said Zeiss, "but I thought you would want to know as soon as possible."

"Thank you," said Katrinka.

"I am sorry, Mrs. Graham."

"Yes," she said. She heard him say good-bye, and forced herself to respond before replacing the receiver. I've lost everything, she thought. Everything in the world I care about. Everything.

561

Forty-Three

Sabrina rolled up the stained cuffs of her sleeves, hiked up her uneven hem, and began shoveling dirt with a vengeance. "Katrinket Abandoned for French Doll" ran the column headline announcing the impending Graham divorce. Her dislike of Katrinka had always been instinctive and irrational. What she saw always was a woman not so different from herself—intelligent, ambitious, from a family with no social clout—who, only because she was beautiful, was able to snare a rich, handsome husband to provide her with a life of unbelievable luxury while she, Sabrina, had only been able to get a poorly paid, second-rate government official who had kept her firmly on the sidelines of the society she longed to command and then had left her. That Katrinka's financial success was the result of hard work, that she was well on her way to achieving it—though perhaps less grandly—long before she met Adam, was something Sabrina could not make herself believe. Nor could she accept that people were drawn to Katrinka not because she was rich, that women cared for her and men courted her not merely because she was attractive, but because she was interesting as well as charming, and genuinely *nice*. Homely, bitter, unloved, *unliked* for the most part, Sabrina regarded Katrinka's beauty as a birthright stolen from herself, and jealousy made her spiteful.

And paranoid. She was angry with Katrinka for any number of imagined slights, from greetings that seemed too brief or too cool to unsatisfactory table assignments at galas.

But, most of all, she was angry at Katrinka for lying to her about Natalie's bolt from Prince Khalid at Ascot. To be able now to get Katrinka and Natalie simultaneously, with Adam Graham thrown in for good measure, seemed a wonderful revenge, and the thrill of it made her particularly vicious. In column after column, she reported arguments that had never happened, conversations that had never taken place, gifts that had neither been bought nor received. Adam had given Natalie a twenty-carat diamond engagement ring ran one story; Natalie had phoned Katrinka and begged to be forgiven for stealing her husband went another; a third reported that Katrinka was running up astronomical bills with her favorite designers and was sending them to Adam to pay. There were stories about Katrinka's neglecting business, seeking psychiatric advice, taking lovers, making unreasonable financial demands. Each of the stories had some remote relationship to the truth. The one about psychiatric help, for example, started with a photograph that appeared in *W* of Katrinka chatting amiably to an eminent psychiatrist at a Metropolitan Opera opening. When she twisted her ankle one night while out dancing with a group of business associates and had to be helped from the floor, the incident made Sabrina's column as "Katrinket's Drinking Worries Friends."

Rick Colins, driven by loyalty, friendship, and, most of all, by his dislike of Sabrina, came like a knight to Katrinka's defense. But other columnists picked up the stories and, with little interest in their truth, repeated them. Newspapers and magazines, even television current affairs programs, ran item after item until Katrinka, who had hoped that the press and public alike would soon lose interest in her and Adam, despaired of ever regaining control of her private life.

Though she made an effort to avoid reading or seeing anything concerning the divorce, it was impossible to escape. If Nina Graham did not phone to report the worst of the reports, Clementine did. And there were some items even her friends thought she ought to see for her own protection.

The invasion of her privacy made Katrinka cringe. For

someone who had always been reticent about her life and problems, seeing them splashed in exaggerated form across the front pages of the tabloid press was excruciatingly painful. Still, she tried to bear it all with some semblance of dignity, taking a page from the Kennedy family's handbook on public deportment and pretending to be oblivious to the scandal. She hired a security guard to shield her from those strange people on New York's streets who attempted to get near her either to shout abuse or offer sympathy. She didn't talk about her feelings, even to her closest friends. After Adam's betrayal, and Natalie's, Katrinka found it even more difficult to trust anyone completely. And she lived in fear of Sabrina's discovering the secret of her illegitimate child and her connection to Klaus Zimmerman's suicide. Would Erica, who felt so guilty about her part in his death, blame Katrinka and talk? Would someone else? Would Paul Zeiss? The thought terrified her.

Hoping to dampen public interest by keeping out of sight, Katrinka spent some time in London, handling the business of all three hotels as much as possible from there, retreating from time to time to St. Moritz to ski, to the Villa Mahmed or to Daisy's farmhouse in Italy to rest. But she was forced to return to New York occasionally for meetings relating to the Praha or the Graham, to consult with her lawyer, deal with Adam, and inevitably to see her mother-in-law, who seemed to dislike the divorce (or at least its notoriety) even more than she had the marriage.

Nina used the excuse of her monthly trips to New York to trap Katrinka into a lunch or dinner whenever they were in the city at the same time, and if Katrinka was available for neither, invited herself to stay at the apartment in order to make seeing one another inevitable. That Adam no longer lived there might have been reason enough for most soon-to-be ex-wives to ban his mother from the premises, but Katrinka was reluctant to do that. It seemed petty, it seemed rude, and it violated her sense of family. Instead, she simply tried to keep out of Nina's way.

Why Nina Graham insisted on seeing her was difficult for Katrinka to understand. Their meetings were no more pleasant than they had ever been. In thirteen years, she had won Nina's grudging admiration but not her affection, though that no longer bothered Katrinka. She had come to understand that Nina had no affection, no love to give, not even to her children or to her grandchildren. The most she had to offer was an acceptance of them as her own, and a fleeting approval of their accomplishments should they happen to meet her high expectations. But Katrinka was not one of her own, and even had she managed to produce the desired grandson, the most she would have received in return from Nina was an acknowledgment that Adam's marriage had not been the complete failure she had expected.

If Adam had left Katrinka for someone more socially acceptable, for someone named Duke or Rockefeller or Elliott, Nina might not have been so upset at the prospect of her son's divorce. But, instead, he had chosen—as Nina put it—a Parisian shopgirl, divorced from an Arab and mother of a half-caste child. She was of the opinion that Adam had completely lost his mind. "Who *is* this woman?" she asked Katrinka repeatedly as if she had not met Natalie often at various social functions. "What does my son see in her?"

"Why you don't ask Adam that?" was Katrinka's usual reply.

Nina did, of course, but thinking it an invitation, Adam brought Natalie to visit her. Even after their two-day stay in Newport, Nina was none the wiser. Natalie's charm completely escaped her, which surprised no one, least of all herself.

"Is this true, do you suppose?" Nina asked Katrinka one morning in May, handing her the copy of *The Chronicle* she had been reading.

They had had dinner together the night before at La Grenouille and Katrinka had hoped to escape to her office early enough to avoid seeing Nina again but, to her infinite dismay, on her way out she had found her mother-in-law awake, seated on one of the library's banquettes, reading the morning papers and sipping her coffee. "What?" asked Katrinka, taking the paper and scanning Sabrina's column quickly.

"Do you suppose that woman really is pregnant?"

Katrinka turned pale. Was it possible? Sabrina seemed to think so. Natalie had been seen shopping for baby clothes. "It's possible," said Katrinka, a knot forming in her stomach.

"Not very conclusive evidence," sniffed Nina.

"No," agreed Katrinka. Her throat was so tight she could barely speak.

"I suppose if she does give him a child all this terrible mess will have been worthwhile."

"For you maybe," snapped Katrinka. "Not for me."

For once, Nina Graham seemed taken aback. "Oh, my dear, I am sorry. I had hoped you were over him by now," she added, thinking five months ample time to recover from a broken heart.

"I am," said Katrinka, though she was not sure whether or not that was true. Her feelings seemed to change from moment to moment, love and anger, loneliness and relief alternating so quickly that she no longer could say with any certainty what she felt about anything. "But that doesn't mean all this doesn't hurt," she continued, waving the newspaper at Nina. "And I don't discuss Adam with you ever again. If you do want to know something, ask him. Not me." Katrinka turned to leave the room but stopped when she heard Nina calling her name. "What?" she said ungraciously.

"I know I've made no secret of the fact that I didn't think you the right wife for my son, Katrinka, but you mustn't think that means I don't care about you. In fact, I rather like you. I always have. You're intelligent and courageous, and God knows you're ambitious and hardworking . . ."

"Why wasn't I the right wife for your son?" asked Katrinka, interrupting.

Nina Graham hesitated, frowning. Why indeed? Her judgment of Katrinka had been made quickly, as all her judgments were, without any real consideration of the evidence, but no one before this had ever expected her to justify herself. "For one thing, there was no child . . ."

"That was later. Why at the beginning?"

She took a sip of coffee, considered the question a few more moments, then said finally, "I suppose it's quite simple really. Diamonds in the rough have never much appealed to me."

"What an impossible snob that woman is," said Lucia over lunch that afternoon when Katrinka repeated the line to her.

It was just the two of them at Le Cirque, making a concerted effort to ignore the curious glances thrown their way, greeting acquaintances with amazing poise, determined not to run for cover because their personal lives happened to be the subjects of a media show. Nick Cavalletti had finally been indicted by the grand jury on various felony counts, including conspiracy to defraud and accessory to murder.

The circle of friends who usually provided a protective shield were, for one reason or another, unavailable. The '90s had made their entrance and, since the art market had taken a dive with the rest of the economy, Alexandra was tied up with accountants trying to close her gallery without losing everything. Daisy was in Fiesole with Riccardo; Margo and Ted had sold everything and moved to Monte Carlo; Zuzka, who had finally left Tomáš, was following the golf circuit with Carla; and Natalie, of course, no one spoke to any longer. Lucia herself was in town only briefly for business before returning to Fiesole to be near Pia.

"She did ruin Adam," said Katrinka, "and Clementine. Neither one knows how to be happy."

"I suppose you're right. She has a way of making everyone, including her children, feel as if they've just tracked dog shit onto her priceless Aubusson carpet." Katrinka laughed, and Lucia, taking another Brie twist, covered it in butter and bit into it without any display of enjoyment. One of those women who ate for comfort, since her life was in a mess, she had increased two dress sizes in the past few months. On someone as short and small-boned as she, the weight gain seemed enormous. "But does anyone really know how to be happy?" she asked.

"All the time? No. But sometimes, just to sit still and enjoy the good things you've got? Why not?"

Lucia dropped the roll back onto the bread plate. "I'm not even really enjoying this."

"We should go to the Canyon Spa Ranch. It would do us both good."

"God knows I could stand to miss a few meals." She looked at the barely touched warm chicken salad on Katrinka's plate and shook her head in bemusement. "But look at you, you don't eat a thing. I can't stop when I'm miserable."

"I'm not miserable," insisted Katrinka. "Not anymore."

But Lucia wasn't convinced. She hesitated a moment and then said, "She's not pregnant."

"No?" said Katrinka, almost ashamed of how eager she was to believe Lucia. Perhaps, if Adam had a child later, it would not hurt so much. But with the divorce still pending, with Adam still in her life, with the wound of his leaving her still so raw, she would feel it now as another cruel blow. "You've seen her?"

"Of course not," said Lucia, sounding as outraged as if she had been accused of treason. "But I had a meeting with Adam this morning." She looked at Katrinka apologetically. "That's why I'm in New York. To show him the sketches for a new yacht we're designing for Rupert Murdoch."

"Is Natalie here, too?"

"No. I get the feeling he doesn't encourage her to come. I don't think he'd enjoy running into you with her on his arm."

"I wouldn't like it either," said Katrinka dryly.

"The minute I walked into his office, he told me he had seen Sabrina's column and there wasn't a word of truth in it. Natalie was buying a gift for some baby shower, that's all." The relief rushing through Katrinka made her feel almost happy. "He wants to know all about you, Katrinka," continued Lucia. "He pumps me for information every time I see him. If you ask me, I think he's sorry he left. I think he still loves you. I think he'd come back if you'd let him."

How comforting it would be to accept Lucia's version of reality, thought Katrinka, but she couldn't. She knew Adam too well. He probably did still love her, in some way, on some level, but that wasn't what his curiosity was about, or the ambivalence Lucia sensed in him. "He might, for a while," she said. "But he would go again. Or I would make him leave. The trouble with Adam is he wants too much. All the money, all the women, all the children in the world wouldn't satisfy him." There had been other women over the years, she had learned since he left, items in the columns confirmed by people whose word she trusted. There would be more in the future, she was sure. She could never stand that.

Her own ambition was different from Adam's. It didn't leave her discontented with what she had while striving to achieve something more. "That's what his mother did," continued Katrinka, returning to Lucia's thought. "She made him believe everyone else is to blame for the shit on the carpet. And all the time, they're the ones who do track in the dirt."

The phone rang in the middle of the night and Katrinka, waking, groggily considered not answering it. Wherever she was in the world it seemed to ring sometime around two, with only the soft sound of breathing at the other end when she answered, followed a few seconds later by a click disconnecting the line. With no real evidence, she suspected it was Natalie, wanting to talk, not daring to, when it came to the point not knowing what to say.

They had talked once, briefly, after Katrinka's return from Prague. Natalie had called her to say how sorry she was, how she had never meant to hurt her, how falling in love with Adam had been an accident, perhaps even a mistake. She said she hoped that some day Katrinka would forgive her and that they could be friends again. Katrinka had hung up on her.

After so many years, it could not have been easy for Natalie to lose such a good friend, and perhaps the fact that she had caused the break in some ways made it worse for her than for Katrinka. Katrinka could understand that, but understanding did not make her able either to forgive yet or to forget.

The phone kept ringing and Katrinka realized that the light flashing was on her private line. Few people had access to that number and most used it only in an emergency. She pressed the button, lifted the receiver, and said hello.

"Katrinka, it's Adam."

"Do you know what time it is?" she replied, instantly irritated. If he had another problem with the divorce papers, now was not the time to discuss it.

"There's a problem with Lucia," he said, his voice tired and concerned. "I want to bring her there. Is it all right?"

"What happened?"

"I'll explain when I see you."

"Come right now."

Katrinka got out of bed, put a blue silk wrap on over her nightgown, quickly washed her face and brushed her teeth, pulled her dark hair back into a ponytail, and went into the kitchen to make coffee and put some water up for tea. Anna, looking dazed and a little scared, came into the kitchen to see what was going on. Katrinka reassured her and sent her back to bed, then put cups, a milk jug, and sugar bowl on a tray, and carried everything into the library. A few moments later the intercom rang, and the doorman announced that Adam had arrived. She went to the door and opened it, standing on the threshold, waiting impatiently for the elevator to arrive.

"What is it? What did happen?" she said as soon as she saw them.

Adam had his arm around Lucia who looked completely distraught. "Someone broke into her apartment," he said.

"It was awful," said Lucia.

"You want something to drink?" asked Katrinka, as she led them into the library. "Some wine? A brandy?"

"No, tea will be fine," said Lucia.

"I'll take a brandy," said Adam, moving to the cabinet to help himself.

They had been out to dinner with the Murdochs, explained Adam, taking off his jacket and laying it across the back of a chair, pulling off his loosened tie. Afterward, they had gone on to a club to listen to some jazz. When he took Lucia home, not liking the fact that, since leaving Nick, she had taken a studio in a building without a doorman, Adam had decided to escort her right to her apartment. They had been arguing about the fact, Lucia insisting that, because she was in New York so rarely these days, she did not need anything larger, and Adam replying that he was not advocating bigger, just safer. And then they had noticed her front door ajar.

Everything inside was a mess, tables overturned, lamps knocked askew, sofa cushions torn, contents of drawers spilled, the refrigerator emptied, packages of frozen pizza and cartons of ice cream lying on the floor. They had called the police, waited for them to arrive, told them what they knew, which was nothing, and did not mention what they suspected, although the cops were smart enough to guess.

"You do think Nick was responsible?" asked Katrinka.

"His friends, anyway," said Lucia. Her auburn hair was disheveled, her eye makeup had run, she looked as if she had not slept in days.

"Nothing was missing," said Adam, certain this confirmed what they thought.

"They're trying to frighten me."

"Why?"

"Nick's afraid I'll testify against him at his trial."

"But you know nothing!"

"Not much, anyway. But I believe he's guilty. That's all they want the jury to see. That I think my husband is guilty." The tears ran down her face in streaks of black mascara. Katrinka sat next to her on the sofa and took her hand.

"She ought to get some sleep," said Adam. "She's worn out."

"I'm too scared."

"Do you have anything?" Adam asked Katrinka.

Katrinka nodded. "In my medicine cabinet," she said, watching as Adam walked down the hallway and into what had once been their room. How strange it looked, she thought, though until five months ago she had seen him do just that several times a day, every day they were in New York.

"He ought to pay for what he's done," said Lucia, though

it was not clear whether she meant to society or just to herself. "But I can't testify against him. I love him. It's a sickness," she added sadly, "and I'm not over it yet."

"Tell him," urged Katrinka. "He'll make them leave you alone."

"Nick wants me to lie for him. I can't do that either."

"Promise him you won't start the divorce until after the trial. The district attorney can't subpoena you if you're still his wife. Promise him you'll stay away until everything is over."

Adam returned with a pill and a glass of water. "Here," he said gently to Lucia. "Take this."

Lucia took the pill and swallowed it, then Katrinka led her to one of the guest bedrooms, took a spare lace-trimmed cotton shift from the built-in lacquered chest, turned down the covers of the bed, and waited until Lucia had changed and slipped into bed. "See Nick tomorrow," urged Katrinka. "If you do want, I'll go with you. That would be better than Adam, I think. They would just argue."

"I'll call him," agreed Lucia sleepily. The pill was already beginning to work. "I'll call him in the morning."

Returning to the library, Katrinka found Adam sprawled on one of the banquettes, holding a refilled glass of brandy, his eyes closed. "She's asleep."

His eyes opened. "It was pretty terrifying," he said. "Even I was scared."

"Are you leaving for Scotland tomorrow?" His secretary had called using that as an excuse for Katrinka's having to sign and return the latest version of the divorce papers immediately. She had, of course, not done it.

"The day after. Why?"

"I do think you should take Lucia with you. You can send the jet on to Florence with her."

"Little Miss Fix-it," said Adam, but affectionately.

"I don't want her hurt," replied Katrinka, annoyed.

"Neither do I. I'll suggest it to her tomorrow."

She picked up the tray from the coffee table and carried it into the kitchen, a signal for Adam to leave so that she could get back to bed. But when she returned to the library, he had not moved. "You do have a driver waiting downstairs?" she asked pointedly.

"I sent him away."

"Why?" she asked. She could not help herself, though she knew it was a stupid question. Had she not told Lucia earlier today that Adam always wanted it all?

"I thought you might let me spend the night here," said Adam.

"Well, you were wrong," said Katrinka. "It's not far. You can walk."

"This is still my apartment," he said sulkily, bitter as usual that he now had to take a suite at the Plaza when he came to New York on business.

She turned back and looked at him. "Adam, I don't want to argue. I just want you to go."

He stood up finally, but instead of putting on his jacket, reached for her and pulled her into his arms. "I miss you," he said.

"Good," she said. "I'm happy to hear it. Now, go away."

"There's so much going on, so much I want to talk to you about."

It was, possibly, the most seductive thing he could have said to her. There was so much she would have liked to discuss with him. She wanted his opinion about various things she was planning. In business, his advice was always invaluable. For a moment, she hesitated. And he kissed her. "You're so beautiful," he said, his hands moving slowly up her back, pulling her nearer, sliding gently around to cup her full breasts.

Katrinka had not made love in almost six months and she could feel the welcome, unfamiliar tremors, the slow melting in her body begin. Then she remembered, and all the hurt and pain came flooding back. She pulled away. "And you're a sonovabitch," she said.

"Don't be like that," he murmured, disappointed, trying to pull her back to him, burying his face in her neck. He did want to talk to her. After. There was no one really he could talk to the way he could to Katrinka, no one else he could tell just how worried he was. Every day there was some new problem with one of the businesses, something going wrong he had not anticipated. Sometimes he felt he was running out of the energy to cope with it all. "I need you."

"You should have remembered that before you threw me away," she said, pushing against his chest, trying to remove herself from his arms. Still he didn't let go, and she was afraid for one sickening moment that the encounter was about to turn into a brawl.

Finally, he released her. "I'm sorry," he said.

"You should be."

He smiled and her stomach did its familiar flip. "Only that you won't say yes," he added.

She didn't reply, and he picked up his jacket and tie and put them on. "You were very good to Lucia," she said.

"So were you."

"She did seem so frightened."

"Still haven't learned your verbs, I hear."

"And you still don't know what's important and what's not."

"You're probably right about that," he agreed. She followed him to the door, and, when he opened it, he turned and kissed her on the cheek. "Good night."

"Good night," she replied, closing the door again as soon as he had stepped over the threshold into the corridor.

Immediately, Katrinka's emotions began seesawing inside her, one moment regret rising, the next satisfaction. Finally, satisfaction won. Three months, perhaps even one month ago, she would not have been able to send him away. But as hard as it had been tonight, she had done it. She was definitely getting over him. Very definitely. Feeling lonely, but proud of herself, she returned to her bed.

Forty-Four

Because he was ambivalent about the divorce, Adam
kept changing the terms. It would have been difficult enough
disentangling their various and separate business interests
without trying to work out compensation for what they
might have contributed to each other's ventures, as Adam
sometimes suggested, but then reversed himself when he
realized what he might end up having to pay Katrinka for
her services to Graham Marine should he make any claim
against her hotels, and then reversed himself again when
settlement seemed too near. For her part, Katrinka would
have been happy to have her three hotels, her clothes and
jewels, and the villa in Cap Ferrat. Adam was welcome to
the New York apartment, the *Lady Katrinka,* and all of
Graham Marine. She would be happy if she never saw
another boat again. But sometimes, seeming almost hurt
that Katrinka was not prepared to fight for the apartment, as
if her lack of interest was a rejection of his taste and their
entire marriage, he offered it to her. Sometimes he was
prepared to let her have the Villa Mahmed, sometimes not,
claiming it as an important cog in his European wheel, the
base from which he ran all his ventures. Actually, he had
never cared much for the villa, finding its Oriental opulence
at odds with his simpler taste.

The Graham divorce proceedings dragged on from month
to month, keeping Katrinka in an unsatisfactory limbo,
neither married nor unmarried, emotionally tied, reluctant

to involve herself with the men who had begun courting her as soon as they heard that Adam had left, unable to get on with the rest of her life with her usual decisiveness.

One of the most eager of her suitors was still Jean-Claude Gillette, and occasionally Katrinka toyed with the idea of going to bed with him. He was rich (and seemed likely to remain so, despite the uncertain world), powerful, charming. Difficult as he sometimes was, Katrinka had always found Jean-Claude attractive, and no less so now that deep lines scored the handsome planes of his face. His body was still slim and youthful, his dark eyes as keen as ever. Sleeping with him might be just what her sore ego needed. And, as if he sensed her weakening, he increased his efforts. Wherever Katrinka traveled, when she arrived, she found her hotel room full of orchids. Sometimes, she found him as well in the same hotel. Not foolish enough to think that such a busy man traveled the world specifically in pursuit of her, she did consider that he might rearrange his business schedule occasionally to coincide with hers and wondered if someone on her staff was feeding him information and, if so, what they were getting in return. She had Robin make a few inquiries, and when the culprit—a junior secretary in the London Graham's executive office—was discovered, Katrinka fired her. It was not possible, at that point in her life, for her to pardon even a minor treachery.

Of Jean-Claude she had expected no better and so she continued to dine with him wherever they met, enjoying his company, his mind, the accuracy of his observations, valuing his assessment of the world's worsening economy. Like Adam, he had the good sense to treat her as if she had a brain as well as a body. It was one of the most likable things about him.

Jean-Claude's business empire by this time was vast and, despite the downturn in world markets, he did not seem to be suffering. Except for opening a Galleries Gillette on Fifth Avenue, he had scaled back his upmarket retailing interests throughout the world and concentrated instead on extending his chain of discount stores, as well as the Gillette Boutiques specializing in moderately priced, highstyle casual wear. When the once well-off were reduced to bargain hunting, he was determined to be in place to take their money. With his gourmet stores expanding to include specialty health foods, he was confident he could survive the recession unscathed, vineyards and stud farms intact.

But Katrinka did not, could not finally, go to bed with Jean-Claude, however attractive she found him. For one thing, he and his long-suffering Hélène were still married, and Katrinka had never forgotten the lesson Mirek Bartoš had taught her. For another, she didn't trust him. How could she? He cheated on his wife.

But her association, platonic or not, with Jean-Claude enraged Adam. It was not simply jealousy, or at least not simply jealousy of Katrinka. The Jean-Claude Gillettes, the Mark van Hollens, the Michael Milkens, the Rupert Murdochs, all the nouveaux riches of the world clawing their way to the top, trying to push him and the establishment rich from the mountain they had occupied for so long, brought out the worst in Adam. It was while negotiating with them that he had earned his reputation for ruthlessness. He had to prove that his blood was not too blue and thin for battle, that luxury had not made him soft.

Whenever an item appeared in Sabrina's column or elsewhere that she had been seen with Jean-Claude, Katrinka got a phone call from Adam, which always ended the same way, with her slamming down the phone. The incidents always amused Jean-Claude, who learned of them from Natalie, with whom he remained in touch.

"Why doesn't Adam mind that you're her friend as well?" asked Katrinka one day while they were lunching in the Caviar Kaspia's chic upstairs dining room overlooking the Place de la Madeleine.

Jean-Claude savored his blini of Russian caviar draped with smoked salmon for a moment, then said, "Do you know, your eyes are the exact color of this room, czarist turquoise, I think they call it."

"Why?" persisted Katrinka.

"I assume because he doesn't know. Natalie isn't fool enough to tell him. And don't you, *ma chère*," he said, waving his empty fork at her.

"I'm not interested in making trouble."

"They have enough of their own at the moment, in any case."

"Oh?" said Katrinka, trying not to sound too interested. Though she knew it would be better for her to remain completely ignorant of what Adam and Natalie were up to, she was driven to know, and Jean-Claude was her most reliable source of information. At times she thought that was the principal reason she continued to see him.

"Adam is not divorcing himself from you fast enough to suit her, I'm afraid."

"Or to suit me," said Katrinka, sighing.

But no matter how she pressured her lawyer, or begged Adam to be reasonable, still he found ways to stall.

The months dragged on. Katrinka traveled constantly promoting the hotels. In one ten-day period in July, she flew to Paris for the collections and was guest of honor at a dinner party given by Dior, one of her favorite design houses; went on to Rome and London for a series of luncheons promoting the hotels; returned to New York to present an award at a charity dinner; back to London to renegotiate the details of a package plan with the head of Adam's cruise ship line; to Hamburg to accept an award from *Condé Nast Traveler;* and on to Cap Ferrat for a fashion shoot for *Chic,* designer gowns photographed against the sumptuous backdrop of the Villa Mahmed. The publicity worked, and her hotels remained at eighty-five percent occupancy, though many were falling below sixty.

Others did not fare so well. Nick was tried and convicted on several lesser charges and sentenced to six years in prison. Alexandra closed her gallery, having lost several million dollars, while Neil held Knapp Manning together with spit and chutzpah as the savings and loan scandal rocked the economy and Wall Street shook with the fall of Drexel Burnham.

For a while, Katrinka believed that Adam, like Jean-Claude, would manage to weather the bad times. The film Tomáš had directed (an action-adventure movie about a group of renegade robot teenagers) had been a box-office hit, and several other more modest successes had followed in its wake, so the condition of Olympic Pictures, while not robust, was at least improved. But not only had the recession hit Graham Marine's luxury boat building and tanker business hard and the end of communism in eastern Europe cut military contracts, but the invasion of Kuwait in August 1990 and the tense situation in the Gulf meant a fall-off in holiday travel and losses for the gambling and cruise ship line. Then one of the cruise ships still operating collided with a tanker off the coast of Greece; the Graham captain, found to have been drinking, was held responsible, and a class-action suit for several hundred million in compensation was filed against Graham Marine.

As soon as he heard, Adam called Katrinka. "It's all falling apart," he told her. "Sweetheart, I don't know what to do."

She had never before heard him sound defeated. "You'll hold it together," she told him. "You'll find a way."

"Have dinner with me," he pleaded and she agreed.

They went to "21"; Adam tipped the maître d' and was given his usual table. He didn't want to talk about either business or the divorce, which limited their conversation to gossip about family and friends. He offered her the use of the *Lady Katrinka* and she accepted, though she was not sure when she would have time to use it. They entertained each other with anecdotes and laughed a lot. It was the strangest dinner they had ever had together, but not unpleasant. Still, when Adam asked if he could go home with her, Katrinka said no. She had gained too much emotional ground over the past several months to relinquish it for the price of a meal.

Her phone rang again in the middle of the night and when she answered, it was Natalie. "Katrinka, is Adam there?" she asked without preamble.

"No," she replied, trembling with rage. "And don't call me again. He'll never be here. Never!"

She dropped the receiver back on its hook. Almost immediately, the phone rang again. "I don't know what to do," said Natalie, crying. "Katrinka, he's driving me crazy."

Katrinka depressed the disconnect button and then took all the phones but the one on her private line off their hooks.

And the next day, when *The Chronicle, The Post,* and *The Daily News* featured a photograph of Adam and herself dining cozily at one of "21"'s best tables, Katrinka realized what an awful fool she had been again. Not that she doubted that Adam had been genuinely upset, but his asking her to dinner had had a more devious motive than the simple need for her comfort. The evening had been a setup, a ploy, one more public-relations move by Adam to convince his creditors that he remained a good risk. What the photograph in the newspapers conveyed, contradicting all the negative press he had been receiving, was that Adam's finances might be as shaky as the economy, but he wasn't scared; he was smart enough and confident enough to turn it all around; whatever he had lost (symbolized by Katrinka in a playful and expensive Ungaro dinner suit) he would get back.

If he had asked outright for help, she would have given it. If he had been honest about what he really wanted, she still would have had dinner with him. It was being manipulated that she resented. She promised herself she would not let that happen again. When, a few days later, he called and asked her to dinner, she told him no.

As Christmas drew near, Katrinka found it more and more difficult to keep her spirits high. Memories of the preceding, terrible holiday haunted her. She relived the scenes with Klaus Zimmerman and Jean-Claude and Adam over and over, constant slow-motion replays of a disaster, a nuclear explosion, a volcano erupting, her life falling apart. She seemed little closer to putting it all back together again.

But the advantages this holiday had over the last, she observed to herself wryly, were that nothing so terrible could possibly happen again, and that, for the first time since her marriage, she would be spared Christmas Day with Nina Graham.

More comforting were the numbers of invitations she received. Various suitors proposed romantic interludes in Rio, in the Bahamas; an Australian suggested Christmas in Sydney. Business associates asked her to their homes in Stowe, Acapulco, Palm Springs, and Santa Fe. Neil and

Alexandra Goodman, who always spent Chanukah with his family, Christmas at their Pound Ridge estate with hers, and New Year's in their house in Aspen, invited her to spend as much or as little of the holidays with them as she chose.

More tentatively, Daisy suggested that Katrinka return to St. Moritz to spend Christmas with her and Riccardo and their families. Lucia, who, confided Daisy, was almost down to her normal weight, would be joining them with Pia, and Margo and Ted would be there as well. "Just the old familiar crowd," she coaxed. "Family. We'd love you to come."

Zuzka phoned to insist Katrinka join her and Carla in Los Angeles. "Martin promised to come for Christmas dinner. Finally, he and Carla are speaking. What a time it has been!"

And no sooner was Zuzka off the phone than it rang again with an invitation from Tomáš to spend the holiday with him and his new girlfriend, the head of her own small but well-respected literary agency, in the house he had just bought for them in Santa Monica.

"It's a long way we've come from Svitov," he said to her.

"Who could have imagined it?" agreed Katrinka.

"Our dreams were bigger than this, zlatíčko," he added sadly. "Much bigger than what we've got. We thought we'd be happy."

"Tomáš, Tomáš, what a way to talk. You'll be happy again. So will I."

"You maybe. Not me. Next I direct a film about geriatric robots who don't want to be junked. They call it 'heart-warming.' Shit, that's all it is."

"You can't give up."

"I wish I had your energy," he said fondly. "Come and cheer me up, zlatíčko. I need you."

But Katrinka politely refused all their invitations. She was in the mood, she found, for none of those things. Instead, on the twenty-third of December, she flew to Prague, hired a car, and drove to the farm, where she spent Christmas with her Aunt Zdeňka, her cousins, and their children.

Though not the big-spending extravaganza common in

the West, Christmas in Czechoslovakia was still the biggest holiday of the year. While the women cleaned and cooked and baked, the children made ornaments, and František cut down a pine tree, which the whole family decorated. The gifts were opened on Christmas Eve: handmade sweaters and scarves, colorful pottery bowls, small items of beautiful Czechoslovakian crystal, skis, ice skates, bicycles. Katrinka had brought makeup and French perfume for the women, jeans and American cigarettes for the men. For Christmas dinner they ate duck with red cabbage and *knenlíky*. There were home-grown vegetables and preserves and baked *koláčky*. The two sisters-in-law, who did not usually get along, put their grievances aside; Oldřich's children, who lived in Brno and tended to lord it over their country cousins, restrained their snobbery. During the day they went skiing or ice-skating. At night they watched television, danced to rock music on the radio, or, with Oldřich and Katrinka taking turns on the guitar, gathered around the fire and sang.

Her friends worried that, instead of going on with her life, she had retreated into the past. But that was not at all how Katrinka saw her decision to spend Christmas in Czechoslovakia. She saw it as returning to her roots, to the source of her strength.

From Prague, Katrinka flew to London for business meetings and was still there when the Gulf War broke out. Immediately she canceled her plans to meet Daisy and Margo in Paris at the end of the month for the haute-couture collections. Given the state of Neil's finances, Alexandra had already decided not to attend. And with the world in such a state of crisis, with the reports of air raids and casualty figures broadcast on radio and television around the clock, it did not seem an appropriate time to spend vast sums of money on clothes (not that many people had such vast sums anymore, and the few who did had become more cautious about spending it), nor was it possible to muster much enthusiasm for fun. The lavish entertaining, the grand parties, which had been dwindling since the October crash of '87, in January of 1991 ground to a halt. If people entertained at all, they did it quietly, small dinner parties for eight at home, a few friends meeting in a restaurant to dine.

Occupancy at the London Graham and the two New York hotels hovered at around seventy-two percent. Revenues in the casino were down. It could be worse, Katrinka told herself, but it wasn't good. Frustratingly, there was little to do about it but wait. If the war was a short one, the damage would not be too great. If long, there was the possibility she could lose everything. Though her debt burden was comparatively small, there was still a limit to the amount of time she could go on absorbing losses.

Transatlantic calls jammed the phone lines while she consulted with her managers and planned what to do. Finally, she did a deal with the commuter airlines and ticket agents, upped the advertising budget for the following months, and peppered newspapers and magazines with glossy ads offering a variety of holiday packages in an attempt to lure not only additional business travelers but those who were worried about going abroad into spending vacation time at the various Graham hotels. It took a few weeks, but gradually the scheme began to work, and, despite the continuing war, occupancy in New York and London began to climb back toward the high seventies.

Katrinka continued to put off her return to the States. It seemed less exhausting to deal with Adam at a distance of at least three and, usually, six thousand miles. Occasionally they spoke on the phone, but usually she left it to her lawyer to try and complete the divorce settlement, which Adam continued to revise. When he passed through London on business, she managed to avoid seeing him except once when he stopped by the hotel unannounced. Jean-Claude had told her that he and Natalie had broken up and that Adam was now dating an actress. Both Adam and Sabrina confirmed it. "I kind of like being single again," Adam confessed as he settled into one of the chintz sofas in her office. Katrinka pointed out that he wouldn't be single until he signed the goddamn divorce papers. "What's your hurry?" he asked. "Don't tell me *you* want to get married again. Who's the guy?"

There was an expression on his face that she didn't like. If she did want to marry someone else, she realized, he would stall forever to stop her. Adam never wanted to let go of anything that he considered his. "There's no one," she said pleasantly. "I just want to get you out of my life."

He lounged back into the sofa, looking very handsome in a new light gray Fioravanti suit, and smiled. "Divorce or no, that'll never happen. You'll never get me out of your life," he promised cheerfully.

When she could get away, Katrinka went skiing. Once, curious about how the Golden Horn was faring, she met Franta and his wife, Ingrid, a stunning Swede who towered over him, in Kitzbühel. Franta had given up racing to manage a team of Formula Three drivers and seemed, if not happier than he had ever been in his life, at least contented with the way it had turned out. Usually, though, Katrinka stayed in St. Moritz, at either the Palace Hotel or with Riccardo and Daisy, who were often there weekends during the season.

The second week in February, Katrinka and Daisy both returned to London to attend a dinner party in honor of Carlos Medina's fortieth birthday. Riccardo, who was preparing for a major retrospective of his sculptures in Milan, refused to accompany them, and Daisy didn't press him. "There won't be any shortage of men there, God knows," she said to Katrinka. "It's lone women Sir Alex is going to need if he wants his numbers even."

"And there are plenty of us around," said Katrinka, laughing, "so I don't think he has much of a problem."

"You don't have to be alone a minute longer than you want to," said Daisy sternly, "and you know it. And if you ask me, you've gone a bit too far with your celibacy routine. How long has it been?"

"I just haven't found anyone who attracts me."

"Do you want to?"

"Of course," she said.

Daisy sighed. "Well, unfortunately, I don't think you'll find anyone straight at Carlos's birthday party."

But she was wrong. The house Carlos and Alex occupied in Holland Park was large, and though the guests could not be called a crowd, there were thirty-six for dinner, a larger party than any Katrinka had been to recently, and a much more varied group than she had expected, though she knew that Sir Alex Holden-White's friends (and now Carlos's) extended through high and low society and the arts.

Carlos, his dark hair threaded with silver, greeted Daisy and Katrinka as if they were royalty, which is to say much as he had the Prince and Princess of Wales, who were also guests. "You look wonderful," he said, admiring Katrinka's upswept dark hair, still its natural color, her perfect complexion, the lines around her eyes and mouth adding character to her beautiful face, her slender body wrapped flatteringly in a short Christian Lacroix dress with a round-necked, hand-painted top and silk chiffon skirt. "Better than I've seen you look in years," he added frankly. He turned to Daisy, looking petite and elegant in a green satin dress by Valentino. "And the same goes for you. Though I hear you're in love, which explains it. What's your excuse?" he asked, returning his attention to Katrinka, curiosity plain on his face. Was there a new man in her life? he wondered.

"Herb tea, plenty of rest, fresh air, and exercise," she replied primly, teasing him.

Carlos laughed, and, taking them each by an arm, said, "Come and say hello to Alex, and meet some of the other guests."

Katrinka had, in fact, met the Prince and Princess before, in Palm Beach, and most of the others at Ascot or the Prix de l'Arc in Paris or at St. Moritz or the south of France. It was rare, these days, for her to attend a party anywhere in the world and not know most of the people there. Usually, she found this phenomenon relaxing and fun. To be always assured of a welcome, never to have to search for conversation, never to feel awkward or alone in a group of strangers, took most of the pain out of socializing. It did not, however, remove the boredom when the faces reappeared too frequently.

Waiters in tails circulated with crystal glasses full of champagne and delicately cut canapés on silver trays. A string quartet played in the corner beside the Adam fireplace in the drawing room. Separating, Katrinka and Daisy moved from group to group, renewing old acquaintances and encountering an occasional new face. Katrinka was introduced to the head of the Royal National Theatre and his wife; to David Bailey, the photographer; to Blair Brown and David Hare; to Neil Kinnock, the leader of the Labor party; to a Conservative MP.

Spotting Anoushka Hempel, the talented designer who owned Blake's, a hotel Katrinka admired, she headed for her to say hello, but was intercepted by a blond giant who murmured *"Dobrý den"* as she passed.

Katrinka stopped dead in her tracks. "Mark!"

"I wondered when our paths were going to cross again," said Mark van Hollen, taking hold of her arm.

"I never did expect to see you tonight," said Katrinka, feeling the same rush of pleasure the sight of him always caused.

"I wasn't going to come," he said, "until Carlos told me you were going to be here. I was supposed to leave tonight for New York." On an impulse he did not quite understand, he had changed his plans.

On close inspection, his thick blond hair was now more than half silver; his tanned face was deeply lined; his body had broadened, though with muscle not fat. Once his looks had not appealed to her because they had seemed almost too perfect. Now, with age, they had acquired character. Like most of the men who crossed her path, he radiated confidence, power, success. But it was his other, perhaps less obvious qualities, that Katrinka had always found so compelling: strength combined with tenderness, compassion with humor. "I'm glad you did stay," she said simply.

They sneaked into the dining room and, like mischievous children, changed the place cards at the tables so that they could sit next to one another. When they sat down to dine, Alex noticed, of course, since he was the one who had spent hours doing the seating plan, and was obviously annoyed, but neither Mark nor Katrinka cared. They were enjoying themselves too much. By the time the evening ended, their relationship had changed from an intermittent social friendship to something more, something still vague and undefined to them both. It was not that either had ever, from their first meeting on the ski lift in Kitzbühel, missed the obvious fact that the other was attractive. But when they had been so in love with other people, it had been a matter of little importance to them. Now it seemed loaded with significance. They were responding to each other differently, they recognized that much, but were as yet unsure why. Both were curious to discover the reason, the idea of a sudden sexual attraction after so many years not really seeming credible to either.

Mark offered to see Katrinka home, but she and Daisy had a car and driver waiting, as did he. "I'll call you tomorrow," he said as he kissed her cheek, then he turned to say good-bye to Daisy.

"How nice to see Mark again," said Daisy as they walked the few feet from the house to the waiting Bentley. "He's looking wonderful, I think. Completely over that awful tragedy. How long ago was it now?"

"Eight years," replied Katrinka, surprising herself by remembering. "But no one does recover from something like that completely."

"I suppose not," said Daisy sadly, for a moment caught up in her own terrible memories. Then she brightened. "But life goes on," she said. "And sometimes turns out well."

"Yes," agreed Katrinka. "Sometimes."

With so many empty rooms at the hotel, Katrinka had seen no point in renting a flat and so was staying in one of the suites, making the commute to her office a short one, down in the elevator to the second floor. When she arrived there the next morning, a large arrangement of roses had already been delivered and there was a message that Mark van Hollen had called. She phoned him back at once and was put through immediately. "You're not in a meeting?" she teased.

"I was waiting for your call," he said. She laughed, and he added, "Truthfully, I had none scheduled today. I told you I was supposed to return to New York last night."

"You do leave today?" she asked, surprised at how much she disliked the idea.

"No, I don't think so. But it depends on you. Can you play hookey?"

"Well . . ."

"Come on, Katrinka, say yes."

"Yes," she said, feeling a wave of pure joy rush through her.

"I'll be there in half an hour."

"But, what we are doing?"

"I don't know yet. But wear something warm. It's freezing out."

She replaced the phone in its cradle, looked quickly through her correspondence file to see if there was something that absolutely could not wait, jotted notes on a few letters her assistant could deal with, returned a phone call to the head of the ad agency that handled the London Graham, then rose from her desk. Luckily, she had no meetings scheduled either, though she suspected she might have canceled them if she had. "I'll phone you later," she said as she left the executive suite.

"Where can I find you?" called her assistant, running after her.

"You can't," she said.

Returning to her rooms, Katrinka changed quickly into a pair of brown woolen Victor Costa slacks, a cream cashmere sweater, and tweed jacket. She checked her makeup, pulled on a pair of warm boots and a brown felt hat, and when her phone rang, announcing Mark's arrival, she was ready. Grabbing her purse and coat, she raced out the door. This is ridiculous, she thought. I feel like a schoolgirl.

It had snowed the week before and, amazingly, the drifts had accumulated to heights of twelve inches and more in London, a phenomenon no one could recall happening in living memory. What remained of it in the city were small gray piles of grit-covered ice, but the fields in the country were still white, and the verges of the road were lined with mounds of snow resembling a line of cumulus clouds stretched along the horizon.

In his rented Jaguar, Mark and Katrinka drove into Berkshire. They stopped in a pub with a thatched roof and ate a traditional ploughman's lunch of cheese and bread. "We can go to the races," said Mark, "if you'd like that."

She would, said Katrinka, and they drove to Newbury, heart of England's racing country, and watched the jumpers from the box Mark kept to entertain business associates. Not particularly wanting to run into anyone they knew, they kept to the box for most of the afternoon, studying the racing form, debating (with complete indifference to their ignorance of the subject) the merits of the horses and jockeys, leaving only to place bets at the tote. Once, Katrinka thought she spotted Prince Khalid in the distance, but, next to Adam, he was the last person she wanted to see, and so hurried Mark back to the box without attempting to say hello.

By the end of the day she had won a hundred pounds and Mark had lost fifty. "You look as pleased as if you'd won a million," teased Mark.

"I do love to win," admitted Katrinka.

"So do I," said Mark, with a smile, "but the day's not over yet. Would you like to go to the opera tonight?"

"We can get tickets?" asked Katrinka eagerly.

"I think I can manage it," Mark assured her with the same confident smile. For some reason, she did not find his assurance offensive, just interesting. She was curious to see where it would lead him, content for the moment to follow, not certain how she would react if he attempted to go somewhere she found too dangerous, wondering where that somewhere might be.

Mark returned her to her hotel to change and picked her up again an hour later, whistling softly in appreciation when he saw her in a short transparent embroidered dress over a satin underslip, no jewelry except for the antique diamond combs in her dark hair and diamond earrings. "Lady, you do know how to dress," he said as he wrapped her coat around her.

So did he. Katrinka returned the compliment and he smiled a little sheepishly. He was wearing a dark Armani suit, with a waistcoat and flowered tie. His style of dressing was casual, unaffected, as if he did not care much about what he put on, yet everything he wore was expensive, stylish, and in the best of taste. Katrinka wondered why she had never noticed before.

Instead of the Jaguar, Mark had a car and driver waiting to take them the short distance through Trafalgar Square, along the Strand, to Covent Garden. "In the movies I saw when I was a kid, the rich always wore fancy dress to the opera," said Mark sadly, surveying the crowd as they climbed the Opera House steps.

"Now, poor people go too," replied Katrinka. "It is more democratic."

"Not at these prices," laughed Mark.

They saw *Cavalleria Rusticana,* with no one either one had ever heard of singing. Afterward, they went to Orso's, which was nearby, for dinner, and Katrinka's heart stood absolutely still for a moment as they passed Sabrina on their way in. She was in a party of people, including the MP Katrinka had met the night before at Carlos's party.

"Hello, Sabrina," said Mark pleasantly.

"Mr. Van Hollen," replied Sabrina, "Mrs. Graham," not quite managing to keep the note of surprise from her voice.

They stood in a group, Mark chatting with Sabrina and the others while Katrinka tried her best to seem completely at ease. Then, what seemed like an eternity later, Mark put his arm around her waist and led her firmly away.

"She is vicious, that woman," said Katrinka with loathing as soon as the maître d' had seated them. "Absolutely vicious."

"You won't be reading about us tomorrow, if that's what you're worried about. You won't be reading about us at all, ever," he assured her.

They argued about that, the only sour note in the day, Mark defending his journalists' right to report what they damned please, Katrinka assuring him that he wouldn't feel so righteous about it if he didn't occupy such a protected position. "How you would like to read tomorrow some nasty insinuation about us in that cow's column?" asked Katrinka.

"I wouldn't give a damn," insisted Mark. "It's you I'm concerned about."

"If you're that concerned, fire her. Because maybe next time you won't be my escort, and then she'll feel free to write anything she likes, true or not."

When neither of them seemed prepared to shift positions, they declared a truce, but the disagreement cast a shadow on the evening, and when Mark took her back to the hotel, he got out of the car to give her a friendly kiss on the cheek, but did not offer to escort her inside. When she reached the door, she stopped and turned to wave, then said good night to the doorman and went inside, surprised at how lonely she felt as she crossed the hotel's busy lobby to the elevator.

There were roses again the next morning, this time delivered to Katrinka's suite. Mark called but knew better than to ask her to play hookey two days in a row and invited her only to the theater and dinner. He had put off his trip to New York another day. "I didn't want to go away with us angry at one another," he explained.

"I wasn't angry," said Katrinka, stretching the truth a little.

"I was," admitted Mark.

They went to see the David Hare play at the National Theatre and then to dinner at Langan's. Annabel's they avoided instinctively for fear of running into too many people who would begin making wild suppositions about their relationship before they themselves were ready to define it. That night when they returned to the Graham, as Katrinka started to get out of the car Mark pulled her back toward him and kissed her. The chauffeur, with that extraordinary sixth sense Katrinka always admired, stood waiting outside, not even attempting to open the door. It was a brief kiss, but it left them both a little shaken. "Why do I feel as if I've been waiting to do that for years?" he asked when he let her go.

"Have you?" He had flirted with her occasionally, but in such a lighthearted, casual way, she had never taken it seriously. Could she have been wrong? she wondered.

"No," admitted Mark with his usual honesty. "Or at least, if I was, I never noticed." He leaned across her toward the door but had no sooner touched it than the driver pulled it open and extended a hand to help Katrinka out.

"Close the door," said Mark sharply, pulling Katrinka back toward him. Hurriedly, the chauffeur did as told, then stepped away from the car and stared fixedly at the mansion at the far end of the street while the doorman turned his attention away from the interesting events in the parked limousine to the couple leaving the casino who wanted a cab.

Mark sat back, his arms folded across his chest, and looked at the startled Katrinka. "Come home with me," he said.

Katrinka had had years of practice refusing sexual advances and was good at it, usually managing to do it without hurting egos, rarely losing men from her circle because she had rejected them physically. And she was about to deliver one of those practiced denials when she stopped herself. For the first time in a long time, she did not really want to say no.

"Look," he continued, when she did not reply immediately, "I know I'm rushing this. I know I ought to be patient and court you, send you flowers, buy you jewels . . ."

"I don't want jewels . . ."

"And I meant to. Last night, when I stopped being angry with you, when I realized how much I wanted you, I told myself, take it slow, there's no hurry. But, goddamnit, I'm no good at taking things slow. Not anymore. Life is so short, Katrinka. Too short. I hate to waste it playing games. I want you. I want to make love to you. And I can't go into that hotel with you, or the whole world will know it tomorrow, and I can see you don't want that."

"It's the divorce," she explained. "I don't want any problems."

"So I'm asking you, come home with me." He unfolded his arms and, leaning toward her, kissed her. "Come home with me," he murmured, his lips against her mouth. She began to tremble. "You want to, you know you do," he insisted. "Say yes," he pleaded.

There was nothing else she could say.

He slid an arm around her waist and settled her comfortably against him as he rolled down the window. "Take us home," he said to the driver who returned immediately to the car, got in, and started the motor. "You won't regret this," said Mark, taking hold of Katrinka's hand, turning his head into the warm column of her throat, letting his lips drift slowly up the tender stretch of skin to her ear. "Whatever else happens, I promise, you won't regret this."

The
Present

———◦◆◦———

1991

Forty-Five

*A*nd she never had regretted it, thought Katrinka, fingering the Cartier leopard pin on the lapel of her suit. Mark had given it to her as he had given her so many things in the nine months since they had become lovers: flowers, clothes, jewels, and—most important of all—his love, the sort of love she had been seeking for years, total, equal, supportive, the sort of love that allowed for differences of opinion, that bowed to greater need, that understood all and forgave all, the sort of love she believed her parents once had shared.

Katrinka had gone to great lengths to protect that love, nurturing it out of the public spotlight, keeping it secret from all but Robin, who arranged their travel plans, Anna, who prepared the quiet meals they ate at home, and possibly Sabrina, who was too intimidated to talk. Mark often accused her of being paranoid, but ultimately he was inclined, as always, to trust her judgment; and Katrinka, who had never forgotten the possessive look on Adam's face at the mere suspicion that she might be involved with another man, more than ever wanted no further delays reaching a settlement. As quickly as possible, Adam had to be put somewhere he could do her no further harm, and that place was anywhere permanently out of her life.

When she had returned to New York in the spring after spending a blissful week with Mark on a small desolate island he owned in the Hebrides, off the western coast of

Scotland, Katrinka had begun cracking the whip in earnest. By June a settlement was agreed upon and signed, granting her the villa in Cap Ferrat and a cash payment for her share of the New York apartment, payable in ten days' time, on December 20, when the divorce would be final. On the twenty-first, Mark and she had planned to marry.

But now . . . She brushed the tears from her face, picked up the Zeiss Associates report and scanned it again. Now . . . Uncertainty gripped her. How would Mark feel about this? Was it really worth jeopardizing her future? After all this time?

The phone rang and she jumped. She picked up the receiver, knowing it was Adam even before she heard his voice. Or rather, his secretary's. "Mrs. Graham, please hold for Mr. Graham," she said confidently, as if no one ever refused Adam's calls.

"You're late," he said. "Where have you been?"

She was tempted to tell him none of his business, but thought better of it. "At the Praha."

"I tried you there. I must have just missed you."

"Yes," she agreed unhelpfully.

"Can we have dinner tonight?"

"I'm sorry, I'm busy."

"You're always busy lately," he said, a note of suspicion in his voice.

"No busier than usual," she replied, her voice even.

"We have to talk," he said. "It's important."

"About what?"

"The settlement."

"Oh, Adam, no. Everything is agreed."

"I'm having a little bit of a problem."

"Discuss it with my lawyer."

"I want to discuss it with you," he said belligerently.

"And I don't want to talk about it anymore. It's over, Adam. Over. Everything is over."

"It's about the apartment. I've had to mortgage it," he said, changing tack, his voice coaxing now. "I need you to give me a little more time."

There was no way she could any longer judge Adam's financial condition accurately. The lawsuit was still pending against Graham Marine, she knew that, and since the economy continued to be weak, she doubted that either the luxury yacht, the cruise-ship line, or the tanker businesses had improved. On the other hand, she had read in *The Wall Street Journal* that the Connecticut yard had just been awarded a military contract and that an Italian company had made an offer for Olympic Pictures. All things considered, she did not think he was in such bad shape. She thought that, as always, he simply did not want to let go. "Sell one or two of the diamonds you did buy your girlfriend recently. That will pay for the apartment."

"You know that's all bullshit," said Adam.

This was a new girlfriend, another actress, not a very successful or, if Tomáš was to be believed, a very talented one. Natalie seemed to be permanently out of his life, according to Sabrina, trying to sell her successful chain of boutiques to a retail-wary Jean-Claude, and involved now with a wealthy real estate developer whose business interests were in Australia and Japan as well as the United States.

"Speaking of jewelry," he continued, "where did you get that leopard pin you were wearing today? Did I buy it for you? Perhaps you could sell it, and use the proceeds to buy me out of my share of the apartment."

"You'll find a way to meet the deadline," said Katrinka sweetly, ignoring his comment. "I do have great faith in you."

"I'm only asking for a couple of weeks."

"No," said Katrinka firmly. "Adam, why you are stalling like this? It's better for both of us to settle everything now."

"Still having trouble with your verbs?"

"It's been almost two years," she continued, ignoring his interruption. "That's long enough to live in limbo. I want you gone, out of my life, forever."

"Never," he repeated, as he had months before, stubbornly refusing to accept the inevitable.

"I'll see you in court," she said, "on the twentieth," and hung up.

How different everything was now, she thought. How different *she* was. A year ago she would have been weeping in pain and rage at the end of a phone call with Adam. Now, she was only mildly irritated, as if he was a problem already solved.

The new problems, the ones yet unsolved, were the ones that concerned her now. Debating what to do for a moment, Katrinka sat still. Then, almost of its own volition, her hand reached out and picked up the phone. It would be about ten o'clock now in Paris, she calculated. Thoughtfully, Paul Zeiss had included his home number. Katrinka dialed, listened impatiently to all the clicks and hisses on the line, to the odd double ring at the other end, until, finally, a woman answered, sounding impatient, as if she found it inconceivably bad-mannered for anyone to call so late. Katrinka told the woman her name, asked for Paul Zeiss, heard her mutter a grudging *"Ne quittez pas,"* and waited what seemed an endless amount of time until Paul Zeiss said hello in his slow and careful English.

"Mr. Zeiss, I got your report."

"Yes?"

Still unable to believe what she had read, terror and joy battling for control of her, Katrinka asked, "Is it true? You did find my son? You're certain?"

"There can be no doubt, Mrs. Graham," Zeiss said confidently.

"Oh, God," murmured Katrinka. Positive when Zimmerman died that she had lost her last chance, Katrinka had stopped hoping, allowing Zeiss to continue with his investigations only so that she could tell herself later she had left no stone unturned. It hardly seemed possible that, after all, Paul Zeiss had found him. It was impossible to believe, and yet she knew it must be true. "And now," she said excitedly, joy at last conquering all traces of fear, "now, what we do?"

"As always, Mrs. Graham, that is entirely your decision."

Mark had left for Australia that morning to discuss buying a newspaper chain and publishing house in Sydney. He expected only to be gone a week, which did not leave Katrinka much time for trying to resolve matters, if only in her mind, before seeing him again.

Wishing as always at times like this that she still had the use of the Graham jet, she phoned Robin and told her to book her on the next flight to Munich. From there Katrinka would drive to Kitzbühel, where, so Paul Zeiss had said, her son was spending the week at the Schloss Grunberg. She packed quickly, ate the dinner Anna had prepared, showered, dressed, and, while Luther carried her skis and luggage down to the waiting car, went over a list of instructions with Anna and then, once in the Mercedes, another list with Robin, who rode with her to the airport.

Used to Katrinka's sudden arrivals and even more sudden departures, Robin didn't find this decision of her employer's at all unusual; she just wanted to get her stories straight. "And what am I gonna tell Mr. van Hollen when he calls?" she asked as the car pulled to a stop in front of the Lufthansa building.

"Tell him I've gone skiing. And give him my number at the Schloss Grunberg."

"And Mr. Graham?"

"Tell him to go to hell," said Katrinka. Then she laughed. "No, better tell him where I am. I don't want any trouble these next few days." She leaned over and kissed Robin's cheek. "Fax me anything urgent. The rest can wait. I won't be gone so long. Call me tomorrow."

"I will. Don't worry."

"Not about you, anyway," said Katrinka, waving as she hurried into the terminal.

The first class compartment was almost empty and, after a glass of champagne, Katrinka turned out her light and drifted into a light sleep, soothed rather than disturbed by the hum of the engines and the murmur of the attendants taking care of their few passengers. The plane touched down in Munich early the next morning. By noon she was in her luxurious white-and-gold baroque room at the Schloss. She changed immediately into her ski clothes and took the gondola to the Horn. After so many years, even with occasional return visits, there were not a lot of familiar faces, but enough to keep her talking, exchanging news while her eyes raked the crowd, not really expecting to see her son, knowing she would have a better chance of finding him later that afternoon in the bar, or later still in the dining room.

She skied until the lifts closed for the day, though conditions were not good. There had been too little snow, and the terrain was icy and terrifyingly fast. Trying to spend as much time as possible with Mark, always in out-of-the-way country places where they would not be noticed, she had not skied as much as usual this year and felt a little out of practice. By the time she returned to her room, she was exhausted. She showered quickly, tumbled into bed, and was sound asleep in minutes.

Luckily, she had forgotten to put the Do Not Disturb sign on the door, so when the maid knocked wanting to turn down the bed, she woke Katrinka just in time for dinner. Asking her to return later, Katrinka slipped into the Christian Lacroix dress she had worn to Carlos's party, the night—as she thought of it—that she and Mark had finally found each other. She considered it her lucky dress.

Entering the dining room, waiting for the maître d', she stood in almost the exact spot where Adam and Alexandra had stood waiting so many years before while Natalie and she had watched them from their table. Anxiously, her eyes searched along the muralled walls, among the potted plants, looking for her son's familiar face. What if he had chosen to dine somewhere else? What if Paul Zeiss had been wrong and her son was not in Kitzbühel at all?

Finally, she saw him. She sighed with relief, and apprehension. He was here, and soon, very soon, she would speak to him. He was with a group of friends, all male. Good, she thought, that made it easier. Determined as she was, wresting him away from a smitten girlfriend might have been difficult even for her.

"Just one, Mrs. Graham?" asked the maître d' in German, smiling as he came up to her. "Or will friends be joining you?"

"Just one, thank you. And, if possible, I would like to sit at that table, against the wall, by the boy and dog," she said, indicating a section of the mural that covered the three walls of the room. The route to the table would take her directly past her son.

"Of course," he said.

Katrinka followed the maître d' across the room, her eyes

riveted on her son's face, willing him to look at her. And, as if aware that he was being summoned, he looked up just as she walked past, in time to catch her smile and the slight nod of her head in greeting. His eyes were puzzled, but only for a moment. Then, he smiled, remembering her. With a great effort of will, she turned her head away and continued on to her table.

If anything, he was more handsome than she remembered him, but perhaps she would think that now. Didn't mothers always believe their sons the most handsome in the world? Then she smiled at herself. Nina Graham was hardly blinded by so much love for Adam.

As she ate, Katrinka tried not to stare at him, limiting herself to an occasional glance in his direction, almost as if she were flirting, which in a sense she was. She watched him lingering at his table, looking at her a little uneasily from time to time, not sure what was expected. Finally, as she was served her coffee, he rose and crossed the room to her, clicked his heels together lightly and bowed. "Mrs. Graham?"

"Yes. And you're Christian Heller."

"I saw you last, when was it? In St. Moritz two years ago?"

"That's right." They spoke, as always when they met, in German. "Would you care to join me? Or do you and your friends have plans?" Luckily, Gerhard Brandt, Christian's usually inseparable companion, was not part of the group, or undoubtedly she would have had both young men at her table.

"No. That is, nothing important. I would be delighted to join you, if you would permit."

He had the polished manners of a European educated at the best schools, in his case, she had learned from the report Paul Zeiss had sent her, Le Rosey in Gstaad. She had seen him many times over the years with the Hellers, before and after she had been formally introduced to them. But never once had she recognized him, never once even suspected that Christian was her son. How could that be possible? she wondered. Always she had believed that she would know her son anywhere, that blood would call to blood.

Christian resembled her, but not enough so that their

603

relationship was unmistakable. He had her dark hair, fair skin, and high cheekbones, but his nose was broader and the color of his eyes was more like Mirek's, or her father's.

"You are here alone?" he asked.

She nodded. "Just for a few days." If she wasn't careful, she knew, he would think she was trying to seduce him. "When no one can come with me, I come alone. I love to ski. I used to own a little inn near here. The Golden Horn."

"Ah, yes," he said, smiling. "My parents used to take me there for tea when I was a child. Sometimes I still go."

"A tradition I started," she said proudly. "Would you like some coffee or a brandy, perhaps?" she asked since he seemed in no hurry to leave and she was anxious to have him stay.

He agreed to both and Katrinka summoned the waiter, placed the order, then settled back to find out what she could about Christian, not the facts, all of which had been stated clearly enough in Zeiss's report, but what he thought, what he felt.

It was easy enough to draw him out. Katrinka was practiced at it, and Christian was young, a little arrogant, committed to the belief that he was interesting and that every woman he met wanted him. She was careful to keep the tone light, but not flirtatious, probing for him to reveal more to her than he would have to a girl he was trying to get into bed.

Much of what Christian told her, Katrinka already knew: that Kurt Heller was a diplomat, and his elegant wife the daughter of a leading German industrialist, founder of an electronics firm, and a great asset as a hostess. As a small child, he had traveled with them a great deal, from one diplomatic posting to another, Argentina, Uruguay, Spain, Holland, until he was old enough to be sent to boarding school. He was still at university, taking an advanced degree in economics, a ticket to top government posts or influential positions with the leading German financial institutions.

"Did you enjoy it, all that traveling?"

He shrugged. "I was too young to appreciate its advantages. And by six, I was in boarding school."

"And did you like that?"

"It's a lonely life for a child, at first. But eventually I made friends."

Why would people adopt a child and then send him away, and so young? she wondered.

"I would have hated boarding school, I think. I hated to leave my parents even when it was time for me to go to university."

Christian grinned. "But perhaps you liked *your* parents." Katrinka sat back in her chair, obviously shocked, and Christian's smile broadened. "Do you think that a shocking thing to say?" he asked. "But it's no secret. Everyone knows I loathe mine."

Katrinka wondered if that was the type of thing young men liked to say to appear interesting. She laughed. *"Ay yi yi yi,"* she said, shaking her head. "Both equally or one more than the other?"

"You don't believe me."

"Not really."

"You will when you know me better. Or know them better. They are quite easy to dislike, take my word for it."

"Dr. Zimmerman seemed to like them well enough," said Katrinka, throwing the name into the conversation to see what response it would get.

"Well, he would. He was a complete opportunist, and my parents are very well connected." He saw the color drain from Katrinka's face and added, "I do hope he wasn't a good friend of yours."

"No," she replied curtly.

"I've upset you. I'm sorry. I suppose if you come from a loving family, it is difficult to imagine one that is not."

He sounded so sympathetic, so mature, that Katrinka felt suddenly as if their roles had been reversed, as if she were the child, and he the adult. Whatever she had imagined, whoever she had expected to find, she had not anticipated a young man quite so determined to surprise, to disturb. "It is not," she said firmly, "difficult to imagine at all."

His friends had left the dining room, but now one returned, excused himself with a slight bow and a click of the heels that made Katrinka suspect he had been at school with Christian, to say that a group of them had decided to go dancing and wanted to know if Christian wished to join them. He hesitated a moment, casting a quick glance at Katrinka, as if assessing his chances if he should stay. But she smiled and told him to go, as she intended to go to sleep immediately. "I get up very early to ski."

He stood, almost reluctantly, bowed, and said it had been a pleasure to see her again. Then he asked what mountain she would be skiing the next day.

"The Hahnenkamm."

"Then perhaps we shall meet."

"Perhaps," she agreed, though she thought it more like a dead certainty since, if he did not come looking for her, she had every intention of finding him.

As she was getting ready for bed, Mark called from Sydney, wanting to know what had prompted her sudden decision to leave for Kitzbühel. "Is anything wrong?" he asked. "Did something happen after I left?"

"I'm fine," she assured him. "Fantastic. I'll explain everything when you get back. What time is it there?"

"Eight A.M.," he said. "I'm just about to start my first round of meetings."

"Good luck."

"I'll keep you posted."

"I miss you already."

"I love you."

"I know," she said. "I do count on it."

She got into bed and turned off the light, then lay awake staring into the dark. Expecting a man to accept the sudden appearance of his lover's, of his soon-to-be-wife's twenty-three-year-old son was asking a lot, even of someone like Mark. She knew that. Suddenly, the terror she had felt on first reading Zeiss's report came rushing back. What if Mark did not understand? What if the simple fact of her son's existence changed everything, completely altered his feeling for her? How could she bear that? How could she bear to lose him?

* * *

Katrinka did not sleep much that night, rose early, drank only a cup of coffee, and was at the lift to the Hahnenkamm in time to catch the first gondola.

Christian was waiting for her. "I knew you meant it when you said you would be up early to ski."

"Did you go to bed at all?" she teased. "Or did you dance all night?"

"I got a few hours' sleep," he said.

More than I, she thought wistfully. She hoped she had enough energy to get her through what she knew would be a difficult day.

"Heller, I didn't know you had a sister," said someone behind them in the line.

Katrinka started and Christian looked at her curiously for a moment. She was wearing black stretch ski pants and a turquoise jacket with a turquoise fur hat on her head. As usual, she wore little makeup, but her cheeks were flushed and her eyes bright despite the lack of sleep. She looked at least ten years younger than the forty-three she was.

"How very flattering," said Katrinka.

"She's not my sister," replied Christian, turning to introduce her to the man who had spoken, the older brother of one of his school friends. "She's a friend of mine," he added in unmistakably proprietary tones. With a skill far beyond his years, Christian crowded the young man out of their gondola and into the one behind, then monopolized the conversation all the way to the middle station.

"I'm going right to the top," she said.

"So am I," he said, following her into the connecting gondola.

"See you later," called the friend as he put on his skis.

Christian waved but did not reply. "Pest," he muttered.

They skied together the entire day, Christian following wherever Katrinka led. He was a good skier, she was proud to see, not as experienced as she, without such good control, but strong and fearless.

"You are terrific," he said to her once as they reached the bottom of a long run.

"I trained for the Olympics once," she told him.

"You never competed?"

607

"I left Czechoslovakia before I could."

"You have to tell me the story of your life," he said. "It sounds fascinating."

"If you tell me yours," she replied.

"I already did."

"You never mentioned your girlfriends," she teased.

He wasn't in the least bit embarrassed. "That's because none of them are important. I've never been in love," he said, almost proudly. He saw the look on her face and added, "Why is it you never believe me when I'm being my most serious?"

"Maybe it's because what you say then is so sad."

At three, Christian suggested that they stop skiing and go to the Golden Horn for tea. Katrinka agreed quickly. She felt the need to talk to him at greater length before deciding what to do. But, as it turned out, Christian took the decision out of their hands.

The Golden Horn had not changed much in the years since Katrinka had sold it. Some of the older furniture as well as the carpets had been replaced and the walls repainted often, but no extensive renovations had been done, and tea there was still a local tradition. Hilde, looking significantly plumper, greeted Katrinka with a cry of pleasure and a motherly hug, sending for Bruno, who arrived moments later to greet her as he always did with a hearty handshake followed by a kiss on both cheeks. They still managed the inn for Heinrich Ausberg, who had bought it from Katrinka.

"You'd think they hadn't seen me forever," she said to Christian as soon as they were seated. "I was here only a few months ago."

"They obviously care about you."

"As I do about them," she said. "They're very good people."

"I don't know many good people," said Christian.

Again, Katrinka felt that slight stirring of unease, an uncertainty about Christian's motives. Was he telling the truth or trying to produce an effect? But a pretty young waitress arrived with their tea and scones and he admired her with such frank pleasure that he seemed suddenly the most ordinary kind of twenty-three-year-old and Katrinka felt foolish for thinking him anything else.

A moment later Hilde returned with a pot of preserves. "Homemade jam," she announced. "Still made from her recipe," she told Christian with a smile. Then, as if she had just noticed something extraordinary, she looked from one to the other, a question forming in her eyes. About to say something, she suddenly thought better of it, and started away, turning back to add, "Let me know if you think it's as good as it used to be."

"You're always worried, and it's always fine," said Katrinka, laughing.

"It's a charming little inn," said Christian.

"Yes," agreed Katrinka, surveying the almost empty room fondly. "But the recession has hit even here. It used to be packed this time of day."

"Mrs. Graham . . ."

"I think you should call me Katrinka," she said, turning back to look at him.

"Katrinka, about last night, what I said about my parents."

"Yes?"

"I know it upset you. And I know I should not have spoken so frankly. I'm not quite sure why I did. That's why I wanted so much to see you today, to explain."

"Really, Christian, you don't have to explain anything to me."

"But I want to," he said. "I would hate you to think badly of me."

"I don't," she assured him. "But why should it matter to you if I did? We don't know each other well. What I think can't be so important."

"But it is. I don't know why. Usually I don't give a damn what people think. But I would like you to like me."

He was drawn to her, she could see that. And she was pleased and horrified at the same time. She had done it badly. He had got hold of completely the wrong idea. He was mistaking her feelings, and his own. "Well," she smiled, stirring her tea, trying to take the intensity out of the moment. "You got your wish. I do. You're an extremely interesting boy," she added, hoping that he got the point and would not begin protesting that he was not a boy, but a man.

But again he surprised her. "You see, it doesn't matter at all what I say about them, what I feel about them. They are not my real parents."

"They told you that?" asked Katrinka, surprised. Why, if Christian had known, had Zimmerman insisted so on secrecy?

"No. Of course not," said Christian, answering her unspoken question. "They would never tell me the truth about anything. I heard them arguing once. When I was quite small. About four, I suppose. That was probably why I was so awful to them."

"At four, how awful could you have been?"

"You have no idea," he said, again with that same strange pride. "Awful enough for them to send me away at six."

"You're exaggerating again," she said.

"I assure you, I'm not."

"If they adopted you, they must have wanted a child very badly. They must have loved you very much."

"They didn't love me at all. And I didn't love them. What they wanted was another status symbol, like the right car or the right address. If you don't have them, and everyone else does, you feel out of it. That's all children are to some people," he added with a cool smile, "a symbol of yet another success."

"Yes, I know." It was so hard to know what to do, whether to tell him or not, to tell him now or to wait. But here was an opportunity she might never get again. "Did you ever wonder about your real parents?" she asked.

"Of course," he said, with a smile. "All the time."

"And did you try to find them?"

He shrugged. "Why would I want another set of parents who didn't want me?" Then he laughed. "I can't imagine why I'm telling you all this."

"Because I'm old enough to be your mother," she said lightly.

"You're not." He seemed startled by the idea.

"And because I'm interested." She picked up a scone, broke it in two, put some jam on it and took a bite. "When is your birthday?" she asked.

"You want to know my birth sign?" She shrugged. "I'm Cancer. June thirtieth."

"I have a son who was born on June thirtieth."

"Oh?" He looked surprised, and not very interested. It was not *her* son he wanted to talk about.

"June thirtieth, nineteen hundred and sixty-eight."

"But that's my birthday!" he said. "I've never read that you had a son. Where is he?"

"I've been trying to find him for a very long time. I . . . I gave him up for adoption when he was born."

"You must have been very young," said Christian slowly, as if trying to make sense of what he was hearing.

"Yes. And very frightened. My lover was married. My parents had just died, suddenly, in an automobile accident. I didn't know what to do, and I made a terrible mistake. One I've regretted ever since."

He looked at her suspiciously. "Why are you telling me all this?"

She smiled. "Because you told me your story. And so that perhaps you'll understand, and maybe forgive."

"Forgive? Forgive who?"

"Me," she said.

His eyes scanned her face as if searching for clues, then, suddenly, he understood. "It's you!"

She nodded. She wanted to reach out and touch him, but was afraid to. "I only found out who you were the day before yesterday. Before then I had no idea, none at all. And I didn't come here to tell you. That was not what I planned. I just wanted to see you, to get to know you a little." She shrugged. "But one thing led to another. If I've upset you, I'm sorry."

"Upset? No. Stunned, maybe." He was silent for a long moment. Then, finally, he said, "I thought I would hate you."

"And?"

"I don't know." He laughed. "God, I thought I wanted to fuck you."

"Don't talk to me like that," she snapped.

He was instantly contrite. "I'm sorry."

"You like to shock too much."

"So do you," he countered.

"No, you're wrong. I don't like it at all."

He stood up. "Excuse me, please. I . . . I really think I must go somewhere and think this all over."

"Wait . . . just a minute." She signaled the waitress and asked for a pen, then wrote her New York phone numbers on a napkin and gave it to him. "I'll be here only until tomorrow. After that, you can reach me in New York. Robin, in my office, will always know where I am. If you call, she'll get a message to me. I hope you'll call," she added softly.

Christian took the napkin from her, stuffed it into the pocket of his parka and zipped it shut, but didn't reply. Clicking his heels together, he bowed slightly. "It has been interesting," he said coolly, his expression wary, guarded, "more interesting than I expected. *Auf Wiedersehen.*"

"*Auf Wiedersehen,*" she said.

Forty-Six

"Do you want me to have some lunch delivered from the restaurant?" asked Robin.

"I'm not hungry," said Katrinka, running down the list of telephone messages that had accumulated in her absence.

"You have to eat something."

Katrinka had had a doctor's appointment that morning, and he had said the same thing. "A salad," she said, giving in, "and black coffee."

"Herb tea," contradicted Robin. "You've been drinking too much caffeine."

"Herb tea, thank you," said Katrinka quickly. She looked up from the pink slips in her hand and said, "There are no other messages?"

Almost at the door, Robin turned, a smile wrinkling her freckled nose. "Those aren't enough for you? I thought you wanted to be out of here early today."

Mark was due in from Sydney that afternoon and Katrinka had scheduled head-to-toe beauty treatments at the apartment—hair, nails, facial, massage—for the few hours before they met for dinner. It was going to be a difficult evening, and she wanted to look and feel her best. "I guess I'd better get started," she said, with a sigh, pulling the phone toward her and lifting the receiver, wishing she could feel happy at the thought of Mark's return instead of apprehensive.

"I'll see about that lunch," said Robin, going out the door, wondering who the hell this Christian Heller was who had

Katrinka in such a state. All she knew about him was that she was to find Katrinka wherever she was, as soon as he called. A new boyfriend didn't seem likely. She was too crazily in love with Mark van Hollen, and who could blame her? Curiosity killed the cat, she warned herself, trying to console herself with the knowledge that if Katrinka didn't trust her with all her secrets, at least she didn't trust anyone else with more.

"Your mother on the line," said one of the junior secretaries as Robin entered her office.

"Oh Christ," she muttered. Now there would be another argument about her moving in with Craig, and it had been six months already. You'd think the woman would be used to the idea by now. "Would you tell the restaurant to send over a tuna salad for Mrs. Graham, Lucy, please," she said. "And buzz me in five minutes with an important phone call."

"But," said Lucy, looking confused, "what if no one calls you?"

"Just do me a favor, Lucy, okay? Buzz me."

Katrinka checked the list again, though she knew she had not missed his name. Christian had not called. Not yet, at any rate. On her last day in Kitzbühel, she had not gone skiing but waited in her room until it was time to leave for the airport, hoping that—after a few hours to think everything over, to recover a bit from the shock—he would be as eager as she to try and establish some sort of relationship between them. But he had not phoned then, nor in the four days since, and Katrinka was beginning to worry that perhaps he never would, that perhaps he had meant what he said about having no interest in a parent who had deserted him at birth.

If he didn't phone, Katrinka was uncertain what she would do. She had found him, and let him know that she cared for him, and that she wanted him in her life. The rest was up to him. He was twenty-three years old, an adult. How could she insist on their having some sort, any sort, of relationship? How could she make him love her if he didn't choose to? But she had spent so much of her life searching

614

for him, she knew it would be hard for her to stop, to let go. To sit back and do nothing was not in her nature.

Katrinka returned her phone calls, sat in on an executive meeting, listened to the rundown of the figures, which, to everyone's relief, were creeping slowly upward, then refereed an argument between the heads of the advertising and finance departments about the need for more money and the lack thereof. She was sleepy and desperately wanted to nap. "I tell you what we do," she said suddenly. "Children of the Streets is planning a Christmas party. We'll let them use the ballroom free of charge, and ask a celebrity—Sylvester Stallone, Luciano Pavarotti, someone like that, to dress up and play Santa Claus. It will be in all the papers, and we'll save a fortune in advertising for the month. Two birds, one stick."

No one bothered to tell her it was "stone," as Adam might have done. They just went with it. "I like it better than a streaker in the lobby," said Michael Ferrante with a grin.

"More class," agreed the head of advertising, who looked as if someone had handed him a sack of gold coins.

The head of finance smiled. He had always thought he'd hate working for a woman, but not only was this, so far and knock wood, the best job he had ever had, but while friends of his were out of work all over the place he seemed likely to stay employed, at least for as long as he did his job well. The Praha was not about to go under.

The hairdresser had arranged her hair in a loose upsweep of curls, but Katrinka decided that with the cream-colored silk Vicky Tiel pajama suit she was wearing she preferred it down. She was combing it out when the phone rang. Thinking it was Mark on her private line, she leapt up from her dressing table, raced to answer it, and heard an unfamiliar voice say her name.

"Who is it?" she answered cautiously.

"You don't recognize my voice," he answered, with mock sadness, in German.

"Christian! Oh, I am so glad you called."

"Didn't you think I would?"

"I *hoped* you would. I wasn't sure."

Though she should have known better, she had always imagined that when she found her son the bond between them would be instant, the problems small and easily worked out. It was not going to be so simple. She knew that already, just from the short time Christian and she had spent together. He was difficult, elusive, with odd quirks of personality that startled her, disturbing flashes of anger and unexpected vulnerability, eager and sincere one moment, striking an artificial pose the next. She felt always as if she was fencing with him. But what else, she asked herself, could she expect from someone who had grown up the way he had? She was determined to make it up to him, if only he would let her.

They talked for half an hour, each describing to the other in awkward, fragmented phrases the confusion of the past few days, the turmoil of their feelings, Christian moving from shock to anger to (the most he was willing to admit) curiosity and Katrinka alternately frightened and hopeful. But the conversation, at least to her, was unsatisfactory. Without being able to see his face, to watch his expressions, it was even harder for her to guess what Christian was thinking, or feeling. In any case, she wanted to see him again, soon. The few hours they had spent together had only given her an appetite for more.

Since the university's Christmas recess had already begun, Katrinka was able to convince him to come to New York to spend a few days with her. When they had worked out the details of her getting his ticket to him, she asked, "What will you tell your parents?"

"Nothing," he said curtly. "I will be with them for Christmas, as I promised. Until then, what I do with my time is my own business."

"Don't you think you should tell them about me?"

"Why? There is nothing yet to say."

When she replaced the receiver, Katrinka felt troubled rather than pleased. Christian would come, she was certain of that much. But when he arrived? She sighed. Building a relationship with her son, explaining everything to Mark, none of it was going to be easy.

She glanced at the clock and returned hurriedly to the dressing table, reached for the gold-plated Canovas makeup case and powdered her face, repairing the damage a few tears had caused. She drew a comb through her hair and turned to see the door open and Mark appear looking tired but happy. Soon after they had become lovers, he had taken an apartment in the same building, the best way to prevent gossip, they thought, and he came and went as he pleased, using his own key. They were rarely seen together in public.

"That's what I like," he said, a smile brightening his handsome face, "to come home and find my woman waiting for me in the bedroom. But naked in bed would have been better."

Katrinka laughed and raced across the room to him. "Oh, I am so glad to have you back," she said, flinging her arms around his neck, as eager as a schoolgirl for that first kiss. How lucky she was to be able to feel this again, the rush of excitement, the surge of pure joy, just seeing the face of the man she loved. And when he touched her! Then her whole body began to vibrate exquisitely, as if in the grip of a small, pleasant earthquake.

"Did you buy the newspaper?"

"Nope. Too expensive. I'm going to wait a bit. Hmmm, these are bigger, I think," he said, fondling her breasts. "Let me see." He pulled the silk top over her head, undid the clasp of her bra, and let her breasts fall free. "They are." He bent his head to nuzzle them. "They definitely are. It's all that rich Austrian food you've been eating."

"Aren't you exhausted?" she teased.

"Exhausted," he agreed, his hands moving to stroke her silk-covered bottom. "Let's go to bed."

"And the delicious dinner Anna's cooking?"

"We'll eat it later," he said, undoing the zipper on her pants, letting the silk fall to the floor. He slipped his fingers inside the thin strip of her bikini panties. "When I've rested."

Later, she lay with him cradled in her arms, his head resting on her breast. "You know, they are bigger," he said sleepily. "I'd swear it." His hand followed the line of her hip for a moment and came to rest on her belly. "You've gained weight. I never would have believed it. This is not a complaint, if you're wondering. I like it."

"You better. I'm pregnant."

He sat up and stared at her. "Is that any way to break news like that to a guy? I could have had a heart attack."

"I did practice how to tell you. I was going to lead up to it gently at dinner. And then you wouldn't eat."

"Not dinner anyway," he said, forcing a smile. He was on automatic pilot, responding instinctively while his mind tried to take in what she had just told him. "You're sure?" She nodded. "How far along are you?"

"Three months."

"Three months! And you just got around to telling me now?"

"I did see the doctor only this morning."

"Oh, honey," he said, leaning down to kiss her.

"For so many years I did try to get pregnant, and couldn't. I didn't realize I was at first." His weight was resting on her, his head buried in her neck. She touched his hair, the pale luster of corn silk and silver mixed. "Are you happy?"

"Happy?" he murmured without looking at her. "Terrified is more like it."

"I do want this baby so much," she said.

He lifted himself on his hands and looked down at her again. "I want to be happy, for your sake, Katrinka. But you don't know what it's like to lose a child. It makes you afraid to love one again."

She pushed gently against him and, when he moved aside, got out of the bed. As he watched her with anxious, unhappy eyes, she went into the bathroom, then returned a few minutes later wearing a silk robe. Sitting on the bed beside him, she smiled and said, "I do understand. I just ask that you try."

"I hate doing this to you, honey," he said. "But I can't lie to you about what I feel."

"There's more."

"There's something wrong with the baby?" he asked, sounding even more terrified.

"No, no," she said quickly. She took a deep breath. "I did know this wouldn't be easy. Any of it."

"For Christ's sake, Katrinka, just tell me!"

"I do have another child. A son."

"You what?" He felt as if he were caught in a rockslide, larger and larger boulders heading right for him, and no safe haven in sight.

"I have a son." She told him the story, from the beginning to the end, from her meeting with Mirek Bartoš to her conversation with Christian a few hours before. The reticence of a lifetime slipped away, all her caution, her need to protect herself. Never before had she been so completely honest with anyone, not even her parents, and if not unafraid now, at least willing to face the consequences. She wanted Mark to know her totally and to love her in the same way. She wanted no secrets between them. It was as if, finally, like Czechoslovakia, she had won her freedom.

And Mark, reeling from the revelations of the night, sitting propped against the pillows of the bed, listened with conflicting emotions, not saying anything, waiting to discover what he felt. By the time she had finished, rising above the fear, the resentment, the anger at Katrinka for concealing something so important for so long, for being less than honest not only with him but with everyone, was pity for the young, lonely girl who had been terrified into doing something she regretted, for the self-protective young woman who was afraid to jeopardize what she had gained. He pulled her close to him again. "Poor little honey," he said. "What a time you've had."

A sob of relief escaped her. "I did have no one to trust for so long. No one, until you."

"Do you like this kid?" he asked. "This Christian?"

"I don't know. I love him. He's mine. But he's a difficult boy. I won't have an easy time with him."

"I'll do what I can to help, if you want."

"Oh, Mark, *miláčku,* I was so afraid. I love you so much. What would I do without you?"

"You'd manage," he said wryly, rubbing her back, enjoying the slide of the silk robe against her skin.

"Not very well," she said, finally managing a smile.

"My sons would be fourteen now, and twelve." He never talked about them.

"We must love each other very much," she said.

"I do." He untied the belt of her robe and slipped his hands underneath, pulling her down against him. "I do love you. We'll get through this together, somehow. I'll try, Katrinka, I swear."

Forty-Seven

hat are you still doing in New York?"

"I was supposed to leave last week," admitted Daisy as she tilted her powdered cheek to receive Rick Colins's friendly peck. "But I decided to stay for Katrinka's divorce. Have you met my husband? Riccardo Donati, Rick Colins. Rick's a columnist," she explained to Riccardo as the two men shook hands, "one of the better ones."

"She means I usually say nice things about her, but who could help it?" said Rick, his warm smile highlighting the deep network of lines in his face, confessing to an age completely at odds with his lanky adolescent body and schoolboy charm.

"Very nice tie," commented Riccardo, admiring the large flowered scarf Rick had tied in an enormous bow under his cleft chin.

"Rick is noted for his ties," said Daisy as the three continued across the Plaza's cream-and-gold lobby, past the Palm Court, where a violin and piano entertained the few guests who had decided on a light supper.

"Are you dining here?" asked Rick, always the inquisitive journalist.

"Yes," said Daisy. "With Katrinka and a few friends, in the Edwardian Room. A dinner party, to celebrate her divorce. You must stop by and say hello. I know she'd love to see you."

He was meeting a friend in the Plaza's Oyster Bar for a quick drink before wandering over to the Cort Theater to see a preview of *Two Shakespearean Actors*. This was a new friend, a professor of mathematics at NYU, of all things, and Rick had high hopes for him. Not that he believed anyone could ever replace Carlos in his life. But the professor seemed interesting and intelligent, attractive, too, though not in the leather and heavy metal sort of way that Rick sometimes found a turn-on. He had a great sense of humor, an important asset given the times they were living in. "I'll do my best," said Rick.

"You're all right, aren't you?" asked Daisy as they reached the door to the Edwardian Room and were about to go their separate ways. Her meaning was unmistakable, as was the concerned look in her eyes.

The question from someone else might have been irritating, but remembering how Daisy had cared for Steven before he died, Rick smiled at her reassuringly. "So far, so good," he said, stooping again to kiss her cheek. She smelled deliciously of Poison. "Thank you for asking."

As she and Riccardo crossed the Edwardian Room's dimly lit interior, Daisy could see that Katrinka had not yet arrived, though Margo and Ted, Alexandra and Neil, Tomáš, Lucia and her escort, Patrick Kates, a noted yachtsman and the first man she had shown any interest in since leaving Nick, were already seated. The men stood as she approached, and Daisy made the rounds, kissing everyone hello, introducing Riccardo to Patrick, whom he had not yet met, then sitting down beside Neil as Riccardo took the armchair next to her. A waiter came, took their order for drinks, and Daisy realized finally what had been bothering her for the past few minutes. "Three empty places?" she said as she surveyed the table. "Who else has Katrinka invited?"

"Just what we were wondering," said Neil. He had lost weight and some of his old arrogance was gone, but he had managed to hold on to his job and to keep Knapp Manning afloat, though the team of federal investigators who had been ransacking the books for months was not doing much for company morale. The audit, and for this he thanked God every day, had so far turned up nothing; that is, nothing criminal."

"Zuzka and Carla aren't still in New York, are they?" suggested Alexandra, though she was certain the answer was no. But really she could not think of anyone else Katrinka might have invited.

"No," said Tomáš, who had flown in just for the dinner from Montreal where he was filming, "Carla had a tournament somewhere." Whatever bitterness he had once felt toward his ex-wife had long since been eased by financial success, a new wife (he had married the literary agent), and a baby on the way.

"Zuzka wanted to stay," said Daisy, "but you know how Carla gets when Zuzka is out of sight."

"She's made quite a success of Carla's merchandising business, hasn't she?" asked Ted.

"It's making a fortune," said Neil. "She's one smart woman."

"Czechs," said Ted, grinning at Tomáš, "you can't beat them for hard work."

"Or imagination," said Neil. "That's what it takes, in business, and everywhere."

"Sigmund Freud was born in Czechoslovakia," said Riccardo.

"Was he?" said Alexandra, surprised. "I always thought he was Austrian."

"Riccardo's right," said Tomáš. "He was born in Příbor, in northern Moravia."

"Maybe it's Rick," said Margo, whose mind could not be distracted from the empty places.

Daisy shook her blond head. "I just saw him. He's meeting a friend in the Oyster Bar."

Lucia turned to Patrick and smiled. "Are we boring you to death?"

"Not that far," he said, returning her smile. His hand, concealed conveniently by the tablecloth, had found its way under her short skirt and was moving slowly up her inner thigh. She was wearing stockings and a garter belt, for which he was very grateful, and when she separated her legs for him just slightly he could feel the silk of her underpants. "I can usually manage to keep myself entertained."

"Talking about all these people you don't know," continued Lucia, wondering if she was falling in love with him. He wasn't really her type. She had always preferred dark, solid men, like Nick. But what a mistake that had been. Patrick was tall and thin and fair, much more the sort her mother used to marry with his thick silver hair and aristocratic face bespeaking generations of privilege. The thought was disturbing. She did not wish to have anything in common with her mother. And hoped that Pia did not feel the same about her.

"Here she comes," whispered Alexandra.

Everyone's eyes turned to the door where Katrinka, wearing a Calvin Klein amber-beaded slip dress, stood flanked by two men.

"Who on earth is that with her?" said Margo.

Katrinka spotted the group and smiled, spoke briefly to the maître d', then followed as he led her across the room toward them, attracting admiring glances as she passed. Her hair, French-braided in back, framed her face in soft curls. Even at a distance, her friends could see the sparkle in her eyes, the lustrous patina of her skin, the radiant glow of pure happiness. It was not the look any of them had expected to see today. They had anticipated a fit of divorce doldrums and had come to dinner with the sole intention of cheering Katrinka up.

"It's Mark van Hollen," said Daisy, her voice full of surprise and curiosity. "The other one, I don't think I've ever seen before."

"What is she up to?" said Margo.

"With Katrinka, who can guess?" said Tomáš.

But Katrinka had reached them, preventing further speculation. Again the chairs brushed softly against the carpet as the men got to their feet and the women swiveled their bodies slightly to say hello. Greetings were exchanged, names murmured in introduction. "I don't think any of you know Christian Heller," said Katrinka, indicating the dark, handsome youth accompanying her. Blatant curiosity was obvious in all their eyes as Christian clicked his heels and bowed slightly, shaking their hands, then took his place beside Katrinka at the table.

The sommelier appeared immediately with a magnum of Roederer Cristal, popped the cork expertly, and poured it into their waiting champagne glasses.

"Well," said Daisy, angling for an explanation.

"Ay yi yi yi," said Katrinka happily, "do I have news for you."

"You're divorced," said Margo. "It's final. No last-minute hitches?"

"None," said Katrinka. "That is over absolutely and forever." Adam had tried several more times to delay the proceedings and she had been afraid, up to the very last, that he might yet find a way to keep the matter dragging on, but at five-thirty the day before, all problems with the mortgaged apartment resolved, the papers had been signed. The divorce was indeed final.

"I hope Adam is taking this as well as you are," said Lucia, with some vestige of loyalty to her old friend.

"I hope so," agreed Katrinka cheerfully. "I do hope he is as happy as I am. And I mean that." Mark had been leaning back comfortably in his chair, watching with some amusement the curiosity in the others' faces, but when he felt Katrinka's hand cover his own, he looked toward her, his rugged face wearing a tender smile. "Mark and I did marry this morning."

"What?" said Lucia, knocking Patrick's hand out from under her skirt.

"Zlatíčko!" murmured Tomáš.

For the first time they noticed the large emerald-cut yellow diamond and wide gold band she was wearing on her left hand.

"Without telling us?" added Alexandra, sounding hurt.

"We wanted to do it quickly and quietly," said Mark.

"How quickly?" asked Margo, a little worried that Katrinka, on the rebound, might have done something very stupid.

The captain approached their table to take their order,

but Mark waved him away. No one had begun to think about food yet.

"We've been in love for a long time," said Katrinka, explaining her fears that Adam might delay the divorce even more had he known. "Maybe I was a little paranoid . . ." she continued, seeing how skeptical some of them looked. But then, they didn't know Adam as well as she.

"Just a little," agreed Mark, smiling.

"But I did want to marry Mark as quickly as possible."

"She wanted the baby to be born in wedlock," said Mark, enjoying himself enormously. "She's full of all sorts of old-fashioned ideas. I tried to tell her it didn't matter, but you know how stubborn she is."

"Baby!" shrieked Daisy, looking in amazement from Mark to Katrinka for confirmation.

"I'm pregnant," said Katrinka.

"Oh, my God," said Margo, "this is all too much for me."

"A baby," said Lucia, her eyes filling with tears. "Oh, Katrinka, how wonderful."

"Oh, my dear," said Daisy, sniffing, "I am so happy for you."

"I don't feel a thing," said Margo truthfully, "but shock. I'm sure I'll delighted tomorrow."

"That's exactly how I felt," said Mark. "But I'm getting used to the idea."

"This calls for a toast," said Neil, looking toward Tomáš.

"Wait," said Mark, "there's more."

"More?" said Alexandra, who felt she had had enough surprises tonight to last a lifetime.

"Christian . . ." said Katrinka.

Their eyes followed her glance to the young man on her left. They had forgotten all about him.

"Christian," repeated Katrinka. Then she hesitated. How could she possibly explain this? She looked at him, studying his face for a moment, but received no encouragement. They had had a difficult few days together, coming closer, but not yet close enough to suit her. It would take time, she knew, to build the kind of relationship she wanted, and patience, a virtue she did not have in any great supply.

Christian returned her gaze, looking neither happy nor unhappy, but wary. Finally, he smiled.

"Christian," said Katrinka for the third time, "is my son. As you can see," she said, smiling, "I did have him when I was very young."

Ted's mouth dropped open and Neil stared at her dumbly. Confusion registered on Tomáš's face, followed quickly by traces of hurt and anger.

Katrinka looked at him and said, "Mirek's son. I told no one. Until now. I was afraid, I think."

Tomáš nodded, trying to understand.

"This is the best dinner party I've ever been to in my life," whispered Patrick to Lucia.

"But how," stuttered Lucia, "why?"

"First, I want you to assure me there are no more surprises," said Margo, a dazed look in her large smoky eyes. "I really can't take any more."

"That's it," said Mark, reassuringly. "All done for the evening."

"I don't believe it," said Ted.

"Just look at them," said Daisy, finally seeing the resemblance. "Of course."

"I'll explain everything," said Katrinka, as Mark turned and signaled to the captain, "but first I think we should order. I don't want you to die of starvation."

"Oh no," said Daisy, laughing, "you'll be satisfied just to kill us with shock."

"How about that toast?" said Neil.

Tomáš pushed back his chair and got to his feet. He wanted an explanation from her, but it could wait. For now, he was content to see her happy again. "This turned out to be a more special night than any of us expected. One we'll all remember with pleasure the rest of our lives." He lifted his glass. "To Katrinka, Mark, and Christian, happiness!"

"Happiness," repeated the others.

"Thank you," murmured Katrinka, reaching out and taking hold of Mark's hand and Christian's. She looked around the table, seeing the smiling faces of her husband and son, of her friends, and thought of how much misery had shadowed all their lives in the past, and how much joy. She wondered for an instant what changes the next few years would bring, what pain and what happiness, then pushed the thought away. This was not the time to worry about that. Here, now, surrounded by the people she loved most in the world, for this moment, however brief, she had it all.

628